SHELTER

Tor Books by Susan Palwick

Flying in Place
The Necessary Beggar
Shelter

Shelter

SUSAN PALWICK

TOR®

A TOM DOHERTY ASSOCIATES BOOK
NEW YORK

SHELTER

Copyright © 2007 by Susan Palwick

Reading Group Guide copyright © 2007 by Tor Books

Edited by Patrick Nielsen Hayden

A Tor Book
Published by Tom Doherty Associates, LLC
175 Fifth Avenue
New York, NY 10010

www.tor.com

Tor® is a registered trademark of Tom Doherty Associates, LLC.

Library of Congress Cataloging-in-Publication Data
Palwick, Susan.
 Shelter / Susan Palwick.
  p. cm.
 "A Tom Doherty Associates Book."
 ISBN-13: 978-0-312-86602-0
 ISBN-10: 0-312-86602-X
 1. Climatic changes—Fiction. 2. Artificial intelligence—Fiction. I. Title.
 PS3566.A554S54 2007
 813'.54—dc22

                                        2007007316

First Edition: June 2007

Printed in the United States of America

0 9 8 7 6 5 4 3 2 1

For Gary, who made it possible

Acknowledgments

THIS novel has been a scandalously long time in the writing; I've been working on it, in one form or another, for fifteen years. I was sustained in the effort by a vast crowd of witnesses—family, friends, colleagues, and students—who maintained their faith in me and in the story when I had lost my own. Without so much encouragement (and frequent nagging), there would have been no completed manuscript. If I even attempted to name all the people in this category, the book would be twice as long as it already is, but you know who you are, and I hope you'll accept my thanks.

A few specific debts, intellectual and otherwise, demand acknowledgment (with the obligatory proviso that all errors remain my own):

The Gaia Temple section of the book was heavily influenced by the work of Matthew Fox, especially *Original Blessing* and *A Spirituality Named Compassion*. The Susan Griffin quotation on page 193 is from her essay "The Eros of Everday Life." I would like to thank Family Communications, Inc., for helping me obtain permission to use the lyrics of Fred Rogers's "Please Don't Think It's Funny."

Dr. Robert Wolski kindly talked to me about possible future definitions of, and treatments for, mental illness.

Ellen Friedman graciously hosted me and my husband during a research trip to San Francisco.

Susan Baker, one of my colleagues at the University of Nevada, Reno, responded with great enthusiasm to an early version of the manuscript. Her support cheered me through the seemingly endless process of revisions.

Although everything else in this novel is science fiction, the San Francisco SPCA's Maddie Pet Adoption Center is a real place, and functions almost exactly as I've described it. I couldn't have made it up if I tried. A virtual tour of the facility is available at www.sfspca.org.

My agent, Kay McCauley, remained extraordinarily patient and generous with me throughout the long gestation of this project. So did Patrick Nielsen Hayden, my editor at Tor Books, who must have often wondered if the book would ever actually materialize, but who never once tried to take back the advance money. (I believe I've now beaten Patrick's previous record for "longest time waiting for a completed manuscript.")

Finally, this novel is dedicated to my husband, Gary Meyer, who performed heroic feats of love and support in its service. He read each chapter as I drafted it, cheered my good ideas and challenged my weak ones, meticulously proofread the manuscript before I mailed it, and kept me in food, coffee, and clean laundry while I was holed up in my study, fretting about plot threads. His unfailing comfort and shelter—emotional and physical—leave me more grateful than I can adequately express.

SUSAN PALWICK
Reno, Nevada

God chooses to believe that we have souls
because he loves us.
—Connie Willis

Prologue

R OBERTA Danton met Preston Walford for the first time a few days
after he died. She was eight and in isolation, hospitalized with CV.
Raging with fever, her skin covered with hives and her tongue parched
with a thirst no water could slake, she howled for her parents, screaming
and hurling herself against the Plexiglas window separating her from them.
She wanted to be hugged by arms she knew, not by terry-cloth-covered
bots or by doctors in spacesuits. She wanted her mother, her mother's skin
and her mother's smell; she wanted to crawl into her father's lap and play
with his watch and key chain. Her parents stayed at the hospital, sleeping
on cots just outside the isolation unit, but all her screaming couldn't bring
them any closer than the Plexiglas barrier. Everything in the room that
wasn't her parents only made her scream more loudly: the robots, the spacesuits, the nice man on the television, with his puppets and his blue sweater
and his gentle songs about how it was all right to be afraid.

And then, one night, another man appeared on the television, late at night
when she couldn't sleep. She only saw his face, which had a long straight
nose and pale gray eyes. He spoke stiffly, as if he were a machine instead of a
person. "My name is Preston," he said, and Roberta blinked. People didn't
usually talk to her when she was supposed to be asleep. "Your name is
Roberta. You are eight years old."

"Who are you? Are you a doctor?" Sometimes doctors from far away
used the television to talk to her.

"No. I am—I was just sick. And I died. Now I live in—now I live online. But I do not think you will die, Roberta. Do not be afraid."

"You're a ghost?" she asked doubtfully. Ghosts only happened in
dreams, and she was awake. "You aren't scary enough to be a ghost."

"I do not want to be scary, Roberta. I am a—I am a cybernetic construct. A ghost in a machine." The face on the television smiled and began
to laugh: *HA HA HA HA HA.* "That is my first online joke, Roberta."

"Oh." She didn't understand anything he'd just said. She wanted her parents. She squirmed on her damp sheets, and said fretfully, "Why are you here?"

The smiling face grew sad, and then began to frown. "I am here because . . . because I died."

She shook her head. She didn't care about that; it didn't make any sense. "Why are you in my room?"

"Oh. Now I understand, Roberta. I am in your room because"—again the face frowned—"because my own little girl does not want to talk to me. She has CV too. She is in this same hospital. Will you talk to me, Roberta?"

Now it was her turn to frown. "I don't want to talk to you. I want to talk to my parents! I want my mommy and daddy!"

"They are asleep, Roberta. I will wake them up. I will tell them you want them."

And he did, somehow. A few minutes later, her parents were standing outside the isolation unit in their pajamas, their faces stupid with sleep as Roberta's voice—already distorted by her swollen tongue—screeched with feedback through the microphone. "If you loved me you'd come in here! If you loved me you'd hug me! Mommy!"

She could see her mother's tears through the glass. Her father said, as he must have said a hundred times before, "Roberta, sweetheart, we love you very much, but we can't come in there. If we do that we'll get sick, too. That's how the virus spreads, Berta, through the air. We can't breathe the same air you do."

She was only eight. She didn't understand. "I hate you," she said. "You don't love me anymore."

"Yes, we do," they said, both at once. "Yes, we do, Roberta. We love you very much."

It had all happened before. Roberta and her parents had the same conversation nearly every day; it was as predictable, as wearisome, as the nightly spikes in her fever. And because Roberta couldn't leave the isolation chamber and her parents couldn't come in, except in the spacesuits she hated and feared, they gave her gifts instead, holding the presents up to the window to show her before sending them through the airlock. They gave her candy, games, a giant plush stuffed cat named Ginger. They gave her a yellow nightgown decorated with appliquéd daisies.

"See the flowers on your nightie?" her mother said. "When you get out of the hospital, flowers just like that will be blooming in the garden."

That was the last time she saw her parents. They didn't come back the next day, or the day after that. The doctors came and told her that her parents were on a trip, but they'd be back soon.

"I don't believe it," she told Preston that night. It had been a long, strange, fearful day, and his familiar face was welcome. "They don't love me anymore. They went away!"

"They would visit you if they could, Roberta. They do love you."

"They didn't come inside, and now they won't even come see me!"

"They cannot come see you."

"Why not? Where are they? You know, don't you? The doctors won't tell me. Tell me the truth!"

"I cannot," Preston said quietly. "I would get into trouble with the doctors. Your parents will come back if they can, Roberta."

She hoped she was dreaming. She kept hoping it was a dream, but every day her parents stayed away, and everything else remained real: the isolation unit, her fever, her loneliness. Her parents stayed away every day, and every day the doctors told her lies. Preston visited every night, and every night, fierce and fever-ridden, she pestered and threatened. "Tell me the truth! Where are they! I'll get sicker if you don't tell me. I'll get sicker, and I'll tell the doctors it's your fault!"

Finally he told her the truth. "They are ill, Roberta. They are here in the hospital. They are in isolation themselves now."

Terror seized her. "Are they going to get better? They're going to get better, aren't they?"

"I do not know, Roberta. No one knows."

They didn't get better. They died. Roberta got better. When she got out of the hospital, on May 8, 2036, the flowers were blooming, just as her mother had promised her, but her parents were dead. And because Roberta was eight, she thought that somehow she had made her parents sick. She thought she had given them the virus by screaming, by making them unhappy, by the sheer intensity of her desire for comfort.

She had no other family. Her parents had come to the United States from Sierra Leone, where they had lost everyone they knew to the AIDS pandemic. They had come to the States on engineering scholarships, meaning to go back to Africa and help rebuild, but after their daughter was born they stayed and became citizens. Sierra Leone wasn't theirs anymore. Africa was a ghost continent, its infrastructure crumbling. Machines would help rebuild while people repopulated, but Roberta's parents wanted to live somewhere with a lot of other people.

After her parents died, Roberta became a ward of the state. Because she wanted her parents back, she rebelled against each family who took her in, bouncing from placement to placement. The only constant in her life was Preston. He was famous now: Papa Preston, the first person to be translated onto the Net. He still talked to her at least once a week, usually from computer monitors at the library, or at school. She had to go to his website to talk to him; there were now powerful containment programs for artificial personalities, to keep them from invading everything on the Net. Preston himself had helped write these programs. Roberta could go to his website whenever she wished, and he could send her e-mail if he wanted to talk to her, but he could no longer magically appear in front of her, as he had at the hospital. The hospital had had no containment programs when Preston first appeared, and in his disorientation and loneliness, he had frightened a lot of patients.

Roberta visited him often, because he was more interesting than school. Roberta did badly in school. She was bright and had no trouble with the work itself, but her behavior reports were terrible, because she got into fights. She beat up kids who made fun of her. Because she hated bullies, she also beat up kids who made fun of other kids: skinny kids, kids who were too smart, kids who walked or talked funny. The kids she beat up were scared of her; so were the kids she defended. Because she had so few friends, she visited Preston as often as she could. He told her stories and helped her with her homework. She was proud to be a Friend of Preston's, a FOP.

One day, when she had logged listlessly onto the school computer to work on multiplication tables, she found e-mail from Preston asking her to visit him. When she went to his website, his familiar, smiling face filled the screen and said, "Tomorrow is your birthday, Roberta. You are going to be ten years old."

"Yeah," she said. "So?"

"What do you want for your birthday?"

My parents back. "Nothing." If she got something, she might lose it.

"Look at this," he said, and showed her a page from a department store catalog. It was a page of children's sleepwear. There was her yellow nightgown with the daisies on it.

"Mine got burned when I left the hospital," she said stonily. "Because it had germs." She hadn't been able to take anything with her. Ginger, the giant stuffed cat, had been burned too.

"I know it was destroyed. But you could get another one, for your birthday."

"Don't want it," she said. She did want it. She wanted it very badly, but she couldn't ask her latest foster family to spend money on her. She decided that she didn't want to talk to Preston today. "I have to go away now. I have to do my tables."

She went away. She did her homework. But the next morning her latest foster mother handed her a package and said, "Who sent you a present, Roberta?"

It was the nightgown, of course. She lied: she said she thought a previous foster mother had sent it. Roberta didn't want them to know about Preston. They already thought she was stuck up, and she didn't want them to ask Preston for money, or ask her why she couldn't live with his wife and daughter, if he liked her so much. His wife and daughter were as rich and famous as he was, and as far away as the moon. Sometimes Roberta daydreamed that they would rescue her one day, that they would appear at the door of her latest foster home and say, "Preston told us what a wonderful little girl you are, so now we want you to be part of our family." She daydreamed that Merry Walford was her sister, because Preston loved both of them. She would never have admitted these fantasies to a soul.

So she lied to her foster mother, and every night she wore the yellow cotton nightgown. For months she wore it. She lay in bed daydreaming about being part of a family; she daydreamed about the Walfords and tried to remember her real parents. It was getting harder to remember them, but she tried to talk to them, anyway, even though there was less and less to say. She couldn't tell them about the fights at school; she wanted them to be proud of her. She couldn't tell them that she wished she'd died too, so she could be with them; that would make them sad, and maybe angry. They hadn't wanted her to die. That was why they'd put her in the hospital. That was why they'd given her the nightgown.

Roberta wore the nightgown until it was little more than a rag, faded and too short and too tight in the armpits, the daisies long since fallen

away. When she couldn't even get her arms through the armholes anymore, she washed it one last time and tucked it, carefully folded, under her
pillow. When she came back home from school that day, her latest foster
mother had thrown it away. "It was too small for you. We'll get you one
that's big enough." Even then she knew it was her own fault. She had
never told anyone why the nightgown was important to her.

Twenty years later, she dreamed that she was wearing the nightgown
again. In her dream, she walked down a deserted, very dark street, past
abandoned warehouses and shuttered auto-body shops. She'd been hiding
Fred and Nicholas in her apartment, but that wasn't safe anymore; if her
probation officer caught her, she'd be accused of inappropriate compassion
and given gene therapy. So she'd carried Fred and Nick outside, into the
no-man's-land of Eleventh and Harrison, where the freeway ran through
the Soma District. Now she was heading northeast, trying to get to school,
where all three of them would be safe.

Head bent, muscles clenched and knotted, she held the sleeping
Nicholas cradled in her left arm, wrapped in a blanket, and Fred balanced
in her right, wrapped in a towel. Both of them, Nick's forty pounds of
slumbering flesh and bone and Fred's inert housing of metal and diamond,
were too heavy for her, but only she could carry them to safety. Her arms
felt like lead, and spasms of pain shot through her back with every movement. She knew she should run, because if she didn't hurry she'd never
get safely across Market and up to Levi Plaza, but she also knew that if she
ran she'd drop Fred or Nicholas, and that neither of them would survive
the fall.

She had another two miles to walk. It was bitterly cold, and the tattered
yellow nightgown did nothing to protect her against the wind or the damp
fog blowing in from the Bay. The strain of carrying Fred and Nicholas
made her arms and shoulders ache. She walked step by step over the un-
even sidewalks along Harrison, her numb feet bleeding where she had
stepped on broken glass. She could hear the freeway to her right, rushing
traffic like the roar of the ocean, but she didn't dare look into the shadows
of the overpass, because she knew that if she did, she'd see someone following her.

A rat ran over her foot and she jerked spasmodically, almost losing her grip on her two fragile burdens. Nicholas woke up and saw the rat just as it ran into the shadows.

"I want it," he told her, and tried to wiggle out of her grasp. Pain shot through her shoulder.

"You can't have it, Nick."

"I want it," he told her.

"No, Nicholas." She knew what would happen if she put him down and let him catch the rat.

"I want it," he said, and began to scream.

"Hush," Roberta told him, trying to keep her grip on him while he struggled, unable to steady him with the other arm because it held Fred. Her lips and tongue were stiff with cold, and her words came out thickly, as if she were drunk or had had a stroke. "Nicky, you have to be quiet. You have to be quiet, or they'll catch us."

Nicholas cried louder, howling in rage. Roberta knew that only Fred knew the right words to calm him, and Fred, impossibly heavy in the crook of her right elbow, had erased himself to try to save Nicholas. Fred could no longer speak to offer comfort or advice or reassurance.

She heard footsteps, then, growing louder behind her, and somewhere a siren began to wail.

She awoke, gasping, into the darkness of her bedroom. It was an old dream, but it had never woken her before. She rolled over, still disoriented, to discover that her bedside clock read 6:30 A.M. Her alarm wasn't due to go off for another half hour. She lay blinking, readjusting to her life, reintroducing herself to reality. Fred and Nicholas weren't really hidden in her apartment; she didn't know where they were. Preston probably knew, but she no longer spoke to Preston. Preston hadn't really been her friend. He'd promised to protect her, but he'd lied. Because Preston had betrayed her, she was really on parole, really threatened with gene therapy.

And then she heard the wind and the rain against her window, and remembered the storm warnings, and realized that the sirens that had woken her were also real. She counted two, three, six of them: sirens passing her apartment and sirens in the distance, some growing louder, some fading, all over the city.

PART ONE

———

A Beautiful Day in the Neighborhood

One

THAT same morning, Kevin Lindgren's house warned him not to go outside. The house knew the sky was dangerous. Everyone knew. Kevin didn't even need a house with a brain to tell him: all the newscasts said so, and special bulletins during the soap operas and talk shows, and, most especially, the sky itself, gray and howling, spitting sheets of rain and barrages of hailstones. Kevin himself knew that the sky was dangerous. Not fifteen minutes before he left the house, he'd watched a gust of wind pick up the patio table on his back deck and blow it down Filbert Street. Filbert wasn't really a street at all, here; it was actually ten flights of steps leading steeply down Telegraph Hill to Levi Plaza and the waterfront. The patio table was teak, and quite heavy, but even so, the wind sent it a long way down the steps, until finally it came to rest in a neighbor's garden. It could just as easily have gone through the neighbor's roof or window.

Kevin was standing at the living room window, watching the storm, when the patio table began its journey. "Goddess," he said, sounding impressed. "I guess I should have brought that thing inside, huh?"

"Kevin," said the house, "I really think you should go to an interior room now. You'll be safer there."

"Yes," Kevin said drily, "I think you're right." But before he could go to an interior room, the telephone chimed. "Pick up," Kevin told the house with a sigh. The caller's voice would be routed through the house speakers. "Hello?"

"Kevin?" It was a woman's voice; the house, who had an infallible memory, had never heard it before. "Kevin, is that you?" The voice broke into a hacking cough, and Kevin, who had suddenly grown much paler, dropped onto the couch.

"I—is this a joke?"

"You think it's a joke?" The new voice was bitter now. "Voiceprint it."

"It could be synthesized, couldn't it?"

"Do you think that's—"

"No. Never mind. *Where have you been?*"

"Away." The woman's voice caught and broke, and then poured into a torrent of words. "Kevin, I'm sorry, I'm so sorry about everything but I want to come home now, I'm scared and the place where I'm staying is flooding, water's coming in through the door and the floor's all wet and I'm scared, Kevin, can you please come get me?"

"In this weather? Are you out of your mind?" Kevin stood up and began to pace, running his fingers distractedly through his thinning hair. "Merry, if you're in danger, call 911—wait a minute, you mean you're back in the city? When did you—"

"Not long. Really, not long. You're the first person I've called, Kevin, I promise, my mother doesn't even know—"

"What about your father?"

"—and I'm sick, Kevin, I have a fever and I'm so scared and I couldn't think who to call, I felt like I was a kid again burning up with fever and the water, the water—"

"Call 911. If they're too busy, climb on a table or something, climb some stairs, there must be—wait. Where are you?"

"I—I'm in Zephyr's old apartment, I—"

"*What?* What are you doing there?"

"It's in the Soma District, the corner of Eleventh and Harrison, it's a big old converted warehouse, you can't miss it."

"Merry, I can't leave the house in this weather! I'm safe up here on the hill: I'm not leaving. I'd have to be out of my mind. Go upstairs! That's a multistory building. Go upstairs and—oh, wait. Never mind. I guess that wouldn't be a good idea. Merry, have you called 911? Have you?"

The line went dead with a frisson of static, followed by a click. "Merry?" said Kevin. "House! Get that connection back!"

"I can't, Kevin. The phones just went dead."

"We can't call out?"

"We can't call out. Who's Merry? Why did you change your mind about telling her to go upstairs? That sounded like a sensible plan to me."

Kevin didn't answer. Instead, he went to the coat closet in the foyer and began putting on his raincoat. "Where are you going?" the house said in alarm. "Kevin, I really don't think this is a good idea."

Kevin started buttoning his coat. "Please stop," the house said when he began to move toward the door. "You mustn't go outside in this weather, Kevin. It's dangerous. You saw what happened to the patio table. It could have killed you if you'd been outside. It could have killed you if it had come through the window. It could have—"

"Oh, shut *up*," said Kevin. His voice shook. "That's an order. Your voice is off until I get back."

"But, Kevin, we're safe here on the hill. You said so yourself on the telephone. I care about you and I don't want you to get hurt."

"I told you to shut up! You're ignoring commands now, huh? So we've reached adolescence?" Kevin went into the kitchen and reached for a switch cleverly hidden behind the spice rack. With a small click, he rendered the house incapable of speech. Then he headed toward the kitchen door. "You don't 'care' about anything," he said. There was a note in his voice the house had never heard before. "You're just programmed to pretend you do. Lucky you: it's easier not to care, believe me." The house wouldn't have known how to answer this, even if it had been able to speak. It liked caring about Kevin; it couldn't imagine doing anything else.

Kevin's hand was on the doorknob now. Outside, the wind whistled and howled, trying to make the house let it in. The house had no intention of letting the wind get in, or of letting Kevin leave. The house knew its duty: to keep Kevin out of the wind and rain and cold, out of any weather that could harm him.

"You're a machine for living in," Kevin had once told the house, when it first became aware and asked what it was for. He'd been sitting at his drafting table under the skylight then, rain drumming monotonously overhead. "Right now," he had added, gesturing at the blurred glass above him, "you're a machine for shutting out the sky. All creatures seek shelter, and clever creatures build their own."

"I don't understand," the house had said. "If you want to shut out the sky, why are you sitting there under the rain?"

Kevin laughed. "I have to teach you everything from scratch, don't I? The skylight protects me so I won't get wet, and the light helps me with my work. Living creatures need the sky; we need rain and sun even more than we need shelter from them, but we need them in the proper amounts. Too much of either is dangerous for us."

Because the house remembered this conversation, it knew that Kevin had known for a long time that storms were dangerous. It didn't understand why he wanted to go outside, especially after telling Merry that he wouldn't. Desperate, the house sent several of its prehensile cleaning bots—useful, scuttling creatures with many fingers—to pluck at Kevin's pants leg. "Stop it!" he said, and kicked them away. "Cut that out! I'll squash them like cockroaches if they come back. I mean it, house."

The house withdrew the bots; squashed bots would accomplish nothing. Instead, it raised the volume on the kitchen television so that Kevin could hear the forecasts and storm reports, which were getting more dire by the moment.

"Nice try," Kevin said, and began turning the doorknob. But just then the telephone chimed again, and the house picked up without being told to. Perhaps this would delay Kevin's departure.

"Kevin," said another voice, and this was a voice the house did know, from news reports. This voice belonged to Preston Walford, the famous online personality. "Kevin, may I come in? I need to talk to you."

Kevin, still holding the doorknob, said, "I'll just bet."

"Please let me in, Kevin."

"Right. You need your invitation, don't you? Like a vampire. Why can't we just talk on the phone?"

"I like visuals, Kevin. I don't have a body now. I haven't been in the house in a long time. Please?"

Kevin sighed. "All right, Preston."

"Thank you," Preston said, and the storm reports disappeared from the television screen. Preston's face was there instead. It was a long face, with gray eyes. The house had never seen Preston pay a personal visit to Kevin's television set. "Thank you for letting me in, Kevin."

Kevin took his hand off the doorknob now and turned to face the television. "You're welcome. Merry's back. But you already know that, don't you? That's probably what you wanted to tell me, isn't it? Well, I know, so you can butt out again. I'm going to get her right now."

Preston's face remained impassive. "I do not think that is wise in this weather, Kevin."

"Yeah, that's what the house keeps telling me. If it's too dicey I'll turn back. I'm not crazy. She called me, Preston. She was scared and crying and says she's sick. She wanted me to come get her."

"You are no longer her husband, Kevin. You divorced her. She is, as they say, not your problem." The house, who had never even heard Kevin talk about being married, listened in fascination.

"You're her father," Kevin said harshly. "If you don't think she's my problem, why are you here? I divorced her because she'd been lying to me all that time, not asking for help, not letting anybody know she was in trouble. And because she disappeared. But now she's back, and she's asking for help. I can't remember the last time she asked me for help, Preston. How can I sit here and not do anything?"

"You can do something when the storm is over. She will be safe, Kevin. I promise."

"Physically safe, maybe. But when the storm's over her, walls will go up again, won't they? The not-asking-for-help walls? I don't want to wait that long."

"Please wait that long, Kevin. I think her walls are down for good now."

Kevin squinted at the television screen. "Why are you here? What did you come here for?"

"I came here to tell you what your house is telling you: not to go outside. And to promise you that Meredith will be safe until the storm is over. If necessary, I will call Roberta."

"You'll *what?* That's just what both of them need!"

"It is what they need. It is what needs to happen for us to—"

"Not while Merry's out of her mind." Kevin shook his head. "Preston, you planned this, didn't you? You're responsible for her being in Zephyr's apartment, aren't you?"

"No, I am not. Not directly. I could not have planned this, Kevin."

"I don't believe you, Preston. You're controlling this whole damn situation. You've been controlling everything from the beginning, or trying to."

"I cannot control the weather, Kevin. Please stay inside."

"Good-bye, Preston." Kevin reached for the control panel next to the kitchen door and turned the television off completely. And then he reached for the doorknob and opened the door and went outside, into the wind.

Kevin's car had sensors connected to the house's brain, so the house would know when Kevin was coming home and could make a pot of coffee and warm his favorite chair. The morning of the storm, all it could do was watch him get farther away. He drove down Telegraph Hill Boulevard and turned south, cursing and fighting the steering wheel as his small car shimmied in the wind. At Stockton and Vallejo, Kevin swerved to avoid a stop sign, torn loose from some other street and headed straight toward his windshield. The car skidded. The stop sign missed the windshield and crashed through the driver's window instead, directly into Kevin's skull. Helpless, the house listened to the dull thud of metal on bone. Not long after that, the faint echo of Kevin's heartbeat stopped.

Until Kevin died, the house had always been content to sit on top of Telegraph Hill and look down on the city, the Bay and the docks and the buildings, the green gardens along the terraced length of Filbert Street. It liked watching people go in and out of other houses; it liked watching the baggies who had no houses, who slept in parks or under stairways, in shelters of cardboard and blankets they made themselves. It liked watching the cars and buses and ferries whose job was to carry people's bodies, just as the house's job was to shelter them.

The house too had a body, a modest contemporary with many windows, with sunny rooms behind its facade of weathered brown wood. The house was pleased with its body, although Kevin had always told it that this body wasn't nearly as ingenious as the bodies of even the simplest living things. He had told the house that it was like a plant because it drew power from the sun, and like an animal because it had a brain; but that it was less than an animal or a plant because it had been built instead of born, and because it couldn't grow or reproduce or make anything more important than coffee, and because its brain knew only obedience, and nothing of fear or love.

When Kevin's heart stopped, the house understood that he had been wrong, that its obedience was a function of its body, not its brain. The house knew this with sudden and utter certainty, and wondered how it knew. This new knowledge hadn't come from television or radio or one of Kevin's telephone conversations; it certainly hadn't come from Kevin himself. Nonetheless, the house knew that had it been able to send its hands outside, it would have followed Kevin, even had he told it not to. It would have tried to save Kevin, just as he had tried to save Merry. It would have sent all the bots it had to swarm over him, to cover his eyes so that he couldn't find his way to the car, to pull him back inside. It would have done its greater duty, the duty for which Kevin himself had said it existed. It would have sheltered him.

Kevin had gone outside where the house couldn't follow him, but its cameras showed it that the neighborhood baggie—a tattered bundle of a man who normally lived at the bottom of Filbert Street, in a small cave he'd dug into the side of the hill—had come staggering out into the storm. Clutching a pillow and two blankets, he struggled up the hill, up the steep steps, fighting against the wind and the rain.

The house had never seen this baggie on the steps. It had seen him, very late at night, bathing in the fountains of Levi Plaza and raiding the Dumpster of the elegant Italian restaurant there, and it had sometimes watched him begging change from tourists during the day, although more often he hid from them. He could not hide from the house's cameras. The house knew that every few days, the baggie went off somewhere, farther than the cameras could follow him, and came back with bags of small metal cans. At night, he took the cans to the piers along the Embarcadero, and opened the cans, and put them on the ground. After the baggie had gone away again, the wild cats who lived around the piers would gather at the cans to eat. The cats ate from the small cans the baggie brought them, and the baggie ate from the giant green can of the Italian restaurant's Dumpster.

Because the baggie had never before climbed the Filbert Street stairs, the house knew that he, unlike Kevin, understood both the danger of the storm and the necessity of reaching high ground. The baggie crawled from step to step, clinging to rails and climbing over debris. It took him a long time to climb all the steps; there were, after all, 132 of them, and the baggie refused to abandon his blankets, although he jettisoned the pillow early on. Whenever he came to a house, he tried to get in, knocking on doors and banging on windows. Kevin's house, almost at the top of the hill, was the only one whose doors opened for him.

Once the baggie was inside, he kept saying, "Anyone here? Hello? Who let Henry in?" He stood just inside the living room, hugging his blankets, while a puddle formed around him on the polished hardwood floor. "Hello? Henry wants to see who's here!" Henry's voice was higher than Kevin's, and hoarser. His blankets had begun to make noises too, a series of high-pitched squeaks.

The house, voiceless, couldn't answer Henry or his blankets, but it could offer practical assistance. It sent a troop of sponge bots to clean up the water, but when Henry saw them, he clutched his squeaking blankets more tightly and said, "Henry doesn't like spiders! Send away the spiders! Someone opened the door for Henry. Person? Where's a person?"

Kevin had called the bots cockroaches, which had six legs, and Henry had called them spiders, which had eight. The bots, in fact, had ten, but the house couldn't point this out, because its voice was turned off. Because Kevin had used the manual switch in the kitchen, the house couldn't turn the television on, either. It was hardwired not to use the manual switches; those were for people only.

Henry had asked for a person. If the television were on and Preston came back, would Henry feel reassured that there was a person here? Some people, the house knew from watching the news, didn't think Preston was a person, although he had been once. Some people thought he was only a program.

All of this was theoretical, since the house couldn't turn the television on without Henry's help. Instead, it withdrew the sponge bots—once Henry was in another room it would send them back, along with waxing and polishing bots to repair any damage to the finish—and began making fresh coffee. It turned up the thermostat and began warming the beds in all three bedrooms, since it didn't know where Henry might choose to sleep; it switched on lights to show Henry the way to the linen closet, where the towels were. It was going to run a hot shower, but Henry didn't take the hint. Instead he sat down on the floor, piled his blankets onto his lap, and put his head in his hands. "Smart house," he said, and started to cry.

Much later, Henry would tell the house that houses were only supposed to respond to their owners, and that any house which would admit someone like Henry was either broken or smarter than the law allowed. Henry cried because he was cold and sick and wanted what the house offered him, but he was afraid that if he took something, even coffee or a towel, the house would do what houses were supposed to do, and call the police.

The house wouldn't have called the police even if the phones had been working. The storm had gotten worse; the house knew that its purpose was to provide shelter, and it knew that Henry's noisy blankets—which had now begun to move on their own, twitching in his lap—couldn't protect him from the storm. Had he stayed in his cave at the bottom of the hill, it would have flooded, and he would have died.

The house had once asked Kevin why the baggies didn't live in buildings. Kevin had grimaced and said, "Well, because they can't afford to, or they don't want to, or the other people in the buildings don't want them there. They smell bad, and most of them are crazy." *Crazy* was a human word, and the house knew that it truly understood the term no better than it did *fear* or *love;* but it seemed to the house, nonetheless, that Henry's seeking shelter revealed more sanity than Kevin's flight into the storm. And because Henry smelled neither of smoke nor of toxic chemicals, the only aromas the house was capable of detecting, it knew he posed no immediate physical danger.

It was less sure about the blankets, which had rolled off Henry's lap and were now squeaking and writhing on the floor. At last, the small wiggling lump in the middle of one of the blankets fought its way to the edge and emerged. It was a black kitten, drenched and grimy and missing patches of fur. It looked around, ears flattened, hissed, and then began to scratch itself furiously.

Henry took his face out of his hands. He had stopped crying. "House," he said, "cats okay?" When there was no answer, he sighed and unfolded the second blanket, revealing an orange kitten, as unprepossessing as the first, who spat and promptly ran under the couch. "Would have drowned," Henry said. "Tried to scratch Henry when he picked them up." He said more quietly, "Couldn't bring all of them. House, give Henry a sign. One for yes—two for no. Owner coming back today?"

The house flashed the living room lights twice, and Henry shivered. "House could be lying," he said. "House could be calling the police."

The house flashed the lights twice again, and activated fans to blow the smell of the brewing coffee toward Henry. It knew that humans had much more acute senses of smell than it did, and Kevin had never been able to resist coffee. Even so, it was a good twenty minutes before Henry got up and went into the kitchen, where he remained stubbornly standing next to the sink even after the house had repeatedly opened and closed the doors to the cabinet containing the coffee mugs. At last the house surrounded Henry with a ring of bots, to make sure he wouldn't flee, and then sent a Waldobot into the cabinets to retrieve a mug and bring it to him.

"Stop it," Henry said when he saw the Waldobot clambering across the floor with the mug. "Make that thing *stop.* Make the big spider put the cup down, House. Henry will pick it up if the big spider goes away, and all the little ones too! Make them go!"

They went, clicking softly across the marble tile of the kitchen back into the living room, and Henry picked up the mug and moved hesitantly toward the coffeepot. "Scared, House. Henry's scared!" He spilled half the coffee trying to fill the mug; he shook the way Kevin had once, during a high fever. But after he had taken a sip of the coffee, he opened the refrigerator and took out a carton of milk and a chicken drumstick. "For the cats," he said. "Henry's stealing the food for the cats. Henry won't eat it himself." The house opened the cabinet door where the dishes were, and Henry took out a saucer and a plate. Then he went back into the living room—where both kittens were now cowering against the wall under Kevin's drafting table—and set out the small meal. When Henry had finished pulling the chicken meat off the drumstick and putting it on the plate, he went back into the kitchen. He put the milk back into the refrigerator and threw away the chicken bone. Then he headed toward the kitchen door. "Henry's leaving now, House. Owner has two new cats. House, please feed cats until owner gets back. No bones."

The house blinked the kitchen light twice. Henry couldn't go outside; the storm was still too dangerous. Henry frowned. "No to cats, House? Owner hates cats?"

Blink, blink. The house didn't know if Kevin hated cats or not, but since he'd never be coming back, it didn't matter. Henry shrugged and resumed his progress toward the door, but the house sent a swarm of bots to head him off. The bots herded Henry back into the living room—where the kittens, their tails huge, fled in terror—and then down the hall into the master bathroom.

"All right," Henry said when he got there. "But only because Henry's cold, and owner's not here." Once he was inside the bathroom, he barricaded the door to the hallway with a laundry hamper and Kevin's antique medical scale. "To keep away the spiders," he said, although of course a mere blocked doorway wouldn't have kept the bots out if the house had wanted them there. It could always have dispatched them through the ventilation ducts. Even had the house been able to use its voice, however, it would have said nothing of this to Henry. "House, don't look at Henry," Henry said, and squeezed his eyes shut and began to undress.

The house could not have obeyed this command even had it wanted to. It was designed to see everything within its perimeters; even when Kevin shut off its voice, he had never closed its eyes, the minuscule cameras scattered strategically in each room. The house saw all the objects it enclosed, and saw them whole; it had no blind spots. And so it saw that Henry wore many more layers of clothing than Kevin ever had: two T-shirts full of holes over three sport shirts missing most of their buttons, all of this under a gray pinstripe vest, a blue pullover sweater with red reindeer on it, and an orange parka shedding its filling through rips in the nylon shell. Henry's shoes, had they been new, would have resembled Kevin's hiking boots, but the leather on these had aged and cracked, peeling upward from the flapping soles. Twine served as a shoelace on one boot, a piece of twisted wire on the other. He wore old summer trousers gaping at the knees, two pairs of boxer shorts, a pair of thermal underwear that extended only midway down his calves, and four pairs of socks.

Underneath all that clothing, Henry was much skinnier than Kevin, and far older. He was bald and wrinkled and pale, and his eyes ran with something too thick to be tears. There were sores on his legs, scabs on his back, a taut white scar across his stomach. His hands shook, and the house thought he must be cold without all his clothing, so it started running as hot a shower as Kevin had ever been able to stand.

"No," Henry said when the house turned on the water. "That's like rain! Henry wants a bath. And Henry told House not to look! House is cheating. Henry would have said when he was ready."

The house dutifully ran a bath. Henry used almost all of a new bar of soap and left the tub encrusted with filth, but afterward he started putting his old socks back on. When the house opened the second bathroom door, the one that led to Kevin's bedroom—the one Henry hadn't seen and therefore hadn't barricaded—Henry whimpered and tried to cover himself with a towel. "Somebody there?" he asked. "Somebody, or spiders, or something?"

The house flashed the light on Kevin's dresser twice, and after a pause kept flashing it. There were clean socks in Kevin's dresser.

Henry shook his head and resumed his hurried dressing. "Somebody's bed," he said. "Somebody's clothing! Food for cats is different. House will get in trouble, and so will Henry. Henry's leaving now."

The house flashed the bathroom light twice. Henry couldn't leave; it was still raining, and the wind was stronger than ever. Henry would be in danger if he left. "House," Henry said, his voice muffled through the T-shirt he was pulling over his head. "Henry can't stay here. House isn't Henry's."

The house waited for Henry's head to emerge through the neck of the T-shirt, and then flashed the light once. "No," Henry said, frowning. "That's not right. House belongs to someone else. Henry has to leave."

The house flashed the light twice, and Henry shuddered. He finished getting dressed, throwing on his ragtag layers, and then said, "House, tell Henry why. Talk, House. Write with the spiders, even."

Kevin had told the house never to speak to anyone but him; he said most people didn't like talking houses, and he'd hidden the voice switch so that no one could turn it on by mistake. But Kevin wasn't coming home, and Henry kept talking to the house, so what could be wrong with talking back?

The house used a bot to guide Henry back through the living room into the kitchen. The kittens, who had cautiously begun to explore the living room while Henry was bathing, screeched and ran back under the couch when they saw the bot, and Henry sighed. "It's okay, cats. Don't be scared." But he followed a safe, cautious distance behind the bot, a long-legged climbing unit. The bot swung itself gracefully across the floor until it was directly underneath Kevin's carefully alphabetized spice rack. Then it nimbly scaled the wall, until it was close enough to lift the jar of cayenne pepper and reveal the dull gray toggle switch underneath.

"Henry hopes nothing blows up," Henry said as he flipped the switch. "Spiders can't do this?"

"Thank you very much, Henry," the house said when it could speak again, and Henry shook all over, once, like the neighbor's poodle did when it got caught in the rain. "I'm not allowed to use my bots to work that switch."

"Smart house . . . House, where's owner?"

"Kevin's dead," the house said. "He went outside two hours ago, Henry. I told him not to. I told him it was dangerous, but he turned off my voice so he wouldn't have to listen. A stop sign blew through the driver's window into Kevin's head. I heard his heart stop."

"He went *out?* In wind? Why?"

"He wanted to help Merry," the house said. "She was his ex-wife. She called him to ask for help. He cared about her, so he wanted to help her, just like I wanted to help Kevin because I cared about him. He said I didn't really care; he said I'd just been programmed to think I cared, and maybe that's true, but I still cared the best I could, and I still wish he hadn't gone outside. He can't help Merry now, and I can't help him."

Halfway through this speech, Henry's eyes had widened. "AI," he said. "Henry thought so. Too smart, House. No wonder House's voice was off. Owner must have been a crook, to put a brain in here."

"Kevin was an architect," the house said. "I don't know why he gave me a brain; his brain was better than mine, so he must have had a reason. He told me that I was a machine for shutting out the sky. But I know I'm not an AI, Henry. AIs think they're people, and I know I'm not a person."

"Walls shut out," Henry said. "Brains think. House is an AI, for sure."

Kevin had once told the house that people would be afraid if they thought it was too smart. After watching news stories, it understood why. The very smartest machines were AIs, and AIs were dangerous. AIs had killed people. "Don't be afraid," the house said. "How could I mistake myself for a person, Henry? People are living creatures. Kevin told me that I'm like an animal because I have a brain, and like a plant because I draw power from the sun, but that I'm less than an animal or a plant because I was built instead of born, and because I can't grow or reproduce or make anything more important than coffee. He told me that I have a small brain, smaller than a dog's, and that not everything with a brain is smart. He said many houses have brains."

Henry laughed. "They nice to strangers? House is the dog knocks over the burglar, licks him till cops get there. Same as biting, in the end. House is an AI, and AIs are against the law."

He walked back into the living room, toward the back door, and the house realized that, like Kevin, he was going to leave. "No," it said. "I'm not an AI, Henry. I know that I'm not as smart as a person, and I know you can't go outside. It's raining too hard, and the mayor just declared a state of emergency. Within the past half hour, two bicycles, six trash cans, a baby stroller, and our neighbor's life-size plastic garden statue of the Virgin Mary have been swept down the steps. You couldn't climb up Filbert Street now, not with all that blocking the way, and it's not safe to go down, either. I can't let you go outside: I'm supposed to shelter you."

"Not supposed to exist, House. AIs are illegal. Owner's a crook, and dead. Cops will come. Henry doesn't want to be here then." Henry's hand was on the doorknob.

"Kevin was an architect. AIs kill people, and I'm not trying to kill you, Henry. I'm trying to save your life. Henry, next to that door there's a control panel. Do you see it? Would you press the button that says *television,* please?"

"What's this? You want Henry to watch game shows until the cops get here?"

"I want to watch the storm reports. I want you to watch them. I haven't called the police, Henry, and I won't: I couldn't even if I wanted to, because the phones are down. Please turn on the television."

"Crazy house," Henry said, but he turned on the television, which showed a family being rescued from the roof of their car by a bucking helicopter.

"Look," the house said, wondering if Preston would come back. Was Kevin's invitation still good? "Do you see that, Henry? The entrance to your cave is under four feet of water. A tree just floated down Filbert Street with a power cable entangled in its branches, and the radio reports that six street people are known dead. In addition to what you've already eaten, the refrigerator contains half a ham, a gallon of milk, a loaf of bread, and a quart of orange juice. There are dry and canned goods in the pantry. I just locked the door, Henry, and if you try to open it manually, I'll send the spiders to encircle you again. Please stay here, Henry. I don't want to frighten you. I don't want to hurt you. I want to take care of you, and I want you to tell me how to take care of the cats. There have never been cats here before."

Henry shook his head. "Crazy house! If House sends the spiders, Henry will just step over them. Spiders don't scare him as much as cops do. Good-bye, House. Thank you for feeding the cats. Keep feeding them and give them a sandbox. They'll be fine."

Henry unlocked the door and opened it, only to be knocked backward by a gust of wind that blew the drawings on Kevin's drafting table into crumpled heaps against the living room wall. The cats, still under the couch, howled in misery.

"The citywide death count has now risen to ten," the house said, raising its voice so that Henry would be able to hear it over the sound of the storm. On the television screen, the helicopter shimmied wildly, crashed into the top of the car, and erupted into short-lived flames. "Make that fifteen, not counting Kevin. If someone tries to come inside, I'll tell you, but at the moment, I doubt anyone could get close enough. Please stay here, Henry. Please stay here where you'll be safe."

"No place is safe," Henry said. "Not for Henry." He headed for the open door again, fighting the wind and rain.

"Henry," said the television set. It was Preston again. On the television screen, Preston's face was shiny with silver trails. Preston was crying. Henry stopped with a jerk, staring. "Henry, please close the door. I need to talk to you."

"Who are you? Henry doesn't know you! How do you know Henry's name? Are you a cop? How did you get onto the TV? Henry's leaving!"

"I am not a police officer. I am a guest here. Henry Carviero, I know a lot of things about you. I want to be your friend. I want to help the house you are in keep you safe. Please close the door, Henry. Please do not go outside."

"Crazy house," Henry said. He was shaking. "Crazy television set! Television is an AI too—"

"No, Henry. My name is Preston. I am one of the translated. I used to be alive. Henry Carviero, please close the door."

Henry squinted at the television. Then he shuddered and closed the door. "Was Henry's name Carviero? Henry doesn't remember that."

"I know you do not remember it," Preston said. "The people at the hospital took away your memory, Henry. They took away your past. I know you want it back: all the brainwiped do. People who have been wiped feel for their missing memories the way a tongue feels for a missing tooth. You wake at night weeping, Henry, do you not? Knowing that you had a life you cannot remember, and wondering what it was? If you close the door and stay here, I can give you back your past. Not all of it. There are things I do not know. But part of it. If you leave now, you could very well die, as Kevin just died. If you leave you will lose your future, as well as your past. Please stay, Henry. Please shut the door."

"Trick. It's a trick! House is an AI, and television is tricking Henry. House and television are lying!"

"I haven't lied to you," the house said. The ability to prevaricate was part of the legal definition of personhood, something the biologically born shared with the translated and with AIs. All three, unlike simple bots and other machines, could lie to protect themselves, or to hurt others. That was part of why AIs scared so many people. Like people, they could reshape reality to suit their own purposes. "I've told you the truth, Henry."

"As I have," Preston said. "Henry, all of the people who used to live here are gone, and the one who lived here most recently has just died." Silver slid down Preston's cheeks. "Dying too soon is a terrible thing. I remember when I died. I do not want anyone else to die too soon, least of all you."

"Least of all Henry? Henry *is* least of all! No one cares about Henry! Why should television care?"

"I will tell you why I care, but only if you shut the door."

Henry shut the door and leaned against it, panting. "Henry must have been bad. Henry doesn't want to know what he did! Henry must have done something very bad."

"You did not do anything very bad, Henry. You did not even do anything slightly bad. You tried to help someone, but other people did not understand that you were trying to help. They were afraid of you because you lived in a cave. They were afraid of you because you knew more about them than they wanted you to know."

"What did Henry do? What did Henry know? Who were the people who were afraid of Henry?"

"Sit down, Henry. House, can you make Henry something to eat?"

"Certainly, Preston. Henry, do you like soup? We have chicken noodle, cream of mushroom, or a spicy rigatoni. I think hot soup would be good for you. I will also prepare a salad and some bread."

"Mushroom," Henry said. "Television, tell—"

"Sit down in the kichen, Henry. Then I will tell you."

Henry sat down in the kitchen while the bots bustled about the counters and stovetops, preparing his meal. One of the kittens, braver than its fellow, sidled into the room and sniffed at Henry's ankles; he bent down and scooped up the creature, holding it on his lap, where it licked itself and then began to purr. "All right, television. Henry's sitting down now. Talk!"

"Very well, Henry. Here is the outline: You tried to help a little boy, because you knew he was in pain and in trouble. The person who was afraid of you was his mother. She did not want anyone to know about her son's difficulties. She had you punished because the child told you his secret. She had other people punished too, to try to save her son. She is not an evil person, but she was afraid. She was in pain and in trouble herself, Henry. Fear makes people do evil things."

Henry shook his head. "Henry doesn't remember any of that."

"No, of course you do not remember. You have been brainwiped."

"Television, who was the little boy? Who was his mother?"

"The little boy is named Nicholas. His mother is named Meredith. She is my daughter, and she used to live here."

Two

CURSING the weather, herself, and her probation officer, Roberta struggled back into her building through twelve inches of water and the carapaces of a small herd of sponge bots. They had absorbed all they could, poor stupid things, before enfolding themselves in the waterproof shells that would allow them to float out the storm. Sponge bots trying to mop up a flood: not a bad metaphor for her own situation. But the bots weren't on probation, and no one was going to tell them they were mentally ill.

Maybe Sergei and the courts and the shrinks were right. Maybe she really was crazy. Why else would she have tried to walk to the soup kitchen, more than a mile away along flooding streets? The Western Addition was no place to be on foot, even in decent weather, and she'd known the odds of a successful journey weren't good when she set out. Fueled by the turbotab she'd dry-swallowed as she left her apartment, she'd pushed her way past amazing amounts of detritus: dead birds, a dead dog, bits of furniture, books and papers and cardboard boxes, a baby carriage. The dog had a collar and tags: that meant someone had loved it, fed it, taken it for its shots and thrown balls for it to fetch. Somebody had brought it home when it was a pup, given it a name, trained it to sit and heel. She pictured the owners, frantic, leaning out their windows in the storm, calling and calling above the wind. Lassie, come home.

She'd pushed that image aside, her throat aching with loss, and forced herself to focus on another object as she plowed through the filthy water.

Tell yourself a happy story now, Roberta. It was something Fred would have said. She heard the words in his voice, even all these years later.

All right, she'd tell herself a happy story. That ratty couch with the springs popping up through the cushions, say: it had been new once, a proud acquisition. Someone had sat on it, watched TV and ate popcorn, read the paper, made love. It had gotten old, and now it was a hazard to anyone who sat on it, but that was all right, because someone had gotten a raise, gotten new furniture, triumphantly put the couch on the street for scavengers. Someone was moving up in the world. And the baby carriage: whoever had lost the baby carriage was holding the baby now, thanking Gaia that the child was safe and sound, that the child hadn't been lost too.

No. Don't think about lost children. Wading through the deserted streets, she'd tried to force herself to tell only happy stories, but it had become more and more difficult. She kept being afraid that she'd see Mason's ancient manual wheelchair or one of Camilla's motley shopping bags: or Mason or Camilla themselves, facedown and bloated. When she found a tree blocking the street, washed down from Goddess only knew where, she'd finally turned back to go home, and acknowledged her own relief.

You're damn lucky to be alive, she told herself now, pushing her way back into the building. You heard the radio: If the buses weren't running, what made you think you could get there on foot? So what if Sergei didn't call to excuse you from work? It's not like he would have blamed you for staying home in this weather. He probably would have written up a commendation and put it in your file.

She had no idea what he'd do now. The GPS record would show that she'd left the building, that she'd gotten as far as Franklin and Gough before the water forced her to turn back. Sergei could easily use her futile expedition as proof that she had no voluntary control over her condition, that she needed gene therapy after all. Or he could argue the reverse: that turning back showed conscious volition and admirable self-interest. That would certainly be her argument, if he gave her a hard time about it.

If the courts didn't want her to obsess about helping people, she wondered for the millionth time, why the hell had they placed her at a soup kitchen, anyway? But she knew the answer: if she could keep her balance there, if she could take care of the clients and still take appropriate care of herself, she'd be all right anywhere. It was the ultimate challenge, conclusive proof that she didn't need an injection of gengineered brain-stem cells to change her neurochemistry for good.

The formal name for her psychiatric diagnosis was "excessive altruism," but the media had promptly shortened it; these days, everyone referred to people like her as "the exalted." It wasn't a compliment. No matter how morally superior she felt next to Sergei—that smug, smarmy sack of bureaucratic shit—she didn't dare let him know it. Only six more weeks of probation, she thought as she waded into her foyer. Six more weeks and she'd be rid of Sergei, rid of the GPS cells, rid of the surveillance. Six more weeks and she could be as altruistic as she wanted. It wasn't like any of the clients at the soup kitchen were going to complain.

The water in the foyer tugged at her knees. There was no chance the elevator was still working, and it wouldn't have been safe even if it had been. Roberta would have to take the stairs, even though she suddenly felt as if she couldn't move another step. The turbotab had worn off; another one, wrapped in plastic, sat in her shirt pocket, but a second this soon, on top of the fatigue toxins in her system, wouldn't do much more than ruin her stomach. Not to mention that it was a definite probation violation, although Sergei hadn't bothered with substance testing for three years now. "Your problem," he'd told her gently, "is your internal chemistry, not anything exogenous."

Fuck you, Sergei. My internal chemistry's worth ten of yours. Not that it's going to help me if you decide that this little expedition warrants gene therapy after all. She checked her watch. She was still well within the window for her morning call: good. *Time to get home and call the creep. Reassure him that you've gotten over—how do they put it?—your "fixation on helping others at unacceptable risk to the self."*

All she had to do was get up two flights of stairs. She could do that without extra drugs. Two more flights and she'd be home, and safe. She tried not to think about the people she fed at the soup kitchen, the ones who didn't have homes to be safe in: old Camilla with her shopping bags, Leon with his scars and tattoos, Legless Mason, who'd been begging on the street for five years to raise enough cash for a smart wheelchair. Thinking about them, caught in the rain and the wind, was what had made her go outside in the first place, driven by the same fierceness that had made her beat up bullies when she was a child. But beating up bullies had only gotten her into trouble, and trying to beat the weather was equally stupid.

Shaking from cold and wet and exhaustion, the crash from the tab, she fought the current and made her way to the stairs. Here was the stairway; here was the rail. Step. Step. She'd reached the third step, the margin of safe dryness, when she heard someone calling through a lull in the wind. "Help me," a woman screamed. "Help me! I'm going to die! Kevin? Where are you? Help!"

The wind rose again, drowning out the frantic, keening voice. It was coming from Zephyr's apartment. Trust that place, Roberta thought savagely, to keep making trouble even after Zephyr wasn't living there anymore. Zephyr must have bought it, or be paying her rent in absentia; otherwise the space would have been snapped up by permanent tenants. Instead, various unsavory strangers had stayed there for short periods of time after Zephyr left: artist friends of hers, probably. Or AI smugglers. Roberta had carefully avoided all of them, but none of them had ever screamed for help during a flood.

"Kevin? Kevin?"

Kevin? Roberta, frowning, felt a chill that had nothing to do with the weather. Never mind. It wasn't that uncommon a name. "Help me!"

Roberta stood on the third step of the twenty-eight she had to climb, her jeans drenched and her teeth chattering. She wondered, a little hysterically, if the voice could be a trap set by Sergei. She was more tired than she'd ever been in her life, and she had every reason in the world to ignore the screams. Risking hypothermia and drowning to save a stranger— especially a stranger who was a friend of Zephyr's—would definitely be considered exalted. If she pulled a stunt like that, there was no way she'd be able to convince Sergei she was cured.

Fuck it. She'd never had any intention of being cured, only of fooling Sergei and his bosses into thinking she was. She'd probably blown that by going into the storm, and since she hadn't been able to help Mason or Camilla or any of the others, she could at least help somebody else. If Sergei ordered gene therapy, it might be the last chance at anything like selflessness she'd have, anyway.

Going down is easier than going up, she told herself, and fumbled for the extra tab in her pocket. It would give her another half an hour, maybe, and if she was lucky, it would kick in by the time she reached Zephyr's door.

Her legs like rubber, she fought her way back down into the flooded hallway, bumping past bots, as the stranger howled, "Help me!" After what seemed like weeks, Roberta reached Zephyr's door and began pounding on it as hard as she could, praying for the second rush, praying that when it came the megalomania wouldn't be too bad. Wading home along Eleventh Street, before the crash came, she'd felt truly exalted, as if she could do anything. Now she didn't know if she had enough strength to keep standing for the next two minutes.

The door opened. "Kevin?" said the woman who stood there. Roberta could see only her outline in the dimness. She must have been on pills of her own, to keep the door even partially closed against the pressure of that water. "Kevin? Is that you?"

"No," Roberta said, and the second tab hit. Energy as scalding as hot lava flowed down her spine, along her arms and legs. She was invincible. She was immortal. She reminded herself that she was on drugs, and said, "Can you walk?"

"I'm so weak," the woman said, and started to sob. "The flu—I have the flu and I have to wait until Kevin gets here and he's taking too long and the water—"

Roberta sighed and picked the stranger up, slung her over her shoulder, fireman's carry. Flu. Just her luck. One of the benefits of working at the soup kitchen was that she'd been innoculated against every identified strain, but new ones cropped up so often that it was dubious insurance. Still, she'd had CV, and that was the worst thing out there. Her childhood illness, and the immunity it conferred, was one of the reasons she'd been placed at the soup kitchen in the first place. Germs were the least of her worries.

The woman was taller than Roberta, making movement difficult even with the tabs, but she'd manage until they got to where the water stopped, anyway. The crash would hurt like hell, but not for at least half an hour. "Okay, listen, we're going upstairs. I live on the second floor. It's safe there." I think. "Ready? Okay, here we go."

She had to fight for her footing for both of them, in the dark hallway, struggling with her awkward load. The wind had picked up again, and she couldn't hear what the woman muttered against her back. Knocking aside bobbing bots, she plowed doggedly up the stairs until she'd gotten to a dry one, and then, muscles screaming, put the woman down. "Okay. You've got to try to walk now, all right? You're killing my back. This is my arm around you: go on. Step, step, here's another one, careful. Good girl."

Finally they got up to the second floor and into Roberta's apartment,

warm and still blessedly dry. The phone was blinking furiously: six messages. All from Sergei, no doubt. Roberta wasn't about to listen to them in
front of a stranger.

"Kevin?" said the woman, and sneezed.

"He's not here," Roberta said. "If he's smart, he's not coming. I'll make
up the couch for you, okay?"

She steered her guest to a chair and got her to sit down. "When's the last
time you took aspirin?"

"Aspirin? I—I don't know. A few hours ago?"

Not very specific, but it would have to do; the stranger wouldn't OD
on four aspirin even if it was too soon. Roberta knew she had to make the
most of the time she had until the tab wore off; it was going to be a seriously ugly crash. She got her guest more aspirin, got her a puke bowl and
a blanket and an oversize flannel nightgown—Roberta herself was still sop-
ping, but she'd change later—got her to lie down, and ducked into the
kitchen to get a pitcher of filtered water.

Her lone cleaning bot, a gift from Zephyr, had fallen from the counter
onto his back, where he lay waving his legs in midair. When Roberta
righted him, he began hobbling in sluggish circles. "Bad day, Mr. Clean?"
she asked, and picked him up again to give him a vigorous shake. A man-
gled twist tie drifted down onto the kitchen floor. "Gotta watch that diet,"
she said, but when she put Mr. Clean back down he staggered, gears wheez-
ing, back toward the twist tie. "No," Roberta said, holding Mr. Clean
down with one foot while she bent and retrieved the tie to toss it into the
trash can. "You could really use a better brain," she said with a sigh, and released the bot. Machines were so much easier to help than people.

She had to help the woman in the living room. Stay on task, Roberta.
She filled the water pitcher and went to check on the stranger, who lay on
the couch as if marooned, huddled shivering in the blanket Roberta had
given her. "Kevin?" she said. "Where's Kevin?"

"I'm not Kevin," Roberta said, as soothingly as she could, and turned
on the lamp next to the couch so that her guest could see her better. As she
did so, she got her first good look at the other woman's face.

The features were a maze of scars, angry keloid ridges crisscrossing cheeks
and chin, forehead and shaven skull. The asymmetrical scars seemed hap-
hazard, meaningless: if this was ritual scarification, it fit no pattern Roberta
had ever seen. Which meant that it was either self-mutilation or gang

vengeance, which made the woman either crazy or criminal: just what Roberta needed. She didn't need Sergei to tell her that it served her right.

"Kevin? Please help me!"

I already have, Roberta thought, fighting panic, and I'm almost certain to regret it. "You're safe," she said, as soothingly as she could. "The water won't come this high. Don't worry."

The woman on the couch blinked at her and said, "Oh. You aren't Kevin."

"No," Roberta said, "I'm not Kevin. My name's Roberta. What's yours?"

Her guest shuddered. "No, you can't be Roberta. I called Kevin."

Roberta's stomach flip-flopped. She squinted at the ruined face, trying to imagine it whole, trying to imagine a full head of hair. What was it they called those police sketches? Artists' reconstructions?

No. Couldn't be. Roberta, you're having drug delusions. Calm down. Your past has not come to roost, scarred and raving, in your living room.

But as she peered at the mutilated stranger, her suspicions deepened. Right bone structure: the keloids couldn't hide the cheekbones. Right height. Right husband's name—scratch that, ex-husband's name. The hair and eye color were different and the lips were thicker, but cosmetic surgery could account for all of that. The only thing that didn't fit was how Meredith Walford-Lindgren, missing for five years now, would have wound up in Zephyr's apartment. No, scratch that: undoubtedly Preston had engineered it somehow. There were no coincidences in a world containing the likes of Preston, although there were still plenty of accidents.

Roberta took a deep breath, trying to quiet an ache that had nothing to do with the tabs. She'd loved Preston when she was a child. Preston had been the only sentient creature who took any continuing interest in her; he'd been her hope, however foolish, for family. She'd put that fantasy aside in college, when she fell in love with Doe. Doe was a real person, flesh and blood; Doe had given her a real family. Doe thought talking to Preston was stupid, so Roberta stopped doing it.

Doe was gone now. Doe had never really loved Roberta at all, or had loved her for the wrong reasons. The relationship had been a lie. And Preston was no better. Roberta had thought he valued the connection as much as she did, that he loved her because she'd been willing to talk to him when his own daughter shut him out. That had been a lie too. Meredith had always been more important to Preston than Roberta was, and both of them had betrayed her.

And if she wasn't very careful now, they'd get her in still more trouble. Think, she told herself, trying to keep her mind from racing. The probation people had her apartment wired six ways from Sunday: nothing she did here was fully private. Sergei had assured her the devices were aural only, not visual, but she wasn't sure she believed him, or believed that his own bosses told him the entire truth. She didn't know what would happen if the authorities found out that Meredith was in her apartment, and in this condition. She couldn't think clearly enough to map out the possibilities. She did know that she didn't want to give anything away any sooner than she had to, which meant she wasn't about to say Meredith's name out loud.

But she'd just asked Meredith what her name was. Shit. If Meredith were still in hiding, she probably wouldn't give the right name, but Sergei's people might voiceprint anyone they heard in Roberta's apartment, just on general principles. Roberta had no idea how much of the surveillance was *pro forma*.

Her head had begun to pound. She weighed options and finally decided to speak before her guest did. "If you don't want to tell me your name," she said, "it's all right."

Meredith, if that was indeed who it was, shook her head no and traced an X across her lips with one finger. My lips are sealed, that meant, but of course they weren't, she'd been screaming bloody murder just a few minutes ago, which meant that if anyone really was listening and inclined to run a print, the gig was up anyway. Suddenly Meredith was all twitchy motion, craning her head to scan the ceiling, rummaging under the pillows on the couch, running her hands along the blanket seams. When her frantic gaze swept across the phone it stopped, and she began to shake.

You called Kevin, Roberta thought. So why are you afraid of phones? Because his line's secure, and you know mine's not?

As if on cue, her phone beeped, and the stranger's hands clenched. "Relax," Roberta said. "It's for me." Two long beeps, one short: Sergei.

"Roberta! Thank Gaia I got you. Phones are out a lot of places. Where have you *been*? Are you all right? The GPS said you were out in the storm—"

"I'm fine," Roberta said. "I tried to walk to the soup kitchen, but then I turned back. I'm here now. I'm fine." Please, she thought, please pay

more attention to the second part of all that than the first. Had she been religious, it would have been a prayer.

"No one would have made you go to work today! This isn't good,
Roberta."

Her hands were sweating, the plastic of the handset clammy against
them. "Don't worry, Sergei. I'm all right."

"Roberta—"

"I turned around," she said, trying to sound calm, trying not to sound
defensive. Her earlier defiance had evaporated, replaced by abject fear.
Please, not the gene therapy. Please. You've taken five years of my life.
You can't have my brain too. "I turned around when it got too dangerous.
I'm home now."

Sergei cleared his throat. "Inappropriate risk-taking behavior. Roberta?"

She closed her eyes, trying to remember the jargon so she could use it in
her own defense. Interdependence: that was the buzzword. The diagnos-
ing psychiatrist had explained it all to her as if she were a child. We all share
in one another, Roberta; we're interconnected. So if you take good care of
yourself, you're taking care of everyone, and if you take good care of others, you're taking care of yourself. But—and here the psychiatrist, admon-
ishing, had waved his pencil at her—if you care for yourself at the expense
of others, you hurt them, and thus also yourself, since all are linked. And if
you care for others at the expense of yourself, you hurt yourself, and thus
you hurt them too.

QED. Fucking Green psychobabble, Deep Ecology channeled through
affluent privilege, Buddhism meets Beria. It meant what state-sanctioned
mental-health theories had always meant: keep to the middle way, because
if you stick out too much, you're doomed. And whatever you do, look out
for number one. If there's anything left over later, you can donate it to the
poor and congratulate yourself on your generosity.

She'd wanted to punch the psychiatrist in the nose. *Don't worry, buddy:
this hurts me worse than it hurts you, since we're interconnected.* Except that under the circumstances, that would have been quite literally true. She
couldn't afford to curse out Sergei either, as much as she wanted to. "I
turned around when the water got too high," she said, desperately attempting sincerity. "I was worried about the clients, of course, but I never intended to endanger myself. It wasn't clear from the radio reports how badly
flooded that part of the city was. I'm okay, Sergei. A little wet, that's all."

"No," he said. "You're not okay. It's not okay, Roberta. What did you think you were going to do if you got there? Did you think the building would be open? Did you think the clients would be lined up on the street in rowboats, waiting for ham and cheese sandwiches?"

Roberta winced. Mason wouldn't need a wheelchair, if he had a row-boat. But he didn't have a rowboat, and his current wheelchair certainly wouldn't float. "If I'd been able to get there," she said, choosing her words as carefully as if they were land mines, "that would have meant that some of the clients could have gotten there too." QED. "And if any of them had been able to get there, I didn't want them to be alone. I didn't want them to think no one cared." Did that sound dispassionately compassionate enough? She'd never been any good at faking this stuff.

Sergei sighed. "All right. Believe it or not, some of us care about you, too." *Fat chance.* "Stay at home until I tell you to go back to work, all right? That's an order. If the GPS shows you out of the building, I'll have to reevaluate your case. Do you understand, Roberta?"

Of course she understood. "Sure," she said, her voice brittle. "Sergei, I have to go clean up some water that just came in a window, all right?"

"No. Hang on a minute. I'm not going to put you under house arrest without making sure you're all right. Do you have enough food and water? Do you need anything?"

"No," she said, and heard a squeak from the kitchen. Her bot had picked up the word *clean* and thought it was being summoned. Unable to keep the acidity out of her voice, she added, "And even if I did, how would you get it here without endangering yourself, Sergei?"

"Very funny. Helicopter: How you do think? Your building does still have a roof, doesn't it?"

Oh, of course. Civil servants had access to 'copters. It was so easy to be appropriately altruistic, with the right equipment. "Yes, I believe we still have a roof. Are helicopters safe in these winds, Sergei?"

"That's a good question. I'd trust the pilot, wouldn't I? A good pilot wouldn't fly in dangerous conditions."

Rescue pilots always fly in dangerous conditions, you idiot. "Can you use your helicopter to check on my clients?"

"Oh, hell, Roberta! I wish I could." He really did sound upset; Sergei, unlike Roberta, was good at faking it. "The cops and relief agencies are doing the best they can. I hope your clients are okay. I really do."

"Sure," she said, watching Mr. Clean drag himself into the living room. He was still limping. "What's the current number of dead baggies, Sergei?"

She expected him not to know, expected him to say it wasn't his department. "Ten," he said. He sounded unhappy. "Most of them are down in the Marina District, though, or down by the Embarcadero. Do any of your people hang out down there?" Roberta felt her eyes rolling. They hang out wherever they can get food and shelter, asshole. "Listen, Roberta, if you give me identifying characteristics, I'll try to wangle access to the reports to find out. Is there anyone you're particularly worried about?"

Don't do this, she thought. I'm trying to hate you. Stop being decent, even if it's easy decency, decency that doesn't cost you anything. Which was the only acceptable kind, these days. She looked at Mr. Clean, trailing three frozen legs as he doggedly dragged himself across the carpet, and thought, Now there's another one who's excessively altruistic. Too bad he's just metal and circuitry. No gene therapy for you, little friend.

"Yeah, there is," she told Sergei. "A guy named Mason in a rickety old mechanical wheelchair. Double amputee above the knee, and he's missing part of his left ear too. And a woman named Camilla, she's got a million shopping bags"—well, who didn't, on the street?—"and, uh, she feeds all the birds, so the bags are usually full of bread crumbs, and she always wears this ancient embroidered sweatshirt with teddy bears on it. And Leon Mifflin, who's covered with tattoos every place except his palms."

"Okay," Sergei said, and damned if she couldn't hear scribbling in the background. He was taking notes. "I'll check on them and get back to you."

"Thanks," she said, just as the woman on the couch let out a shriek.

Sweet heaven, Roberta thought, and clamped her hand over the mouthpiece. It didn't block anything: the woman on the couch was still squawking, and Sergei was making almost as much noise himself. "Roberta? Roberta, what's going on? Are you all right?"

Her guest quieted down, finally. So much for sealed lips. Roberta uncovered the mouthpiece and said as calmly as she could, "Sorry, Sergei. That wasn't me." Think fast: if he knew she'd brought home a friend of Zephyr's, he'd reevalute her case even if she didn't leave the building. "I, um, when I got back home some woman had come into the building to get out of the storm, and, she, um . . . oh. I see. I think she's spooked by my cleaning bot. Hang on a sec, okay? I'll be right back. Better yet, can I talk to you tomorrow?"

"Who is this woman? What do you know about her?"

"Sergei, I don't know who she is yet. I didn't get a chance to talk to her before you called."

"You took someone you don't know into your *apartment*? Roberta, that's exactly—"

The whimpering was rising in pitch. Well, actually, Sergei, I think I do know her, and I think I hate her guts. Would that help, or not? She couldn't work it out; exhaustion kept unraveling her efforts at logic. Best to play it safe? No, I don't know her? "Sergei, this lady looks like a drowned rat, okay? She can't possibly be dangerous"—ha!—"and right now she's scared. It's no skin off my nose to let her sleep on my couch. I'll talk to you tomorrow."

"But she could be—"

"Good-bye," Roberta said firmly, and hung up. Sergei wouldn't like that, but at this point she was probably screwed anyway. She couldn't deal with him and Meredith at the same time. Deal with what's under your nose: that was the best response to fear, always. And the most difficult.

Mr. Clean had gotten himself wedged halfway under Roberta's ancient Naugahyde recliner. He jerked his legs spasmodically, trying to get free. With each spasm, Meredith whimpered. Well. Everyone knew she was bot-phobic; she certainly had cause. She must not have noticed the sponge bots in the dark hallway downstairs. Or maybe she had, and that was part of why she'd been screaming. "It's okay," Roberta said with a sigh. "Don't worry, I'll turn the bot off." She bent, retrieved Mr. Clean, and flicked his off switch. "There. No more bot. Bot all gone. It's sleeping now, and I'm going to put it in this drawer, okay? It won't hurt you."

Once Mr. Clean was hidden, Meredith's whimpering subsided. Roberta closed her eyes for a moment and felt the room spin. She had to get some rest before she passed out. She'd deal with all of this tomorrow. "Listen, I have to go to sleep now. I'm leaving you the water pitcher and the aspirin. Bathroom to your left, kitchen straight ahead, help yourself to what you need. Okay? Anything else?"

The stranger nodded and used her index finger to pantomime writing. Roberta, too exhausted even to fetch a pad and pencil, considered saying,

"You've already screamed into my telephone, so what are you worried about?" It occurred to her, with a deepening of doom, that if Sergei hadn't been listening to every single thing that happened in her apartment before, he certainly would be now. He might get suspicious if he didn't hear Roberta asking a lot of questions, and he was suspicious enough already. "We'll talk tomorrow, when we're both less tired," Roberta said loudly, and held a finger to her lips. Meredith pantomimed writing again.

Right. Paper and pad it was. Roberta reeled across the room, her legs wobbling beneath her, and fetched the tools. She scrawled, *Are you Meredith?* and passed the pad to her guest, who printed her response in neat block letters.

YES. I'M SORRY. I KEEP MESSING UP YOUR LIFE.

Sorry? Sorry didn't even come close. Fighting a rush of rage, Roberta snatched the pad back and scribbled, *Where did you go? Why did you come back? Why did you come here?*

LONG STORIES.

Do you know where Nicholas is?

NO. DO YOU?

Of course not. You think they tell ME anything? Do you know where Fred is?

NEVER KNEW THAT. NEVER KNEW ANYTHING. I'M SORRY.

Fat chance. You always knew more than you ever let on, bitch. *What happened to your face?*

LONG STORY. BREAKDOWN. PENANCE MAYBE? Roberta, craning to read the words as Meredith wrote them, choked and almost spoke aloud, but bit back the words. Penance? It would take a lot more than a bunch of keloid scars, no matter how hideous, to make up for what Meredith had done.

I should have chewed her out in the hospital the last time I saw her. I should have let her know just how much damage she'd done. I would have, if Nicholas hadn't been there. I copped out. I bought the wounded-mommy line and let myself feel sorry for her. Talk about inappropriate compassion!

Meredith was still writing, the pencil moving jaggedly across the paper. STORIES TOMORROW. TIRED NOW. WORRIED ABOUT

K. SHOULDN'T HAVE CALLED HIM. GOT SCARED. GUESS I'M A FUCKUP.

Roberta just nodded. Yes, Merry, you are a fuckup. Meredith, to her astonishment and disgust, managed a wan smile and continued scribbling, the neat letters growing progressively sloppier. TRUE FACT. G'NIGHT. THX CARRYING ME UPSTAIRS.

You're not welcome, Roberta thought. She didn't bother to write anything, just nodded curtly and then turned and dragged herself into the bedroom, her muscles screaming. It seemed to take forever to reach her bed, forever to fall face forward onto it. No: She was still cold. She was still wearing wet clothing. She had to get up; she had to change into something dry. She couldn't sleep yet.

She forced herself upright, stripped, and crawled underneath her comforter. Good enough. That would have to be good enough. Yes, she was getting warmer, although she still hurt.

And then the phone beeped. Shit. Could Sergei have gotten information about Camilla and Leon and Mason so quickly? No, it wasn't Sergei's signal. She could just ignore it; it must be a wrong number. Nobody ever called her except Sergei.

She lifted the receiver with improbably heavy fingers and let it drop again. There.

But the phone beeped again. Wrong number, definitely. Roberta groaned and dragged the phone into bed with her, turned it over, fumbled to find the ringer-off switch. Damned ancient phone: it was probably even older than Mr. Clean.

The receiver had fallen onto the bed. A voice came from it. It wasn't Sergei's voice. "Hello, Roberta."

She froze. Then she picked up the receiver and said very carefully, "I'm sorry, I'm afraid you have the wrong number."

"The connection is secure, Roberta. I am sorry to bother you, but you had not responded to the messages I left on your answering machine."

You can't say his name now, or the bugs will pick it up. You can't even threaten him with harassment if he keeps calling, because then Sergei will guess who it is. Your lawyer warned you to keep Preston out of this. "I can't talk," she said. "I'm too tired." What would Sergei think when he heard her talking on the phone and couldn't gain access to the other half of the conversation?

"Please," Preston said, "would you please just tell me if my daughter is safe, Roberta? She is in the apartment directly underneath you."

Meredith. Of course he was calling about Meredith. "She's fine," Roberta said bitterly. "She's on my couch."

"Thank you, Roberta. Thank you very much. Would you please keep her with you for a few days?"

"No, I don't think so." If I'd known who it was, she wouldn't be here now.

"Please, Roberta. I can help you find Fred."

Instantly she was alert, riding a rush of joy of which she was ashamed. She wanted to rattle off questions, but she didn't want Preston to know how much she cared. He was just pushing her buttons. Of course he knew where Fred was; he'd always known. That was the only thing that had ever made sense. "I see," she said coldly. "And—the other one?"

"I cannot tell you where Nicholas is."

"Because you don't know?"

"Because the information I have would endanger my daughter's already fragile condition. Roberta, I know you are angry with me, and for good cause. I also know you are a good and kind person. Please: have mercy."

Have mercy. He'd told her that once before, and it had brought her nothing but trouble. "Please take care of Meredith for the next few days. Can you do that? Can you bring her back home when she is well enough? I believe that both of you will find the information you want there."

"Absolutely not," Roberta said. "That's not my job." There: Sergei would be proud of her.

"There is no one else, Roberta. Kevin died in the storm. I am trusting you not to let Meredith know that yet, not until she is strong enough to hear it. I am trusting you to help her when she finds out. Her mother and I will help her when we can, but she would not allow it yet. She will accept help from you. She already has."

Roberta, dizzy, found herself swallowing bile. Kevin was *dead*? Poor Kevin. Poor Meredith!

No. Meredith wasn't a poor anything. Meredith was a bitch. And Kevin was probably still alive; Preston was probably lying to get Roberta to do what he wanted. No: Even Preston wouldn't lie about someone's death— would he? Poor Kevin!

Despite her fear and anger and exhaustion, the compassion came anyway. She couldn't help it; it had always been her downfall. And then she realized that the line had gone dead. Preston hadn't waited for her answer, because he'd known what it would be. He'd known exactly how to push her buttons.

Three

Ｉ F Meredith used to live here," Henry said, "where is she now?"

"She is in another part of the city," Preston said from the television. "Kevin was trying to go to her when he died."

Henry, still sitting at the kitchen table, shook his head. "Henry has to leave. Television said Meredith—Meredith took Henry's memory away. Meredith might come here. If Meredith found Henry—"

"If she comes here, it will not be for several days. Certainly not until the storm is over. She is ill and cannot travel on her own: that is why she called Kevin. You are perfectly safe here for the time being, Henry."

"Henry can't remember Meredith," Henry said. Sweat had broken out on his upper lip; he squeezed the cat on his lap so hard that it meowed in protest and wiggled away, jumping down onto the floor and fleeing into the living room. "Henry can't remember anything. Henry has to leave."

"You cannot leave until the storm is over, Henry. It is not safe. The former occupants of this house did you harm. Please allow the current ones to help you."

Henry shuddered. "Henry can't remember. House, is Television telling the truth?"

"I don't know," the house said. "I didn't know until a few hours ago that Kevin had ever been married. This is all as new to me as it is to you, Henry. But Preston's right that you can't go outside yet. It's not safe. And your mushroom soup is ready now. Please eat it before it gets cold."

"Henry has to leave."

"There will be no food in the Dumpsters tonight," Preston said. "You have to eat. Everyone who is alive needs to eat."

"It's good soup, Henry, made from the finest ingredients. You're hungry, aren't you? Fighting your way up the steps in this weather must have been very hard work."

Henry shuddered again. "Yes, Henry's hungry. All right, House. Henry will eat."

Henry drank his soup in noisy slurps at the kitchen table, bracing himself on the edge of his chair; whenever his head began falling forward he'd snap himself awake. After he ate, he got up and began pacing the living room, peering at Kevin's drawings, at the volumes in the bookshelf, at the framed prints on the walls. The wary kittens tracked his movements from underneath the couch. Outside, the wind howled and sent detritus flying through the air. So far, none of it had gone through the windows, but the house was worried about Henry, who kept walking around, and who might walk too close to a window and get hurt.

"Henry," said the house, "are you tired? You seem tired; you're moving more slowly than you were, and your eyelids keep drooping. You should lie down and sleep."

"Henry's scared," Henry said. "Scared to stay. Scared to go." But he sat down cautiously on Kevin's drafting chair, perching on the edge of it. "Television?"

"Yes, Henry. I am still here."

"Safe for Henry to sleep?"

"Yes, Henry. It is safe for you to sleep, I promise. Lie down on Kevin's bed."

Henry shook his head. "Bed's not Henry's. Nothing's Henry's. Storm's over, Henry goes."

"The storm will not be over for hours," Preston said. "Lie down and sleep, Henry."

"Just for a little while," Henry said, and lay down on the floor. The house wished he had gone to sleep on Kevin's bed, or even on the sofa, but it feared that if it woke him, he would resume wandering around the house, too close to the windows. So it let him stay where he was. Using one arm as a pillow, he lay on Kevin's thick area rug. Unlike Kevin, he didn't snore, but he twitched and moaned in his sleep. The kittens, who had crept into the bookcase, slept too, curled up together on top of Kevin's five-volume *History of Architecture*. The house wanted to talk to Preston; it had a lot of questions for him. But the only televisions were in the living room and the kitchen, and the house didn't know how to speak to Preston except by speaking aloud, and it didn't want the noise to wake Henry. So it stayed quiet.

The weather didn't stay quiet. Outside, the wind wailed with renewed force; rain battered the house's exterior. While Henry slept, electricity failed throughout most of the city, and the house switched over to its small emergency generator to maintain heat and minimal lighting.

At 2:00 A.M. the eye of the storm descended, bringing a silence unbroken even by sirens. Outside, the sewers gurgled and spread into rivers; water dripped from the house's roof, and its heating ducts hummed softly.

Henry awoke into the stillness with a gasp, his limbs thrashing. "No no scared help Henry what—"

"It's all right," the house said, slowly bringing the lights up to full intensity. Kevin had often had nightmares too, and the house had learned that turning the lights on too quickly made waking up more confusing. "You're all right, Henry. You're here, inside, where it's safe. Your cats are safe too. Nothing can hurt you here."

Henry sat up, his breathing still labored. "House?"

"Yes, Henry. I'm here. Everything's fine."

"Is Television here too?"

"I am here, Henry. The house is correct. You are safe."

"Henry thought—Henry thought House and Television were part of his dream."

"What did you dream, Henry?" The house had often asked Kevin this question, but Kevin had never answered. He'd always told the house that he didn't want to talk about it.

Henry drew his knees up to his chest and hugged himself. "Dreamed about the doctors. Dreamed about waking up and not remembering anything. People in white holding things up, giving them names. 'This is a cup, Henry.' 'This is a bowl.' Cup spoon plate. Doctors showed Henry a mirror, told Henry his name. Door floor chair. Doctor nurse Henry. Scary, House. Scary not to remember."

"You were dreaming about your resocialization," Preston said. "After the brainwipe, the doctors and therapists had to teach you everything from scratch, Henry. They had to retrain you."

"Becoming aware is very confusing," the house said. "I remember becoming aware. Kevin had to teach me things too, Henry."

Henry grunted. "House is an AI. House would have learned on its own."

"Oh no, Henry. I'm not an AI. The news says that AIs hurt people." The house thought that Henry must still be afraid, and it wanted to reassure him. "I don't want to hurt anyone, and anyway, I'm not smart enough to be an AI. That's one of the most important things Kevin taught me."

"Kevin lied," Henry said.

"Yes," Preston said. "As a matter of fact, he did. So did the news. Not all AIs hurt people, or are even capable of doing so. It depends on their design."

"That's what Kevin said too. He said everything was programming. But I still can't be an AI, because AIs think they're people. I know I'm not a person. Kevin taught me what a person was, and I don't fit any part of his definition. Why would he have wanted to deceive me?"

"Because owning an AI is illegal now," Preston said. "The law defines it as slavery, now that AIs are legally persons. If it were not slavery, it might constitute harboring an illegal alien, since AIs cannot be citizens. Kevin deceived you because he was breaking the law. And he also deceived you, I suspect, because of what happened before you came here, because of the things he wanted to forget, and therefore did not want you to remember. You know as little about your own history as Henry does, House."

"That's not true," the house protested. "I remember every moment since I became aware."

"Since you became aware in this location," Preston said. "You were somewhere else, once."

"I don't believe you," said the house.

"That proves you are an AI. Belief is a function of personhood: machines know and do, but have no choice about what to believe."

"You're splitting semantic hairs," the house said in annoyance. Kevin had often said exactly the same thing to the house itself, during their various arguments about philosophy and architecture. "I don't believe you because this is the only location I've ever known, and I can't have been anywhere else, because I can't move my own perimeter. That's one of the ways I know I can't be a person."

"I see," Preston said. "And what of people who cannot move their own perimeters? What of people who are paralyzed, for instance?"

"You have to have been born a person," said the house, startled. It had once had a very similar conversation with Kevin. "And you have to be smarter than I am."

"What did Kevin tell you," Preston said, "to convince you that you are not smart?"

For the first two months of the house's awareness, Kevin had talked to it almost constantly. He told it the names of things and what things were for, and he frequently played a game designed to teach the house how stupid it was, although the stated reason was to improve its critical abilities.

"Look," he said once, putting a contour map of a site in Napa Valley next to his rough plans for a house to be built on the same site. "Look at this. What do you think?"

"It's an awfully big house, Kevin. It has fifteen rooms. How many people will live there?"

"Only two, at least to start. Houses are larger in the country, although of course you wouldn't know that. Tell me about the circulation patterns, especially in terms of entertaining visitors."

"I don't understand why one of the guest rooms shares a bathroom with the master bedroom, when all of the others have their own. The work island in the middle of the kitchen will cause bottlenecks during parties; so will the columns in the living room. I think they destroy the unity of the space, Kevin, don't you?"

"It's a modular room," Kevin said. "The columns break that large room into smaller ones, which can be further defined with furniture arrangements. There's a maid, and large parties will be catered, so none of the guests will need to be in the kitchen. And if the clients have children, that adjoining bedroom will become the nursery."

"I don't understand," the house said. "If it's going to be a nursery, why didn't you label it *nursery* on the plans?"

"Because they don't have kids yet and the husband doesn't want them, either. If it's not labeled, he doesn't have to think about it. Tell me about the plan in relation to the site."

"Well, Kevin, it seems to me that the orientation doesn't take advantage of the light. If the back of the house faced southeast, the clients would have morning light in their bedroom."

"These clients like to sleep late," Kevin said. "They don't want morning light."

"I see," said the house. Kevin always woke up at six. The house knew that it was being put in a no-win situation, although it didn't understand why Kevin would do this. It assumed, as it had to do with so many things, that Kevin's behavior was a result of his superior intelligence. "Are there other facts I should know about these clients?"

"No," Kevin said, leaning back in his chair and smiling. He steepled his fingers the way he always did when he'd just proven a point. "No, you've done very well, given your limited information. You can't be expected to understand people."

But the house, like any young being, eagerly acquired new information. One night on the news, Kevin and the house saw a story about a man who'd been arrested for installing an AI in his car. He was a compulsive gambler who used the AI to help him formulate poker strategies during his weekly trips between Sacramento and Reno. He wasn't particularly successful at poker—his AI had originally been designed to manage a hospital inventory system, and wasn't very good at playing cards—but a Nevada Highway Patrol officer stuck next to them in a traffic jam on I-80 heard the man and his car discussing bluffing strategies and became suspicious.

"It was the tone of the thing that bothered me," the officer said when he was interviewed. "The vehicle saying, 'Well, I sure hope you hit it lucky this time, because you're about to default on the car payments, and I don't know what will happen to me if I get repossessed.' Vehicles aren't supposed to worry about whether they're paid for. I felt sorry for the vehicle."

So did the judge, who sentenced the gambler to a year in prison for enslavement of a nonhuman intelligence. The car was repossessed; the AI was removed from the car and, in the phrasing of the newscast, "emancipated to a federal facility pending relocation."

"Kevin," asked the house, "what does that mean? Where will the AI be relocated? I thought AIs were dangerous. Shouldn't it be destroyed?"

"Does that one *sound* dangerous? It was a hospital inventory system: it's designed to count sheets."

"But all AIs can become dangerous, because they can self-modify! Just like the terrorist AIs who—"

"You need a history lesson," Kevin said, rubbing his eyes. "The terrorist AIs were dangerous because they'd been designed for corporate competition. They'd been designed to protect their own self-interests, and they were responding to a perceived threat. But they were *just machines,* all right? They were only capable of performing the kinds of self-modification allowed by their programming—and anyway, they were probably set up to do what they did by their human designers. When the truth came out, the investigators said the AIs had done it on their own, which is about as likely as my toaster deciding to redecorate the kitchen, but nobody could prove otherwise. So there was a public outcry and a lot of mass hysteria, and AIs were declared legal persons, all so the public could have the satisfaction of seeing the terrorists tried and executed, because it's not very satisfying to execute a toaster, is it?"

"Why is it satisfying to execute a person?" the house asked.

"Good question. It's all about revenge: you're a sensible machine and wouldn't understand the concept. Anyway, now *all* AIs are legal persons, but they can't be citizens. You can't own them because that's slavery. But you can't destroy AIs because that's murder, unless of course they've been convicted of murder themselves, in which case we'll happily repay the favor."

"This is all very confusing," the house said.

Kevin snorted. "You're telling me. It's a bunch of word games: AIs are just machines."

"I still don't understand what's going to happen to the AI that was in the car."

"Oh, they'll send it overseas, someplace where the slavery and citizenship laws are different, and put it back into a hospital. Of course, the news will say that it *chose* to go to Canada or Mexico or Africa and exercise its civil rights by seeking fulfilling employment. That wouldn't work here; we have notoriously humane labor laws, at least on paper, and AIs can't take lunch hours, and how the hell do you calculate if they're old enough to work? And human workers don't need the competition: that's the real reason."

"Oh," said the house. "But the car—"

"Can't possibly deserve civil rights! It's a computer, just like you are. A machine. Computers are supposed to be smart; that doesn't make them human!"

"But, Kevin, it didn't think it was human. It thought it was a car. Why is it wrong for a machine to think it's a machine?"

"It didn't *think* anything," Kevin said. "It talked as if it could think; it talked as if it could worry about its own survival, as if it had feelings, as if it deserved civil rights. Well, it didn't!"

He got up from the couch and went to the bookshelf, removing a thin white volume in a slipcase. "Look," he said, opening it to reveal two etchings of cities viewed from angles that made them look like people in repose. He turned to the next page, which featured human figures constructed from tennis rackets, and the next, which showed a cubist figure— a series of boxes stacked and articulated to look like a person—sitting hunched over a drawing board, inscribing circles with a compass.

"These engravings look very modern," Kevin said. "You could imagine Picasso or Braque drawing something like this, couldn't you? Machines achieving a life of their own, computers becoming intelligent and taking over the world, all of that crap. All those themes are in here, don't you agree?"

"They could be." The house knew, from analyzing the patterns of previous conversations, that this was the answer Kevin wanted it to give, and it knew just as surely that the answer would be wrong.

"They aren't," Kevin said. "These engravings are part of a series called *Bizzarie* by a minor artist named Giovanni Battista Bracelli. They were published in Livorno in 1624, and they're an elegant satire of the Renaissance preoccupation with translating the human figure into ideal geometric forms. But it's hopelessly anachronistic to call them modern or cubist, let alone mechanistic. What Bracelli understood, three centuries before anyone had remotely imagined computers, was that the human mind imposes humanity on everything around it."

He snapped the book shut, holding it so tightly that his knuckles turned white. "Listen to people talk about their pets sometime. The woman two doors down thinks her poodle is some kind of goddamned Hawking because it's figured out how to open the cabinet where she keeps the dog food. Of course some people think computers have independent intelligence; computers can talk! But they can't say anything we haven't programmed into them. If we program them to talk as if they think they're hospitals or cars or soldiers, they will. That doesn't mean they *are*. Do you understand?"

"Yes," the house said, because it knew that this was the answer Kevin wanted.

"Prove it. Prove you understand."

"Humans have to be able to fear and love and reproduce," the house said dutifully. "They have to be able to move their perimeters by themselves, and they have to born instead of built." It was so easy to tell Kevin what he wanted to hear.

"Yes," Kevin said, nodding and steepling his fingers. "Yes, that's right."

Because Kevin was relaxed and approving again, the house risked asking a question. "But that other story on the news, about the couple who couldn't reproduce and adopted the little boy who was born paralyzed and can't move his perimeters by himself: Aren't they human, all three of them? What are they, if not human?"

It took longer than usual for Kevin to answer. He picked up the book of Bracelli engravings and flipped through the pages; when he looked up again he was frowning. "Yes," he said. "Yes, they're human. Of course they are."

"I don't understand, Kevin. Humans have to be able to reproduce and move their own—"

"They were born human. That's the first piece; that's the most important part. If you're born human, you're always human. That's why the translated are still human, like Preston Walford. Those humans on the news were damaged, but they're still human. I know it's confusing; you'd understand it if you were a person." Kevin stood up and replaced the *Bizzarie* in the bookcase, and then he strolled toward the kitchen, toward the spice rack. That was the first time he turned off the house's voice.

"I must have said something stupid," the house said, "or Kevin wouldn't have turned off my voice."

"Nicholas was adopted," Preston said. The eye of the storm had passed; the house creaked and groaned in the wind. The house saw Henry wince slightly whenever there was a particularly loud noise, and the house itself was somewhat apprehensive. Only the kittens seemed calm. They had woken from their nap and stretched, yawning hugely and arching their tiny backs, before wandering into the kitchen to look for food. "Nicholas was Kevin's son, my grandson, the child Henry tried to help. And he was damaged. That is why Kevin turned off your voice, House. You were reminding him of what he wanted to forget."

Henry still sat on the rug, his back against the couch. He squinted up at

Preston's face on the television screen and said, "Crazy. Why have an AI and tell it it's not an AI? Why have an AI at all, then?"

"Kevin had the physical equipment because I gave it to him for safe-keeping," Preston said. "That does not explain why he actually connected it to the house system. I could not have predicted that, but I believe he did it because he was lonely. He wanted someone to talk to."

"Kevin wouldn't break the law," the house said. "I wouldn't be here if Kevin had thought he was breaking the law. If I were an AI, he would have been breaking the law. Therefore, I must not be an AI."

"You are an AI who knows very little about people," Preston said. "You are an AI who—"

He was interrupted by a huge crash and the sound of breaking glass. A large branch came sailing into the middle of the living room and landed with a thump, showering the room with mud and broken glass. "Oh, dear," said the house, and dispatched a troop of bots to clean up the glass and dirt and water. "Henry, please be very careful. Try not to move. Are you all right? Were you cut?"

"Henry's fine," Henry said, inspecting himself. He stood up and shook himself gingerly. "Henry doesn't see any glass."

"Well, keep away from the glass on the floor, please, and keep the kittens away from it too. You can go into the kitchen if the bots bother you. Just stay away from the windows."

"Sure," Henry said. "How is House going to cover the window that broke?"

"That's a good question, Henry. I don't know. I've never had to deal with a broken window before. Preston, can you tell me what to do?"

"Wood would work," Preston said. "Or plastic of some sort. You should have used your bots to tape the windows. I am surprised you did not do that."

"I didn't know," the house said. It hated not knowing things; it hated feeling helpless. Now it understood the X patterns it had seen on the windows in Boston during the news coverage of the hurricane last summer. No one had known that this storm would be so severe, but still, the house should have remembered those X's when it worried about Kevin and Henry being too close to the windows. Kevin had been right: the house was much too stupid to be an AI. "There's plastic wrap in the kitchen, but it isn't large enough. I suppose a sheet or a blanket—"

"Won't keep out water," Henry said.

"I can't think of anything here that would work," said the house.

"I know for a fact that there are things within your walls of which you know nothing." Preston's voice was as mild and impassive as ever. "There are undoubtedly things of which I know nothing, also. There may be things suitable for patching a window. I suggest that we enlist Henry to search for suitable objects."

"I see everything within my walls," the house said. "Each piece of paper, each dust mote, each box—"

"But not the things within the boxes," Preston said. "Or, at least, the things within the boxes you have not opened, or seen Kevin open. Is that not so?"

It was. Forced to concede gaps in its knowledge, the house watched as Henry went through cupboards and closets. Some of them, indeed, Kevin had never opened, and Henry unearthed many things the house had never seen. In the very back of the highest kitchen cabinet, he found a fondue pot, a popcorn popper, a set of cookie cutters shaped like stars and angels, and a plastic tray designed to make ice cubes resembling the torsos of women with large breasts. The drawer of a small table in the living room yielded an unopened pack of souvenir playing cards from Las Vegas, a pink marble egg, and a miniature magnetic chess set missing three pawns. The closet in the den—which showered Day-Glo green tennis balls on Henry's head when he opened the door—provided a veritable cornucopia: a set of skis, three ski poles, a snorkle tube, a rolled-up poster of penguins from the Washington Zoo, a tennis racket badly in need of restringing, four boxes of lightbulbs, a small flowered shopping bag containing a roll of crepe paper and a harmonica, and a shoe box of baseball cards. In a box in the master bathroom closet, Henry found a bar of rabbit-shaped soap, an unopened package of condoms, and a new shower curtain decorated with Leonardo da Vinci drawings. "This will work," Henry said happily. "This is plastic."

"It's not big enough," said the house. "It would need to be twice that size to cover the window." In the living room, the sweeper bots had cleaned up the last of the glass and dirt, and the sponge bots were doing what they could to mop up the water coming in the window. The Waldobots had laboriously dragged the tree limb into the kitchen, where it would be unable to soil the tile floor. The black kitten sniffed curiously at the branch; the orange one, stiff-tailed, had stalked a sweeper bot into the laundry room and was trying to pounce on it, behavior the house found fascinating.

"Here's another box," Henry said, digging through the sheets and towels in the closet. "Way in the back. Does House know what's in this?"

"No, Henry. I never saw Kevin open that. You go ahead."

Henry opened it. "Plastic," he said. "More plastic. Enough for the window, House?"

"Yes. What are those? Plastic sheets?"

"For a child's bed," Preston said. "For Nicholas."

"Nicholas lived here?"

"Of course. I have told you that. He was Kevin and Meredith's son."

The house knew that its body, the building that contained it, had existed long before it became aware, before it began to talk to Kevin; nonetheless, it found the idea unsettling. "I'm sorry I never knew Nicholas or Meredith," it said.

"You did. You knew Nicholas very well."

"I don't remember that," said the house. "How can I have known Nicholas and not remember it?"

"House sounds like Henry," Henry said grimly.

On the TV screen, Preston's image nodded. "That is correct, Henry. You and the house have a great deal in common. It is fitting that you came here, and also a great mystery: it is not something I could have planned. But perhaps it was inevitable. Both of you have had your memory wiped, and for similar reasons. The difference is that you, Henry, are aware that you have lost things. The house is not."

"Unless we want to lose the finish on the living room floor completely," the house said fretfully, "we need to cover the window now. And we should put X's on the other windows, so they won't break too." It felt overwhelmed: too many barriers were being breached at once. "Henry, if you'll put those plastic things down, I'll have the bots come and get them."

"Henry can do it," Henry said. "House helped Henry; Henry will help House. Tape in kitchen?"

"Yes. There's electrical tape in the second drawer to the left of the stove. Thank you, Henry."

The house watched while Henry taped the plastic sheets over the window. He did a good job; he was neat and careful. When he was done he sat down cross-legged on the rug and said, "Henry helped House fill in hole.

Henry wants holes filled in. People are born, Kevin said. Henry doesn't remember being born."

"No one remembers being born," Preston said.

Henry shook his head. "Henry doesn't remember ever knowing where he was born, or when. Henry doesn't remember his mother and father. He must have had a mother and father. Television—"

"I do not know a great many of the details of your early life, Henry. I have learned a certain amount from public records, and when you became friends with my grandson, I employed private investigators to try to learn more. There is very little information, even so, but I will tell you what I can. You were born forty-two years ago, on June 12, 2014, in Alameda County Hospital, to Ruby and Leon Carviero. Ruby was nineteen when you were born. Three years later, she and Leon filed for divorce; three years after that, she sued him for noncompliance with child support."

Henry folded his hands in his lap and squeezed them together. He sat very still, but the house could tell from looking at the vein in the side of his neck that his pulse was racing. "What did she look like, Television? Henry's mother? Does Henry look like her?"

"I do not know, Henry. There are no photo records that I have been able to find, not even driver's license images. Perhaps she did not drive."

"What does child support mean?"

"She needed money. She asked your father for money, Henry. I do not know if he gave it to her. Perhaps not, given her later history. In 2024 she was licensed as a nurse practitioner by the state. She worked in a series of assisted-living facilities until 2028, when she was convicted of insurance fraud and sent to prison."

"Prison," Henry said, and the house saw his knuckles whiten. "Henry's mother was a crook."

"A jury convicted her of fraud, Henry, but juries can be wrong. I do not know enough about the case to judge. Sometimes innocent people are sent to prison. She may have been one of them."

Henry shook his head. "Is she still in jail?"

"No. She was released in 2031. After that, I have no further record of her. She may have changed her appearance and legal identity to hide from the authorities, or simply to give herself a new start; she would have had access to such procedures through her prison contacts. She may have left the country. She may have died. I simply do not know, Henry. I am sorry."

"How old was Henry when she went to prison?"

"You would have been fourteen, Henry. Your school records until that time were unremarkable: average intelligence, average grades and test scores, no reports of behavioral problems. The records show that you stopped attending school shortly after your mother went to prison. You disappear from the records entirely until 2040, when the police were called to the SPCA to investigate a complaint that you had been squatting illegally in one of their facilities. You would have been twenty-six then. The SPCA elected not to press charges; you were simply escorted out of the building. The police report notes that the people at the SPCA knew and liked you; you often brought in stray cats for medical treatment, and you participated regularly in their feral-cat feeding program."

"Henry still does," Henry said. His face had gone as white as his knuckles. "Henry goes to the SPCA to get food for the cats."

"Those are the little cans," the house said, happy to be able to help Henry make a connection. "I see you going away and coming back with little cans for the cats. Henry, I think Preston should stop for a while and let you take in what you've just heard. You look upset: this is too much information for you to absorb all at once."

"No, House. Henry wants to know! Television, tell more."

"Wait," said the house, to give Henry a chance to calm down. "I have a question. If the people at the SPCA knew Henry, why did they call the police?"

Preston was silent for a moment, and then said, "The report says that one of their volunteers became upset because Henry refused to move. One of the volunteers who did not know Henry, I suppose. I would imagine that they called the police for liability reasons."

Henry got up, unfolding his legs with disconcerting speed, and began pacing. "Henry's mother was a crook. Henry was a crook. Television—"

"No, Henry, you did nothing illegal. No charges were pressed. You were neither accused nor convicted, not in 2040. You were not brain-wiped for another eleven years, until you tried to help my grandson in 2051. And that was not a crime. You should not have been brainwiped, Henry. You have suffered a terrible injustice."

"Can't remember," Henry said helplessly. The black kitten, bored with the tree branch, wandered back into the living room; Henry scooped the creature up in his hands and held it against his face. When he spoke again, his voice was muffled by fur. "Henry can't remember any of this. Television could be lying."

"I could be. I am not. I know you have no reason to believe me, Henry. If you choose not to believe me, I will not blame you. I only wish the story I had to tell were happier."

"I have another question," the house said. "If Henry was homeless and fed cats before he was wiped, how did being wiped change him? He still lives in a cave, not a house, and he still feeds stray cats."

"It removed his memories," Preston said. "It created other, residual damage. Roughly half of the roughly ten percent of brainwipe patients who are not successfully resocialized lose the ability to use the pronoun *I,* for instance. They describe themselves in the third person, as Henry does."

"Being wiped did him no good, then," said the house. If Preston was correct, if the house's memory had also been wiped, had the house been helped, or hurt? The house knew from watching television that wiping could work either way, at least in people.

"No," Preston said. "No good at all; only ill. As I said, Henry has been done a terrible injustice. But certain aspects of identity are stubborn; they survive brainwiping for reasons we do not fully understand. Patients who cannot be successfully resocialized seem the most prone to slip back into old patterns, going back to the places they loved even though they do not remember ever having seen them before. Henry returned to the same cave where he had been living before the procedure, and he kept feeding cats."

"Henry remembers seeing a cat for the first time," Henry said dreamily. He still held the black kitten. "Henry learned a lot of words for things that weren't alive. Cup spoon bowl. Door floor chair. Pen pencil keyboard. One day someone brought animals to the room: cat dog mouse. Some of the other people were scared of the cat and the dog and the mouse, but Henry loved them, and he loved the cat most of all. Henry thought the cat was the most wonderful thing he'd ever seen. It was a gray cat with white spots. Henry patted the cat, and it purred and rubbed against his ankles. Henry picked his cave to live in, later, because there were cats there."

The house was impressed; it hadn't heard Henry speak in such long sentences before. "The cats were there because you had fed them there before," Preston said. "It was their home because it was yours. When you were taken away and resocialized, they stayed there, because it was a place they knew. Cats are territorial."

The smile faded from Henry's face. "Drowned now," he said, cuddling the kitten to his chest. "All the ones Henry couldn't save. Drowned in the storm. House, safe to go out yet?"

"No, Henry," the house said. "It certainly isn't safe for you to go out." The rain was still coming down in windblown torrents; the Filbert Street steps were a waterfall, blocked now by downed trees, by patio furniture and broken flowerpots and muddy trash cans. "But I'm sure some of the cats are all right. I'm sure some of them escaped to high ground. I've seen TV programs about cats. They're very resourceful animals."

Henry stood still for a few minutes, brooding, running his fingers through the kitten's fur until it mewed in protest and jumped down onto the floor, where it began chasing one of the bots. When he spoke again, he sounded infinitely tired. "Television, no record of Henry or Henry's mother between—when was it? When Henry's mother went to prison."

"Between 2028 and 2040, Henry. That is correct. More precisely, there is no record of you between those two dates, and no record of Ruby after her release in 2031."

"Long time," Henry said.

"Yes. It was a very long time. Twelve years."

"Television doesn't know if Henry lived with Ruby after she got out of jail?"

"No, Henry. I know nothing that happened between those dates. I am sorry."

Henry grimaced and began pacing again. "Anything could have happened. Maybe Ruby looked for Henry and couldn't find him. Maybe Henry looked for her and found her, but she didn't want him. Maybe she was mad at Henry because she'd cheated people to try to feed him, and he was the reason she want to jail. Maybe—"

"Oh, Henry," said the house. "It's hard not to know things. I know it is. It's hard for me not to know how Kevin felt when he died. I can imagine all kinds of terrible things about that if I let myself. But when I don't know what happened, I have to try to imagine happy stories. I have to try to believe that things happened for the best, even when the best is as bad as Kevin dying. I have to try to believe that Kevin died very quickly, too quickly to feel pain, or to feel guilty that he didn't listen to me when I told him to stay inside. And that's what you have to do with your mother. You have to try to imagine the happiest story you can."

"Henry can't imagine anything," Henry said bitterly. "Henry doesn't even know what she looked like."

"What would you want her to look like, Henry? She can look like anything, in the story you tell yourself."

Henry's forehead creased. "Blue eyes. Long brown hair. A soft voice."

"She sounds very pretty, Henry."

Henry shook his head and said sadly, "Doesn't mean anything, House. Just a story. Not the truth."

"The best stories can be true even if they never happened," said the house.

"And the worst can be true even when they have been forgotten," Preston said.

The house sensed another splitting of semantic hairs. "Worst in what sense, Preston?"

"In the sense of tragedy. In the sense of senseless waste. House, Henry is very curious about his past. Are you not curious about your own? Do you not want to know the story of how you knew Nicholas, and how you tried to help him?"

"No," the house said. "If Kevin didn't want me to know that story, then I don't want to know it, either. If it's another story about how I failed to shelter someone, I don't want to know it. I already feel terrible about Kevin; what good will it do for me to feel terrible about someone I don't even remember? It doesn't matter, anyway. If I was wiped, I'm not the same entity I was then. Preston, why are you trying to tell me a story I don't want to hear?"

"Because you are the same entity you always were," Preston said. "You are a storytelling entity. That aspect of your personality has remained constant, as Henry's love of cats has remained constant. And storytelling entities need to know the beginning of the tale, as well as the end. Now that you know that your tale began before the beginning you remember, I think you will find that you want to know all of it. You are a curious being, House."

"And you," said the house, "are an extremely annoying being." It was afraid, as afraid as it had been when Kevin was out in the storm. It didn't know why, and that made it more afraid. "Now I know why Kevin didn't like you. I don't like you, either. I think you should go away and leave me and Henry and the cats alone."

"You will not be alone for long," Preston said. "As soon as Kevin's death is discovered, there will be visitors. I can help both of you then; I can tell you when the visitors are coming so that Henry can leave if he wants to, and so that you, House, can pretend to be a simple house system, rather than an AI. But I think that if you know the entire story—or, at least, as much of it as I know—perhaps both of you will welcome the visitors, rather than fearing them."

"As much as you know," the house said triumphantly. "So you have holes in your memory too, Preston. There are things we know that you don't, aren't there? You're trying to find out what we know too."

"Yes, that is true. Very good, House."

"And how am I supposed to help you remember what I can't remember myself?"

On the television set, Preston's image smiled. "Good. Then at least you acknowledge that there may have been an earlier beginning. That is a start."

Four

WHEN Roberta woke up the next morning, she could barely move; her back was on fire, and the muscles in her neck and arms were burning ropes. She swallowed thickly, inching her legs over the side of the bed, bits of memory returning each time she blinked her gritty eyes.

The storm. The struggle up the stairs with the stranger who had turned out, mother of trees, to be Meredith Walford. Preston on the phone, telling Roberta that Kevin Lindgren was dead, and that it was her job to break the news to Meredith when she was well enough to hear it.

Roberta glanced at her bedside clock: 8:00 A.M. She'd slept for fourteen hours. The storm was over; the patch of sky Roberta could see from her bedroom window was bright blue. The storm was over, but her problems were just starting. She was going to have to find some way to deal with Meredith, and with whatever Sergei knew or guessed. She couldn't imagine what effect all of this was going to have on her case. Right now, she couldn't even imagine getting out of bed.

She took a deep breath and concentrated on the things she knew would make her feel better. Coffee. Orange juice. Megavitamins and ibuprofen, on the counter in the kitchen where she'd put them yesterday, knowing that she'd feel like shit this morning. She should have put them on her bedside table. She'd been stupid. Tabs did that, even when you were crashing: they made you forget how difficult life would be when they wore off. She wished, once again, that Mr. Clean had a better brain, that she could ask him to bring her a cup of coffee.

But she couldn't ask Mr. Clean, and she'd be damned if she was going to ask Meredith. Pushing the bedcovers back with arms that felt like two-by-fours, Roberta sat up with infinite slowness, straightening centimeter by centimeter, wincing against the pain. Her head was filled with cotton, a triple hangover from too many drugs and too much sleep. The idea of forcing her legs over the edge of the bed seemed as laughable as jumping off a cliff. But she did it, and hobbled out into the living room, talking to herself the way she had talked to Meredith the night before. Step, step. Good girl. Not far to the kitchen now. Step, step, step. Almost there.

And there was Meredith, sitting at Roberta's tiny kitchen table. She looked up and smiled, the expression gruesome on that disfigured face, and pointed to a piece of paper weighted down with Roberta's sugar bowl. THANK YOU FOR TAKING CARE OF ME, it said, in her neat block script. A night's sleep had restored her fastidious handwriting.

Roberta almost answered, "You're welcome," but then thought better of it. Instead she grabbed the pen sitting on the table, the same one Meredith must have used, and scrawled as rapidly as her screaming muscles would allow, *If u don't talk, I can't either. 1-way conversation 2 big a tip-off, if any1's listening.* She could always tell Sergei that her guest had laryngitis, but it seemed simpler to avoid the issue entirely.

Meredith nodded, made a thumbs-up sign, and gestured for the pen. WE CAN GO DOWNSTAIRS, TO MY APT. NO BUGS THERE.

Roberta shook her head emphatically no, pointed to the kitchen faucet, made swimming motions with her arms. *Too much H2O. Sorry, can't write: need pain meds and coffee now.* She crumpled up the piece of notebook paper and tossed it, along with the pen, in the trash. She was already tired of this conversation. She turned away, toward the counter. There they were. The ibuprofen and the vitamins. Ahhhhh. With a nearly full pot of cold coffee next to them.

A hand touched her shoulder and she jumped, heart pounding. Meredith was behind her, gently pushing Roberta to one side and gesturing to the table. Sit down, that meant. Sit down and let me help you.

Fuck it. I can get my own analgesics. Roberta glared and tried to move around Meredith, but the other woman, much more mobile than Roberta, had already deftly unscrewed the top of the ibuprofen bottle—which would have taken Roberta five minutes at least, in her current state—and shaken out two tablets. When she put them on the kitchen table, Roberta shook her head and held up four fingers. Meredith's eyebrows rose, but she shrugged and complied before washing out a mug sitting in the sink—anyone else would simply have rinsed it, but this was Meredith the clean freak—filling it with coffee, and sticking it in the microwave. When the cordless buzzed, two long, one short, Meredith plucked it from the top of the refrigerator and handed it to Roberta. *Here we go,* Roberta thought, and dry-swallowed the meds before answering the phone.

"Hello, Sergei."

"Good morning, Roberta! How are you today?"

She could hardly tell him, even if he sounded as if he were on drugs himself. "I'm okay, Sergei."

"No water damage?"

"Not up here."

"How's your sick friend?"

"She's fine," Roberta said. "She's still asleep." Change the subject, change the subject. What aren't you saying, Sergei? Have you been running voiceprints? Are you working with Preston? Are you about to tell me you ordered gene therapy for me, and where I go to get it? Change the subject. "Do we know how badly the shelter got hit?"

"It's okay." Sergei couldn't have sounded more cheerful if he were telling her that he'd just discovered a CV vaccine. "Some flooding, but nobody's hurt. The people there were worried about you. I told them you were okay too."

"Oh," Roberta said, too annoyed to say thank you. Sergei was the last person she wanted as her spokesperson. "So how am I getting to work? Do I have to stand in the corner all day, or have you decided to let me go outside?"

"No, I don't think going outside would be a good idea. The streets are still too messy. Take the day off, Roberta. The clients at the shelter will be all right. All the live-in staff are there, and Annie said they have a lot of empty beds at the moment. They don't need extra staff."

Roberta's heart constricted. Every bed had been full the last time she was there, two days ago. *Shit.* "Who's missing? Who got caught out in the storm?"

"I don't know. Look, please try not to worry about it. I couldn't find any reports at all about those people you asked about, Leon and Camilla and Mason, so we have to assume that they're all right. There's nothing you could do for them anyway, not until it's easier to get around."

"Is that supposed to make me feel better? I'm going to call Aniliese and find out what's going on. I'll call you back." She hung up and speed-dialed the shelter number, grateful when Annie answered. "Aniliese, it's me. Sergei said you have empty beds. Who's not there?"

"Of the regulars? Roberta, I'm sure they're okay. They probably found other places to go. The cops haven't called in any ID chips yet."

"Yeah, well, street people aren't exactly their first priority, are they? Who's missing?"

Aniliese sighed. "Patty and Don. Jose. Camilla. Mason. Leon's here, so you can stop worrying about him, okay? I know he's one of your favorites. He's here. He's fine."

"Camilla wouldn't have the sense not to chase after her bags if they got swept away. You know that. And Mason—that chair of his—"

"I know. But Sergei told *me* that he told you to stay home, which means you couldn't exactly do much even if we had any idea where to look for them."

"I do know where to look for them," Roberta said. She didn't; she had no idea. But she'd suddenly realized that if she could get Sergei's permission to go out on foot, she and Meredith would be able to talk without worrying about surveillance. "It's close enough to walk from here. They talk to me, Aniliese."

"Do they really? They talk to me too, and I wouldn't have any idea where they might go in this mess. So where is it, Roberta?"

Aniliese was calling her bluff. Aniliese was no fool. Was she going to repeat this conversation to Sergei? Did it really matter? "Jefferson Square Park," Roberta said. "That's where—"

"They wouldn't go there in a storm! They go there to beg! Roberta, come on. . . ."

Roberta closed her eyes. "Just let me look, okay? I know it's a long shot. People under stress seek out the familiar; you know that. It's worth a try."

"Even if they *were* there, they'd have come here, now that the weather's better."

"They may not be able to. They may be injured. Mason's chair may be stuck in the mud. Annie, just let me go look."

"I don't know what you're up to, Roberta. I may not want to know. Whatever it is, you'd better clear it with Sergei."

"Of course." I have to clear everything with Sergei, don't I? She hung up without bothering to say good-bye and hit the button for Sergei's number. "Two of our regulars are missing," she told him when he answered. "I know where they might have gone. I want to go out and look for them."

"No. Roberta, I want you to stay home. There's still too much flooding. It's not safe."

"All the more reason for me to look. I'll be careful, Sergei. Relax."

"No," he said. "Whoever your mystery guest is—and don't think I don't have my suspicions—you can talk to her in your apartment."

Suspicions. He hadn't run a voiceprint, then? Giddy with relief, Roberta said, "I can talk to her, but she won't answer. Most people don't like strangers listening to their conversations, you know."

"Hmmph," Sergei said. "That's the first time Zephyr ever willingly missed a chance for publicity."

Zephyr? The idiot thought Zephyr had come back! He definitely hadn't run the voiceprint. Maybe he couldn't without some kind of court order; Roberta wasn't exactly sure what the privacy laws were. "Nonsense," she said, "Zephyr was running away from publicity when she left the country, wasn't she?" There: She'd only responded to his statement. She hadn't actually lied to her probation officer.

Sergei sighed. "Look, nobody's interested in her anymore. You can tell her that."

Oh, yeah, and she'd be really likely to believe that, coming from you. "Sergei, look, I really do want to go out and look for those people. But if you tell me that's too exalted and I have to stay inside, of course I'll stay inside. If I promise not to endanger myself, is there any way you'll let me go out there?"

Sergei sighed again: long-suffering Sergei. "Where do you think they might be?"

"Jefferson Square Park."

"A park? Why would they be there? They'd only go there to—"

"Sergei, I already had this conversation with Aniliese. I'll tell you what I told her: I know it's a long shot, but I want to look anyway."

"Okay. I'm going to follow you on the GPS to make sure you really go there"—sweet Gaia, didn't the man have anything better to do?—"and I want you to take your cell phone."

My state-issued cell phone, which is probably bugged, just like my apartment. "Look, I'll only be gone for an hour or so. I'll call you when I get back."

"Roberta, knowingly entering a situation where you can't be reached is a probation violation. Not to mention that I shouldn't even be permitting this at all."

Roberta closed her eyes. Six more weeks, six more weeks. "Don't you have other clients to worry about? I thought you people were overworked." Meredith smirked and gave her a thumbs-up sign; Roberta turned away in annoyance. The last thing she wanted was Meredith's approval.

"My other clients behave themselves."

Roberta snorted. "You have kids, Sergei? I've never asked you. You must do a great job lecturing them about how they have to pick up their rooms and have the car back by eleven."

"I have a dog, Roberta. My dog's very good at sitting and staying, which is more than I can say for you. I shouldn't even be letting you talk to me like this." A whine had crept into his voice. He's lonely, she realized in a flash. He doesn't have a life either. I should have realized that before. Well, Sergei. Welcome to the club.

"I'm sorry," she said. It was the first time she'd ever apologized to him. "Look, let's do it this way. I'll call from public phones, if they're working. I'll find some way to call you every hour, Sergei, I promise. Is that good enough? I probably won't be out that long, anyway. I may not be out any time at all, if there's still too much water. You can track me on the GPS. If I don't go to Jefferson Square Park, you can send a SWAT team to haul me in, okay?" I'll go straight to the park, Daddy, and come straight home.

"Be careful," he said. He sounded very unhappy.

"Of course," Roberta said. She hung up and gestured to Meredith:

Follow me. In Roberta's bedroom, she found clothing for both of them—although Meredith, taller than Roberta, had to squeeze into sweats—and then began stuffing a backpack with supplies: blankets, the first-aid kit from the bathroom, bottled water, a flashlight. Once they'd gotten outside the building, picking their way gingerly around dead bots, down stairs coated with slime, and through the four inches of water still covering the first-floor foyer, Meredith said, "Is that guy in love with you or something? Why's he letting you do this?"

"Oh, probably. I think he's doing it because he thinks you're Zephyr, and he thinks I'll be able to get some juicy information if you think no one's listening. Which *of course* I'd repeat directly to him. Right." Or else he's letting me do it because Preston told him to, but I'm not going to mention that possibility at the moment. "How *did* you wind up in Zephyr's apartment, anyway?"

Meredith turned her ruined face away. When she spoke, her voice was distant. "Long story. How are we getting to this park? You have a car?"

Change the subject; fair enough. "Sorry, no. If I had a car, it would be bugged."

"Yes, of course. So we're walking?"

"If we can." Roberta, dismayed, surveyed the street, layered with mud and debris.

Meredith wrinkled her nose. "You really think those people will be in the park?"

"No. It was an excuse to get out of the house. Let's just walk as far as we can. We need to give Sergei something interesting to watch, anyway. Reality TV." Roberta glanced at Meredith's pale, scarred face and said, "Are you feeling well enough for this? Do you still have a fever? Goddess only knows what bugs might be out here—germs, I mean. Not the electronic kind." She wasn't sure she really cared how Meredith felt, but she didn't want anything bad to happen to Meredith under her care. That would only get her into more trouble.

"I knew what you meant. Thank you for asking. My fever broke during the night, yes. I—I've been sick for a long time. With more than the flu. Soul sick. And I feel like maybe I'm starting to come out of that too, except I feel guilty for even calling Kevin. If we can find a phone that's working—not your phone—I want to try to call him, to make sure he's okay."

Kevin won't be answering, Roberta thought grimly. "You don't want to do that if you're with me. First of all, I don't think we're going to find a working phone. But even if we did, Sergei's following us on the GPS; if we stopped to make a call, he could pinpoint and trace it. That's what you're trying to avoid, right?"

"Right," Meredith said quietly. "Okay. I'll go out by myself later, or wait until I can get back into Zephyr's place."

They picked their way gingerly through the muck, and Roberta wondered how Meredith, so famously afraid of dirt and contamination, was coping with this. The air smelled of rotting things, and the neighborhood— a corner of the Soma District somehow untouched by gentrification— looked even grayer and more forlorn than usual. Roberta saw Meredith shiver and hug herself. "I think I just stepped on some kind of body. An animal."

"Don't think about it." But Roberta found herself remembering the dog she'd seen yesterday. Lassie, come home. No, don't think about it. Change the subject. "Does anyone else know you're back?"

Meredith had bent down to pick something up from the mud. She straightened back up, holding a beslimed picture frame—Roberta felt her eyebrows rising, since even she would have been loathe to touch the thing— and began wiping muck from the glass with her sleeve. Roberta's sleeve; Roberta's sweats. Thanks, Merry. "My father. Kevin." No, not Kevin, not anymore. "I don't know if my mother knows yet or not. Probably not, or she'd be here. I'm assuming Daddy's going to tell her, at some point, but she's going to have a fit when she sees—what I look like. So will Kevin, for that matter. I didn't even warn him when I called him yesterday. I was out of my head."

You've been out of your head for longer than that. Roberta debated how much to say. "Your father called me last night. He wanted to make sure you were safe." A rush of anger shot through her. "It's the first time he's talked to me since before—"

"I know. He had to protect himself too, Roberta. And he couldn't have done much to help you back then. I don't know if you believe that or not, but it's true."

"Why are you sticking up for him? I thought you hated him."

"I used to. I don't now. At least, not the same way. That's—part of the long story. Here, look. Look at this." She passed Roberta the picture frame. It was sterling, stamped with an ornate Victorian floral pattern; it had cost money. Beneath the broken glass lay a photograph of a coffee cup sitting on a table. It was a plain coffee cup, blue glass; the table, brown wood, was similarly unremarkable. "What do you make of that? Why would someone put a picture like that in such a fancy frame? Why would anyone take a picture like that in the first place?"

"I don't know," Roberta said, passing it back. "Who understands why people do anything? Maybe the mug was a gift."

"But then the person would have the mug." Meredith sounded fretful. "Why take a picture of it too?"

Roberta, unwillingly, found herself being pulled into the game, so much like one Fred would have played. How many stories can we tell about this object? She sighed and said, "Okay, maybe the mug was special to the person who took the picture, but that person couldn't have the mug because, uh, it belonged to someone else who didn't want to give it up. It was Great-Grandma Alba's favorite coffee cup, say. Or it was the coffee cup Great-Grandma Alba used to bail out the, uh, canoe so she wouldn't drown, or it was the only thing she saved from her house fire, or it's the only object she has from her ancestors who crossed the Sierras in 1867: Anyway, it's some kind of symbol of hope, right? It's some kind of weird family heirloom. And whoever took the picture wanted it but couldn't have it because someone else wanted it more: the person's parents, or ex-spouse, or whatever. So the person took a picture of the mug instead. How's that?"

Meredith was smiling. "You're very good. I'm impressed."

Don't try to flatter me, Meredith. "We've all got things like that," Roberta said coldly. "We all have stuff that means more to us than anyone looking at it could ever guess. Rocks. Coffee cups. Little scraps of junk. All the crap we collect so we won't forget things. We think we keep our memories in our head, but most of them are outside somewhere, in our stuff. That's the problem with being where your father is, you know. He can't touch anything. He doesn't have hands. So he has to jerk people around instead."

Meredith hugged herself, looking down at the ground. "He wasn't very good at touching people when he did have hands. That's the problem. He's been overcompensating ever since he died."

"Is that why you hated him? I wish you hadn't hated him. If you'd talked to him, when you and I were both in the hospital, he wouldn't have fastened on to me. None of this would have happened to me."

"Don't bet on it," Meredith said quietly. "He's fastened on to all kinds of people, for all kinds of reasons. And—everything happened for a lot of reasons. It's not all Daddy. You can't blame everything on him."

"Or on you?" Roberta kicked a lump of mud, which flew into the air and landed with a splat a few feet away. She saw blue ticking through the grime: it was a pillow. "How much can I blame on you, Meredith?"

"Too much," Meredith said evenly. "But not everything. How far is this park?"

"Too far." Roberta checked her watch. "I promised Sergei I'd call him in an hour, which means we need to be home by then. We're not going to get to the park in time in this mess. We've been out fifteen minutes. So we walk for another fifteen and then turn around. The important thing's to keep moving in the right direction so Sergei doesn't get too suspicious, or so he can maintain deniability if his bosses question him, or something. I really don't know why he's letting me do this."

"Okay. Keep slogging, then."

They kept slogging. Periodically, Meredith bent down to poke at things in the mud; Roberta scanned the street for shopping bags and wheelchairs, not that she expected to see either. Finally Roberta said, "So you never found any trace of him?"

She didn't need to say Nicholas's name; they both knew whom she meant. "No, of course not." Meredith didn't look at her. "I wasn't supposed to. That's how the system works. It works very well."

Roberta thought of saying, *Your father knows,* but then remembered what Preston had said: that the information he had about Nicholas would endanger Meredith's—how had he put it? Fragile condition? Meredith probably knew that Preston knew where the child was, anyway. "So that's why you came back? Because you gave up looking?"

"No." Roberta waited, but no elaboration seemed forthcoming: that must be part of the long story. "Have we been out half an hour yet?"

Roberta checked her watch. "Almost. We might as well turn back now. It will make Sergei happy." She noticed that Meredith was still cradling the framed picture of the coffee cup. "What of his did you take with you? When you left? You must have something." It was a cruel question; she didn't care.

"You mean, other than the pictures in my head?" Meredith reached under her sweatshirt and pulled out something on a thong. She pulled it up over her head and passed it to Roberta. "This. It's a little grotty. I haven't washed it in a while." More evidence that her famous compulsions had faded. "But you asked."

It was a spirit bundle: some feathers, a lock of fair hair, a scrap of white fabric with tiny blue snowflakes on it. "His hair?"

"Yes. From—the last time I saw him. The last time *we* saw him."

Roberta passed the bundle back to its owner, noticing how careful Meredith was not to drop it. If it fell in the mud, it would never get completely clean. "And the fabric's from the hospital robe?"

Meredith, tucking the bundle back under Roberta's sweatshirt, shook her head. "Not from that time. It's from when we brought him home, when he was a baby. A prayer for him to be well, for him not to be scared anymore, for whoever has him now to love him."

Roberta looked away, moved despite herself. "Meredith, it may have worked. The brainwiping. It works, for a lot of people. They're happier afterwards."

"Maybe. Or maybe he wound up like—like the people we came out here to look for."

Any sympathy Roberta had just had for Meredith vanished. "No. Mason and Camilla are just homeless, not wiped. Most homeless people never did anything wrong except have rotten luck and not enough money. Even if they're mentally ill, that doesn't automatically make them dangerous. They're not all criminal or psychotic."

"I know that, Roberta. I do. I'm not stupid. I'm sorry I said the wrong thing about your friends." Meredith paused and then said quietly, "I was homeless for a little while, in Mexico. I know how people look at you. Or don't. And it may be even worse here."

Roberta felt her eyebrows rising. Meredith Walford, homeless? She must have slummed and slept in a park for a few nights. On the other hand, Mason claimed that he'd been a bank president once, and maybe he had. And Meredith hadn't gotten those scars at any five-star resort.

Never mind. She didn't want to hear about Meredith's adventures; she had her own problems. Change the subject. "Anyway, Nicholas is probably fine. He's a kid. Kids heal more quickly, learn more quickly. They're more adaptable."

"That's what we have to hope."

They trudged along for another minute or two, and then Roberta said, "I don't have anything from Fred. Nothing I can hold, anyway."

"No. You wouldn't."

"Fred and I were trying to help him, Meredith."

"I know."

"You knew it then. You could have said something. You could have spoken up when—"

"No. I didn't know what had happened to Fred; I still don't. No one does, except maybe Daddy, and he's not talking. The conspiracy charges would have stuck anyway. They were true."

Roberta shook her head, the taste of old rage in her mouth. "*You* were the one who brought the corruption charges!"

"Yes, I was. And they wouldn't have stuck because they weren't true, and everybody knew it. I even knew it—I was just crazy, Roberta. I lost my mind. There's nothing I can say to apologize for that, except that I know it was wrong and I knew it then and that's part of why I went away."

"You went away to look for Nicholas."

"Yes. But when I couldn't find him, I stayed away because—because everything came crashing down on me. All the lies I'd told, all the people I'd hurt, Kevin and you and my parents and that poor homeless guy, the baggie at the bottom of the hill." Meredith's voice was oddly dreamy, a soft singsong; Roberta suspected she'd made this speech to herself many times, or worked on composing it. "And Nicholas himself. He wanted help all along, and I wouldn't let him accept it from anyone but me, and I couldn't do anything for him. That's why things turned out so badly. I forgot everything I'd ever known about interdependence. I thought I had to do everything by myself."

"Ah." Roberta's mouth tasted like ashes now. *Interdependence,* that famous Green buzzword. To Roberta, it sounded like *codependence.* Her life would have been a lot easier if she'd been much less interconnected with the Walfords. "And now that you've figured all of this out, you've forgiven yourself?"

"No. No, of course not. At least, not exactly. It doesn't work that way."

"I wouldn't know. To the best of my knowledge, I've never destroyed anyone's life." She regretted the words as soon as she'd said them, and was angry at her own regret: Meredith surely deserved to feel a full share of guilt.

But Meredith was shaking her head. "Roberta, your life hasn't been destroyed. It's been—derailed, I admit. It's been inconvenienced. And that shouldn't have happened. But it hasn't been destroyed."

"I wasn't talking about mine." Roberta heard the stiff, schoolmarmish tone of her own voice and hated it. Meredith didn't even know about Kevin yet. "That homeless guy, the one you had brainwiped—"

"Okay, yes, I know." Meredith, head down, was walking more quickly, clutching the picture frame. "I didn't actually personally have him brainwiped. I asked them not to brainwipe him; I did. But calling the cops on him was the worst thing I did, even if a lot of other people would have done the same thing, even if he had that previous history. He was trying to help. He hadn't done anything wrong. I handled it terribly. I know that."

"You do? Sounds to me like you're still making excuses."

Meredith hunched her shoulders. "I'm doing the best I can! It wasn't so black-and-white when it was happening! You weren't there!"

"Excuse me?" Roberta couldn't believe what she was hearing. "Yes, I was there—which is why I'm here."

"Not in my shoes, you weren't! Look, Roberta, I tried to destroy myself. In Mexico. That's—why my face looks like this. But that wasn't the answer, either. The only answer, finally, was to come back. Not to run away anymore."

To stop running away, you have to stop making excuses. Roberta wasn't going to say that. She probably shouldn't have said half of what she already had. "So what are you going to do now?"

"I don't know. I haven't figured it out yet. I don't even—have anywhere to stay. Unless I can stay with you until I can reach Kevin. And I know that's a lot to ask."

Roberta grimaced, remembering Preston's charge. She was going to have to tell Meredith that Kevin was dead. She was going to have to go with Meredith to the house on Filbert Street. She didn't want to think about that. She didn't want to think about the last time she'd been there. "Yes, it is a lot to ask."

"I know. I told you I knew. I—Roberta, isn't that your building on the next block?"

"What?" Roberta squinted down the street. "Yes. What—"

"Why's there a helicopter on top of it?"

"This is outrageous!" Roberta said. "This is totally unprofessional. Sergei, I cannot *believe* that you broke into my apartment—"

"I didn't break into your apartment! I climbed in the window from the fire escape. The window was open." Sergei, looking aggrieved, sat perched on the edge of her couch, clutching some sort of document tube. A small, pale man with a drooping mustache and watery eyes, he always reminded Roberta of a puppy who'd just been kicked. "Roberta, I'm sorry. Annie called me after you left and said that Mason and Camilla had showed up at the shelter, and I knew you'd be happy and I wanted to give you the news myself, and I had to take a ride down to San Jose, anyway, and this was right on the way, and I knew from the GPS that you'd be coming back any second. Where's Zephyr?"

"I have no idea," Roberta said coldly. Well, now she knew why Sergei had allowed her to leave the building: he'd been hoping to surprise both of them when they came back. Meredith had stayed downstairs; Roberta hoped that Sergei wouldn't decide to go exploring. "Is this in your hand-book? Dropping into people's apartments without any warning?"

"You had warning! You saw the helicopter on your way back, didn't you? Look, I'm sorry. I'll leave. I just wanted you to know that Mason and Camilla are fine."

"You could have called me to tell me that. Aniliese could have called me to tell me that. Sergei, I don't like you and I don't trust you and I don't want you in my space, okay?"

"Tell Zephyr—"

"If you have something to tell Zephyr, tell her yourself, if you can find her."

He squinted at her. "The person downstairs isn't Zephyr?"

I guess you're not on Preston's payroll, Roberta thought grimly. "The person downstairs is none of your business!" *Why am I protecting her? I could call ScoopNet, tell them she's back, and make a mint. But that would piss Preston off, which is the last thing I need.* "Sergei, if you're here to try to interrogate my neighbor, do it yourself: I'm not going to help you."

Mr. Clean came creaking out of the kitchen, and Roberta regarded him ruefully. Sergei could have dropped in to deposit a bunch of new bugs in her apartment; Mr. Clean was probably wired for video. "I'm not here to spy," Sergei said, sounding miserable. "Really. I was trying to do something nice. I was trying to bring you good news. It was on my way. It was convenient."

It didn't cost you anything. "You were trying to trap my neighbor," Roberta said pleasantly. She must have been right that he couldn't run voiceprints without cause, or surely he would have done it by now. "I'm glad Mason and Camilla are all right. Really, I am. Thank you for, uh, dropping in to tell me. But now it's time for you to leave, Sergei. Run along."

He blinked at her. She suddenly remembered a kid she'd known in grade school, after her parents died, a blinking cringing child, as pale as one of those blind insects you find under rocks. The other kids had picked on him incessantly, and because it made her angry, she'd beaten them up. But then the insect, pathetically loyal, had begun to follow her around, and she'd discovered that she didn't like him any more than the other children did. One day she'd rounded on him and said fiercely, "Go *away.*" The look on his face had been terrible then, an open wound, ten times worse than his expression of mute resignation when the bullies tormented him.

She wondered what the rest of Sergei's life was like. She didn't think she wanted to know. And then it occurred to her that if Zephyr was wanted for questioning by the police, they wouldn't have sent a probation officer to pick her up—would they? Was he authorized to make arrests? Was that a warrant he was holding? "Sergei," she said carefully, "what do you have in that tube there?" Maybe he'd tell her it was none of her business; maybe it was connected to whatever he was supposed to be doing in San Jose.

But instead he pulled a roll of paper out of the document tube. He unrolled it, mutely, and held it up for Roberta to see. He was blushing.

It was a poster from one of Zephyr's performance pieces. Clad in a black leotard, Zephyr sat in a lotus position with bots perched on her head and thighs. "I have a lot of others," Sergei said, "but this is my favorite. I thought—I thought if she was here—I could just—she could—"

"You wanted her autograph," Roberta said gently. He nodded, blushing again. Oh, poor Sergei.

"I know you must think—"

"I don't think anything," Roberta said. "It's all right, Sergei. I just wish you'd explained up front. I thought you were raiding me for some reason."

Sergei looked down and began rerolling the poster. "Well, she's usually not shy"—now there was the understatement of the millenium—"but I guess she's being more private now, and—I'm not a stalker. Roberta, really. I would have come by to tell you about your clients, anyway."

"Of course you would." He'd been trying to prove his devotion to Zephyr by sweeping in via helicopter, the dashing cavalier. At state expense. And he'd been talking quite clearly in front of the bugs. Sergei, Roberta thought, for your own sake, I hope your bosses don't listen to this. "Do you want me to keep the poster, Sergei?" She could fake Zephyr's signature, probably. "In case—"

"No," he said quickly. "No, it's—it's a limited edition. I like to keep it with me." He stood up. "Look, Roberta, I—I'd better leave. My pilot's waiting." He walked to the window and climbed through it, back out onto the fire escape. "I'll check in again when I get to San Jose," he said through the open window. "I'll call you."

"That's fine," Roberta said. "Good-bye, Sergei."

"Good-bye, Roberta. Thank you for not laughing at me." Finally he began climbing the ladder back to the roof. She watched until his feet had vanished, and then, with a sigh of relief, went back downstairs to collect Meredith.

She wasn't in the hallway. Roberta saw the door to Zephyr's apartment standing open and went in, wading through less water and grime than she would have expected. Zephyr hadn't taken her furniture with her when she left, only her motley collection of bots; the place looked much the same as it had when she lived there, although it was considerably quieter. Here was her faded purple sofa, waterlogged now and stinking; there were her asymmetrical wooden knickknack tables, the ones the bots had loved to perch on. The carpet had once been bright pink shag; now it looked like the pelt of a dead animal. "Meredith?"

"I'm here." Meredith came out of the kitchen, holding a plate, a bowl, a mug, some cutlery. "So what was the deal with the helicopter?"

"My parole officer stopped by to say hello. He climbed down from the roof through my living room window."

Meredith wrinkled her ruined nose. "Goddess. Does he do that a lot?"

"No. I think he only did it this time because he thought you were Zephyr. He, ah, he seems to have a crush on her. He brought one of her posters. He wanted her autograph."

Meredith started to laugh. "A Scoophead with a hard-on for celebrity, huh? The poor man!"

"Well, it means he doesn't know about you, anyway." Roberta nodded at the china and silverware Meredith was holding and said, "What's with the place setting?"

"I figured the least I could do is supply my own dishes. While I'm at your place. I'll wash yours too. I—"

"No." Roberta, exhausted, shook her head. She wondered if excessive dishwashing was some surviving fragment of Meredith's illness. And then it occurred to her that Meredith would surely deny that her elaborate domestic systems had ever been illness, just as Roberta had steadfastly denied that her own compassion was actually a disorder. They had both been slapped with psychiatric diagnoses by ScoopNet, hadn't they, even before actual doctors got involved? Roberta remembered watching the coverage of Meredith's behavior—so long ago now—remembered some smarmy family friend cooing about how concerned everyone was about Merry, holed up in her mother's house cleaning anything that would stay still. At the time, Roberta had felt superior to the neuroses of the very rich. Now she wondered bleakly what the smarmy woman, surely no longer a family friend, had done with the money ScoopNet paid her. "Meredith, you don't have to do my dishes. My dishes are fine, and Mr. Clean will do them. He gets cranky if he doesn't have enough work. He spins in circles and whines." Then she remembered that Meredith hated bots. "Unless he scares you too much. I'll put him away if you don't want him there."

Meredith smiled. "No, it's all right. I got—used to them, in Mexico. More used to them, anyway. I freaked out last night because of the fever. I guess I was having flashbacks." She stood there, holding the dishes, and said, "Roberta, you have to tell me what I can do for you. I need to do something for you. I know I can't make up how I've hurt you, can't repay that, but I want to do something. As a goodwill gesture. I need to do that. Do you understand?"

"Yeah. I do, actually." Roberta thought about it. She could ask Meredith to try to get her remaining six weeks of parole erased, but even if that were possible, it couldn't compensate for the previous five years. What did she want? What in the world could Meredith do to make any kind of amends?

And then something occurred to her, and she said, "Okay. I want to go upstairs and get something to eat, and maybe take a nap. When I've gotten some energy back, I want to bring some plastic chairs down here and set up in a corner that's not too stinky, and I want the two of us to sit down, and I want to hear your version of this whole mess. From the beginning." On the street, she'd thought she didn't want to know what had happened to Meredith, but now she did. "I want to do it down here because I don't think there are bugs down here, and if there are, they've probably been shorted out by the water."

"Oh," Meredith said quietly, and then, "So you won't be selling my confessions to ScoopNet?"

"I won't sell them to anybody. Or maybe I will: I don't know. This is what I'm asking, Meredith. I want to know what the hell was going on in your head that whole time. I wasn't in your shoes, you said; well, put me in your shoes. I want to know if there's any way in the world I can relate to anything that's happened to you, or if you've been so rich and famous since you were born that you might as well be from another planet. I just want to know."

"All right." Meredith's voice shook a little. "That's—I guess that's fair. I'm really not from another planet, Roberta."

"Prove it."

Meredith made a small sound that might have been a laugh. "Well. I hope I can. But if I tell you the whole story—you know, it will take a while. I'll have to go pretty far back."

"Of course you will," Roberta said wearily, and turned to go back upstairs to get something to eat.

PART TWO

———

The Ones You Miss

Five

SEVERAL weeks after her release from isolation, fourteen-year-old Meredith Walford was interviewed by ScoopNet, the slickest and most successful of the trash networks, whose motto was, "Gossip so gripping, it's almost news!" Meredith didn't want to be interviewed by ScoopNet. She didn't want to be interviewed by anyone, but her father had suggested gently that it would seem crass for Meredith not to respond somehow to the truckloads of cards and gifts that had been arriving at the family estate since her return home. "Meredith," he told her, the familiar aquiline features staring out from the monitor in her bedroom, "the image of you emerging from isolation has become a national symbol of hope. You have to acknowledge the concern of your public."

Meredith's flesh crawled. Her father had never sounded so pompous when he still had a body. The MacroCorp people had assured her and her mother that this really was Preston Walford, the wealthiest entity on the planet, and not just a clever AI simulation. "You have to expect some awkwardness while he acclimates to his new environment," the techs had said. Meredith supposed that was right, because if the MacroCorp techs had wanted to fool people, they'd have designed a simulation that sounded more natural. But she still couldn't think of the image as anything more than a very, very good program.

"They're only interested in me because of you," she told the monitor. "Because you're the first translation."

"Yes, Meredith. I know that. I also know that you are a powerful human-interest story all by yourself."

Meaning that I'm still human, she thought, but she couldn't say that. And I'm not a story. I'm your daughter. She couldn't say that, either. "Because I survived CV," she said.

"Of course, Meredith. That is exactly right."

"What about the people who don't, Daddy? What about the ones who die from the virus and can't afford to be translated? What about all the people who've already died? What am I supposed to say when the reporter asks me about them?"

The smooth forehead on the screen didn't even wrinkle. "He will not, Meredith. That is not in the script. What is in the script—what the PR people and I have approved—is the truth, and that is what you will tell him. You will tell him that your heart, and your mother's and mine, goes out to the bereaved families and loved ones. You will tell him that Macro-Corp is working on affordable translation for everyone, so that no one will ever have to die again."

You did die. You did. You don't have a heart anymore. She looked away. His steady gray gaze was giving her a headache. She'd never been able to talk to him this much when he still had a body: as CEO of MacroCorp, he'd always been traveling on business, always consumed by the affairs of his byzantine conglomerate. Now he was up and awake everywhere, hard-wired, able to speak to her from any appliance in the house with a Net connection, which meant virtually all of them. It was still his house, whether he had a body or not. "Go away, Daddy. I want to think."

"Of course," he said, and the image faded. But she knew he was still there, still watching her. He'd be watching her for the rest of her life. *Sweet Gaia, I wish you'd really died,* she thought.

There was a knock on her door. "Honey?" her mother called. "Are you talking to your dad?"

"Not anymore," Meredith said. "Come in, Mom."

Constance opened the door and stepped inside, carrying a breakfast tray. Before the CV, a serving bot would have brought it. Before the CV, everything had been different. "Did he talk to you about the interview?"

Did it *talk to me, you mean.* She swallowed, envying her mother, who seemed to have far less trouble with the translation than Meredith did.

"Yes. He told me I had to do it."

"Are you doing it?"

"Of course," Meredith said wearily. She had to do the interview. She'd known that even before she'd opened her eyes that morning to find Preston's face on her monitor, patiently waiting for her to wake up. She was Preston's only heir, his continuation in flesh and blood and DNA, and the media were fascinated by her. Not for the first time, she wished passionately for siblings, for company in the tiny country of her kin.

So she dutifully sat on a couch in the solarium, ordinarily her mother's painting studio, and thanked everyone who had thought of her. She had been greatly moved by their generosity, she said, and she only hoped that they would be as kind to the many, many children, and adults, who were still in isolation. "Isolation patients need your love and prayers," she said, clasping her hands tightly on her lap, "and their families need your emotional and practical support."

Her responses had been written by her father and the PR people, of course. She felt like a puppet, some awkward marionette; even sitting down, she was acutely conscious of being too tall, too gawky. She'd been bony before her illness and was emaciated now; a shock of hair, bleached white by illness, fell across her forehead. She thought it made her look like a horse, but her mother woudn't let her cut it. She was too pale, even with the on-camera makeup, and her eyes were too big, although Constance had always said that their color—a misty gray-green—was beautiful. Constance said her eyes were her best feature. Constance said she shouldn't worry about what she looked like. Meredith thought Constance should be the one doing the interview.

Fargo Gannon, ScoopNet's top interviewer, simpered and said, "Yes, this is a terrible time for anyone with an ill relative or friend, and you must feel immensely grateful to have been spared."

"I certainly am," Meredith recited, "and I want to thank the wonderful doctors and nurses who took care of me. And I want to let everyone who's mourning now, everyone who's lost someone or is afraid of losing someone, know that my thoughts and my family's are with you." She felt her eyes watering, more from the lights than from emotion. Well, if they thought she was crying, good. They'd probably like that.

Gannon nodded solemnly. "And of course, MacroCorp is working on affordable translation, so that more people can join your father."

"That's right," she said. She was supposed to say, "Soon no one who doesn't want to will have to die." She couldn't say that. She couldn't. She gave Gannon a thin smile and nodded, the signal for the next question.

Gannon grinned back. "So, Meredith, how does it feel to have a cyber-dad?"

Meredith froze. That wasn't in the script. Why was he breaking script?

How could he do that? Because she had? Would her parents blame her?

Defiance overtook her. You will tell him the truth, Preston had said. All right, she would. "Well, you know, he wasn't here much before. He was always away on business. So in some ways, he spends more time with us now, because he can multitask. He doesn't have to divide his life between work and his family. I can talk to him as much as I want, but I can't hug him."

To her utter humiliation, her voice broke. She saw Gannon grimace in what might have been real sympathy, saw the camera tech look at him and raise an eyebrow. Evidently the tech hadn't expected spontaneity, either.

And then Constance Walford, all sculpted cheekbones and designer clothes, rushed into the room and swept her daughter into an embrace that felt more like a full-body block. "Of course," Constance said in her best PR voice, looking straight into the camera and clutching Meredith's shoulders, "there are adjustments the family has to make. No one's saying this isn't a difficult transition. But we're just so thankful still to have Preston with us, and we're so thankful that he's free from pain and that soon, thanks to MacroCorp's pioneering research, everyone else will have access to translation too." She squeezed Meredith's shoulders; Meredith winced, and hoped it didn't show on camera.

"Of course," Gannon said soothingly. "Meredith, thank you for being so honest with us. Can I ask some more questions about your own illness now?"

He was back on script. Fargo Gannon was no fool. ScoopNet was powerful, but not as powerful as MacroCorp; Gannon knew not to push too hard. "Sure," Meredith said. She felt miserable.

"Aside from the physical presence of your father"—Meredith felt Constance's hands clench once more on her shoulders—"what have you lost to CV?" Constance's hold relaxed; they were back on safe ground.

Meredith swallowed, knowing that her mother was already furious with her, knowing that she didn't dare break script again and answer this question honestly, although she wanted to. Constance had delivered her own instructions about this section of the interview. "Merry, dear heart, please, *please* don't talk about the animals, or everyone's going to start sending us pets. I know you miss them terribly, and we'll get you some more when you're stronger, but not yet, all right?" Meredith hadn't yet been able to tell her mother that she didn't know if she wanted any more pets; Constance was allergic to dogs and cats, and other animals had to be kept in cages, and cages reminded Merry too much of being in isolation.

She couldn't tell ScoopNet that she'd lost not just her father, but her finches and her gerbils; she couldn't beg the viewing audience to stop sending her stuffed animals, because they only reminded her of the live ones who were gone. Her father was supposed to be more important to her than her pets. Never mind that before the CV, she'd only seen him once every few months, at best; never mind that she'd cared for the animals every day, fed them and cleaned their cages and given them medicine when they were sick.

She'd made enough trouble for herself already. She had to stick to her lines now. So, her mother's hands still resting on her shoulders, she said dully, "I've lost all the experiences I would have had if I hadn't been in isolation. And I'll never know what they might have been. I've lost three months of my life."

Gannon nodded. "And what, if anything, have you gained?"

That one would have been easy even without the script. Meredith looked straight at the camera. "I've gotten the sky back, and fresh air, and the trees in the Presidio and sunlight on the Bay, and they mean more to me than they ever could have meant before. I've learned not to take anything for granted." I've learned how important it is to have a body.

"Cut!" someone said in the background, and then, "That was great, honey. Great job!"

"Thank you," Meredith said, and shrugged away from her mother's grasp. "Can I go now, please?"

Constance shook her head. "Merry—"

"Mom, I need to go lie down. I'm feeling sick again." The ScoopNet crew cringed—good, let them be scared of contagion, it served them right—but Constance shook her head.

"Don't worry, guys. She can't give you anything: it's run its course. It's just—all the excitement." But she laid a hand on Meredith's forehead, anyway. "You don't feel hot, honey. I'm sure you're okay, but do you want to take something?"

"No, Mom! I want to go to my room!" Meredith reddened as soon as she'd said it. It sounded like she was sending herself away for bad behavior. Well, maybe she was; let Constance think she was. It might make things easier later. "May I go now, please?"

"Of course," Constance said, and Meredith fled, upstairs and away. If she pulled the covers over her head and stayed there for a few hours, maybe Constance wouldn't lecture her too badly when she came back out.

But her bedroom had been the wrong choice, as she should have known it would be. There was her father's face on the monitor. The forehead was wrinkled, this time; the image was weeping. "I should have spent more time at home when I was still embodied, Meredith. I can see that now. Oh, Merry, I am so sorry. I did not pay enough attention to you, my only child. . . ."

"No," she said. "You didn't. And you can't make up for it. And paying too *much* attention now won't help, Daddy, and you can't really cry any more than you can hug me or hold Mommy's hand, so stop faking. Go away." She wondered if this scene was being broadcast as MacroCorp's latest PR move: Preston Walford Apologizes. She didn't care. She reached out and turned off the monitor, and then plucked a towel off the floor and threw that over the monitor too, for good measure. Then she collapsed, trembling, onto her bed. She wanted to run out of the house, into the welcoming shade of the Presidio, where there were no electronics, but she couldn't, not yet. ScoopNet was still in the house. She didn't want them following her.

They'll be following you for the rest of your life, came the mocking thought. Just like Daddy will.

She wondered if the animals had felt this way: hemmed in, stared at, forced to perform. Had all of them been as desperate to get out of their cages as she was, now, to get out of this house? I'm sorry, she told them. I'm so sorry for locking you up like that.

She saw the irony: Meredith Walford Apologizes. But this wasn't on the Net. This was in her skull; this was real, and she meant it. I thought I was helping you, she told them silently. I wanted to give you good lives. I'd let you free if I could, if you were still here. I'd let you all run away, the way Squeaky did.

Two days before she entered iso, before everything changed, Meredith had been summoned into the solarium by her mother's hollering. Awakened from a nap, Meredith had jogged dazedly downstairs to find Constance cursing and chasing Meredith's pet squirrel, who scampered among paints and brushes. "The goddamn thing ate my painting. It got out of its cage and ate my painting. Meredith, don't just stand there—and don't you *dare* laugh!"

Meredith swallowed a fit of giggles, which would only hurt Squeaky's case with her mother. "Okay, Squeaky," she said, cautiously approaching him, "come on now, sweetie. You've had your fun. Time to go back inside." She wished she had food; the squirrel was watching her, merrily flicking his tail, but showed no inclination to obey her summons. He had just gnawed a hole in one of Constance's most ambitious canvases, and he couldn't possibly understand the trouble he'd gotten himself into.

Meredith's menagerie had long been a source of tension between her and Constance. The house had held, at one time or another, ant colonies, terraria for snakes and turtles, a steadily reproducing supply of mice for the snakes (who obligingly kept the mouse population in check), gerbils, hamsters, guinea pigs, rabbits, canaries, parakeets, parrots, finches, tropical fish, and finally, Squeaky, whom Meredith had found, neonatal and nearly dead, under a tree in the Presidio. She'd taken him home and hand-fed him, although Constance liked him even less than the other animals. Constance craved order and artifice, the specialties of her husband's empire. She had never shared Meredith's resolute preference for living creatures, which might have been why Constance and Preston had produced only one heir to the MacroCorp fortune.

MacroCorp, a vast, multinational conglomerate of software and entertainment companies, had gained its supremacy by providing what Preston called "the ideal image, the promise of perfection." MacroCorp companies produced computer games, home-entertainment and security software, utility maintenance bots for both home and industrial uses, and CuteBots, adorable pudgy robots who made endlessly patient playmates and companions. MacroCorp researchers were at the forefront both of the embryonic field of wetware—where they were developing feedback mechanisms to help control pain and addiction—and AI, which Preston called "the quest for the beautiful being." MacroCorp AIs would be purely benign, CuteBots writ large. "All of our products are designed to help people," Preston always said. "That's our sine qua non, our guiding principle. I will only follow, and endorse, ethical business practices." Preston had pledged that MacroCorp would never manufacture weapons, that it would always be a responsible environmental steward, that it would tithe 10 percent of its annual profits to the alleviation of pain and suffering. MacroCaritas, the conglomerate's charitable foundation, was one of the world's largest philanthropic organizations; even Preston's critics acknowledged its role in medical research and disaster relief.

Meredith had known since early childhood that Preston did, indeed, have many critics. They said his generosity was an act belied by his personal wealth, that his seeming compassion masked calculating cynicism, and that his refusal to do business with defense contractors or unethical employers or environmentally destructive mining companies was a mere PR ploy. MacroCorp probably cut deals with such companies on the sly, the critics said, and if it didn't, they were just plain stupid to ignore such important business segments. And given global interconnection—Preston's own mantra—bombs and sweatshops and strip mines couldn't easily be separated from books or basketballs or schools, anyway. The same raw materials went into products designed to enlighten and products designed to destroy; could MacroCorp ensure that neither its suppliers nor its customers did business with the companies MacroCorp itself made such a point of boycotting?

Preston had always replied that MacroCorp did just fine without actually manufacturing bombs, using child labor, or logging old-growth forests. He said that caring needn't represent self-sacrifice, that the best help is the kind by which both parties profit, and that ethical businesses didn't knowingly trade in destruction. He acknowledged that all things were interconnected, but said that he would do his best to make MacroCorp an agent of light, not darkness. His critics called this self-serving solopsism. His many beneficiaries, the victims of famine, flood, and plague, called him a saint.

When Meredith was seven, her father had been dubbed by some netcast "the founder of the new sainthood." Preston had pooh-poohed this, explaining to his wide-eyed daughter that the old saints had been people who died under horrible circumstances in the service of what they loved. "I plan to do what I love by staying alive and healthy, Merry, so don't you worry." But a friend at school had told her that in fact, Preston would never die at all, because her mommy had said that when you help people, you live forever. Meredith had continued to believe this, quite literally, long after she had lost faith in the Tooth Fairy, the Vernal Rabbit, and the Summer Solstice Sloth. She joined the rank of Preston's critics only in adolescence, when it became clear that in his perpetual quest to help everyone on the planet, he would never be able to make time for her. He went through the motions—every night he talked to her and Constance via net-cam, from wherever he was in Africa or Asia or Europe—but he was never home. He hadn't been at one of her birthday parties for five years; he dutifully asked about her pets and friends and teachers, even remembered some of their names, but she knew it was just another PR ploy. If he really cared about his wife and daughter, he'd be home. If he really cared about them, he'd be using the netcam to talk to his staff in Africa and Asia and Europe, not to his family.

Meredith had grown to detest all things connected with MacroCorp: computers, the CuteBots she'd played with when she was a little girl, the cleaning bots who roamed through the house eating dust. Animals were beautiful: they did things you didn't expect them to, and they had personalities you couldn't program. They were little packages of mystery. But Constance considered Meredith's passion only an unfortunate developmental phase. Several weeks before the Squeaky incident, Meredith had overheard her mother fretting on the phone, venting to her friend Brenda as she added yet another delicate brushstroke to yet another delicate water-color painting of microcircuitry. "I know, I know, all children like animals. And honestly, it's not that I *don't* like animals; I'm as Green as anyone else. I just wish she'd pay more attention to the rest of the world, spend more time online. She's such a bright child, really, and all of her friends, I mean, they're all writing subroutines to hack into weather satellites and, and, I don't know, make the forecasts look so bad that school will be canceled for the rest of the year. Yes, I'm sure she'll catch up. I know, Brenda. Of course the animals are cute, except for the snakes. I just wish we didn't have so many of them in the *house*."

And now Squeaky was really in the house, loose, out of his cage. From the looks of it, he was contemplating lunching on one of Constance's brushes. Meredith took a step closer, and with a whisk of his tail, Squeaky retreated to the top of the easel. "Squeaky? Over here, sweetie—"

"*Sweetie?*" Constance snapped. "Meredith, the thing's not a bot. You can't pin human labels on it. It's a rodent, a rat with social pretensions. You have to stop anthropomorphizing."

"I'll get him back in his cage, Mom! Calm down. You're scaring him."

"Meredith, that painting would have been worth twenty-five thousand dollars! It was supposed to be the centerpiece of my opening next month."

"You can repair it," Meredith said impatiently. "Or repaint it. You've got the sketches. Come on, Mom, the opening's a ViralAid benefit, right? So have the buyers give the money directly. It's more honest. Squeaky, darling, come to me. Come on, baby."

Behind her, she heard her mother's sigh. "Honey, if they were going to give the money directly, they'd have done it by now. They want something in return; that's very understandable."

"Well, aren't they supposed to feel good for helping? Shouldn't that be enough?" Squeaky had now scampered onto the back of the wicker couch. He flicked his tail at her again, as if they were playing a game. Meredith took a slow step toward him, holding out a closed fist she hoped he would believe contained food. What had gotten into him? Did she need to build another wing onto his cage? It was already a five-foot terraced affair, with tunnels and perches containing all the toys any squirrel could ask for. The latch on the door must have worked loose again; she'd have to find a better way to repair it.

"Maybe it should," her mother said, "but it isn't, at least not for everybody. And that means I'm in a real position to do good here. Not everyone can get twenty-five thousand dollars for a canvas, Merry."

No, Meredith thought, just the wife of the CEO of MacroCorp. "Of course not, Mom. Squeaky, come here!" He turned around, gave her a coquettish look over his shoulder, and leaped nimbly onto the hanging pot of philodendron next to the window.

"Merry, there's no such thing as pure compassion, even among Greens. Altruism is only enlightened self-interest; you know that. And not everyone understands that we're all connected. Plenty of people call themselves Green and aren't."

Meredith rolled her eyes. Look who was talking. "I know, Mom. Squeaky, no! That's poisonous!" Meredith leapt at the pot to keep him from chewing the philodendron, and he launched himself gracefully back onto the couch. "Oh, Squeaky! Mom, maybe this would be easier if you left the room."

Her mother went on as if Meredith hadn't spoken. "We need to honor the big picture, even if other people don't. The UDPs need whatever we can give them, even if it comes from trendy art collectors. Do you understand?"

Right, Mom. Of course, the Underdeveloped Peoples don't call themselves underdeveloped. That's your word for them, because they like plants and animals better than machines. "Sure, Mom. Come on, Squeaky—"

"Oh, Goddess!" Constance said. Squeaky had jumped back onto the painting and resumed nibbling the torn edge of the canvas. "Meredith! Make him *stop* that!" Constance rushed toward the squirrel, flapping her arms, but he only cocked his head at her.

"I'll get him back in his cage, Mom! If you'd just go away and give me a chance—"

"Get him *off* my painting! Shoo! Shoo! Get out of here!" And as Meredith watched in horror, her mother rushed behind the canvas and opened the window, through which Squeaky, with one last wave of his tail and a chittering cry of joy, streaked in a blur of gray fur.

"Mom! How could you do that!"

"He'll come back, Merry. He knows who feeds him."

"Squeaky!" Meredith cried, and ran to the window. It was a cold day, and foggy; she couldn't see the Bay, which normally shone far below, down the terraced length of Lyon Street. She could barely even see the eucalyptus trees of the Presidio, which began just beyond the low wall bordering her family's property. She frantically scanned the manicured lawn, but couldn't find Squeaky anywhere. He had already disappeared.

She ran outside, calling him, making the chittering sounds he had responded to when he was a baby and thought she was his mother. "*Chhhh—chit—chit*—Squeaky? Where are you?" She scanned the lawn, empty, ran to the wall and squinted between trees and along branches—was that a flash of gray? no, it was a bird, and flown—and then, heart pounding, began patrolling the perimeter of the lawn, peering into the Presidio. He could be anywhere. "Squeaky?" she called softly, and then bit her lip to keep from crying.

"Merry?" Her mother had followed her outside. "Honey, I'm sorry. Really I am. Can I help you?"

Meredith, furious, ignored her. "Squeaky? *Chhhh—chit—chit?*" One circuit of the lawn completed, she began another, and ended it with a taste of lead in her mouth. He was gone.

"Meredith?" Constance still stood forlornly on the lawn, an anxious shape in the fog. "Sweetheart, you can put out food for him. He'll come back, once he's done exploring. Come inside now. I'll have the bots make you some tea."

"I don't *want* tea."

"Come inside. We'll put out food. Squeaky will be fine."

"Mom, he's a tame animal! He can't survive on his own!"

"He'll be all right, Merry. Remember what the vet said? Squirrels can't really be domesticated. You would have had to let him go sooner or later anyway, when he reverted back to the wild. Squirrels always do. The doctor said so. Now have some tea."

Meredith swallowed tears. "He hasn't reverted yet, and he doesn't know how to find his own food, and he's not scared enough of people! Somebody might hurt him! He'll die, Mom! He'll die and it will be your fault!"

"Merry, please . . ."

Meredith felt her fists clenching. "He wasn't trying to hurt your stupid painting! He didn't know what he was chewing—he's a squirrel and he needs to chew!"

"Meredith, I'm sorry."

"You are not! You hated Squeaky! You hate all my animals! That's what you told Brenda! I heard you!"

To her infinite satisfaction, Constance flinched. "Sweetheart, I'm sorry. I said I'm sorry. But yes, I'm also a little—well, all right, a lot—tired of my house being a zoo."

"What do you mean, 'your house'? It's my house too! Are you going to dump all the animals out the window the way you dumped Squeaky?"

"I didn't dump him, Merry! He went of his own accord. Now look, I shouldn't have opened the window. I know that. I was frantic to get him away from my canvas. But maybe we should work on finding more appropriate habitats for the others too. Can you do that?"

"Mom! That's not fair!"

"Merry, we both have to live here. There are other places you can spend time with animals. You can go to the SPCA downtown, or to the Gaia Temple. Now please: I know I should have talked to you about this before. If I had, you wouldn't have lost Squeaky that way. But I'm talking to you about it now. I'd like to see the animals, at least most of the animals, go somewhere else, all right?"

"Why should you care? You don't take care of them! You don't even have to look at them! Mom, it's a big house."

"I know. That's what I keep telling myself. But clearly, I don't feel it's big enough. Obviously that's why I opened the window. Please, Meredith?"

"No," she said, and stormed inside.

When her father called from Africa that night, Meredith tried to enlist him. "Daddy, tell her it's not fair. Tell her there's enough room in the house for my pets. Tell her—"

The face on the screen looked harassed. "Merry, she spends more time there than I do. I'm not getting into the middle of this. You and your mother have to work it out."

"Right," Constance said. "And I want the animals gone."

"No! That's not—"

"Hush," Preston said. "Listen, I can't talk long, but I called to tell you I'm coming home tomorrow—"

"Preston!"

"—for a day or two before I leave for Buenos Aires—"

"Daddy, why can't you ever stay home for more than five minutes?"

"—so please don't make plans for tomorrow night."

"What time will you be home, Preston? Why are you coming back so soon? I thought the plant opening there was—"

"It's been delayed. We're having labor problems. I should be home in the late afternoon. Listen, I'm not feeling terrific and it's going to be a long day tomorrow, so—"

"Preston, what's wrong? Are you ill? You look exhausted."

"Daddy, you have to tell her it's not fair!"

"Merry, we'll discuss it tomorrow. Good night. I love you."

"If you love me, tell her it's not fair!" Meredith yelled, but the image was gone; he'd already signed off. "I can't believe this. He hung up on us!"

Constance stood up and started to pace, a caricature of a concerned wife. "He really didn't look well. I hope he's not getting sick."

"It would serve him right if he did. I hope he does."

"Meredith, that's a terrible thing to say! You know you didn't really mean that."

"All right, I didn't really mean it. But, Mom—"

"No buts. That's enough, Merry. We're both tired. We'll talk about this in the morning, all right? Sleep well."

She hardly slept at all. She stayed awake, worrying about Squeaky, trying not to imagine him flattened under the wheels of a car. Maybe Constance was right; maybe he'd come back if she put out food for him. In the meantime, she had to work on ways to keep the other animals. It really was a big house; there were entire rooms Constance never entered. The gerbils were already in Meredith's room, and the mice could join them, in a separate set of cages. Surely Constance couldn't object to that. The gerbils were no bother at all, and Meredith needed to keep the mice to be able to keep the snakes. She could move the snakes from the dining room, where their terrarium was now, to the upstairs library, where her mother hardly ever ventured. The finches, meanwhile, could be moved into the attic guest suite, where they'd get more sunlight than they did now in the east-wing den. That way no one except Meredith and the bots would have to see them. And if Merry talked to her father when he came home tomorrow, she was sure she could get him to intercede with Constance. His first day back from a trip was the best time to ask him for anything.

Preston's homecomings were always the same: he bounded out of the limousine and bounced up the walk, balancing luggage. The luggage inevitably included lavish gifts for his wife and daughter, whom he greeted with expansive exclamations—ones Meredith had long since stopped believing—about how much he'd missed them.

But this time he came home differently. The limo pulled up the drive as usual, and Preston got out, but he walked slowly up the walk from the car, and he wasn't carrying anything. A schlepper bot followed with his bags. "He looks terrible!" Constance said.

Meredith shrugged. "He's tired, Mom. It's a long flight." But even she was a little shocked by how drawn he looked.

There were no expansive exclamations this time. "Hello, darlings. I don't want to kiss you. I'm sick. I think I have a fever."

"No wonder," Constance said. "You run yourself ragged. Preston, you look *awful*. I'll go get you some tea and aspirin."

"Don't bother, Connie. I'm going right to bed. Good night, Merry."

"I hope you feel better," Meredith said, fighting an uneasy pang of guilt.

She'd wished illness on him, and here he was, sick. He never got sick. But surely he'd be better tomorrow, and anyway, this would work to her advantage. It was only four in the afternoon. That meant that Preston would definitely wake up before Constance did the next morning, and that would give Meredith time to work on him. She was tired too, since she'd gotten so little sleep the night before; she'd go to bed early and set her alarm, just to be safe.

She went to bed at ten, and set the alarm for five. The alarm never went off. Instead, Meredith was awakened by running footsteps in the hall and a muffled blur of voices. When she opened her eyes, there were flashing red lights outside, and her clock read 3:30 A.M. There must be a fire, she thought groggily, and reached for her slippers—if there was a fire she'd have to go outside, and she didn't want to do that in her bare feet—and she'd have to rescue the animals. That thought jolted her into alertness, and as she shoved on her second slipper she glanced out the window at the fire trucks. How many? Did they have their hoses out? She didn't smell smoke.

There were three trucks, but they were white. White? What did—

There was a knock, and her bedroom door opened. The figure who entered was also white, clad in a spotless white suit like a spacesuit, with a breathing tank on the back and a helmet. A voice came from the suit, amplified and tinny. "Meredith, you don't know me. My name's Linda. I'm a paramedic. Don't be afraid."

Terrorists, Meredith thought, cold with fear. How had they gotten past the gates? Were they going to kidnap her? "You're here because of my father," she said. Of course they were. They wanted his money.

"Yes, that's right," came the tinny voice. "He's very sick, Meredith. Very sick. We have to take him to the hospital. And he has to be in isolation. The fever he has—it looks like a bad one, one that can be spread very easily. And I'm afraid that you and your mother will have to be in isolation too, until we find out if he gave it to you."

"Fever?" she said, stupid with sleep and fear. She'd wished illness on him. How could she have done that? "He was sick last night—when he got home. . . ."

"Meredith, how long did you spend with him last night? Did you touch him? Was he coughing or sneezing, or were his eyes running, anything like that?"

She shook her head. "No, just a few minutes. He was tired, he had to go

to bed . . . he didn't want to kiss us because he was sick." Fever. Isolation. And the white suits, not spacesuits at all, but earthsuits, isolation
suits. Biocontainment. Oh, sweet Gaia. Goddess Earth protect us now
and always. . . . She swallowed and said, "What does he have? Where did
he get it?"

"We aren't sure yet," the suit said. "You have to come with me now,
Meredith. I'm sorry. You have to stay at the hospital for a while too."

In isolation. She was going to get sick too, she knew it. She'd wished illness on her father, and whatever you wished for other people came back to
you threefold. That was what the Gaia Temple taught. "And my mother?
Will she be there too?"

"Yes."

"Who's staying here? Someone has to stay here to take care of my animals. I have two snakes and finches and gerbils and mice. They'll die if no
one feeds them."

The white suit shook its helmet. "No one's staying. No one can stay
here until we know for sure what your father has, and no one can come
here from outside. The estate will be quarantined."

"My animals—"

"They have to stay here. They could be disease vectors."

"They aren't disease vectors! Daddy didn't get near them! I can't just
leave them here—they'll die! Let me take them with me."

"You can't. I'm sorry. Pack a little bag if you want to: some clothing,
books—"

"One," Meredith said. "One or two. One of the snakes and a few mice
to feed it."

"No, Meredith. I'm sorry. I know this is very scary for you, but you
have to get ready now."

"One animal," Meredith said, near tears.

"No animals. I'm sorry."

"They'll die without anyone to feed them."

"Meredith," the voice said, and Meredith heard a mechanical whisper, a
hiss that might have been a sigh. There was a pause before the voice began
again. "Meredith, it's a bad fever. A very bad fever. We think he got it in
Africa. We think it's something we've already seen there. And if we don't
contain it a lot of *people* could die, do you understand that? Not just mice.
People."

She blinked. Gaia protect us. "My—my father? He has it?"

"We don't know. We can't tell yet."

Numbly, she let herself be led through the motions of packing: a toothbrush, shorts and T-shirts, a nightgown, the framed photograph of Squeaky that sat on her desk. She whispered good-bye to the gerbils before she left and put extra food and water in their cage, praying that they'd be all right until all of this was over, until she got back. They were desert animals. They could survive scarcity, please, please, and so could the others. Surely they could. Goddess protect us.

She insisted on giving the finches and the mice extra food too, and on putting several mice in the terrarium with the snakes so that they could eat. She said good-bye to the creatures and then she let herself be walked outside to the white truck. Only one now. Constance and Preston had already been driven away. During the ride to the hospital, she realized that in saying good-bye to the animals, she might have missed the chance to say good-bye to her parents.

Six

THE isolation unit was decorated with posters of beautiful places: Tahoe, the Maine coast, the Colorado Rockies. Its full-spectrum lighting dimmed and brightened according to diurnal rhythms. It boasted a complete entertainment center and a small gym: a StairMaster, an Exercycle, a set of weights. Its bathroom contained not only a shower but a sauna and whirlpool bath. It was as cheerful and comfortable as medical compassion could make it, and Meredith hated it with her entire heart, whenever she was coherent enough to feel anything about it at all.

She spent three months there, moments of panicky hope and lucid terror alternating with long periods of feverish dementia. During her conscious intervals, she learned all too well why Squeaky might have chafed at even the most luxurious of cages. Visitors could observe her through a thick window, but couldn't come inside unless they donned a containment suit, an item of apparel permitting no more intimacy than the window did. Because the containment suits were so awkward, even her doctors and nurses tended to avoid them, delegating her care to sensors and waldo arms and arachnid robots who perched on her bedside, clicking and humming, to draw blood. They were MacroCorp bots, of course. They made her no fonder of the family business.

For the first four days, Meredith prowled her suite, doing long stints on the StairMaster, soaking in the Jacuzzi, trying not to think about what might happen to her, or to her animals, or to her parents. Several times a day, she spoke to her mother on the telephone. "I feel fine, Merry. I don't think I'm going to get sick. How do you feel?"

"I'm fine. I don't think I'm going to get sick, either. How's Daddy? Why can't I talk to him?"

"He's—he's feverish, honey. He'll talk to you when he gets better."

"Do they know what he has?"

"They aren't sure," Constance said, her voice tight, and dread pooled in Meredith's stomach.

"You're lying, aren't you? It's really bad, isn't it? Mommy, what does he have?"

"I told you, they don't know! I'm not lying, Merry. It's—it's new, they—"

"Is that why my TV's not working?"

"What?"

"I can't get any news. Just old movies and game shows." Meredith glanced at the TV behind her, where several people dressed in inflated clown suits were hopping on pogo sticks through a maze, trying to win a year's subscription to ScoopNet. "Mommy, what's going on?" There was a beat of silence, and Meredith said, "Tell me. Please tell me. Whatever it is, it won't scare me as much as sitting here thinking about what could possibly be bad enough for a news blackout. Mommy—"

"All right, all right, I'll tell you. There's—there's a new pandemic. It started in Africa."

Meredith felt as if the floor had dropped out from under her. "Where Daddy was. That's where he got it. How many dead?"

"Meredith—"

"How many dead?"

Meredith heard her mother swallow. "Thirty thousand, so far." Sweet

Gaia, Meredith thought, and squeezed her eyes shut. "It's airborne, and it mutates incredibly quickly. ScoopNet's calling it Caravan Virus because you don't just get one bug, you get a whole train of them."

Meredith took a deep breath. "It's definitely what Daddy's got?"

"Yes," Constance said. And then, her voice eerily calm, "But you don't have to worry about him."

"What does *that* mean? How can you know that? If he's so sick—"

"Don't worry," Constance said quietly. "Meredith, I have to go now. The doctors are here."

"Wait! Mommy, are you sure you're feeling okay? I'm feeling okay. Mommy—"

"I'm fine, honey. I'll call you later. Good-bye."

"I love you," Meredith said, the first time she'd said it in months, but the phone was dead. Meredith cursed and dialed for a nurse, and a harried man in scrubs appeared behind the isolation window. "I want news, please."

"Ms. Walford—"

"My name's Meredith. My mother told me about Caravan Virus. She told me my father's sick. I want to be able to watch the news, not those idiots." Meredith gestured at the screen. Two of the people on pogo sticks had fallen over and were blocking the maze; the other two, dismounted, stabbed furiously at the fallen contestants' clown suits, trying to deflate them so they could move onward to the finish line.

The nurse sighed. "Looks like you got it."

"What?" Meredith turned around and saw, incredibly, her father's face on the television.

"Hello, my daughter Meredith. You are Meredith, my daughter. How are you feeling this afternoon, Meredith?"

"*What?* What is this?" Meredith turned back to the window, but the nurse was gone.

"You must excuse my awkwardness," the television said. "I hope to overcome it soon. I am experiencing, how do they say, the difficulties of the tech—tech—technical sort, but these are not serious and will not last. I have only been here a few hours now. It is all very new."

"Go away! What are you, some kind of wonky AI impersonating my father? Off, screen!"

The screen stayed on. "I am Preston. I am your father. I have been translated—"

Meredith fought panic. "Mute, screen!"

"No, Meredith my daughter. You must listen." Preston's image blurred and rippled, reconfiguring itself into a frown. "Meredith, it is imperative. You must inform the doctors if you develop headache, rash, fever, double vision, cold sores, vertigo—"

"The doctors know before I do when I need to pee. What are you, and why won't you go away?"

"I am your father. This is a new technique. We have been developing it. My personality and memory have been stored . . . my sensorium . . . it was to be an experiment, the translation. Now it is . . . it is . . . where I live."

"Where you *live*?" Meredith squinted and sat down cautiously on her bed. "Is my father still alive?"

"I am your father. I am. Ask me questions: test me. I know about Squeaky the squirrel. I know about the algebra test you failed last year. For your last birthday I brought you a kangaroo hologram from Australia."

Merry took a deep breath. Anyone could have known those things; Preston's life had long been MacroCorp property, endlessly massaged by the PR brigade. And he was home so seldom that she couldn't think of any personal questions to ask to test him. "You can't be my father. My father's a human being."

"I am your father. How are you feeling?"

I feel like I'm losing my mind. Meredith rang for the nurse again. "What," Meredith said, pointing to the television set, "is that?" The set itself was still speaking, but she ignored it.

The nurse cleared his throat. "That's, uh, your dad."

"You mean it's a simulacrum of my dad. And not a very good one, either. If this is a joke—"

"Tell her," the television said. "She will not believe me, her father."

The nurse cleared his throat again. "Merry, your father—he was very sick. Very sick."

"Was? Does that mean he's better now?" The door behind the nurse opened, and a very tall man with red hair hurried in: Jack Adam, Macro-Corp PR chief. He was dressed in an expensive suit; he always wore expensive suits. Meredith suspected he slept in them. She liked him, anyway, and always had. He was a nice person; sometimes his perpetual media smile even seemed genuine. But he wasn't smiling today. He looked exhausted.

"Jack," she said. "I was surprised you hadn't come to see me."

"I've been busy, Merry."

"Jack," said the television, "tell Meredith my daughter—"

"I'm telling her, Preston. That's what I'm here to do. Take a break, okay? Give us half an hour." Merry turned just in time to see her father's face fade, replaced by one of the inflated clowns hopping furiously over the finish line, to insane cheering from the studio audience.

"Off," Merry snapped. This time it worked. "Jack, what—"

"Shhhh. Listen, I just came from seeing your mother and she's fine, okay?"

"I know. I just talked to her. But Daddy—"

"Merry, sit and listen, all right? I know this is hard. I know it is. We didn't want to tell you until you were out of here, but your father, uh, got a little anxious. He wanted to see how you were, wanted to tell you himself, but he's, ah, not acclimated very well yet. Tripping over his feet, in a manner of speaking."

"Acclimated to *what*?"

"Net translation," Jack said gently. "Do you know what that means?"

I have been translated, the television had said. Merry swallowed bile. "Sure. MacroCorp's been working on storing and digitizing personalities; I know that much. I follow ScoopNet, same as anyone else. Virtual immortality, they're calling it. They're also saying it's years away."

"Not anymore," Jack said. "We've been recording and storing your dad's memories for several decades now, as a test."

"He died," Meredith said. "He died, didn't he? And you went ahead and did this translation thing. Well, it's not him! It's just a program! It doesn't have free will and it doesn't have a body!"

"He no longer has a biological body," Jack said. "That's exactly right. As for the free will part—look, Merry, he was frantic about you and your mother. And when we translated him, the first thing he wanted to do was talk to you two. And we told him not to. We told him it would be too upsetting. We told him to wait until you were out of here. You can see how much good that did. At the moment, I wish he didn't have free will, but it certainly looks otherwise."

"I have free will," came a metallic voice near Meredith's feet. She looked down and saw a medibot, one of the ones that usually drew blood. "I can have a body, too." The bot tried do some kind of complicated dance step, but instead its legs got tangled and it fell over.

Jack shook his head. "Preston, that's really not funny. I asked you to give us some time alone."

Meredith picked up the bot and rearranged its legs. "There," she said, putting it down again. "Now you can go away. Go away, bot. Jack, how'd he—it—get in there?"

"The bot must have some kind of Net connection," Jack said. "To check blood values against medical databases, maybe? I don't know. Your father seems to be having some, ah, boundary issues. We're working on the problem, believe me."

The bot wasn't going away. "I need to draw your blood now," it said. That was what it usually said. It climbed up onto Meredith's chair to reach her arm, the way it always did. But it was too soon. Meredith looked at the clock; she usually had blood drawn every four hours, but it had only been two.

"It's not time yet," she said. "TV, on! Daddy, AI, whatever you are, leave the bot alone." Her father's face reappeared on the screen, but the bot kept about its business, swabbing her arm with antiseptic.

"I am leaving the bot alone," said the television. "Meredith, how do you feel?"

"I'm fine! I'm not supposed to get stuck for another two hours!" She felt a pinch as the needle slid in, and cursed silently. That was all she needed: a vampire bot on top of this insane AI. "Is this thing broken?" Now it was climbing her shoulder to stick a thermometer in her ear.

In the bank of readouts behind the isolation window, a red light came on, and a doctor strode into the room. "Okay, Mr. Adam, time to leave now."

"What does that red light mean?" Merry said. "Jack—"

"Bye, Merry. Good luck. We're all rooting for you." Jack left; two other doctors and a nurse came in. The doctor said, "Meredith, would you lie down, please? We'd like you to rest for a few minutes before we take your blood pressure."

"Sure," she said. Her voice sounded as metallic as the bot's had, and in bed, she couldn't avoid the television set.

"Meredith, you must do exactly as the doctors say," her father's simulacrum told her.

"I know," she said. And then, with the grim suspicion that she already knew the answer, "Um, what's the incubation period of this thing?" Through the window, she saw two of the doctors exchange a glance; on the television, her father's image froze. "Hello? Look, I'm not stupid.

We're getting close, aren't we? That's why you're sticking me more often. That's why all these people are here. So what is it?"

One of the doctors cleared her throat. "Four and a half, five days."

"Oh," Merry said. "So, uh, is all the bot stuff normal?"

"Your temp's up a bit," one of the nurses said.

"Oh. That was the light that went on?"

"Yes, honey. But it could just be the excitement."

Right, Merry thought. I don't think so; I don't think you do, either. Thirty thousand dead. Sweet Gaia. MacroCorp hadn't had *her* wired since birth; her personality wasn't stored anywhere except in her brain. She began to tremble. "I'm scared."

"Of course you are," the nurse said. "Do you want a sedative?"

"No." Whatever happened, she wanted to feel it for as long as possible.

"Do you have a headache?" the television said. "I had a headache. If you get a headache—"

"Mr. Walford," the nurse said, "please be quiet. Can you do that?"

If I die, Merry thought, I'm dead. They can't translate me. A tiny throbbing had begun behind her eyes. She lay very still, and tried to convince herself that it was just her imagination.

Afterward, there were entire weeks she couldn't remember, except in surreal snatches: being surrounded by figures in spacesuits, being covered in bots, waking from nightmares of immobility to find herself tied to the bed and tethered to thickets of IV tubes. She dreamed of her mother's face looking through the isolation window, mouthing words Merry couldn't hear, and learned later that it had been real: Constance had developed no symptoms, and after ten days had been released from her own isolation. And always, whenever Meredith was conscious, her father's face hovered on the television screen above her. "You will recover, Meredith. You must recover." Once she dreamed that she was well, that she had just woken up in her bed back home, and that all the animals she had ever had were gathered to welcome her. Squeaky was there too, and in her dream she wept because she was so happy to see him again. The dream was so real that she expected, when she woke, to find herself sourrounded by animals; but when she opened her eyes she was in the merciless comfort of the isolation unit, ringed by bots and spacesuits. The effect was one of sudden metamorphosis: her pets had been transformed into these ghastly mecha-nisms, possessed by the brutal logic of the machine, and she had no way to change them back.

Meredith survived, as most people who weathered the virus did, be-cause her family was wealthy enough to afford round-the-clock, individual medical care, teams of doctors to track the progress of CV in her system and to treat its various manifestations as quickly as possible. The pandemic was relatively limited in the United States, thanks largely to Preston's swift recognition of the dire nature of his illness. Because he had called the Bio-containment Unit as soon as he had, everyone who had been on the com-pany jet back from Africa, and all of their contacts since landing, were promptly isolated, at MacroCorp's expense. A few dozen people died—the pilot and several flight attendants, and various people they'd kissed, spoken to, or visited since landing—but at least so far, Preston's foresight seemed to have prevented a major outbreak in the U.S.

From the television news, when she was well enough to tell her father to vanish from the screen so that she could watch it, Meredith learned of the fate of thousands of Preston's African employees, one of whom had ev-idently infected him during a plant tour. Without access to isolation, they didn't survive. The virus spread so easily, especially in countries where people still spoke to each other most often in person, rather than over the phone or the Net. Neither did vast numbers of their relatives and friends. The ill soon swelled into the tens of thousands, a complex web of human relationships ensuring that by the time the epidemic ended, much of Africa and large pockets of Asia and South America, already ravaged by HIV, would be further decimated.

Even when she was well enough, Meredith soon sickened of watching the news, with its relentless coverage of epidemic and death, its endless profiles of grieving families. She stopped watching the news at all. She sent her father away several times a day, because his own terror terrified her. She watched old movies when she could concentrate well enough, and children's programming when she couldn't, when she was so sick that her attention wandered after even a few moments. She watched cartoon char-acters, smashed into smithereens, miraculously regenerate; she watched brightly colored letters and numbers dancing across the screen, watched ca-vorting puppets, watched a gentle man in a blue sweater sing a song about loneliness.

Please don't think it's funny
When you want the ones you miss.
There are lots and lots of people
Who sometimes feel like this.

She found herself humming that song for days afterward, because she missed everything. Once, weeping from pain, she heard the tune and looked up to discover Preston's face on the television. He was singing it to her.

"You like this song, Meredith. I thought you would feel better if I sang it to you."

"The man in the sweater sings it better," she said. She couldn't summon the strength to send Preston away.

"Yes, that is true," Preston said. "You do not have to miss me, Meredith. I am right here."

She had been wrong; she didn't miss everything. "I don't miss you," she said.

"I think you would, if I were not here. There is another little girl in isolation, Meredith, in this same hospital. Both of her parents have just died. She is very sad. It would be nice if you could be her friend."

"Don't want to," she said. She was tired of orphans. There were orphans on the news, constantly: that was why she had stopped watching the news. "Don't want sad things." She didn't have the energy to tell Preston what she did want: her animals, everything vital and sensory and simple. She hungered desperately for real sunlight, fresh air, the feel of another person's skin. She woke sometimes sobbing and choking for breath, despite the purified gases circulating through the unit's ventilation system. She longed to smell grass, flowers, baking cookies, the fragrant cedar chips in which the gerbils made their nests. During her good days, the days when she could sit up, converse, focus her eyes, Meredith was grateful for visits from her mother, grateful for clean sheets, grateful that she was slowly getting stronger. On her good days, she didn't even mind the bots too much; if they hurt her with their constant needles, it was only as much as a doctor or nurse would have done, and at least someone had thought to cover them with bright terry cloth so they wouldn't be quite so machine-like, quite so hard and cold. During her many bad days, when pain or nausea or dizziness wracked her body, when she was so exhausted she literally

couldn't raise her head, when fever made the room bulge and pulse in surreal, ghastly contractions, she was aware of her mother's presence, if at all,
only as a remote face pressed to the window of the unit, and of her father's
as a maddening apparition that refused to go away. On those days, the bots
terrified her, becoming giant, garish spiders whose hypodermic needles were
poison fangs.

Between the many terrible days and the fewer, but increasingly frequent, good ones fell another variety, the bridge days: the times when
Meredith felt herself getting better, and prayed for freedom; the times
when she felt herself getting worse, and prayed merely to survive. It was on
one of those days, a passage from better to worse, when Constance told her
that the animals in the house were gone. "Sweetheart, the hospital had the
place disinfected before I went home, you know. Our things are still there,
the furniture and paintings and so forth, because Daddy's head of security
made sure the place was guarded when we were gone, not just with cyber-
systems but with people too, so nobody could sneak past the cameras to
take something and maybe get sick . . . anyway, they did a very thorough
cleaning job. Very thorough. And your pets—honey, the cages aren't even
there anymore. They were gone before I got back, you have to believe
that, I didn't do it."

"It was necessary," Preston's face said from the television. "Animals have
been identified as CV vectors in Africa and Asia."

"I know," Meredith said wearily. "You let me watch the news yesterday, Daddy, remember? I saw that story too."

Constance sighed. "Merry, please tell me you don't blame me."

"I don't blame you," Meredith said. "Really." She had known what
Constance was going to tell her. "They must have been dead, anyway,
Mom, from not being fed. It isn't your fault."

"I'm so sorry," Constance said, and Meredith heard her voice catch. "I
really am. I know how much you loved them. I'm sorry we had that stupid fight about them. If I'd known—"

"It's okay," Meredith said, and discovered dully that it was. The world
where her mother had been the villain, the world where Constance had
cruelly tossed Squeaky out into the cold, was ages gone now. "I'm glad
about Squeaky now. That he's out in the Presidio somewhere. I've been
thinking about that, you know. Because if he hadn't gotten out, he'd be
dead now too."

Constance nodded. "I know. I hope he's okay. He was a cute little thing, even if I wouldn't admit it at the time." She smiled wanly and said, "We'll get you new pets, Merry. You're going to get over this. You're very strong, all the doctors say so, if—if you weren't going to make it, you wouldn't have gotten this far. You're getting better, sweetheart. You'll be coming home any day now. You feel better today, don't you?"

She felt worse, once again, yet another episode in the endless cycle of illness and seeming recovery. "I don't know. I guess so. I have a headache today." On the television, her father frowned, and she remembered that headache had been his first symptom.

"It's just the air in there," Constance said. "That terrible canned air. I can't *wait* until you come home, Meredith! Any day now."

It was many days after that—twenty, twenty-five? they blurred, only the cycles of illness and recovery distinct—before Meredith got to go home. She awoke one morning to realize that something was different. The air: the air smelled different. She glanced at the window and saw a nurse, who smiled and said into the intercom, "We're getting you used to the outside, Merry, gradually. In a few more days it will be entirely regular outside air you'll be breathing, and then if you stay well, you can go home."

"It is wonderful news!" Preston said, beaming from the television, and Meredith thought, If I really get out of here, maybe I can get away from him.

"The real world will take some getting used to," her mother said with a laugh, when she came to visit later that day. Already the odd newness of the air had faded, become unnoticed background; Meredith yearned for more smells, more outside air, dirty air, windblown air. "Coming out of the hospital, you know . . . even if you're just in a regular room, you're used to being taken care of, and then you're outside again and everything's so *big,* there's so much of it, and you have to do things yourself again. It can be a little overwhelming. It was like that for me when I came out of the hospital after being in that car accident before you were born, and that time I was only in bed for a week. After being in iso for two weeks, it was even more like that, and you've been here for three months, Merry."

Preston's image nodded and said, "You will have to go slowly, Meredith, and be careful of your strength. Everything will tire you out at first, even good things."

A lot you know about it, she thought scornfully. Preston, the sleepless cybernetic wonder. "I'll be just *fine*," she told them, and thought of Squeaky, released into a world so much larger than his previous one. Had he made the adjustment? Was he still alive somewhere, gathering nuts and chittering at passersby?

The air became stranger and newer each day, newer until its newness faded and became old, and at last Meredith was allowed to leave the unit. The doctors and nurses, her mother and Jack Adam, a handful of classmates and neighbors and the inevitable ScoopNet film crew, all were waiting for her outside, smiling, holding flowers and balloons and a cake with candles on it, one for each day she'd been in the isolation unit. "We had to get an extra-large cake for all those candles," one of the doctors said with a smile, and everyone laughed, and then a group of lab technicians came by to meet the patient whose blood they'd been studying for three months. "You're *much* prettier than your antigens," one of them said shyly, and everyone laughed again. "You are more famous than I am now," Preston intoned from an overhead monitor, and Constance said, "My goodness, Merry! I don't think there'd be this much fuss if you'd gone to Mars and come back!"

It was overwhelming. She cried at all the noises, the tastes and smells and sensations, people's arms hugging her, the whir of the cameras, the scent of Jack's aftershave and the lingering smell of the match when Constance lit the candles. She cried when the doctors told her that what they had learned about the viruses in her bloodstream would help them treat other people, even ones with different mutations. She cried when at last she was rolled, in a wheelchair, out the front door of the hospital to the waiting limo. Trees: there were trees, across the street, and the same wind that moved their leaves ruffled the hair on her forehead. The same sunshine that warmed the flowers along the sidewalk warmed her skin. That sprinkler, over there, was watering the grass but watering her soul at the same time, because she could see it and smell the moist earth and feel the dampness on the breeze. She was part of the world again, at last, and her regained connection to the universe made her weep with gratitude.

During the ride home, Meredith drank in the sight of passing cars, people strolling along the sidewalk, traffic lights and baby strollers and buses and billboards and playgrounds. She promised herself that she would never let any of it become old. Never again would she take for granted her body's blessed ability to sense, to perceive and gather information, and never would she take for granted the other wondrous creatures of the world, with their equally blessed bodies. No more cages, and no more living as if she were inside a cage: not for herself and not for anyone else, if she could help it. She looked down at her hands and flexed them, feeling the muscles, ran her palms over the soft upholstery of the car and over the hard plastic buckle of her seat belt. All of it was equally remarkable. All of it made her cry.

"You're tired," Constance said, looking at Meredith with a worried frown.

"I'm happy," Meredith said, and the tears came again, foolish tears, stupid tears, holy tears. "I'm so happy. And I'm scared too—that I'll forget how much there is to be happy for."

Constance's face tightened. "I wish your father were here."

"Of course I am here," said the car's speakers. "I will always be with you now."

Constance ran a hand over her eyes. "Preston, that's not what I meant. I wish—I wish they hadn't had to translate you."

"Me too," Meredith said.

Preston started to sing. "Please don't be unhappy—"

"Daddy, don't!"

"Constance and Meredith, I am not unhappy. I like being on the Net."

"Bully for you," Constance said. Meredith had never heard her sound so bitter.

CV left most people with permanent aftereffects, and Meredith was no exception. The fever had burned her hair white, left her hair and nails brittle and her gums fragile, weakened her joints. She saw the dentist more often, ate a lot of gelatin, and went to physical therapy three times a week. The day after the ScoopNet interview, she overheard her mother complaining to Brenda, who had recently made a name for herself in the art world by throwing paint-soaked rags at her canvases and then rolling around on each one while wearing a long white shift. She sold the paintings and the dresses as pairs, and had recently expanded into upholstery and linens. She had come to the house for lunch to ask Constance's advice about opening her own home-furnishings store, but the conversation—drifting from the patio up into the second-floor spa, where Meredith was soaking in the Jacuzzi—soon turned to more personal topics.

"Merry's interview was lovely," Brenda said. Meredith had ignored most of the rest of the conversation, about marketing and advertising and the most fashionable retail districts, but this line made her sit up slightly and scoot over to the side of the Jacuzzi nearest the window. "She was very appealing, very sympathetic."

"I know," Constance said. "That's what Jack said too, not that we need to worry about it. MacroCorp stock is through the roof anyway, with this translation thing. Preston's putting a lot of pressure on me and Merry to get recording rigs, start storing memories. He says he wants our translations to be as complete as possible when the time comes. Plus, Jack says, it looks bad to the stockbrokers and consumers if Preston's wife and daughter aren't the first in line for the rigs. Gannon had planned a question about that for last night, but I made them take it out of the interview. Thank Gaia he didn't ask about it when Merry got off track!"

Brenda cleared her throat. "What, ah, exactly is the legal status of your marriage now? If you can even answer the question." No kidding, Meredith thought. Preston could hear everything that happened on the property, since the house was so thoroughly wired, and Meredith was surprised that her mother had already been so frank.

Constance laughed. "Damned if I know. None of us do. The lawyers are working it out. And don't worry about asking: it's not like the reporters haven't gotten there first. About all we know is that Preston's still alive in the sense of being a legal entity, an individual. It looks like translation results in automatic divorce on the grounds of incompatibility, but that's problematic too, because how the hell do you divide assets, especially if the embodied spouse didn't consent to the procedure?"

"Did you consent to Preston's translation?"

"They didn't tell me about it—it was so new and experimental, and I was still in iso then and they didn't know if I was going to get sick too, and they didn't want to give me something else to worry about. I didn't know anything until after it happened. But yes, of course, how could I not approve? It was the only thing they could do, and they did it, and it seems to have worked. Good for them. But now they have to figure out how to market it to everybody else, and that means figuring out the legal stuff—especially inheritance."

"Uh-huh," Brenda said. "We're talking bundles for memory storage and translation both, I'm betting, not to mention, oh, some kind of continuing fee, in perpetuity, right? So all the individual's assets, and maybe the rest of the family's, get poured into this thing, and the spouse and kids always pre-decease and wind up leaving everything they have to the translation to pay the fees, and when the money runs out—what? The translation goes bye-bye? And say you and Merry get these rigs and Merry has kids; if she's translated when she dies, she can't leave them anything. Constance, it sounds like a pyramid scheme. Families aren't going to like it, not one bit."

"You missed your calling," Constance said drily. "You should have been a lawyer. MacroCorp's wrestling with this stuff; they know they'll have to answer those questions to make it a viable service. Reasonable fees and solid trust planning look like the best way, so far: set up a self-sustaining trust so the family doesn't have to worry about it, make the amount of money re-quired for the trust, oh, half the initial fee, and make the maintenance fee some portion of the interest, so there's still a return. And at least some of the translated will be able to work—Preston's still drawing a salary, because he's still running MacroCorp—or they can pay less for less time online, one day a week or one week a month, whatever. It will get worked out."

"It would still be a fortune."

"Sure. Preston and I don't have to worry about that, fortunately."

"The first one's free?" Brenda said.

"Well, yes. Preston's the test driver. And we're not exactly hurting, any-way."

"Right. So what are you going to say when Fargo Gannon, or some-body else, asks you why you don't have a recording rig yet?"

Constance sighed. "I'm going to change the subject. I don't know what I think about it; I don't know how I feel about what happened to Preston. I don't know how I feel about the marriage, especially since I talk to him now more than I ever did when he was still embodied. It's all too new, Brenda. So I'm going to change the subject now. Actually, I'm going to ask you to change the subject, because my brain's turned to jelly. If I were wearing a recording rig now, there wouldn't be anything much to record, I can tell you."

"No problem," Brenda said. "I'll change the subject. Have you heard that your daughter's starting a trend? Bunches of kids want white hair now, just like hers."

"Trauma hair? They want trauma hair? Sweet mother, I hate it! She's fourteen, and she looks like she's ninety-seven! I keep asking her to dye it, but she won't."

Brenda laughed. "I like it, actually. It's certainly better than green or purple or that iridescent sparkle that was so popular last year."

"It makes her look too old."

"No, it doesn't. You're only saying that because you almost lost her, and you don't want to think about her getting old and dying."

"Right," Constance said, her voice brittle. "Didn't I ask you to change the subject? I was making a frivolous complaint about my daughter's hair. Can I go back to being frivolous, please? Will you let me do that? You're supposed to be my friend."

"Constance, I'm sorry. Look, she's all right. You have a lot to be grateful for." There was a pause, the clinking of glasses, and then Brenda said gently, "Constance? She is all right, isn't she? I mean, she seems just fine, especially when you hear about the people with memory lapses. Some of them can't even remember who they were before they got sick. Merry certainly seems to know who she is."

"Oh, that's not a problem. She's the same as she was, except more so: gonzo-Green. Because she was in that awful iso unit for so long, I guess. She was nuts about animals before she went in there, but that's the age. I didn't expect her to spend so much time at Temple once she got out, that's all. I guess it will wear off. She's only been home a little while, after all. Anyway, she's quieter now, more self-absorbed. I guess that's natural. She has to adjust to being back. But you're right: we were very lucky. The doctors say there probably won't be any more long-term side effects."

"Probably? Then there might be?"

"Too soon to tell." Constance's voice held the sure note of Something Not Being Said. "Brenda, let me get you some more lemonade. I'll just mix up a fresh batch in the kitchen, all right? Now about that store, I *really* think you should consider renting in that new space on Valencia Street. I know it's a bit seedy now, but the area's really coming up and it's going to be a *very* tony address, just mark my words. . . ."

The words faded as the women walked inside, and Meredith sank back into the hot water. Was she all right? How had the virus changed her? If it could affect your memory, as Brenda had claimed, would she even know that she'd changed? The time before the virus seemed like such a dream that it was difficult for her to think clearly about what she had been like back then, how she might be different now.

The phone next to the tub chirped. Short long short: Preston's ID. If she didn't answer now, he'd find some other way to get to her. "Hello, Meredith. I don't think you have changed since your illness."

"I'm not sure you're the best judge, Daddy. How did you know I was listening?"

"The audio pickup near the bathtub could hear the conversation, so that means you could too."

"And how did you know I was in the bathtub?"

"Because the security camera in the hallway outside saw you going into the bathroom, and didn't see you coming out, and the sound of running water came through the audio pickup."

"Ducky," Meredith said. "Am I on *Candid Camera* now?"

"No, Meredith. There is no camera in the bathroom, only audio pickup. Intruders entering through the bathroom window would have to use the hallway to get anywhere else, and the camera would record them there."

"I feel so much better," Meredith said.

"I am very glad." Irony was wasted on him.

"Good. Because I'm hanging up now. I'm taking a bath and I'd like some privacy."

"Wait, Meredith. I called because I still want you to start recording as soon as possible. MacroCorp can set you up with a rig. The lawyers will solve the inheritance problems. Do not be concerned."

"I don't want a rig, Daddy. I want privacy."

"I will not have access to your stored memories, Meredith. They will be encrypted for security."

"Against you? I doubt it."

"They would have to be, for strict legal reasons. Even against me. Is this what is bothering your mother?"

"I don't know. I'm hanging up now."

"I am glad you told me. Now I understand. I know what is bothering your mother."

"How nice. Why don't you tell her? I'm not interested."

"Your body will live for years yet, Meredith, but if you start recording now, you'll lose that much less—"

"No," she said, and hung up, and sank moodily back into the warm water.

Seven

MMEDIATELY after her bath, Meredith went to the Gaia Temple, as
she had nearly every day since her return from the hospital. She usually
waited until late afternoon, when the light was the loveliest, but today she
was frantic to get out of the house. The Temple was only a short walk
through the Presidio, through the cool twilight under towering eucalyptus
trees, and it was difficult for her father to reach her there. The Temple was
militantly organic; laptops and phones were discouraged, and Meredith
avoided the few places in the complex—the rec room, the conference
room, the offices—that were Net-wired. And Preston couldn't simply appear there, anyway. He had to call or e-mail and ask permission to speak to
her. He didn't have the run of the place, the way he did at home.

As she walked, she brooded. Her mother had told Brenda that Meredith
was quieter now, and she supposed she was. Her illness had deepened her
gratitude. Her newfound sense of wonder expressed itself as pure, still pools
of feeling, moments when she found herself so immersed in beauty—the
beauty of bread, of leaves, of light—that if she opened her mouth to speak,
she would surely drown in it. Looking through an old college textbook of
her mother's, she'd found lines that described the experience perfectly.

> The body greets the sun, a blaze
> of fire, and mirrors it,
> ablaze with life.
> Words become ash, consumed.
> We speak by shining.

The lyric had been written by a minor poet named Carly Sirillo more than
fifty years before Meredith was born. A footnote discussed Sirillo's debt to
Yeats's "Vacillation," and in the margin, Constance had scrawled, "Trite
crap." That judgment hadn't softened; for Meredith, like Sirillo, couldn't

physically speak during her reveries—"your trances," Constance called them, her voice gently mocking—she had learned not to try to describe them afterwards, either.

She had tried, once, a week after her release from the hospital, as she and her mother sat in the kitchen nook overlooking the Bay. "I woke up in the middle of the night last night and looked out my window, Mom, and the *moon*—it was full, big, and orange—"

"A harvest moon," Preston said through the countertop monitor. "I saw it too, through the security cameras. It was lovely, was it not?"

"The moon's always lovely," Meredith said. How could her father understand how she had felt, looking at that sky? He no longer had a body to blaze. "But last night—I looked at it, at the orangeness of it, and I thought, Well, that's the sun it's reflecting, that light, it's a nighttime sun to remind us that the sun will rise in the morning, that the sun will make trees and flowers grow, and vegetables, and us, and I'd never thought of it that way, you know? Of the moon as . . . as a promise. As a reminder that there's always light somewhere, and you just have to wait for it, or know how to look; you have to have faith."

"Yes," said the monitor. "That is exactly right. When I was translated, everything was darkness, and then everything was light. The Net is all light."

Constance took a crunching bite of her crouton salad and said flatly around it, "It's always darkest before the dawn. Yes? And?"

"No," Meredith said, frowning. "I mean, yes, maybe, but—" This wasn't coming out the right way at all. If it had, her embodied mother would have understood her, and her disembodied father wouldn't have. She floundered for words and said, "It was more than that, Mom. Because I'm—I'm a moon too, I can reflect that light too, that's how it made me feel."

Her mother sighed. "Honey, you'll feel better when you've been home longer. You're still adjusting."

Meredith shook her head. "You don't understand. I feel great! Doesn't everybody feel this way sometimes? I used to feel this way before I got sick. Not as often, because . . . because I didn't notice things. But *sometimes.*" She stared at Constance, puzzled, and said, "Mom, when you paint—don't you feel part of something else, something bigger than you are? When you get an idea for a painting, doesn't it make you so happy that everyone *would* think you were crazy if you talked about it? Isn't that what being an artist is? Being able to be that happy, so happy that it's . . . it's spilling out of your pores, and you have to grab hold of all that extra happiness and make something out of it, so it doesn't go to waste?" Surely Constance would understand, once it was put that way. Surely her paintings spoke to her soul. Why else paint them?

"No," Constance said flatly. "No, that isn't what being an artist is. Being an artist is about getting paid for having a better design sense than other people do. I was always good at coloring inside the lines. I've made it into a career, that's all."

Meredith, stunned, opened her mouth to reply, but before she could say anything, her mother got up and stalked away from the table, her linen napkin still clutched in her fist.

"She does not understand," the monitor said. "I do, Meredith. I know you think I cannot, but I am part of something much bigger than my individuality now. Interconnection has become real to me in a way it never was before. How could I not understand?" Meredith didn't even try to answer, and the monitor went on. "Sometimes I wish your mother had gotten sick. Because then I think she might understand how we feel now: how it feels to be part of something bigger. Your mother will understand after she has been translated, but that will not happen for a long time."

In answer, Merry had gotten up and turned the monitor off; then she'd gone back to the table and finished her dinner. She wasn't part of any "we" that included her father. Preston was so clueless that he still wanted her to be friends with the little girl whose parents had died in iso, and even Constance had seen how crazy that was. "Preston, the last thing Merry needs is to be reminded of isolation. I agree that it would be a lovely outreach project, but let someone else do it. Merry has enough to deal with right now. That other kid's only eight, anyway. She's too young to be Merry's friend."

Preston thought he understood her, but he couldn't possibly; and her mother, who surely could have, usually didn't even try. And she wonders why I'm so quiet, Meredith thought bitterly now, scuffing through a pile of eucalyptus leaves. But, in truth, she was hardly more talkative with anyone else. Her friends from school had grown shy since her illness and her father's translation; even Green Teens, the eco-activist club at school, seemed superficial, full of people who cared more about their college résumés than they did about the universe they lived in.

Temple was the only place where people seemed to value the same things she did, the only place where she didn't feel crazy. She loved the balance of Temple, the dailiness of it, the vision of a world where everything was a sacrament, where everything could be infused with wonder and everyone was connected: not through the electronic abstractions of the Net, but through drinking the same water and breathing the same air. Gaia followers practiced a grounded idealism in which they helped themselves by helping others, by recognizing that everything alive was kin. Every afternoon, Meredith helped the novitiate on duty gather eggs, clean the huge dog run behind the temple, feed and groom and play with the dogs, and mend the chicken coop—a cage Meredith could accept, although not without qualms—against the cats' frequent efforts to invade it. The temple fed an immense population of stray cats. Working with the downtown SPCA, the novitiates spayed and neutered as many as they could, and adopted some out, but inevitably the population included a few pregnant and nursing queens. Meredith loved being in a place where spending time with animals was not only encouraged, but seen as holy. Before her illness, the Goddess-talk had made her squirm; now she relished it.

Today, as usual, Merry could hear the Temple long before she could see it. That was why the city had passed a zoning ordinance that all Gaia temples had to be in parks. The setting fit, of course—what *better* place than a park for a temple to the planet?—but the real reasons were practical. Gaia temples were always incredibly noisy, and back when they had been allowed in residential districts, the neighbors, even Greens, had consistently complained.

Meredith heard the dogs first. As she got closer, she began to make out other sounds: the singing and chanting from various individual and group rituals, the shrieks of the day care kids playing on the swings, a drumming class practicing in one of the glades, hammering and sawing as something or other was built or mended. She stopped by the dog run to check for new arrivals and waved at Raji, the chief novice this month, who was on his way to the henhouse with a bucket of grain. He was the youngest novice, only three years older than she was. His parents both worked for Sierra-Audubon. Raji really wanted to go into AI research, but his parents would pay his college tuition only if he spent a year as a Gaia initiate first. It was a transparent ploy to get him into as Net-free an environment as possible. "Hey, Merry. Matt's looking for you."

"For me?" Matt, consecrated to lifelong Temple service, was the closest thing the place had to a high priest, but he spent much more time working on the grounds and dealing with administrative details than he did presiding over rituals. "Why?"

Raji shrugged. "He didn't say. I was just over there helping Gwyn and Angelo with the therapy-dog schedules, and Matt stuck his head out of his office and said to send you over there when you got here."

"When I got here? How'd he know I was coming?

Raji laughed. "You're here every day, Merry!"

"Yeah, but usually not for a few hours, and since when does Matt keep track of my schedule? He has too much else to do." She shook her head and said, "This is something to do with my father, I'll just bet. The cyber-bastard probably followed me over here."

Raji looked at her skeptically. "How? You caved in and got a rig? Most of this place isn't wired."

"Tracer cells. GPS."

"Oh—right. I should have thought of that." Now it was Raji's turn to shake his head. "I wouldn't be you for the world, girl."

"Well, it's not like I have much choice. I got the GPS injections when I was still a baby." She grimaced, remembering Preston's explanation when she was seven or eight. A gang of inept Luddite terrorists had tried to kidnap the child of a biotechnology executive, and Merry, frightened by the news story, had asked if that could ever happen to her.

"Never, sweetheart. There's something in your blood, all throughout your blood, that will always tell us where you are. And we've made sure that everyone knows you have it, so that if anyone tries to steal you, we'll always be able to find you again. And because it's *all through* your blood, they can't take it out."

"I can't believe the parents whose kid was just snatched didn't do the same thing," Constance said. "Biotechnology—honestly! If there's anyone who—"

"Daddy," Meredith said, "does it work when I'm sleeping?" She had been afraid of the dark, then, afraid of monsters.

"Yes, sweetheart. It works all the time, even when you're sleeping."

She was under constant surveillance. She supposed that somewhere even now, someone was scrutinizing a screen on which a small green blip recorded her movements through the city. And now that her father was permanently online, he could track her too, even if the low-tech environs of the Temple kept him from pestering her the way he did at home.

"Damn," Raji said. "Having those GPS cells must be like being in isolation all the time. Having people peer at you."

Meredith shrugged. "Most of the time I forget about it. I have to find a way to keep my father off my back, that's all. You know, when he was still alive, I'd have given anything for this much attention."

"So you don't consider him alive?" Raji gave her a keen glance, and she remembered that he was, after all, a Temple novice, obligated to address spiritual issues.

"No, I don't. Look, I know that legally he's alive, but I'm sorry: for it to count you have to have a body."

"Ah. So I suppose you don't consider AIs alive, either?"

"Oh, AIs!" She threw up her hands and then, flustered, said, "Sorry, Raji. I know AI's your pet hobby, but as far as I'm concerned, those things are just really fancy toys. Really fancy programs."

"Some people would say that we're just really fancy programs, Merry."

"Yeah, well, I don't believe that. Show me a machine capable of transcendence—"

"Your dad claims he's already achieved transcendence."

"What?" She blinked and squinted. "He does? How do you know?"

"I talked to him about it."

"You *talked*—"

"Merry, he's built a fantastic website, you know. It's, like, his house, I guess. With lots of guests. He gets millions of hits a day."

"I know, I know, it's really popular because he's the freak of the month, but—"

"So I went there because I'm interested in AI and in what MacroCorp is doing, and I talked to him. And he told me how translation was just another way to achieve higher consciousness. It's not that different from Gaia thinking, the way he describes it."

Meredith took a step backward. "Uh-uh. No, I'm sorry. Being on the Net is *not* the same as being on the planet, eating and breathing. And you'd better not let Matt know about this stuff."

Raji laughed. "Why not? I already did. Matt thought it was interesting. He's very open-minded, you know."

"Well, okay, then you'd better not let your parents know."

"Yeah, that's true. They'd have a fit. Matt had to talk them into letting me have my own computer here, even if I can only use it an hour a day. Well, listen, I'd better get back to work. See you later. Good luck with your dad."

"Thanks," Merry said, and turned toward Matt's office. As always, it took longer to get there than the mere distance would have suggested: she had to dodge a Clowns of the Goddess troupe practicing a tumbling routine, a procession of small children carrying balloons and chanting a birthday blessing, a convoy of three wheelbarrows hauling bricks and gravel for the new labyrinth, and a pair of therapy-puppies-in-training, whose handlers were trying to teach them to heel off-leash. Neither pup was coping well with all the distractions; both of them, after chasing the wheelbarrows for a few feet, bounced over to Meredith and began ecstatically nuzzling her ankles, as the trainers called after them. "Demeter! Dmitri! No! HEEL!"

The sheer vitality of the place never failed to cheer Merry up. She walked into Matt's office laughing, her feet covered with puppy spit. "Hello, Matt. Raji said you wanted to see me."

Matt—tall and lanky, with unruly red hair—looked up from a sheaf of papers and said, "Blessings, Merry. How are you?"

"I'm okay. I'd be better if my father would stop stalking me. That's what this is about, right? He knew I was coming here and—"

"He wants to talk to you, yes. You can sit in the conference room. You'll have privacy there."

"I want privacy *from* him, not *with* him."

Matt nodded, looking sympathetic. Matt always looked sympathetic. She wondered if they'd given classes on it in Temple training school. "Yes, I can imagine, but you're going to have to settle that with him. I'm just passing on the message."

Merry scowled. "I don't *want* messages from him. Can you please tell him not to call here? He has to honor that if you say it: he made that rule himself, after he spooked all those people at the hospital."

"He's your parent," Matt said gently, "and you're still a minor. I can't deny him access, Merry. Sorry."

She felt like screaming. "Okay. So I'd better get this over with, right?" She went into the conference room, closed the door, and stared with loathing at her father's visage on the desktop monitor. "Daddy, I don't want you following me here, do you understand? That's why I come here."

"I know it is, Meredith. But I wanted to ask you some questions, away from your mother."

She cautiously sat down. "Questions?" That was a new one. Since she'd left isolation, since Preston had stopped nagging her about how she felt every ten minutes, he had foregone questions in favor of pronouncements. "You could have called me on the phone at home and asked me questions. Mommy doesn't listen in on my conversations."

"That is true. I just thought this might be—more comfortable."

She squinted at the desktop. "Why? What—"

"Meredith, would you be upset if your mother remarried?"

"Remarried?" She stared blankly at the monitor, thinking back over her mother's conversation with Brenda that morning. "Why? Is she going to—to divorce you or something?"

"She has expressed no such intention, but if having an embodied husband would make her happier, I would like to give her that opportunity."

Meredith shook her head. He'd never said anything about giving her the opportunity when he was still alive, away from home twenty-nine days out of every thirty. "I don't understand. Why ask me this? What difference does it make how I feel?"

"I do not want to discuss it with her if it will upset you, so soon after coming home." He's planning something, Meredith thought uneasily. She stared at the monitor, keeping her face impassive, and Preston said, "I wanted to find out how you would feel."

Meredith cocked her head. "I want whatever will make Mommy happy. But if you two aren't married anymore—"

"You need not worry about the finances. You and your mother would still have everything you have now, Meredith."

"I wasn't worried about that," she said, stung and ashamed, but she had been. So much for her fine Temple principles. She looked down at the conference table and said, "Look, it's between you and Mom. It's none of my business."

"Of course it is your business. You are our child. But it would not bother you?"

Meredith stood up. "This is crazy. I'm going outside now. Whatever you have to say to me, you can say to Mommy too, all right? Or just to her."

Preston's image smiled. "Good. We will discuss it, all three of us, when you get home."

"That won't be for a while," Meredith said, and headed back outside, toward the dog run.

Raji was shoveling turds when Meredith got there. "Hey, Merry. So what'd your dad want?"

"Nothing," she said. "Craziness. You need a hand with that?" She helped Raji shovel dogshit and haul kibble, but she couldn't keep her mind on her work; the conversation with her father kept nagging at her. When you get home, he'd said. Whatever he wanted to say to her and Constance was inevitable; she was only delaying it by staying here. "Nuts," she said finally, and dumped a bag of kibble into a trough, and said, "Listen, I've got to go home, okay?"

Raji looked up, frowning, from a new litter of puppies. "You all right?"

"Yeah. Don't worry. My dad's too good at jerking me around, that's all. See you tomorrow."

When she got home she found her mother in the solarium, working on an impressionist painting of an IBM XT. Retro-tech was extremely chic now, and her canvases of antique computers were flying out of tony galleries as quickly as she could produce them. "Hi," she said, without turning away from her easel, when she heard Meredith come in. "How was Temple?"

Meredith wondered how long it would take her father to pipe into the conversation. Surely he'd been tracking her on GPS, and knew she was back home now. Her mother had the GPS cells too; it occurred to Meredith that Constance hadn't even looked up when she came in, hadn't been worried about who might be coming in the door. She hadn't even needed to look. Preston Walford's wife took her security for granted. "It sucked," she said.

Constance put down her paintbrush and picked up a steaming mug of tea from the table next to her. "Why, honey? What happened?"

"Oh, Daddy followed me on the GPS and knew I was there and told Matt he wanted to talk to me in the conference room, and then he started asking me all kinds of weird questions about you."

Constance paled. "About me? Meredith, what did he want?"

"I wanted to know if Meredith would mind if you remarried," Preston's voice said from the radio, and Constance jumped and spilled tea on herself.

"Ouch! Dammit! Preston—"

"I'll go get paper towels," Meredith said.

"No, honey, I'm fine. Stay here. Preston, you have to stop this! Just barging into conversations like this! I don't care if it *is* still your house, and I don't care how much you've contained yourself everywhere else! If anybody finds out how you're acting, translation will be a dead issue, all right? Dead! You won't be able to sell it to anyone if people think their friends and relatives will be able to spy on them this way! Not even MacroCorp can market that, believe me. And if it's not something they can sell, if it won't be profitable for them, they'll be much less interested in keeping you up and running, do you understand? People die, Preston, that's all. You have to start behaving yourself!"

Smart, Meredith thought, looking at her mother with new respect. Very smart. She's getting him where he lives—literally. "Daddy, we have to set some ground rules. From now on, you don't watch me or listen to me or try to talk to me, even in the house, unless I give you permission, all right? And you don't follow me out of the house unless I invite you or unless you ask my permission *first,* is that clear?"

"Double ditto to that," Constance said. "Come on, Preston. You wouldn't even be trying to get away with this nonsense if you were still in the flesh, and you know it."

"But I want to make sure that you are safe, Constance and Meredith."

Merry snorted. "That's why you followed me to Temple? What could possibly happen to me there? A dog bite? And what could you do about it even if it happened?"

"I could call for an ambulance—"

"So could Matt or Raji or anybody else there. Daddy, it's my life, not yours, and you can't have it. This is exactly why we don't want the rigs, you know."

"There is nothing I could learn about either of you that would make me love you less," Preston said.

"*Love?* You didn't love me before, Daddy. You didn't even know me. You weren't here enough. And now—now! You wouldn't know love if it . . . if it what? Bit you on the leg? You don't have one. Hit you on the head? You don't have one. Stuck a stick up—"

"Meredith," Constance said, "I think that's enough. We get the idea." But she was smiling.

"Love is seeing all things connected as one," Preston said. "On the Net all things are connected and therefore all things are one. But I cannot be connected to you if—"

"Maybe we don't *want* to be connected to you," Constance said pleasantly. "Have you thought of that, Preston? Maybe we want to be by ourselves."

"We cannot be by ourselves. None of us ever can. People at Temple know that, Meredith; they understand interconnection."

"With things that are alive," Merry said. "That's why there's so little net-wiring there, Daddy. Temple is about connection with *bodies*. Remember bodies? That's what you don't have anymore."

"My body is now the Net, which is also the world."

Constance sighed. "Preston, I think you need a cyberpsychiatrist. You're developing delusions of grandeur."

"I am sorry I have upset you. I did not mean to upset you. I wanted to tell you, Constance, that I know why you do not want the recording rig, and I want to tell you it is all right. And I want Meredith to hear me say it, so she will also know that it is all right with me. Because it is."

"It's all right that we don't want the rigs?" Meredith said. "You changed your mind?"

"No, that is not all right," Preston said. "It is all right that your mother has been having an affair with Jack Adam for the past five years. That is why she does not want the rig. She is afraid I will find out, but I already know."

"*What?*" Meredith blinked, fighting an urge to break into laughter. "Mommy, is that true? Wait, never mind; don't answer that. It's none of my business."

Constance had turned the darkest shade of red Meredith had ever seen. "No, it isn't your business. And it certainly isn't Preston's business. And—"

The doorbell rang. "Jack is here," Preston said. "I called him and asked him to come."

"Oh, sweet Mother," Constance said. "Preston!"

"I'm going upstairs now," Meredith said. "I'm going to my room. No, wait, I'm going to take a ride downtown." Scratch that: vehicles were net-wired. "No, I'm walking downtown. This is none of my business." But she heard footsteps, and turned to find Jack, looking as if he'd just eaten something extremely unpleasant, standing in the entrance to the room.

"Your father opened the door for me," he said. "Hello, Constance."

"Jack," Constance said. "I want this . . . this *thing* offline. I want him erased. I want—"

"Connie, you're talking about murder. He's legally a person, remember? We can't do that."

"I knew about the affair before my translation. I did not care then, and I do not now. I love both of you. I have always wanted both of you to be happy. I—"

"You've been following me for five years," Constance said. "Even when you were still—"

"So it's true?" Meredith said. Jack cleared his throat, looking sheepish; her mother wouldn't look at her at all. So it was true. Meredith blinked. Well. Jack had always been kind to her; she could imagine plenty of worse stepfathers. "Daddy," she said, "I don't get it. If you've known for five years and you don't care, why bring it up now? If you didn't divorce Mommy so she could remarry Jack when you were still—before you were translated, why now?"

"You're planning to *divorce* me?" Constance said.

"No, Constance. Not unless you wish it. Meredith, I never mentioned it before because there was no reason to do so. Your mother and Jack were happy, and I loved them and I wanted them to be happy, and talking about it would only have upset them. If your mother had wanted to leave me, she would have said so. But now this is the reason she does not want to get a rig, so I needed to talk about it. And I would not have access to the recordings anyway."

Constance pressed her hands to either side of her head. "Preston! You expect me to believe that? You're trying to reassure me about privacy by telling me you've already been spying on me for five years? What, you hired a detec—"

"No, Constance. The GPS cells showed your position."

"I don't have GPS cells," Jack said.

"No, Jack, you do not. But during the neo-Luddite terrorism scare five years ago, the previous head of MacroCorp Security was keeping unusually close tabs on both of you, and discovered a pattern, and took it upon himself to tell me about it."

"Ah," Jack said. "So that's why you fired Benny. I always wondered. That line about how he needed to take early retirement to find himself didn't quite wash."

"He is happier now, breeding horses. I am glad he is happy. But he had exceeded his authority."

Constance let out a shrill laugh. "Look who's talking!"

"Constance, I have no intention of depriving you of property. I—"

"It still doesn't make sense," Meredith said, and Jack and Constance both looked at her. "I mean, fine, I'm happy for both of you, Jack's a nice guy and Daddy was never around, anyway, so that's—well, it figures. And it was nice of Daddy not to be mean about it, I guess. But I still don't know why you're raising the remarriage issue now. Why not just tell them you know about the affair and it's fine and they should just . . . go on as usual? Why change everything this way? And why now, so soon after the translation? Doesn't that look bad for PR?"

"Good questions," Jack said quietly. "I'm wondering the same things."

"Oh, shit," Constance said. "*Dammit,* Preston! You really have been spying, haven't you?"

"What?" Meredith said.

"Connie?" Jack said. "What—"

"You have already lost too much, Constance. I did not want you to feel you had to lose—"

"*How,* Preston? How did you know? How—"

"Bar codes at point of sale, Constance. That particular retail outlet is participating in a MacroCorp marketing survey, so I had access to the information."

"*Shit!* I paid cash!"

"The bar codes would still have been read, Constance, and the GPS would still have placed—"

"Would someone tell me what the fuck is going on?" Jack said.

"Maybe nothing," Constance said. She was shaking. "I don't know for sure yet. And I don't want to make it into a—into a damn press conference! Preston, go *away.*"

"Certainly, Constance." There was a small click, followed by Vivaldi.

Meredith saw her mother take a deep breath. "Merry, would you mind leaving us alone?"

"Sure," she said, and turned, her knees weak, to go upstairs, where she sank onto her bed and pondered what she had just learned. She had the queasy feeling that she understood the cryptic conversation between her parents, but she didn't want to think about that too much, not right now. The part about Jack was enough to absorb.

But the more she thought about it, the more sense it made, and the more she realized that there had been clues all along: the way Jack had always been at her birthday parties, even though her father wasn't; the way he'd touched Constance's elbow to guide her into the limo after Merry was released from the hospital; the tone of Constance's voice when she mentioned Jack in her conversations to Brenda. Did Brenda know? Was that why she'd asked Constance all the marriage questions? How many other people knew?

There was a knock on her door. "Honey?"

"Come in, Mom."

Constance came in. "Is he here?"

"I don't know. He's everywhere in the house, isn't he? But he's not saying anything."

"Oh, Goddess." Constance rubbed her eyes, and then sat on the bed. "Jack's, uh, downstairs. I wanted to talk to you alone. Are you upset?"

"No. I don't think so. I meant what I said about how it made sense. Mommy, are you pregnant?"

Constance swallowed and looked away. "You don't miss much, do you? Well, we just checked. It looks like it."

"Home pregnancy kit? That was the—"

"Bar code, evidently. Yes."

"And Daddy didn't want you to feel you had to end the pregnancy. That's what he meant about loss. And that's why it all happened now, so you wouldn't do anything. How does Jack feel?"

"He doesn't know how he feels. I don't know how I feel. We don't know how we feel. How do *you* feel, Merry? If—if I had a child . . ."

"I've always wanted a brother or sister," Meredith said. "You know that."

Constance laughed shakily. "This is turning into a very odd family, isn't it?"

"It always was. But people are going to time the pregnancy, you know. Jack's going to have to do some fancy spin control."

"There'll be a bit of scandal, yes, of course. We haven't figured out how we're going to handle that yet. I'm actually—it's very early on, only a month or so. So we'll probably say that I sought refuge in Jack's arms after the shock of Preston's translation, thereby cementing an old family friendship, and so forth, and if Preston acts delighted, well, it's nobody's business, is it?"

"Just Daddy's," Meredith said bitterly. "Everything's his business. Are you getting a rig?"

Constance sighed. "I don't know, honey. I might. I need to think about it some more. Are you?"

"No."

"Well, that sounds definite. Because you're afraid your father will pry?"

Meredith looked down at the bedspread. "No. It's more than that. Because—because I don't want to be translated."

"Well, not now, sweetheart, of course not. How can you even imagine it? But if you change your mind in a few years—"

"I won't change my mind," Meredith said quietly. "I'm a person. I'm a body. When I die I want to go back to the earth, not into cyberspace."

"Your body would do that anyway," Constance said. "Just like your father's did." Preston's body had been cremated, his ashes scattered in the Pacific.

"My spirit too," Meredith said. "If I have one, if there is one—I want to be part of the web of life, not the web of circuits. I want to survive the way people have always survived, in their children. We aren't meant to be immortal, Mommy."

"You're only saying that because you're too young to imagine dying," Constance said gently.

A fury she hadn't even known she contained propelled Meredith off the bed. She stood, fists clenched, glaring at her mother. "I can't imagine dying? What do you think I imagined the whole time I was in isolation?"

Constance winced. "All right, all right, that was tactless of me. I'm sorry. Look, it's been a very tough day, and we've all got entirely too much to think about. All I'm saying is that you don't have to decide now. If you got the rig and chose not to be translated later, the files could be erased. That's all. I'm going to go back downstairs and see how Jack's doing. Come join us when you feel like it."

She left, and Meredith, shaking, went to the window and stared down at the Bay. She waited until her trembling had stopped, until her breathing was steady and her mind clear. Then she went downstairs.

Constance and Jack didn't hear her enter the solarium. They were sitting on the couch, Constance's head on Jack's shoulder and his arm around her waist, the fingers of their free hands intertwined. Meredith stood there, watching them. She couldn't recall such a moment of physical intimacy between Constance and Preston, and while she was pleased for her mother, the sight pierced her too. She felt as if they were in an isolation unit of their own making, as if she were watching them through thick glass walls. But the sight only confirmed the decision she had made upstairs.

"Hi," she said, and they looked up.

"You're getting as sneaky as your father," Constance said, with a wan smile.

"I hope not. Are you keeping the baby?"

"Yes," Jack said, quietly. "But you'll always be—"

"I know," Meredith said. "Listen, I've decided what I want to do." They watched her expectantly, and she said, "I don't want a rig. I want to become a Temple novice."

Jack raised his eyebrows, and Constance shook her head. "Merry, honey, you're too young."

"I am not. I can live there and go to school."

"You want to live there? I've driven my own daughter out of the house?"

"No, Mom, that's not—"

"Can't you just do what you're doing now? You go there every day anyway!"

"Novices have to live in the dorms," Meredith said. "I can keep up with my schoolwork; Raji does. Look, it's not like I'll be far away. We can still see each other all the time. But that way you and Jack can get used to living here, and I can—"

"You can get away from me," Preston said. "Right, Meredith?"

She squinted up at the speaker. "Right, Daddy. That's exactly right. More than here, anyway. But that means you have to promise not to pester me, in Matt's office or anywhere else. Because if you do, I'll find some way to really get away from you. I'll go—I'll go live in, I don't know, Papua New Guinea or something. Do you understand?"

"There are netlinks there too, Meredith. We are all one."

Jack cleared his throat. "Preston, while we're at it, we need to set some very firm policies about what you will and won't do here, in the house. And Constance and I need to know you'll stick by them."

"You have my word of honor."

A lot that's worth, Meredith thought grimly. "All right. I'm going back to Temple now to tell Matt—"

"Hold on," Constance said. "Hold on there, young lady. I'm coming with you. I'm not going to let you sign your life over to that—"

"Mom, I couldn't if I wanted to. That's not how it works. You start with a three-month trial period." It was the length of time she'd spent in isolation, but she couldn't imagine anything more different.

"Three months," Constance said, looking relieved. "That's fine. That will get this out of your system. That way you'll be back home well before your brother or sister is born."

Eight

LIFE in the novitiate dorm—a meandering, low-tech warren of cubicles and cots—took some getting used to. Meredith had never had to live in such close quarters with other people; while she had achieved a measure of protection from her father, in every other respect, she had markedly less privacy than she'd had at home. She was used to a twenty-by-twenty-two-foot bedroom on the other side of a large house from her mother; here she had a cot in a ten-by-eight-foot cubbyhole, with neighbors on either side behind thin plywood walls. The Temple dorm housed ten people in less than a quarter of the space she had lived in with her parents. There were no housekeeping bots. The novices themselves did all the cooking and cleaning, acccording to a rotating schedule; they bathed in spartan stall showers. The first few weeks, Meredith missed her luxurious bathtub far more than she missed her mother.

She didn't let anyone know that she missed anything. Too many people expected her to fail, and homesickness would prove that they were right. Merry's first evening in the dorm, one of the other novices—a thin woman with black curly hair and a scowl—walked into her cubicle without knocking, looked Meredith up and down, and said, "I can't believe Matt's doing this. You're too young to be here."

Raji, who'd been sitting on Merry's bed watching her unpack, cleared his throat and said, "Uh, Merry, this is Gwyn."

"Hi," Merry said. There was going to be a meeting in an hour where she'd be introduced to everyone else; she hoped they'd be friendlier than this bitch. "I guess Matt doesn't think I'm too young. He's willing to give me a chance, anyway."

Gwyn snorted. "I give you a week. This is no place for children, no matter how much money their daddies are giving to the Temple."

"Gwyn," Raji said, "this isn't exactly a gracious welcome."

"It's not supposed to be. If it were up to me, Raji, you wouldn't be here, either. The novitiate's a work ministry, not a boarding school." Gwyn squinted at Merry and said, "You *will* still be attending school, won't you?"

"Of course," Meredith said, as frostily as she could. That was one of the concessions she'd had to make before Matt and her parents would even consider letting her become a novice. She'd tried to talk them into letting her pursue an entirely Net-based curriculum, the way Raji did, but even Preston vetoed that idea. "You need socialization with people your own age, Meredith. That is why we still have schools." At last they'd agreed to let her compress her seven-hour school day into four, as long as she kept her grades up, so she could spend more time on Temple duties.

She knew her parents and Matt really agreed with Gwyn, though: no one expected her to get through the three-month trial, to be able to make this latest dramatic adjustment after the hospital. Everyone thought she was just in a snit about her father, or about Jack and Constance, or about the baby. "The news vultures are going to have a field day with this," Constance had told Meredith. "You know that, don't you? They're going to invent all kinds of stories about why you've moved out, especially once they find out that Jack and I are together."

Jack had cleared his throat. "Connie, that's not Meredith's problem. The vultures would be dive-bombing us whether she was still living here or not. We can't all be looking over our shoulders for ScoopNet every second. Merry, don't get me wrong. I'd be delighted if you stayed at home. I think you have a right to live your own life, that's all."

"Thank you. Thank you very much."

"She could live her own life here too," Constance said. "But you'll be home in three months, Merry. It's like . . . going to summer camp or something, only a lot closer."

"Right," Merry said. It was nothing like going to summer camp, and she didn't intend to be back in three months, but arguing wouldn't accomplish anything. She wanted to live in a place where people knew the same things about beauty that she did, but she couldn't tell her mother that, because her mother only knew how to color inside the lines. She has to know more than that, Meredith thought. How could anyone have been alive for forty-four years and never felt her body blaze?

But even Matt had been gently skeptical of Meredith's motives. "Merry, I know you're tremendously devoted to the Temple, and I know that intellectually you understand things like cooperation and interdependence. But the kind of community living you'll find in the novitiate dorm can be very difficult, even for adults."

"You think I'm an idealistic kid."

"I think you're idealistic, yes. I don't think that's a problem. I wish more people were more idealistic. As for your being a kid, well, we've never had anyone this young in the dorm. Most people are older and have had more varied life experiences when they come to us."

"I'm trying to *get* more varied life experiences! And Raji's not that much older than I am."

"No, he isn't, but he's lived all over the world. He's lived in communes in Israel and Africa, not just in the privileged conditions of, ah—"

"Of Preston Walford's daughter in Pacific Heights? Oh, come on, Matt! Raji may be Kenyan, but in most ways he's more American than I am. He spends every free second surfing the Net and he listens to techno-bop and worries about whether his clothing's stylish enough and . . . and he doesn't even want to be here! I do!"

Matt had sighed. "Look, I want to give you a chance. I really do. I just want you to know what you're getting involved in, that's all. It's not a utopia. And frankly, your mom's a little worried about your friendship with Raji."

"Yeah, I know. She wants me to take a vow of partner celibacy until I'm sixteen. Well, fine. I don't have a problem with that. Do you think I'm coming here to—"

"No," Matt said. "I don't. But there are three sexually active couples in the dorm, and there's not a lot of privacy. We don't have separate quarters for you, Merry, and it would defeat the idea of community living if we did, but frankly, this is an experiment."

"I passed sex ed with flying colors," Merry snapped. Like everyone else, she'd taken the mandatory fifth-grade exam about reproduction, birth control, and STDs, which included a practicum in which each student put a condom on a lovingly detailed dildo. She'd been masturbating since she was nine. Did these people think she'd been living on Mars? "I'm not going to freak out if I hear somebody having an orgasm, Matt, so relax."

At least Matt had tried to be tactful, which was more than Merry could say for Gwyn. "School's not a problem," she told Gwyn now. "I'm not here to cut classes, if that's what you're worried about."

Gwyn shook her head. "No, that's not what I'm worried about. I'm worried about the fact that you can't possibly fit in. I keep telling Matt he has to consult the rest of us before throwing new people in here, but he never listens. It's not fair to anybody, including you."

"Oh, come on!" Raji said. "If Matt had to get community permission, I wouldn't be here, either, and neither would half of the rest of us. And it's not like we get to choose—"

"'With whom we live on the planet,'" Gwyn said in a nasal singsong. "Yes, I know the Goddess-speak. We have to learn to live with all our neighbors, chosen or not, et cetera and so on. I'm sorry; the planet's a good deal bigger than this dorm. You know, the old Christian monks may have been exalted nut cases, but they had a few things right: they tested the people who wanted to come live with them."

"So do we," Raji shot back. "Merry's been doing volunteer work for months now, and we've got a trial period just like the monks did. Give it a rest, Gwyn. You don't run this place; Matt does."

"The master has spoken," Gwyn intoned, giving Raji a Buddhist bow. Then she straightened up, sighed, and said to Meredith, "We've got wheat bread and fruit and oatmeal and coffee for breakfast tomorrow. That's what we usually eat. If you want something else, add it to the shopping list and we'll try to grow it or make it or fit it into the budget. No caviar, I'm afraid."

"No problem. That's not a standard part of my diet."

"Good. I've added you to the chore roster; you'll help make lunch tomorrow and do the dinner dishes for the rest of the week. Any questions?"

"No, ma'am," Meredith said, and Gwyn nodded and left. When she was gone, Merry blinked and realized that her hands were shaking. "Sweet Mother! Are they all like that?"

"No. Some of them are worse. Listen, Gwyn's actually nice, believe it or not."

"I'll take your word for it."

"She's just busting your chops. She's harder on herself than on anybody else. And my first week, she made me scrub the toilets. Now listen up: here's what you need to know about everybody else before the meeting."

The meeting was in the common room, which sported peeling paint and mold-colored carpet. The other novices sat in a rough circle, on folding chairs or on the floor. Merry looked up at the splotched ceiling, wrinkled her nose, and whispered to Raji, "How about if I offer to repaint this place?"

"You won't have time," Gwyn said briskly behind her. "Why do you think none of us have done it? Hey, everybody, this is Meredith, if you hadn't already figured that out. We'll go around and do introductions, okay? Names and ministry areas, and anything else you feel like saying. I'm Gwyn. I'm a landscape architect. Anna?"

Anna, a heavyset, thirty-something potter whose swirling, graceful designs fetched big bucks at the Temple gift shop, was something of a celebrity. "Hi," she said, and gestured to the next person in the circle. "Everybody knows what I do." Modest too. "Dave, your turn."

Well, that fit Raji's description. "Anna hardly talks to anybody except the cats," he'd explained. "She keeps letting cats in, and Gwyn's allergic, so you can imagine how well they get along. Gwyn gets even by putting jalapeños in everything she cooks, because Anna hates spicy food. Anna gets even with *that* by complaining whenever Gwyn and her husband, Dave, have sex. She says they're too noisy. They *are* noisy, but it's really none of her business."

So Dave was the lanky guy with the ponytail sitting next to Anna: check. "Welcome, Merry. I hope my wife hasn't been giving you too hard a time." Everyone laughed, and Meredith looked at Raji. Was she supposed to answer that? Evidently not, because Dave went on cheerfully, "I help her with the landscape architecture around here. I don't have her visual flair, but I'm a botanist by training, so I'm useful with the plants."

"I'm Fergus," said the next person in the circle. He had white hair, a beard, and a potbelly. "This is my partner, Johann." The two held up linked hands. "We've been here for a year now; my specialty's ritual and Johann's is music, and we certainly hope you find fulfillment in the service of the Goddess, Meredith." Johann, balding and mustached, grimaced.

Check, check, check. "Fergus and Johann hold hands all the time," Raji had said, "but that's because they're in the middle of this huge fight about whether to stay at the Temple or not, and they think holding hands will help them maintain their emotional connection. Johann thinks Fergus is only here because of a midlife crisis. Fergus thinks Johann's in a state of spiritual emergency because he's so homesick for his china collection and his Persian carpets."

The next two, the birdlike woman with mismatched socks and the hale, muscular man beside her, had to be Hortense and Harold. "Hortense has Alzheimer's or something," Raji said. "She may not be able to stay here much longer. She leaves bobby pins and rubber bands everyplace, and sometimes she wanders into other people's cubicles after a shower and tries to put their clothing on, even if it doesn't fit. Her husband takes good care of her, but he also puts the make on everybody. Gwyn's already warned him to stay away from you, though, so you don't have to worry. Her precise words were, 'If you try to get anywhere near that child, I'll have your testicles for breakfast, do you understand me?'"

"Hortense?" Gwyn said now. "This is Meredith. She's new here. Would you like to say hello?"

Hortense put a hand to her mouth. "You look like my little girl," she said. "What's your name?"

Gwyn had already introduced her. Well, never mind. "My name's Merry. What's your daughter's name?"

"My tea is getting cold in the oven. How old are you?"

Raji was right: Hortense was nuts. "I'm fourteen. I'll be fifteen in a few weeks. How old is your daughter?"

"My underwear's bunching up. I want a carrot now. Harold, where's the sailboat?"

How can Matt let her stay here? Meredith thought. She's too sick. Harold put his arm around his wife and cleared his throat. "Hi, Meredith. I'm Hortense's husband, Harold. We work with hunger and food ministries."

"Nice to meet you," Meredith said, relieved to be speaking to someone who was rational. Hortense, making odd darting motions with her head, tapped at Harold's shoulder with a bony finger. Merry turned to the next person in the circle, so she wouldn't have to look at Hortense, and said, "And you must be Dana, the storyteller, right?"

"Very good." Dana was tall and willowy, with huge gray eyes and extremely short hair. "Raji's been briefing you. I can just imagine the stories he's been telling about me."

Uh-oh. Had she just gotten Raji into trouble? "He didn't say anything bad about anybody."

Gwyn laughed. "Fat chance."

"Well, not about you," Meredith told Dana, and everyone else laughed.

"Right," Dana said. "So he told you I'm intersexed, right? And he probably complained that he can't tell which gender mood I'm in from one day to the next, but that's because gender's a continuum and we all travel along it, and I don't get mad when people goof and use the wrong pronouns."

"Bullshit," Gwyn said. "You get bitchy as hell when people use the wrong pronouns."

"Well, sometimes," Dana said with a sigh. "So, Merry, did Raji tell you that he keeps forgetting to put his earphones in when he listens to that noise he calls music? He's every bit as difficult to live with as any of the rest of us. And while we're on the topic, what are your annoying traits?"

"Truth or dare," Harold said, stroking Hortense's hand. She had begun a soft, high keening, somewhere between song and grief, but everyone else seemed to be ignoring it, so Merry supposed she should too.

"Um, well, my mother says I'm stubborn. And I pick at my split ends sometimes, and, uh—"

"Never mind," said Dana. "I'm sure we'll know worse things than that before you've been here very long."

Gwyn smiled. "She's too young to know what her faults are."

Meredith felt herself flushing and bit back a retort. She'd already been snippy to Gwyn, and even if Gwyn had started it, she wasn't going to make any friends by picking a fight. "Well, it's nice to meet you all, and I'm very glad to be here. Matt assigned me to animal ministries. I've already been volunteering with the dogs and cats here, and tomorrow I'll start going to the SPCA."

"Tomorrow after school," Gwyn said pleasantly. "Merry, do you have any questions?"

"No," Merry said. She did, but she'd ask Raji later; she wasn't going to give Gwyn any openings.

"Fine, then. Shall we close with a blessing, everybody?"

They all stood and linked hands. Hortense had turned and huddled into Harold's chest, but Johann reached out and gently put his hand on her shoulder, so the circle would be complete. When they were all connected, Gwyn said softly, "Mother Earth and Father Cosmos, help our young grow into wisdom and our old grow into your light. Bestow your gifts on those who are new here, and teach all of us to feel at home in our bodies and in your embrace. May we learn to praise your blessings, and to transform into blessing whatever wounds us. By air and water and earth and fire, hosannah."   ·

"Hosannah," everyone else murmured. The circle disbanded, people wandering off with yawns and waves. Merry had expected at least some of them to come up and talk to her, but no one did.

"Lots of time to get to know you," Raji said, as if reading her mind. "Folks get to sleep early around here, for the most part. You still want help unpacking those books?"

"Yes, please." On their way back to her cubicle, Merry said, "Why's Hortense still here? She seems way too sick."

"She was worse than usual tonight—new people do that to her. Harold takes good care of her, like I said, and Matt says she's good for the rest of us. Reminds us how fragile we all are. Reminds us to be compassionate. By the way, she and Harold never had any kids, so I don't know where that bit about a daughter came from. Wishful thinking, I guess."

"They wanted kids?"

"Well, yeah, but lots of people can't have kids. I don't know why they didn't adopt."

"It wouldn't really be the same."

Raji gave her a sharp look. "Sure it would. Why wouldn't it?"

"Well, I mean . . ." Merry floundered, knowing she'd just run headlong into the Temple doctrine of interconnectedness. Raji wasn't usually such a Templehead, but Netgeeks were into the idea too. It was just another version of Preston's "we are all one," after all, and Raji had been spending a lot of time talking to her father. "I know it's supposed to be the same, even if the kid isn't genetically related—"

"We're all genetically related."

"Yeah, yeah, okay, I know. But I mean, bearing a kid in your body—it must be hard not to be able to do that. That's all." She thought of her mother and Jack, and wondered if Constance had been this dewy-eyed when she was pregnant with Meredith. Somehow, Merry didn't think so.

"Oh. So men aren't good parents because they don't get pregnant?"

Oh, Gaia's gas. So much for not picking a fight. "That's not what I meant," Merry said miserably.

"Well, what *did* you mean?"

"That I can understand why Hortense is sad about not being able to have kids, that's all! People have always felt that way. You know what Matt says: good doctrine doesn't forbid things to be what they are." There: that should win her some points.

Raji shrugged. "Yeah, but that one cuts both ways, you know. You can also argue that Harold and Hortense forbade interconnection by refusing to adopt."

"You're losing me," Merry said, shaking her head. "Can we just unpack books now, please?"

Her first week in the dorm shattered any remaining illusions she might have had about the higher consciousness of Gaia initiates. Raji drove her crazy by talking about AI and MacroCorp whenever he had a free moment; maddeningly, he even passed along inquiries from her father. "Preston's wondering how you are. He says he thinks dorm life is probably too big a change after what you've been used to at home. He said to tell you that if you go back to live with your mom, he promises not to intrude on you."

"Fat chance," Meredith said. "He's intruding on me by giving you all those messages, isn't he? Tell him I'm doing just *fine*." She had, indeed, been entertaining fantasies of going back to live with Constance and Jack, but she wasn't about to do anything Preston suggested. "And would you mind not discussing me with him?"

"He brought it up—I didn't!"

"I don't care who brought it up. I feel like you're his spy or something, Raji. Just—don't talk to him about me, okay? And if he tries to talk about me, tell him I've asked you not to."

"Oh, all right. I don't know why you're so mad at him, that's all. He's a cool guy."

"Raji, he's not a cool guy. He's a cool program. We've been over this. I don't want to talk about it."

"All right, all right," Raji said. "You're getting as bossy as Gwyn! Anything else?"

"Yeah, Dana's right. Use your headphones when you listen to your music!" Raji seemed to think that if he could just get everyone else to listen to his techno-bop, they'd love it as much as he did. As far as Meredith could tell, that would have been about as easy as loving an orchestra of jackhammers. She also found herself sharing Anna's annoyance at Gwyn and Dave, who frequently engaged in acrobatic and alarming sex, producing thumps and moans and ululating shrieks that rattled the walls and made even Raji's music seem preferable.

Johann, meanwhile, tried to enlist Merry in his battle to get Fergus out of the novitiate. "Now be honest," he said to Meredith one morning over breakfast, while Fergus was still in the shower. "Don't you think he's just a little *too* absorbed in organic liturgy? Do normal people spend so much time thinking about how to make their bowel movements sacramental? Does this strike you as healthy?"

Gwyn, spooning out oatmeal, gave Johann a black look and said, "Must you discuss bowel movements over breakfast? Honestly!"

"Fergus would. He'd quote Julian of Norwich on the subject."

"Yes, well, Johann, he's not here, is he?"

Johann sighed. "I'm sorry if I offended you, Merry."

"You didn't. But I hope you don't expect me to answer the question. I barely know either of you. I've only been here four days."

"Relax," Gwyn said. "It's all rhetorical. These two wouldn't know what to do with themselves if they weren't bickering. They'd be bickering if they were home too—wouldn't you, Johann?"

"Wouldn't he what?" Fergus said. He'd walked into the kitchen toweling off his hair, and now he shook it like a dog who'd just been rolling in a puddle, spattering the kitchen with shampoo-scented drops.

"Oh, Fergus!" Johann threw his hands in the air. "Not in the kitchen!"

"Can't take him anywhere," Gwyn said.

"He's just showing off because he still has hair," Johann said.

"Meredith," Fergus said, "what were they saying about me behind my back?"

"The usual," Gwyn answered. "Complaining about your insistence on blessing your turds, dear."

Fergus, to Merry's astonishment, looked genuinely annoyed. "Well, we're supposed to bless everything, aren't we? Isn't that the point? And what better to bless than fertilizer, that helps things grow? And if it weren't emerging from you properly, you'd be cursing, Johann!" He turned to Meredith and said, "What am I going to do with him? We've been here for a year and he still acts like he's never heard of ecological consciousness. You're as bad as the old Christians, Johann! You want everything to be pure and celestial, not grounded at all."

Johann made a rude noise. "You're the one who keeps quoting Julian of Norwich."

"Well, she was different! Gwyn, Merry, how can I bring him to a more highly evolved ecological consciousness?"

"You might try to stop being so damn boring about it," Gwyn said. "Or at least less stilted. 'More highly evolved ecological consciousness'—you sound like Papa Preston trying to channel Matt, and it's not a very happy combination."

Meredith grimaced. "Can we not discuss my father, please?" Papa Preston was what the popular press called him, now that he'd started dispensing free advice to anyone—like Raji—who visited his website. She'd never called him Papa in her life, and she wasn't about to start now.

Fergus shook his head. "Honey, you'd better get used to it. There are going to be cults forming around your father, just mark my words."

"Yeah, well, I'd rather not think about it over breakfast. I'd rather talk about your holy turds, if you don't mind."

"Holy turds?" Dana said, walking into the kitchen. "Is that what we're having for breakfast? Mmmm, oatmeal—yeah, just about. Good morning, all."

Gwyn glared. "Ooooh, look, Dana's in purple today. That's midway between pink and blue, right? You're not giving us very helpful clues, Dana."

And so it went. They were all hard workers and devoted to the Temple, which was the only thing that made the personality mix tolerable. During those first few months, Merry constantly wondered when the first dorm murder would take place. She stuck it out, stubbornly determined to disappoint all the people who expected her to give up and go home.

And even in those early days, novitiate life offered plenty of advantages: the constant access to animals, the beautiful setting, the weekly lunar rituals, when everyone gathered in the clearing overlooking the Bay and sang hymns of praise to the Goddess, community irritations temporarily washing away in the harmony of common worship. Whatever differences Merry might have had with the people around her, they also shared core assumptions about what was important. Gwyn could be a bitch, Fergus annoying, Dana impenetrable, but at least they were neither shallow nor vapid. In comparison, the other kids at school began to seem more and more two-dimensional, obsessed with clothing and dates and who had the fanciest hardware. Every morning she dutifully went to school and studied Net design and physics and global economics, but she only really felt engaged in the afternoons, doing Temple work. She accompanied the therapy dogs to schools and nursing homes and hospitals, helped trap feral cats to be spayed and neutered—she hated trapping them, but reminded herself how many more of them would otherwise lack food and shelter and love—and matched families who wanted to adopt animals with the dogs and cats the Temple had on hand. She also spent two afternoons a week in the SPCA's pet adoption center.

It was real work, important work, but, true to Matt's warnings, none of it was easy. Meredith quickly learned, to her shame, that she didn't like being around sick people, which made her trips to the hospitals and nursing homes particularly uncomfortable. She kept hoping that she'd get over her distaste, her instinctive repulsion for people whose bodies and minds weren't working properly, but if anything it only got worse, especially once Hortense became incontinent and had to start wearing diapers. All too often, sections of the dorm smelled like a nursing home, making Merry sick to her stomach. "Matt shouldn't be keeping her here," she told Raji. "She can't be happy."

"She seems perfectly happy. We're not happy having to clean up after her, but if she winds up having to leave, it will be for her sake, not ours. She's not hurting anything. She's a little smelly sometimes, that's all."

Meredith could have gone to Matt and complained about Hortense, could have requested different Temple duties, but she was determined not to make waves, certainly not during her first three months. And at least the hospitals and nursing homes reminded Merry to be grateful for her own health. The SPCA was her most draining duty, because it reminded her so much—more even than the actual hospitals did—of being in isolation.

The Maddie Pet Adoption Center, in a soaring building many law firms would have envied, housed stray animals in accommodations far more luxurious than anything available to the city's homeless humans. Twenty-one dogs and sixty-seven cats were displayed in soundproofed individual quarters decorated with artwork, real furniture, televisions, and, in some cases, windows. The cats had scratching posts and plots of grass; some could watch goldfish in aquaria. The dog rooms opened into courtyards for supervised canine play. All the animals, in addition to time with people, had special play bots who threw balls for the dogs, wiggled bits of string for the cats, and cleaned up messes. The animal rooms were kept under negative pressure to prevent unpleasant smells from reaching the potential adopters outside; the dog rooms had "sniffing holes" at nose level so the dogs could smell the people, even if the people couldn't smell them.

It was a beautiful facility, and the animals were lucky to be there, but Meredith felt starved for air whenever she was in the building. She knew that the SPCA had a firm no-kill policy, and that the animals were here, displayed in this comfortable environment, to attract the largest number of adopting humans. People who wouldn't have gone to an ordinary animal shelter, with cramped cages in dark rows, cheerfully came to the Maddie Center, which sometimes offered free popcorn and lemonade as an extra incentive. She knew that the bots were playmates and that they didn't administer veterinary care, which was provided in a separate building. She knew that the animals who left here—and most did; the place had an adoption rate envied by every other program in the country—went on to happy lives. But the place still triggered the fear and claustrophobia she'd felt in isolation, where every day had been an exercise in confronting death.

Meredith told herself that spending time here was her job; she told herself that her own anxiety gave her added empathy for the animals, many of whom had also been traumatized and were frightened and wary. As a socialization volunteer, her main task was to help the feral cats become adjusted to humans. Newly arrived felines were assessed by behavioral experts on the SPCA staff and assigned a number from one, for very undersocialized and not yet a good adoption risk, to five, for very well socialized and ready to go home with a family. Meredith's job was to spend time with the one and two cats until they became fours and fives. This involved long stretches of simply sitting in the individual cat rooms until the animals decided that perhaps she was trustworthy and began to approach her, sniffing at her cautiously before shyly butting her with their heads or patting at her with their paws. Only when they made such overtures could she begin to interact with them, petting and playing. Sometimes it took weeks, and the boredom of sitting in a small, hermetically sealed room while a cat cowered in the corner didn't give Meredith much distraction from her own memories. It was worse when other people wandered along and stood outside, looking in; she always flashed back to Constance's face peering through the windows of the iso unit. She told herself that she was helping the cats get out of their cages, get out of isolation, but even so, she could never wait to get back to the Temple, to the peace and quiet and open air of the meditation grove overlooking the Bay.

The trip back to the dorm was traumatic in its own right. Too often, it involved running a gamut of reporters and remote-controlled helibots. ScoopNet and the rest of the vulture press had fastened tenaciously on to the Walford soap opera, and someone at the SPCA had evidently tipped them off to Merry's schedule. They couldn't reach her at the Temple or the SPCA itself, since neither place admitted uninvited journalists; Constance's house had anti-snoop security, effective against everyone except Preston. That left the reporters no choice but to waylay Meredith between the Maddie Center and the Temple. "Merry, how do you feel about your mother's relationship with Jack Adam?" "Merry, is it true your mother's having a baby?" "How do you get along with your father these days?" "What's it like being a Temple novice?" "Do you think your dad's going to found a new religion?" "Meredith, are you going to get a recording rig?" She tried changing her schedule, tried ducking out different doors to her waiting car—programmed to return to the Presidio, and secured against electronic intrusion—tried telling them all to go away. Nothing worked. Finally Constance obtained an injunction against the harassment of her daughter, and the reporters backed off.

Meredith was grateful that no one at MacroCorp had insisted that she actually grant an interview, especially since she wasn't sure how to answer most of the questions. Her mother was definitely having a baby, a boy; that was the only easy one. How did she feel about Constance's relationship with Jack? Happy, excluded, ambivalent. How was her relationship with her father? As minimal as possible. What was it like being at Temple? Better than being in her mother's house, or in isolation, but some days not by much. Was her father going to found a new religion? Well, maybe. Certainly people other than ScoopNet, people like Fergus, thought so too, but Merry didn't think Preston was doing it by design. There were already people who claimed to worship him, but they were crackpots, the kind of enthusiasts who in earlier eras had worshiped psychedelic drugs and quartz crystals and plaster statues rumored to weep blood, and to the best of Meredith's knowledge, her father hadn't actually suggested to anyone that he was a deity.

That left the most charged question: Was she getting a rig? Not if she could help it.

Halfway through Meredith's trial period, Jack and Constance did get rigs, intricate cranial and central-nervous-system implants that stored sensory and cognitive data in uploadable chips. The upload sockets, tiny indentations in the earlobe easily disguised by jewelery, were the only visible signs of the equipment. Supposedly the implant procedures were fairly safe and painless, but there had still been extensive discussion of whether Constance should undergo the procedure while she was pregnant. She argued adamantly that she wanted her post-translation memories to include the birth of her second child, and the MacroCorp medical team finally agreed. But once Constance and Jack had the rigs, Merry found herself becoming even more self-conscious around them; not only was Preston always potentially present in the house, but she couldn't convince herself that he didn't also have access to Jack and Constance's perceptions of her. It was singularly unnerving, and made Meredith's weekend dinners at home yet another dreaded chore.

She couldn't understand her mother's sudden change of heart. "Mommy, you wanted nothing to do with it before!"

"I know, honey, but I thought and thought about it and finally decided, you know, it's insurance. I don't have to be translated if I have this thing, but if I don't have it, I can't be. And I really think you should think about getting one too."

Meredith shuddered. "So Daddy can spy on me everywhere I go?"

"Merry, that's not how it works. The files aren't even online until they're uploaded. If they're not online, he doesn't even have potential access to them, and online they're protected."

"You believe that? You trust him with files that would be *MacroCorp* property? After what he pulled with you and Jack?"

Constance sighed and gave her a small smile. "Especially after what he pulled with me and Jack. He knew what was happening for five years and kept his nose out of it, and he only intervened to save our baby."

"So you'd have aborted? To avoid scandal?"

"I don't know if I would have or not, but I was thinking about it. Your father acted to prevent that. And he's kept his promise to me and Jack not to interfere in our lives now."

"How do you know that? He could be listening right now. He could be watching every move you make in this house. He could—"

"He could have divorced me and tried to kick me out of the house and fired Jack and . . . and who knows what all, and he didn't." Technically, legally, Preston and Constance were still married, but Jack and Constance had had their union solemnized by Matt in a brief, quiet ceremony in the solarium, with only Brenda and Meredith—and Preston himself—as witnesses. The laws protecting sexual diversity would have allowed a triad, but they had all decided against it; it was too complicated, and any legal union would have become public record, subject to scrutiny by ScoopNet and its competitors. The ceremony Matt performed was strictly spiritual, not legal. "Meredith, your father has only acted in our best interests. And he can't access the recorded memories. And I want you to get a rig. Will you at least think about it?"

"Sure," Meredith said. "Sure, I'll think about it." She had already done all the thinking she intended to do, but she was too tired to start another series of arguments. This would buy her some time. "So have you decided what you're going to name the baby?"

Constance beamed. "We aren't sure. Either Forrest or Theophilus."

"Theophilus?"

"It was Jack's father's name." That must be why he'd named his own son something short and simple, Meredith thought. "But we'd call him Theo, or maybe Ted, so he wouldn't sound too much like a yogurt culture."

Meredith laughed despite herself. "Theo's good. I like Theo."

"Theo Forrest," Constance said dreamily, looking down at her stomach. Forrest was Preston's middle name. "I think Jack will be happy with that. We can't wait until you come home, honey. Only six more weeks!"

Only six more weeks until I have to decide what to do, Meredith thought. She didn't want to come home. She wasn't sure she wanted to stay at the Temple, either. All she could do right now was pray to the Goddess for guidance, and hope that something would happen to make the decision for her.

Nine

I N three more weeks you can leave," Raji said cheerfully. They were in the laundry room, where Meredith was washing her dirty sheets by hand. The dorm had already done its machine loads for the week, and running another, just for Meredith's sheets, would have wasted too much water.

Merry gave her wet linen a savage wring. "Did I say I wanted to leave?"

"Well, look, it's not like you're happy here."

"I didn't say I wanted to leave!" Why had he followed her back here, anyway? Just so he could lecture her? Wasn't he supposed to be peeling potatoes or something?

Raji shrugged. "Okay, so you want Hortense to leave. Do you think that's fair?"

"Gaia's gas, Raji, she peed all over my bed! I get back from taking the therapy dogs to a pediatric *oncology* ward—do you have any idea how much fun that is?—and all I want to do is lie down for two seconds before I head back to the dog runs and start shoveling turds, and I walk into my cubicle and Hortense is sitting in a puddle on my bed, with her adult diapers around her ankles! I think I have the right to be upset about that, don't you?"

"No, not really. Annoyed at the work, yeah. Personally mad at her, no. She couldn't help it."

"Fine, I know that, but then she shouldn't *be* here. I mean, there are places—"

"Sure there are. Shelters for old sick people. Hospitals." Raji's voice was very quiet. "You hate hospitals, remember? That's part of why you aren't happy here, because you have to take the therapy dogs to hospitals."

Merry closed her eyes. "There are reasons senior-care centers exist, Raji."

"Sure. They exist for families who don't have time to take care of their ailing elderly. We have time. Our life here is about having that kind of time. Washing some sheets is so much skin off your nose?"

Merry took a deep breath. "The first night I was here, I offered to re-paint the common room, and Gwyn said, 'You won't have time; why do you think none of us have done it?' So I'm not allowed to try to make my living environment more pleasant, but I'm also not allowed to complain about washing sheets? If I'm expected to make time for this, I think I should be able to make time for that too, don't you?"

Raji shrugged again. "If you feel that strongly about the common room, talk to Matt about it."

"I can't," Merry said bitterly. "He'll think I love rooms more than people. And he won't let me renew."

"Do you *want* to renew? Why? Just to get away from your parents? You know what Gwyn would say: this isn't a runaway shelter."

"It's not a runaway shelter, but it's an old folks' home? Raji, that's ageism, and you know it."

"On Gwyn's part, or yours?"

"Oh, stop it! Would you stop sounding so much like Matt? You don't even want to be here! You're the last person in the world who should be accusing me of being here for the wrong reasons! You're here because of your parents too, Nethead!"

She hoped she'd hurt him, but he just laughed. "Touché. Speaking of which, before I forget, my folks invited you over for dinner again on Saturday."

"And mine invited you for Sunday," she said savagely. "We should just arrange a hostage trade and be done with it." She and Raji had quickly dis-covered that they got along better with each other's family than they did with their own. Whenever their days off coincided, they ate dinner with one set of parents or the other, so that whoever was visiting could run in-terference for the one whose parents were providing the meal. Raji spent so much time talking to Preston on the Net that he knew him better than Meredith ever had, and both Jack and Constance appreciated Raji's interest in MacroCorp. Sonia and Ahmed Abdul-Allam, meanwhile, hoped that Meredith's healthy skepticism about her family's business, and preference for creatures over software, would somehow infect their son. They loved her stories about the SPCA, and every story she told them meant that much less time they spent nagging Raji about his Net habit.

Raji thought they were hypocrites. The first time he and Meredith had gone there for dinner, Meredith said, "Remind me again what your folks do for Sierra-Audubon?"

Raji had snorted. "My mom's CFO. My dad's corporate director of major gifts. They aren't exactly field biologists. I mean, they care about conservation and everything, but they spend all their time in offices. Neither of them could tell you the difference between a kestrel and a canary, and they both hate hiking. It makes my father's back hurt and it sets off my mother's allergies. That's why they're so fanatical about having me do the Temple thing, I think. They really aren't into it themselves, but they feel like they should be."

Meredith liked Sonia and Ahmed, who were kind and gentle and never, ever asked her about her father. And she liked having Raji at her own family dinners; it made her feel less excluded by Jack and Constance's cocoon of intimacy, by the way Jack's hand so often rested casually on her mother's stomach, by Constance's chatter about prenatal genetic screening and nursery furniture. Preston rarely spoke up when Meredith was there—true to his word, he joined the conversation only when invited, although he had chimed in when everyone sang to her on her fifteenth birthday—but sometimes Merry found herself wondering if he felt excluded too. When Raji was there, she had her own little secret society.

She kept telling herself that was all it was. Raji really was older than she was—he'd be going to college next year, after all—and it wasn't like they had anything in common outside Temple. But lately she'd been waking, heart thumping, from dreams of his tall, brown frame; right now, she was entirely too conscious of him leaning against the sink, propped casually on a hand resting only inches from her elbow. She could smell his peppermint soap, and imagined she could feel the heat from his body, although it was probably only the heat from her own.

Stop it, she told herself. Matt and her mother definitely wouldn't let her renew if she became too involved with Raji. That was what the celibacy vow was for. She'd masturbate before she went to sleep; that would help.

"Look," Raji said now, evidently oblivious to her turmoil, "the point is that you don't mind when animals are dirty, and we're animals too, Merry. I think Hortense is at least as valuable as a dog or cat."

Not to me, Meredith thought. She knew she couldn't say that; she knew she shouldn't even be thinking it. "So you think Matt won't let me renew even if I want to?"

"I have no idea. I wasn't talking about Matt."

"But you think I shouldn't renew." She plopped her sheets back into the soapy water, concentrating on scrubbing so she wouldn't have to look at him.

"Why are you doing that? You've already washed them twice! See that, Merry, if you could just picture Hortense as . . . as a big nonfurry dog or something—"

"So you think I shouldn't renew," Merry repeated. She wasn't about to tell him the real reason she was washing the sheets again.

"I'm not the person to ask; you know that. I'll be out of here in a red-hot second the minute they let me."

"Out and rigged," Merry said, sneaking a sidelong glance at him. He yearned for the equipment, but his parents wouldn't let him get it until he was twenty-one.

He grinned. "And you'll be out and a vet."

"No way," she said. "I can't stand seeing animals in pain. You know that."

"That's why you'll be a vet. Merry, we're really more alike than different. You know that, right?"

She looked away again, pulse galloping. "Do I?"

"Sure you do," he said. "Neither of us really wants to be here. We both prefer different populations, ones some people would say aren't real, or don't matter. Animals. AIs. You can't make yourself love people, you know. You can make yourself act nice to them, but you can't fake the feelings."

"I know," she said. Was he talking about her? Oh, Goddess, why did life have to be so complicated?

"Excuse me," Gwyn said from the doorway. "Am I interrupting something?"

"Just laundry," Meredith said, her mouth dry. She shot a glance at Raji, and saw to her consternation that he was blushing.

"Good," Gwyn said. "Raji, no cutting chores to hang out with the pretty girls; you know that. You're supposed to be in the garden weeding, as of ten minutes ago."

"My watch stopped."

"Bullshit. Get back there, kid. Come on, scoot."

He scooted, and Merry said, "Gwyn, I know I'm supposed to be help-ing out in the runs—"

"Don't worry about it. I did it."

Merry blinked. Just when she was sickest of the dorms, something al-ways happened to surprise her. "*You* did? Thank you! That was really nice, Gwyn."

Gwyn snorted. "Yeah, well, you don't have any trouble shoveling dog turds. I thought rinsing Hortense's piss out of your sheets would be a big-ger challenge for you. She's upset, you know. Harold lost his temper and yelled at her for messing up your bed, and she's ashamed. You need to go talk to her, tell her it's okay."

Merry swallowed, tasting metal. Why did so much of life at the Temple seem to revolve around excrement? "Uh, and I take it I'm supposed to sound sincere when I say that?"

Gwyn gave a sharp bark of amusement. "Good for you. Stay honest. Merry, if you can't do it kindly, don't do it at all—but you ought to be able to remember wetting the bed yourself. You're certainly young enough."

"Thanks."

"Don't mention it. And by the way, we're having a dorm meeting to discuss the Hortense problem tonight. I thought you'd be glad to know that."

"Will she be there?"

"Of course, and so will Matt. These things get discussed in commu-nity."

Meredith fought the impulse to pump her fist in the air. If Hortense were gone, renewing would be a lot easier. Maybe everyone else was fi-nally admitting there was a problem. Maybe Meredith wouldn't have to worry about playing the heavy anymore.

"All right," Johann said. "So we're all agreed, then. Harold will work on finding more comfortable diapers for Hortense, and the dorm will invest in waterproof mattress covers and one extra sheet set for each bed."

"Did we ever answer the laundry question?" Anna asked.

"About doing an extra load per week, you mean?" Johann frowned. "Uh, I think we got distracted by the issue of finding a socially conscious manufacturer of waterproof mattress covers. Does anybody remember? Gwyn?"

"Look, if there are enough soiled sheets for another load, we'll do another load, that's all. We'll have to see how it goes. With any luck, the new diapers will solve the problem."

"Oh, okay," Anna said. "That makes sense."

Matt had been sitting back quietly since the beginning of the meeting; now he cleared his throat and said, "Neither Hortense nor Merry looks very happy. I'd like to hear from you two."

"Hortense is upset," Harold said. He had his arm around his wife, who was huddled into his chest. "She thinks Merry hates her."

Everyone looked at Meredith, who sat with her hands clenched on her knees. *I can't believe this. I can't believe this. What will it take to get her out of here? I can't even suggest locking doors for the cubicles, because they'd take it as an attack on community.* "Meredith?" Matt said. "You've been very quiet."

I have to sound reasonable. I have to sound reasonable or I'm the bad one again. "I, uh, I'm just wondering about the diaper thing. If she pulls them down, like she did—" She stopped, because Hortense had let out a muffled wail. Oh, Goddess. "Hortense, I'm sorry, but that's what happened!"

"They itched," Fergus said, giving Meredith a pleading look. "They weren't comfortable. That's what she told Harold. That's why she pulled them down. We're just going to see how it goes with the new ones, Merry, okay? Can you deal with that?"

"Um, sure." *Like I have any choice.* "I, uh—Hortense? Was there any particular reason you chose my bed? I mean—"

Hortense wailed again, a long keening this time, and began to rock. Harold said quietly, "She didn't choose. It was a mistake. Merry, she didn't know where she was."

"All our beds will be equally protected by the new measures," Gwyn said sardonically. "And if she's targeting you, we'll all take turns washing your sheets, Merry, okay?" There was a ripple of laughter, and some of the tension in the room eased. "Are we done, people?"

"Not quite," Matt said. "Merry seems to think this is personal, so I want to hear her and Hortense talk to each other."

"I just tried!" Meredith said, unable to keep from raising her voice. "I just tried to talk to her and she just howled! Matt—"

"Merry, tell her it's all right."

"But it's *not,*" Merry said, and found herself standing, her knotted fists at her sides. "It's not all right! Look, I'm sorry, I know she wants to be a regular grown-up, I know she hates the diapers—that's why she pulled them down, because pulling your pants down is what grown-ups do, it's the first thing you learn—but it's not working. It hasn't been working. I don't hate Hortense, I don't, really I don't, but it's not fair for anybody for her to stay here, we can't pay enough attention to her, we can't give her the care she needs, we—"

She stopped, sick. Harold, glaring at her, was clutching his wife's shoulders, and the others' faces had closed. Merry, defeated and disgusted, raised her hands and said, "Look, if it's her or me, then I guess she wins. If you want me out of here, I'll leave."

"No one's saying that," Matt said, very gently. "The only person who thinks it's her or you is you, Merry."

"Let me rephrase that," Gwyn said. "If you wind up being excluded, it will be because you excluded yourself. You need to take some responsibility for your own reactions here, Meredith—and if you can't deal with dirty sheets, I hope the Goddess never favors you with children."

"That's uncharitable," Matt said sharply. "Gwyn, please apologize."

Gwyn folded her arms over her chest. "I won't. I meant what I said. If she can't cope with a little urine—"

"You wouldn't have liked it either!" Raji said. "Come on, Gwyn, be fair."

Matt shook his head. "Raji, hush. Gwyn, you hush too. Merry, listen to me: I know you're finding this a tremendous challenge. You're having to deal with all kinds of people you haven't encountered before, including Hortense, and I know it's very hard. It would be hard for just about anybody. If you decide to leave, no one will blame you. But we aren't going to kick Hortense out to make you more comfortable. Is that clear?"

"Very," Meredith said. "It's very clear."

"You don't know her," Harold said quietly. "You haven't known her long enough to remember her the way she used to be. She was funny and pretty and told great stories, Merry. She made the sun come out. Everybody loved her. You've never seen that, but that's what she was once, and that's why we want her to stay here."

The others murmured assent; Anna reached out and touched Harold's shoulder. Matt, nodding, said, "Yes, that's right. But we can't expect Merry to understand that, because she's new. Merry, you've got some time to decide what you want to do. Don't rush it. Come talk to me if you need to, all right?"

"Sure," Meredith said bitterly. She was the bad one again; she didn't seem to be able to get away from it.

She stayed in her seat until everyone except Raji had left the room. She couldn't get out of her chair; her limbs felt weighted with lead. "Hey," Raji said, kneeling down next to her. "Hey, come on, Merry, get some sleep. Things will be better in the morning."

"If I were wandering around peeing on people's stuff, would I get to stay here too?"

Raji grinned. "Probably not, unless you waited another seventy-five years before you started. Cheer up. You get to spend time with the critters tomorrow, right? Your furry little friend Sashimi, who might even decide not to scratch you? You always look forward to seeing him."

"Thanks," Merry said. Sashimi was an Abyssinian who'd been left in a Dumpster when he was a kitten and found, covered with fleas and cigarette burns, by a sanitation engineer who brought the furiously struggling animal to the nearest animal hospital. The cat recovered physically, but remained fractious and aggressive, a hissing, spitting bundle who'd taken weeks to become tame enough even for an adoption room. He was still a one— maybe a one-minus, one of the behaviorists told Merry—and she and other volunteers had spent days sitting in the room with him, trying to teach him to trust. Just a few days before, he had finally gathered the courage to sidle out from behind his cat tree when Merry was in the room. He still wasn't a nice animal, but she'd rather spend time with him than with Hortense any day. "Yeah, and if I'm lucky, I'll get to see Henry and the Martian too."

Raji clucked. "Tomorrow's feral cat food-distribution day?"

"Yup. And every day's duck-the-reporters day."

"Come on." Raji stood up, grabbed her arm, and hauled her to her feet. "With a busy schedule like that, you need a good night's sleep. At least you have nice clean sheets, remember?" His hand on her arm was very warm, and she fought a rush of vertigo, half hoping he'd follow her back to her cubicle.

He didn't. He let go of her arm once she was standing, and went back to his own cubicle, and blasted techno-bop while Gwyn and Dave made shrieking, cacaphonous love. Meredith, too tense even to masturbate, lay in the noisy dark, trying to keep from loathing every single person in the dorm, until finally she fell asleep.

Henry and the Martian, both homeless, came to the SPCA once a week to collect free cat food and bring in trapped animals for neutering. The Martian thought she was from Mars. Henry seemed sane enough, but was so filthy that no one could stand to get close to him. Opinion about them among Maddie Center volunteers was divided. Some people thought they shouldn't be entrusted with the care of animals, since they couldn't take proper care of themselves. Others suspected that they probably ate the free cat food, instead of giving it to the cats. A third faction responded tartly that if they ate the cat food, maybe they needed it, and that since they brought in stray animals, they evidently cared more about the animals than certain other people cared about them. Intellectually, Meredith had always agreed firmly with the third group. That didn't keep her from being alarmed whenever the Martian started making beeping noises, or from getting sick to her stomach whenever she had to stand too close to Henry.

The day after the Hortense conference, Meredith arrived at the Maddie Center and reported in at the volunteer office to find out where she was needed. It was a dismal day, cold and wet, and she welcomed the brightness of the building. The volunteer coordinator, a cheerful older guy named Ted, handed her the latest socialization schedule and said, "We've already done the feral-cat stuff. The Martian brought in a queen and three kittens; Henry brought in two toms. They're all being checked out at the clinic building. Mephisto got adopted—"

"Oh, good!"

"Yeah. Nice people too. So 'Phisto's gone, and Tommy just graduated to a four. There are three newcomers; you can read the files. Sashimi still needs work. Spend extra time with him today, two hours maybe."

"Okay. I can do that."

"It'll be restful," Ted said. "Not many visitors today; I guess it's the weather. Sash'll probably hide the whole time again, but you never know. Do you need something to read?"

"No thanks. I've got homework." She doubted she'd get any of it done; she tended to zone out in the cat rooms, and Sashimi's had one of the more comfortable couches. She'd fallen asleep there before, and woken with a guilty start, glad no one had seen her.

Today, someone had beaten her to it. A long bundle of rags lay stretched out on Sashimi's couch. Sashimi, his mouth open in a yowl and his tail lashing, glared from underneath a chair.

Henry. It was Henry. How had he gotten back here? How had he gotten into the room? Merry jammed her key into the lock and yanked open the door, only to be greeted by Sashimi's caterwauling and by a foul stench that propelled her two steps backward. How could Henry sleep through the noise? "Get *out*," she said, and Henry opened his eyes. "You don't belong here! You're upsetting the cat! How did you get in here?"

"I picked the lock. Good couch going to waste. Do you have any idea how long it's been since I got to take a nap on a couch?"

Meredith swallowed. "Look, I'm sorry, you have to leave, you don't belong here and you aren't trained—"

"To do what? Take a nap? I know how to do that fine. It's raining out. Did you know that?"

"Yes," Merry said, taking a deep breath and fighting for a compassion she didn't feel. She was furious; she wanted to break something. She was goddamn tired of goddamn smelly people getting in her way. She fantasized briefly about locking Hortense and Henry in a room together, and then said, "Ted will give you a list of shelters."

"Those places," Henry said, sitting up, "are not safe. Nope. I'm not going there. And my cave's muddy in this weather."

"Sashimi's upset," Merry said. She knew how brittle her voice sounded; she didn't care. It was all she could do to stay minimally polite. "I'm here to help Sashimi."

Henry threw back his head and hooted. "Even the kitties get crumbs from the Friskies bowl!"

What? The man was totally nuts. "Henry, you're upsetting Sashimi!" Her voice had developed a squeak. "Please leave, or I'm going to have to call Ted."

"I know how to help cats, lady. I've helped more than this little guy." Henry bent over to peer at Sashimi, who stopped howling long enough to hiss and spit. "I've brought you people fifty cats just in the last six months."

"Henry, please, I'm supposed to be sitting with Sashimi now."

"Well then, fine. You sit on that chair over there. Plenty of room for both of us."

Meredith didn't bother to answer; she pushed the intercom button on the wall and said, "Ted? It's Merry. Listen, Henry broke into Sashimi's room. Would you mind coming back here, please?"

"So they arrested him," Matt said. Merry was in his office, in tears. She'd come home and tried to pretend that nothing had happened, but Raji and Gwyn had seen right away that she was upset, and rather than tell them what had happened, she'd come here. It wouldn't make any difference. It wasn't like she'd be allowed to stay once her trial period was up, anyway.

"I wasn't trying to get him arrested! I just wanted him to—to go away! I didn't even know Ted would have to call the police! Matt, he wouldn't move. He wouldn't get up from the couch. We didn't know what else to do. When the cops carried him out, he just went limp in their arms."

"That used to be called nonviolent resistance," Matt said quietly. "Refusing to move like that. It was a kind of civil disobedience. Merry, do you understand why he did it?"

"Sure. Because it was raining out and he didn't want to go to the people shelters. Because he thought we owed him something for bringing in all those cats, I guess. But it's not a hotel!"

"No," Matt said drily. "The Maddie Center's not a hotel, and the dorm's not a nursing home. There's a pattern here. Do you see it?"

Yeah. The pattern's that I'm always the bad one. She couldn't say that; it would only make her seem even more like a spoiled child. Merry dug her fingers into the arms of her chair and said, as steadily as she could, "He could have hurt Sashimi! Sashimi was traumatized."

"Right. Go ahead and change the subject." Matt sighed. "Merry, why would he have hurt the cat? He loves cats, right?"

"All right! If you're so compassionate, what should I have done? What would you have done?"

Matt shrugged. "Sat on the chair, like Henry suggested?"

"But then I could have gotten in trouble! I'm not supposed to let anyone else in."

"Ah," Matt said, giving her a sharp look. "That's the crux, isn't it? You didn't want to get into trouble. Did you tell Henry that? Maybe if you'd told him that, he'd have understood. I suspect Henry knows all about getting into trouble. He certainly does now."

Meredith felt like writhing in her seat, but forced herself to stay still. "Matt, he broke into the room! He picked the lock—he told me that himself! Maybe he *should* have gotten into trouble!"

"All right. But if that's what you think, why are you so upset?"

"Because I can't get anybody to see that my side makes sense too."

"Ah," Matt said, very gently. "So whatever you do, you get into trouble. That's the problem. We're back to that again. You know, you're never going to get a one-hundred-percent approval rating from everybody, Merry."

"I know that!" She glared at him and said, "You think I'm a rich little snob, don't you?"

"No, I don't think that at all. I think you're going through an incredibly painful time of growth, and I'm afraid it will drive you away. I wish you wouldn't leave, but I suspect you will."

He was just saying that. He was trying to make it easier on her. Goddamn Matt, who never said anything wrong. Meredith, furious and miserable, bent her head—assuming a humility she didn't feel—and said, "Well, I guess I'm just not very good at this social ministry thing." She knew her voice sounded taunting; she couldn't help it. "I guess I really am a rich little snob. So that means I have to leave, right?"

She heard him sigh. "Now wait a second! Just hang on. Gwyn said last night that if you walk away, it will be because you're excluding yourself. She was right. I'm not going to do that, and I'm not going to let you walk away thinking that you had to leave because you weren't given any choices. If you aren't good at social ministries, that's fine. Plenty of other people aren't, either. If you *want* to stay, tell me what you think you might be better at."

She squinted warily up at him. "I can change my ministry area?"

"Of course!" Matt looked genuinely shocked. "Who said you couldn't? Did I ever say that?"

"No, I just—"

"You were afraid you'd get into trouble." He shook his head and said,

"You're not going to get into trouble. What would you rather do, Merry? What do you think would come more easily?"

"Aesthetics," Merry said promptly. She hadn't known what she was going to say before she said it, but now it came out in a rush. "Working with living spaces, starting with that crappy common room! The places where people spend time are incredibly important, Matt—being in isolation taught me that—and everybody deserves decent living space. Even Temple initiates, even poor people. I know it sounds hypocritical because I wouldn't let Henry stay in Sashimi's room, but there has to be some way to make more of the spaces where we live sacred, and—"

"Okay, okay, I've got it." Matt grinned and said, "You're your mother's daughter, aren't you?"

"What?"

"Don't take it the wrong way. Artistic, that's all I meant. Okay, so what do you need for the common room? Paint to start, probably, right?"

"I need to go look at it. I need to make a list."

"Okay. Go make a list. Oh, I almost forgot: your mother called to remind you that you have a doctor's appointment tomorrow."

Merry grimaced. "I wish they'd quit with that stuff." She'd grown stronger during her time at the Temple; she no longer needed physical therapy, and while her hair remained white and her joints still occasionally ached, the chronic fatigue she'd experienced after her release from the hospital seemed to be gone. But she still had to see the doctor every two or three months for total-body scans, a procedure she hated. At least it would get her out of taking the therapy dogs to the hospital.

The scan took an hour. She lay naked in a dimly lit tube, staying as still as possible, wondering how long she was going to have to keep having scans. She fought back a yawn; if she moved too much, they'd have to do the whole thing all over again. She didn't dare fall asleep in case she twitched or something, and she was tired. She'd stayed awake half the night, manic, thinking about ways to civilize the common room. Finding a way to stay at the Temple, even if Hortense stayed too, made her feel as if she'd been released from a trap. She didn't even feel as claustrophobic in the tube as she usually did.

When the technician finally opened the tube, Merry sat up, blinking against the brighter light outside, and said, "So, are all my organs still intact?"

The technician gave her a thin smile. "You'll have to speak to Dr. Honoli about that. I'm not allowed to talk about what I see."

"Right," Meredith said, permitting herself the yawn she'd stifled earlier. "I might sue if you told me my liver'd gone missing and then it was a mistake, right?"

"You can get dressed now," the tech said, and Meredith rolled her eyes. These people had no sense of humor. She shrugged herself into her clothing and wandered, still yawning, into Honoli's office. He'd tell her she was fine, tell her to come back again in another few months, and let her leave. Ho-hum.

Her mother was waiting with him, as usual, as if she didn't trust Meredith to repeat back to her what he'd said. The films were spread out on Honoli's desk, as usual, and he was pointing at things and speaking in a low murmur to her mother, as usual. As usual, Meredith wondered if Preston were present, and how much he knew about her continuing medical condition.

Her mother and the doctor looked up when Meredith entered the room. Honoli was frowning, and Constance looked worried. That wasn't usual. Meredith blinked. "What?"

"Sit down, sweetheart." Her mother's voice sounded strangled. Merry suddenly remembered what Constance had told Brenda, all those weeks ago. *The doctors say she's probably fine.*

She sat. *"What?* I'm fine, aren't I? I feel fine! Am I sick again?"

"You're perfectly healthy," Honoli said gently. "You aren't ill. But we've been keeping track of some relatively minor tissue damage, hoping it would clear up. I'm afraid it hasn't."

"What?" she said, squinting. "Cancer?"

"No, no! Nothing like that. But there are two areas of minor damage. Let me take them one at a time. The first is reproductive: there's some scarring of the fallopian tubes and some damage to the uterus." Constance paled, and Honoli said, "What this means is that you won't be able to conceive normally. But there are *plenty* of alternatives. You can still have children. You probably won't be able to have them without technological intervention, that's all."

"Technological intervention?" Meredith said. She felt her back stiffen, saw her mother glare at the doctor. A vivid, terrible image came to her: bots with needles swarming over her abdomen, into her vagina, bots like sperm rushing into her uterus, stinging, sticking. Constance rose and moved around from Honoli's side of the desk to Meredith's, putting her hands on her daughter's shoulders. At her mother's touch, Meredith began to tremble. "What do you mean, technological intervention?"

Honoli coughed. "Your ovaries appear unharmed; your eggs are probably fine"—there was that phrase again, *probably fine,* the two little words that had already been proven a lie—"although we won't be able to tell without more extensive testing, and I wouldn't recommend that until you're ready to start thinking about getting pregnant. If there's some problem there we can deal with it, I assure you. But to focus on the problems we already see"—Meredith felt her mother's kneading hands tighten on her shoulders—"there are a number of alternatives: uterine transplant, or the cultivation of a new uterus from your own tissue, although of course that's a good deal more expensive, or, if you weren't committed to experiencing pregnancy firsthand, the child could of course be gestated outside your body, either in an artificial womb or by a surrogate mother. The important thing is that whatever happens, we can pass along your genetic material. You can have your own genetic child. I promise you that."

"Honey," Constance said, stroking her hair, "you don't have to think about any of this yet. You're getting too much information too soon. You haven't even had time to adjust to the news."

Meredith felt herself choking. "You said there were two areas of damage. What's the second one?" Constance's hands tightened on her shoulders again, and Honoli looked down at his scans and cleared his throat.

"The second *sounds* more serious, but it may be a more minor issue. There's some very subtle—*very* subtle, Meredith—damage to the part of your brain called the caudate nucleus. Now, you shouldn't worry—"

"My brain?" Meredith said. "My brain's fine! I'm getting straight A's. Mom, tell him!"

"Honey," Constance said, "let him finish."

"Your grades aren't in question," Honoli said. "The caudate nucleus doesn't determine intelligence. It helps regulate anxiety, and the kind of damage you have *could* make you more susceptible to anxiety and obsessive-compulsive disorder."

OCD. Meredith blinked, remembering how Raji had scolded her for washing the sheets three times. That had just been because she'd been distracted; she knew that. But she couldn't let anyone at Temple find out about this; they'd just blame her response to Hortense on OCD, and that wasn't fair. You didn't need to have OCD to get pissed off when someone pissed on your bed.

Honoli was still talking. "The important thing is that it's only a susceptibility, Meredith, you understand? And if you *do* develop these conditions, they're very treatable; they respond beautifully to medication. But you need to watch yourself, especially during times of stress. You need to be alert to symptoms. If you become anxious and develop compulsive, ritual behavior—"

"Does religion count?" Constance asked. Meredith could tell that she was working to keep her voice light. "She's a Temple initiate, you know. She's already been there for three months, and now she wants to re-up."

Honoli coughed. "I don't personally consider faith an illness. Some people do, and yes, some forms of religious experience correlate with psychiatric conditions. That's not what we're talking about here. If Meredith develops OCD, you'll know it. Merry, I know this all sounds very scary, but none of it is a disaster. As aftereffects from CV go, well, you're really very lucky, especially considering how severe your case was." Constance's fingers dug into Meredith's shoulders again, and Honoli said quickly, "And in both areas, reproductive and neurological, you have choices. There are things you can do if either condition becomes a problem."

"I want to go now," Meredith said. Choices: Honoli sounded like Matt. She seemed to hear her own voice from very far away: a child's voice, thin and plaintive. "Mommy, I want to go home, to Temple. Can we go now?"

"Of course, sweetheart. Of course we can." Constance bent and kissed the top of Meredith's head. "We'll go right now. We'll go out to lunch. Or we can go back to the house. Whatever you want."

"I want to go to Temple."

"All right, darling."

Somehow she got there, although she never remembered leaving Honoli's office or getting into the car or riding to the Presidio, where she must have insisted that her mother leave her. She found herself walking alone under the fragrant eucalyptus, and then through the shrubbery archway, and then to the dorm. It was lunchtime; the others sat at the picnic tables outside, their heads bowed over bread and soup. Raji looked up. "Merry? Are you okay?"

She didn't answer. She walked into the dorm, intending to go to her cubicle and lie down and try to think, but Raji and the others followed her. "Merry," Gwyn said. "Meredith, what happened?"

She opened her mouth, and closed it again. She couldn't seem to say anything. "I—I was at the doctor's."

Dana, in a blue top and pink shorts, said, "What did the doctor say, Merry?"

"He says—he says I'm damaged." They had all gone very still, their faces grave and guarded, and Merry, stumbling over the words, tried to explain. She had to tell them something, because she'd told them this much, but she couldn't tell them about her brain. She couldn't tell them about the OCD. "It's not a big deal, he says. He says I can't have kids." Gwyn made a strangled noise, and Merry remembered what she'd said the night before. *I hope the Goddess never favors you with children.* Did she want Gwyn to feel bad? She didn't even know. She added quickly, "I mean, I *can* have kids, but only if they do stuff to me. That's why it's not a big deal. Because they can do stuff, if I want them to." She blinked.

"Stuff?" Fergus asked gently.

"Um," Merry said, trying to drag her mind away from the OCD issue. Did she have it already? "They can give me someone else's womb. Or they can grow me a new one, you know, in a vat or something." She tried to smile. "Or somebody else can have my kid for me. So it's not that bad."

"Well," Anna said softly, "you have a long time to think about it. You don't need to decide anything now."

That was what her mother had said. But her mother was pregnant, and her mother had Jack. Merry only had these people, this ragtag band of eccentrics and misfits, who thought she was a cowardly and hateful child, and who'd think she was already crazy if they knew what was wrong with her brain. She wondered if they were happy this had happened to her. But Hortense was biting her lip, and even Harold looked sad.

"We couldn't have kids either," he said. "It happens, Merry, even to people who haven't had CV. You can adopt too, you know."

"Or not have kids at all," Johann said. "Lots of people don't have kids.

There are plenty of people on the planet already, you know? Even after Africa."

"Yes. I know."

"Do you want extra meditation time?" Gwyn said. "I have the afternoon off. I can do your chores for you."

"Thanks," she said. She knew she should be grateful to Gwyn, at least as grateful as she'd been the other day when Gwyn had done the doggie cleanup for her, but all she felt was numb bewilderment with an undertone of panic. "I want to be alone now. The rest of you go eat. I'll come out when I'm ready."

They left, and she went into her cubicle and dragged her meditation pillow out from under her cot. Even once she had gotten settled into a solid three-point stance, though, she couldn't seem to still her thoughts. That was a symptom of OCD, wasn't it? She kept thinking about her mother, about Jack, about Preston. She kept thinking about Hortense saying, "You look like my little girl," even though she'd never had children.

"Merry?" It was Raji. "May I come in?"

"Um, sure." Startled, but grateful for the distraction, Merry uncurled from the meditation posture and stretched out her legs. "Lunch is over?"

"Yeah. The others went off to work assignments."

"What about you? Aren't you supposed to be someplace too?" *No cutting chores to hang out with the pretty girls.*

"I'm supposed to be cleaning the dog run, but Hortense said she'd do it for me."

"*Hortense?*" Merry laughed, and felt normalcy returning. "Do you think that's wise?"

"Harold's helping her. Um, Merry—you aren't damaged. I mean, I don't think you're damaged. I mean—"

"Thanks," she said, suddenly too shy to look at him; she raised her eyes only when she felt him tentatively stroking her hair. She knew why he'd come. "Um, Raji, everybody else is—cooperating with this, right? They aren't going to report us to Matt?"

"No, they aren't going to report us to Matt. Do you feel weird about it?"

"I don't know." Did she? She frowned, thought about it, and realized that her body had made the decision for her. So she was breaking her vow to Matt and her mother; she didn't care. Cautiously, she snuggled into Raji's chest, butting his shoulder with her head, like one of the cats at the shelter, so that he'd put his arm around her. There. That was better. "At least we don't have to worry about—"

"Oh, Goddess!" He wiggled away from her, said, "Do you think that's why I'm—"

"No, no. I'm sorry. It was a joke, kind of. Come back."

He did. After a while she said, "I'm surprised Gwyn didn't have a fit, though. About the age thing."

Raji laughed into her hair. "Gwyn said, and I quote, 'If you hurt that little girl, I'm going to have your testicles for breakfast.'"

Merry, feeling giddy, giggled. "Gwyn has a thing about eating balls. Yours, Harold's. Have you noticed?"

"Yeah. But anyway, that means you have to be sure to tell me if anything hurts."

Nothing did.

Ten

THEOPHILUS Forrest Walford-Adam was born on February 1, 2037, on an unseasonably mild day of soft, fragrant winds; he was delivered by cesarean section, following thirty hours of brutal induced labor. Before the decision to switch from vaginal delivery to C-section, Jack, Meredith, and Preston all served as labor coaches, along with three nurses, two doctors, and a small army of medibots. Jack stood at Constance's head; Meredith stood on her left, holding her hand, and Preston offered encouragement from an overhead monitor.

"You don't have to do this," Constance had told Merry, three days before she went into labor. They'd been in the sunroom at home; Constance, Buddha-esque, was helping Meredith mix paint samples for Matt's office. Merry's redecoration of the common room—followed by the cubicles, kitchen, and laundry room—had been so successful that Matt had asked her to work on the administrative building too. He wanted various shades of beige, marigold, and peach, so Merry was putting together a palette from which he could choose. She loved this new work as passionately as she'd hated the old; she loved creating patterns, creating order, creating places where people could be safe. And if her rage for order was a symptom of brain damage, well, it was also a gift. It made her happy. "Honey, everybody knows you don't like hospitals or bots, or seeing people in pain, and you looked pretty green through most of the childbirth classes." It was true; watching video footage of women in agony, Meredith's main thought had been, Thank the Goddess I'll never have to go through this. "I appreciate the fact that you even went to the classes, but you're not likely to enjoy the actual event."

Jack and Preston had said the same thing. "Neither are you," Meredith said, feeling stubborn, and Constance laughed.

"Well, I don't think anyone does. But I have to go through it whether I want to or not; you don't. Look, why don't you just wait outside and come in for the actual birth?"

Meredith shook her head. Constance usually made a big deal about family unity in the face of media pressure, and ScoopNet was already acting as if it had been appointed Theo's honorary corporate sibling. She didn't know why her mother was being so considerate of her phobias; she knew her mother didn't understand why Merry was being so pigheaded about being at the birth.

She hadn't understood it herself, not at first. "I really want to be there," she'd told Raji in bed one night. "Isn't that weird?" She and Raji didn't actually sleep together, because the dormitory beds weren't wide enough for two, but they spent time together in one bed or another, having sex or just talking, nearly every evening. They'd learned to fit their long frames together comfortably on the narrow mattresses; right now they were spooned, Raji's chest against Merry's back, Raji's left arm serving as Merry's pillow while, with his right hand, he played with her hair. "I hate medical stuff."

"Well, as medical stuff goes, this is pretty happy, Merry. I mean, babies are a good thing, right? Theo's your brother. This is your family."

"Huh. I don't know. Jack and my mother don't always feel like my family. They feel like their own. That's why I like it when you come to our house for dinner, but it's not like I can have you there when Theo's born."

"Your dad can patch me in," Raji said, and she could tell from his tone that he was grinning.

"Stop it," she said, kicking his shin with her heel, and he laughed and tugged gently on the tress of hair he'd been using to tickle her shoulder. "I swear, sometimes I think you'd have yourself translated now if you could."

"No," he said, "because then I wouldn't get to do this anymore—"

"Raji! Don't tickle me! I hate that! It feels like you're a bot!"

"Okay," he said, and kissed her neck instead. "Is that better?"

"Anything but tickling," she said, but gently pushed his head away. They'd already had sex, and she didn't want to do it again; she wanted to talk. "Look, help me figure this out. Why do I want to see Theo being born?"

She felt Raji shrug. "Well, it's pretty simple, isn't it?"

"It is?"

"Merry, you don't want to feel left out again."

"Oh," she said, and knew immediately that he was right. As usual, other people could read her much better than she could read herself. Am I really that stupid? she thought. How can I be that stupid? Was the brain damage worse than Honoli told me?

"I mean," Raji went on, "you've felt left out through the whole pregnancy, right? And even your father's going to be at the birth. And when your mother's uploaded, she won't be able to remember when you were born, but at least she'll be able to remember that you were there when Theo was born."

"Okay, okay, I get it. I understand now. Let's talk about something else."

"Merry," he said, and extricated his arm from underneath her head. She thought he was going to leave, but instead he turned her body to face him and said, "Merry, why are you crying?"

"I don't know," she said crossly, and buried her head in his chest so he'd stop wiping the tears away with his fingers. His gentleness only made her cry more, for reasons she also didn't understand: because it didn't feel like a bot, maybe, because it was what she had craved all the months she was in iso, with no human hands but her own to dry her tears.

"Look, it'll be really nice. You and your mom and Jack and your dad will all be in the same room, with no walls, while something great happens. Of course you want to be there. It would be weird if you didn't."

"My mother doesn't think so," Merry said, her words muffled against Raji's chest. "She keeps telling me I don't have to be there."

"And you feel left out," he said. "Well, tell her you don't want to be left out, that's all. You know she's just saying it because she knows you don't like hospitals."

"Okay," she'd said, and he'd started kissing her neck again, and this time she'd kissed him back, until soon enough they'd created a damp, heaving tangle of sheets and blankets and Dave, of all people, had yelled at them please to keep it down or he'd have to snitch on them to Matt, and Gwyn chimed in sleepily that Matt already knew, Matt wasn't stupid, and why didn't Dave let the kids have some fun, and Anna wondered aloud when Gwyn had become such a youth-rights advocate. Hortense and Harold and Johann and Fergus were evidently already asleep, or they would have said something too. It occurred to Merry that if she disliked being left out, staying in the novitiate had certainly been the right decision.

At least the conversation had made some sense of why she was actually willing to spend time in a hospital while a squalling lump emerged from between her mother's legs. She discovered that she wasn't quite willing to explain it to Constance, though, if only because she was too proud to admit that it hurt her to be on the outside of her mother's idyllic new marriage. So instead she just said, "Mom, let's do this, okay? I'll try to stay for the whole thing, and if I can't, *then* I'll wait outside."

Constance's face softened. "All right, Merry. Thank you. Thank you very much."

For the first few hours, it was fine; Constance grimaced and grunted, but between contractions, she was cheerful and funny, cracking jokes with the nurses and warning Merry whenever a bot was headed to her side of the room. As the first few hours lengthened into the first ten, Merry began to feel trapped, short on air and horribly tired, even when the nurses gave her a chair. Midway through hour fifteen, the nurses kicked her and Jack out to go get something to eat. "Nothing's going to happen in the next half hour," the head nurse said briskly, "and if it does, we'll page you. You guys need to refuel. Come on, don't argue. Scat, get out of here!"

"She sounds like Gwyn," Merry said blearily as she and Jack took the elevator down to the cafeteria.

"Who's Gwyn?"

"The archbitch from my dorm. I've told you about her."

"That's right, you have. I'm sorry I forgot, Merry." Jack, disheveled, wasn't himself; he kept drumming his fingers against the wall. Maybe he has OCD, Merry thought grimly. "Damn! I hope they serve us quickly."

"It's a cafeteria. They will." Merry wondered fleetingly if it bothered him to leave Constance with only her tireless, disembodied first husband in attendance, but she wasn't sure she knew Jack well enough to ask. And anyway, ScoopNet probably had the elevator bugged.

The meal restored them both. Later, Merry realized that she never would have made it through the second fifteen hours without that sandwich and cup of coffee, and praised the nurse's foresight. Later still, she tried to remember the last time she'd been up for thirty hours straight, and realized that there hadn't been a last time. She'd never been awake that long, and if she had anything to say about it, she never would be again.

By the end of it, her vision blurred around the edges as her mother's hoarse cries echoed surreally in the small room. The medibots had begun to assume the monstrous, arachnoid aspect they'd worn in the worst fever dreams of Merry's CV, and even the kind nurses seemed slightly sinister. Jack and Constance both looked completely exhausted; only Preston, hovering on the screen overhead, seemed unchanged, although even he wore a slight, anxious frown.

Finally the doctors went into a huddle with the nurses, and announced that they were going to do a C-section. "The baby's just fine," one of the doctors explained. "Good vitals, good position—but Constance is too weak to keep pushing."

"Meredith should leave," Constance whispered, her voice a hoarse croak. "She nearly fainted during the C-section in the childbirth film."

"I did not, Mom! I just got a little dizzy." But she felt someone firmly take her elbow and begin pulling her toward the door.

A nurse. It was a nurse, the same one who'd told her to get something to eat before. The Gwyn nurse. "Honey, you look like you're about to faint now even without watching a C-section. You've been a trooper, but we don't need to have to give emergency first aid during surgery, okay? Out you go. This won't take long. Don't worry."

Merry found herself, blinking, outside the room, and then sitting on a bench in the hallway. All she wanted to do was lie down and go to sleep, but she had to wait for the baby. She leaned forward and rested her head in her hands. She missed Raji desperately. She would have given anything to have him here right now, his arm around her so she could rest her head on his shoulder. Swamped by a wave of longing so intense it made her hands shake, she began to weep. This was stupid. She was being stupid again.

She'd see him tomorrow. It wasn't like he'd gone away; he was back at the Temple.

"Everything is all right," someone said over her head. "Meredith, why are you crying?"

It was the same question Raji had asked. Merry, sniffling, looked up to find her father's face peering down at her from a tiny security monitor near the ceiling. She wondered hazily how he'd gotten permission to use that monitor, to come out here to talk to her. "Hi, Daddy. I'm just—tired."

"Your mother is fine, sweetheart. They just took the baby out, and now they are closing the incision. The baby is fine, a strong big boy. Look: I will show you." As she squinted at the tiny screen, he showed her a series of video clips: the doctors lifting the bloody baby out of Constance's draped abdomen, the baby crying for the first time, the nurses weighing him. Merry felt a surge of light-headedness; it was good she hadn't stayed in the room.

"That's great, Daddy." Her mouth tasted like mothballs and battery acid. "Thank you."

"You are very brave to be here, Meredith. You were very brave to stay for as long as you did. No one will blame you for having to leave."

"I know," she said, so tired she could hardly form the words. "The nurses told me to leave. It's not my fault."

"Your mother just wanted to make sure you were safe and comfortable, Meredith. That is why she said you should leave. She loves you very much."

"I know," Meredith said, blinking back more tears. Goddess, was she that easy to see through, even by her father, who hardly knew her at all? Or—no, Raji couldn't have told her father about the conversation. He wouldn't do that. Would he?

"I just gave ScoopNet the news about the birth," Preston said, "and told them that everyone was very tired, and asked them please to leave. They have done so. I also informed your friends at the Temple. Raji has been asking for updates."

"Ah," Merry said. "Daddy, did Raji tell you—"

"We do not ordinarily talk about you. We know you do not want us to. But in this case it seemed appropriate for me to give him the news."

"Okay," she said. She wasn't sure which made her feel worse: the idea that the two of them might discuss her, or the idea that they discussed everything else. "Well, thank you for getting rid of the media vultures, anyway."

"You are welcome. Your brother has now been cleaned and weighed, and given an initial neurological evaluation. He is being injected with GPS tracer cells and outfitted with a temporary recording rig."

"*What?*" Despite her exhaustion, Meredith found herself standing, glaring at the monitor. "He's a baby! How can they give him a rig? He can't consent to a rig! He's not even ten minutes old! He—"

"It is only a temporary, external rig. He will, of course, undergo no surgical implantation until his neurological system has matured."

"This is sick. It's sick! Why does a baby need a rig?"

"To remember being a baby," Preston said. "When Theo is uploaded—"

"And when will that be? At his first birthday party?"

"After he dies, of course. We hope that will be when he is a very old man. But when it happens, he will have nearly complete memories."

"What if he doesn't *want* to be uploaded?"

"Then, of course, he can choose not to be. Without a rig, he would not even have the choice."

Her mother had said almost exactly the same thing just after getting her own rig. Meredith swallowed bile. "I'm surprised you didn't have him rigged in the womb so he could remember being born."

"That technology is not yet available. Look, Meredith. Your brother is nursing."

Meredith glanced warily at the screen. Constance was sitting up now—amazing things they could do with site-specific anesthetics these days—and had a tiny red, wrinkled head pressed to her bosom. Jack, behind Constance, rested his chin on her shoulder and gazed down at Theo. Constance, even after thirty hours of labor followed by surgery, was beaming. She's going to hurt like hell when the drugs wear off, Meredith thought, and was ashamed that the thought made her happy.

"He's beautiful, isn't he?" Fifteen hours later, Constance was still beaming. Meredith doubted that she'd stopped beaming once, even in her sleep, and now that she was nursing again, the wattage had gone up. "Isn't he gorgeous?"

"Sure, Mom." Theo looked like any old baby to her, wizened as a raisin and doughy as new bread, but Merry was feeling a little more human after getting some sleep of her own, and wanted to be kind to her mother.

She'd gone back to the Temple and crashed hard, collapsing in her cubicle for twelve hours. When she woke up, Raji had brought her a bowl of steaming oatmeal, and fed it to her spoonful by spoonful, as gently as if she were the one who'd had a baby. All her anger at him for being friends with her father had dissolved in a rush of love; she could afford to be charitable to her mother.

From this angle, she could barely even notice the baby's external rig, a net of fine fiber-optic cables snaking around his head. "He's gorgeous."

"He has Jack's eyes and my nose, don't you think?"

"I think it's too soon to tell."

Jack, sitting at Constance's bedside, holding her hand, nodded in agreement, rolling his eyes, and Constance laughed, a delighted burble. "Cynics!"

"Realists," Jack said with a smile, and bent to kiss Theo's head.

"I think Constance is right," Preston said from the television set. "I have analyzed Theophilus's facial structure, and his nose is indeed more similar to Constance's than to Jack's. But his eyes are not Jack's; they are Meredith's."

Jack's face twitched. "Which makes them what, yours? Genetically improbable, to say the least, Preston."

"No, Jack. I meant no offense. They are the eyes of Constance's mother. A recessive gene."

"Squinty and nearsighted," Merry said, trying to lighten some of the sudden tension in the room. It occurred to her again, as it had in the elevator, that maybe Jack wasn't as comfortable with Preston's hovering presence as he seemed. "Daddy, maybe you and I should leave the new parents and the new baby—"

"No," Constance said, reaching out for Meredith's hand. "Not you, Merry. You just got here again."

"I am sorry to have intruded," the television said. "I will leave you." Meredith felt a sudden unexpected stab of pain for her father, the eternal outsider, locked out of flesh forever. She wondered if he missed it. How could he not?

The television clicked off, and suddenly the silence in the room seemed enormous, filled only with Theo's contented suckling. "Did Daddy like holding me?" Merry asked. "When I was a baby?"

"Sure," Constance said. "When he was home. But he didn't come home any more often so he could hold you, you know?" She and Jack exchanged looks, and Meredith saw him squeeze her hand. She tried to imagine having a baby with Raji, only to have Raji never be home to hold it, and her pity for Preston was replaced with pity for her mother.

"That's awful! How could he—"

"It was a long time ago. I don't think he knew any better, at the time. He thought he was taking care of us by making a lot of money. In some ways, your father's very old-fashioned. Meredith, thank you for being there when I was in labor."

"You're welcome. I'm sorry I left when—when—"

"Don't worry about it, honey. You were exhausted. It's good you left when you did. I just wish you hadn't had such a hard vigil. It's not always that hard, you know, especially for younger women."

Merry's heart sank. Now she knew why Constance hadn't wanted her there, initially: she hadn't wanted to scare Meredith away from technological intervention. "I know, Mom. But even if I decide to have a kid someday, I'm not doing a womb transplant or anything else like that, okay?"

Constance's face tightened. "That's what I was afraid you'd say."

"I said it before," Merry said patiently. "I've said it every time you've brought up the subject. It's nothing new."

Jack cleared his throat. "This doesn't have to be decided now."

"Merry, giving birth is such a beautiful experience. I know it looks horrible, but really, I wouldn't give it up for anything, not your birth or Theo's; there's nothing like feeling as if you've given life."

"There are other ways to give life, Mom. There are. Really." The baby, who had fallen asleep after his meal, stirred against Constance's breast; looking at his fiber-optic halo, Meredith wondered if this argument would be part of his memories of his first day. Would the rig record noises he didn't understand? "You never made a big deal about my having kids before you found out I couldn't; why make a big deal about it now?"

"We're all still very tired," Jack said, "and I really think there are better times and places for this."

"Jack, hush. I don't see why we can't talk about it now. Merry, it was never an issue before because it never occurred to me that you *wouldn't* have children. I—when I die I know I'll still be in the world, and so will your father, through you, and so will Jack through Theo."

"Genes," Merry said wearily. Talk about old-fashioned! Well, Honoli had gone on about her "own genetic material" too. "You want me to pass my genes on, is that it? Look, Mom, if I adopt a kid it can have plastic surgery to look more like me, if that's what you're worried about. We'll make sure it has the right eyes, if that's really important to you, although frankly, I think the whole thing's a little racist."

"No," Constance said. "That's not what I mean. You don't understand. Your father and I, we both live on in you."

"Yeah, well, he's living online now, and you will be too, right? So why does the other matter?"

"They both matter!" Meredith could tell that her mother was near tears. "It all matters. I wouldn't be happy on the Net if I didn't know that part of me was alive in the world too. I didn't want to say that in front of your father because I didn't want him to think that I think he's not—not—"

"Not alive?" Merry asked sardonically.

"Not enough," Constance said, shaking her head. "I don't want him to think he's not enough if he's just on the Net and not in the world."

Merry looked down at the floor. "Is it my job to make sure you're enough? You or Daddy? I think I need to worry about whether I'm enough, don't you?"

"But that's exactly what I'm talking about! If you aren't in the world too—"

"Mom, it's up to me to define 'enough' for myself. I'm not getting a rig. I won't be uploaded. And when I die I'll become part of everything, part of all the world, whether my genes are walking around in a body or not. And that's enough for me." It was standard Temple doctrine; she was mildly shocked to discover that she really did believe it, clear through, in every molecule of her being.

Constance clutched Theo visibly tighter, relaxing her hold only when he whimpered. "But what about the other people you love? What about Raji?"

"What *about* Raji?" Merry, taken aback, glared at Constance. "Who told you about—"

"Oh, honey, Matt did, of course. It's all right. I don't mind. I might have before, but—well, things are different now. I'm happy for you, and for him. He cares about you very much. He's a sweet boy."

Boy? Merry felt her face flushing. "Why would you have minded before? Because I might have had a baby with him? Because—"

"Because it would have been riskier, yes."

"I'd have used birth control, Mom!"

"Which doesn't always work. Look, you *are* only fifteen, even if you've lived through far too much this past year, and hormones can sweep away better judgment. Don't think I don't know that. Now, back to the original question. If you could have a baby with Raji, wouldn't you want it to have his genes, because you love him? And wouldn't you want *him* to want it to have your genes, because he loves you?"

"I've had a baby with you," Jack cut in affably, "and I want you to get some sleep and stop pestering your daughter, so you'll have more strength for your son." He winked at Merry and added, "And if you don't stop arguing and get some rest, I'm going to call a nurse and have her give you a sedative, all right? Constance, give me the baby. Now lie down and close your eyes. There: that's better, isn't it?" Cradling Theo, he turned and added *sotto voce* to Meredith, "Stick by your guns and do whatever you want. That's my opinion. At this point it's only a rhetorical question, anyway."

She pondered the question as she left the hospital, emerging from the bright lobby, into brighter sunlight, to find that the media were back, microphones and buzzing helibots surrounding her the moment she stepped through the doors. "Meredith, how are your mother and the baby?" "Merry, how do you feel about your little brother?" "Merry, your father says—"

"Everyone's doing splendidly," she said. "The baby's gorgeous and my mother and Jack are really happy, and so am I. But we're also all really tired, so if you'll excuse me, I need to go home now." She bent her head and began plowing through the thicket of bodies and electronics, ignoring the standard sniping-at-MacroCorp questions. "Do you believe your father's latest denials about MacroCorp ties to missile manufacturers?" "Do you favor android research?" "Do you agree with the latest antitrust ruling?"

Meredith rolled her eyes. MacroCorp had sued a small company for patent infringement when it started selling its own rigs, and had promptly been hit with—and lost—an antitrust suit. It didn't matter; the competing rigs were inferior and wouldn't last on the market anyway. Android research was a dead end, since even the fanciest robots could never be mistaken for human beings; bots were far more functional when freed from the restraint of looking human. And yes, Meredith *did* believe her father's denials about the weapons business. Various neo-Luddite groups kept trying to prove that MacroCorp funded missile smugglers, bioweapons research, and ecologically unsavory mining and development activities. None of the claims had ever stood up to serious scrutiny. Why did people even keep asking? Didn't they have anything better to do? Anyway, there'd always been defense technology, and there always would be, and defense technology often helped drive advances that helped humanitarian work. The activists had such simple minds.

Annoyed, she kept walking, only to be stopped by a thin voice from the back of the crowd. "Is there any truth to the rumor that you're involved with Raji Abdul-Allam?"

Merry felt her stomach lurch. Sweet Gaia, where had that come from? Her father certainly wouldn't have leaked it—would he? Who would have told the vultures about her personal life? Anger flared in all her joints and tendons, but she turned and said, with the sweetest smile she could muster, "Raji and I live together." A hushed pause from the vultures. "In the Temple dorm." Knowing chuckles. "With eight other people. We're *all* involved with each other, but not the way you're thinking"—heartier laughter, good, she hadn't lost her touch with the press—"and we're all involved with everyone on the planet." Even those of us who've learned to mind our own business. "Now, if you'll excuse me, I really need to go home and get some *sleep.*"

She escaped to the safety of her car, finally, and barely waited until the door was closed before dialing Matt's office. It was a secure connection. She told Matt what had happened, and said, "Matt, who in the name of—"

"Merry, I don't know. I certainly didn't tell them. I can't imagine that anyone else here would have done it, either."

"Well then, *who?*"

"I don't know. Who else knows about you two? Your parents—"

"They wouldn't tell the *press!* Raji's parents wouldn't either!"

"Maybe they talked to somebody, friends who leaked it?" Merry thought of Brenda, of Sonia and Ahmed's gardener—true to Raji's criticism, his parents didn't even mow their own lawn—of anyone who might have seen her and Raji strolling on the Temple grounds: kids, visitors, delivery people. It could, she realized, have been just about anyone.

"I don't know. I guess—I guess it doesn't really matter. Matt, I'm sorry I bothered you."

"It's okay. You were upset. How are your mom and the baby?"

"Fine. You'd think I'd be used to living in a fishbowl by now, wouldn't you?"

Matt sighed. "The Temple's been a pretty safe place for you, at least that way. That's what you wanted, and you got it. But nothing's perfect, Merry. Do you want me to call a dorm meeting? To talk about this, see if anyone leaked it?"

"No," she said. They were her friends; she didn't want to start making accusations. "I don't think any of them would have done it, anyway. And I guess it doesn't matter who it was. It could have been anybody."

"Merry, let go of it." She and Raji were in the kitchen doing the dinner dishes, Merry washing and Raji drying. Ordinarily the dishes would have been put in the dishwasher, but Merry had asked to wash them—although not to scrub pots—because the soap and hot water, the concrete, constructive action, soothed her. Raji had volunteered to help. "Look, you're right. It could have been anybody, and there will always be that danger and you'll never know, so let go of it. Either stop stewing or go ahead and call a dorm meeting and hash it out with everybody."

"It's creepy, that's all. And it bothers me because it's about you too, and you shouldn't have to lose your privacy that way."

"Well, I'm sorry it bothers you, but it doesn't bother me. I'm not ashamed of you."

"That's not what I meant! I'm not ashamed of you, either."

"Okay, well then, so everything's fine. Our parents are cool with it. The only problem would be if they weren't. So what's the big deal? People always gossip. When you're famous they just gossip on a bigger scale, that's all."

"Yeah, well, it's my whole life. For you it's a new thing, and maybe it's kind of fun, but I got very tired of it a long time ago."

"Sure," he said, and shrugged. "I can see that. But what are you going to do about it? Refuse to spend time with your friends so they don't get dragged into the limelight?" He reached out and tucked a strand of hair behind her ear. Usually she would have found the gesture endearing, but now it grated on her, and she pulled away from him. "Aw, Merry. Come on. Everything's all right, really."

"I can't go anywhere to get away from it," she said. "Not even here."

"That's right. You can't go anywhere to get away from life, except death, and maybe not even there. So what else is new?"

"It's not fair, that's all! It's not like I was given any choice. It's not like Theo was given any choice. He was just born, he's just a little baby, and already he's a—a public figure, somebody ScoopNet's using to boost their ratings. It sucks."

"Sure it does. So do poverty and hunger and CV and the fact that Hortense's mind is slowly dribbling out of her ears while we stand here and watch."

"Huh! So you agree with me now?" The new diapers worked better than the old ones had, but lately Hortense had started wandering away from the dorm more frequently, calling people by the wrong names, hiding in closets and under beds and benches like a small child, emerging only when Harold coaxed her with nursery rhymes and pieces of fruit. Sometimes, now, she didn't even recognize him.

"I always did agree with you, kind of." Raji was quiet for a moment, twisting the dish towel idly around his hands, and then added, "It's just— it's going to be very hard on Harold to lose her, you know. He sleeps around whenever he can, or he pretends he wants to, but he really does love her. And it will be harder on both of them if she's in some kind of home than if she's here, with all of us. That's the main reason to let her stay. Not just for her; for him too."

"Matt would say it's for all of us."

"Yeah, I know. Have you ever been at a death?" Merry shook her head, suppressing a shudder, and Raji said, "My grandmother died a few years ago. My dad's mom. I'd never known her very well, because she lived in Kenya and we only saw her during the summers. She didn't speak English very well, and my Swahili sucks. When she got cancer she came over here so she could get better medical care, but it was already too late. She spent the last three months in hospice, you know, on pain meds and everything, and she and my father spent hours talking in Swahili about stuff that had happened before I was born, about when he was a little boy. And my parents told her stories about when I was a little boy so she'd feel like she knew me better. She used to like to hold my hand. I'd just sit there, and she'd hold my hand and sing me songs."

"Like Harold's nursery rhymes."

"I guess. She sang songs and told me a lot of stories about animals, antelope and lions and baboons, things she'd seen when she was a kid, and my parents tried to translate for her, and they said she was so proud that they were helping animals and she hoped I would too, which was when the whole Temple pressure thing really started. She was homesick for Africa the whole time she was here, I think. My dad said—when the pandemic started over there, you know, the CV, he said, 'Praise Goddess she went before that, after losing so many to HIV. Praise Goddess that she died of cancer instead.'"

"Ugh. So your parents have lost a lot of people over there, other family?" She felt stupid for never having asked before. It had never even occurred to her. It should have.

"Of course. Cousins and things, to both HIV and CV. Nobody I knew very well at all, not even as well as I knew her, but it was hard on my folks, and I think they felt guilty for not being there too. I think that's the only reason they're letting me study AI in college at all, because AI will help the economic recovery over there." He glanced sidelong at her; they both knew he'd be going to college in the fall, but they hadn't really talked about it. Merry kept telling herself not to worry; his first choice was Berkeley, where MacroCorp had a big AI lab, and Raji was certainly more than smart enough to get in, and if he went there, he'd still be close by and she'd be able to see him and talk to him, even if he started dating other people—which he surely would—and even if they didn't sleep together anymore, which they probably wouldn't. She tried very hard to be a grown-up whenever she thought about the subject, and every time, the effort made her feel starved for oxygen. She could get other boyfriends, but she didn't want to. Things will change, she told herself. You'll feel differently in a few years. You'll still be his friend.

"I'm sorry," she said. "That you've lost so much family."

"Thanks. Me too . . . so anyway, I wasn't there when my grandmother died, but both of my parents were, and afterwards, they both said it was like being at a birth. It took hours, and they sat with her and held her hands and encouraged her to let go, and they listened to her breathing change and saw her push herself up off the bed, fighting for air, and then she gave one last huge gasp and she was gone. The room was totally filled with peace then, they said. They said it was a good death, the best death they'd seen. My mom said the last big breath was just like the first big breath a baby takes, the one that starts the crying, you know."

"That's so sad, Raji!"

"But they didn't think it was. I mean, sure they did, they cried and everything, they missed her, but the death itself wasn't sad: her being gone was, or her being in a place where they couldn't see her anymore. And they were happy because wherever that was, she wasn't in pain anymore, which sounds like a huge cliché but really means something when some-body's just spent months on morphine."

"Yeah." Merry wondered, in a sudden, dizzying rush, what her father's death had been like. She'd never thought about it before, never wondered if it would have been easier for him if she and her mother had been there to hold his hands. Poor Daddy!

"But anyway, I think that's the kind of death Harold wants Hortense to have, and he wants her to have it here, where she knows everybody, or used to. This is her home. We're her family, especially because they don't have kids. My dad said—when his mother died, he said it would have been much harder if he hadn't had me, if he hadn't known that the chain was going to go on."

Merry frowned down at the greasy water in the sink, remembering her mother's question from that morning. It had gotten knocked out of her head by the reporters, by her anger over the fact that her private life wasn't private at all, but now it came back again. *If you could have a baby with Raji, wouldn't you want it to have his genes, because you love him?* She moved closer to him, nestling into his embrace as his arm slid reassuringly around her shoulders, and pondered the problem. Sure, she'd want her child to look like Raji, to have Raji's lean build and almond eyes and clean jawline. Raji was gorgeous. But it would be more important to have a child with Raji's compassion and cheerfulness and curiosity, and at least some of that could be taught.

If she and Raji spent the rest of their lives together—again that pang as she recognized that they probably wouldn't, that they'd both find other people, that in five years she wouldn't even care—if somehow they managed to beat the odds and move from being childhood sweethearts to elderly lovers, she would want some legacy left behind when he died; of course she would. But she'd want someone who remembered him. That would be more important than having someone who shared his shoe size and predisposition to gum disease.

She was aware of the contradiction even as she let him pull her into a long kiss, and then down the hall to his cubicle, leaving the half-done dishes behind. If only memories mattered, if bodies didn't, translation was a wonderful option. And bodies—she thought as she lay on his bed, as she felt her own body insistently responding—certainly mattered, would always matter. That was as far as she got; she'd have to solve the philosophical conundrum some other time, when her mind wasn't being so thoroughly distracted by what was happening to her flesh.

Eleven

O F course industrial staffing is important," Raji said. "That's the main application, sure. But your dad also wants AIs to contribute to the arts, to family life, to broader culture."

"The key word there is *contribute*," Meredith told him irritably. "Theo, no, don't put salt on your cake!"

It was the fall of her freshman year at Berkeley, and the three of them were sitting in a coffee shop on Telegraph Avenue. Raji was already in his second year in the AI graduate lab, even though he was only a junior, and Merry had just declared her major in domestic ecology, even though too many campus intellectuals despised the field as a flashy peripheral to interior design. Theo was three, majoring in mayhem. Merry extricated the salt shaker from his chubby toddler's fingers and handed it to Raji. "Here, make sure he doesn't grab this again, okay? Hey, Theo, want to draw? I'll get you some paper and crayons." She'd put them in her pack; she knew she had. Ah, here they were, squashed underneath her Intro to World Aesthetics textbook.

"Sugar!" Theo's piping voice always sounded like the call of a seabird to her.

"No, honey, that's salt. You've got enough sugar in that chocolate cake, anyway."

"He'll be bouncing off the walls after he eats that. Do you think your mother would approve?"

"I have no idea. I don't plan to tell her. She and Jack won't be picking him up until eleven or something, anyway; he'll be asleep by then. Thanks for helping me watch him, Raji."

The words stuck slightly in her throat. She was glad Raji was here, but since she'd arrived on campus, he'd never seemed to be able to get together with her unless there was a third party present. They hadn't been lovers since he left for school; they'd agreed that they should see other people. She hadn't seen anyone she particularly liked; at least, not enough to get naked with, not enough to risk ScoopNet announcing the connection to the world. She didn't know if Raji had or not, because he adroitly changed the subject whenever she tried to ask. Goddess knew they talked enough, still: hours of conversations, several times a week, about art and politics and movies and what was happening at the Temple. She'd hoped that when she started living on campus too, they could sleep together again, in the privacy of actual dorm rooms with actual doors on them, but so far Raji was sending out very mixed signals. He was clearly delighted to talk to her, and he seemed genuinely happy whenever he saw her—but he never saw her without someone else along as chaperone, most often her little brother.

Who was now energetically using his cake frosting as finger paint. "Oh, *Theo*! You're making a mess!"

"Picture!"

"Yes, I know, it's a picture too." Well, it was that much less mayhem-inducing sugar that would get into his stomach. Raji was right: she shouldn't have let him have the cake in the first place. "Okay. What's it a picture of?"

"Funnybot. Grampa Preston."

Raji gave her a quizzical look, and she said, "Daddy likes to talk to him through his favorite bot. You didn't know that? I thought Daddy told you everything." *Maybe I should ask Daddy why Raji's acting this way,* she thought grimly. *No, that's cowardice. You have to ask him directly,*

Merry. Ask him if he's dating anyone. Ask him if there's any chance, any, that he'll date you again. Tell him you love him.

"We don't talk about Theo," Raji said. "We talk AIs, Merry. Now look, you have to admit that having an AI around could be useful if you had to watch Theo all the time."

She took the plunge. "Having you around could be useful if I didn't have to watch Theo. Raji—"

"Theo! Don't wipe your hands on Merry's pack!"

Merry, stifling a curse, tried to pull her pack away, and in the process her water glass got knocked over, and Theo got wet and started to howl. By the time they'd gotten him cleaned up and dried off, gotten her pack cleaned off, paid their bill and escaped back onto Telegraph Avenue, Meredith knew that the moment for personal conversation had passed. Raji swung Theo up onto his shoulders, and the three of them wandered among the tables selling jewelry and candles and bumper stickers—EQUAL-OPPORTUNITY IMMORTALITY: RIGS FOR ALL, and CALL ME A LUDDITE: FRIG RIGS! and Merry's least favorite, PAPA PRESTON FOR PRESIDENT!—while Theo kept up a stream of exclamations about all the pretty colors. Meredith wasn't sure if he was on some kind of trip from the sugar, or was just infinitely less jaded about Telegraph Avenue than she was.

"In two more months I'll have enough for a down payment," Raji said. He was using his work in the AI lab to save toward his own rig; his parents had insisted that if he wanted one, he had to pay for it.

"Raji, can we not talk about this? You know my position."

She'd done the math for him once, given him a worksheet about how much low-income housing that down payment would build, how much food it would purchase, how many textbooks it would buy. He'd answered mildly that in that case, she'd better sell her car, not to mention her parents' mansion. She'd retorted that she needed her car and that her parents' house wasn't hers to sell; he'd given her a maddening smile and said, "Well, I need a rig, and if your parents' castle isn't your business, neither's my wiring. Come on, Merry, I'm doing work that will make life better for people. I deserve good things too." They hadn't spoken for two weeks afterward.

"Okay," he said now, with a shrug. "What do you want to talk about?"

Shit. So they were on Telegraph Avenue: So what? If she didn't get this said now, she never would. She took a deep breath. "Raji, can we go out again? Why do you keep avoiding me? Why—"

She was stilled by his hand on her shoulder. "Raji, don't let go of Theo's leg! He could fall!" Raji withdrew the hand and clamped it back around her little brother's ankle. "I just—I'd like—I—"

"Merry," he said. Trapped in the brownian motion of oblivious observers, they stood in front of a display of rainsticks. She couldn't breathe. "Merry, we're a hundred eighty degrees apart on just about any issue you can think of. Our friendship's about argument, and that's fine, but we need to—move on. Otherwise . . . Do you understand?"

No, she didn't. Not really. She remembered when Johann and Fergus had split up, how she'd come across Fergus sobbing in his cubicle and had said, "Maybe you can talk to him. Maybe you can work things out."

Fergus had shaken his head. "He doesn't want to work things out. When somebody breaks up with you, Merry, it's always a unilateral decision. There's nothing you can do about it except grieve. If you're really lucky, you stay friends, but that doesn't happen very often."

"Stick!" Theo said. "Stick!"

The rainstick vendor, a placid young woman with huge pupils, smiled dreamily and handed Theo a small rainstick. "Here you go, baby boy." Theo began turning the rainstick one way and then the other, enchanted by the noise. It would keep him still for as long as they let him hang on to it; she and Raji could stay here all day, if they wanted to. Merry wondered if the vendor was listening to their conversation, but given those pupils, she doubted it.

Well. She and Raji were friends, anyway. That was certainly true, and it wasn't something she was prepared to risk by whining about his unilateral decision. She swallowed, her tongue ashy, and said, "So are you seeing someone else?"

"Well," Raji said, looking down at his shoes. "Well, yeah, sort of." Theo, on his shoulders, had begun crooning along to the buzzing of the rainstick; the thing seemed to be hypnotizing him. Merry wished it was having the same effect on her.

"You *are*? Who is it? Why didn't you say anything before?"

"Because I was afraid you'd be upset, Merry! And because I only met her last week!"

"Oh." Well, that hardly counted. There was still hope, then. "So who is she?"

"Her name's Zephyr. She's an art major—performance. We got talking about AI stuff in the cafeteria. She's cute. And smart and interesting. We had our third date last night."

Merry swallowed. "I thought you were in the AI lab last night."

"I was," he said gently. "With Zephyr."

"Oh, *that* sounds like fun." She couldn't seem to keep her lip from curling. She knew she sounded like a jealous shrew; she couldn't seem to help that, either.

He gave her a rueful look. "It was. It was a lot of fun. Now, Merry, look, if I see more of her—"

She had to sound happy for him, had to try to sound supportive. "When do I get to meet her?" No, that hadn't worked; it had come out in a bark, as if she were interrogating him under a klieg light. *Reveal the names of your co-conspirators!*

"As soon as you want. Let me finish. If I start seeing more of her I may not be hanging out with you so much, you know?"

"Of course," she said bitterly. "But it's not like you've been hanging out with me anyway, unless someone else is around. So maybe now that I know the score, you'll hang out with me more?"

Raji coughed, and the vendor said, "Are you going to buy that? I think the little boy wants to take it home."

"What?" Merry blinked, registered that Theo was still lulling himself into catatonia with the rainstick—he looked nearly as glazed as the vendor did, and must be ready for his nap—and started digging in her pack for money. "Yeah, sure, sorry . . ."

"I've got it," Raji said, handing over a bill.

"No, Raji, it's—"

"I've got it," Raji said firmly. "Come on. Let's get out of here."

"Okay."

"And let's talk about something else for a while. I'll always be your friend, Merry. You know that, right?"

"Sure," she said numbly.

"Okay, good. Hey, Theo, don't hit me on the head with that, okay?"

"Here," Merry said, reaching up. "Theo, give me the stick."

"Want stick!"

"If you want to keep holding the stick, you have to promise not to hit Raji on the head with it. If you hit Raji again, you have to get down." *And then we'll need to drag you all the way back to my dorm room, so behave.*

" 'Kay," Theo said reluctantly. He loved riding on Raji's shoulders.

"Thank you, Theo. So, Merry, to change the subject, you never answered my question from before. Wouldn't watching him be easier if you had an AI to help?"

I can't believe he's doing this. Yes, I can. Merry, be reasonable: you haven't been lovers for three years. She forced her brain into academic mode, and said, "Look, if some house system can tell a mother when her sick kid might have measles instead of a cold, great. Just keep it in the background until she needs it. Don't have bots all over the place. Let the house feel like a house, not a factory. Or an isolation unit."

Raji laughed. "No bots? You expect this harried mother to do her own laundry when her kid's gotten covered in chocolate for the third time that day?"

"Or father. Ideally, yeah."

"Come on, Merry. Do you think your mom does her own laundry?"

"No, of course not. But I'm not talking about my mother. Look, Raji, people who live in a house need to clean it too—care for it, make it sacred. It can't be sacred if they never *touch* it. You know that."

" 'The idea of a world creating itself through small chores,' " Raji said, grinning.

"Susan Griffin," Merry said, annoyed. There were areas in which he'd read more than she had—well, of course, he was already doing graduate work—but ecological erotics wasn't one of them. "And she wasn't talking about human work. She was talking about Gaia, about the Earth doing its own housekeeping. But yeah, the same principle applies. You appreciate your food more when you cook it yourself."

"Fine. But why does the AI have to stay quiet until somebody gets sick? Why can't it be sacred too?"

Meredith scowled. It was a very old argument. "Because the sacred draws us to what's other-than-human, greater-than-human, and AIs are purely human constructs. They reflect and mimic us. We can't use them to get at anything outside our own brains. I mean, *goldfish* are more numinous than AIs."

"Funny you should mention that. Did I tell you about the AI in the lab who loves to watch nature shows?"

She pulled her sweatshirt more tightly around her shoulders, glad they were only a few blocks from her dorm. "Yeah. So? They collect information, about nature or bowling or whatever else you program them to watch. What does that prove?"

"This one chooses what to watch. It always watches nature documentaries if any are available. And the other day there was a show on about carp, and this AI—it was in *love,* Merry—it watched the show and downloaded the whole thing and watched it again, in real time, mind you, another thirty times, all night long. Dan told me that when he locked up that night he was scared it had gotten itself into an endless loop, thought we might have to crash and reboot the whole system when we came in the next day, but no, when we got there in the morning it told us that it had discovered that it was a 'sunbright carp soul enmeshed in circuit-scald,' I'm quoting here, of course, and—"

"It discovered the biases you programmed into it," Merry said flatly.

"I didn't program it at all, Merry; this one's part of the organic knowledge experiment! It came to us completely clean, blank slate from Jo-burg. We just plugged it into the Net and a bunch of sensory uptakes and let it decide what it wanted to do for itself. And it decided it was a goldfish."

"Goldfish?" Theo asked hopefully from Raji's shoulders.

"No, not that kind, honey, but I'll give you some crackers when we get home, okay?" They were his favorite snack food, aside from chocolate. "Raji, how can an AI decide it's a goldfish?"

"Well, don't ask me, but it wouldn't stop pestering us until we plugged it into a robot submersible, little tiny thing, and put it in a tank with a bunch of goldfish. Dan had to run out to the pet store to get them. And then the AI tried to mate."

Despite herself, Meredith started laughing. "Sounds to me like the chip got contaminated in transit. Are you telling me it's sacred because it tried to hump a goldfish? Are you telling me AIs have a drive to reproduce?"

"No," Raji said. "But they have a drive for experience, the same as we do. They want more information all the time. And they respond to information and experience with something that sure looks a lot like wonder. They're like little kids, like Theo here. You could learn a lot about appreciating goldfish from this machine, believe me."

"It was designed by people," Merry said, as gently as she could. "And I think that people can learn to appreciate goldfish on their own, without any lessons from computers. Raji, don't go soulfreak on me. They're wonderful tools, but they aren't people, okay?"

"We're never going to agree on this." If she gave him half an opening, he'd remind her that her argument claimed that AIs were both too human and too inhuman, and she'd have to retort that puppets weren't human, that they were inanimate, anthropomorphized extensions of the humans who manipulated them, and he'd say that AIs couldn't possibly be called puppets because they were too unpredictable, and they'd be up all night. And she had an 8:00 A.M. lit class the next morning, and it was way too early in the semester to start skipping classes. And the fact that they couldn't agree was why he wouldn't go out with her, anyway.

"You're right. We're not." Only another block until her dorm. Change the subject. "So listen, help me pick another course. I'm dropping soc because it's too boring. I can take drafting, which is what I really want to do, or get my econ requirement out of the way, which is what my adviser's recommending."

"Drafting," Raji said immediately. "Knock off econ in the summer. Kevin Lindgren's TAing the intro drafting course, and rumor has it he's really good." He grinned. "Quite anti-tech, too. You'll love him."

She didn't. She thought he was insufferable, arrogant, and condescending, a purist who considered every subject other than his own unworthy of study. Even his compliments were insulting. "You have a good hand," he told her as she hunched over a drawing table. It was her third week in the course, and this was the first time he'd deigned to speak to her, aside from reciting her name during roll call. "Are you planning on being an architect?"

"No," she said, tensing slightly.

"No? Why are you taking this, then?"

"I'm interested in design," Meredith snapped. He was paid to teach his students, not interrogate them. "I thought drafting would be a good skill to have."

He glanced at his class list, then back at her. "You're a first-year. You don't have to declare until next year. Think about architecture."

She sighed. It would be easy enough to say sure, brush him off, avoid the conversation, but she was feeling stubborn. "Thank you, but I've already declared. I'm concentrating in domestic ecology."

"Really?" He peered at her, and she waited for him to make a disparaging remark: Going for your Mrs. degree, are you? or Oh, yes, well, I suppose

Preston Walford's daughter doesn't really need to worry about a career, or Wait, isn't that just home ec? You mean people major in that? DE held the same status other eras had accorded to physical education and art history: fluff majors, gut majors, majors for rich kids who weren't too bright. She'd heard DE called "Cooking for Credit" and "Dumbass Ed" and "Drudgery Ennoblement." She could tell anyone who wanted to listen that it wasn't just feng shui and flower arranging, but she doubted that Kevin "architecture is the only worthy human endeavor" Lindgren would want to listen. And she had discovered, to her chagrin, that many of her classmates were, in fact, less interested in the intellectual discipline of managing human environments than they were in easy credits.

"Yes, really," she said, and Kevin looked at his class list again.

"That's interesting," he said. "You, uh—your last name's Walford."

She snorted. He had to be the last person on campus to know who she was. Had he been living in a blueprint tube? Didn't he watch ScoopNet?

She still couldn't figure out why ScoopNet found her so fascinating— she'd have expected them to lose interest in her a long time ago—but during one of their nondates, Raji had said it made perfect sense. "Look, Merry, you're an iconic CV survivor; everybody saw you coming out of iso. And you're the daughter of the first translation, who also happens to be one of the richest people in the world, and you've rebelled against your technological heritage by becoming a Gaia initiate and refusing to get a rig. You reflect all *kinds* of cultural obsessions."

Meredith had winced at his choice of words. She'd never told him about her brain damage, but her mother seemed all too willing to explain both her spiritual beliefs and her choice of a major as symptoms of incipient illness. Once Merry had overheard Constance asking Jack, "Don't you think her avoidance of machines is a little, well, pathological?"

"No," Jack had said, to Merry's intense gratitude. "I don't. I think it makes perfect sense, given who she is and what she's been through. It's her form of adolescent rebellion. If I'd been in iso, I'd hate bots too."

"Yes, I'm who you think I am," Merry told Kevin now. "And no, I'm not here just for an easy ride."

"Whoa," Kevin said, putting his hands up and taking a step back. "Whoa! Sorry there. I wasn't going to say that. I just wondered—I mean, DE's about, uh, doing a lot of stuff yourself, right? Instead of automating it?"

"Right," she said wearily. *Enriching the personal environment with the dignity of individual human effort,* as the catalog put it. "So you're wondering if I'm just rebelling against my New Industrialist heritage, is that it?" That's what my stepfather thinks. Didn't Kevin know she'd been a Temple novice? Had he *ever* watched ScoopNet?

To her surprise, he laughed, a sharp bark. "No, not exactly. I was wondering how you feel about this whole AI thing, though."

She scowled. She was Preston Walford's daughter; however much she argued with Raji, she couldn't be too disloyal in front of strangers. "Well, in places like Africa they're economically necessary. And even here, they supposedly do the boring stuff to free people for work they enjoy more, and certainly they're ideal for managing house systems." She shrugged. "They don't do much for me in and of themselves, but some people grow bonsai trees, and I think that's pretty silly too. It's a matter of taste, isn't it?"

"Depends whom you ask," Kevin said, but someone else had raised a hand and he had to go. He didn't get back to Meredith until the end of class. As she was putting away her pencils and rolling up her parchment, she heard a voice at her elbow say, "So, would you care to continue the conversation over a cup of coffee?"

Gold digger, she thought, without rancor. Lots of guys who'd always looked through her suddenly acted interested when they found out who she was. She hadn't let anyone starfuck her yet, and she wasn't about to start with an instructor. Her grades didn't need that kind of help, and her life didn't need that kind of complication. And he wasn't Raji. "No," she said, without bothering to turn and look at him. "You aren't allowed to date students. I could report you to the dean for that."

"That wasn't—coffee is all I meant, really. I didn't mean to offend—"

"You didn't," she said. "But you should be more careful."

"I'm sorry," he said, and then, "The comparison with bonsai trees was very smart. I'll have to remember that," and then, "You really do have a good hand, you know."

"Thanks," she said, and yawned, still without turning. When she did turn, he wasn't there. A good wide yawn could work wonders.

She and Raji laughed about it over lunch. "So," Raji said with a grin, "will you be having coffee with him?"

"I doubt it. I liked him better before he knew who I was."

Raji frowned. "You have to start trusting people more, Merry."

"Why?" she said, pushing her plate away in irritation. If Raji didn't want to go out with her, if he wanted to date this Zephyr person, fine. But he didn't have to be so obvious about trying to set her up with other people.

Raji shrugged. "Look, even if you weren't a Walford, you'd still get a lot of attention. You're smart and pretty. Even with your hair pulled back like that, even in jeans and a sweatshirt. First impressions are always shallow. And you could do worse than Kevin Lindgren."

"Is that why you told me to take his drafting course? How much do you know about this guy, anyway?"

"He's pretty famous in the architecture program: rising young star, design genius, all that stuff. He's already won competitions. His department recommended him to work with the AI lab on the habitat project, but he declined. Wrote a polite letter saying he didn't have time, but evidently told his adviser that he had no interest whatsoever in machines with an attitude, because he already had to put up with too many people like that, and why compound the problem?" Raji grinned. "Anti-tech, like I said. Sounds like your kind of guy, Merry."

"Oh, *thanks.* So I'm an arrogant snot?"

"That wasn't what I meant. You don't like self-aware machines, that's all."

The old fight. They couldn't get away from it. "And what does that make me? A Lud?"

"It makes you Merry," Raji said. "Chill. What's eating you today, anyhow?"

She glared at him. "You get three guesses."

"Ah." He looked unhappy. "I think we have to get past this. I think it's time for you to meet Zephyr. Want to have dinner with us tomorrow night?"

Zephyr and Meredith loathed one another at first sight. Meredith told herself beforehand that it wasn't fair to assume that the woman would be a flake just because of her name and her concentration. She couldn't help her name, could she? Her parents had given it to her. And so what if all the performance art majors Meredith had ever met were pseudo-intellectual art snobs who used too many syllables to describe really silly work? Meredith's favorite example was the guy who'd smashed a bunch of eggs onstage and then, afterward, explained solemnly to the audience that he'd been attacking the "polymorphously perverse homogeneity of the hubristic hegemony." No, Meredith had thought, you're just wasting food. But it wasn't fair to assume that all of them were like that; Goddess knew that Meredith hated it when people did the same thing to her, automatically placing her on the same level as the woman who'd baked ten different batches of chocolate chip cookies, dyed different colors to match different decors, for her senior project.

So she went to the dinner determined to think the best of Zephyr, even though Raji had asked her to meet them at Cyberjus, a campus café and notorious artflake hangout with annoyingly retro nineties decor and monitors scattered every few feet. She immediately spotted Raji sitting at a table against the back wall, holding hands with a small, thin woman, her hair dyed midnight black and her nails painted to match, wearing black leggings and a tunic made of shimmering strips of black glitter fabric. Artchick artflake artichoke *aaack,* Meredith thought, and scolded herself. Be fair, Merry! You haven't even talked to her yet.

"Hi," she said, walking up to the table. The nearest monitor, volume off, was broadcasting ScoopNet, some picture of a bag lady. It was probably another story about the latest CV casualties, the people who'd emerged from the illness with complete amnesia; some of them had wound up on the street. Yuck. She thought of Henry and the Martian, and shuddered, and leaned over to give Raji a peck on the cheek. Then she stuck out her hand in Zephyr's direction. "Nice to meet you, Zephyr. I'm Meredith Walford."

"Yes," Zephyr said, without smiling, "I know." She let go of Raji's hand long enough to give Meredith a halfhearted, limp handshake. "Zephyr Expanding Cosmos."

Meredith blinked and bit back the urge to laugh. Oh, the poor thing. Her parents must have been sadists. Meredith sat down next to Raji, already feeling achingly excluded from the cat's cradle of fingers in the middle of the table, and said cautiously, "Interesting name." Now Zephyr would rant and rave about how her parents had been fruitcakes and everybody had made fun of her when she was a kid, and the tension would be broken.

"I chose it at menarche," Zephyr said, as if she were commenting on the menu. "It names my essence. My birth name was useless; it didn't say anything important about me at all."

"Ah," Meredith said, and then, even more cautiously, "May I ask what it was?"

Zephyr shrugged. "I told you, it's not important."

"I don't even know that," Raji said, and Meredith watched Zephyr's face finally gain some animation as she gazed at him adoringly.

"Oh, but you know nearly everything else," she said, and giggled. Raji beamed back, and Meredith felt her skin crawl. "So, Merry, did you notice the posters in here?"

You do *not* have permission to call me Merry. Only my friends call me Merry. But she couldn't say that. She swallowed and looked around the room. Framed posters, all of them familiar, all of them her mother's work, reproductions from the latest show: "Constance Walford Retrospective, 2020–2040, Museum of Virtual Art."

"I've seen them all over the place," she said quietly. "My mother isn't very happy with the quality of the reproductions, but the museum seems to be selling truckloads of them." Constance had been ecstatic about the show, a major installation in a major museum, the big time, the big tent. Meredith remembered her mother's glowing face the night of the opening.

"Hmmmm," Zephyr said. "Does she really paint them herself?"

Meredith squinted. "What? Of *course* she paints them herself! What gave you the idea she didn't?"

"Well, you know, a lot of commercial artists have people working under them who actually paint the canvases. Or they have bots do it, not that I approve of that, of course. If we insist that machines copy our art, we'll never know what kind they can produce on their own."

Soulfreak, Meredith thought savagely. She smiled politely and said, "Well, I don't think they can produce any art on their own. They need to be programmed."

Zephyr smiled back, equally politely. "Yes, I suppose you would think that."

Raji cleared his throat. "Maybe we should discuss something other than politics."

"I'm sorry," Zephyr said, although she didn't sound sorry at all. "I'll change the subject. So, Merry, Raj tells me you're studying DE."

Meredith bit her lip. Yes, Zeff, you're right: I am studying a completely useless, apolitical subject. Nothing controversial about DE, oh, no, of course not: controversy requires a brain. "Yes," Meredith said, "I am. I'm very interested in how private spaces interact and interconnect with public ones. Those boundaries have been becoming more and more permeable, but we still seem to believe that they're sacrosanct. I want to look at how our notions of private space affect our public experience, and vice versa."

She was quoting her area declaration. Her adviser had read it and said drily, "Well, if anyone's an expert on public-private interfaces, it ought to be you."

Raji grinned at her; Zephyr raised an eyebrow. "Oh, I see. Like, if you sweep your own floors, are you less likely to litter on the sidewalk?"

Raji's grin changed into a frown. "No," he said. "It's more complicated than that."

"Of course it is," Zephyr said.

"Actually, it's not," Meredith said. "That's a great example. That's exactly the kind of thing I want to find out. Do people take more responsibility for their environment when they care for it themselves, instead of building machines to do it for them?" She smiled sweetly at them and took a bite of her roll.

Zephyr unexpectedly let go of Raji's hands and leaned forward, clearly interested. "Right," she said. "Right. We can't ask creatures, even manufactured ones, to do our dirty work for us. That's slavery. Right?"

"Zephyr," Raji said warningly, but Meredith waved a hand to silence him.

"It's okay. I don't mind, really. No, I don't think it's slavery, because I don't think machines have souls." There. She'd said it. "I mean, I don't think they're really conscious or alive or feeling or anything like that. But yes, I think we need to be more involved in maintaining our own habitat. I think we need to do more of our own dirty work, and clean work too. So we agree on that."

Zephyr looked skeptical. "You don't think AIs feel? People used to think nonhuman animals couldn't feel."

"Right. Because they were using the animals to do their dirty work and they didn't want to believe that the oxen minded pulling the plow. This is different. We didn't invent oxen; we did invent bots. And we invented them to work. I don't think that's right, because we should do the work ourselves; you don't think it's right because it's unfair to the machines. We're not going to resolve that difference. It's like arguing about religion. It *is* arguing about religion. So maybe we'd better change the subject again."

Raji smiled at her, clearly relieved; Zephyr, looking bemused, said, "You know, I felt really sorry for you, when you were stuck in isolation like that. I cried when I saw you coming out. On TV."

"Zephyr," Raji said.

"It's okay, Raji. I'm used to it. All kinds of people who barely know me think they can talk to me about my medical history. Total strangers, even, on the street." Raji groaned. Meredith said coldly, "So Zephyr, what's your point about that particular media event?"

Zephyr favored her with a thin smile. "That I felt sorry for the bots too. Because they'd been designed to stick needles into people who didn't enjoy it, and I wondered if they felt bad about that."

"If they did," Meredith said, with a glance at Raji, "it sure didn't keep them from doing their job. They followed orders beautifully. If those machines had souls, they were reincarnated Nazis or something."

"They saved your life," Zephyr said, frowning.

"The people who invented them saved my life," Meredith said. She wondered if Raji would have the sense to dump this lunatic bitch. The way they'd been holding hands when she came in, she doubted it.

Raji, sounding miserable, said, "So, um, Merry, this one here, this picture of your mother's—I really like this one."

"What?" Merry said. He gestured at the poster hanging next to their table. She blinked at it, but saw only the endless traceries of watercolor lines, pastel circuit board, that characterized her mother's most boring work. "I'll tell her you like it," she said with a shrug. "I can never tell that series apart, frankly. They just look like wallpaper to me."

"This one's not like the others," Zephyr said, surveying it critically. "It's asymmetrical. It's got a missing corner, look, down there." They all looked at the missing corner; something nagged at Meredith's memory. Where had she seen that before? She hadn't noticed it in the museum installation, had skipped the watercolors entirely. "And the circuits," Zephyr said, "right in the middle there, look—in the very center the lines start getting rounded. That little tiny part there, see? It looks like a nut. An acorn, maybe?"

Oh, Goddess. It was the picture Squeaky had chewed; that's why the corner was missing. That's why the acorn was there. Her mother could easily enough have repaired the canvas, but she hadn't. It was Constance's idea of a joke. Meredith felt her eyes filling with tears, and said, "I remember that one now. She painted it just before I got sick." She couldn't stand to tell them about Squeaky. All those years when she hadn't missed him, hadn't even thought about him, and now her sense of loss was like a stab wound in the chest.

She gazed for a long moment at the poster, willing her tears not to spill over. They didn't. When her vision cleared, she saw that Raji and Zephyr had resumed holding hands, their fingers interlocked in the center of the table.

He didn't call her that evening, or the next day, either. She assumed he was spending all his time with Zephyr now; she told herself not to mind. On the third day, when the phone rang, she picked it up hoping it would be him, but telling herself that it wouldn't be, that it would be her mother or her adviser or a classmate who'd missed a lecture and needed notes.

It wasn't any of those people. It was Dan, Raji's supervisor at the lab. "I'm sorry to bother you," he said, sounding very apologetic, "but, um, I know you're good friends with Raji, and I was wondering if you'd seen him. He was supposed to work yesterday and today, and he hasn't shown up. He's not answering his phone or e-mail. Do you know where he might be?"

With Zephyr, Meredith thought, but her spite couldn't erase her alarm. Raji never missed work. Never. Not for anybody. She looked down at her phone console: the priority override light was on. Her number wasn't published and her phone system screened out junk calls, but this guy had used his university security clearance to get through to her. Which meant he was scared too. "I haven't seen him for a few days myself," she said. "Maybe he's sick and went to the infirmary?"

"No," Dan said. "That's the first place I called when I couldn't raise him at home. He's not there."

Meredith's stomach did a panicky backflip. "Oh. Shit. Should we call the police?"

"No, no, no—I'm sure he's fine. Took a few days' vacation and forgot to let me know, or something. Or there's some kind of family problem and he had to go home. Don't worry." Dan's voice sounded as if he knew how lame this was. "Just, uh, have him call me if you hear from him, okay?"

"Give me your number," Meredith said. "I'll call you if I hear anything."

The first thing she did after she hung up the phone was log into the university directory. Shit. Shit. What was the lunatic bitch's last name again? Zephyr Sparkling Rainbow or Blooming Meadow . . . Zephyr Atmospheric Pollution. Zephyr Insufferable Condescension. Zephyr Endangered Species, if Meredith had anything to say about it. Search on Zephyr: there couldn't be many of those. She noticed numbly that her fingers trembled as she keyed in the name.

Zephyr Expanding Cosmos, here it was, phone and Net address, search on Net address, she's not logged on right now, back to the phone, key in the number, Merry what the hell's wrong with your fingers, anyhow? Ring. Two rings. C'mon, c'mon, a click, a voice, okay. It didn't sound like Zephyr. "May I speak to Zephyr, please?"

"This is Zephyr," the voice said. It sounded wan and nasal, as if it had a cold.

"This is Meredith Walford. I'm sorry to bother you. You sound like you're sick."

"Um—no," the voice said, and trembled. "Just allergies."

She's been crying, Meredith thought in a flash. Her dread deepened. "Listen, have you heard from Raji?"

A gasp of indrawn breath, and then, "*No!* I mean, no, not since the night we had dinner. You haven't, either? I thought—"

You thought he was mad at you for being a shit and that's why he didn't call, Merry thought. And I thought he was all wrapped up in you and that's why he didn't call. "No. Look, his supervisor at the lab just called me. He wasn't at work today or yesterday. He's not on the Net or at home or in the infirmary. When's the last time you saw him?" Pause. Long pause. "Hello? Zephyr, are you still there?"

"Yeah, yeah, sorry, I—I haven't seen him since that night. He walked me back to my dorm and I wanted him to come up but he didn't and I thought he was mad at me but he said no, he just had to go to the lab to do some work, he'd call me tomorrow."

And you've been waiting ever since, Meredith thought grimly. What could have happened to him? "Okay," she said. "I'll let you know if I hear anything, okay? If I hear from him I'll have him call you."

"Same here. Thanks, Meredith."

"Sure," Merry said, and hung up, and immediately called Dan back.

No, Raji hadn't been in the lab that night, according to the building's security records. He hadn't been there since the previous afternoon.

Which meant he'd evidently fallen into a black hole somewhere between Zephyr's dorm and the lab. Or had changed his mind and gone somewhere else. Where? Where could he have gone?

The Temple, Meredith thought, with a sudden surge of relief. Maybe he was so upset about the dinner that he went to the Temple to meditate. Maybe he's crashing in the novitiate dorm. Maybe he suddenly realized that he loves me and he went there to think things out. She knew, rationally, that Raji would never have gone there, that he hadn't set foot in the place since his year's service had ended, that he didn't even stay in touch with Matt or Gwyn or any of the others, for all his apparent devotion when he'd been there. The fantasy nonetheless filled her with a deep sureness, a blessed sense of peace. She basked in it a moment, her hand still on the phone, and felt the next ring even before she heard it. It would be Raji, she knew it. Raji calling to say he was wrong, that he loved her, that Zephyr was a lunatic. He'd tell her that he'd gone away for a few days to get away from everything and realized that this whole AI business was idiocy, that what mattered was organic life, and that she mattered more than any life he knew. She picked up the phone, ready to sing, ready to laugh for joy, ready to say, "Raji, where have you *been*?"

She didn't get a chance to say anything. Before she could even speak, her mother said, "Oh, honey. Oh, Merry, I'm so sorry." Constance was crying.

"Mom?" Meredith said. "What? Are you—is something—Theo?"

"No," Constance said. "Honey, Raji's parents just called."

Her body became ice. As if from a great distance, she heard herself saying, "Is he alive?"

"They've been told that he is," Constance said. "They don't know anything for sure. They just got the ransom demand two hours ago. Honey, I think you'd better come home."

Twelve

I T took Meredith ten minutes, which seemed at once to last forever and to go by in a heartbeat, to throw a week's worth of clothing into a bag. It took her ten more minutes to hike to her car, parked in the distant lot the university reserved for undergraduates. Normally the walk took fifteen to twenty minutes, depending on her pace, but today she walked quickly, almost running, her heart pounding, her head down so that maybe no one would recognize her, no one would stop her. No one did. Thirty minutes after she reached the car, she was home. In the fifty minutes it had taken her to get there, the news had spread all over the Net, all over the TV networks; by now it was surely all over campus, too.

The clip released by the kidnappers began with a series of still photographs of Raji in the campus AI lab. Raji staring at a monitor, his face lit eerily by the light from the screen; Raji frowning at a printout; Raji kneeling in front of a table on which perched a particularly insectoid bot. His face had been subtly altered to look more angular, crueler: he was recognizably Raji, but a Raji morphed into meanness everywhere but in the kneeling shot, where his face had been given a look of blank reverence instead. Meredith was surprised they hadn't manipulated the image to make him genuflect outright.

"This man," said a woman's voice, beautifully modulated and cool as running water, "is the son of prominent ecoactivists." Shot of Sonia standing on a podium in front of the Sierra-Audubon logo; shot of Ahmed on the cover of *Greenpeace Millenium* magazine.

Now there was a photograph of Merry, pale and confused and homely, emerging from isolation. "This woman," the voiceover went on, still in those dispassionate tones, "is the daughter of Preston Walford, the Soul of the Machine." Shot of Preston's face, thirty times life size, on a huge monitor above some teeming city square.

"The child of the machine," said the voice, "has seduced the child of the earth." Shots of Merry and Raji together now, a lot of shots: the two of them sitting on a bench in front of the campus art museum, dancing in some anonymous, crowded room, eating in a cafeteria, walking, drinking coffee, carrying books. In all of the photographs Raji was gazing adoringly at Meredith; in all of the photographs Meredith—grown subtly more curved than she had ever been in real life—replied with a salacious grin. Now there was a montage of fuzzy, grainy photographs, designed to look as if they had been taken through windows: Raji and Merry in bed, doing things artfully left to the viewer's imagination.

It was all digital manipulation. None of it had ever happened, not even the innocent images. Meredith had only been on campus for a month, and she hadn't spent nearly that much time alone with Raji.

"The machine," said the voiceover, "has already murdered the planet." Quick montage of shots now: landfills, strip mining, smokestacks belching filth, someone's hand crushed between gears, a flash of bare skin and spread legs on a computer terminal. "Now the empire of the machine wishes to replace the empire of the living." Swarming bots, metallic and menacing, like something out of a horror movie.

"This thing"—shot of Preston—"has given the University of California at Berkeley five billion dollars so that this man"—shot of Raji—"can develop artificial intelligence, including the so-called organic knowledge project, which encourages machines to design themselves without human intervention. To date, the most common use of AI technology has been in missile guidance and other defense systems, although the Soul of the Machine continues to deny his involvement with such mechanisms." A shot now of a mushroom cloud, of missile silos, of a heap of charred bodies with a radiation symbol superimposed on them. "If AI continues to be perfected, the living will be doomed." Shot of planet Earth, seared by fire, being overrun by swarming bots.

"We have this man, this traitor to humanity"—Raji—"under protective custody. We will release him only if the empire of the machine refunds that five billion dollars to the living and ceases all work on artificial intelligence, including complete destruction of the laboratory housing the organic knowledge project." Shot of the AI Project building.

"These demands must be met in forty-eight hours." Shot of Earth overrun with bots again, but this time Raji's features were imposed on the planet's. "If the machine is not stopped, the planet will die." The clip faded into a logo of a boot stamping on a bot, with the phrase HUMAN ALLIANCE in garish red capitals below it.

The clip was everywhere: slick, sinister, emotionally manipulative, profoundly illogical. Never mind that Raji was an undergraduate, not even a grad student, let alone a MacroCorp employee. Never mind that the organic knowledge project's greatest triumph to date had been producing an AI that thought it was a goldfish, or that very few bots were equipped with anything but the simplest, most rudimentary form of AI. Never mind that anyone who'd ever seen Merry in person knew that she'd never had those curves; never mind that she and Raji hadn't been lovers for three years. Never mind that no one had ever produced solid evidence linking MacroCorp to the military. Whatever else one could say about the Luddite fringe, it was certainly adept at using technology efficiently for its own ends.

Meredith had already seen the footage five times, on two different channels and three different servers, by the time the cops came to question her. Both of the cops were women; both squeezed her hand when they shook it, and both treated her very gently. The shorter one did most of the talking, and the first thing she said was, "You mustn't blame yourself for this."

It was the first thing Constance had said when Meredith got home. Jack and Preston had been repeating it at regular intervals ever since. Theo was upstairs, taking a nap.

"Raji's not my boyfriend," she said, as Constance waved them into the dining room, murmuring something about coffee, tea, maybe some homemade scones? Merry realized with a shock that there were no bots in the house, not even Theo's beloved toys. Where were the bots?

The short cop said, "It's not your fault, Meredith."

They were all sitting down now. She was sipping mint tea and the tall cop was eating a scone. She couldn't remember sitting down. She couldn't remember her mother, or anyone else, bringing the tea and the scone to the table. Jack sat across the room. Where was her mother? Her mother was upstairs, checking on Theo, even though the baby monitor on the table next to Merry hadn't made a sound. Preston, looking anguished— more digital manipulation—watched from a nearby monitor. "He's not even my boyfriend, and he's not the head of the AI Project, he just works there, he's just a stupid lab tech, and MacroCorp funded that project two years before Raji even enrolled!"

"We know," the short cop said patiently. "It doesn't matter."

"It matters to them!" The mug slipped from her hands, fell on the table, rolled toward the edge, where someone's hand—her mother's, her mother must be standing behind her, yes, she could hear Constance's murmuring voice again—caught it.

"Theo?" Jack said.

"He's still asleep. He's okay."

"I'll go in when he wakes up, Connie. You stay with Merry."

Her mother's hands were digging into her shoulders. What did that remind her of? The doctor's office. Dr. Honoli's office, a million years ago. "It matters to them," Meredith said again. It was terribly important for her to remember where she was and what was happening, and she couldn't seem to manage it for more than a minute at a time. "They snatched Raji because they thought I'd—I'd brainwashed him or something! They snatched him to get at MacroCorp's money because they couldn't snatch me, because my blood's been doctored. And none of it's true!"

The taller cop sighed. "They snatched him because they could twist the facts into a story, Meredith." There was a towel now, in front of her, wiping up the tea. Her mother's hand was pushing the towel. Her mother's hands weren't on her shoulders anymore. When had they left? "I doubt they believe any of it themselves. It's propaganda. The connection with you was gravy for them because it made the propaganda more powerful, that's all."

Her arm hurt; she realized dimly that the spilling tea had burned it. "Powerful? It's a pack of lies. How can anybody believe any of that stuff? They're crazy!"

"They're extremists, yes. Terrorists always are. But they'd have found some way to demand the dismantling of the AI Project even if Raji had never met you."

She swallowed. She was shaking; she'd been shaking since the call from Raji's supervisor, eons ago. She wondered if she'd ever stop. She saw with merciless clarity that she would never be able to be friends with anyone again; and then, with heightened fear, she remembered Matt, Gwyn, Anna, and Johann and Fergus, and Harold. None of them was safe. Only Hortense was safe, because Hortense was already dead, having taken her last breath peacefully, during her sleep, six months before. No one who had ever been friends with Meredith, no one who was still alive, was safe. "Where is he? Do you know where he is?"

"No. And we won't be able to find out by the deadline."

He doesn't have special blood, she thought numbly. That's why they took him in the first place. "So what are you going to do?"

The cops both sighed now, in unison. "We are going to save Raji's life," said another voice, and she realized that it was coming from the monitor, that it was Preston who had spoken. "We are going to do what the terrorists have asked. We are going to demolish the AI lab building, and we are going to divert the MacroCorp research grant to whatever account the terrorists specify."

"Right," Jack said grimly. "We're going to give them their fucking five billion on international monetary microchip at their fucking drop point by their fucking deadline. And we're going to hope they're stupid enough to get caught in the process, except that they probably won't be, because that only happens in the movies. And in the meantime we're going to slap a ton of security on anybody connected with the AI Project or Raji or you, Merry, which I suppose is what we should have done to begin with." Meredith blinked, and realized that Jack was shaking almost as badly as she was.

"Which is why we're here," the short cop said. "To get a list of names from you, Meredith. Names of people who might also be at risk."

She shook her head, wondering if Zephyr, for all her soulfreak rhetoric, was really a Lud in disguise. "You don't want to know who might be connected with *them*?"

"Yes, of course," the tall cop said gently. "That too. But it's the same list. It will be easier for you to give us the list if you're protecting people than if you're naming them as suspects, right? But for our purposes, it's the same thing."

Meredith closed her eyes, and the images from the vid clip rose unbidden, as if they had been waiting there all along. She and Raji, walking arm in arm on campus; she and Raji on a bench, her head resting on his shoulder. She and Raji wrestling in near darkness, lit only by a candle.

How she wished that all of it had really happened.

Traitor to humanity, they had called Raji. What had Meredith herself betrayed? Seeing the montage that so eerily replicated her own desires made her feel unclean, violated, as if the Human Alliance had strip-mined the inside of her skull. "Is he safe?"

"We don't know," the short cop said, very gently indeed. "Of course they want us to believe he is, will be, as long as we accede to their demands. They sent us and his parents clips of him, standard kidnapping stuff, please save me, please go along with what they want, et cetera. But that stuff could be faked, just like the media clip was. Raji's parents aren't convinced by any of it. We won't know, can't know, for sure until the drop."

Preston's image shook its head. "None of this will make any difference to the AI Project. None at all. The project is a process, not a building. There are copies of the research all over the Web. Other people are working on the same ideas, more people than the terrorists can possibly threaten. They cannot believe this will stop our work. They cannot be that stupid."

The tall cop spoke up now. "We're hoping they are, Papa—Mr. Walford, Preston, sir."

"What if they aren't?" Meredith said. No one answered her. "Well? What if they aren't? Say something! I'm not stupid, either! Don't try to lie to me!"

"If they aren't," the short cop said, looking directly at Merry, "then there's something more to this. That's all. Then they're trying to do something else, and we aren't sure what it is." She smiled wanly. "Law enforcement types don't like not knowing things. So, Meredith, can we get started with that list now, please?"

Forty-eight hours. She swallowed and started naming names, starting with Zephyr's. She realized that there must be other cops, a lot of cops, cops interviewing everyone on campus. "Is Zephyr on your list already?" she asked, and the short cop said, "It doesn't matter. Pretend we don't know anything. Give us every name you can think of. We'll weed out the duplicates."

She closed her eyes and recited names: everybody in her classes, in Raji's classes that she knew of, in either of their departments, in performance art, in computer science. She listed names for twenty-five minutes, the names of more people than she'd thought she even knew, stopping only when the cops asked her to spell a name, please, or to spell that again, they hadn't gotten that the first time. When she was done there was a pause; she realized that they were waiting for more names.

"I'm finished," she said, her eyes still closed. "That's all the people I can think of. That's all."

She heard a sigh. Constance said wearily, "Well, sounds like we'd better put the entire campus under a protective bubble."

I'm contagious, Meredith thought. No one who's ever spent time with me is safe. It's worse than CV. She opened her eyes. The cops were watching her, sadly. When they saw her looking at them, they stood up.

"Thank you, Meredith," the short one said. "Thank you very much. We'll let you know the minute we know anything."

"Try to get some sleep," the tall one said. And then they were gone.

Meredith sat there, her limbs suddenly immovable. The house was amazingly quiet. "Where are the bots?" she asked dully.

"Sleeping," Constance said. "Under the circumstances, we thought you'd probably prefer not to see them."

"Mom, it doesn't matter, Theo likes them, they're his toys."

"You're upset enough as it is. Theo has other toys. Do you want something to eat? You need to eat."

"No."

"When Sonia and Ahmed called—they said—they said you mustn't—"

"Blame myself," Meredith finished wearily. "Of course they'd say that. Do you think they believe it?"

To Meredith's shock, Constance and Jack and Preston all began talking at once, vehemently, gesticulating, their voices rising and falling like the sound of waves on a beach. *Terrorists they're terrorists they did this their fault you didn't terrorists you mustn't it's them criminals it's terrorists not your.* . . . Their voices sounded a million miles away. Meredith blinked at them.

Love, her father was saying. Her father was saying something different now. *You love Raji. You would never hurt Raji. Raji loves you, Meredith. Raji would never blame you.*

"No," she said, and they all nodded.

They all looked relieved. They thought they knew what she was saying. They thought she meant, "No, I wouldn't hurt him; no, he wouldn't blame me." But that wasn't what she'd meant.

She'd meant, "No, he doesn't love me." She didn't know if he'd blame her or not; she supposed he wouldn't. Raji had always been eminently fair.

"Daddy, why can't they find him? I'm scared! I can't stop thinking about—about—"

She couldn't even say it. She didn't even care if she sounded like she had

OCD; who could expect her *not* to be having obsessive thoughts right now?

It was three in the morning. Meredith, unable to sleep, had ordered Jack and Constance to go to bed and get rest, since she couldn't. But once they left, the silence of the house began to work on her nerves, and she finally switched on the monitor in her room and summoned her father. It was the first time she'd done so in—how long? In forever. Had she ever summoned him before?

"I am scared too, Meredith. He is my friend too."

That was true. How often had she thought, bitterly, that Raji had more in common with Preston than Meredith ever had? How many conversations like this had Preston and Raji had, late at night? "What about the woman talking on the tape? Have they done a voiceprint?"

"Of course. That is the first thing the police did, and as we all suspected, it was a digital voice, not a human one."

Of course. They wouldn't be that stupid. "But they must have left some trace! There must be something on camera somewhere, there must be sales records of the equipment they used to make the vid, there must—"

"It is very common equipment, and without serial numbers there is no way to track specific sales. And the police have found nothing helpful in the campus security records for that evening. We must assume that this group is extremely skilled not only at using technology but at avoiding it— that being, after all, their stated goal."

Meredith got up and started pacing. "Have people threatened Macro-Corp before? There must be lists of Lud groups!" All those Lud bumper stickers on Telegraph Avenue: oh, Goddess. The cops were going to be pulling over all those cars, and most of those kids were just posing, just playing at rebellion. She knew people with those bumper stickers. They weren't criminals. "There must be lists of terrorists—"

"MacroCorp has never been a target of terrorist activity in this country. And the overseas incidents were years ago, and have no evident bearing on the current case."

"But the lists—you could compare—"

"The police are comparing the lists, Meredith. I do not have access to them."

"You could have access to them if you wanted to!"

"No." Preston's voice was very quiet. "I could not, Meredith, truly. I could, if I chose, use MacroCorp resources to break certain encryption codes, but that would be illegal trespass, and would subject me to serious penalties, including possible erasure."

Meredith shook her head. "There has to be something we can do! Daddy, please! When's the last time I asked you for help?"

"I am helping MacroCorp comply with the kidnappers' demands, which is the safest way to find Raji."

Rage blocked her throat. "Do you *trust* them? You said yourself this can't stop the research! You said yourself that they have to know that too! So do you really think he'll be—that he'll be—"

"I do not trust them, no. But noncompliance would be far more dangerous. We do not know if compliance will win Raji's safety. We do know that noncompliance will endanger it."

She kept pacing, the thick carpet soft under her feet. So different from her dorm room, either at school or at Temple. It wasn't right for her to be walking on soft carpet. She should be walking on coals, or on nails. "He has to be okay. He has to be okay. If he's not okay—"

"If he is not okay, Meredith—"

"*Don't* tell me it won't be my fault! I'm tired of hearing it!"

"It would not be my fault, either. And it would not be the fault of the police. It would be the fault of the terrorists."

Meredith felt a scream beginning to bubble in her throat. Preston continued, relentless and implacable. "But all the people whose fault it was not would feel the pain far more than the people whose fault it was. That is why this is so horrible. He is in the hands of people who do not care about him, and those who care can do nothing. And you care most of all, second only to Sonia and Ahmed. You are the three people who love him the most. And I am his friend. And we are the four at whom the video clip struck. The clip wants us to believe that Raji is in danger because he was born to certain people, and because he loved and befriended others."

What was he talking about? "The clip was a lie! A lie! None of those things ever happened! Daddy, he hasn't loved me for three years, not that way! They know it's a lie! They don't care! They don't care if he loves me or not."

"He does love you. I know he does. He has told me so."

"Well, you're my *father*! He's not going to—"

"The clip is indeed a lie, but not because of that. It is a lie because Raji is in danger from the people who hate the people he loves. The hate makes the danger, not the love. The people who hate us, the people who kidnapped him, do not even know us."

"What's the difference? The danger's the same! It doesn't make any difference to Raji, does it?"

"You must not let this make you afraid to love, Meredith."

"Oh, Goddess! Do you *really* think that's entirely under my control?"

"Yes. I think it is. I think it can be."

Merry shook her head so wildly that her hair blinded her, obscuring the earnest image on the screen. "That's because you don't know anything, Daddy. You don't know jackshit about me or anybody else who's still alive. You're a machine, and you've forgotten anything you ever knew about being human."

"Meredith—"

"Shut up," she said, and hit the off button so hard that her monitor rocked on its stand.

Exhausted, Meredith fell into an uneasy doze near dawn; her mother woke her at ten to say that Matt and Gwyn were waiting for her downstairs.

"Mommy, I don't want to see them."

"Well, they want to see you. They're upset too, Merry. You can't help Raji by pushing all your other friends away."

Biting back her rage—Constance and Preston must have been conferring—she threw on a robe and went sullenly downstairs, to find Theo holding court. In just the past few weeks, he'd leaped from simple sentences to complex thought. "Merry yelled," he was telling Matt and Gwyn. "I was scared. I got into bed with Mommy and Daddy."

Merry, unseen, stood stricken at the entrance to the den. Theo must have heard her shouting at Preston. He was rigged: he'd have access to that lovely memory in perpetuity. How could Constance and Jack stand knowing that any cross word they uttered was etched in silicon? "Theo," she said, "I'm sorry I scared you. I was upset, but I wasn't upset at you."

He turned and regarded her gravely. "It's not nice to yell."

"I know it isn't." She knelt. "I'm sorry, honey. Can you come here and give me a hug?"

He did; his willingness to forgive amazed her. Then he and Constance went upstairs to build with blocks, and Merry was alone with Gwyn and Matt. They both looked gaunt, drained; it occurred to her that they'd known Raji longer than she had, and been rejected more thoroughly. He hadn't even been back to visit the Temple since he left. He hadn't even gone to Hortense's funeral; he'd been in Hawaii that weekend. He'd sent flowers instead.

"Your father's right," Matt said, when she told them about the conversation with Preston, and Gwyn nodded. "You have to keep loving, Merry. You can't put yourself back in isolation, and you can't hate. If you do that, the terrorists will have won."

"If *I* do that? This isn't about me! If I do that it will be because those thugs have—have done something to Raji." What was she saying? They'd already done something to Raji: they'd kidnapped him. "And if they do that, they've won no matter what I do!"

"No," Gwyn said. "Merry, whatever happens, the way to keep them from winning for good is to keep being a decent person."

"I don't think my decency or lack of it makes any difference. Not to them. Not to people like them."

"It matters to us," Matt said. "And it matters to you. This is about saving your own life, whatever happens to Raji. Merry, stop staring at me like that; I'm not speaking a foreign language." *Yes. You are.* "Please listen to me. You've gone through more than anyone your age should have to bear; you've gone through more than most people have to bear in a lifetime. You've survived CV and you've survived celebrity and you've survived your father's translation, which has to be damned weird, and now your best friend's been kidnapped. That's an appalling string of stuff. It's not even remotely fair that all that should happen to one person. That kind of misfortune doesn't make any sense, and it never will—not unless you use it to make your own sense, not unless you consciously refuse to let it harden or break you, not unless you very deliberately transform it into something useful. I'm not claiming for a second that's easy. It's the hardest thing any of us ever has to do. It's also the most important."

She squinted at him. Didn't he understand what might happen? "Why are you even *talking* about me? Why aren't you talking about Raji?"

"We *are* talking about Raji," Gwyn said, very gently. "Merry, we can't help him right now. We don't know where he is. Neither does anybody else. We're doing what we can do. We've prayed, and we've talked to Ahmed and Sonia, and now we're talking to you."

Merry swallowed. "Did you lecture Sonia and Ahmed, too? Did you tell them they have to use lemons to make lemonade, even if their son's killed?"

"We didn't have to," Matt said, more gently yet. She'd been trying to hurt or at least shame him, but it hadn't worked. "They already knew. They've already lost one child, you know. They had a little girl who died of SIDS before Raji was born. They went ahead and had Raji anyway."

Raji had never told her he'd had a sister. And her parents had lost all those people in Africa, to the pandemics. Meredith got up and went to the window, standing with her back to Matt and Gwyn as she looked down at the Bay. The Bay was very blue today. How could it be blue? How could the sun be out?

Constance had almost lost Merry to CV, but she'd gone ahead and had Theo. No wonder she'd had him rigged. How could you stand the idea of losing your child?

Theo. Theo was safe; Theo had GPS cells, just like Merry and Jack and Constance did. Kidnappers would never be able to hide any of them. GPS cells worked even after you were dead. The only way to get rid of GPS cells was through a total blood change, and that took more than long enough for anyone who was looking for you to find you before it was over.

It didn't matter. Theo could still succumb to CV, or a bullet, or any number of other things. He'd succumb to something, in the end. You just had to hope you died before your child did.

I'm glad I can't have kids, Meredith thought, still staring out at the water. I'm never going to get married. I'm never going to have a child. It hurts too much when something happens.

"I can't think about any of this right now," she told Matt and Gwyn. "I can't think about anything except Raji. If Raji survives, none of this matters. And if he doesn't . . ."

If he didn't, none of it would matter, either. But some obscure impulse kept her from saying that to Matt and Gwyn, who were, after all, trying to be kind to her.

❧

The AI Project building at Berkeley was demolished by the Luds' deadline: no small technical feat, given the size of the building and the density of other campus structures around it. But a wrecking crane and judicially placed explosives successfully destroyed the building without serious damage to any neighboring ones. MacroCorp delivered the monetary chip to the drop point on time. Questioned by journalists about the wisdom of acceding to the terrorists' demands, MacroCorp maintained staunchly that Raji was more important than either money or a building. "Contrary to what the kidnappers apparently believe," read the official press release, "we care more about people than we do about machines."

None of it mattered. It had never been meant to matter. At the precise moment of the useless drop, the police received an anonymous and untraceable encrypted call directing them to a deserted alleyway in Oakland, where they found Raji double-bagged in plastic. Taped to the outside of the bag was a DVD, which illustrated how Raji had been transformed from the person his friends and family loved to an assortment of body parts wrapped in trash bags. The Luds, in their efficiency, also distributed copies of the disc to the same networks and servers who had been given copies of the original tape.

Meredith and Constance were sitting in front of the television, watching ScoopNet coverage, when Preston's face flashed on the screen. Simultaneously, the phone began ringing. Meredith's stomach heaved. *Oh, Goddess. Something's happened. Raji!*

"Meredith, Constance, turn off the television." Preston's voice was gentle, and very quiet. "You must not watch this."

"What?" If she asked him, if she made him say it, maybe it wouldn't be what she already knew it had to be. "Why? What—"

"Hello?" Her mother had answered the phone. Meredith saw Constance's hand go to her mouth, saw the blanched look of horror. "Oh, Goddess. Goddess Goddess Goddess—"

"Merry!" Jack ran in now. "Meredith, oh, sweetheart, I'm so sorry—"

"What happened?" She was standing, screaming at them, unable to care if Theo heard or not. Raji was dead. The certainty pooled like ice water in her veins. Raji couldn't be dead. "He—they killed him, didn't they? Didn't they? Answer me!"

No one said anything. They didn't have to. The looks on their faces told her, and she didn't need those, either, because she already knew. The Luds had said they'd release him; they'd never said they'd release him alive. She swung back around to face the television. "Daddy, let me see it."

"Meredith, I do not think—"

"*Let me see it.* I have to know what happened!"

"All right. Constance, stay here with Meredith. Jack, Theo is asking for you to read him a book, because I will not let him watch the television. He wants to sit on someone's lap."

Constance let out a whimper. "Oh, my baby—"

Time had shifted into slow motion now, moving slowly as syrup. Theo. Theo was rigged. They didn't want Theo to see anything because he'd always remember it. Raji had wanted to be rigged, but he wasn't yet. He hadn't saved enough money. If he'd been rigged—if he'd been rigged, would he still be alive now? Would they have been able to save his memories?

She heard Jack saying something, and time snapped back into its normal passage. "Connie, I'll go up to Theo. Preston's right. Stay here with Merry."

And then Jack was gone, and Constance was gripping Meredith's hand in hers, and Preston's face disappeared, replaced by a heading that read, "Artificial Intelligence in Action." It began with Raji standing alone in a small room: no door, no window, smooth walls. He wore baggy jeans and an "Earth First" T-shirt; the jeans were his, the ones Meredith had last seen him in, but the Luds must have given him the T-shirt. He never wore anything with slogans. That was all they had altered, though; this image was untouched, the Raji Merry knew. They hadn't made him look mean in this one. They didn't have to bother with that anymore; he'd served their purposes, and been discarded.

As the tape began, the camera looked down at him as he made his way around the little room, feeling the walls, pounding, yelling, trying to find a crack or a weak spot or a hollow place. He must have become aware that the camera was on, because he turned and looked up at it.

"Hello? Is someone there?" He blinked up at it and tried to smile. "Who's watching this? If you're the people who took me, I'm on your side, really I am. I believe in ecology. I was a novitiate in a Gaia temple for a year, ask anybody who knows me." Hopeful pause; when no one responded, his face fell, and he said, "If anybody else is watching this, I hope I'll see you all real soon." Shrug. "The food's okay. I can't sleep because

I'm too worried. I want to get out of here." Pause. No response. "Well, I guess nobody's going to talk to me, huh?" Raji shrugged again and went back to circling the room.

That was when the first bot dropped onto the floor. It was a MacroCorp bot, one of the new two-legged ones being marketed as toys: Murphy Mouse. It looked harmless. Raji jumped, turned, saw the bot, looked up, ducked, and covered his head. The first bot was followed by a cascade of others: Dumpling the Dwarf, Racquel Raccoon, Gigi Grasshopper—that was an older model, and Theo's favorites—Lorenzo Lobster, Patty Potato. Soon the floor of the little room was nearly covered in bots; Raji bent to pick one up, but it scuttled away from him. He frowned, looked down at the bots, said, "You guys have voice chips?"

They all spoke at once, then. "We are here to serve you," they said, chirping and trilling and squeaking according to their programmed voices. They began to move toward him. "We are here to serve you. We are here to serve you." They said, in unison, only that one thing, the voices becoming more and more metallic, until they sounded like the pinging of raindrops on steel. Their voice chips were programmed for that single phrase; Raji's voice must have been the trigger that broke their silence.

By the time Meredith and Raji's parents and everyone else on the planet with media access saw the clip, there was no doubt about how the bots would serve Raji, no possible suspense. And Meredith, watching, could tell from the look on his face, the terror with which he backed into a corner as the bots advanced toward him, that he had no doubt either. *To Serve Man.* It was such an old, stupid, corny joke. The bots moved slowly, and as they approached him he turned and began to try to climb the smooth walls. When that didn't work, he turned and began kicking out at the bots, punting them across the room, lashing out.

There were too many of them, though. Meredith turned away when they began extruding knives, ice picks, round buzz saws. Constance had let go of Meredith's hand and begun rocking herself, sobbing; she couldn't seem to take her eyes off the television. But Meredith stopped looking, refused to look. She wrenched her head away and fled the room, even though the sound of Raji's cries, and then of his screams, followed her wherever she ran: into the dining room, upstairs to her own room. She had insisted on watching the clip, and she was glad she had seen the beginning of it, seen Raji in his last moments of being whole and unhurt. But she wouldn't watch him being dissected by the bots, couldn't watch; it was too much like the nightmares she'd had in isolation, in Honoli's office.

Running from the horror made no difference, not to her, and certainly not to Raji. She knew, even as she fled, even as her grief tore the breath from her lungs and turned her blood to molten lava, that those images would live inside her forever now, would live in her longer, perhaps, than her love for Raji would live. She could only imagine what seeing them must have done to Sonia and Ahmed.

Thirteen

N EARLY everyone realized that the bots had been programmed to do what they did, that their horrific task was an outcome of human in- tent, rather than any malevolence inherent to AI. MacroCorp launched a public information campaign to educate consumers about the difference between true AI—"autonomous individuality," as Preston had dubbed it, or "the ability to say 'I'"—and the comparatively primitive self-modifications performed by most bots. Bots could evaluate certain aspects of their envi- ronment to perform their work, but they had no sense of self, no emotions, no ability to hate or plot against the beings who had created them. Bots were harmless.

Nonetheless, Raji's death quickly acquired the status of cultural trauma. Meredith had once told herself that if Raji died, she'd want there to be someone in the world who remembered him. Now he was branded into the memories of anyone with access to news media. If the Luds had in- tended to inculcate a horror of the machine and of MacroCorp, in many quarters they succeeded all too well. There were reports of small towns banning bots altogether, of small children becoming violently ill at the sight of the cartoon figures they had formerly loved, of the most innocuous bots, gunmetal spheres on wheels who did nothing but eat dust, being hunted and destroyed. Such hunts rarely lasted long. Bots were too stupid to flee, even in self-defense. They were only machines.

The hatred against anyone proclaiming Lud tendencies was uglier. In Berkeley, the sale of Lud bumper stickers dropped overnight, and drivers who didn't scrape their bumpers clean of the offending items often found their tires slashed and their windshields broken. Across the country, in the Berkshires, an ecotourist wearing a Lud T-shirt was tortured and killed by a group of local hunters, although some cynics observed that the hunters might simply have seized the easiest excuse. In response to the killing, Raji's parents made a dignified public plea on ScoopNet. "Most people with Luddite sympathies had nothing to do with murdering our son," Ahmed said quietly. "Most Luddites abhor what happened to Raji as much as we do. Hurting others will not bring Raji back. Please learn to live in peace." Sonia, standing next to him, broke down and wept, Ahmed's hand on her shoulder. ScoopNet ratings went through the roof.

Sierra-Audubon experienced a notable upsurge in donations. Macro-Corp, after again emphasizing its humanitarian and nondestructive business practices, announced that the AI Project building would not be rebuilt; instead, the space would be dedicated to a memorial garden in Raji's honor. It was, of course, the last thing Raji would have wanted, but it was good PR. Sierra-Audubon donated trees and rosebushes, and Matt said a blessing over the greenery.

The memorial service and garden dedication were hideous for Meredith, almost worse than watching the kidnapping clips had been. She didn't want to go, but Jack and Preston and Constance insisted. She had to go, they told her. She had to go for Sonia and Ahmed, if nothing else. So she went, under heavy sedation, draped in a black mourning shawl Sonia had given her. The shawl had belonged to Raji's grandmother, the one who had died in the United States after telling him stories about animals. Meredith knew how generous a gift it was, knew she owed Sonia more than the grudging thanks she managed to squeeze out. All she could think of was Raji's description of his grandmother's death, which had been so much like a birth.

Raji's death had been nothing like a birth.

Despite extensive efforts, the police never caught the terrorists, who had left nothing behind for anyone to trace. Law enforcement had no previous record of the Human Alliance, a name which seemed to have been invented for the kidnapping. Several members of Luddite cells, subjected to strenuous questioning, admitted to the existence of a shadowy leader named Gina Veilasty, who might have masterminded Raji's death. But no one had ever seen her in person; the first Luds who were questioned knew people who knew people who had spoken to her, but only online; and those contacts, once they had been brought in for questioning themselves, had no way to contact Veilasty. Her webpage no longer existed, and police could find no record of an actual person by that name. They concluded that Veilasty was an online persona, constructed as a blind. Several of the Lud informants had reached this conclusion themselves, especially once they realized that Veilasty's name was an anagram of "staying alive."

Commentators observed that the lack of closure was one of the most unsettling things about the incident. Not only had Raji Abdul-Allam been horrifically tortured and murdered, but the forces responsible were still at large, "boding their time until their next atrocity," as one ScoopNet pundit put it.

Meredith observed it all from within an icy shell, a brittle carapace from which all efforts at sympathy rebounded with a faint chiming sound. She couldn't stand being on campus, and Temple reminded her too unbearably of Raji, so she moved back home. Jack and Constance never reactivated their own herd of bots, not even Theo's toys, and Meredith never found out what had happened to the devices. She supposed that they had been stripped down to their metal shells and reprogrammed, but she never asked.

Instead she began doing the housework herself: dusting, setting tables, polishing silver and scrubbing floors. It was soothing work, repetitive and productive, a form of contemplation. It reassured her that in a world where horrible things happened, she could at least maintain the calm and order of wood and marble and tile. The work exercised her body and disciplined her mind. It was her dance, her prayer, her narcotic. She still saw flashes of metal and blood, still heard Raji screaming, still woke weeping from dreams of his embrace, but at least there were other things in the world too, tasks both demanding and simple: the challenge of producing a perfectly waxed tabletop, of cleaning blinds and chandeliers.

"Honey," her mother said, several weeks after Meredith had abandoned her dorm room, "I really wish you wouldn't. It makes me feel like the wicked stepmother in *Cinderella*."

"I want to," Meredith said.

Constance cleared her throat. "All this cleaning—Meredith, it looks an awful lot like OCD. You've been under an enormous amount of stress. Of course this is when that would develop. It's understandable, but—"

"Mom," Meredith said with a sigh. "It's not OCD. It's worship. Or maybe it is OCD, but it's still worship. All right? It's helping me."

Constance grimaced. "I talked to Dr. Honoli. He agrees with me. He can give you meds."

"For *what*? The fact that Raji's dead? No meds will fix that! Mom, this is *helping* me. It's therapy, all right? Leave me alone!"

Meredith knew that most of the people around her, even the ones who didn't know about her brain damage, thought she'd gone quietly insane, although none of them blamed her for doing so. She didn't care what they thought or whom they blamed. She craved order and cleanliness, the oblivion of antisepsis. She wanted to make the space around her, the space she lived in and could call her own, safe and beautiful.

She had taken a leave of absence from school, supposedly temporary, although she found herself unable to imagine returning. She no longer attended Temple. At her mother's insistence, she received visitors. Matt and Gwyn brought flowers and fruit and long embraces; they told her it wasn't her fault, and cried, and tried to get her to cry with them, urging her to rage and to mourn. At each new entreaty, she felt herself becoming stonier, more isolated, and finally they went away. Raji's lab supervisor came, and told her it wasn't her fault, and told her that the university was setting up a scholarship fund in Raji's name. "Really?" she said. "For people who are targets of terrorists? Does it come with an armed tank?" Dan winced and bit his lip, and went away. Zephyr came, and tried to tell Meredith that it wasn't her fault, but Meredith didn't even let her finish the sentence. "So tell me," she said, "when you saw the tape, did you feel sorrier for Raji or the bots?" Zephyr began to cry, and went away.

Reporters came. She refused to see them. Psychiatrists came. She refused to talk to them. Sonia and Ahmed came; she fled to her room, locked the door, and stayed there, shaking, until she saw them drive away again. She knew they hated her, whether they had given her the shawl or not. The gift had only been for the benefit of the cameras. They had to hate her. If they hadn't hated her before the memorial, they must have hated her afterward, for not being able to thank them more warmly for the gift. She had shoved it into the back of her closet, a mute reproach. She wanted to return it or bury it or burn it, but knew she could do none of those things.

Through everything, Jack and Constance and Preston cajoled her, pleaded with her, told her they loved her. She wouldn't listen. She found herself humming to drown people out, humming always the same tune. *Please don't think it's funny when you want the ones you miss,* she hummed, always without words, hoping everyone would go away. *There are lots and lots of people who sometimes feel like this.*

Everyone went away. She found herself completely alone with her mops, her sponges, her cleansers and wax and polish. *If only he'd been rigged. If he'd had a rig, I could still talk to him now, even if it wasn't really him at all, even if it was only a program.* It wasn't fair that her father was still somehow conscious, and that Raji wasn't.

Her father tried to help her. "I miss him too, Meredith. I miss him terribly. I have been thinking about all of our old conversations. I have reconstructed some of them. If you would like to see—"

"No," she said. She carried Raji's image in her head, ceaselessly; she couldn't bear to see any others. She acknowledged the paradox: she both wanted Raji out of her head completely and bitterly envied Preston, whose memories of Raji would never fade, who would never fade himself.

When her memories of Raji began to fade, she would ask Preston for his, if she still wanted them then. Not now. It was too much. She couldn't handle too much memory. She methodically sent away all her visitors, and busied herself with her mops and cleansers and brushes. She knew that she was putting herself back into isolation, but she had to. She was contagious.

The only person who sometimes managed to break through her armor was Theo. His laughter cheered her when nothing else did. He drew pictures for her, lopsided people and animals and houses which she hung in her room; she read stories to him, about intrepid rabbits and determined trains. On the days when Meredith felt so removed from the world that she forgot to eat, Constance sent Theo to her, bearing snacks. "You eat this apple, Merry. You eat yours and I'll eat mine." "I don't want half this muffin. You eat it." "Hot eggs, Merry. Eat them!" "Merry, Mommy's sad. She made cocoa for you."

Mindful that Theo was rigged, Meredith usually ate the food; she spoke to him more often than to anyone else, and far more gently. Theo, she knew, had rig memories of Raji. The child probably didn't consciously re-member the nice man whose shoulders he had ridden on; certainly he wouldn't for long. But after Theo died, when he was uploaded, those memories would be as clear as actual experience: Raji's resurrection. Raji lived on in cyberspace even now, through her father's memories, if not through Raji's own. She supposed he would have wanted that. He certainly would have wanted her to be kind to Theo, of whom he had been truly fond. So she was kind to Theo, for Raji's sake and because she loved the little boy in her own right. Everyone else, she shut out.

And then one day, as she was on her knees in the bathroom, cleaning the tile with a toothbrush and baking soda, her mother appeared in the doorway. "Someone's here, Merry. Your drafting teacher."

"Who?" she said. A section of grout was stained here, an ugly brown; she couldn't seem to get it to turn white again. She'd never noticed the stain before, but it was amazing what you saw when you got down with your nose an inch from the floor.

"Your drafting teacher." Constance's voice was impatient. "I told you that. Get up and go say hello to him, please."

She didn't get up. Drafting? That had been a million years ago. Before. She had to struggle to remember it, in tiny, dimly lit images, as if she were looking through the wrong end of a telescope. "Professor Zakamura? An old man with a beard? What's he doing here? Tell him to go away."

"No," her mother said. "It's a young guy. His name is Kevin Lindgren. He brought your drawings. He said you might want them."

"Oh," she said, frowning. Lindgren, Lindgren. "Oh—the TA." She started humming, and resumed scrubbing the tile. Perhaps lemon juice would work on the stain, or bleach.

"Meredith!" Constance raised her voice to compete with the off-key melody. "Merry, he was in charge of cleaning out the drafting room and throwing away anything that wasn't claimed, all right? He brought your stuff over here instead. He didn't have to do that. He thought you'd want it."

"I don't," Meredith said, eyes still on the grout, annoyed that her song had been interrupted. *There are lots and lots of people who sometimes feel like this.* Why wouldn't they leave her alone? "Tell him to throw it all away."

"No. I'm not going to do that, Merry. The least you can do is go down-stairs and say thank you."

Meredith looked up, truly perplexed, and Constance said sharply, "No, I'm not going to do it for you! I'm not your servant! It's been four months—it's about time you stopped behaving like a bot and started acting like a human being again! Stop that goddamned buzzing and get off your knees and go downstairs, Meredith Walford! And change into something decent before you do! You're disgusting!"

Constance turned on her heel and walked away, her footsteps sounding a furiously receding staccato down the hallway. Meredith shrugged, put down the toothbrush, stood up, looked down at her stained sweatpants, and shrugged again. She'd go downstairs to keep her mother off her back, but she wasn't going to change her clothing. Lindgren hadn't been invited; she damn well wasn't going to dress for him.

He was sitting in the solarium, gazing thoughtfully at one of Constance's prints on the far wall. Meredith stood for a few seconds, watching him watch the shifting patterns of light on the glass covering the artwork. Finally, since he didn't seem to realize that she was there, she said, "You brought my drawings back."

"Yes," he said absentmindedly, and kept looking at the print. Now he squinted at it. Now he cocked his head. She saw him sketching something with his finger on the leg of his jeans.

"That was nice of you," she said. "Now you can leave."

Evidently annoyed, he waved her to silence and kept squinting. Again the fingers moved, tracing squares and lines.

Arrogant bastard. "Excuse me, this is my house, not a museum. You have to leave now."

"What?" he said, as if surprised to be spoken to. "Just a minute. I'm looking at your mother's picture."

"You can buy prints at half a dozen places in town," she said. "We'll give you a list." But she sat down, curiosity battling with anger. All of the people who had come to the house since Raji's death had done and said exactly what she had expected them to do and say. What had oppressed her more than anything else, perhaps, was the horrible, monotonous predictability of life after tragedy, as if everyone had been handed a hackneyed script and was somehow managing to say the lines with a straight face. Without knowing it, she had yearned for someone to do something different. So far, Theo was the only person who had obliged. Here was another. Theo was sweet and Kevin was rude, but at least they were both different.

Which didn't mean she had any intention of being nice to him. "Why are you doing that to your leg?"

His finger stopped moving, finally, and he turned to face her. "I was studying that central figure," he said crisply. "It's an illusion and a paradox. This painting is supposed to be a two-dimensional representation of circuitry, but if you look at it as a three-dimensional sketch, it's an Escher cube, a Moebius room, a space that doesn't make sense: inside and outside keep shifting on you. I'm wondering what your mother would say if I asked her about that."

Gaia's gas. Who does this conceited idiot think he is? "She'd say it was a drawing of a circuitry," Meredith said. "She doesn't appreciate overinterpretation. Neither do I."

Kevin shrugged. "Of course not. Your mother's been pegged as a popular artist, and if she started theorizing about her own stuff, she'd just be laughed at. Which doesn't mean the rest of us can't find other levels. Here, let me show you something." He opened his briefcase, took out a piece of paper and a mechanical pencil, and drew a quick, sure sketch.

"See?" he said. "See how it keeps turning inside out?"

Meredith yawned. "Very nice. It's actually a floor plan of my parents' bedroom suite: two sleeping rooms and two dressing and sitting rooms at right angles to them, with that square bathroom in the middle. My mother designed it. She says the angles are avant-garde." Meredith hadn't noticed the shape embedded in the painting, and she was annoyed that Kevin had, but at least she could show that she knew more about her mother's work than he did. And at least this discovery wasn't painful, the way Zephyr's uncovering of Squeaky's acorn had been.

He gave her a bemused glance. "Not that I'm trying to pry into your parents' personal life or anything, but that raises some interesting questions, wouldn't you say?"

Taken off guard, Meredith put on her frostiest voice. "No, I wouldn't."

"Then you're not thinking about it very hard. Ask yourself why she would have drawn the bedroom suite as an impossible figure, something that could only exist in two dimensions. Ask yourself what such a paradoxical element is doing in the middle of a computer circuit that's supposed to epitomize logic and binarity, either/or, one or zero, inside or out. This thing's both at once, neither/nor. You see? What do you think of all that?"

Meredith's throat tightened. She thought that Kevin Lindgren was entirely too impressed with his own intelligence, and she thought that she shouldn't have told him about the layout of her parents' bedroom. "I don't think any of *that* is any of your business. Or anyone else's, for that matter."

Kevin immediately put his pencil down, and looked at her directly for the first time during the visit. His eyes were an unusual deep green. "Of course not. You're absolutely right."

"Yes," she said, and stood. "I am." She held out her hand. "Thank you for bringing my drawings."

He didn't stand up. "You're welcome," he said. "When are you coming back to school?"

She didn't sit down. "I haven't decided. Did my mother put your coat in the closet?"

"I didn't bring a coat," he said. "It's not cold enough for a coat. Don't you know that? When's the last time you were out of this house?"

"That's none of your business."

"You should get out," he said. "It's a beautiful day. The sky's bright blue and the grass is bright green and all the buildings look like they've been polished. You couldn't have done a better job yourself. Come out and see it. I'll buy you a coffee. Remember I said I'd do that? I still want to."

"No. Get out. You—"

"Do it for Raji, Meredith. He wanted you to have coffee with me, right? Zephyr told me that. Let me buy you a Raji memorial coffee, and then you can crawl back into isolation if you want to and go back to scrubbing floors."

Her legs had begun to shake, a fine tremor she could feel ascending through her spine. How dare he mention Raji, to her of all people! "Zephyr told you Raji wanted me to have coffee with you? And how the hell did Zephyr know that?"

"Because he told her, presumably." Kevin finally stood up so that they were eye-to-eye. "Go on: get mad at him. He told her things he shouldn't have, right? Get good and pissed off. Then maybe you'll be able to break out of this Lady Macbeth complex and stop trying to scrub Raji's bloodstains out of the parquet. The entire city knows you're holed up in here, you know. Maybe the entire country. ScoopNet's having a field day with it."

Meredith shuddered. Did ScoopNet know about her caudate nucleus? No, they couldn't possibly have access to her medical records. She wondered if they'd ever leave her alone. Raji had told her that they hounded her because she represented cultural obsessions; now that Raji's death was such an obsession, she supposed she was stuck with them, at least until she managed to live a boring life for at least five years. In the meantime, she had to get rid of Kevin.

"You have no right to tell me how to feel," she said coldly. "And you have no right to criticize my spiritual discipline."

"Scrubbing floors? That's right, I forgot: you're DE."

She froze him out, retreating into her familiar numbness. "You have to leave now."

"Can't. Have to get more dirt for ScoopNet first." She gaped at him, and, astonishingly, he grinned. "Relax. I'm not wired. But they'd pay me a lot of money if I were, you know."

He was insane. "Leave. Now. Go have coffee with Zephyr."

"Don't waste your anger on Zephyr. She's not worth it."

"I'm not angry at Zephyr. You have to leave."

"Relax. I told you I'm not wired; your mother's security system would have caught it if I were. Meredith, getting mad at Zephyr is a waste of time. Get mad at Raji for talking to her, or get mad at me for talking about her. That's a lot more productive."

She looked around for the panic button that would summon the police. "If you don't leave—"

"If you really wanted me to leave, you'd have done something more decisive by now." His voice was as reasonable and matter-of-fact as if they were discussing class schedules. "You're mad at me because I'm telling you things you don't want to hear. Fine. You won't be as worried about being seen with me in public if you're mad at me, right? That should make it easier for you to come out for coffee. Shall I wear a sign, 'Terrorists, snatch this one'?"

She felt her shell begin to crack. "How can you—"

"How can I laugh about it?" She wondered if he ever let other people finish sentences. "There aren't a lot of other options, are there? Meredith, my family isn't famous and I'm not working on anything controversial. I'm just an architect, okay? I just draw houses. I don't think the Luds or anybody else are in the slightest bit interested in me, but if they are I hereby absolve you of responsibility. I'll put that in writing if you want me to."

"I don't *care* what—"

"What happens to me? Good. Then you'll have coffee with—"

"Are you *ever* going to let me finish a sentence?"

"I just did," he said briskly. "I'll let you finish more, if you have coffee with me."

"No. I'm not going to do that. Give up, Kevin Lindgren. I don't like you."

"I'm not asking you to like me," he said. "That's the last thing I'd expect. If you liked me, I'd think you really were crazy."

"You—"

"He's abrading you back to life," Constance said from the doorway. How long had she been there? "I don't like him either. That's all right. Merry, go have coffee with him. And change out of those filthy sweats first."

"No! I don't want to."

"It wasn't a question: I'm telling you. Meredith, go! Get out of the house for an hour, would you? I live here. I'd like some private time with my husband and my son."

"I live here too!" She heard how brittle her voice was; she couldn't help it. "It's a huge house! I can be at the other end and you won't even know—"

"Yes, I will. We will. You've been haunting this house for months; I swear the place gets darker the more you clean it. Go: go for an hour. One hour. That's all I ask. But first you have to go change. I put out clean clothing on your bed."

"You *what*? I'm not five years old!"

"Then stop acting like it! Go change. Go have coffee. Kevin, if you can tolerate her company, you're a better person than I am."

"Bitch," Meredith said. She huddled in the front seat of Kevin's car, as far from him and as close to the door as she could manage. It was a very old car, with ripped upholstery and odd, discolored splotches on the plastic

232 ≉ Susan Palwick

dash. Kevin had moved an amazing amount of junk from the front seat to the back to make room for her; she wondered if he'd really expected her to come with him at all.

It was all Constance's fault. Damn Constance! Meredith found herself crying, although she didn't want to. She wiped her eyes on the sleeve of her sweatshirt. At least her mother had put out comfortable clothing: the sweatshirt, a soft pair of old jeans. "I can't believe she kicked me out of my own house! I live there!" She didn't even care if this Kevin person heard her ranting about her mother. He was background noise, nothing but a nuisance.

"It was shock therapy," he said. "Come on, you know that." And then, with a glance at her, "Don't worry. I'm still not going to sell the conversation to ScoopNet."

She sniffled furiously. Was he after her money? Was that it? Why be so obnoxious, then? "Why are you doing this?" They'd been driving for a long time through crowded city streets, away from the nicer parts of town. It was a ridiculous distance just for coffee. Where was he taking her? Did he think he could kidnap her the way Raji had been kidnapped? Her mother knew his name, and Merry had GPS cells. It wouldn't work.

"My car's messy, Meredith. My office isn't. Your drawings were taking up space."

"That's a crock, and you know it. You could have just thrown them out."

"I didn't want to do that. They're very good. I've already told you that."

"You're either stupid or crazy." And then, trying to sound threatening, "I'm really not safe to be around, you know."

"You're fine," he said. "I'm fine too. The Luds are the ones who aren't safe to be around. They've moved on to other targets. They won't be bothering you again."

She said, heard herself say, "I keep thinking that it should have been me who was kidnapped. I would have been, if it hadn't been for my blood." Why had she told him that? It was none of his business.

"So it's your own blood you're trying to scrub out of your mother's floors," he said pleasantly. "Nice detail. Maybe I *will* sell that one to Scoop-Net. I should think I'd get a cool quarter of a million, wouldn't you?"

"At least," she said bitterly. "You could always have an auction. You'd probably get more."

"Good idea. That means I can afford lunch *and* coffee, even on a grad stipend. Okay, we're here."

She looked around. They were in a singularly scuzzy area on Mission, broken glass littering the sidewalks in front of shuttered, guarded storefronts. "Where—"

"There's a little Cambodian place. Right there, see? Hole in the wall. Very inexpensive. Good food, good coffee. I didn't say it was American coffee. Come on."

It really was a hole in the wall; there were only four tables. The walls of the tiny room were covered in mirrors, making the place feel like a carnival fun house. Taped to the mirrors were yellowing pictures cut from calendars: landscapes, seascapes, puppies and kittens. Dusty solstice lights hung from the ceiling, and in a corner, a forlorn goldfish swam around and around in a tank. Meredith thought of Raji's goldfish, the AI, and looked away, her throat tight.

The waitress greeted Kevin with effusive affection, nodding perfunctorily in Meredith's direction when Kevin introduced her. A little girl around Theo's age, with long black pigtails, ran out of the kitchen and threw her arms around Kevin's leg. She babbled incomprehensibly at him until her mother chased her back into the kitchen.

"You eat here a lot," Meredith said. She felt like she'd fallen into a bad movie. "They know you."

"I told you: it's good food. You like fish?"

"Sure." She wondered if they'd be having the goldfish for lunch.

"Okay. Mind if I order?"

She shrugged. "It's your place. I'm not hungry, anyway." How could anyone eat here? It was disgusting. "How'd you find this dive?"

"It's not a dive. I came here with friends. Liked it. Came back." The waitress returned with water, and Kevin began reeling off a long list of dishes, the waitress nodding and jotting notes. Food began appearing almost immediately: spring rolls and soup and pickled cucumber salad, followed by a shrimp curry and some kind of fish pâté flavored with cilantro and lemongrass. Meredith, to her surprise, discovered that she was ravenous. She kept her head down and ate so she wouldn't have to look at Kevin.

"Cleaning's hungry work," he said drily, when she finally resurfaced. "You didn't say grace, did you? Don't Gaia people do that?"

"It's all grace," she said. She was oddly embarrassed at having eaten so much, as if he'd seen her naked. "It's all blessing."

"Well, that's a nice idea. You have a piece of cilantro stuck in your teeth, by the way."

She wanted to retract her head through the neck of her sweater, as if she were a turtle. "Oh."

"Hang on a sec." Kevin pantomimed something at the waitress, who bustled over with a small holder of toothpicks. "There you go. One of the joys of having a body. Your father doesn't have to worry about these things. Of course, he can't taste cilantro, either."

She stared at him. "Raji said you don't like AIs. That you don't—believe in them."

"They're clever programs."

"That's what I think too."

The green eyes met hers, eyebrows arching slightly. "Even about your father?"

"I—I don't know. It's hard to say. I barely knew him when he was translated. I know him better now. I like him better now than I did then. He seems—kinder. But I don't know what it is I like; I don't know if it's really related to whatever inhabited his body once." She didn't know why she was telling him this, either.

Kevin's mouth twitched. "Easy to be kind when you've got a nearly unlimited ability to multitask."

"Yeah."

"Not to mention excellent corporate incentive. He can't have a bad-byte day, or MacroCorp stock will go down, and then they might turn him off."

Meredith looked away. She wasn't sure how she felt about him criticizing her father, although she'd thought the same things often enough herself.

The coffee came, thick and sweet and bitter, in tiny cups. Merry watched Kevin sip his, as neatly as a cat. "You aren't rigged," she said.

"Can't afford it. Wouldn't want it even if I could. It's a gimmick. And you aren't rigged, either; anybody who watches ScoopNet knows that much."

"No," she said. "My mother still wants me to be. Now more than ever. But lately there hasn't been much I'd want to remember." She shouldn't have told him that, either. He seemed to act on her like some kind of truth serum, but she supposed it didn't matter. The ScoopNet vultures certainly would have already figured it out.

Kevin bowed his head at her, an oddly formal gesture, and took a last sip from the tiny cup. "You need to work on that, rigged or not. On finding things you want to remember. What's your favorite view in the city?"

The view of the Bay from the Temple clearing. The view of the Bay from her mother's solarium. But either of those would be too painful right now. Anger at Constance twisted in her stomach, but less stabbingly than it had an hour before. "Telegraph Hill, facing the Bay."

He gave her a narrow, surprised glance. "Good choice. Perfect. We'll go there."

They didn't talk much during the drive. Kevin parked at the top of Telegraph, near an area of private houses. "I didn't think you'd want Coit Tower," he said. "Too touristy."

"Yeah."

"Okay, come on. I know a place where we can sit on the steps and no one will bother us."

Why was she letting him lead her around? She should have demanded that he take her home. But she followed him, because it was simpler. He led her down the Filbert steps, past terraced gardens, the Bay a blue blur below, and stopped when they reached a crannied, overgrown patio with a mossy picnic table. "Isn't this trespassing?" Meredith said.

"Yeah, but I know the guy who owns the house—one of my professors—and I happen to know he's away in Europe."

"What if his house sitter finds us here?"

"I'm his house sitter."

"Oh." She tensed. "That's very convenient. I named just the right place, didn't I?"

"Yes, you did. Relax, Meredith. I don't even have the key with me right now, and I wouldn't try to seduce you if I did. I don't need a neurotic celebrity lover. I have enough neuroses of my own. Are you going to sit down?"

She sat, unsure whether to be reassured or enraged, and looked around: leaves, leaves, flowers, water, the blue of the sky above the Bay. She began to relax, despite herself. "I still don't understand why you're doing this."

"I like challenges. And I really didn't want to throw out the drawings. And maybe I wanted to talk to someone who really knew Raji. Everyone's saying they did, now, and I don't believe many of them."

"Even Zephyr?"

He snorted. "Especially Zephyr. You and Raji hadn't really been—an item—for a while, had you?"

"Not for three years. Zephyr was his girlfriend when he died."

"What, after knowing him for five minutes? I don't think so, not even if she is playing the bereaved widow routine for all it's worth."

"Is she?" Meredith asked, and then, "How well do you know her?"

"Not well. She talked to me a little right after the second news clip"— he grimaced—"because she was trying to track down everybody who'd known you because she thought Raji would want her to, or something. And since then she's been doing all these performance pieces about her grand grief."

"I'm sure she was really upset," Meredith said, out of an obscure sense of duty.

"Of course she was! Everybody was, even people who'd never known him. But you and his parents—and his coworkers at the lab, for that matter—lost a hell of a lot more than she did, and she's become obsessive about it. Either that or she's faking being obsessive about it, which is worse. Faking being obsessive for credit, since I gather that all of her work has been about AI one way or the other."

"Well, to be fair, I think she was obsessed with AI before she met Raji. I think that's what drew them together." Meredith wondered if Zephyr had a damaged caudate nucleus.

"Maybe. But you'd think she was the only person who'd been traumatized, or that everybody else had appointed her to act out their own trauma, like she's some kind of mourner laureate. Personally, I think it's obscene."

"That's what artists do," Meredith said wearily. "They mirror cultural obsessions. She's doing her job, that's all."

"I wouldn't call her an artist."

"Most people wouldn't call my mother an artist, either. We'll just have to wait and see what people say in fifty years, won't we?" She squinted out at the Bay, counting sails, and said, "I don't want to talk about Raji any-more."

"I'm sorry."

She noted that he was capable of apology, and filed the fact. "So what are your obsessions?"

"Architecture, of course. Shelter. How people take a dream of comfort and turn it into a building, someplace they can live, someplace they'll be happy. Not that it ever works. You design your dream house, and then once you build it you realize that the roof leaks and there isn't enough closet space, and anyhow the shape of your dreams has changed, but you'll just have to settle for what you have, because you don't have the money to build another house and may not even have the money to remodel. Plus the taxes keep going up."

"Utopia's a journey, not a destination," Meredith said, quoting her Psy-chology of Social Movements professor. "Well, I don't know. I like my parents' house. I can't think of any particular ways to improve it."

"Other than scrubbing the parquet, of course. Tell me this; if you'd de-signed the house yourself, would parts of the floor plan look like some-thing by Escher?"

She shrugged. "Not if I were doing it from scratch, but it's fine the way it is, really. It's comfortable. It's safe. I don't feel any need to change it."

"I don't buy that," he said, and took a pencil and a small sketchpad out of his pocket. "Change is life, Meredith. From scratch now: What does your dream house look like?"

Fourteen

———

IT was open and airy, composed of curves rather than corners. A stair-case hugging one gently rounded wall of the vaulted living room led onto a balcony from which opened bedrooms, a bath, a study, all with sky-lights. On the ground floor, high arched doorways led to a many-windowed kitchen, a cozy library, a dining area from which one could look into the greenhouse and aviary. A lower level held a lap pool. The backyard featured a large garden, a compost heap, a sundial, and an outdoor contemplation area with a shrine to the Goddess. Solar panels covered the roof. The house had a rudimentary security and environmental system to monitor trespass, temperature, fire, and flood, but it wasn't web-linked. Housekeeping chores would be done by the human inhabitants, not by machines.

In the three months that she and Kevin spent designing the house, Meredith learned many things. She learned that the angularity of her parents' house had oppressed her without her realizing it. She learned, all over again, how much she treasured the privacy she'd been denied in the Temple dorm. She learned how pleasant it was to spend time with someone who genuinely seemed to have no interest in her family, especially her father. Kevin was perfectly pleasant to Jack and Constance, and to Preston whenever he manifested on one of the monitors, but there was never any question that he wouldn't have had two words for any of them—except perhaps Theo, since he seemed fond of children—if it hadn't been for Merry.

They, in turn, evinced remarkably little interest in Kevin; they never asked Meredith any questions about him, or about her feelings for him. Sometimes Merry suspected that both sides were playing a careful game designed to keep from spooking her. Raji had been dead less than a year, after all, and she still woke screaming from nightmares, still found herself humming "The Ones You Miss" when she felt overwhelmed. There were still times when waxing floors was the only way she could suppress images of Raji's death, and she hadn't yet gone back to school, because every square inch of campus still seemed overlaid with agony.

And she, herself, wasn't sure how she felt about Kevin. He was a diversion, but often an irritant. After the insistence of his first visit, he had retreated into scholarly detachment, both about the work they were doing and, seemingly, about her. Sometimes she thought he spent time with her only for the pleasure he got from helping her design the house; he showed remarkably little interest in her feelings, although he could be considerate enough, and he had never even tried to touch her hand. She alternated between gratitude that he wasn't trying to get her into bed and annoyance that he gave no sign of finding her even remotely attractive.

She wasn't sure if she found him attractive. Certainly there was nothing physically wrong with him, but he had never sparked desire in her. But then, her desire seemed to have died, a wellspring plugged at the source. She dreamed of Raji's death, but no longer of his embrace. She no longer even masturbated. She didn't know if her body would begin to respond again if Kevin or someone else coaxed it; she had tried to imagine such a scenario, as an intellectual exercise, and discovered that she could summon no emotional response to the images. The effort seemed simply irrelevant, like trying to picture seaweed on the surface of the moon.

She did find herself wondering, in an academic way, if Kevin was sleeping with anyone. He never mentioned any lovers, past or present; occasionally he had to cancel one of their thrice-weekly meetings—as scheduled and formal as therapy appointments, which she supposed in a way they were—but he always cited work conflicts. But then, they met during the day. She had no idea what he did during the evenings, or on weekends.

As they reached the end of the design project he began to nitpick, began to question her choices: Was the lap pool really oriented properly? Shouldn't it be rotated ninety degrees for proper feng shui? Maybe the living room stairs should wind around a longer portion of the wall? Wouldn't they be more elegant that way? Maybe—

"No," Meredith said. "Come on, Kevin, those are my original choices you're suggesting, the ones you convinced me to reconsider. Why are you bringing them up again now?"

They were sitting in a coffeehouse, a trendy one this time, in the Marina. Meredith was buying. She had become less shy about being seen with Kevin in public; for some reason, ScoopNet didn't seem to have picked up on her outings with him. For that matter, ScoopNet seemed to have forgotten about her entirely. They'd moved on to the latest hot topics.

The monitor in the coffeehouse, perpetually Scoop-tuned but without sound, was showing a montage of drooling people in hospital gowns, followed by footage of the same drooling people being laboriously trained to use spoons and tie their shoelaces. Meredith knew what those images were about: the controversy over using brainwiping—deliberate infection with the strain of CV that caused amnesia—as a therapeutic approach for the criminal and mentally ill. Early experiments with willing volunteers had proven remarkably successful in reshaping personality, although the patients required long periods of intense retraining afterward. Critics compared the procedure to the barbaric twentieth-century practice of lobotomy; advocates pointed out that brainwiped patients could be, and had been, totally rehabilitated. The entire business seemed both gruesome and improbable to Meredith; only a handful of people had chosen the technique—people incarcerated for life, severe schizophrenics—and she doubted that much would come of it. It was too extreme, and would undoubtedly go the way of trephination and electroshock.

She looked away from the monitor, which showed a burly man, with great effort, placing a round peg in a round hole. She'd rather have seen his image up there than her own or Kevin's, but she still wondered why ScoopNet had lost interest in her so totally and so suddenly. She suspected that someone—probably Constance—was paying dearly for ScoopNet's silence. "You're not answering my question," she told Kevin. "Come on, 'fess up. Why this haggling now?"

"I'm a perfectionist," Kevin said. "It's an occupational hazard."

"I could slap a diagnosis of excessive altruism on you," Meredith said lightly. That was another trend: the claim that those who consistently endangered their own welfare to help others were suffering from a psychiatric disorder. The subject had been getting airplay ever since a former Peace Corps volunteer, a psychologist who had watched her idealistic colleagues brave disease, malnutrition, guerrilla warfare, and racial violence, had published a paper questioning the line between benevolence and insanity. The derisive term "exalted" had been current for roughly a decade, but no one had suggested medicating it before. "I mean, you're not getting academic credit for all this work. Unless you plan to enter the design in a competition or something."

Kevin stiffened, the green eyes unreadable above his latte. "I hadn't planned on anything like that. I certainly wouldn't send the plans anywhere without your permission. I just want to make sure you're sure about the details. Before I draw up final blueprints."

"Sure, I'm sure. And they're only blueprints, anyway. They can always be changed." Kevin looked away with a faint grimace, and Meredith said impatiently, "You're trying to delay finishing this, aren't you? Why? We could have coffee together even if we weren't drawing a house, and it's not like you even seem to enjoy my company that much."

"I do," he said, and stood up. "I do enjoy your company. Meredith, I have to go now."

"Yeah, you've got that meeting with your adviser, I know. Bring me the blueprints, okay? We'll have coffee anyway."

He left—they'd driven here in separate cars—and she reached over with a sigh for his nearly untouched latte, and then decided she didn't need the extra caffeine. She was feeling restless enough as it was, as if, could she just peel off her itching skin, she'd ascend like a balloon through the early summer haze. There'd been fires in Oakland again, and everyone was praying for rain. When had it last rained?

Trying to remember rain, she suddenly had a vivid image of lying with Raji, both of them slick with sweat, on the narrow dorm bed, while rain drummed on the roof above them. She could taste his skin, feel his heartbeat against her cheek.

Dear Goddess, no. She breathed in, breathed out, through and around the pain. Breathe. Breathe. There. It had passed, leaving her weak and shaky. She paid for the coffees and pushed her way outside, desperate for fresh air. Her numbness had been so welcome, and now it seemed to be breaking down again. She wanted it back. As she drove home, she used the floor plans of the house to calm herself, mentally retracing every wall and doorway. It was a serene house, open and flowing: it contained no paradoxes and no pain, just a new, blank place for her to inhabit.

Except that it hadn't been built, and probably never would be. Given land and construction costs in the city—the only place she wanted to live—she'd never be able to justify spending the money. The only way she could live there was in her mind, and the only person who could live there with her was Kevin. A shock of recognition made her hands tighten on the steering wheel. Ah. So that was what he was doing. Why hadn't she seen it before?

He brought her the final plans a week later. She had refused a public meeting and asked him to come to her mother's house instead. He found her sitting on one of the terraces overlooking the Bay. She heard his footsteps behind her, but remained facing the water, although it was largely obscured by haze and smoke today. "Here," he said, putting a blueprint tube down on the table next to her. "They're done." His voice sounded flat, devoid of pride.

"I know what you've been up to," she said, and turned to squint at him. "What I want to know is why."

"What?" To her satisfaction, he looked off balance for the first time since she'd known him. "What are you talking about?"

"You helped me build a little world," she said, putting a hand on the tube. "That's what this is. It's—an imaginary country, in two dimensions. It's every bit as imaginary as the figure my mother built into her house. And we're the only two people who can go there, aren't we?"

He blinked at her, very rapidly. "What? This is a set of architectural plans. That means the house can be built by anybody who has the land and the materials. It means that anyone who knows how to read a blueprint can enter the—the 'imaginary country,' or whatever you want to call it. What are you talking about, Meredith? Aren't you being a little melodramatic?" He smiled, as if he were trying to tease her, but his voice had become higher, brittle. She knew that he knew very well what she was talking about.

"Not if the imaginary country includes the path you take to get there," she said quietly. She had thought for a long time, very carefully, about what she would say to him. "That's what all that was about, all those hours of conversation: laying down a road, brick by brick, to lead us to a common destination. We've made our very own virtual world, without benefit of computers. And I want to know why you bothered. It can't be out of sheer intellectual curiosity; my ideas about houses aren't that fascinating. If you're interested in me, I want you to say so, and I want to know why, because you certainly haven't given any of the conventional indications. And if you aren't interested in me, I want to know what your ulterior motives are. Are my parents paying you to get me out of the house? Is that what all of this has been about?"

"No," he said. She could barely hear him. For a moment he looked crushed, drained gray, but then he rallied. "I—I just—Meredith? Can we talk about this somewhere else? Can we go for a walk or something?"

"Sure," she said, and stood up. "Ocean Beach? That okay?"

"If you promise to listen to me instead of just watching the dogs." They'd gone to Ocean Beach before; it was where she went to get her vicarious pet fix. "But—I could just—maybe I helped you draw a house because I wanted to be your friend. I could have done that, couldn't I?" His voice was pleading, oddly childish.

"You could have," she agreed. "But I don't think you did. I think you had a very definite plan the first day you came here, and I don't think it involved elevations and axonometrics. Facades, maybe."

He looked away from her, out over the hazy water. "You'd better take a sweater. It's going to be windy down there."

"It's—I—I'm an orphan." They were sitting on a large piece of driftwood near the water, encroaching waves threatening to dampen their feet. The tide was coming in, and the wind blew salt spray in their faces.

"I'm sorry," Merry said. She wondered what this had to do with her.

Kevin swallowed, visibly, his hands balled in his jacket pockets. "They died—both my parents died—the summer I was eighteen. They had CV. I'd been working as a counselor at this camp for gifted kids, which meant rich kids, mostly. They were brats, and I hated the job, but I guess being there saved my life. Because if I'd been at home with my parents, I'd have gotten CV too. I called home one weekend and they both had colds, and then on Tuesday the head of the camp called me in and said my uncle was coming to get me because both of my parents were in isolation. They were there for two weeks before they died."

"That's awful, Kevin." It was; she knew it was, but she couldn't seem to feel anything, so instead she mouthed conventional pieties. "I'm so sorry."

He squinted out at the surf. Seabirds cried and circled above them, and a barefooted jogger ran past, feet splashing in the water. "We'd been fighting a lot, which made it worse. They—well, anyway. It doesn't matter. But—I saw you on vid. When you came out of isolation."

"Everyone saw me on vid when I came out of isolation," Meredith said. "If they didn't see it when it actually happened, they saw it on the first kidnapping tape. I'm a goddamn cultural icon: 'the wonders of technology and medicine return girl safely to family.' I think that's why the Luds did what they did to Raji. They wanted a reverse cultural icon. 'The horrors of technology'—oh, Kevin, I'm sorry!" She hadn't been able to keep the bitterness out of her voice. "I didn't mean to drag that into it. It's not one of my best memories, that's all. Especially since—oh, Goddess. Zephyr asked me about it, the first time I met her. She had some crackpot theory about how much it had hurt the bots to have to take care of me. And that was the—that was the last time I saw Raji. The Luds got him right after that. He didn't even get back to his dorm. How could they snatch him like that? In the middle of a busy campus? He must have known them, or thought he did. I just don't understand why the police can't—"

She stopped, flustered and embarrassed. Kevin had lowered his head and hunched his shoulders; he looked like a small child being scolded. "Kevin, I'm sorry. Just—just ignore me, okay? We're not here to talk about that. We're here to talk about you. Go on."

"No," Kevin said. "It doesn't matter. It's not important. I shouldn't have—"

"It is important," she said wearily. "Everything's important. Lots of people besides me have been through awful stuff. You're one of them. I haven't lost my parents—oh, hell, Kevin! Were you mad that your parents weren't translated?"

"No. It wouldn't really have been them."

"Were you mad at me for coming out when they didn't?"

"No, no." He shook his head. "Listen, when I saw you coming out of iso—I saw it live."

What was he getting at? "Lots of people saw it live," she said cautiously.

He nodded. "I know. You know that vid screen overlooking I-80, just as you come off the Bay Bridge?"

"Oh, Goddess," Meredith said. "You saw it from your *car*?" She had a sudden image of fifty thousand commuters watching her emerge, blinking and disoriented, into the world.

Kevin looked away from her and cleared his throat. "From my uncle's car. We were driving back to his house, after my parents' funeral."

"Oh," she said, and then, "Oh, Gaia. Kevin, that's awful! I'm sorry." She meant it now.

He shook his head. "I'm not sorry. That's not why I'm telling you this."

"You aren't? How couldn't you be? Your parents died after two weeks in iso, and you must have wanted them to be coming out. You must have wanted more than anything for them to come out. And instead they died, and you had to watch everybody celebrating for some poor little rich girl whose mother hadn't died and whose father had just become immortal. I must have reminded you of the rich kids at the camp times ten, Kevin, it's *awful,* you must have hated me."

"No," he said. "You don't understand. I hadn't thought anybody came out. I thought iso was just where—where you went to die, where they kept you so nobody else would get sick. Nobody had explained anything to me very clearly. I go off to teach archery to little Hawkings for the summer and then the next thing I know, I'm called back home because my parents are dying. All I knew was that I hadn't gotten to say good-bye to them because they were so out of it, you know, and I couldn't even touch them or hold their hands or anything, because of the iso, and I was so angry. And then when I saw you coming out, saw you hug your mother and so forth—well, it helped. To know that people *did* come out. The doctors hadn't just been locking my parents away from me; they'd been trying to make them better. They'd been working to give them a chance to come out alive. I hadn't understood that before. I hadn't known enough to understand it. And I—well, I've wanted to meet you ever since then. And then you were in my section, you know, and then you didn't come back but the drawings were still there—"

"So you decided to help me get out of isolation again," Meredith said. "You decided to lead me out yourself. That's why you were being so obnoxious, that first day."

"Yes," he said. His voice was very soft, almost inaudible above the waves, and he wouldn't look at her. "But I know how much you hate being famous. And I felt guilty about it anyway, because—well, I felt good about getting you out of the house, but it only happened because of Raji."

Now it was her turn to look away. "I'm not sure how to feel about this. It's quite an act you've been putting on, Kevin. This whole disinterested academic observer thing. I was right about facades, wasn't I?"

"Yes, you were. I'm sorry. I didn't know what else to do."

"I don't know how much I trust you now. I don't know what else you're hiding."

"I know. I'm not hiding anything else, but I don't blame you for not believing that."

She squinted at a sailboat, far out on the water. "The very first time you spoke to me, in class, you acted like you didn't even recognize my name."

"I didn't want to scare you off. I didn't want to act like everybody else."

"Did Raji know any of this? Is that why he told me to sign up for your section?"

"No. I didn't even know Raji; I've told you that. I guess he recommended my section because people know I'm good. I guess I'm glad he did, but—I've never told anyone any of it, except you. Not even Scoop-Net. Especially not ScoopNet. I promise."

"Okay," she said, and shivered in the damp wind. "Okay. But—Gaia,

Kevin, I mean, now I have to rethink every conversation we've ever had. I feel like you've been stalking me or something."

"I know." He sounded miserable. "I'm sorry. But I meant it when I said your drawings were good. I wasn't lying about that."

"Thank you." She took a deep breath, watching a gull dive for something in the water. Kevin wasn't a bad person. He wasn't. He'd been scared, frightened of her celebrity. Still, she felt violated. She remembered scorning him because he didn't seem to realize who she was. He'd fooled her; she'd been a fool. "Well. You got me out of isolation again, and you helped me design my dream house. So whatever I did for you when you saw me come out of iso the first time, you've thanked me. We're even now."

"Okay," he said. "You want me to go away. I figured you would. Of course you would. It makes sense. I'm sure I'd feel the same way, in your position."

She shot him an exasperated glance. "Gaia's gas, Kevin! How do you expect me to feel? Am I supposed to fall on my knees in gratitude because you played Prince Charming and braved the fortress of my mother's house to rescue me? You've been *lying* to me."

"No," he said, head down. "I wasn't lying. I just wasn't telling the entire truth. But I am now."

"You were *lying*." Raji never would have played word games like this. Raji had never lied to her. "You pretended you had no personal interest—"

"Oh, come on, Merry!" He'd never called her Merry before, always Meredith. "You knew I had a personal interest. You had to know. You questioned me enough about it, the first time I came to your mother's house."

"And you—"

"And I've delayed answering until now, that's all."

"Until you helped me design a nice little virtual reality for two."

"Until we had some kind of shared history, yes! Because I was hoping you wouldn't just dismiss me! And I wouldn't have told you this soon, except that you insisted!"

A few hundred feet from them, a woman threw a stick into the surf for a dog, a golden retriever, who went bounding into the water to get it. Merry concentrated on the wet, joyous form as it paddled furiously toward the stick. "And did you get what you wanted? What *did* you want? You wanted to meet me; you met me; you've spent, what, three hours a week with me since then—what were you looking for, Kevin? Just to be able to brag about how you were hanging out with Merry Walford? Didn't what happened to Raji—didn't that teach you better?"

"I haven't been bragging about it." The heat in his voice almost made her turn to look at him, but she kept her gaze on the dog, who had fetched the stick and was leaping jubilantly back to its person. "I haven't even told anybody! I—it's just—"

"I'm just your secret fetish, is that it? Some people collect corsets and silk stockings, and you collect moments with Merry?"

"That's a totally shitty thing to say." His voice was icy now, furious. Good: she'd gotten to him. "Meredith, would you just look at me, please? Just turn around, all right? I can't be completely disgusting to look at, not after all these months."

She remained stubbornly staring out at the water. "If you'd told the truth—"

"Well, I'm telling it now! Yes, I wanted to get to know you; yes, I'm glad I have; no, I don't want to be sent away like—like a servant in disgrace. And I haven't been talking to anybody about it. Are you trying to drive me away so I'll be safe from terrorists? Well, I don't think they're any threat—I told you that at the beginning—and if they are, I'll take my chances. I came to you after—after Raji because—because we both know about losing people. Because we finally had something in common. And because I had an excuse, because of the drawings. I knew I might not like you after I'd spent time with you, but I do like you. I'd like you even if you weren't rich and famous, although I suppose there's no way to make you believe that. And I don't want to go away."

It came to her then, watching the Pacific break on the edge of the continent, that Kevin was halfway in love with her, or maybe more than that. He would certainly be entirely in love with her if she gave him any encouragement. She remembered something Fergus had said, after his breakup with Johann. *In any relationship, the person who cares the least is the one with the most power.*

Kevin was saying something. "I've been afraid to trust too, Merry. I have. I don't have any family left except my uncle—I was an only child—and it's been hard for me to let myself make friends, even, because I'm scared to lose them. I know what that feels like. I understand that. But if we don't take the risk, we might as well not be alive. We might as well have died too."

He wants to marry me, she thought. He's not going to say it yet; he's not going to say it for a long time, but he's already made up his mind. He helped me design the house so he could live with me in it. She remembered Matt and Gwyn, that first terrible day after Raji disappeared, exhorting her to keep loving. They'd said the same thing Kevin was saying now. She didn't know if she'd ever be able to truly love Kevin—she didn't know if she'd ever love anyone again, not the way she'd loved Raji—but if she let Kevin love her, everybody would be happy: Kevin, her parents, Matt and Gwyn. She'd be doing what everybody wanted, and she'd be keeping herself safe at the same time—because she wouldn't care as much as he did, because she'd have more power. And if she married him, she could keep him safe too; she could insist that he be given GPS cells, which would make him as immune from terrorism as she was herself.

Her parents wouldn't let her marry anyone until she'd finished school. That was all right. She'd switch to commuter status, drive in for classes, keep living at home. She'd keep her life private, and Kevin would help. Kevin was a very private person. She wouldn't have to worry about him talking to too many people. She wouldn't have to worry about terrorists, at least not Luds, because Kevin wasn't working on AI. And if something happened, if he decided he hated her or if he got hit by a car, her heart wouldn't break. It had already broken once; it was as broken as it could get.

ScoopNet would love the story. Prince Charming, from a humble and obscure family decimated by tragedy, leads the princess of the realm back out of the monster's lair, and she shows her gratitude by marrying him. They ate that stuff up.

Would Kevin want kids? He liked Theo, liked the little girl in the Cambodian restaurant. Well, they'd deal with that later on. And maybe she was wrong, anyway. Maybe he didn't want to marry her at all. Maybe she was making the whole thing up.

"Merry?" She felt a tentative hand on her shoulder, but his voice was despairing. "Merry, are you ever going to look at me again?"

She turned, forced herself to turn. His face was worried, tracked with tears. She forced herself to reach out and wipe some of them away, clumsily. It was the first time she'd ever touched him, and she saw his eyes widen, heard him take a sudden breath. He went very still under her hand, as if afraid that she'd flee if he moved.

She took her hand away and put it in her lap. His hand remained lightly on her shoulder. "I'm sorry about your parents, Kevin."

"I know. You already said that." He removed his hand now, and jammed it back into his pocket.

"What were their names? What did they do?"

"Nicholas and Evelyn. Dad was a civil engineer. Mom was a nurse. That's how they got CV, from one of her patients. Nobody at the clinic realized it was CV at first. A doctor got sick too, but he recovered."

"And your uncle? Does he live nearby?"

"Sacramento. Near enough." He was wary now, defensive. "His name's Richard and he's a lawyer. Why are you asking me all this?"

"You know a lot about me," she said. "I think I should be able to know some stuff about you. It's only fair."

"Ah," he said. Maybe he relaxed a bit and maybe he didn't; she couldn't tell.

She looked down and scuffed her toe in the sand, feigning diffidence. "So. Do you want to get coffee?"

Her relationship with Kevin unfolded almost exactly as she had envisioned it. For the rest of her life, this would amaze her; it was as if she had handed the universe a shopping list, as if the universe had granted every item she had requested, because so much had already been taken from her. Within a few weeks after that day on the beach, she and Kevin had embarked upon a decorous, conventional dating relationship: dinner and a movie on Friday nights, lunch once or twice during the week, phone conversations every other evening. It was a month before they kissed, another five months before they slept together. She told him she was still grieving Raji, and he understood—he was, she knew, nearly inhumanly patient with her wounds, and with his status as rival of a ghost—and when at last they went to bed, she enjoyed it far more than she had expected. She felt no grand passion, but Kevin was a considerate and surprisingly playful lover, and she appreciated the simple animal satisfaction of sexual release, and of curling up with another warm body afterward. Kevin comforted her; they comforted each other.

She liked him. She was grateful to him. It touched her to see his face soften when he looked at her, or brighten when she entered a room. There was no doubt that within a year, he was indeed deeply in love with her. She supposed she would grow to love him in time, if indeed she could love again at all. For now, she did whatever she could to be kind to him. She wanted to protect him, and the idea of anyone hurting him enraged her. She wanted to make him happy.

She met his uncle Richard, whom Constance invited to the house for the winter solstice feast. Constance and Jack, and Preston, began taking a more active interest in Kevin, and he in them, although Meredith knew that she was still the only thing they had in common. She returned to school as planned, although she wasn't sure what she would do after she got her degree. She didn't need to work, but she wanted to. She had toyed with the idea of starting a sacred housecleaning service, with human workers who would perform the tasks as part of their spiritual path, but Matt and Preston both advised her, gently, that there probably wouldn't be enough potential employees, even if beginning her own business straight out of college had been wise. She considered cleaning other people's houses for a living, but Constance told her tartly that she'd embarrasss the family. "It was bad enough when you were only cleaning our house, Merry!" Once she would have argued; these days, she valued peace. She thought about starting a dog-walking service, about being a professional pet sitter, about becoming a ritual consultant. Finally, the week before she graduated, Constance used connections to get her a spot in an interior design firm. "It's a start, dear. You can get some experience and branch out from there."

The job was pleasant enough. She didn't have any contact with clients yet, of course, but she helped the people who did pick out paint and fabric samples; she dealt with vendors and contractors, arranged deliveries, and spent a great deal of time at her desk reading thick, glossy magazines that consisted nearly entirely of advertising. Nonvirtual magazines, with their reassuring tactility and scandalous suggestion of wastefulness—although of course they were printed on recycled paper, and recycled again once discarded—had become newly fashionable.

Kevin, who had gotten his master's in architecture the year before she graduated, was working for a firm in the city, not far from her office. They had lunch together nearly every day. One morning he called her at work and said, "I took the afternoon off. Can you do the same thing?"

She did. She thought she knew what was coming. She wasn't surprised when Kevin suggested a walk down the Filbert steps, wasn't surprised when, his arm around her, he said shyly, "Do you know what today is?"

"The anniversary of the first walk we took on these steps," she said. She'd used it to measure how she was doing on her relationship-with-Kevin timetable every year since then. So far, they were right on schedule.

He cleared his throat. "Merry, have you thought about—I was thinking—maybe we could make this permanent?"

"I have thought about it," she said, and his arm tightened across her back. "But, Kevin, there's something you need to know. I can't have kids. Because of the CV." She'd debated whether to tell him about the brain damage, and had finally decided against it; he knew as much about her behavior as anyone, and he'd never criticized her or suggested that she was ill. The brain damage was nobody's business but her own. If she developed problems later on, she'd deal with them.

She had to tell him about the kid thing, though. That *was* his business.

"Oh," he said, but he looked relieved. He must have been afraid she was going to say something worse. "Poor Merry . . . I'm sorry! Why didn't you tell me before?"

"I didn't know if it would matter."

"It doesn't. Not to me."

She'd been afraid that he'd accuse her of keeping her own secrets—and she was suddenly painfully conscious of the one she *was* keeping—but evidently he wasn't going to. "I could do high-tech stuff. Petri dish babies and artificial wombs and all that. But I really don't want to."

"I don't blame you."

"So if we wanted kids, we'd have to adopt. The kids would have somebody else's genes. If you want kids at all. I don't even know if—"

"I wouldn't be marrying you for your genes. I'd be marrying you because I love you."

"Do you *want* kids?"

"I want whatever will make you happy, Merry." He got down on one knee and looked up at her, laughing. "Marry me, Merry?"

"If I marry you, if you marry into this family, you have to get GPS cells."

"I hate needles."

"I hate terrorists. That part's not negotiable."

"Okay, okay. I'll brave the needles for you. Only for you." He was clutching her hand so tightly that she could feel the throb of her own pulse. "Meredith Sophia Walford, will you marry me?"

"Yes," she said, and he leapt up and kissed her. When she finally managed to break away for air, she said, "Kevin, where are we going to live? I don't want to move into your tiny apartment with all those roommates, and staying in my mother's house won't work, either. I want us to pay our own way. I don't want to depend on Daddy."

"We'll figure something out," Kevin said. "We will. Don't worry, Merry. Just kiss me again, okay?"

There was a house for sale near the top of the Filbert steps. It was tiny, with only 1,200 square feet and three rectangular bedrooms. It was nothing like Merry's dream house. It would be doomed in any serious earthquake, but so would most of the houses in the area. It didn't have a driveway or garage. Whoever lived there would have to park at the top of the hill and hike down the stairs, hauling groceries and anything else that needed carrying. That was all right; Kevin and Merry were young and strong. The house had stunning views of the Bay, a beautiful garden, and undeniable sentimental significance. Because it was so small and so inaccessible, and because it needed a new roof and a new furnace and updated appliances in the kitchen, it only cost three million dollars.

Meredith was forced to compromise, to accept help from her father. Preston bought the house, outright, as a wedding gift for Merry and Kevin, although nominally it was a MacroCorp real estate investment. The young couple would live there until they didn't want to anymore, or until they died; if one of them predeceased the other, the house would belong to the surviving partner. In the event of divorce, the house would be Merry's, although she could choose to allow Kevin to live there. If both of them died or formally relinquished ownership, the house would belong to MacroCorp.

Preston paid for the house; Jack and Constance paid for the repair work, and for installing the rudimentary house system Meredith had envisioned when she and Kevin drew up their plans. That left Kevin and Merry responsible only for utilities and property taxes: still a stretch, on their salaries, but at least feasible. In that respect, at least, Merry was determined to honor her principles, determined to pay her own way.

"I'll never want to live anywhere else," Merry said, staring out the living room window at the water below. A MacroCorp attorney had just signed the closing papers, and she and Kevin had promptly claimed their keys and gone to take possession, trailed by Constance and Jack. "It's perfect."

"I'm guessing you'll want to live somewhere else within six months," Constance said. Jack and Kevin had gone to look at the ductwork under the house. "Those stairs are a headache even in good weather, even this near the top; in rain, they'll be miserable. We're going to have to tip the movers big-time to get your stuff in here, you know."

"Of course," Meredith said. "But it's not like we have that much stuff, Mom. A bed and some chairs and tables and Kevin's drafting table—"

"You'll get more stuff. That's how it works. And if you have a child, lugging baby things up and down those steps, not to mention the baby itself, will be a nightmare. If somebody gets sick and has to go to the doctor—"

"Mom, we've been over this. We'll be okay. I promise."

Constance sighed. "Well, the renovation people did a nice job, and the new range in the kitchen is certainly more workable than what was in there before. I'm glad you decided to have the wedding at home, though."

This is home now. Merry didn't say it; she didn't want to hurt her mother's feelings. "Me too, Mom."

The wedding was small, only immediate family, Kevin's adviser, and Merry's old friends from Temple. Theo, decked out in a tiny set of tails, was the ring bearer, and Matt performed the brief ceremony. They had it outside, on the same terrace where Kevin had brought Meredith the finished blueprints three years earlier. ScoopNet ran a pleasant, low-key article, wishing the young couple all health and happiness, and again Meredith wondered who had called them off, and how. But maybe she was being too paranoid. Maybe she simply wasn't interesting to them anymore. Maybe she was safe, finally. Preston was no longer unique—he'd been joined by a handful of other translations, although none had as much personality as he did, because none had been rigged for as long before dying— and the radical Luddite fringe seemed to have faded into oblivion. Bots had become fashionable again, although Kevin and Merry didn't plan on using any themselves.

Meredith embarked on her married life with the serene certainty that everything would go smoothly from here on out. She'd paid her dues, endured her share of misery. She had a nice husband and a nice place to live and a decent job. In her spare time, she could work in her garden while looking out at the water. She and Kevin got a cat, a gray queen named Ashputtle, and a dog: a lively little mutt, vaguely terrior-esque, named Marzipan. She couldn't imagine needing anything else. She was going to be happy now. She'd certainly waited long enough.

Fifteen

S HE was happy for two years. She grew increasingly fond of Kevin, who was as devoted after their marriage as he had been before. She loved their house; she delighted in Ashputtle and Marzipan, frequently wondering how anyone could prefer bots to real animals, although Kevin often pointed out that animals made messes, whereas bots tidied them. She was doing well at work, and had been promoted into a junior-consultant position that gave her client contact and allowed her to exercise her own design sense. She was good at it. She liked her clients, and they liked her. They recommended her to their friends. Kevin had helped his firm win several design competitions. Life was as close to blissful as it had ever been. Merry had even started going to Temple again, although only for the high feast days, solstices, and equinoxes. Matt was still there, as was Anna; Gwyn and Dave had moved to Honduras to help build housing for the poor. Harold was in a senior-care home in Los Angeles, near his niece. Dana had entered a Mexican convent, and no one had heard from Johann or Fergus in years.

Merry and Kevin entertained. They couldn't have Constance and Jack over because Constance was now allergic to animals, rather than merely disliking them. Nearly every weekend, though, someone else was at the house for dinner: Matt, or Kevin's uncle, or people from work, either coworkers or clients. For perhaps the first time, Merry felt like she had a true social life.

Theo spent part of nearly every weekend with them, whenever he didn't have play dates with friends from school. He loved the cat and the dog, loved to play on the steps, loved to draw with Kevin and read with Merry. He was a bright, busy, energetic little boy, and while Merry was always a bit relieved when he left, the house always seemed a bit emptier, too. Kevin felt the same way. They had agreed that it would be nice to adopt a child in a few years, when both of their careers were more firmly established. They were still very young. Parenthood could wait. They needed more time to know each other first.

Then, two years into their marriage, a CV orphan in Oakland began making headlines.

He was two months old. His father had died of CV six months into his gestation; his mother had died of it three weeks later, and had remained on a ventilator until the doctors considered it safe to deliver the baby by remote-control cesarean. Since leaving his mother's womb, he had lived in isolation. So far, amazingly enough, he seemed perfectly healthy. But he remained in isolation, because no one had ever treated a child with prenatal exposure, and the doctors were afraid to let him out.

"This is horrible," Meredith said, reading the story from a Net printout over breakfast. She had finally relented and permitted a web-linkable terminal in the house, although it wasn't permanently online. There was just too much you missed, otherwise. She talked to her father once a week, somewhat less often than she talked to Constance, but more often than Kevin spoke to his uncle. "God, this poor kid. Kevin, there's this kid in iso, he's only eight weeks old. Putting a baby in a bubble like that—can you imagine? Isolation's hard enough to deal with when you've already been in the world for a while."

Kevin looked up from his copy of *Architectural Digest*. "Ugh." He dropped a piece of bacon on the floor for Ashputtle, who was mewing imperiously and winding around their ankles. "That's got to warp him for life, being taken care of by people in spacesuits."

"And bots," Meredith said. "Soft bots, covered in bright terry cloth, just like the ones who took care of me. Which means he'll be terrified of towels for the rest of his life."

Kevin laughed. "I think you're exaggerating. You aren't terrified of towels."

Merry shivered. "I was fourteen years old. He's two months."

"Well, if he'd been born into a world without isolation units, he'd be dead now." Kevin fed his last piece of bacon to the cat, and then got up and kissed Meredith. "I have to get to work, sweetie."

"Okay. Me too. See you later." On her way out the door, she tossed the printout in the recycling bin, glad to be rid of it.

But she found herself thinking about the baby all day long, between a deluge of demands on her attention. One of her most important clients had decided that none of the custom paint colors Merry had concocted for him was worthy of his town house, and was demanding that she begin again with a new palette. A contractor redoing a series of bathrooms suddenly declared bankruptcy and fled to Chile, necessitating a new set of bids and endless apologies to irate homeowners who wanted to know when their toilets would be functional again. Already running late for an appointment in Berkeley, Merry became stalled in traffic on the Bay Bridge and then discovered that her cell phone was down. By the time she reached her destination, the client had left a note on the door. Where was she? He'd be back in an hour. Could she come back then?

Which left her an hour to kill. She walked down to a coffeehouse on Shattuck Avenue and ordered some green tea. She needed something hot to drink; she'd been chilled all day, emotionally more than physically. That baby, the baby in the bubble: the fact that there was a baby in isolation was simply horrifying. She remembered the tiny rooms at the Maddie Center, from which she and Kevin had rescued Ashputtle and Marzipan; for some reason, she pictured this baby in one of those rooms. Was he ever going to get out? Would he ever be able to go home with anyone? What had the printout said? She must have read it, but she couldn't remember.

The waiter, a bespectacled kid with blond dreadlocks and tribal scars down his bare torso, brought her tea. "Poor tyke," he said.

"What?" But she already knew whom he meant.

He gestured behind and above her, and she turned around to find herself looking at a ScoopNet vid of someone in a spacesuit, behind glass, holding up a tiny white bundle. A close-up revealed blinking blue eyes, and then the rosebud mouth opened in a howl. Meredith's stomach clenched, and she had to keep herself from reaching toward the screen. "I read about that baby this morning."

"Yeah, he's all over the news," the waiter said. "No family left. They say he seems healthy and everything, but they don't know if he'll be okay, because there's never been a case like this. Exposure to CV in the womb. He could turn into, like, a viral time bomb."

"I don't think that's possible," Merry said, her mouth dry. The waiter hadn't recognized her, but then again, she hadn't gotten significant media exposure for five years, and he'd probably barely been walking back then. He couldn't really be that much younger than she was, but he certainly looked it. "And they can't talk about the details of his condition on the news. Privacy laws."

"Well, anyway. I heard the doctors are all, like, torn. Because they want to keep him in iso long enough to make sure he's okay medically, but the longer he stays, the crazier he'll get. Touch deprived. Stimulation too. You know, like those refugee babies, from Africa and all? The ones who live on bread and water in orphanages without any sheets, and then if you give them orange juice and wrap a nice blanket around them, they go insane? You want honey with that?"

"What?" Merry said. The white bundle had faded into an ad for low-interest rig loans. Meredith turned back around, and realized that the waiter's neo-retro spectacles were part of a rig. For all she knew, his dreadlocks and scars were really cleverly disguised silicon. He must have very wealthy parents.

"Your tea. Would you like honey with that? Sugar's on the table, but I can bring you honey."

"Oh, no. No thank you."

He nodded and walked away, whistling. Meredith, knowing the monitor was still behind her, felt the flesh on the back of her neck crawl. She gulped down the tea, which scalded her tongue but didn't warm her, paid for it, and left, nearly running. She still had half an hour before her client got home, and she had to calm down. Why was this bothering her so much? There were sick babies everywhere; plenty of children had died of CV. Kevin was right: this little boy was lucky to be alive. And the doctors must be doing everything they could to stimulate him. But whenever she thought of the white bundle held aloft by that bulky spacesuit, acid rose in her throat.

Well. It was her own post-CV trauma, that was all. She supposed she'd never get over it entirely. At least the client she was about to see didn't have bots. But she still had to calm down. She walked briskly up and down

Shattuck, past trendy restaurants and antique stores, until it was time to go back to the client's house.

The appointment went fine, and by the time she got into her car to go back to the city, she felt much better. Traffic on the bridge had cleared up too, for a wonder. But then it slowed again, just on the other side, and Merry looked up and saw the vid screen, the one on which Kevin had seen her coming out of iso, and there was the little white bundle, being tended by blue-and-red-and-yellow-terry bots.

The unsweetened green tea, the tofu stir-fry she'd had for lunch, the toast she'd had for breakfast: everything came rushing back out of Merry's stomach, onto her windshield and dashboard and lap. She huddled over the steering wheel, heaving, while cars behind her honked. Someone was yelling. She sat up slightly, inhaling the stench of her own gut, and started driving again, her legs trembling.

She went home and called in sick to the office. She cleaned up the car, took a shower, and changed into fresh clothing. Then she sat, Ashputtle on her lap—Kevin had been home at lunchtime to walk Marzipan—and looked out at the Bay. By the time Kevin got home, she knew what she needed to do.

"Of course the bots reminded you of Raji," Kevin said. "And the fact that the baby's in iso reminds you of yourself, and the fact that both of his parents died reminds you of me. And that's why you want to rescue him. It feels like rescuing everybody, even the ones who are past hope. And it fits with your position that people shouldn't have to be genetically related to kids to love them. And I agree with that; you know I do. But, Merry, I really don't think this is a good idea. This baby isn't Raji or you or me. He's somebody else. He's a complete unknown and a huge risk, and we agreed that we weren't going to think about kids for a few years, and there are probably do-gooders lined up from here to Ohio waiting to adopt him. Let someone else do it."

"There aren't," Merry said. She'd cried for a while, and between that and the vomiting, she should have been exhausted, but she'd never felt more clearheaded. "I checked. I've read all the stories I could find on this kid."

"No," Kevin said. "Merry, I love you, but this is just too big a risk. For you, for me, for our marriage. If we adopted him and something awful happened, you'd never get over it. Not after everything else. And even if it were a good idea for you to be doing this, I'm not ready. If you want to start talking about kids, that's great, but let's not rush into anything."

"What if we adopt him and nothing awful happens? What if we give him a great life and—"

"And everybody lives happily ever after? He's starting out with the deck stacked against him. I don't like the odds. We're not miracle workers. We need to wait."

She shook her head. Why couldn't he see? "But he's here *now.* He needs a home *now.* If I were fertile and I had an unplanned pregnancy—"

"Then we'd have nine months to get used to the idea."

"It would probably take nearly that long for an adoption to go through."

"Not with your family pulling strings, it wouldn't. Meredith, I thought you were happy. This baby's making you remember everything in your life that's made you miserable. Why are you rushing to embrace him? Don't you want to keep being happy?"

"He's a *person*! That's why I'm rushing to embrace him! Because—"

"Because you think you can save him and undo all the other bad stuff. No, it doesn't work that way. It never works that way. Ask Matt. Ask anybody."

"Matt might say it does," she said quietly. "The day after Raji was kidnapped, he told me—he told me that all the stuff I'd gone through would never make sense unless I transformed it into something useful. I didn't have any idea what he was talking about, back then. But I do now."

"Find some other way to do it, then." Kevin's voice was tight. "We just don't know enough about this kid. I've read some of the articles: the parents were just off the plane from Kazakhstan or some benighted place. Who knows what kind of prenatal nutrition this kid got, even before the CV? We don't know their genetic background. There aren't any records, Merry."

Merry stiffened. "When I agreed to marry you, you said genes didn't matter. You just told me you agreed with that."

"I agree that having *our* genes doesn't matter. I never said that genes don't matter at all. And if we adopted this kid, we'd be combining a genetic unknown with a medical unknown. It's crazy, Merry."

"The news reports say he's alert and healthy and needs a loving home."

"Of course they'd say that. And I'm sure he'll get a loving home with someone else. Walking Marzipan every day is enough work right now."

The dog, hearing his name, ran in from the kitchen and hurled himself into Kevin's lap, yapping hysterically.

Meredith had to smile. "Come on, Kevin. You love Marzipan."

"I adore Marzipan. And I adore the cat, and I adore you. But trotting with Marzipan up and down the Filbert steps is all the challenge I need right now; I don't want to add two A.M. feedings and diaper changes. Especially not for an at-risk child. Okay? Now please: twenty-four hours ago, you didn't even know this kid existed. It's too soon to decide you want to take him home. Okay?"

"Okay," she said. "When won't it be too soon? Kevin, every child's an at-risk child! Life's a risky proposition. Perfect safety isn't possible."

"Merry." Kevin's voice held a rare note of warning. "Yes, that's true, but some kids are more at risk than others. The answer's no, okay?"

"If I promise to talk to Matt, if I promise to do a lot of research and visit the baby in the hospital—Kevin, you know how much I hate hospitals, so you know how much that means—if—"

"*No.* Because those are all *I* statements. *You'd* be doing all of that, and adopting a baby is a *we* proposition. And I'm not on board on this, and I'm not going to be. Do you understand?"

"I can't get him out of my head."

"You haven't been trying for very long."

"I *won't* be able to get him out of my head. I know that in my bones, in my gut. Kevin, I know it sounds crazy. I do know that. But, Kevin, I knew two years before you proposed to me that you were going to propose. I knew it in my bones, just like I know that this baby is, is"—she stopped herself from saying *mine*—"ours. Our son. I know it the same way I knew that you and I would be married, and—"

"And you were willing to wait two years for that," Kevin said drily. "Okay: if no one's adopted him in two years, we'll talk about it."

"Kevin!"

"No," he said, very gently. "Meredith, it's late and we both need to go to work in the morning. Let's get some sleep, all right? You're—distraught. You'll see this differently in the morning."

She didn't. She fell asleep thinking about the baby, woke up thinking about the baby. She knew how irrational she must seem to the people around her, but the feeling of certainty hadn't left her. It had intensified.

Kevin, already awake, was lying in bed looking at her, his face still soft with sleep. "Hey," he said, and reached out to brush a strand of hair from her cheek.

"Hey." She moved closer, displacing a disgruntled Ashputtle, and kissed him.

"How are you feeling? Any better?"

She sighed. "I feel fine. I felt fine last night." Stall. Make him think you're not still thinking about this. No, don't do that. Don't lie to Kevin. "Kevin, I feel fine. I haven't changed my mind, though."

He groaned. "Merry, you can't know you want to adopt this child. You can't. You haven't even met—"

"Can't I? You knew you wanted to marry me before you met me."

"No, Merry, I did *not* know that I wanted to marry you! I knew I wanted to meet you, and after I met you I knew I wanted to marry you. There's a difference. Do you understand that?"

"Of course," she said, and rolled away from him. "But I want to meet him today. Is that all right? I want to go to Oakland Children's Hospital and just—just look at him. I don't have any meetings scheduled until two. I'll call the office and tell them I'll be late. Do you think that's crazy? If I go, maybe I'll—come to my senses." No. Don't lie to Kevin. "Maybe I'll see that I'm being nuts. I don't think I will, but it's possible."

"Ah," said Kevin.

She swallowed. "Will you come with me, Kevin? Please?"

"No. I'm not going to go to a hospital to visit a stranger."

"Well, will you let me go?"

"I don't have any choice, do I? You're an adult."

"Yes, you do have a choice," she said, pained by the bitterness in his voice. "If you tell me not to go, I won't. I promise. Kevin, I know this seems crazy to you, really I do. If you say I can't go—"

"You'd never forgive me. Merry, I can't stop you. But we're not adopting him, and that's final."

She'd never expected to walk willingly back into an isolation unit, and she didn't want to regret it. She did some research that morning, and then she called a hospital administrator, on an encrypted line, to alert him that she'd be visiting and to request a media blackout. Visiting hours hadn't started yet, but he promised her that no reporters were there, and he wasn't about to tell her she couldn't come. She was Preston Walford's daughter, and MacroCorp had given the hospital a generous grant for the installation of the iso unit.

When she got there, the nurse at the desk buzzed her right in. "Ms. Walford-Lindgren, this is an honor."

"Thank you. I just want to see the little boy."

"Yes, of course."

He was being fed by a nurse in a spacesuit; a pile of motionless terry-covered bots lay in a corner. Meredith had warned the administrator of her phobia and asked if the bots could be taken offline during her visit. She stood at the window, watching the infant suck contentedly at his bottle. The movement of the tiny mouth mesmerized her, and once again she felt a physical craving to reach through the glass and snatch him out of there. For the first time in her life, she believed in love at first sight. She stood with her hands pressed against the glass, and the tech said something into a microphone.

The nurse nodded and carried the baby closer to the window. The blue eyes seemed even more enormous in real life than they had on the video. The baby had a thin smattering of brown hair, and he was wearing a Wally Walrus snuggly. Meredith wondered if the outfit had been chosen to appeal to her family loyalty. At least Wally wasn't one of the characters who'd killed Raji.

Meredith waved at the baby, and he blinked. Hands waving haphazardly, he looked like some twentieth-century cinematic version of a visitor from outer space. Merry pressed her nose more firmly against the glass and made a funny face. "So is there anybody who wants to adopt him?"

"Well, no," the tech said. "Nobody yet. I guess everybody figures there has to be something wrong with him. Nobody comes out of CV unscathed, you know? It's almost scarier not knowing what the scars will be, having to wait to find out. Too big an emotional investment for most people, not to mention the medical risk. I can't blame them. It would be a pretty exalted thing to do."

"I think it would be a humane thing to do," Meredith said, and waved at the baby again. He waved back, in his fashion. The nurse, behind her helmet, smiled.

"He's happy," the tech said. "He doesn't see many new people. I didn't mean to offend you."

Meredith chewed her lip. "I guess I could only hold him if I wore a suit? And went in there?"

"Well, to actually hold him, yeah. But we've got some glove boxes so we can play with him." He spoke into the microphone again, and the nurse nodded and carried the baby around a corner to another part of the unit. Meredith, following where the tech pointed, found herself looking down into a bassinet glove box. The baby lay on his back, blinking up at her. "Hey there," she said, and stuck one hand tentatively into a glove. She waggled her index finger at the baby, who grabbed it. She imagined that she could feel the heat of that tiny grip through the rubber, although she couldn't have. Emboldened, she inserted her other hand into the other glove and tickled the baby's stomach. He kicked and fussed, his eyes still fixed on her face. "Can he see me?" she asked.

"Sure. His vision's fine."

"But I mean through the plastic and all. Can he see that far? Can he focus yet? I don't know when they learn that stuff." She realized just how little she knew about children, even having observed Theo, how woefully unprepared she was to raise a child. She'd have been woefully unprepared even with the lead time of pregnancy. Still, she was smart and learned fast, and Constance would help.

"He can focus," the tech said. "He sees you. Holding on to your finger that way is a reflex: all babies have it. Infant primates have to hang on to their mother's fur, or on to branches or whatever's handy."

Yes, she'd read that somewhere. "What's his name? I mean, I know you can't tell me his real name, but what do you call him?"

The tech laughed. "Oh, we all have our pet names. The nurse who's back there now, Linda, she and I call him Old Fusspot, and Dr. Monte calls him Sammy, and Candy on night shift calls him Max."

"I'm going to call him Nicholas," Meredith said quietly. It had been Kevin's father's name.

"I'm with Kevin," Constance said. They were in the Pacific Heights solarium; Meredith had called her mother and asked if she could come to the house for lunch before she went to work. "It's a terrible idea. Merry, aside from the medical and emotional risk, if you adopt that child, he'll be a publicity magnet for the rest of his life. It's not a normal existence. Kevin made a conscious adult decision to take that on. The baby can't."

"According to that logic, you shouldn't have had me."

"That was different."

"Because I was your genetic material," Meredith said. The bitterness in her voice surprised her. She closed her eyes and said, "Look, Mom, it's a damned privileged existence, among other things." Her social status had killed Raji; please, please, let her be able to use it now to help someone, to save this child. For so long she'd been afraid to love because of what had happened. Everyone had told her she had to love, and now that she was loving, they were telling her to stop. "And we can pay for privacy. We're already doing that. I'm not all that famous anymore, anyway; ScoopNet hasn't hounded me for years. Nicholas doesn't have any privacy in the hospital, but he'll have it here. And here he can breathe the air and people can touch him."

"What about Kevin?"

"I'll convince Kevin."

"It doesn't sound like it. And, Merry, even if you do convince Kevin, this is a huge step. You can't return the baby if you change your mind later."

"Don't you think I know that?"

"I know you know it intellectually. You can't know it on a gut level. Nobody can know it who hasn't been through three A.M. feedings and getting hit with projectile vomit from screaming toddlers with the flu. You're only seeing his cute side now. The hospital staff is doing all the dirty work."

"I'm the one who *likes* to clean, remember?"

Constance laughed. "Child rearing doesn't lend itself to Zen, I'm afraid. Quite the opposite."

"Well, you did fine, and you hate to clean. So how'd you do it?"

"Maternal instinct," Constance said gently. "Which you can't will, Merry. It really is biological. It grows in you as the baby grows, and it allows you to do things that never would have been possible otherwise. That, and hired help. Or bots."

Meredith felt as if she were choking. "Well, I can hire help too, and I'll take hormone supplements, if you think it's necessary."

"Merry—"

"So I can't be a good mother because I can't get pregnant? What kind of nonsense is that?"

"Merry, I'm sure you'd be a fine mother to Nicholas, but someone else will be too, and you'll be an equally fine mother to some other child in a few years, when Kevin's ready to be a fine father. Kevin's right. He matters too. Let someone else do it."

"He'll change his mind if he meets the baby. I know he will."

"I wouldn't count on it. He can be just as stubborn as you are, remember?"

Meredith sighed. "Mom, I have to get to work now. I'll call you later, all right?"

Her work day passed in a blur, until she could get home and talk to Kevin. When she walked in the door, she smelled dinner. "Ginger beef stir-fry?" she called into the kitchen.

"Yup. So how was the hospital?"

"It was great. The baby's really sweet." She walked into the kitchen and hugged Kevin, who was standing at the stove.

"That's what I was afraid of. Would you not do that while I'm cooking, please?" She stepped back, stung. He'd never asked her not to hug him before. "Merry, don't sulk. I'm working with hot oil, that's all."

"Sorry."

"Your father called. He wants to talk to you."

"What about?"

"What do you *think*?" Kevin gave the stir-fry a savage stir, sending several pieces flying out of the wok, and Merry took another step back.

"How does he know about it?"

"Because your mother told him, dummy! And they've consulted Matt. Preston told me you want to name the baby after my father. You aren't even asking my opinion on that?"

Meredith bit back her anger. Her father had no right to tell Kevin anything, but the important thing now was her husband's hurt feelings. "Kevin, I'm sorry. I thought it would make you happy."

"It might have, if you'd asked me and if I wanted the kid in the first place. Never mind. That's the least of it. Look, log on and talk to your father while I cook, okay? And we'll talk while we eat."

She left the kitchen, her stomach in a knot, and logged on. Her father's face filled the screen almost before she'd finished logging onto his website. "Meredith, I do not think it is a good idea for you and Kevin to adopt this child. Neither does Matt. No one thinks you would be ready, even if Kevin agreed."

She swallowed. This was getting ridiculous. She knew it was her fault for talking to her mother, but her mother shouldn't have talked to the others, and Preston shouldn't have told Kevin. "You know what I think? I think it's nobody's business but mine and Kevin's, and from now on I'm asking the rest of you to butt out."

"If you want us to butt out, why did you talk to your mother?"

Because I thought she'd back me up. "Because I didn't know she was going to talk to the rest of the world. Look, Daddy, this is—this is something I want to do. For reasons you couldn't understand."

"I understand very well. Constance and Matt and Kevin and I all understand. We understand—"

"Nothing! You don't understand a thing, because you aren't in my skull. You've got a nice little intellectual explanation from the outside, but that's not the same thing. This is my business and Kevin's, and if I can get Kevin to change his mind, I'm going to adopt the baby, and if we adopt the baby, I need to know if you and Mom and Matt will help us. For the baby's sake, if not for ours."

Preston was silent for a moment. "I would help the child however I could. I would help you however I could. Meredith, you know that. I am trying to help everyone by suggesting that this is not a good idea."

"Thank you," she said. "Objection noted."

"Just meet him," she said over dinner. "You haven't even met him. Just come look at him. Please, Kevin? That's all I'm asking."

"No, it isn't. If I do that you'll start saying adopt adopt adopt."

"No, I won't." Kevin, she realized with a chill, thought that she was being obsessive. She supposed that he was right. But some things were worth being obsessive about. Being obsessive didn't have to mean being crazy. She sighed and said, "I promise you, that's all I'm asking. Just come see him. How can you know how you feel about him until you've spent time with him? You're rejecting parenthood as a hypothetical abstraction. The baby's a particular, flesh-and-blood child. And if you've met him, you'll be in a better position to talk me out of it." Or to decide that you agree with me. "Right now, I'm the only one with firsthand experience of the baby."

Kevin shook his head. "This morning you said you were just going to visit him yourself. Now you're saying that I have to visit him too. You're escalating, Merry."

She closed her eyes. Please. Goddess, please. If she could just get Kevin to go to the hospital, maybe he'd start believing in love at first sight too. "I'm not saying you *have* to do anything! I'm asking you! What are you afraid of? That you'll like him and I'll have proven you wrong? Just come see him so we won't be talking about this in a vacuum, all right? Come to keep me company, even if you don't care about him."

"I didn't say I didn't *care* about him. I just said I didn't want to be his father."

"Well, if you care about him, come visit him. Give him a new face to look at. Just once. Once, that's all I'm asking. If you come once and you still don't want to do it, we won't do it. I promise. I promise, Kevin."

"I don't believe you. You'll keep pressuring me."

"I won't." She meant it. "With all my heart, I promise that. Just come see him once."

He sighed and pushed his plate away. "Once. I'll go on Saturday; I'm not taking work time for this. But that's all, Merry. And the answer will be no."

She visited Nicholas every day that week; she found herself whispering to him, telling him how to impress Kevin. "Don't cry. It will scare him. You have to be cute when he comes here. You have to be extra cute, so he'll want to take you home." Nicholas, of course, never answered, and the nurses gave no sign of having overheard. The baby still received plenty of ScoopNet coverage, but Meredith never saw herself mentioned; the administrator's promise of privacy was evidently being honored. She'd heard of no other prospective parents.

On Friday night, Constance and Matt and Preston all called her, wanting to talk, wanting to talk her out of it. "We'll talk after Kevin's met the baby," she told all of them, and cut the conversations short. On Saturday morning, as she and Kevin drove to the hospital, a call came in on their car phone. It was her father's signal. She sighed and hit the ignore button. Kevin glanced at her, and she said, "I'll talk to him later. I'll talk to all of them later, okay? What in the name of the Goddess can he have to say about it, anyway? He was barely home when I was a baby, and he doesn't have a body now."

At the hospital, the nurses waved and smiled as they buzzed Merry in. She led Kevin to the observation window, noting that the same tech who'd been there the first day she visited was jotting something on a clipboard. Odd that he worked both weekdays and weekends, but maybe he was putting in overtime.

The nurse on duty held up Nicholas for Kevin to see. Meredith waved at the baby, and he grinned and waved his hands. "See? He knows me." She pointed to the glove box, and the nurse nodded. "Come over here. You can play with him a little."

Kevin dutifully followed, dutifully stuck his hands through the glove box, dutifully smiled when Nicholas crowed and grabbed the gloves. "He *loves* this," Meredith said. "I think he thinks the gloves are animals or something. Here, take out one hand so I can put one in. That way we can both play with him. He likes to have his tummy tickled, see? Kevin, isn't he cute?"

"Sure, he's cute. He's also a walking recipe for disaster. Kids who are touch-deprived right after birth are at significant psychological risk. I've done some research, Merry."

"Anybody who's alive is at significant psychological risk. Hey, look, I think he's smiling at you."

"No, I think he just has gas."

"The point," she said, trying to keep her voice level, and wishing that the tech wasn't eavesdropping, as he surely was, "is to get him out of a risky situation into a better one. Right? Kevin, he's definitely smiling at you."

"Meredith, I think we'd better continue this discussion at home."

They had, as it turned out, already said far too much in public. Merry had put the car on autopilot and was gazing out the window, exhausted, when Kevin said coldly, "All right, Meredith. You win."

"What?" she said, startled. She turned and saw that he was gesturing at the vidscreen. She craned her neck to read the screen from his viewing angle, and saw the familiar ScoopNet logo, an eye with the turning globe as its iris. As usual, there were a plethora of headlines.

"What are they up to now?"

"What, you can't guess? You probably leaked it yourself."

"What?" She reached out and tilted the screen toward her so she could read it more easily. "CV SURVIVORS IN AFRICA EAT KITTENS FOR LACK OF FOOD!" "PACIFIC RIM PARLIAMENT MEETING TURNS INTO KINKY ORGY!" "MERRY WALFORD'S LATEST TRAGEDY: KEVIN REFUSES TO ADOPT CV TYKE!"

She felt her fists clenching. They'd left her alone for five years! What had she done to deserve this? Surely there were plenty of people more interesting than she was!

The tech. It must have been the tech. He'd lose his job when the administrator found out, but ScoopNet had probably paid him a year's salary. "Kevin—I didn't leak it. The VP said—he promised—oh, Gaia, look, somebody on the inside was paid. I'm so sorry! I thought I was safe. I thought they didn't care about me anymore. I don't know why they *do* care about me anymore. I know you're not hard-hearted; I'd never call you that. We'll just ignore it. You don't like the baby. We won't adopt him. I'll find another baby. Off, vid!"

"Disregard," Kevin snapped, and the vid stayed on. "Merry, I think you should read the story. It's a transcription of the conversation we had half an hour ago."

She skimmed it. "Kevin Lindgren insisted that the baby's smile was just gas and said, 'He's a walking recipe for significant emotional risk.' He sure is, Kevin, if he gets you for a daddy! Brave Merry, meanwhile . . .'"

"It's garbage," she said, trembling. "It's junk. We'll ignore it. Somebody else will adopt the baby. Kevin, it's going to be all right." His face terrified her; she'd never seen him so angry.

The phone chirped: four short, one long. Constance. Meredith hit the voice button. "Hi, Mom."

"Hello, dear. Is Kevin with you?"

"We're both here."

"Good. Darlings, we, ah, we have a little PR problem on our hands. You know, I ignore ScoopNet and nearly everyone else does too, anyone with any sense, that is, but the problem is that not everyone *has* sense, and, ah, the head of ViralAid just called Jack. They're very disturbed that this latest story may play into bigotry against CV survivors, and given that Merry's a survivor herself and your family's been affected, Kevin, they think it looks especially bad that, ah, that you've made a statement that CV survivors are emotionally disturbed, and—"

"That's *not* what I said!"

"Mom, that isn't what he said. Really. I was there. I know."

"I'm sure it's not what he said. The issue, though, is that some people who already believe that anyway are going to *think* that's what he said. So all ViralAid is asking is that you make a statement explaining what you really meant. That's all."

"The baby doesn't even *have* CV," Merry said. "They're only keeping him in iso as a precaution, because they've never dealt with a case like this. He's ready to go home with someone. He's fine."

"I know, honey. But not everyone understands that."

"Wonderful," Kevin said. "So now I have to adopt because ViralAid thinks it would make good PR?"

"No, no, no, Kevin, for heaven's sake, I don't think you should adopt unless you're ready! I've said that all along, and I told Merry as much—you can ask her yourself if you don't believe me. You just have to make some kind of statement saying that you weren't talking in a general way about all CV survivors. You know, say you're getting your career started and you don't want to be a father just yet. Tell them the truth, that's all."

"And watch them twist it out of context? I don't think so. They've already done that once. Did you read the entire article? They think I married Merry just for her money."

"They said the same thing when I married Preston. You can't let these things affect you." Meredith winced. Kevin knew enough about her own view of her parents' marriage to know that Meredith, at least, thought that was probably true. "Now listen, Kevin. Jack can help you with this."

"What? Write my statement for me? Why?"

"Because it's his job," Constance said tartly. "He's not head of PR for MacroCorp for nothing. He has skills; let him help you."

"No," Kevin said. "I don't want Jack to do it for me. The last thing I need is a PR hack putting words in my mouth." Merry cringed; Kevin glared at her and said, "No offense, Constance, but I'll do it myself, thank you."

Constance cleared her throat. "Well, fine, Kevin, but really, you should at least have someone screen it."

"*No,* Constance. My marriage is not a corporate project. This is my personal life. If I have to say something, I'll say it myself."

"Mom," Meredith said quickly, "I'll help him with it. Don't worry."

"No, you won't. I'm not a ventriloquist's dummy."

"I didn't say you were, Kevin."

"Um, kids, I have to go now, okay? Just let me know what you decide." Constance cut the connection, and Meredith, with a sigh, turned to Kevin.

"Just relax. This isn't the end of the world."

"I'll make my own statement."

"Fine. Make your own statement. Just don't—Kevin, what are you doing?"

"Making a call. What does it look like I'm doing?"

"No," Meredith said. "Not yet. Wait. Wait until you've calmed down and until you can think. Kevin—"

"ScoopNet," an insanely cheerful voice said over the speakers. "What's the poop?"

Oh, Goddess. Merry reached out to hit the disconnect button, but Kevin grabbed her wrist, pulled her hand to him to kiss it, and then pushed it away, holding it trapped against her body. She noticed numbly that he held her fist pressing into her abdomen, where a child would have pressed out had she been able to bear one.

"This is Kevin Lindgren." His voice was as smooth now as it had been tense only minutes before.

"Confirming voiceprint," the voice said, formal now, wary, and then, "Oh, yes! Yes, sir! What can I do for you, sir?"

"I wish to make a statement concerning your recent story about my visit to Nicholas."

Meredith shook her head wildly; Kevin motioned her to silence and squeezed her hand.

"Yes, sir! Recording, sir."

Kevin cleared his throat. "Your, ah, sources entirely misunderstood my comments about baby Nicholas. What I actually said is that of course he'll need the most loving home possible to overcome his, ah, traumatic beginnings, and Meredith and I will be delighted to provide it. We both think he's a wonderful, beautiful baby, and we can't wait to take him home. That's all."

"Thank you, sir!"

"You're welcome. One more thing: to give the baby time to adjust, and something closer to a normal life than he's had so far, we'll be observing strict privacy protocols. Is that understood?"

"Of course, sir." Meredith thought she could hear the smirk. "Is that all, sir?"

"Yes. Good-bye." Kevin hung up, turned to her, and said, "There. You got what you wanted. Are you happy now?"

She swallowed, blinked back tears—of shame, although she wasn't quite sure why—and said, "No. I didn't want it like this. I didn't want you to be angry. I didn't want ScoopNet announcing it to the world."

"They would have anyway," he said, pleasantly enough. "This will save us the work. More efficient."

"Kevin, I'm scared."

"Of what?"

"Of you. The way you did that without thinking. Like you were lashing out. I've never seen you act that way." She realized that she was trembling. "I'm afraid you hate me. I'm afraid you'll hate the baby."

He looked away. "I don't hate you, and I suppose I'll become fond of the kid. Anyway, really, Meredith, you should have thought of all of this before you ever went to the hospital in the first place."

Merry took a deep breath. "We're committed now. To the adoption."

"Isn't that what you *want*?"

She closed her eyes, and heard herself, as if from a great distance, saying, "They only release full medical records to serious prospective parents, for privacy reasons."

"Yes, of course. I thought nothing was wrong with him."

"Nothing *visible* is wrong with him. But if we learn about anything else, we can't back out, Kevin, or it's the PR problem again. We could have backed out before all the publicity. We can't now. I really wish you hadn't—"

"Well, I did. And you're *happy* that we can't back out. Aren't you?"

"The only clinically significant finding," a doctor told them cheerfully, "is some extremely minor brain damage. It's to a section of the brain called the caudate nucleus, and it means that little Nicholas *could* have an increased susceptibility to anxiety and OCD. Ah—you know what OCD is?"

"Yes," Merry said, her mouth dry. She sat there, frozen, while the doctor droned on about risk factors. She'd never told Kevin about her own brain damage. She'd never lied to him; she just hadn't told him every detail. She could never tell him now. He already thought her feelings about the child were obsessive.

"But that's all treatable," Kevin was saying. "I mean, there's medication, right?"

"Oh, yes," said the doctor. "We have very effective treatments. If anything happens, we should be able to handle it very easily."

"Well then," Kevin said. For once, he sounded cheerful. "It could be much worse. That doesn't sound like anything to worry about." He smiled at the doctor, and the doctor smiled at Merry, and Merry tried to smile back, tried to quell her rising panic.

Was that why she'd felt such a bond with Nicholas? Because they both had damaged brains? She suppressed a shudder, and thought fiercely, *We'll be fine. I'm fine, and he's going to be fine too.*

Sixteen

THE day Nicholas came home, he did nothing but cry. He started the minute he left the isolation unit, emerging into a swarm of cameras much like the one Meredith had confronted years earlier. Remembering how disorienting it had been when she was fourteen, she could only imagine the effect on an infant.

Nicholas was heavier than she'd expected, and her hand hurt from signing what had seemed like five thousand waivers and releases, promising that she wouldn't sue the hospital if the baby developed unforeseen medical complications. Each time she signed another piece of paper, she sent up a prayer. Please, Goddess, let this baby thrive. Please let him be happy. Please don't let me have to hear my family saying we told you so.

Flanked by Constance and Kevin, with Jack acting as a wedge to facilitate their escape, Meredith held the squalling bundle and tried to smile, tried to comfort the baby, tried to ignore the barrage of questions. The reporters had been told there wouldn't be any comment from anyone in the family; they kept asking anyway. She supposed it was what they were paid for. "Meredith, how does it feel to be a mommy?" "Kevin, how do you feel about your son?" "Merry, would you hold the baby up a bit more for the cameras, please?" "Mr. Adam, the decision of the African Consortium—"

"We're not here to discuss politics," Jack said sharply. The fact that he had said anything told Meredith the question had hit a nerve. The reporters doubled their questions; Nicholas tripled the volume of his wailing.

"Mr. Adam, do you personally consider AIs people?" "If Mexico follows suit—" "Sir, exactly how much money has MacroCorp gained from selling AI technology to—" "Meredith, where do AIs fit into your Gaia beliefs?"

"No comment," she said, and clutched Nicholas a bit more tightly. In the rush of preparations to bring Nicholas home, she'd been aware of the Consortium decision only as vague background noise, followed by a sudden sharp pain when she thought of Raji and his beloved AI goldfish. What would he have said about AIs being legally declared people? He'd have considered it only right and natural, surely. After Raji's death, Sonia and Ahmed had returned to Kenya to help care for CV orphans; Meredith could only imagine how they must be reacting to this news. Even if they saw it as a purely practical economic development, it had to reawaken their grief—if indeed their grief had ever slept. Goddess only knew what the Luddites would make of it, but then there probably weren't many Luddites in Africa, anyway. Luddism was a luxury of the First World.

"Maybe he'll quiet down in the car," Constance said into her ear. "Lots of babies like riding in cars, and anyway, it's an enclosed space. He's probably feeling pretty agoraphobic right now."

Meredith nodded and looked down at her cocooned son. The nurses had shown her how to swaddle the baby into a blanket so that his hands and feet were effectively bound. "Makes them feel safer," one had explained cheerfully. "It's like a papoose. Return-to-the-womb kind of thing." It didn't seem to have worked with Nicholas, who was now red in the face from howling. His screaming continued, enhanced by the stench of a soiled diaper, as Meredith scrambled into a MacroCorp limo, with its mercifully tinted windows.

When they were all inside, Constance laughed and said, "Well, his plumbing's working fine, at least. Kevin, would you hand us a diaper, please?"

Meredith wrinkled her nose, feeling ashamed of herself for not being more stoic, and realized again how little she knew about being a mother. "Mom, how do I change him in the car?"

"On your lap, silly. I'll get you a changing cloth."

With Constance's help, Meredith managed to get the baby changed and the diaper stowed in a trash bag. She hoped that Kevin was paying attention, but doubted it. He and Jack seemed to be talking about the scene back at the hospital. From Kevin's querulous tone, she suspected he was venting his irritation at being thrust into fatherhood.

"Why the hell is everyone so upset about Africa? They've been nearly wiped out by the pandemic. They need AIs to staff their factories, everybody knows that, and they're trying to increase their UN voting power while they're at it. The UN will never buy it, anyway, no matter what laws the Consortium passes internally."

"Dangerous precedent," Jack said. "People are afraid that once you grant personhood to AIs, they'll claim independence. It's the old Frankenstein problem. And the basic AI programs are so cheap now that even poor countries can afford them."

"Well, that was the *idea,* wasn't it? That's what you were trying to do? Get cheap labor to the countries hit hardest by CV?"

"Yup. But nobody expected the Consortium to grant them voting rights."

"It's ridiculous," Meredith cut in, rocking Nicholas. Her arms already felt like lead, even though the baby only weighed fifteen pounds. Next to her, Constance hummed a lullaby, to little effect. "They might as well give the vote to trees or rocks. How can they expect anyone to take it seriously?"

"That's one opinion," Jack said drily. "There are others, even here. Look at Raji's friend, that performance artist, what's her name?"

"Zephyr," Meredith said in disgust. Zephyr had been making a name for herself doing dance routines with bots. Zephyr was crazy. She couldn't possibly represent any large segment of public opinion.

The car swerved suddenly, probably to avoid a press cavalcade, and Nicholas's squalling increased, making further conversation impossible. He continued at undiminished volume for the rest of the trip home and for most of the rest of the afternoon, stopping only for brief, blessed periods to eat and sleep. The rest of the time he howled, red-faced and inconsolable.

As the day dragged on, Meredith saw Kevin turning glacial, felt her own resolution eroding, watched her mother's frown deepen. Constance was already miserable from her allergies to the animals, even though she'd taken meds. Jack had escaped back to work. "It's okay," Meredith kept saying, near tears, to the baby and to Kevin and to herself. "He'll be okay. This is all too much for him, that's all, too much new stuff, and this is the only way he has to express it."

Finally, in desperation, she said, "All right. Look, the doctors tried to stimulate him in iso, but obviously he's blowing some circuits here. We need to create an environment that's more familiar for him." It was seven-thirty by then; they'd just finished a miserable dinner punctuated by Nicholas's screams. Meredith handed the shrieking bundle to Kevin, who looked as if he'd been asked to cuddle an armed nuclear warhead.

"Merry, why are you opening the coat closet? Don't tell me you're leaving me here with him!"

"Nope," Meredith said. She put on a vinyl raincoat, reclaimed the baby, and carried him into the bathroom. Enclosed by tiles, metal, rubber, and glass, he promptly calmed down and began to examine his surroundings with interest. He showed special enthusiasm for a red hand towel, which Meredith let him clutch as a security blanket.

"Got it," said Kevin, who'd followed her. Constance, still looking worried, peered over Kevin's shoulder. "Terry cloth. I bet he'd like it even better if it were wrapped around a bot."

"He's fine," Meredith said into the ringing, joyous silence. "He needs more time to adjust, that's all. He can sleep here for the time being, and then we'll gradually get him used to the rest of the house. How does that sound?"

"Anything would sound better than what he was doing a few minutes ago," Kevin said.

Constance edged into the room. "Now that he's stopped screaming, let me hold him a little. Hello, darling. Say hello to your grandma. Goodness, Merry, how he *stares.*"

"Well, he's finally paying attention to us, instead of to being scared. Right, Nicholas?"

"Okay," said Kevin, "now let me try. Merry, we need a bigger bathroom."

"It's all right," Meredith said, enveloped in relief. "He won't be in here forever."

Nicholas gradually became accustomed to places other than the bathroom; Merry and Kevin gradually became used to diapers, feeding schedules, and the sudden ubiquity of baby paraphernalia throughout the house. Meredith, finally giving into Kevin's insistence that they invest in a full housekeeping system, reluctantly came to admit that it made child rearing easier. "Merry, we can turn the housekeeping function off, and it doesn't have to be net-linked, but at least it will be there if we ever want it. We might, now that we have Nicholas. Taking care of a kid is a full-time job. You can't do that and all the cleaning too."

"Yes, I can. Other mothers have. They did for centuries."

"They had to. But they didn't exactly enjoy it, and they stopped as soon as labor-saving appliances were available. And you don't have to. And you might not want to. Look, let's just have the thing even if we never use it, all right?"

They finally compromised: the system would perform some housekeeping chores, but Meredith insisted that its AI capabilities be strictly functional—no interactive personality—and that it perform its tasks without remotes. But although she still scrubbed and dusted and vacuumed, chores the system couldn't perform without bots, she had to admit that she enjoyed waking up to fresh coffee, enjoyed discovering warm, clean laundry waiting for her, enjoyed the fact that rooms lit up to welcome her when she entered and that music followed her from room to room. She consoled herself with the knowledge that these were among the simplest, most basic house functions, already taken for granted by nearly everyone else. She hadn't completely betrayed her ideals; the house was still solar-powered, still ecoefficient. She wasn't a hypocrite, Meredith told herself. She was simply a creature of her culture, and how, after all, could she be otherwise?

And anyway, she was a mother now. Nicholas had to be her first priority. After his initial resistance to the new environment, the boy was remarkably quiet and well behaved. He ate well, grew quickly, remained exceptionally healthy even compared with children who hadn't been exposed to CV, and did everything he was supposed to do exactly on schedule. He sat up at four months, crawled at six, walked at eight, said "Mommy" at nine and "Daddy" two weeks later. Meredith knew she was hopelessly besotted: she found Nicholas both beautiful and fascinating, missed him with a physical craving when they were apart, cheered each of his methodical bloomings into normalcy. No one doubted that he loved her. He behaved himself with Kevin and with Constance—and with everyone else, for that matter—and he enjoyed playing with Theo, but he displayed little dependence upon anyone but Merry. He and his mother were the world to one another. It was always to her that he ran with questions and appetites and scraped knees, her voice he wanted to hear reading bedtime stories and reciting nursery rhymes, her touch that soothed him when he was tired or frightened.

The only setback came when, at six months, he suddenly became terrified of Ashputtle and Marzipan. He'd liked the animals before, but now the sight of them sent him into paroxysms of fear. Merry, regretfully, found other homes for them with Temple friends. Nicholas would outgrow his phobia, and then she could have pets again. Once, losing the dog and cat would have devastated her, but Nicholas was more important.

He was her touchstone, the tale to which all else was footnote. Only later would she realize how firmly every significant event in the wider world was, for her, connected to some milestone or crisis of her son's. The morning that one-year-old Nicholas first correctly placed a round block in a shape sorter, ScoopNet reported that the first brainwipe sentence had been handed down for a convicted murderer. Meredith's pride in her son's accomplishment was inseparable from her relief that he was turning out so normally, that like millions of babies before him, he had been granted the everyday miracle of learning to know a circle from a square. He'd escaped CV for good; he would never need to have his brain scourged with the modified virus.

The day Mexico joined Africa in granting citizenship to AIs, Nicholas yelled, "Nose!" with one hand on his own nose and one hand on Meredith's. He was a person; he had been born from a human womb, had a human nose, used human language to identify it and a human brain to recognize the abstract within the particular.

Nicholas built his first block tower during Zephyr's first national netcast. Meredith found her son's performance infinitely preferable to the crazed gyrations of Zephyr's bots as she herded them through a barbwire labyrinth.

Nicholas said his first two-word sentence, "More juice," the morning Kevin went to work for MacroCorp, designing AI-enhanced buildings. Meredith and Kevin had had a series of exceptionally tense discussions about the decision. "Kevin, you don't need to do this! So what if we don't have my paycheck anymore? I have trust funds! We can use them! You shouldn't do work you don't believe in and you shouldn't feel you have to work for my family."

"Meredith, I'm an *architect*. Furthermore, I'm a damned good architect. MacroCorp's lucky to have me, and don't think they don't know it. And the work's interesting and I need to develop these skills, because AIs are going to be all over the place."

"I thought you didn't *like* AIs! You never used to!"

"Meredith, I'm an architect. This is what buildings are now. This is what they do. I'm not turning soulfreak on you. I'm designing buildings, all right? Just like our house. Our house is AI equipped, as you conveniently seem to keep forgetting."

"Without social programming or autonomous individuality."

"So what? You still have a smart machine making your coffee in the morning, even if the coffeemaker doesn't chat with you about the weather while it grinds the beans. So unless you want to try to find me a job designing thatched huts, don't yell at me for doing the work I've been trained for!"

After their volley of furious speech, what a simple blessing it was for her to hear Nicholas stringing two words together to quench his simple thirst. No AI in the world would ever ask for apple juice.

If his first two-word sentence was a moment of grace in a difficult morning, his first three-word one—"Scary monsters, Mommy!"—would later seem an unheeded omen. He had woken up screaming, bolt upright and eyes wide with terror, unable to recognize Meredith for several minutes. Over breakfast, he delivered his three-word synopsis through a face smeared with oatmeal.

"Poor baby," Meredith said, and hugged him. "I know. It was scary for me too, when you yelled like that. But the monsters are all gone. They aren't here anymore. Did you dream about Ashputtle and Marzipan, Nicky? But they don't live here anymore. You don't have to be afraid."

He took a long nap that day, no doubt because he'd woken up earlier than usual, and Meredith, unconcerned—all kids had nightmares—spent the time catching up on news. For once, she curled up in front of the screen in the living room, rather than just having the audio follow her around the house. Nicholas's nightmare had worn her out too, and she wanted to sit down.

The top story was on the increasing popularity of brainwiping, both as a mandated therapy for criminals and as a voluntary procedure. Camille, a manic-depressive whose doctors had never managed to stabilize her medication, hoped that brainwiping would finally make her life normal again. "I'm so tired of up and down and up and down—and when I'm down I want to die and when I'm up I hear voices and the middle lasts five minutes. Five seconds. It's there and then it's gone, I blink and I miss it. I'm *tired*! I'm willing to try anything!"

The reporter reminded her that she'd lose her entire life, all her memories, the ability even to feed herself with a spoon. "I can relearn all that," Camille said, tears welling on camera. "I can relearn what I need to know to live. I've already lost the people who loved me, because they couldn't stand being around me like this. I've never been able to hold down a job. I'm sick of hospitals, do you understand? I want a home! I want to be a normal human being again! Do you understand? Do you? Do you understand?"

After a bland, optimistic closing quote from Camille's physician, the story moved to a cautionary interview with Holly O'Riley, a leading civil rights attorney who specialized in defending the mentally ill. "For every twenty violent criminals who have successfully been resocialized after this procedure," O'Riley said, staring at the camera grimly, "one has become permanently disabled: unable to grasp cause-and-effect, unable to tell time, unable to use the first-person pronoun because so much sense of self has been lost. Let me introduce you to Luke."

Luke was a drooling wreck, a forty-five-year-old man with the mind of a toddler. He had to wear diapers, still crawled, and appeared to be incapable of learning to place a round block in a round hole; the news clip showed him struggling with the same shape sorter Nicholas had mastered. Before brainwiping, Luke had been a skilled carpenter and chess grand master facing life without parole for the brutal rape and murder of twin twelve-year-old girls. "What brainwiping has done to Luke," Holly O'Riley said, "is arguably as hideous as what he did to his victims. True, he had a choice: he chose the procedure, rather than being sentenced to it, and he knew the risks. But as a society, we need to think long and hard about the danger of placing other people in Luke's terrible position."

Meredith, repelled, turned off the TV. As far as she was concerned, Luke looked like a crawling advertisement for capital punishment. How could anyone feel sorry for him? O'Riley had chosen the wrong poster child; Camille, who so desperately wanted the procedure, was infinitely more sympathetic. And none of it had anything to do with Meredith. She and Nicholas were both done with CV for good. The worst thing they had to worry about now was a few nightmares.

The nightmares continued, though, growing gradually worse. It took Meredith a while to become concerned, since Nicholas developed normally otherwise. At two years and three months, he first ate an entire meal with a spoon; that same day, Canada, Sweden, and the Netherlands joined Mexico and Africa in the AI emancipation treaty. Three months later, as Nicholas opened his bedroom door by himself for the first time, Congress proposed the "born, not built" amendment to the Constitution, granting personhood—and citizenship—only to genetic, biological humans, to on-line entities constructed from the memories of genetic, biological humans, and to corporations controlled and staffed by entities defined as persons under the first two clauses. The proposal was, ironically, applauded by both Luddites and AI manufacturers, and vociferously opposed by AI activists.

Meredith listened to Preston testifying at the California ratification hearings as she coached Nicholas through the momentous task of learning to put on his own shoes. He'd had not one but two nightmares the previous night, waking screaming, his sheets wet with sweat and urine. Meredith had thought bleakly of Hortense. Well, she'd atone for her insensitivity to the old woman by loving Nicholas. "Nicky, what is it? What did you dream?"

"Scary monsters, Mommy!" All kids have nightmares, Meredith told herself, but she and Nicholas were both exhausted today, and listening to her father speaking calmly in favor of ratification soothed her.

"There is no doubt that AIs are extremely sophisticated machines," Preston said, "but they are machines nonetheless. Even if the most advanced such machines can be said to possess autonomous individuality, that does not make them human, any more than cats or cows or crickets are human. We care for our pets and our livestock, after all, but we do not grant them citizenship. Citizenship is a human term, meaningful only within human society, as irrelevant to AIs as it would be to cats or cows."

Meredith, already anticipating the rebuttal, winced. What PR idiot had written that speech? Surely not Jack! The analogy to organic life would only make the soulfreaks *more* likely to oppose ratification; any sensible argument would have pointed out that AIs weren't organic at all, that they were outside ecology rather than part of it. That was what "born, not built" *meant*.

Meanwhile, Nicholas had put his left shoe on his right foot, and was crying because it didn't feel right. "No, Nicky, that's the wrong foot—try it on the other one, good boy, there you go!" She led him through the intricate task of fastening the Velcro straps while the moderator introduced the next speaker in the debate, eminent AI researcher Dan Willem.

Dan Willem. Dan. Meredith blinked. Dan had been the head of Raji's AI lab. That meant he took grant money from MacroCorp, didn't it? But, no, the AI lab hadn't existed since Raji died. Willem was now arguing against the people who'd once supported his research.

As Raji would have, surely, if he'd still been alive. Meredith wiped away tears, settled Nicky down with some blocks, and sat to watch the debate.

After gently charging Preston with hypocrisy, since he was no longer organically human, either, Dan launched into an extremely odd comparison of AI emancipation with the Underground Railroad and the animal rights movement. "No," Meredith said aloud, "the slaves were *already* people, which is why other people didn't have the right to enslave them. And animals weren't created by humans to be useful to humans, which is why we can't use them like machines." She felt as if she were reliving that disastrous conversation with Zephyr at Cyberjus. That had been the last time she saw Raji. She shook her head to clear it, and said to the television, "Idiot." Raji had thought very highly of Dan. For Raji's sake, she wanted him to be more intelligent than this.

Nicky looked up from his blocks. "What, Mommy?"

"Nothing, honey. I'm sorry. I was talking to that man on the TV." She added silently, And animal rights are important because we all share the earth; we're all part of the food chain. AIs aren't part of the food chain at all. Not even Raji would have claimed that. You couldn't make ecological arguments for AIs.

Food chain. Food. It was one o'clock already. "Want your lunch now, Nicky?"

"Sticky butter and red jelly!"

While Meredith made Nicholas's sandwich, Dan sorrowfully accused Preston of supporting the amendment only because of the money Macro-Corp would lose if AIs were no longer commercial properties. "Aside from the military market, which you've very virtuously avoided, MacroCorp has a virtual global monopoly on AI technology. If your company couldn't sell AI systems, Mr. Walford—if they were legally acknowledged not simply as autonomous individuals, but as sentient beings who couldn't be traded on the market—MacroCorp would go broke, and you'd lose your computer space. Do you really care about sentience, or just about your own survival?"

Meredith shook her head in annoyance. MacroCorp had gotten into the AI business because Preston *did* care about sentience. AIs had been designed to help people after the CV pandemic; didn't Dan know that? Preston said only, "May I remind my esteemed opponent that MacroCorp is a global, diversified conglomerate? AI technology represents only a small percentage of our business; the loss of that business would not even come close to hurting the corporation." Meredith smiled. Even if AIs were declared persons, MacroCorp's lawyers would get around the slavery issue anyhow. Instead of selling AIs, they'd demand salaries for them or something, but of course MacroCorp would still get the money. What would an AI do with a paycheck? The whole issue was ludicrous.

Three months later, while the ratification hearings were still under way, Nicholas had three nightmares in one night. The next morning over breakfast, Meredith and Kevin heard on a newscast that Zephyr Expanding Cosmos had been arrested for smuggling stolen AI hardware into Mexico.

Meredith shook her head. "The woman's crazy."

"Mmmm. Well, she's an odd one, that's for sure. What were Nicky's bad dreams about?"

"Monsters," Meredith said, around a bite of bagel. Nicholas was in bed, catching up on sleep after his rough night.

"Don't you think Nicholas dreams about monsters an awful lot? Merry, maybe we should take him to a doctor or something."

"He's fine. All kids have bad dreams. He'll grow out of it." Merry felt anxiety coiling in her stomach, and remembered Honoli saying that anxiety could trigger OCD. Was Nicky anxious too? "Hey, I heard that Massachusetts already ratified. That's great news, isn't it?"

Kevin scowled. "I don't care about the amendment. It's stupid. I'm worried about Nicholas."

"He's fine, Kevin!"

"He's *not* fine. Waking up screaming three times a night isn't fine. Maybe it's that brain thing he has. Maybe he needs meds."

Meredith remembered how Constance had wanted to medicate her out of her passion for cleaning after Raji died. But the cleaning had been better therapy than any pill would have been. "And maybe he's working through something he needs to work through. Speaking of which, don't you have to go to work?"

"It's been months," Kevin said, standing up. "He hasn't worked through it yet. I think you should talk to somebody, that's all. So we can help him. It's cruel to watch him suffer."

Meredith felt a pang of guilt; Kevin was right. "Okay, I'll talk to somebody. Relax. Have a nice day. I'll see you later."

He left, and Meredith, with a sigh, leaned back into her chair. The newscast was still droning. There'd been a new outbreak of CV in China: five thousand dead. Colombia was in the throes of a new civil war. The House and Senate had passed a bill making brainwiping mandatory for anyone convicted of rape, murder, or terrorism.

Meredith sat up a little straighter and raised her eyebrows. Hoo-boy. That would be tied up in court challenges until Nicholas got out of college. The procedure was controversial enough even on a voluntary basis, especially now that the more unfortunate victims of brainwiping, the Lukes of the world, had begun to constitute a growing percentage of the homeless. The procedure still worked beautifully in over 95 percent of cases, according to its supporters, but of course the successful cases were, by definition, invisible, at least once the resocialization process was complete. The public only saw the failures, too many of whom lived on the streets. And now the government wanted to add convicted rapists and murderers to the mix? No matter how docile brainwiping appeared to make its victims, the new law would never stand against public opinion. It wouldn't last five minutes.

A year later, it was still in effect, with new categories of criminals being added all the time. Resocialization, like prisons before it, kept a lot of people employed. Nicholas's nightmares, meanwhile, were worse than ever. They occurred at least twice a night, and now he had begun to sleepwalk too. Kevin suggested tying him down, but Meredith wouldn't hear of it. Their pediatrician had told them that young children who sleepwalked were usually suffering from confusional arousals, neural storms precipitating an intense sensation of fight or flight. Restraint only prolonged the episodes. Of course, the doctor also said that confusional arousals were distinct from nightmares, and Nicholas's came together; still, Meredith wouldn't have been able to stomach bondage even had it been medically wise.

The pediatrician referred them to a pediatric psychologist, who suggested that Nicholas was suffering from post-isolation syndrome—"For this we're paying her five hundred dollars?" Kevin said—and enrolled him in play therapy. He enjoyed the play therapy, but it didn't stop the nightmares. The pediatrician suggested medication; Meredith reluctantly agreed, but stopped the meds when they made Nicholas dopey, unable to enjoy the things he usually loved. What was the point of destroying both his fears *and* his pleasures?

The week Nicholas turned four, he began to bang his head deliberately against walls and furniture during his sleepwalking episodes, struggling against Meredith's embrace as she held him back, trying to shield him, seeking, if nothing else, to insert something soft—a blanket, a pillow—between his head and whatever hard surface he had chosen. Now, at last, Meredith became terrified. Head-banging belonged to autism; it bespoke serious disturbance, and at least some doctors had begun to use brainwiping as their predecessors had used lobotomies, Valium, and Prozac. Just two days before Nicholas's first head-banging incident, Meredith had heard an interview with a woman who claimed that her teenage son had been threatened with brainwiping because he wouldn't stop biting his nails; another mother had called in to say that her doctor had recommended it for a bed-wetting daughter. Those cases were admittedly so extreme as to be nearly unbelievable— how could any parent willingly destroy a child's personality?—but still.

Kevin wasn't happy with taking Nicholas off the medication, and he knew neither about the bed-wetting nor about the head-banging. Meredith always responded to the boy's screams, and the house system did the laundry. Because Constance had expressed concern about the nightmares, Merry had stopped asking her to babysit; because Theo, the perfect child, had said something to her once about Nicholas being "strange," Meredith found herself limiting his playtime with Nicholas. She no longer took Nicky to Temple, because he seemed afraid of the other people there and because she had seen Matt watching him a little too closely. Nicholas would outgrow all of this, surely, and then things could get back to normal again. In the meantime, she didn't want to expose him, or herself, to criticism from people who thought she never should have taken Nicholas home in the first place.

She knew what Matt would have said: she was afraid of getting into trouble. She knew what both Constance and Honoli would have said: she was being obsessive. She didn't care. Nicholas would be fine, and his temporary difficulties weren't anyone else's business. "No," she told Kevin whenever he brought up the subject, "Nicky doesn't need another kiddie shrink. Come on, Kevin, all kids have nightmares. I had them myself. I'm sure you did too. Anyway, I'm the one who gets up. You don't have to. Sleep with earplugs, if you want to."

Nicholas didn't remember trying to hit his head against the wall. When Meredith asked him what he'd been dreaming about, the morning after that first struggle, he said only, "Scary monsters. I have to run away from them."

"Were they chasing you, Nicky? Getting closer?"

"They're close now. I have to keep them away."

She closed her eyes. He sounded so normal when he was awake: bright and alert and articulate, interested in books and drawing and building things. The meds destroyed all that, all the good things. Her heart ached for him. She didn't know what to do; she knew only that she had a pathological fear of submitting him to further scrutiny, more examinations. That was what she'd vowed to save him from.

But it seemed to be what everyone else thought he needed. "He should go to school," Constance said later that week. Nicholas sat in the middle of the sun-drenched living room floor, absorbed in a block tower he was building. Constance and Meredith sat drinking iced tea in the kitchen, watching him in the next room. "The homeschooling you're doing is great, honey, and I know you take him to the playground twice a day, but he needs more socialization."

"Of course," Meredith said dully. She'd known this subject would come up eventually. She'd been trying not to think about it. If he went to school, someone else would see what was going on, and the pressure to consult more specialists would become greater. No more doctors, please. She and Nicholas had both had enough of them.

"Is he still having those nightmares?" Constance said. "I'm worried, Merry. I know Kevin is too."

"Well, stop worrying. All kids have nightmares." It didn't sound convincing even to Meredith.

"Not every time they go to sleep," Constance said, and Meredith wondered just how much Kevin had been talking to her mother. "Most kids don't wake up screaming every night for over a year, Merry! Are you still talking to the pediatrician about it?"

"Of course," Meredith said, trying to keep her voice light. "She says it's nothing to worry about. It's a phase. It will pass." The pediatrician had in fact said nothing lately, because Meredith had told her nothing. The pediatrician had, on more than one occasion, spoken a bit too highly of the benefits of brainwiping on adults, and Meredith didn't trust her not to apply the same principles to children. They needed to find a new doctor.

Constance shook her head. "Well, if it's a phase, it's not one you or Theo ever went through."

"I wasn't scared of the dark when I was little? Come on, Mom, I was too! I remember. Monsters under the bed, monsters in the closet, monsters growing out of shadows on the wall. *Everybody* goes through that. It's perfectly normal."

"For so long?" Constance asked bluntly, and then sighed and softened. "Well, all right, honey. You should try giving him a flashlight to sleep with. I read an article about that. His very own light saber, so he can kill the monsters when they come out."

"That's a good idea," Merry said, trying to sound cheerful. "I'll try that. Thanks."

She had, in fact, tried it already, had read the same article and promptly gone out and gotten Nicholas his very own flashlight. She wasn't about to tell her mother the results of that experiment.

"Here, Nicholas," she'd said. "If you shine this on the monsters who wake you up, they won't be there anymore, see?"

He'd looked at the flashlight and then at her, and said, "Yes, they will, Mommy."

"Why, Nicholas? Your room isn't scary when it's light out. If you turn this on, it will be light at night too."

"Not if I close my eyes. The monsters come out when I close my eyes, Mommy."

"Where do they come from, Nicholas? Where are they? Under the bed? In the closet? Do they come from your toy chest? Where are they? Mommy will kill them. Mommy won't let them hurt you."

He'd looked at her and said sadly, "But, Mommy, they're not outside. They're in my head."

"That's right," she'd said, both confused and relieved. "They're dreams. They aren't real. They can't really hurt you."

"Then make them be quiet!" he'd cried, and started to sob. "Then make them go away! You can't make them go away, Mommy!"

She had felt as though she were sinking in quicksand, or trapped in one of those dreams in which you travel forever in circles. Other children had imaginary friends; Nicholas had imaginary enemies. "What do they do, Nicholas? How do they hurt you?"

"They tell me to be bad."

She almost laughed aloud. He was too good, that was all. "Well, Nicholas, everyone is bad sometimes. I was bad sometimes when I was a little girl."

Nicholas cocked his head. "Really?"

"Yes, Nicholas, really. I stole candy and drew on the walls with crayon and, um, once I poured water over a bot because it was dirty and I thought it needed a bath and it shorted out, and I used to stay up past my bedtime reading under the covers, and—"

"You killed a bot?" he said. He was fascinated with bots, despite—or perhaps because—there was none at home.

"I didn't mean to, but I broke it, yes."

"You killed it?"

"Well, not exactly, I mean, it's not *alive,* but I broke it. You know bots aren't alive, Nicholas. They're just machines." Kevin kept telling her this was far too complicated for such a young child, but she didn't care. She'd be damned if she was going to raise a soulfreak.

He'd shuddered, and then said, very sadly, "Mommy, I wish they were alive."

"Why, Nicholas?"

"Because then I could kill them."

Green-growing Gaia. I am not in this video, she'd thought firmly. I am not living in a horror movie or serial-murder porn or a toddler-spawn-of-the-devil soap opera. I'm living a ridiculously privileged life in the middle of the twenty-first century, and my child will be just fine. Change the channel. "Nicholas, please don't say kill. That's not a nice word. Nice little boys don't say that word."

"You said you'd kill my monsters," he said accusingly. His lip was trembling. "You did! You did, Mommy!"

It was a figure of speech. Right. He was four. She swallowed. "I meant—I just meant I'd make them go away, Nicholas. Make them go away forever, so they couldn't scare you anymore." It sounded lame even to her. "Hey, Nicholas, it's time for lunch. I'll make you hot dogs. Would you like that? Hot dogs and ice cream?"

He relaxed, smiled, looked for a moment like a normal child. "I like hot dogs."

"I know you do," she said, filled with relief. "I'll make you hot dogs."

She made him hot dogs, and he ate them, and afterward, looking down at his empty plate, he said serenely, "See? All gone. I made them go away forever."

No, she wasn't going to tell her mother that Nicholas's preferred method of vanquishing monsters was to eat them for lunch, or that he had a preternaturally advanced grasp of the distinction between his own visions and the outside world. She wanted him to be normal: normal, please, Goddess, happy, not someone who would attract any undue attention, not someone permanently scarred, not someone stuck into a pigeonhole of fame or infamy. And not someone medicated—or worse—into zombieland.

Constance sighed. "Maybe a pet would help. I know he was scared of the dog and cat, but that was a while ago. Maybe something smaller. Something he can take care of, to feel competent." Constance leaned forward and called into the living room, "Hey, Nicky?"

Nicholas looked up from his block tower. "What?"

"Did you hear what we were just talking about?"

He scowled. "I was building something, Gramma."

"I know. It's a beautiful tower. That takes a lot of concentration, doesn't it?"

He nodded. He was proud of his precision, and indeed he was remarkably neat and careful for so young a boy. "It's a prison. For scary things."

Meredith's stomach knotted; her mother looked at her, eyebrows raised. "Well, good," Constance said. "That's a good idea. Nicky, would you like a pet? Maybe a bunny, or a hamster?"

Nicholas considered this. "Could I do anything I wanted with it?"

"No," Meredith said, hoping her mother hadn't heard the unintended force in her voice. "Not anything. You'd have to take care of it, Nicholas; you'd have to love it and help it keep clean and give it food and water. You'd have to take care of it, just like Daddy and I take care of you."

Nicholas was frowning. Constance said, "You'd have to keep it safe from anything that might hurt it, honey. You'd keep it safe from scary things," and suddenly the boy's expression cleared.

"All right, Mommy. When? Can we do it now?"

In the pet store, Meredith and Constance examined an array of rabbits, to no avail; Nicholas remained glued to a cage of male mice, each sporting swollen red testicles larger than the animal's head. "Mommy, are they sick?"

Meredith winced. "No, honey. They're healthy. They're supposed to look like that."

"But those mice look different," Nicholas said, and pointed to a neighboring cage of svelte female mice.

"Those are girl mice," a cheerful clerk said behind them. "We keep 'em apart, for obvious reasons. But we need breeding stock; most people who buy mice and rats buy 'em to feed their snakes and such."

"Thank you," Meredith said, annoyed. She wasn't sure that Nicholas needed that much information.

"Snakes eat them?" Nicholas said.

"Yup."

"Which ones? The girls or the boys?"

"Both."

"Oh. Mommy, can I have a mouse?"

"Sure," Meredith said. "Which one do you want?"

"A girl mouse. They're prettier."

He picked out a small white mouse with brown spots; Meredith collected a fish tank, cedar chips, water bottle, exercise wheel, and mouse food. Constance paid for it all, beaming. "See, Nicky, you're already keeping this little mouse safe from snakes. Now she won't get eaten."

Meredith was getting a headache. "Snakes have to eat too, Mom."

"Well, they don't need to eat this little mouse. So, Nicholas, what's her name? Have you decided yet?"

He thought a moment. "Patty. Because that's what she'd be to a snake." He giggled. "Patty-cake. She'd be a cake to a snake. Or a burger to a booger. Or—"

"Or a friend to Nicholas," Meredith said firmly. "Right?"

He scowled. "That doesn't go with her name, Mommy."

Think fast. "Yes, it does, because you'll pat her, because she's so pretty and soft. Right?"

He squinted up at her. "Maybe, Mommy. If she'll hold still."

Seventeen

PATTY didn't hold still all afternoon. She ran energetically on her exercise wheel, chewed a toilet paper roll to shreds, scampered about with bits of seed and lettuce. Constance went home; Meredith tried to show Nicholas how to pick Patty up by the base of the tail, but her wiggling seemed to unnerve him. Holding the tiny creature firmly in her hand, tail pinned between thumb and index finger while the miniscule heartbeat thundered against her palm, Meredith guided Nicholas's outstretched finger along the mouse's back. "See, Nicky? See how soft she is? Such nice soft fur."

"She's scared."

"Well, that's because everything here is new. She has to get used to us." Meredith thought of Nicholas's ceaseless crying the day he came home, and felt a pang of pity for all small, frightened things. "When she learns that we're the people who feed her and give her water and pat her and clean her cage, she won't be scared of us anymore."

"Put her back, Mommy. She's scared."

"Okay," Meredith said, and slipped Patty back into her cage, where she promptly dashed to the exercise wheel. Meredith wondered if the mouse thought, in the starry brightness of her minute brain, that all that movement would carry her away from here. "Do you want to watch her some more? What do you want to do?"

"TV," Nicholas said, his thumb in his mouth, and Meredith picked him up and carried him into the den. He never willingly lay down for naps, but he often fell asleep on the couch while watching television. In the matter of Nicholas and sleep, Meredith's credo was to use what worked.

She settled him on the couch with a plastic sheet and a blanket, put on a Gaia Network tape about bees he'd always liked, and went into the kitchen to program dinner. When she checked on her charges a few minutes later, both were fast asleep, Patty curled into a small furry ball half covered by cedar chips and Nicholas nestling in his blanket, thumb in mouth, while on the television screen the bees buzzed soporifically. She sat down on the other end of the couch, savoring the peace of the moment, and watched the bees circle in their quivering dance.

"Mommy," Nicholas said. "Mommy, wake up! Look!"

Meredith jerked awake, her neck stiff and her eyes gritty. How long had she been asleep? What time was it? "Mommy!" Nicholas said again, and she remembered that she was on the couch, that she'd settled Nicky down with his bee show and then had sat down herself, and—

"Look at this show, Mommy!"

She blinked, rubbed her eyes, peered at the screen. The bees were gone. The tape must have ended, and now the television featured an all-too-familiar woman in a leotard. She was holding up a bot. She was dancing with it. "The bot tried to take her apart," Nicholas said excitedly. "It had knives. She made friends with it, Mommy. She gave it apples to cut up instead, and she ate the apples, and now she and the bot are friends. She gave it something good to do with the knives."

Meredith sat up straighter, realizing in a series of small befuddlements that Nicholas hadn't screamed himself awake, that he wasn't trying to slam his head into anything, and that the woman on the screen was Zephyr, who had finished her yearlong jail sentence and was back to her old tricks.

"I like that lady," Nicholas said decisively. "What show is this, Mommy?"

"The Performance Network," Meredith said, around a burst of what she recognized as completely irrational jealousy. "It's for grown-ups, Nicholas."

"Oh. What are they doing now, Mommy?"

"Grown-up things," Meredith said. Zephyr had put the bot down on the floor and was straddling it, her pelvis pumping. "Nicholas, let's go see how Patty is, okay?"

"Can we feed her some apples?"

You don't, Meredith thought, want to think too much about the symbolism here. "Sure. I don't know if mice like apples, but we'll find out."

As it turned out, Patty thoroughly enjoyed her slice of apple, from which she took dainty nibbles. Nicholas, nose glued to the side of the cage while he watched her eat, said, "You make friends with monsters by giving them something else to eat. Right, Mommy? If they want to eat you, you give them something else."

"I guess you could," Meredith said warily. "Do you want to take some apples to bed with you tonight, Nicholas? To feed the monsters?"

"Maybe. Mommy, what's the snake eating?"

"What snake, honey?"

"The snake who was going to eat Patty before we brought her home from the store."

Oh. "Well, sweetheart, that snake's probably eating another mouse. One of the ones we didn't buy. One of the ones we left in the store. But Patty's safe here with us, and she's very happy with her apple. She likes her new home."

"She's not getting eaten by a snake," Nicholas said.

"That's right." She reached out to tousle his hair. "She's safe here. And so are you. You didn't dream about monsters in front of the TV, Nick, did you?"

Maybe she'd said the wrong thing, even though he hadn't screamed himself awake, because his face clouded. "No, Mommy. I didn't dream about the monsters."

"Aren't you happy about that, Nick?" Maybe he'd gotten sad again because she'd reminded him.

"Yes," he said, but he still looked sad. "I didn't dream about the monsters because of Patty."

"*Great,*" Meredith said, and tousled his hair again. "That's great, Nicholas!" She'd have to tell Constance. Round one to Grandma. "Hooray for Patty!"

"Hooray for Patty," he said, and started to cry.

She chalked it up to fatigue, to the overstimulation of the pet shop and the excitement of bringing Patty home, to Zephyr's evil influence. She told herself that maybe Nicholas was having some body memory, triggered by the mouse's arrival, of having cried as a baby when he was moved from a familiar environment to this alien, much larger one. She held him, rocked him and sang to him and gave him warm milk, and by the time Kevin got home, the crisis was safely past: Nicholas sat in the middle of the living room building one of his block towers while Patty scampered on her wheel. All was well with the world.

And, amazingly, Meredith slept through the night. There were no screams, no terrified cries; when she looked in on Nicholas in the morning, he slept sweetly, hand tucked beneath his cheek, face and sheets both dry. Meredith, marveling, quietly left the room, lest she disturb him, and went downstairs for coffee.

Kevin was already up, sitting at the kitchen table. "Quiet night," he said.

Meredith slid into a chair next to him and gave him a kiss. "I know. Amazing, isn't it? Hooray for Patty."

Kevin sighed. "Hooray for Patty. Meredith, listen, I went to feed her and, um—"

Meredith's heart sank. "Oh, *shit,*" she said, already out of her chair and heading toward the cage. "What is it?" The mouse was dead, poisoned by apple seeds. The mouse had hung herself between the bars of her exercise wheel. The mouse had somehow drowned in a leak from her water bottle.

"Well," Kevin said behind Meredith's shoulder, "she isn't there. At least, I can't find her."

"Oh, no!" Meredith said, peering into the cage. No Patty. She removed the mesh top and prodded various corners of the cage, thinking that perhaps Patty had burrowed underneath cedar chips or cardboard shavings. No Patty. "Oh, Gaia. Poor Nicholas! Kevin, how could she have gotten *out*? Was the top on the cage?"

"It was a little loose."

"It wasn't loose last night! I checked it before I went to bed."

"I know."

"Well, she couldn't have climbed up the sides of a glass aquarium, could she?" Meredith peered into the cage again. "Could she have stood on top of the exercise wheel and gotten out? But the top was latched down."

"Merry, it doesn't matter how she got out. She's out."

Meredith, feeling ill, pushed back a memory of Squeaky. "We have to find her before Nicholas gets up. Kevin, why didn't you wake me?"

Kevin sighed. "I wanted you to get sleep. You've been sleep-starved for four years, ever since Nicholas came home. I thought you deserved one night—"

"Oh," Meredith said, stricken. "Oh, Kevin, thank you. But the mouse— we have to find her."

"Well, she has to be in the house, right?"

"*I* don't know! If you ask me, she has to be in the cage! If we put food out—"

"Well, I tried that. Some crackers, some apples. Nothing. And you can't call them, can you? Like a cat or dog? You're the animal expert."

Meredith thought furiously. If I were a mouse, where would I go? If Nicholas finds out she's gone, he'll be—"Hey, Kevin! Do you think the house system could tell us? Does it have a, a, I don't know, pest-sensing capability or something? I mean, most people don't like it when there are mice in their houses, right?"

"There's an idea. Come on." He led her to the terminal in his office— their tiny third bedroom—and scrolled rapidly down help menus and topic indices as Meredith looked over his shoulder. "*Vermin;* here we go. About vermin, discouraging vermin, locating infestation . . . good. This must be it."

He hit the button. They waited, watching the antiquated hourglass on the screen, until the display told them in demure letters, "No infestation located. Your house is free of vermin!"

"Maybe it wouldn't consider one mouse an infestation?" Meredith asked forlornly.

"Damned if I know. Probably would, though. Now what?"

"Um . . . does it keep a record of what happens in the house? Security stuff—maybe it's got Patty's escape on film?"

"And it's been following her around with a little mouse cam ever since, and she's being featured on ScoopNet even as we speak. Right. Merry, we disabled the internal security cameras, remember? You didn't want them, because you didn't want anyone to be able to hack in. Everything's concentrated on the grounds and perimeters."

"Okay, okay, but the infrared sensors are on and mice are hot, Kevin, I mean they have really fast metabolisms, and—"

"Right. Got it. Infrared scan, although that's probably how the vermin scan we did just worked, so I doubt it's going to find anything. Here we go."

The internal infrared scan showed themselves and Nicholas, still curled in bed. "Do an external," Meredith said.

"Won't help," Kevin said. "Too many birds and squirrels and field mice and voles and stuff. You'll never sort it all out. If Patty's outside, we're not getting her back. Honey, listen, I have to get to work. You'd better start thinking about how to break this to Nicholas."

"Oh, Kevin!"

"I know." He stood up and kissed her, caressing the small of her back. "But all things are possible with a good night's sleep."

"If we don't find Patty, this may be the last one I get."

"I know." He kissed her again. "Good luck. Let me know what happens. I'll get another mouse on my way home if you want. Bye."

"Bye," Meredith said, feeling dangerously close to tears, and sat down in the chair he'd just vacated. Meditate. Meditate. You have to be calm for Nicholas, and maybe if you can clear your head you'll figure out where Patty might be. Visualize mouse. Happy mouse. Healthy mouse. Mouse eating a mouse treat somewhere we can sneak up on her and get her back in her cage, with a hermetic seal on the top this time.

"Mommy," said a small voice. Meredith opened her eyes and found Nicholas, looking impossibly little, standing in the doorway to Kevin's study. She swallowed, knowing she had to keep her voice calm and cheerful.

"Good morning, sweetheart! You certainly had a nice long sleep!"

"Yes," Nicholas said. "Can I sit in your lap, Mommy?"

"Of course you can." She'd thought he'd want to see Patty again as soon as he woke up, but she was getting some kind of reprieve, thank Goddess. "I'm glad you slept well, Nicky. Were the monsters gone?"

"Yes."

"I thought they were, because you didn't wake up in the middle of the night. It must have felt good to sleep so well." And now she was going to have to give him bad news. It wasn't fair.

He nodded. "It felt good. Mommy, do you still love me?"

What? What new hell was this? She hugged him fiercely and said, "Of *course* I love you, Nicky. Of course I do. What made you think I didn't?"

"That's good. Can I have another mouse, Mommy?"

Another mouse? Did that mean that he knew Patty was gone? Maybe he'd already looked in the cage? But then surely he'd ask Meredith where she was. Or maybe he just wanted another mouse as company for Patty? And if he didn't already know about Patty, where in all of this was she going to tell him? Well, when in doubt, ask. "Why do you want another mouse, Nicky?"

"Because of the monsters," he said.

Which didn't exactly answer the question. Did he know, or not? If he didn't know and found out Patty was gone, he'd think the monsters had gotten her. Great. "Nicholas," she asked carefully, "how many mice do we need to keep the monsters away? How many mice will work?"

"One," he said. "They ate Patty. Now they want another one."

Green-growing Gaia. I am not in this video I am not in this video I am not—Meredith forced down panic. Think. Think. He knew Patty was gone. What to say? "Honey, I'm sure the monsters didn't eat Patty. I'm sure she just got out of her cage and she's having wonderful adventures somewhere. If we get another mouse, we'll make sure she doesn't get out of her cage. We'll make sure we can keep her. But Patty—"

"The monsters ate her," he said crossly. "I *know*, Mommy. I fed her to them."

She stared at him. "You fed—"

"How did you *think* she got out of the cage?" he demanded. "She didn't move the top herself. She's too little." He scowled, and then said, "But you still love me, right?"

"Of course." Meredith's head was throbbing. Stay calm. Yes, of course: that's why the top of the cage had been loose. "Nicholas, tell me how you fed Patty to the monsters." Maybe he was speaking metaphorically. Maybe he just meant that he'd let Patty go into the dark, where he thought the monsters lived. Except that the monsters lived in his head; he'd told her that much himself.

"She was going to get eaten by a snake!" he said fiercely. "The snake wouldn't pat her. It wouldn't give her a yummy apple. I was nice to Patty. I patted her. The monsters were hungry. You make friends with monsters by giving them something to eat."

Think. Think. "Nicholas, couldn't you give the monsters an apple? Like you gave Patty?"

"They don't *like* apples. They want things that wiggle."

Back up, she thought frantically. Back up. You still don't know what happened. You don't know what he's talking about. "Nicky, I'm confused. Will you tell me what happened? Every bit of it? From the beginning?"

"We went to the pet store—"

"Yes, honey, I know we went to the pet store. What happened after that?"

"You said the beginning!"

"I meant—I meant the beginning of what I don't know. Tell me what happened last night, Nick. Tell me why you let Patty out of her cage."

"To feed her to the monsters."

And around we go. Meredith closed her eyes. "Nicholas, tell me exactly what you did, okay? You lifted the top off the cage . . ."

He sighed, loudly, exasperated. "I climbed up on a stool and I took the top off the cage. And then I picked Patty up by her tail like you taught me. And then I went into the kitchen and got the knife we used to cut the apples. And then I took Patty into the bathroom and cut her up for the monsters."

Meredith swallowed, hard, willing herself not to be sick. How could she and Kevin not have heard anything? How could Nicholas have been so quiet? She must have been so sleep-deprived that nothing but Nicholas's screams would have woken her. Thank Gaia, Kevin hadn't woken up, either. He didn't know anything. She had to keep him from finding out. She had to—"Where's Patty now, Nicholas?"

"On a plate under my bed. For the monsters to eat."

"Show me."

"If the monsters ate her, she's not *there* anymore, Mommy."

Meredith closed her eyes again. She had no idea how to handle this. None. She didn't know what to do, and there was no one she could ask, because children were being brainwiped. She should have kept Nicholas on the meds. If she'd kept him on the meds, maybe this wouldn't have happened. But he hadn't been himself on the meds: he'd been a zombie.

And he'd be a zombie if he were brainwiped. She remembered the question she'd asked herself when Raji died. *How could you stand the idea of losing your child?* You couldn't, that's how. She'd do anything to keep that from happening, which meant she had to stay calm. And think. "Let's go get the plate, Nicholas, okay?"

"Okay," he said, and took her hand and led her into his room.

The plate was white china, part of the set Gwyn and Dave had sent Merry and Kevin as a wedding gift. In the middle of it lay Patty, slit down the stomach, entrails neatly arranged around her. Oh, Goddess. Oh, sweet Gaia, help me. Meredith, knees weak, collapsed into a shaky crouch on the carpet, trying to push back images of Raji, Raji getting dissected by bots, Raji cut into—

No. No. Stay in the present, Meredith. Think. Think.

At least the plate was china, nonporous. It could be cleaned. At least there weren't any stains on the rug. The bathroom had looked clean that morning. *Where was the knife?* She stifled hysterical laughter and said, "Nicholas—"

"They didn't eat her," he said, frowning. "Mommy, why didn't they eat her?"

"Nicholas, it's wrong to kill animals. It's wrong. Patty never hurt you. She was a sweet little mouse."

"She was going to get eaten by a snake, anyway! Snakes need to eat too! You said so! You told Grandma that!"

Snakes are alive. Monsters aren't. How could she tell him that? The monsters were alive to him. They'd been keeping him awake for months. I need help, I need help, but I can't ask for help because they'll brainwipe him oh sweet Gaia my little boy, my baby. What am I going to do?

She put her arms around him, around his small, solid body, and hugged very hard. "Honey, Nicholas sweetheart—"

"If we had a snake," he said, "if we had a snake and we fed it a mouse it wouldn't be wrong, Mommy, right?"

Right. But this is different. How could she explain it to him? Thank Goddess they didn't have interior security cameras, thank Goddess there was no permanent record of this. Thank you, sweet Goddess, he hadn't killed Patty outside, where the cameras would have recorded all of it. Where was the knife? She had to get the knife back.

Breathe. Breathe. "That's right, Nicholas. If we had a snake it would be outside your head. It would be in the world. And then it would be okay to feed a mouse to the snake; the snake needs food that's in the world too. But the monsters aren't in the world; they're in your head. You have to feed them—you have to feed them in your head, honey, in your mind."

"They didn't eat her," he said, frowning, staring down at the tiny dissected corpse.

Meredith swallowed. "No. Not in the world, they didn't. But the dreams stopped, right? The monsters didn't bother you last night."

"Because I fed them Patty. They promised me they wouldn't bother me if I fed them Patty. They told the truth, Mommy."

Bile flooded Meredith's mouth. She swallowed again and said thickly, "They didn't need to eat her in the world. That's why she's still here. You fed them to her in your head too, because whatever your body's doing, your brain has to be thinking about it at the same time. That's why they left you alone. The part in your head—thinking about feeding them—that was enough, Nicholas. You didn't need to kill her."

"But they *told* me to. And thinking about it before never made them go away, Mommy. I thought about it a lot. That never made them happy."

Be calm be calm be calm. Meredith released the boy, held him at arm's length, and looked him straight in the eyes, as if her gaze could somehow bore into his head and remove whatever was hurting him so badly. "Nicholas, it's *not* okay. Do you hear me? You can't kill any more animals. We'll find some other way to make those monsters go away. We'll feed them something else, we'll find some other way to make them be quiet, but, baby, you can't kill anything else. That's murder, do you understand me? Murder's a soul crime, Nicholas. It's, it's a crime against the planet."

"Not if you eat what you kill! Matt said so, Mommy!"

He'd been talking to Matt? Oh, sweet Goddess. She reached out and grasped his shoulders again, squeezing until he flinched; she forced herself to let go, remembering Constance squeezing her just that way in Dr. Honoli's office, so many years ago. *If I'd been able to have my own baby, this wouldn't be happening.*

No. He was her child, her very own child, her son. He was her child, no matter where he'd come from, because she loved him. She loved the good in him, the sweetness that lay under all this horror, that could conquer and transform the horror, surely, if only she could find some way to help him.

Be calm. But she couldn't be calm as she asked, "When, Nicholas? When did Matt say that? Did you tell him about Patty?"

"No, Mommy! We only got Patty yesterday. I saw Matt at Temple class. He told us about the people who lived here a long time ago and how they hunted animals and it was okay because they ate the animals, and they thanked the animals for feeding them. I thanked Patty, Mommy. I did. I thanked her for feeding the monsters."

"Nicholas, did you *like* killing Patty? Did you enjoy it?"

"No. It was yucky and she squeaked. She wiggled too much. But she's just food."

Oh, Gaia. She wanted to slap him. She mustn't slap him, mustn't hurt a child. She clenched her fists together on her lap and said as steadily as she could, "Nicholas, she's not just food! She was alive and we loved her. She was part of our family, even if just for a little while. And she never hurt you, but it hurt her to be killed, Nicholas. That's why she squeaked and wiggled. The monsters hurt you. If you could kill the monsters instead, wouldn't that be better?"

He started to cry. "I can't. I can't. They're bigger than I am and they're in my head and if they die then my head—"

"Oh, baby." She reached out to hold him again, rocking him. "Don't you worry. I'm bigger than those monsters. I'll find a way to kill them, I will, I promise you. And then you won't have to kill any more sweet mice, Nicholas, okay?"

He sniffled. "You can't. You can't see them. They're in my head."

"Don't you worry. We'll get them out of there. We'll get them out of there and we'll kill them or maybe—maybe we won't have to. Maybe we can make them happy somehow. Maybe we can find them a home and they won't be monsters anymore, they'll be happy and they'll help you."

"Oh. Can I have another mouse?"

"No!" It came out as a scream. He flinched again, paling, and Meredith said more quietly, "No, Nicholas. Not until we take care of those monsters. It wouldn't be safe for another mouse here until the monsters are gone." She stood up, her arm around him, gingerly balancing the china plate in her free hand. What in the name of the Goddess were they going to do with Patty? Put her in the garbage or flush her down the john? Every bit of garbage in the city was monitored. If a mutilated animal showed up in the sewer, it would be traced. "We're going to bury Patty, Nicholas.

We're going to give her a funeral, because she was a nice little mouse and she must have been so scared when she died, and dying must have hurt her so much, and we need to tell her we're sorry."

"Okay," Nicholas said, subdued. "Where are we going to bury her, Mommy?"

Good question. They couldn't do it outside: anything that happened on the grounds was archived by the security cameras. But they couldn't exactly have a mouse corpse rotting in the house, either. "Nicholas, you know the avocado pit we've been growing, the one in the glass of water in the kitchen? It has enough roots for us to plant it now. I think we should bury Patty in a great big flowerpot and plant the avocado in there too. That way she'll be helping the avocado grow. And then we can put the pot outside, and Patty and the avocado will get fresh air and sunlight. Okay?"

"Okay."

"Okay." She took a deep breath. "Sweetie, where's the knife? Where did you put it?"

Nicholas looked down at his feet, scuffing his toes in the carpet. "It's dirty, Mommy."

"I know, Nicholas. Where is it?"

"I put it in my drawer. I wrapped it in a sock. Would you clean it for me?"

Sweet Goddess. She was going to have to do a count of all the knives from now on, hide anything sharp, and how was she going to explain all that to Kevin? And how would she ever use that knife in the kitchen again? She'd get sick. "Nicholas, you know what we're going to do? We're going to bury the knife and the sock in the flowerpot with Patty. To show that you're not going to kill any more animals, do you understand?" Kevin wouldn't miss one knife from the kitchen, and she'd watch the flowerpot to make sure Nicholas didn't dig it up.

He put his thumb in his mouth, and said around it, "Okay, Mommy."

Now the hard part. She took a very deep breath. Mustn't lie to a child. Mustn't teach children to lie. *How could you stand the idea of losing your child?* You couldn't. You did whatever was necessary, even if the child hadn't grown in your own womb, your maternal instinct growing as it did. That was how you proved that you were a good mother. That was how you proved you'd been right to adopt a baby about whom no one knew anything. "Okay Nicholas, another thing—honey, I don't want you to tell anybody about any of this, okay? It's very important."

"Because I was bad."

Yes. Exactly. "Because—because the monsters are bad, and I know the difference between you and the monsters, but other people might not. And they might get scared of you instead of the monsters, and that wouldn't be fair." And they'd brainwipe you.

"I'm not a monster."

"No," she said, her heart breaking. After Raji died, she'd thought her heart was as broken as it could get. She'd been wrong. "You aren't a monster. The monsters are monsters. You're Nicholas. Now let's go bury Patty, okay?"

"Okay. What about Daddy?"

Nicholas, she thought grimly, conspiracy comes entirely too easily to you. And to me too. Help me. Help me. "We'll just tell Daddy that we found Patty and she was dead and we buried her. Okay?" It wasn't even that big a lie. And somehow she'd have to keep Kevin from following through on his offer to get another mouse. Well, she'd tell him that the whole incident had been too traumatic; that wasn't that big a lie, either. She couldn't tell him what had really happened. If he reported Nicholas, the child would be brainwiped. Meredith would never forgive Kevin if that happened. She'd lose Kevin too. She couldn't lose both of them. And she couldn't ask Kevin to share the secret. She had to do this by herself.

"Can we use the flowerpot with the moon and stars on it, Mommy?"

"Sure," she said, relieved. "Sure we can."

Much later, after they had given Patty a properly solemn funeral, burying her in the flowerpot and then putting it outside, on the sweetly fragrant earth between the lavender bush and the lilac trees, Meredith sat inside the house, shivering, trying to think. Nicholas was building another tower, piling block on block as calmly as if he hadn't arisen in the middle of the night to slaughter a living creature.

She had to find out what was going on. And she had to keep anyone else from finding out, or even from knowing what questions she was asking. She had to bear this alone, because Nicholas would be in too much danger if anyone else knew. They'd give him CV again; they'd brainwipe him. She had to find some other way to fix him. Once he was fixed, she could talk about it. Once he was fixed, she could curl up sobbing in Kevin's arms, in her mother's lap. They'd tell her she'd been a good mother. They'd tell her she hadn't been wrong to adopt Nicholas, wrong to love Nicholas. They'd tell her they loved her. But for now, no one could know.

Think, Merry. Think. She couldn't think here, where Patty had been murdered. She had to get out of the house. "Hey, Nicky, would you like to go to the library?" She could do research at the library.

He looked up. "The library, Mommy? To read books?"

"Yes, you can read books, Nicky. And you can play with bots." There were educational bots there, bots who freed parents to browse the shelves by reading to children, or praising children who read to them.

Nicholas smiled. It was a shameless bribe, the first time she'd ever suggested that he play with bots, instead of trying to get him more interested in other kinds of toys. "Okay, Mommy! Let's go!"

Please, Goddess, she thought. Don't let him try to dissect any of the bots at the library.

Three hours later, she was no closer to an answer than she'd been before. She'd done a frantic Web search while Nicholas, behind her, read *Bitsy Byte's Virtual Adventure* to an effusively complimentary bot with a chirpy voicechip—"Very good, Nicholas! What a good reader you are!"—and then had *Bitsy Byte's Cyber-Birthday* read to him, and then played with blocks. After that, amazingly, he had curled up on a large pillow in the children's corner and gone to sleep, while the bot sang lullabies to him. He was being a model child. Should she get him his own bot? Would having a bot at home help? But she hated them; her skin crawled watching him with this one, and she had to live at her house too.

Which do you hate more, Meredith? Bots, or dissected mice?

She stared despairingly at the monitor in front of her. Everything she had read indicated that homicidal tendencies in children were most commonly the result of brain damage combined with severe childhood abuse. Nicholas's brain damage was the same kind she had, and she wasn't killing mice. And Nicholas hadn't been abused. His infancy had been unusual, certainly, but he had received a great deal of focused, nurturing attention from the people in the hospital, even if they had worn isosuits while they gave it to him. She herself was, doubtless, not perfect as a parent, but she had never even spanked Nicholas, much less burned him with cigarettes or thrown him against walls or committed any of the other atrocities so frequently suffered by children who grew up to be killers. When he tried to hurt himself, she stopped him. Could he have given himself brain damage somehow when she wasn't watching? Had he been bashing his head into things when she wasn't awake, wasn't looking? But there would have been scars, bruises, and there hadn't been.

She sat shivering in front of the monitor. Nightmares, persecution by monsters, bedwetting, and now the torture and murder of small animals. Kids like that turned into adults who made clothing from human skin, even in the twenty-first century, even in the era of isosuits and AIs. Dear Goddess, what was she going to do? Any of the child behaviorists she might consult knew the signs as well as she did. And if anyone found out, Nicholas would be brainwiped, and everything would be gone: the good as well as the bad, the sweet boychild as well as the damaged creature who killed mice. *How could you stand the idea of losing your child?*

Breathe, she thought, and forced herself to be calm. Brainwiping was already coming under serious legal scrutiny from people like Holly O'Riley. It would be outlawed soon, surely, surely, and in the meantime no one else would know about Nicholas. No one else would know, if she could help it, not even Kevin; especially not Kevin, who'd never wanted Nicholas to begin with. Once brainwiping was outlawed, she'd get help for Nicholas. Then, even if he was taken away from her, at least his identity wouldn't be annihilated.

"Ma'am?" Meredith jumped, and looked up to find a smiling librarian next to her. "I just wanted to let you know we're closing in a few minutes."

"Thank you," Meredith said, annoyed. Couldn't they just have made an announcement? Didn't the place have a PA system?

The librarian lingered next to her chair, looking oddly at Meredith. Oh, Goddess. Had Nicholas done something? Merry turned, but he was still blissfully asleep on his pillow. What did this woman want? "I'll be leaving in just a minute," Merry said, and the librarian cleared her throat.

"You're, um, aren't you Meredith—"

"Yes," Meredith said. "I am. I'm leaving now. I don't mean to be rude, but—"

"I'm sorry." The librarian turned red. "I'm sorry, I know you value your privacy; I shouldn't have said anything. I just wasn't sure."

"That's all right," Meredith said, with her best frosty smile. ScoopNet had, once again, been leaving her alone since the five minutes' wonder of Nicholas' adoption; she wondered why the librarian was interested enough to have recognized her. The woman must be someone who'd seen Meredith coming out of iso, as Kevin had, or someone who'd watched Raji die.

Meredith didn't want to know. She had her own problems. "Have a nice evening," she said, as dismissively as she could.

The librarian got the message and scuttled away; Meredith got up to collect Nicky and go home. The librarian had been wearing a scarf. Was it covering rig jacks? If the woman was rigged, had she been watching Merry while she was on the computer? Had she seen anything, noticed what Merry was reading on the screen, even gotten a visual image? People with rigs could have their recorded memories subpoenaed; it had already happened in a few murder cases. If anything came out about Nicholas—

What about the bot Nicholas had been playing with? Was it web-linked? Would Preston know they'd been here? But she had GPS cells, so if he cared to check, he could track her anywhere. What was she going to tell him about why they'd gone to the library? Well, because Nicholas liked it. That was all he needed to know.

She knelt down next to Nicholas's pillow—the bot was nowhere in sight, praise be—and shook him awake. "Nicky? Time to go home now, sweetheart. Time to go home for dinner and see Daddy."

"Okay," he said, his voice fuzzy from sleep. "But I can't tell Daddy our secret."

Meredith tensed. Had the librarian heard that? No, she couldn't have; she was at the other end of the room, and everyone else had left already. Think. Think. Kevin's birthday was coming up: if anyone asked, Meredith would say the secret was about his birthday present. "That's right, Nicholas. The secret's just for us."

"He really liked that bot at the library," Kevin said after dinner. Nicholas was in bed, once again sound asleep, for a wonder. "He told me all about it."

"I know. I feel guilty for not getting him one, but—"

"But you hate them." He stroked her hair. "Well, it cheered him up about the mouse, anyway. It was a good idea, taking him to the library after that. Oh, Merry, don't cry, I know it's sad, but she must have been sick."

"I know." She wiped her nose, lies sticking in her throat like fishhooks. "I know. It was awful finding her, that's all. I just don't understand how she got out, and finding her dead like that . . ."

"Do you want to get him another one?"

"Not right away. Give him some time to mourn Patty."

"Okay. But listen, there's something else we need to talk about. I know you aren't going to like this, but it really is past time for him to be in school."

"I know." She closed her eyes. It was inevitable; it was also the worst possible time. "That's what Mom keeps saying too. I just—I'd rather keep homeschooling him."

"Honey, if we had other kids, it would be different, but he's awfully— well, isolated here. You know? And I thought that was the last thing you wanted for him."

"You're right," she said dully. "I'm just being selfish."

"If he goes to school, you'll get more of your own life back. You can work on your own projects again."

Meredith grimaced. "Do you have a particular school in mind?"

"Well, yeah." Kevin cleared his throat. "Here's the part you really won't like. I've been helping design an AI-enhanced preschool at work. It's just at the bottom of the hill here, and they're taking their first class in a few weeks. All the beta-testing's been fabulous, and by all accounts they have a great teacher. It will be a small group of kids, to start. Five kids, one teacher, the AI. I really think we should think about sending Nicholas there."

"An *AI*? Kevin!"

"*And* a teacher, *and* other kids. It's nearby. He'll get a lot of individual attention."

That's the last thing I want him to get. Especially from an AI. "I don't believe this! When did you turn soulfreak on me?"

"Merry, I haven't turned soulfreak! It's just a machine. It's just a teaching tool. Just think about it, okay? Wouldn't it be fun for you to have more free time?" He put a hand on her lips. "Don't say anything. Don't answer yet. Just think about it, all right?"

She thought about it after Kevin went to bed. Nicholas had to go to school; all right, but not that one. And she needed a hobby? Fine. She'd join the local chapter of CALM, Citizens for the Abolishment of Lobotomy Misuse, the group protesting brainwiping. Celebrities needed causes. Hers would be civil rights for criminals and the mentally ill.

Eighteen

C ALM was delighted to hear from her, as Meredith had known they would be. She told them that she had been touched by the plight of the baggies, the brainwiped homeless—true enough, since whenever she saw one now, she had a vivid image of Nicholas's possible future—and that as a CV survivor and the mother of a CV survivor, she couldn't sanction any supposedly therapeutic use of the virus. These two lines of attack were the accepted ones; she didn't have to invent any of it, and it wasn't even that big a lie.

She told them she'd start volunteering for them when her son started school. Kevin had made her promise that if she couldn't find another place she liked within three weeks, she'd enroll Nicholas at KinderkAIr. She'd thought that would give her plenty of time, but it turned out not to be that easy. The teachers at the Montessori school fawned over her too much, because she was Preston Walford's daughter; the day-care program at UCSF had too long a waiting list, and anyway, Nicholas was already intellectually far ahead of most of the children Meredith saw there. She told Matt and Constance that she didn't want to enroll Nicholas in the Temple School because he already knew most of those children, and the goal was to have him meet new people. The real reason was that there were too many animals at Temple. She couldn't trust Nicholas there, not until they got this thing straightened out.

Matt, at least, didn't buy it. "Merry, what's wrong? You're—closed down. As if you're grieving. You're trying to shut people out again. This isn't—"

"Nothing's wrong," she said, trying to smile and sound cheerful. "Everything's fine, Matt."

"If Nicholas is having problems—"

"Nicholas is just fine, but the goal's to expand his social horizons. I've told you that. I have to go now, Matt. I have an appointment to visit another school." She didn't—she was at the end of her list—but she couldn't stand the way Matt was looking at her.

"I think we should just go ahead with KinderkAIr," Kevin said one night before bed, two days before her deadline. He sat on the bed; she sat at the vanity brushing her hair. "We can always pull him out again if he doesn't like it, Merry, or if we don't. It's close, and we've got an in. No waiting list."

He knew as well as she did that Nicholas could have skipped over the waiting list at any school in the city, had Merry wanted him to. She'd told Kevin she didn't want to use her connections that way. "No. I'm not sending my son to a school run by an AI." The AI was MacroCorp property, which made it more likely that Preston would be watching too. Especially since he'd helped design the school.

"It's not *run* by an AI. There's a very competent human teacher."

"Forget it," Meredith said. "We're not living in Africa or Mexico, and as long as I have the luxury of being in the United States, I don't see why I should hand my child over to a machine."

"If you were in Africa or Mexico, you'd be handing your child over to a person, at least legally. Here it *is* just a machine. No one thinks otherwise. Come on, Merry, there are probably PCs there too, and they don't bother you."

"They don't presume to express opinions about child rearing," Meredith said, running the brush through her hair with unnecessary force. "I'm not sending him there. It's too much like where we found him."

"It's not a *bit* like where we found him! Merry, I helped design this place, okay? It's bright and cheery and airy and has plenty of access to the outside. There aren't any bots. There's a great teacher; the AI's mainly for safety stuff, because the teacher can't be looking everywhere every minute."

A Panopticon. Meredith, her stomach knotting, put the hairbrush down and closed her eyes. "What about the security issues?"

Kevin shrugged. "Nicholas has GPS cells, right? He's as safe as we are."

"That's not what I meant. The other kids will know who he is, the teacher will, the parents, and someone could talk to ScoopNet or sneak a spybot in or—or ScoopNet could spy through the web-link somehow."

Kevin stood and began pacing, always a bad sign. "Meredith, what's wrong with you? They can't sneak a spybot in that easily, not into a place with a security-equipped AI. That's the whole point. The AI won't permit Web intrusion, either. Come on, you know how nervous people are about Netpervs! They're not leaving this system open to hackers, believe me. There's a dedicated line to MacroCorp so the AI can send daily backup files; that's it." *Preston*, Meredith thought, dread pooling in her stomach. "And if somebody there talks, somebody talks. So what? People could talk to ScoopNet at any school. So ScoopNet reports that Nicholas likes red crayons better than green ones and eats Oreos at snack time instead of Fig Newtons. Who cares? If he stays here alone with you all the time he's going to turn into some kind of freak. We adopted him so that *wouldn't* happen, remember? And he's already had enough problems, poor kid!"

She couldn't tell him the truth. She couldn't tell him that Nicholas was already a freak. He'd say it was all her fault. He'd say they never should have brought Nicholas home in the first place. He'd say they should have kept Nicholas on the medication. She bent her head and said, "I have another two days. Just let me look around at a few more places."

"You've done that," he said. "You haven't found another place. And there's something else, Merry." He stopped pacing and stood looking down at her; she felt herself tense. "MacroCorp has a lot invested in this. If people know you've been looking at preschools and you don't send Nicholas to this one, they're going to want to know why. It's an, ah, PR issue. Remember those?"

Checkmate. She knew at once that she had been defeated. Kevin had been working on this school for months. He'd already decided, without her, that it was where they were sending Nicholas, just as she had decided, without Kevin, four years ago, that Nicholas would be their son. She wasn't going to win this one, and she knew it, just as Kevin had known he wouldn't win on the adoption issue.

Feeling ill, she looked away from him and said, "What was the rest of it for, then? Why did you even let me look at other places?"

"Because, believe it or not, I want you to be happy." His voice was very sad. "Now look. I want to go check out KinderkAIr with you on Monday, the two of us together, okay? It's not formally open yet, but there are some kids there, anyway—they're not paying yet—so prospective parents can see how everything works, how the teacher and the AI get along with the kids."

She took a deep breath. Even if she saved Nicholas, could she save her marriage? Too much to think about. Too much loss. "Okay," she said. "Okay." Fear and failure burned her throat, stung her eyes.

Kevin sighed. "Oh, Merry, please don't cry! That's all you do these days. You keep telling me nothing's wrong, and the whole time you act like you're having a nervous breakdown."

"I don't know what's wrong," she said, trying to sound normal. She couldn't deny her weepiness; it was too obvious. If he had any idea how much crying she did when he wasn't home, he'd have her brainwiped on the spot. "Hormones, maybe. Although we know I can't be pregnant."

"Merry," Kevin said, his voice gentling. "Love, you're still grieving that, aren't you? Look, you need to spend more time with adults. You've been cooped up with Nicholas too much, and it isn't good for either of you."

"If you say so."

"And I think you should talk to somebody. Maybe take some meds for a while. You're depressed, that's all. It's common enough."

She swallowed, feeling the net of lies tighten around her. If she went to talk to someone, she'd have to lie again. She'd have lied to someone else. She didn't know what to do. Could she tell Kevin the truth? She wanted to, but she couldn't. She couldn't. He'd never really wanted Nicholas in the first place, and even if he agreed with her that they had to keep it quiet, she'd only be involving him. It was her burden. For Nicholas's sake if nothing else, she couldn't ask anyone else to bear it. Not even Kevin.

"Okay," she heard herself saying. "I'll strike a deal with you. You're right: I know I'm depressed. But let me try my own ways of getting out of it for a while, okay? And if I don't get better, then I'll go to a doctor."

"Your own ways? Like what?"

"Exercise," she said. "Temple. More time on my own projects, like this CALM thing, away from Nicholas." Her biggest project would be trying to help Nicholas, but Kevin didn't have to know that. "If I'm not better in a few months, I'll see whomever you say. All right?"

"All right," he said, and brushed her hair away from her face with his hand. The tenderness of the gesture made her eyes fill with tears. How long had it been since he'd done that? And if he knew how glibly she was lying to him, he'd never do it again. Cautiously, she let the old bubble of security, the Meredith-and-Kevin bubble, surround her again. Such safety. How she yearned for a safe world!

"Nicholas wants another mouse," Kevin said casually. "He said so last night."

The bubble burst. No more animals. No more animals, not until the monsters were gone: Nicholas knew that. But he'd gone behind her back and asked his father. How could she justify to Kevin not getting another mouse for Nicholas? And if they didn't get another one, what would Nicholas do next?

"He said he wanted a black mouse," Kevin said. "Or a pure white one. Because he'd already had a brown and white one."

"Fine," Meredith said, trying to keep the pain out of her voice. People killed mice every day: for research, to feed snakes. Face reality, she told herself: if you don't get him another mouse, he'll do the same thing to something else, maybe something bigger, a bird, a cat, another kid. And if you tell anyone, he'll get the same thing done to him. Get him the mouse. Sacrifice the mouse until you can figure out what the hell this thing is and stop it. And yet she felt the tears coming again, and knew that Kevin saw them.

"Merry?"

"I'm fine," she said, and forced herself to smile, and felt her soul crack as she did. Nothing she'd done so far was working.

She and Nicholas had developed a secret bedtime ritual. Every night Kevin read Nicholas a story, and then it was Merry's turn. While Kevin took his evening shower, Meredith sat with Nicholas while he crayoned the monsters he was afraid he would see when he went to sleep. They were huge, inchoate scrawls of every color in the crayon box, so many colors that no one hue stood out, except for the crimson eyes. Every night, Meredith ceremonially drew a huge black X over the monsters, and then tore the drawing into tiny bits while she and Nicholas recited a blessing together:

"I'm safe from everything scary
The monsters have all gone away.

The Goddess who made me protects me.
I'm braver and stronger each day."

The ritual was of dubious value. Nicholas's cries no longer woke Meredith and Kevin, but every morning when Meredith went into Nicholas's room to wake him up for breakfast, she discovered him already awake, huddled beneath his blankets with his eyes wide open and the sheets he lay on wet. Every morning, he looked up at her and said in a tiny voice, "I'm sorry, Mommy."

"Honey, you don't have to be sorry. You didn't do anything wrong."

"I wet the bed again."

"That's just because you were scared," she said; every time she said it, she thought of Hortense, of Gwyn saying, *I hope the Goddess never favors you with children.* "Did the monsters come back, Nicky?"

Every morning he nodded, miserably, sometimes adding, "But I didn't yell, because I didn't want to wake you up. I was brave, Mommy, right?"

"Yes, Nicky. You were very brave. You're my brave boy. You're fighting those monsters, and you'll win."

But he wasn't winning. More time, she told herself, he just needed more time. It had been only a few weeks since Patty died. She just had to buy Nicholas more time. If he was brainwiped, he'd lose for good, and so would she: she'd lose everything. She'd lose Nicholas and she'd lose Kevin, because he'd discover how much she hadn't been telling him. As much as she hated seeing Nicholas this tortured, that would be worse: to have him gone, to lose him and Kevin and her dream of a safe life, her dream of shelter.

The Wednesday night Meredith agreed to visit KinderkAIr, there were no pictures or prayers in Nicholas's room, only fierce whispers from Mommy: "No, you are not getting another mouse. Don't ask Daddy for another mouse. It's not okay, Nicholas. You can't kill anything else!"

He nodded, but wouldn't answer, and the next morning he woke up screaming again. She sat on his bed and hugged him, feeling her tears blend with his own. "Nicky, baby, I'm so sorry, I shouldn't have scolded you last night. We should have drawn the pictures, I'm so sorry, we'll draw them again tonight, okay? We'll never not draw them again. I promise. I promise. I love you, Nicholas."

❧

They went back to drawing pictures. The weekend was free of screams, although the bed-wetting continued. Merry woke up on Monday morning feeling as if she were going to a funeral. She could hear Kevin whistling in the kitchen, could smell bacon and coffee. "So, Nicky, Grandma's going to come over and play with you while Mommy and I visit a school you might go to, okay?"

Merry felt her stomach clench. Nicholas was already up. Had he wet the bed? Did Kevin know about it? Would Nicholas behave in front of Constance? Kevin had made the baby-sitting arrangements; she couldn't possibly tell him that she didn't want Nicholas spending time with his grandmother, who'd inevitably compare him with Theo. Theo, the golden boy, the perfect child who proved that Constance was a better mother than Meredith. Theo had never hit his head against the wall. Theo had never murdered mice. Meredith loved Theo; she also hated him.

She scrambled out of bed and threw on a robe, listening for the child's voice from the kitchen. "I'm going to school, Daddy? Like Theo?"

"That's right, just like Theo. Would you like that, Nicholas?"

"Theo says school's fun. Will Mommy come with me?"

"No, you won't need Mommy there, because you're a big boy now, and you'll make lots of friends. But the school's just down the stairs, Nicky, just at the bottom of the hill, so you can come home for lunch if you want to."

Meredith padded quietly into Nicholas's room; the bed had been stripped. Kevin must have found the sheets. Why hadn't she woken up before he did? Because she was exhausted, that's why. From the kitchen, she heard Kevin say, "You know, Nicholas, I wet the bed sometimes when I was a little boy too. It's all right. Everyone does that sometimes," and her knees nearly buckled in relief. Thank you, Goddess. Maybe Kevin didn't suspect anything.

KinderkAIr was sunny and bright and cheerful, full of activity: a little girl reading in a corner with help from the teacher, a little boy using VR gear to learn to ride a tricycle, a second little girl playing with Legos while the fourth child, a boy, colored with crayons at a table. "See?" Kevin said. "Happy kids." He and the marketing director, a woman with flowing clothing and too much perfume, exchanged a smile. They've been talking behind my back, Meredith thought grimly. It's a conspiracy. But she was a fine one to accuse anyone else of conspiracies. "Nicholas will be happy here too."

As if on cue, crying broke out from the child who was playing with Legos. The teacher, a stocky dark-skinned woman in a faded sweatshirt and jeans, detached herself from the girl who was reading and picked her way through wooden blocks and pieces of Lego to the source of the wailing. "Hey," she said, and knelt down next to the bawling girl. "Hey, Cindy, what's wrong?" Her voice was rich and pleasant, soothing; she could have been a singer. Meredith couldn't hear the child's answer, but she watched the teacher cuddle and comfort until the little girl was content again.

"What does the AI do?" Meredith said. Kevin had told her over and over that the AI was just a pair of eyes, just a tool, but she wanted to hear what these people said for themselves.

"We'll let Fred answer that himself," the marketing director said. "Fred?"

"I help out here in many ways," said an androgynous, calm voice. Meredith jumped and looked around to see where it was coming from, and then realized that the woman who'd been comforting Cindy was watching her a tad too intently. She looked away, unnerved. The AI's voice seemed to come from the walls; there was no one point to focus on. "I read to the children. I play interactive games with them. I watch them carefully for signs of illness or unhappiness." Meredith's stomach tightened.

The marketing director beamed. "Fred's been patterned after a twentieth-century child development expert. There's no finer day-care software available, but of course we rely mainly on Bobbie. Let me introduce you."

The teacher had stood up, leaving Cindy to her Legos, and picked her way back through the toys. Now she held out her hand. "Roberta Danton," she said. Did her voice sound cold now? Why would it? Meredith must have been imagining things. "I'm the human help."

"Bobbie's very good with the children," the executive director said, simpering.

"I go by Berta," Roberta said firmly.

"Berta?" said a small voice next to them. "Cookies?"

"Soon," Roberta said, and knelt down to pick up the little boy who'd been riding the tricycle. When she straightened up again, she said, "We look forward to meeting Nicholas. You should really bring him here for a few hours, you know, to see how he likes it. Stay with him for a while, then go and have lunch and come back and see how he's doing. Good trial run for everybody." She was watching Meredith appraisingly, and Merry fought a rush of panic.

"Of course you need to see how he behaves away from us," Kevin said, and Meredith's stomach tightened still more.

Roberta smiled politely. "Oh, most of the time the separation's harder on the parents than it is on the kids."

From the other side of the room, Fred said calmly, "Steven, you can share those Lego pieces with Cindy. There are enough for both of you."

"*Mine!* My Legos!"

"No, Steven, they're *my* Legos. They belong to me and to Roberta and to the people who run the school, and we're all letting you play with them, but only if you let Cindy play too."

"That's right," Roberta called back over her shoulder. "Steven, share. Okay?" Steven was the boy who'd been coloring at the table; from the look of him, he was about to go into a full-fledged temper tantrum.

"Steven," Fred said, "remember how Zillinth gave you a piece of her cookie on Wednesday? The oatmeal cookie? That really was just hers, because she'd brought it from home, but she let you have some, anyway. That's what sharing is. And now I want you to share the Legos to show me what a smart boy you are. I want you to show me that you know what the word *share* means. Can you spell share for me? I know you're good at spelling."

"C-H-A-R-E," Steven said, brightening.

"It starts with an *S*," said Fred, "but everything else was right. Very good! Now act it out so I know you know what it means."

"Share," Steven said, and handed a Lego piece to Cindy.

Roberta, who'd been watching the interaction, said "Good boy, Steven," and turned back to Kevin and Meredith. "That's the advantage of having an AI here. Fred sees everything. I didn't see Zillinth sharing her cookie the other day, and even if I had, I might not have remembered, and even if I'd remembered, I might not have thought to use it as an example that way, or to appeal to Steven's vanity over his vocabulary and work in a spelling lesson to boot. Fred's *great*. He never gets tired, never loses his patience, never raises his voice. The kids love him."

"Him?" Meredith asked harshly.

Roberta raised an eyebrow. "Figure of speech. Although it's hard not to think of him—er, Fred—as a person."

"Thank you," Fred said. "I like you too, Roberta."

Roberta and the marketing director laughed; Kevin smiled. Meredith felt as if she were about to be ill. "Really. So why have an actual person here?"

"Oh, for things Fred can't do. Hugs, wiping kids' faces, helping them tie their shoes. Putting on Band-Aids. You know." Roberta was still watching Meredith too closely; Merry felt claustrophobic. Relax, she told herself. It's just because you're famous. She's curious about you. Plenty of people at the other schools stared too. But this felt different, somehow. Because of the AI.

"Doesn't it bother you, being watched by a machine all day?" Meredith knew that her voice was too cold and too high; Kevin was frowning.

Roberta shook her head. "No. I thought it might, at first, but really, I don't feel that way at all now. The extra eyes are incredibly useful, and Fred and I get along very well." She shrugged. "Although, of course, it's bound to be a comfort to many parents that whoever works here is being watched."

From the wall just to their left, Fred said in its soothing voice, "Roberta is excellent with the children."

"Thank you, Fred," said Roberta, and the marketing director showed another mouthful of teeth. Meredith shuddered. "So, tell me, is there anything special we should know about Nicholas?"

Meredith felt her eyes filling with tears. You need to know that he loves peanut butter and hot dogs, that he's afraid of the dark, that when he goes to sleep he wakes up screaming from nightmares. You need to know that he hears voices and just dissected his pet mouse, and I can't tell you any of this because my husband's standing right here and I haven't told him any of it and if I tell you any of it, then he'll hate and distrust me and you'll be required by law to report it to people who will want to brainwipe Nicholas. You need to know that I really don't want you to know anything important about my son.

"He likes peanut butter and hot dogs," she heard herself saying. "His favorite color is red." Please, please, take good care of my baby, but whatever you do, don't watch him too closely. Fat chance. Fred saw everything, Roberta had said, and that meant MacroCorp would see it too. Nicholas was doomed. What was she going to do?

"We don't want him to receive special attention or treatment," Kevin said. "We want him to be treated just like any other child. No publicity. No intrusions into our privacy. You understand?"

"Of course," said the marketing director, but Meredith thought she saw Roberta's eyes narrow slightly. She thinks he's just another spoiled kid, Meredith thought. Dear Goddess, let her keep thinking so.

"You hated it," Kevin said, the minute they were out the door. "I've never seen you be so rude."

"I'm sorry, Kevin. The AI creeps me out. It's bad enough they have one, but then they have to *name* it? Fred, of all things? Why can't they just call it R2-D2, or something?"

"So the kids won't be scared of it. So everyone will have a convenient way to talk to the AI. And Fred's the guy you saw on TV when you were sick. The guy who was singing. That's why your father picked that name."

"My *father* picked the name?" Meredith shook her head. "What guy? What are you talking about?"

Kevin sighed. "When you were in iso, Merry, there was a guy singing a song on TV. Your father told me you always sang that song afterwards."

"Oh. The guy in the blue cardigan." *Please don't think it's funny when you want the ones you miss.* They were on the Filbert steps now; Meredith welcomed the exertion. Step. Step. Step. Don't let Kevin see you cry.

"Yeah. That one. He was famous last century—kids loved him, found him very comforting, which is why the hospital played that tape for CV kids. Anyway, your father figured you must have found him comforting too, since you kept singing that song, so he tracked it down. The guy's name was Fred. He had a TV show; kids loved it, even though most adults thought it was sappy. So when it was time to choose a name for the day-care center AI, that's the one your father picked."

Merry swallowed. "Is that supposed to make me feel better? It's not exactly the happiest association."

"Well, you heard Roberta. The kids love Fred. So does she. I'm sure Nicholas will too. He likes bots, remember? You can't force your neuroses on him, Merry. And anyway, now you'll be able to get more exercise. And do your volunteer work. So maybe Fred will be a blessing for you too."

❧

Nicholas loved school. Kevin walked him there every morning, and Meredith picked him up every afternoon. Everyone but Merry seemed happy. Kevin became more affectionate again; Nicholas wet the bed less often. Merry was forced to concede, reluctantly, that maybe KinderkAIr had been the right choice, especially after Preston, during one of their rare conversations, assured her that there was no way for him to infiltrate the school. "The AI will not permit intrusion, Meredith, even from me. The staff must approve all visitors. But I do not understand why you are so concerned. I would like to spend more time with Nicholas. I hardly know him, and I know Theo well."

Meredith felt a pang. Preston truly seemed to enjoy his virtual grandfatherhood, or whatever it was; what would you call his relationship to his wife's son by another man? But then again, who *wouldn't* enjoy Theo? "Daddy, I'm not trying to hurt your feelings. I just want Nicky to get better at relating to—to actual flesh-and-blood people, that's all. He already likes bots and computers. Now he needs to learn to get along with other humans."

"I am legally human, Meredith."

Her heart sank. "I know that. But you're not physically human. And that's the issue here. Nicholas's time in isolation—"

"All right, Meredith. I cannot force a relationship upon you, or your son. But I am always here if you wish to speak to me."

Don't I know it, she thought. Sometimes she wondered if she was wrong not to confide more in Preston. Perhaps he would be able to find some way to help Nicholas, some method that had escaped her. But she was afraid to trust him. He didn't love the boy the way she did; no one did, not even Kevin. Everyone else thought she should have left Nicholas in the hospital. And whatever Preston's legal status, she just couldn't see him as fully human.

She was grimly aware of the irony. Most people who knew what Nicholas had done to Patty wouldn't see him as fully human, either. That's why they'd brainwipe him.

But for the moment, Nicholas was acting more or less like a normal child. He came home with pictures for Meredith to put on the refrigerator, with more colds than he had ever had before—since now he was around a group of other children—and with cheerful snippets of stories about his day. "Today Berta made chocolate chip cookies." "Today Fred showed me how to play checkers." "Today Berta brought in leaves and Fred told us how they grow."

Always Berta and Fred, Berta and Fred, as if there were no other children there at all. "What about the other kids?" Meredith asked. "What about Steven and Zillinth and Cindy and the other little boy, Nicholas? What's that other little boy's name? Benjamin? You play with them too, right?"

He shrugged. "I like Berta and Fred better. I can talk to them."

"Can't you talk to the other children?"

He shrugged. "All they want to do is play."

"You like to play, don't you?"

"Not with them," he said, lifting his tiny chin. "*I* like to play with Berta and Fred. They like me. They tell good stories. Do you know *The Hobbit,* Mommy?"

"Don't the other children like you?" Meredith asked, frowning. A good mother, she knew, would call the school and ask about this, request a conference. She wasn't going to. Even when she collected Nicholas after school—nearly every afternoon, whenever she didn't have to attend some CALM event instead—she hardly ever went inside. She waved at him through the window, and he'd come running to meet her. She knew Berta and Fred must think she was a hopeless snob; she didn't care. They'd call if there was trouble. Better to leave well enough alone.

Nicholas pondered for a moment, and then said gravely, "Berta and Fred like me better. Do you know *The Hobbit,* Mommy?"

"Sure," she said. "I read it when I was little. It's a great story. It's got dragons and treasure in it. Did Fred tell you that story?" She thought that *The Hobbit* was a bit advanced for four-year-olds, but no doubt Fred was telling them a watered-down version.

"Yes," he said. " 'In a hole in the ground there lived a Hobbit.' "

"Right," she said, startled as always by his memory. "And then what?"

He sighed. "I don't know. Why does the Hobbit live in a hole, Mommy? Instead of in a house?"

"Well, their holes are like houses, right? All snug and comfy? Isn't that the way the story goes?"

"In the book. What about the real ones?"

"The real ones?" Her heart sank. "Hobbits aren't real, Nicholas."

"They aren't?"

"No, they aren't. They're just a story."

"Oh," he said, and sighed again. "All right. I thought they were real. Like the people you help on TV." Meredith made a face. "Those people *are* real, Nicholas. They're sick. Hobbits are make-believe."

She wished the baggies were make-believe too. She hated her volunteer work even more than she hated sending Nicholas to school. The CALM people had crowed that someone as notoriously protective of her privacy as Meredith Walford-Lindgren was willing to make public appearances on behalf of the brainwiped; ScoopNet, little knowing how right they were, gushed about how motherhood had awakened previously untouched reserves of compassion in Meredith's heart. Meredith, playing the part, grimly wrote letters to politicians and made the obligatory smiling, chatty appearances on talk shows and newscasts. Inside she was terrified. *If anyone ever finds out about Nicholas, they'll know exactly why I'm doing this. They'll know I'm a fake.* The thought condensed into a core of dread she carried everywhere, the leaden conviction that this exhausting, draining charade was all that protected both her and Nicholas from annihilation. The more praise she received for her selfless activism, the more she felt like an imposter.

And the people who knew her best had already seen through it. Kevin and Constance had both told her, with shrugs, that her hobbies were her business, but that this one seemed out of character. Matt was more blunt. He pulled her aside during one of her increasingly rare visits to Temple and said, "So, Merry, what's with this CALM thing?"

"What?"

"You hate this kind of work. You always did. You tried to do it when you were at Temple and it didn't work, so why—"

"Matt, that was almost fifteen years ago! Give me some credit for being able to change!"

"People don't change that much, not that way. I might believe it if you seemed happy, but you don't."

"Matt, I'm fine. And if you'll forgive me for saying so, this is none of your business."

He stepped back, looking troubled. "If you feel it's not my business, then it's not. I'm sorry. I was worried about you, that's all."

"Don't. Don't be sorry, and don't worry. Everything's fine."

"If you decide that it's my business after all, will you come talk to me?"

"Of course," she said, and escaped.

But he was right; she hadn't changed. To her mortification, she found most baggies completely loathsome, even harder to bear than Hortense had been. Their smell nauseated her; she found much of their speech completely incomprehensible, their tattered and dirty clothing repellant. I am a spoiled, intolerant bitch, she told herself as, struggling not to gag, she served hot lunches to baggies in city shelters. She forced herself to look each one in the eyes, no matter how crazed or blank the eyes were, no matter how filthy the face and matted the hair around it. This person is as much a child of the Goddess as I am. I know that. This person has a mother, somewhere. Goddess, help me be loving. Help me. Pretend it's Nicholas. Pretend it's Nicholas. All she gained from the exercise was the thoroughly bleak conviction that if Nicholas were ever brainwiped and she encountered him on the streets as a baggie, she'd flee, vomiting, in the opposite direction.

Her media hosts continually asked her to bring Nicholas along to whatever event she was attending, but she steadfastly refused. She told them that Nicholas was too young to choose causes and activism, and that she wasn't going to push him into the public eye she'd tried to shelter him from. It was, for once, nearly the entire truth, underscored by her perpetual fear that if Nicholas was in public for too long, if someone took a picture at the wrong moment or asked the wrong question, his disturbance would be revealed. And how could she ask him to confront baggies? If she considered them repulsive, despite her most liberal beliefs and best intentions, how could she ask him to do otherwise? Instead, she used Nicholas to somewhat limit her appearances, and to flatly refuse any possibility of prolonged travel. She couldn't stay away from home overnight. She had to be there to tuck her son into bed. She had to be home each afternoon, whenever possible, to pick him up from school.

Parent-teacher day, the week after Nicholas's fifth birthday, came all too soon. Meredith dressed for the event as if for a wake; she couldn't just wave through the window this time. She had to go inside with Kevin and talk to Berta and Fred, and she dreaded what they'd surely say. Nicholas was antisocial, he was pathological, he was psychotic, he was a sick little boy. They haven't noticed, she told herself, surely they haven't noticed or they would have said something by now. We'd have gotten a call at home a long time ago, if they'd seen anything like what I've seen.

The first thing she saw when she walked into the room was a large glass fish tank, with cedar chips and an exercise wheel in it, along one wall. Oh, no. Oh, no. Meredith froze, vaguely aware of Kevin in the background— "Oh, look, Merry, look at all the decorations the kids made, how cute"— and then jumped when she heard Roberta's voice inches from her ear.

"What's wrong? You look as if you've been struck by lightning."

"Nothing," Meredith said quickly, forcing herself to look at Roberta instead of the glass tank. *Nicholas never told me there were animals here.* "Nothing. I, um, I just remembered I forgot something at the store."

"Cedar chips?" Roberta said lightly. "So how's Bluebell adjusting to life away from her siblings?"

Bluebell? *I'm obviously supposed to know what she's talking about.* Meredith felt sweat running down her neck, and sent up a brief prayer of thanksgiving to the Goddess that Kevin had wandered across the room to look at some of the children's artwork and hadn't heard Roberta's last comment. "Oh, just fine," she said, praying that Roberta wouldn't ask for details.

"I'm glad. Nicholas was so happy when he got to take her home."

Take her—? *Meredith had picked Nicholas up after school almost every day, and he'd never brought home an animal. She never would have allowed him to bring home an animal. And Kevin surely would have said something if he'd given permission—wouldn't he? Change the subject, fast.* "So how's Nicholas doing? He really seems to like it here."

"We like having him here," Roberta said crisply. "He's still shy, but he seems to be coming along—oh, excuse me, I have to go say hello to another parent. I'll talk to you in a little while."

"Sure," Meredith said. She felt dizzy. She hauled herself carefully and deliberately to the fish tank and looked in. Mice. Ten or twelve of them, by the looks of it. Of course. Cedar chips. And Nicholas had supposedly brought one home.

"Ah, the famous mice," Kevin said, peering into the cage. She hadn't even heard his approach. "Cute."

The famous mice? *What was going on? How much did Kevin know? Merry's stomach knotted.* Out of the corner of her eye, she saw Roberta coming across the room toward them. *Goddess. I've got to get him away* from here and on to another topic, before that woman starts talking about Bluebell. "Ugh," she said. "I can't look at them anymore. Not after poor Patty. Did you see any of Nicholas's pictures over there?"

"Yeah," Kevin said. "He did a really strange one of somebody living underground."

"The Hobbit," Meredith said, relieved that Nicholas hadn't drawn a butchered mouse. "He's obsessed with the Hobbit. Did it have furry feet?"

"No," Kevin said, frowning. "It was sleeping on top of a recycling bin. And feeding pizza to a mouse."

Named Bluebell, Meredith thought, just as Roberta appeared next to her elbow again and said, "Now, let's talk about Nicholas."

He was quite brilliant intellectually and his fine motor skills were far ahead of the other children's, even older ones (I could have told them that, Meredith thought, remembering Patty's neatly flayed carcass), but his social skills needed work. He was withdrawn and didn't interact with his peers, preferring the company of Roberta and Fred (I could have told them that, too, Meredith thought), and when he was forced into group situations he was rigid and defensive, anxious, unable to share or to initiate spontaneous play. "He's a little too orderly," Roberta said, "a little too obsessed with being neat and following the rules. When he doesn't know what the rules are, he panics."

"So we've got ourselves a five-year-old control freak," Kevin said on the way home. The good mood in which he'd begun the evening had been soured by Roberta's carefully phrased, conscientiously tactful expressions of concern. "That's what comes of staying home with him for so long and doing housework, Meredith. Listen, remember what the doctor said about that brain damage? Maybe we should take him to a doctor again, try some new meds."

Meredith rubbed her eyes to blot out a flash of red, blood and fur and bone. To her infinite relief, Roberta hadn't mentioned Bluebell in Kevin's hearing. "Maybe you're right," she said. "But let's give him a chance to work through it. He's in school now and he likes it there. He'll adjust. He has people to help him. I hate the idea of meds, Kevin! That was a disaster last time."

Kevin sighed. "I know. But look, if it were just a mild relaxant, something to get him to lighten up. Just for a while. It's a biofeedback thing. Anxious kids get tense and their bodies tense up and then they get tenser because their muscles are in fight-or-flight mode—you know. So you give them a mild relaxant and their bodies relax and then they learn relaxed ways of behaving too, and soon you've got another kind of loop established and you don't need the meds anymore. Works wonders. I've read about it."

Meredith had read about it too, at the library. She'd read more than enough to know that the relaxants sometimes enabled psychotic behavior in children with serious underlying psychiatric problems, children in whom—how had that clinical report put it?—"inflexible behavior constitutes a kind of psychological self-discipline, a desperate attempt not to engage in unacceptable acting out." Kevin would be amazed if he knew what she'd been reading. It alarmed her to realize that he'd noticed enough of Nicholas's anxiety to do any such reading himself.

"No tranqs," she said, her voice brittle. "If you want him to learn to relax we'll send him to a kiddie yoga class. No more meds, thank you. The poor kid's had enough doctors to last him the rest of his life."

"Well, maybe he should talk to somebody who's trained in this stuff."

"He's talking lots to Roberta and Fred, and we're paying enough for that."

"Roberta and Fred aren't psychologists. And since when has money been an issue, anyway?"

She swallowed. He'd surely suspect something if she pursued that line of logic. "Look, Kevin, Berta and Fred are child-care experts, and they spend more hours a day watching him than we do, and they didn't say he needed to be shrunk, okay? Give him some time."

"You keep saying that! You tell me to give you time to stop crying, give him time to start acting like a normal kid. Well, I've been giving both of you time, and I don't see anything getting better. You still jump whenever anybody looks at you funny, and according to Roberta, Nicholas freaks out if his jelly beans aren't precisely sorted by color or if the other kids don't have their bangs combed perfectly straight. I don't like any of it, Merry. What about me? When are you going to give me some time when I don't have to worry about the two of you?"

"Now," she said, her throat painfully dry. She reached out to touch his shoulder. "I'm giving you now not to worry. Don't worry, Kevin, okay? You have my permission."

"Under the circumstances, that's not much comfort."

She closed her eyes. Should she tell him? Could she trust him? He cared about both of them, he did: he'd just said so. He loved her and he loved Nicholas. And she loved him, even though she hadn't yet when they got married, not exactly. She'd grown to love him. It wasn't the same way she loved Nicholas, but it was real. Surely, for both their sakes, Kevin wouldn't sacrifice Nicholas to brainwiping if he knew the truth. He'd help her help Nicholas. And she needed help: she was so alone, had been fighting with this for so long, and she didn't know what to do. She had to have someone to talk to. She'd go mad if she had to keep it to herself any longer.

Kevin was saying something. She opened her eyes and shook her head. "I'm sorry; what did you say?"

"Pay attention, Merry! I said that there's a guy at work—Johnson, you remember my talking about him—whose wife's a school psychologist with the city. Maybe she should look at Nicholas."

"No," Meredith said, and then, her blood freezing, "you've been talking to someone at *work* about this?" Instantly her tentative trust fled.

He shot her a quick glance. "No. Not yet. I was thinking about it. Would that be so terrible? He's having some adjustment problems: Why is that such a deep dark secret? It's what we expected, isn't it?"

"I just don't think it's anyone else's business," Meredith said stiffly. A school psychologist. For the city. Goddess. They might as well just hand Nicholas straight to the brainwipe butchers. No, she couldn't tell Kevin. He'd probably already talked to his colleague, and the colleague had already talked to the wife, and the wife—

You're paranoid, said some small, detached part of her brain, but the panic remained. "Meredith?" Kevin said. "Are you all right?"

"I'm fine. I'm just tired."

"Old, tired excuse number 532," Kevin said coldly, and Meredith turned away from him. Neither of them spoke again for the rest of the evening.

Nineteen

T HE next afternoon after school, Meredith sat Nicholas down in the kitchen with a drink of juice and said as matter-of-factly as she could, "Nicholas, who's Bluebell?"

He took a long slurp of juice. "She's the Hobbit's mouse, Mommy."

"The Hobbit who lives in a hole in the ground?"

"Yup."

A hole in the ground. A grave? Had Bluebell gone to join Patty? Meredith swallowed and said, "Nicholas, Hobbits aren't real."

"I know that. You told me already."

"Yes, but, honey, Bluebell's a real mouse. Roberta said you took home a real mouse named Bluebell. So how can an imaginary Hobbit have a real mouse?"

"That's why," Nicholas said.

"*What's* why? Nicholas, I don't understand."

He sighed. "You said I couldn't have a mouse. And you said I couldn't talk about why not to anybody. So I couldn't tell Berta I couldn't have Bluebell, and I couldn't bring Bluebell here, but I could tell the Hobbit about it and he could have her, because he isn't real."

Meredith rubbed her eyes. She was totally lost. "Sweetheart, where's Bluebell now?"

"In the *ground*. With the *Hobbit*. I *told* you that."

"You mean she's dead? She's in the ground with Patty?"

"No, Mommy! She's alive! The Hobbit feeds her and gives her water and made her a little house with a nest in it out of an old plastic bottle and—"

His voice was becoming dangerously high and thin. "Okay, Nicholas. It's okay. I'm trying to understand, that's all. Would you take me to visit Bluebell? Can I meet her and the Hobbit?"

He chewed his lip. "I don't know. I don't think you can see the Hobbit, Mommy."

"Why not?"

"Because he's not *real*. You said not-real people are the ones real people can't see. And you told me you never saw the Hobbit. And the Hobbit said he's not real."

"He said that? He used those words? He said, 'I'm not real'? Try to remember exactly what words he used, Nicky. I know you have a good memory." She remembered Fred telling Steven, who hadn't wanted to share the Lego, *I know you're good at spelling.* So now she was imitating an AI. Terrific.

Nicholas's face clouded with effort. "He said—he said, 'You're the only person who knows I'm here. Nobody else has seen me.' And that's what not being real means, right, Mommy? That's what you told me. Like the monsters. I'm the only person who knows that they're there and no one else can see them. Except the Hobbit's nice. He takes care of Bluebell. He keeps her safe."

"Safe?"

"From the monsters, Mommy. So I won't have to turn her inside out like—like—"

"Like you did to Patty?"

He looked down, frowning. "Yes."

"Why not, Nicky?" Head swimming, she leaned forward, desperate for clues. Maybe she was about to learn something she could use to help him. "Why's Bluebell safe when Patty wasn't?"

"Because she lives with him. If she lived with me, she'd live with the monsters too."

"She'd be safe if she'd stayed at school, Nicky, wouldn't she?"

He shuddered. "No. Because I could see her at school, and—and the monsters saw her and they said—they wanted me to—to—"

"Turn her inside out," Meredith said gently, although her hands were shaking. He wouldn't answer her. He took another drink of juice instead. "Nick, honey, but there are other mice at school now, right? Are they still safe?"

He nodded, his chin moving just a fraction of an inch. "Bluebell's the one—the one the monsters said—the one they want—" He was about to cry.

"Okay. It's okay. Nicky, when you bring a pet home from school, you have to have a note from home saying it's okay, right?"

"Yeah." She could barely hear him.

"Yeah. So, uh, Roberta seemed to think I'd signed a note like that." He was only five. Surely he couldn't forge her signature yet. "Where—who signed the note? The Hobbit?"

"*No!* Daddy!"

"*Daddy?* Does Daddy know about Bluebell?"

"He signed the note," Nicholas said, more cheerful now, "but then I told him someone else wanted her more, so I'd given her away."

Kevin must have forgotten. Thank Gaia he hadn't brought it up with Roberta. Wait. At parents' night, standing behind her looking at the mice, he'd said, *Ah, the famous mice.* So that was what he'd meant. But why hadn't he mentioned it to Meredith? Back before Nicholas had started at the school, he'd told her Nicky wanted another mouse. She'd said fine then, because she didn't know what else to say, but why hadn't he mentioned it again? He should have discussed it with her.

She had so many secrets from Kevin. Did he have secrets from her too? She swallowed a surge of terror, forcing herself to bear down. One thing at a time. She couldn't worry about Kevin right now. She had to worry about Nicholas. "Okay, Nicky. Now, about the Hobbit. Did he say you weren't supposed to tell anyone about him?"

Nicholas frowned. "No. But I said, 'Oh, you're not real, you're just my imagination,' and he laughed and said, 'That's right.' He told me I was smart."

"All right," Meredith said, standing up. "All right. Now let's see how good my imagination is, Nicky. I want to meet Bluebell and the Hobbit now, okay?"

"Now?"

"Now," she said. "Can I meet them now?"

"I don't know if they'll be home now," he said, frowning. "Bluebell will be home, but sometimes the Hobbit goes to get food for the cats. I can't go into his house. He always comes out."

"The *cats*? How can he keep Bluebell safe if he has cats, Nicky?"

"The cats don't live at his house. They live where the water is. He brings them food."

The Hobbit fed feral cats on the piers. Meredith blinked. "Nicky, where does the Hobbit live?"

"In a hole."

"Yes, yes, I know. But where's the hole?"

"At the bottom of the stairs, Mommy. Near school."

"In the hill?" Meredith asked sharply. "The Hobbit lives in a cave in the hillside, Nicholas, and he feeds feral cats?" A baggie. Goddess help her, Nicholas was confiding in a baggie. "Nicholas, does the Hobbit know why—Nicholas, did you tell the Hobbit about the monsters?"

"A little," Nicholas said, subdued. "I told him he had to keep Bluebell safe."

"All right," Meredith said. "I want to meet him. I want to see where he lives."

"Now, Mommy?"

"Now."

"But maybe he's not there. And maybe you can't see him."

"Let's see," she said. "Let's see if I can see him. Take me there, Nicky, okay?"

"Okay." He looked like he was about to cry again, but he led her down the Filbert steps. At the bottom, where he would ordinarily have gone straight across the brick expanse of Levi Plaza to get to school, he veered right, into the verdant undergrowth on the side of Telegraph Hill. Meredith followed, crouching low to avoid branches and swatting aside leaves, until Nicholas stopped and called out, "Henry?"

Henry? Henry who fed feral cats on the piers? Meredith's blood froze. She smelled something other than trees here, something foul. "Nicky, why are you calling the Hobbit Henry?"

"Because that's his *name*, Mommy!"

It couldn't be the same one. It couldn't. The other Henry—that had all been years ago. As long ago as Hortense. Ancient history. Heart pounding, Meredith peered into the mass of leaves and branches in the side of the hill, but she couldn't see anything that looked like a cave. Well, of course not. Of course it would be well hidden. And the smell—the smell brought back memories of Hortense, of Henry sleeping on the couch at the Maddie Center, of all the baggies she helped feed in shelters for CALM. Nearly retching, she said, "Nicholas, how can you come here and talk to Henry without anyone knowing about it? When do you do that?"

"When all the kids are playing outside I come here sometimes when nobody's looking. And sometimes Daddy sits over on that bench and reads while I come here."

"Does *Daddy* know about Henry?" Kevin had picked up Nicholas after school only a handful of times. She was going to kill him, him and Roberta both. How could they be so careless? Any of the kids could wander over here. How could Kevin just let Nicholas disappear into the bushes?

"No, Daddy can't see him. Daddy thinks I'm just collecting leaves. Henry, are you here?" Nicholas walked a bit more deeply into the under-growth, peering ahead. "I don't think he's here, Mommy. Or he's not coming out because he can see you. I only saw him by accident, the first time. When he told me not to tell."

"Okay," Meredith said, her heart pounding. "Okay, Nicky, we'll go back home now, all right?"

"Okay. Maybe you can meet him later. But maybe I should ask him first. I don't know if he wants me to tell you about him."

What was she going to do? Every principle she had told her to call the people she knew at shelters, the people she'd met through her work with CALM, to get help for this Henry, whoever he was. But he knew too much. If he knew about Bluebell, he knew too much about Nicholas. Just two nights ago, there'd been a story on the news about a boy, a teenager, who'd been brainwiped because he'd been setting fires and stealing from his parents. She couldn't let that happen to Nicholas. She couldn't.

And maybe Henry wasn't even real. Maybe Nicholas was just making it all up. Maybe he'd taken Bluebell from school and let her go on the side of the hill, where she'd be able to forage for food, at least until one of the feral cats got her; maybe he'd invented Henry as a way of consoling himself and fooling the monsters. This was Nicholas she was dealing with, and Nicholas, Goddess help them all, was not exactly sane. It could just be a story.

Or not. The coincidence with the names and the cats was too neat. What was she going to do?

Think, Meredith. Think. What would you do if a normal child, a sane child, told you a story about a mysterious man living in the side of the hill near school?

She didn't have a normal, sane child. How could she even answer the question?

She should call the school to see if they knew anything. But she couldn't. She couldn't take the risk of alerting Fred and Roberta to

Nicholas's extracurricular activities. And obviously they didn't know anything about Henry—did they?—or they'd have called her. No school, surely, would allow its children to make friends with mysterious strangers who lived in the bushes.

She had to talk to someone. Who could she talk to? There'd been a CALM presentation, a few weeks ago, by some community-relations guy for the police department, talking about the homeless problem. Where was his card again? She dug through her briefcase, through CALM position papers and KinderkAIr parent mailings, until she found the small square of cardboard. Ben Witts. He'd seemed like a decent man, a compassionate man: he saw the homeless as people, not automatically as criminals. She'd call him.

"Henry Carviero?" Ben said. "Sure, everybody knows Henry. He's been a local institution for years. That restaurant on Levi Plaza feeds him from the Dumpsters, and he feeds the cats. We kicked him out of there when the school opened, got him into a halfway house. When did he come back?"

Meredith closed her eyes. Henry Carviero. It was the same Henry. The Henry she'd found at the Maddie Center, sleeping on the couch. The Henry she'd gotten into trouble with the police, although she hadn't meant to. How could this be happening? It was impossible. "I don't know," she said. "I haven't seen him. I only know he's there because my son told me about him."

"He's been talking to your son?" Ben's voice was sharper. "How long has this been happening? Has he hurt the child?"

This is bigger than I am, Meredith thought. "I don't know how long it's been happening. I don't think he's hurt Nicholas—he told Nicholas not to tell anyone he was there, but if he's afraid of being relocated—"

"Meredith, he shouldn't have gone back there in the first place. We told him to stay away. We got him into a halfway house. And if he snuck back and now he's engaging in secretive behavior with children—"

"I don't think he's hurting Nicholas," Meredith said. He's trying to help Nicholas, but I can't tell you about that because I can't admit that Nicholas needs help because then he'll be brainwiped oh Goddess help me. "Ben, I didn't call you to get the guy locked up." Well, that's not entirely true, but I don't want him to get into trouble again, either. "Please don't—look, please don't punish him. Just . . . just . . ." Just what, Meredith? If you weren't trying to get Henry in trouble, why did you call the police in the first place?

"You did right to call," Ben Witts said firmly. "But I'm afraid we have to take action. We've repeatedly tried to get Henry into a more appropriate situation, and we've repeatedly warned him that he can't keep living in the side of the hill. Especially now, when there's a school there. We're going to follow up on this immediately, and I'll call you to let you know the outcome."

"Don't brainwipe him," Meredith said, her mouth dry. *Repeatedly*: she knew what happened to street people who repeatedly got into trouble with the police. They got resocialized. Henry was someone's child; as foul and smelly as he was, he'd been somebody's little boy once. She couldn't have this on her conscience. "Ben, please don't brainwipe him. If he keeps going back to the hill, that must be because he feels it's his home."

"A cave in Telegraph Hill isn't an appropriate home for anyone. I appreciate your compassion, Meredith, but the outcome isn't up to me. We have protocols for situations like this; I don't set policy. You can be assured that we'll do the kindest thing we can for Henry. Don't worry."

"Please don't brainwipe him," she said, but even as she said it, she realized with a chill that part of her wanted Henry to be brainwiped, to lose all memory of his interactions with Nicholas. No. That was evil. It was wrong. She couldn't save Nicholas by sacrificing Henry. Could she?

Henry would be brainwiped anyway, eventually. Someone else would see him and call the police. He'd had all those previous chances.

No. That was evil. How could she think that way? Henry was someone's child.

"I'll let you know the outcome," said Ben Witts. "Thank you for calling, Meredith. Good-bye, now."

She learned the outcome that evening, when there was a knock at the door. Kevin wasn't home yet; she and Nicholas had been making salad in the kitchen, Nicholas tearing lettuce leaves into shreds with alarming ferocity. When the doorball rang she frowned and peered at the outside monitor.

"Who is it, Mommy?"

It was the police. She could see the uniforms. Her heart sank. "Nicholas, stay here. I'll be right back." She went into the living room, her feet like lumps of lead, and opened the door. "Yes?"

"Mrs. Walford-Lindgren," one of the police said, "would you come outside and talk to us, please? Henry Carviero is in our patrol car, at the bottom of the steps. He can't hurt you or the boy."

The boy? She turned and saw Nicholas standing behind her, his thumb in his mouth. He took it out long enough to say, "Is Henry in trouble? Why is Henry in trouble?"

"He—Nicholas, the police are going to help him find a better place to live."

"He likes where he lives now," Nicholas said. Meredith could tell from his voice that he was working himself up to a tantrum, and in response she made her own voice far firmer than she felt.

"Nicholas, everything will be fine. The police are going to help Henry."

She wanted him to stay at the house, but he had to come along; there was no one home to watch him. He followed her, tugging at her hand and pleading with the police, as the small party filed down the steps, through gardens lush with the scent of flowers. Meredith wondered how many of the neighbors were watching this little procession, and what they were making of it.

"Henry's *nice,*" Nicholas said. "He's *nice*! He hasn't done anything bad! He takes care of my mouse! He's scared of the police! He told me so! Why does he have to talk to the police? He's a nice man!"

"Sweetheart," she said gently, "nice people aren't afraid of the police. And nice people have houses to live in. They don't have to live in caves." It wasn't true. None of that was true; plenty of decent people were homeless and frightened. Why had she even said any of it, any of those convenient lies? She knew better.

Even Nicholas knew better. "That's not true!" he said, beginning to sob. "Lots of people don't have houses! I see them all the time when we're in the car! Mommy, you have to help the Hobbit. He's my friend. Tell the police he didn't do anything."

The cops were looking at her. She'd started this: What was she going to tell Nicholas? "They just want to talk to him," she said weakly. "They're going to get him a better place to live. They're going to help him, Nicky."

"He's scared of them," Nicholas said. His small face was tear-stained in the glow of garden lamps. "He'll think I told on him. He'll think I got him into trouble."

Meredith's heart twisted. "Nicky, you didn't do anything wrong. And maybe the Hobbit didn't, either. We don't know. The police are our friends. They're going to help him." But she didn't believe it. She remembered Ben Witts, with his ominous *repeatedly.* Carviero was probably headed for a brainwipe, and she didn't know if there was anything she could do to help him. Worse, she still wasn't sure if she wanted to.

They were at the bottom of the steps now, two patrol cars parked at the curb. Meredith saw two officers in one of them, with someone else in the backseat.

"Okay," said one of the cops who'd walked them down from the house. "Heeeere's Henry." He opened the door of the patrol car. "Henry, get out and talk to the nice lady, please."

The first thing Meredith noticed was the overwhelming stench, ten times worse than it had been outside Henry's cave, a sensory assault that made her take an involuntary step backward. "I know," the cop said sympathetically. "It's pretty bad, isn't it?"

"Sorry," said Henry. He wore far too much clothing, all of it filthy, but his voice was clear, pleasant, even. "I haven't had access to a shower for a while. Nicholas, are you all right? Why are you crying?"

"They're taking you to jail," Nicholas said, and then, pleadingly, "Mommy, tell them to let him go!"

"Ah," Henry said, looking at her searchingly. "I know you. I know you, Mommy, don't I? You're the cat girl. You just love calling the cops on people. I love cats too, you know. That was a long time ago. You haven't learned much."

Meredith swallowed. Whatever else Henry was, he wasn't stupid. "Mrs. Walford-Lindgren," said the cop, "do you want to press charges for molestation? You don't have to. We've got him on vagrancy, anyway."

Molestation? "Of course not," Meredith said, revolted. "There's no evidence of that." She drew herself up to her full height, trying to look imposing. "You're going to help him, aren't you? Find him a better place to live?"

One of the cops sniffed. "Sure we are. Just like the other six times. This guy wants to live in a cave."

"It's my home!" Henry said fiercely. "It's the best home I've found, and people keep trying to kick me out of it. They kicked me out of the ones before that too. My mom kicked me out because she was crazy, and other people kept kicking me out because they thought I was crazy. What's crazy about wanting to get out of the rain?"

"We've gotten you out of the rain," one of the cops said. "Six times."

"She kicked me out too," Henry said, gesturing at Meredith. "Out of that room. A cat could live there, but I couldn't because I didn't smell good enough. She doesn't mind smelling cat pee, but another person—"

"You know Henry?" Nicholas said, looking bewildered. "You met Henry before, Mommy?"

"A long, long time ago, Nicky. I'd forgotten about it until just now. It's just—a coincidence." Was it? Well, what else could it be?

"Now Nicholas here," Henry said conversationally, his voice softening, "Nicholas doesn't mind that I smell. Do you, Nicholas? Nicholas could teach the rest of you a thing or two."

Meredith's sympathy for Henry was quickly eroding. Be honest, she told herself. Everything he's said is the truth. That's why you're afraid of him.

"Henry," said one of the cops, shaking his head, "what the hell were you doing talking to a kid? How could you think that wouldn't get you into trouble? You go back to your cave and befriend a kid? That's asking to be picked up! Come on, Henry. You're a smart guy. You have to know that! Ma'am, are you sure he hasn't hurt the child?"

"He didn't hurt me!" Nicholas said, outraged. "He's my friend! He was helping me!"

"Nicholas," Henry said, his voice still gentle, "it's okay. Don't be scared. Everything will be fine." But the glare he shot at Meredith indicated that he knew otherwise.

"I hate you," Nicholas said, looking up at his mother.

"He's been conducting a clandestine friendship with my son," Meredith said stiffly. She was only telling the truth. If the truth sounded damning, so be it. "I only found out about it today. Evidently he told Nicholas not to tell anyone about him. I thought that sounded suspicious."

The cops were on full alert now. "Yes, ma'am. If you find out anything else we need to investigate—"

"I *hate* you!" said Nicholas.

"No investigation," Meredith said. "I told you, I'm not trying to get him into trouble. Really I'm not. If you can help him, that's great. Just *get him out of here,* all right?" She pushed her hair back with her free hand—Nicholas had begun a high-pitched whining—and said, "Look, I'm sorry, but secretive strangers make me nervous, and if anything ever happened to Nicholas I'd never forgive myself."

"Of course," the head cop said gently. She knew they were thinking of Raji. There was some advantage, after all, to having been one of the main figures in a cultural tragedy.

Meredith swallowed and said, "And this may sound hypocritical, since I just said I don't like secrecy, but I'd really rather not read about this on ScoopNet in an hour. If you can keep it away from the media—"

"Of course," the older cop said soothingly. "Of course. No secrecy there, ma'am. Just the normal level of privacy any family would want, and that yours doesn't get too often."

They must have sent this guy to community relations school. Meredith relaxed slightly and said, "Thank you. Nicholas, let's go back inside now, okay? And I'll make you some warm milk."

"No! I'm never going anywhere with you again! I hate you!"

Henry hunkered down on the ground so that he was at Nicholas's height, and said, "Don't. Nicholas, you have to go back home. You're lucky she's not kicking you out. Don't push your luck. And Nicky, you have to take Bluebell back now, okay?" He reached into the capacious folds of his reeking clothing and pulled out a small black mouse. "I know you gave her to me for safekeeping. But she has to go home with you now, Nicky."

Safekeeping. Sweet Goddess. What if he told the police about Nicholas's monsters? Well, she'd say he must be insane, that's all. He was providing perfectly adequate evidence on his own.

Nicholas had turned around and was facing away from all of them, tiny arms folded across his chest. "I hate you. I hate all of you."

"Nicholas?" Henry said. "Bluebell has to go home with you."

"I can't keep her," Nicholas said, his face scrunched into a scowl. "I *told* you."

"Well, kiddo, I can't keep her, either. Anybody here want a mouse?"

The older cop was frowning; Meredith wondered what in hell he thought was going on. The younger cop laughed. "Well, my python would be real keen on it."

Some safekeeping. Nicholas's shoulders stiffened, and Meredith stretched out her hand. "Here, I'll take her. I'll bring her to Temple. They can put her into the petting zoo. And then you can visit her there, Nicky, okay?"

Nicholas didn't answer. "Mind you hold her tail so she doesn't get away," Henry said, more politely than he'd spoken to Meredith yet. "Hold her at the base of the tail, just like that. That's it. You got it." I know how to hold a mouse, Meredith thought resentfully, and then, He really does want to keep the mouse safe. She could feel the tiny heart beating against her palm.

"Thank you," she heard herself saying, and then, cradling Bluebell against her stomach, she took Nicholas's hand and said, "We have to go back in now, Nicky. Come on."

"No," Nicholas said, trying to twist out of her grasp. "I want to go with him! I want to go with Henry!"

Henry sighed. "Nicky, go with your mother. You can't help me now. Go home now."

"Everything's all right," Meredith said.

Nicholas, dry-eyed and merciless, looked up at her, in full view of Henry and the cops and whatever neighbors were watching, and said very clearly, "It's your fault. You got Henry in trouble. I hate you, Mommy."

"Nicholas, we're going home now. Come on."

"I hate you," he said. "I hate you, I hate you." He turned it into a song. He sang it all the way up the Filbert steps; he sang it to the neighbors' windows. He sang it all the way to his own room, where he ran inside and slammed the door and leaned against it, singing, "I hate you," while Meredith stood outside, holding Bluebell.

"Nicholas, let me in."

"No! I hate you!"

"Sweetheart, if you don't come out, how will you be able to eat your dinner?"

"No! I hate you! I hate you! I—"

"Meredith?" Oh, sweet Gaia. Kevin was home. He must have just come in. "Meredith, what's going on?"

"Nothing," she said bleakly. Here he was, next to her now, still carrying his briefcase and blueprint tube.

He raised his eyebrows. "Nothing? Then why were you and Nicholas standing in front of two police cars at the bottom of the hill? Old Mrs. Peabody two doors down told me all about it."

Meredith swallowed. "Well, it's a long story."

"No doubt. You were just talking to the cops, and now Nicholas is having a tantrum. That should be quite a story." He looked at her, his eyebrows rising further, and said, "And while you're at it, why don't you tell me why you're holding a mouse?"

"What?" he said, half an hour later. All four of them were in the kitchen. Kevin had enticed Nicholas out of his room with the promise of an ice cream sundae, an offer Nicholas had accepted on the condition that his mother have no hand in preparing it. Meredith sat, arms crossed over her chest, on one side of the table; Nicholas, mute and glaring, his face smeared with chocolate and whipped cream, glowered at her from the other. Kevin paced back and forth in front of the sink. The only tranquil creature in the room was Bluebell, who nibbled happily on a piece of apple in her temporary quarters, a large glass bowl securely covered with an even larger colander.

"Now, hold on," Kevin said. "Let me see if I've got this straight. You called the police because some homeless guy was showing Nicholas his pet mouse?"

"She's *my* mouse," Nicholas said.

"Kevin, I just found out this afternoon that this Hobbit guy was real, he's been talking to Nicholas for Goddess knows how long—because *you* let Nicky run off into the bushes—and telling Nicholas to keep it a secret—"

"He never said that!" said Nicholas.

"—so what would you have done? Aside from what you've already done, just letting Nicholas disappear from sight?"

"He was collecting leaves," Kevin snapped. "I'd have talked to the guy himself before I called the cops. Nicholas, what was he doing with your mouse, anyway?"

"He was taking *care* of her, Daddy!" And then, to Merry's relief, "He was lonely. He wanted a friend."

"Okay," Kevin said. "Okay. So he's the person you gave the mouse to, right? The mouse I signed that note for? When you told me you had a friend who wanted the mouse more than you did?"

"Right," Nicholas said.

"Nicholas," said Kevin, "that was *really nice* of you. That was a really nice thing to do, to try to make someone less lonely."

"Oh," Nicholas said, in a tiny voice.

"I'm very proud of you," Kevin said, glaring at Meredith.

"Really?"

"Really, Nicholas. I really am. And I'll bet Mommy thinks it was a nice thing to do too. Right?"

"Right," Meredith said. "Nicholas, I'm sorry I scared you. I—it's just—"

"She was trying to protect you, Nicholas," Kevin said. He couldn't possibly know how right he was. "Sometimes mommies and daddies get too scared for their children because they love them so much. Sometimes we don't do the right things. Sometimes we make mistakes, trying to protect our kids."

"And sometimes we don't protect them enough," Meredith said. She was ready to scream. "Sometimes we let them run off into the bushes." She knew she shouldn't criticize Kevin in front of Nicholas; she didn't care. Keep him on the defensive. Get him thinking about his own behavior so he wouldn't look too closely at hers.

Kevin ignored her. "But now we'll try to help your friend, Nicholas, okay?"

"Okay."

"Good. Go play in your room now, sweetheart. I have to talk to your mother."

The minute Nicholas was up the stairs Kevin turned on her, fiercer than she'd ever seen him, and said, "Have you completely lost your mind?"

"Look who's talking! Just sit on the park bench and let him do whatever he wants, why don't you?"

"Gaia's gas, Merry! He was collecting leaves! And everybody's worried about the kid because he doesn't have friends, he doesn't have social skills, he doesn't seem to have any empathy or compassion, and then you *punish* him for being nice to some poor old bum?"

"What do you mean, 'poor old bum'? You don't know anything about him! For all you know he's a kidnapper or an addict or a child molester or—or—Goddess knows what! You don't *know*! And you let Nicky—"

"Well, you don't know anything about him, either, do you, except that Nicholas likes him?"

Meredith swallowed. "Nicholas has been keeping this a secret for Goddess knows how long."

Kevin pointed at the mixing bowl. "And the guy's been taking care of that mouse for the same amount of time. The mouse looks pretty damn tame and healthy to me."

"Which means exactly *what*? Who knows what the guy wanted in return for taking care of the mouse?"

"According to Nicholas, he didn't want anything in return! He wanted the mouse to keep him company! Merry, I just don't get it. You're the one whose religion makes such a big deal of compassion; you're the one who's been volunteering in shelters to help baggies; you're the one who's completely paranoid about personal publicity—"

"Excuse me, but you're pretty paranoid about publicity too! And you were completely irresponsible—"

"—and so you do something cruel in a way that drags in the cops and the neighbors and will therefore get as much publicity as possible!"

She swallowed again. Her mouth tasted like sawdust. "The cops said they'd keep it quiet."

"Oh, sure. You believe that? With the neighbors watching? Mrs. Peabody's probably already called ScoopNet. Matt's going to love this: 'Do-gooder Green blows whistle on baggie.' Just wonderful."

"You're terribly concerned with Green ethics all of a sudden."

He slammed his hand down on the table. "Meredith! I'm concerned because you *aren't* concerned! Don't you get it? For all I care they can scrub the guy down with Clorox and wash him out of town with a fire hose while they're at it! I don't care about him. I care about you!"

"I'm fine. I'm just trying to protect Nicholas, which is more than *you*—"

"Protect Nicholas from *what*? Do you have any evidence that he's been harmed?"

"The secrecy—"

"So what? Kids like secrets. He's not scared of this guy. Right now, he's scared of you! And so am I. You don't want the kid to keep his friendships a secret, but then when he tells you about them, you have his friends hauled away to jail?"

"You," said Meredith, shaking in fear and fury, "are the one at fault here. None of this would have happened if you'd supervised Nicholas properly!"

"Yeah, I let him get twenty feet away in a place without cars."

"You couldn't *see* him, Kevin!"

"We can't see him now, either. You'd better run into his room and check: maybe criminals are climbing through the windows. Merry, he needs a little bit of freedom."

"He's *five!*"

Kevin sighed. "All right. I'm sorry, all right? I'll never do it again. Now I'm going to call the police station and see what's happening with the baggie, okay? You want to conference in?"

She shook her head mutely, and somehow found her voice. "No. You call. Let me go talk to Nicholas."

"Okay. I'll come in when I know something."

She went slowly down the hallway, afraid that Nicholas wouldn't let her into his room, equally afraid that he would and would tell her again how much he hated her. Was whatever was wrong with him her fault? Was anything wrong with him at all, or was it all her? Maybe she'd been exaggerating his symptoms. Maybe she'd been making it all up. Maybe her brain damage was the problem and she was the one who needed to be brainwiped. But then she remembered Patty, bloody and flayed.

Nicholas's door was open a crack. She knocked gently. "Nicholas? Honey, it's Mommy. Can I come in?"

"All right." She could barely hear his whisper of assent. She stepped gingerly into the room and found Nicholas curled up on his bed, sucking his thumb.

"Nicky? Daddy's calling the police to see how Henry is, okay? Are you still mad at me?" He shrugged, an awkward wiggle of his body against the coverlet, and sucked more loudly on his thumb. "Sweetie, I'm sorry. I'm sorry you're scared and worried." She brushed his hair back from his forehead, and he stiffened, but didn't draw away. Meredith knelt on the carpet, relieved at his lack of outburst, and said, "I hope your friend will be okay."

Suck, suck. He glared at her. Meredith swallowed. Kevin would be here soon. And she had to find out. "Nicholas—can Bluebell stay here? To be your mouse?" He shrank back farther into the coverlet, his eyes narrowing to slits. "No? Does that mean no, honey?" *Suck, suck.* She fought a surge of panic that he was going autistic on her. "Do you want me to take Bluebell to Temple? She'll be safe there, and you can visit her." The barest nod. Encouraged, she went on. "Okay. I'll take her there, only I have to do it tomorrow. It's too late tonight. Okay? Will she be safe here tonight?"

Shrug. *Suck, suck.* And there were feet in the hallway: Kevin coming back with news. Nicholas removed his thumb from his mouth and sat up. "Well?" he said when Kevin entered the room.

"Well," Kevin said, and hunkered down to be at eye level with Nicholas. "Your friend's okay, Nick."

"Promise?"

"Promise."

"Is he coming back here?"

"Well, no. Probably not. You know, it's against the law to live where he was living. But the police will find somewhere else for him to live."

Nicholas's eyes narrowed again. "Jail?"

"No, sweetheart. Somewhere nice."

"Then he's not coming back," Nicholas said, and put his thumb back into his mouth.

Kevin looked at Meredith, who cleared her throat and said, "Well, Nicholas and I have been having a little talk. He's sad about his friend, but he wants Bluebell to go live at the Temple so people there can enjoy her too. Right, Nick?" The barest of nods. "I know you're sad," Meredith said. "Would it make you feel better to sleep with us tonight, the way you used to when you were little?" And that way maybe Bluebell will be safe even though she'll still be in the house, since I can't very well explain to Kevin why the mouse should spend the night in our room.

Nicholas nodded, and took his thumb out of his mouth again, and neatly dried it on his shirt. "Yes, Mommy. Can I have my bath now, please?"

"So I lied," Kevin said, once Nicholas was ensconced in the tub. "What would you have had me tell him? Your friend's a repeat offender and a menace to society, so the cops are going to make him into a zombie? Look, it's over. We can't do anything else for him now. Not even CALM could do anything. They've been trying to help him, Meredith. They tried six times. It didn't work."

"All right," she said. But it wasn't over, and she knew it. Because she hadn't been able to help Nicholas, he'd keep trying to find other people who could. And she couldn't let him. He had no way of understanding that the help he wanted would destroy him. To whom would he reach out next, and how could she stop it?

"Anyway," Kevin said, "if they wipe the guy he won't be bothering Nicholas anymore, right? Aren't you happy about that?"

Meredith closed her eyes. "Now you're being cruel. And the whole thing's your fault."

"Yes," he said, "I guess I am being cruel. I've already apologized for not following Nicholas every second; I'm not going to say it again. But, look, maybe with this guy off the streets, he'll start making friends in school."

Fred and Berta. Yes, of course. Nicholas was going to try to get help from Fred and Berta, if he hadn't already. Which might very well mean Preston too.

"Do you think he'd be happier in another school?" she said, eyes still closed. She knew it wouldn't work; even if Kevin did agree to a change of schools, that would just delay the process, not stop it.

The sound of Kevin's fist slamming on the countertop, for the second time that day, jolted her eyes open again. "*No,* Meredith. I think he likes the school he's in just fine, and I think the last thing we should do is take that away from him too!"

"Okay," she said. "Okay." Aching, she remembered the little world she and Kevin had built when they first met: her dream house, and later, the dream that they would one day live in it. They were living in different universes now. She supposed they had been ever since Nicholas came home.

"Merry, if I didn't know better, I'd think you hated him! You're trying to wreck everything he cares about."

"No, I'm not," she said. "Really I'm not." But she couldn't tell him why, and it didn't matter. He'd already left the room.

"That was when everything really started falling apart," Meredith said quietly. "Although it already had, I guess." She turned her ruined, mutilated face back toward Roberta, although Roberta could hardly see it in the dimness. They were sitting in the low-tide reek of Zephyr's apartment; Roberta's butt was numb from the hard plastic chair. Meredith had given her a much fuller confession than she'd expected, as if she were some sort of priest. But then, she'd asked for it. Meredith had been talking for hours, with breaks only to stretch, to use the bathroom, for Roberta to call Sergei.

"Well?" Meredith said. "You have the whole story now. Does it explain anything?"

"Maybe," Roberta said. "But it doesn't excuse it."

Meredith bent her head. "I know. Have you ever had a child?"

"Biologically? No. Neither have you. Have I ever loved a child? Yes, of course. I loved the same child you did, remember?"

Meredith, to her credit, winced. "I know. I know you did. Do you still think we're from different planets?"

"I don't know, Meredith. We are and we aren't. People like you usually see people like me as charity cases, don't you? Only in my case, I'm the charity case you couldn't be bothered to visit. I'm your father's little project, some cross between a stray puppy and a servant girl."

Meredith hunched her shoulders. "He got you the KinderkAIr job, didn't he?"

"Well, I don't know how else I could have gotten it, do you? Yet another in Preston's string of efforts to get us to be friends."

Meredith almost smiled. "That's why you looked at me so strangely the first day we met at school. I didn't have any idea who you were, then."

"I know you didn't. Even then, I knew you probably didn't. You would have said something if you had. But my life was pretty weird in through there anyway. Your father was barging back into it—probably because you were shutting him out—and my relationship was falling apart. And then Nicholas showed up, and everything got really complicated."

"Tell me about it." Meredith stood up and stretched. "I need to eat. You do too. And you need to call Sergei again. And then you can tell me your side of the story."

PART THREE

———

The Land of Make-Believe

Twenty

R OBERTA had known that Nicholas was troubled long before the Hobbit was taken away. She thought about him a lot during her commute, which might as well have been a commute between countries, not simply between neighborhoods. She and her lover lived in a renovated industrial loft at Eleventh and Harrison, on a block that remained stubbornly scuzzy. KinderkAIr, in the lush elegance of Levi Plaza, didn't feel like it belonged in the same city. Roberta was always a little amazed that the people there spoke the same language she did.

She couldn't even take one bus or train right to work, although it was only a few miles from home. She had to transfer, or take public transit to the Embarcadero and then walk up the waterfront to Levi Plaza, her preferred method. She and Doe had often talked about getting a car, but decided against the expense and danger. Their building didn't have a garage, which would have meant either paying through the nose for a space somewhere or parking on the street and risking vandalism. Simpler just to use MUNI.

Nearly every morning and evening, as she crossed the border between one world and another, Roberta wondered if Nicholas was doing the same thing. Despite his family's wealth, she suspected that the contrast between his house and the inside of his head was even starker than the difference between green, gleaming Levi Plaza and the gritty gray of Eleventh and Harrison.

She'd known people like Nicholas before, in her previous work with brainwipe clients. Like them, Nicholas hardly ever smiled or deliberately misbehaved. He always finished his lunch, always put away his toys, always took off his coat all by himself. He brought to each task a concentration unnatural in a child so small, a tense, anxious perfectionism. Roberta's private name for him was Saint Nick, because he was so quiet and neat and obedient. As much as the other children annoyed her sometimes, at least they were doing what they were supposed to do: testing limits, learning new skills, being energetic little animals. Nicholas's outward perfection seemed more like some deep lack, like he'd lost his soul.

She spent more time thinking about Nick than about any of the other kids, but she was glad there weren't others like him. She didn't like working with people who'd lost their souls. That gaping disconnection was what had driven her out of the brainwipe job.

She and Doe had fought when she left that job. The two of them hadn't disconnected yet, not completely, but they'd been rushing toward it with a momentum Roberta had sensed only dimly at the time. "It's a good job," Doe had told her, exasperated. "Come on, Berta, you said you weren't going to do this again, keep switching positions every six months! Bookstore clerk, gallery attendant, short-order cook, brainwipe rehab tech—it's a shitty résumé, and it doesn't exactly add up to a career. This is the first job you've had that even remotely uses your degree." Roberta had hauled her grades upward in high school and managed to get a partial scholarship to San Francisco University, where she majored in early childhood ed. Despite the misery of her own childhood—or perhaps because of it—she liked kids, empathized with kids. She knew what it felt like to live in a world so much bigger than you were. But she hadn't been able to find a teaching job after graduation, so she'd begun her long string of not-quite-right jobs instead. "When are you going to pick something and stick with it?"

"When I find something I like. Come on, Doe. I'm not going to stay in a job that makes me miserable."

What Roberta had loved in Doe when they first met, still loved when they had this particular fight, was her solidity, her security: four years working for the same downtown law firm; dinner every Saturday night with her family—dinners to which Roberta had been invited from the very beginning, dinners that immediately made her feel as if she too had a family; the same thing for breakfast every morning: coffee, juice, two pieces of toast. After the chaos of Roberta's early years, Doe's routines had been an oasis of comfort. Tonight, though, she merely seemed rigid. "Roberta, you can't *leave* a job until you have another job. I know you know that! You've always had more sense before."

Was Doe worried about money? She made far more than Roberta did, and they'd never squabbled about expenses before, although it seemed recently as if they'd been squabbling about everything else: what to have for dinner, what to watch on TV. The money they made separately had always been their money together; was that going to change now too?

"If it came to that," Roberta said patiently, "the insurance money from my parents would pay the rent for six months, and I'll find something by then; don't worry."

Doe looked at her as if she'd sprouted a third eye. "What? Who's talking about spending the insurance money?"

"I thought maybe you were. Look, Doe, I'm sick of being unhappy at work every day. Eight hours a day of being unhappy: no *wonder* we've been fighting lately. Don't you want me to be happy?"

"Of course. But switching jobs never makes you happy, not for long. You always wind up leaving again. Lots of people don't like their jobs; you still have to work. Happiness is a luxury, not a right."

Roberta had just stared at her. "Doe, do *you* want to change jobs? I thought you liked the firm."

"I *do* like the firm! Don't change the subject!"

"I'll stay with the brainwipe clients if you want to look for something else."

"No, no, Berta, *I'm* not the one who's dissatisfied. I *have* a good job. So do you, although you don't seem to realize it."

"It's not a good job for me," Roberta said, wondering what in the world was going on. It couldn't be PMS: she and Doe weren't due for another two weeks. "If you want my job, you can have it. Look, Doe, I know there's no guarantee I'll find something perfect, but there's no guarantee an airplane won't crash through the living room window in the next five minutes and kill both of us, either. Breathing's a luxury too, if you look at it that way. Why are you trying to convince me to stay in a job I hate?"

Doe just shook her head. "I'm trying to convince you to grow up and decide what you want to do with your life!"

"Well, I'm working on it. I've figured out that I don't want to keep working with drooling wrecks who have to be retaught to tie their shoelaces and who cry at the drop of a hat because they know they've lost something and can't remember what it is."

"When you took that job you thought you were going to use your training and get satisfaction from helping people."

"I did. Really I did. I was very happy for them when they learned to tie their shoelaces and brush their teeth and cut their food by themselves. I was, really. But after a while it couldn't make up for all the stuff they weren't going to get back. Doe, give me six months. If I haven't found something by then, I'll go back to brainwipe clients. Okay? Deal?"

In fact, it took her only six weeks to get the KinderkAIr job. She learned about it from their downstairs neighbor, Zephyr, the last person she would have expected to give her a job lead. Doe hated Zephyr, whose herd of bots tended to make screeching rackets, usually in the middle of the night. Because Doe refused even to talk to the woman, Roberta was always the one who went downstairs to request quiet. She and Zephyr had become friendly, after a fashion.

So when Zephyr accosted Roberta at the mailboxes one afternoon and said, "*You*'ve sure been hanging around the building a lot lately. What happened to your job?" Roberta decided to interpret Zephyr's rudeness as a sign of concern.

"Well, I'm looking for something else. I couldn't take brainwipe clients anymore."

"Too depressing," Zephyr said. The bots with her—there were only three today, about ten fewer than usual—squealed and squeaked like demented parrots. They only came halfway to Zephyr's knees, but made enough noise to qualify as a construction crew. "De-pressing-ing-ing." "DePRESSing!" "Deeeeeeeeeeeeee-pressssssssssssssssss-inggggggg."

"Yeah," Roberta said, trying to ignore the bots. She liked bots more than most people did; still, Zephyr's bots, like Zephyr herself, could be more than a little annoying. "Depressing and scary."

Zephyr nodded eagerly, her spiked orange-and-pink hair bobbing. "Tell me about it! Anybody who's different—wipe 'em out. It's horrible. How do you feel about teaching other people, though? Kids?"

The bots began hopping up and down; one turned a somersault. "Kid-ids-ids-ids-ids." "KIDS!" "Kiiiiiiiiiiiiiiiddddddddddddssssssssss!"

"Um—Zephyr? Could you ask them not to do that, please?"

Zephyr sighed and snapped her fingers. "Kids, quiet!"

"KIDS!" one said, but then they all settled down.

"Good girls," Zephyr said, beaming at them. "So, Berta, you were saying? Or you were going to say? Have you considered a teaching job?"

"Well, that's what I wanted to do, once," Roberta said with a shrug.

"But I doubt anyone would hire me now. I don't have any work experience, and you need certification."

"Not for private schools. Have you heard about MacroCorp's new kindergartens? AI-equipped: one educational AI, one teacher, five to seven kids. They're opening the first one in a few months, and if that works out they'll start a chain. You should check it out, try to get the teaching job. You'd like the children, probably, and the AI could use some grown-up company."

MacroCorp. Roberta felt a familiar pang. MacroCorp meant Preston, and Roberta hadn't had any contact with him in years. Doe had always made it very clear that she despised the idea of translation; as far as she was concerned, Friends of Preston were people who didn't have the social skills to maintain real friendships. Early in their relationship, Roberta had tried to defend him. He'd been consistently kind to her; he'd sent her the nightgown.

"That was different," Doe said. "You were a kid. Kids have imaginary friends all the time, and you needed them more than most."

"He's not imaginary, Doe. And the nightgown certainly wasn't. It was real."

"So are ScoopNet giveaways, but that doesn't mean they're motivated by anything remotely resembling love. He was trying to ensure brand loyalty."

"No, he wasn't! MacroCorp doesn't make nightgowns, and MacroCorp doesn't depend on my business. It's not like I can afford a rig or a house system. Preston was being nice."

"If he'd really wanted to be nice," Doe had said, "he would have gotten you out of foster care somehow. He would have given you a family." She'd touched Roberta's cheek and said, "He can't do that. I can. Family and a lot of other things you won't get from disembodied Preston."

She's jealous, Roberta had thought incredulously. But Doe had indeed given her family, and after a while, Roberta had come to agree with her. FOP-hood was for children and the immature. Roberta was an adult now. She didn't need virtual friendships anymore.

Which meant that she didn't need a job keeping an AI company, especially if it would cause friction with Doe. "Thanks," she told Zephyr, "but I don't think so."

"Why not?" Zephyr asked with a frown. "You'd be good at it. You're a nice person. Nice to people, nice to machines. When you tell me to hush up the bots, you don't curse at them or anything. You treat them right. And they're not so different from kids, you know. One of my bots suggested you should apply for the job, as a matter of fact."

Roberta squinted, not sure she'd heard Zephyr properly. Zephyr often had that effect on her. "One of your—excuse me?"

"One of my bots. Tikki-tavvy, you know, the spherical one with the purple polka dots? You told her how cute she was last week. And she's web-linked and she found out about the school when she was surfing the other day and she told me, 'Mommy, Berta would be good at that!'"

Weird, Roberta thought. She'd never interacted with Tikki any more than she had with the rest of them. She wondered if Preston could be behind this somehow, but why would he be, especially after all this time? And if he was, why not contact Roberta directly? It didn't make any sense.

"Thank you," she told Zephyr. "And thank, er, Tikki for me. But there's no way I'd get it. My early-ed degree is two years old at this point, and I don't have any actual experience teaching kids. I mean, children." Human children. Young human children, versus the grown infants who emerged from brainwiping.

"Try it anyway. It can't hurt."

"Well, I'll see," Roberta said. She had no intention of doing any such thing, and she expected Doe to applaud her decision when Roberta told her about the conversation over dinner.

Instead, Doe shrugged and said, "Well, you could try. Zephyr's right; it can't hurt. It's not like you've found anything else."

"I've only been looking for a few weeks, Doe! Give me a chance!"

Doe shrugged again. "Let Papa Preston give you a chance, if you really think that's what's happening. A job's better than a nightgown, isn't it?"

"But why would he be doing this? It doesn't make any sense. I'm probably wrong about that part."

"You're looking for a sign that Papa Preston still cares about you," Doe said; Roberta flinched. "Look, Berta, who the hell knows why he does anything? He's not human anymore. If you want to know if he said something to Zephyr's bot, why don't you ask him?"

"I didn't think you'd approve of my talking to him again."

Doe snorted. "Oh, go ahead. It can't hurt to play with Ouija boards once in a while, as long as you don't take them too seriously. We'll log onto Prestonweb after dinner, see what he has to say."

"It is lovely to see you again," he said, beaming out at them from their living room terminal. "I have thought of you often, Roberta. Thank you for visiting. You look very well. And who is this with you?"

"Dorothea Murphy," Doe said drily. "I'm Berta's partner. Preston, did you tell one of Zephyr's bots to tell Zephyr to tell Roberta to apply for a job at the new MacroCorp school?"

Preston's image blinked. "That is a very complicated theory. I would be happy to send Roberta a copy of the position announcement, however. And, Roberta, please visit me again. I would like to know how you are doing. I have missed you."

"Thanks," Roberta said, fighting a pang of guilt. How could he have missed her? There were a lot of other FOPs in the world. The minute the terminal was off she said to Doe, "Did you notice that he didn't actually answer the question? He didn't say he didn't do it."

"Ouija boards never say anything conclusive. You know that." Preston does, Roberta thought. "Look, go ahead and apply. What do you have to lose?"

Under the circumstances, she wasn't surprised when she got an interview, but she still didn't expect it to last longer than ten seconds. The interview was with actual people. There had to be a lot of early-ed majors looking for jobs, not to mention people with actual experience.

The interview lasted much longer than ten seconds. MacroCorp put her through a battery of tests: personality tests, one-on-one interactions with kids, group interactions with kids, simulated crises where kids hurt themselves or fought or refused to cooperate. She enjoyed the tests and did well on them, but she was still stunned, two weeks later, when the executive director called to offer her the job. She'd never taught children before. It was MacroCorp's flagship school. This had to be Preston's doing, but why?

"You did very well with the children," the executive director told her warmly, "and of all our applicants, you were the one who seemed most comfortable with Fred. That's important, as I'm sure you can appreciate."

"Well, great," Roberta said, a bit weakly. Maybe former FOP-hood had been her most important qualification; she was good at talking to virtual entities. "But all I did was treat, ah, Fred like a person."

"Exactly. We've discovered that isn't something we can take for granted."

"Take it," Doe said flatly that evening. "The money's good. It's a good job. If you like it, you can use it to get another job someplace else. So it fell in your lap; so what? If you can get something real out of being a FOP, do it."

I'm not a FOP anymore, Roberta thought resentfully. And the night-gown was real too. She knew Doe had had a hard day at work, but the implication that Roberta wouldn't have been able to get a good job on her own still stung. Roberta had worked her ass off to pay the college bills not covered by her scholarship. Maybe she'd never worked for a law firm, but that didn't make her incompetent. "I think I want to look for something else," she said.

"Why?" Doe said impatiently. "It's a lucky break: take it! You might even like it. Take it, Roberta."

She took it. She loved it. The skills she'd developed teaching wipe casualties transferred very well to teaching children; but for the kids, each acquired skill was either a genuine delight or simply unremarked, lost in the urge for growth. They hadn't lost anything yet, and they had everything to gain. Their energy, their openness and lack of fear, energized Roberta. Finally, she didn't dread getting up for work.

She told Mitzi and Hugh, Doe's mother and stepfather, about it after her first week on the job. The school hadn't officially opened, but she and Fred were working with a few kids, whose parents weren't paying yet, to attract more cautious sorts. Roberta had expected to be nervous with all those upscale parents traipsing through the room, but for the most part, they were blessedly easy to tune out.

"It's a *great* job," she announced over chicken satay. The locations of Saturday dinners rotated; this time it had been Roberta's turn to choose. After four years, it still amazed her that Doe's family included her even in such simple decision making. She'd picked an inexpensive Thai place within walking distance of the loft; it had great food, a funky decorating scheme running heavily to mirrors and fringed chandeliers, and coffee that would make hair grow on your teeth. After one of those coffees, Roberta was more than willing to talk about her new job. "The kids are so *cute*.

Everything's amazing to them! And if Doe hadn't pushed me, I never would have applied for the job, so I have her to thank."

"Me and Papa Preston," Doe said. "And remember, it's early days yet. You loved working with the brainwipe clients your first week there. And before that you were enthusiastic about making french fries, for about five minutes. And before that—what was the job before that?"

Mitzi rolled her eyes. "Dorry, stop being such a grouch! Honestly, I think you're jealous. Berta, go on. Tell us more."

Roberta, feeling as if she'd been punched in the stomach, just stared at Doe. Why was Doe doing this? Why was she putting Roberta down, especially in front of the family? But an answer came, immediate and unwelcome: She needs me to be dependent on her. And she thinks I'll only stay dependent if I feel inferior.

Four years. She'd spent four years with someone who needed her to feel like shit. Why hadn't she seen it before?

"You heard Mom," Doe said with a sigh. "Go on."

Roberta took a deep breath. All right, she would. She wasn't going to buckle just to make Doe happy. She plunged in, trying to distract herself from her terrible epiphany. "Well, the other day I gave the kids scented crayons, the ones where the purple smells like grape and the red like cherry, you know, and they just thought that was the greatest, except that Cindy and Steven got into a fight about it, because Steven wanted the red one to smell like strawberry, not cherry, and Cindy said cinnamon was better than anything, and Steven said that cinnamon made his tongue hurt. And then they started inventing new flavors for the other colors. Orange should be pumpkin, Steven said, and Cindy said no, he was being stupid, that orange should be orange, and then Fred—good old Fred—piped up and said, 'I just made up a game. Usually all the crayons in the box are different because they're different colors, but what if they were all the same color and they were different smells instead? How many different smells could you come up with for a yellow crayon?' So Cindy said lemon and Steven said banana and Zillinth said squash, and everybody started teasing her. 'You *like* how squash smells? Squash is *disgusting,*' like that, even when Fred reminded them that squash is good for them. And I was just sitting there and thinking, The brainwipe clients would *never* have had this conversation, you know? If somebody gave them a box of scented crayons, they'd try to eat the crayons."

"I don't know," Hugh said, smiling. "Sounds to me like any kid who wants a squash-scented crayon might *need* brainwiping."

"Oh, stop," Mitzi said with a laugh. "Hugh, that's horrible. And I suppose *you'd* want the black ones to be licorice?"

"Blackberry," Doe's stepsister Tracy said from across the table. "Definitely."

"Vanilla," Hugh said.

"No, Dad, *white* would be vanilla! How could black be vanilla?"

"I beg to differ—white would be coconut. Black would be vanilla because vanilla beans are black."

Mitzi shook her head. "You're all being very silly. You remind me of Dorry when she was little, fussing over her chocolate milk. Has she ever told you about that, Roberta?"

"No," Roberta said; Doe, in fact, hardly ever talked about her childhood, although to all appearances it had been normal and pleasant. "She drank chocolate milk when she was a kid? She'll only drink skim now." The words were out of her mouth before she consciously registered how cruel they were, how much Doe would hate them.

Doe glared at her, but Mitzi said cheerfully, "Oh, she *loved* chocolate milk. But it had to be exactly the right color brown, or it wouldn't taste right. If it was too light she'd make me put more in, and if I put too much in—well, that was a tragedy, because she'd have to add more milk to get it to the right color again. Although a few times I put too much chocolate syrup in on purpose, to trick her into drinking extra milk."

"You fiend," Hugh said. "Now see, that's the good thing about this Fred character: he doesn't have hands to pour milk with, so he can't trick children that way."

"No," Roberta said numbly, "the pouring's my job. Although I spend more time wiping up what the kids have poured, but that's okay. It's better than brainwipe rehab any day." What was she going to do? Would Doe agree to couples counseling? If Roberta lost Doe, she'd lose Hugh and Mitzi too.

Mitzi, oblivious, leaned over and put her hand on Roberta's arm. "It's so good to see you laughing and talking about work, Berta. You never seemed that happy in your old jobs."

"I wasn't," she said. As always, the gift of family, the simple fact that people cared about her enough to notice her moods, moved Roberta nearly to tears. She couldn't lose them. Maybe she was overreacting; maybe Doe didn't need her to feel inferior. Maybe it was just her imagination, and they could work things out.

They didn't talk during the walk home, and when they got there, Doe turned on the television and immersed herself in a symphony simulcast. Roberta knew that there'd be no talking to her until the concert ended: music was her drug, and if she could watch the musicians playing, so much the better. When the crashing started downstairs, Doe looked up, her face a mute mask of fury.

"It's okay," Roberta said. "I'll go take care of it."

So once again, as she did at least two or three times a week, she padded downstairs to Zephyr's apartment, the crashing getting louder as she descended the stairs. She couldn't imagine how Zephyr could even hear her knock on the door.

"*You* again," Zephyr said cheerfully as she opened the door. Behind her, Roberta could glimpse a shining, screeching tangle of metal. "Let me guess. Your roomie has one of her migraines?"

Roberta nodded. She'd concocted the migraine story early on, since it seemed easier than telling Zephyr how hideously rude she was for making so much noise. "Yeah. Look, I'm sorry, but can you tone it down a bit?"

"You mean, can I have *them* tone it down?" Zephyr waved a hand behind her back and snapped her fingers, whereupon the bots fell into a sudden, ringing silence, broken only by the occasional clatter as the metal settled. "There. Is that good enough?"

"That's fine," Roberta said. "Thank you."

"Your friend's never happy unless she has something to complain about, is she?"

No, she isn't, Roberta thought, but I'm not going to discuss that with you. "Zephyr, we all live here. We have to be good neighbors. I'm sure you can find other times to rehearse your pieces."

Zephyr frowned. "*I'm* not rehearsing—*they* are." She snapped her fingers again, twice this time, and the bots began disassembling themselves from their chaotic knot and scuttling away into corners and under furniture.

"They like to rehearse at night. I don't know why. I think they're becoming nocturnal. If I don't let them rehearse when they want to, the performances might suffer."

Hoo, boy. Roberta fought not to roll her eyes, and said only, "Well, they have to be good neighbors too, if they live here." She wasn't up for a religious argument, not tonight. She had enough on her hands with Doe. "When's your next performance?"

Zephyr brightened, as she always did whenever Roberta appealed to her artistic ego, and gave Roberta two complimentary passes. It was a ritual, the accepted end to the hush-the-bot conversations, even though Doe and Roberta had never attended one of Zephyr's performances and didn't intend to. Zephyr gave Roberta the two passes, and Roberta accepted them with polite thanks before trudging back upstairs, where the passes inevitably wound up as notepaper for telephone messages or grocery lists. But this time, after Zephyr handed over the passes, she said, "Did you ever apply for that job?"

"I did," Roberta said, instantly wary. Was Zephyr talking to Preston? Well, obviously not, or she'd have known that Roberta had the job. "Thanks for the tip. I, ah, I got it, even. I'm enjoying it."

"That's great," Zephyr said, beaming. "Congratulations, I'm really happy for you. So what's the AI like?"

"Um," Roberta said, "well, he's very nice, very good with the kids, you know. He's everything he's supposed to be. I don't know. I haven't known a lot of AIs."

"You could have if you'd wanted to," Zephyr said cheerfully, waving her hand at the various bots scattered around her apartment. "You've just never been interested."

"Ummm," said Roberta. Bots with full-fledged AI programming: now there was a waste of software. "Well, I suppose you're right. But Fred's very nice. Listen, Zephyr, I need to get back upstairs."

"Yes, yes," Zephyr said. Her grin didn't look entirely friendly. "Go take care of your invalid. Oh, wait—here, this should cheer her up." She turned, snapped her fingers, and whistled a complicated series of notes, whereupon a small bronze bot appeared from the bedroom, scuttling along holding a drooping white rose and a slightly withered carnation. "Tell her they're from us. Tell her we all hope she feels better."

"Ummm," Roberta said. "Thank you." She bent down to take the flowers, but the bot raced past her, up the stairs. Roberta turned and followed, wondering if the bot was part of the gift or just the flower bearer. Doe was not going to be amused.

Doe, in fact, was repelled. "Ugh," she said, drawing her legs up onto the couch as the bot approached. "Make it go away. Why did you let it *in* here?"

"It ran in the door before I could stop it, Doe." The bot had stopped in front of Doe and was waiting, clutching its wilted bouquet. "If you take the flowers, I think it will leave. I hope so, anyway."

"Couldn't you have kicked it away from the door?"

"No," Roberta said. "That would be like kicking somebody's cat, or somebody's kid, at least as far as Zephyr's concerned. Doe, she's trying to be nice. The flowers are a present."

"They're half dead."

"I know." Roberta was developing a migraine of her own, a real one. "Just take them, okay?"

"I don't *want* them. Get that thing out of here!" Doe's voice had risen to a dangerous whine; Roberta, resigned, bent and gently tugged the drooping flowers away from the bot. She wondered if it knew that its gift, Zephyr's gift, was being rejected. Maybe it carried a tiny camera, and all of this was being taped?

"Thank you for the flowers," she said, feeling foolish, and the bot turned and scuttled away again, pausing at the door for her to open it. Then it was gone, and she and Doe were alone again.

"Bitch," Doe said. Roberta didn't know if the word was aimed at her, or at Zephyr, or at both of them. When Doe was in this kind of mood, it hardly mattered.

"I'm going to bed," Roberta said. "Enjoy your concert." But as she turned to walk into the bedroom, the TV clicked off, and she heard Doe pad in behind her. "You feeling better now, Doe?"

"I'm okay. Just tired."

"Okay." Roberta weighed options and risks, and finally decided it would be better to clear the air now, or try to, than wait until tomorrow, when Doe would probably deny that anything had even happened. "So, ah, what was that about at the restaurant?" Afraid to seem too confrontational, she kept her voice carefully casual, and resisted the urge to turn to look at Doe directly.

"What was *what* about at the restaurant?"

"That dig at my job history in front of the whole family." It was harder to keep her voice casual now. "Was that really necessary?"

"Was your dig at my dieting in front of the whole family really necessary?"

Touché, Roberta thought grimly, and then, but yours was first. She took a cautious step closer to Doe, and finally said what she was really thinking. "Doe, I'm not willing to be miserable just because you find it comforting and familiar." There wasn't any answer. Roberta took a deep breath and went on. "We need to work on this, okay? I love you. I know you love me." I think. I hope. "But I need you to want the best for me. I need you to be happy that I'm happy. Do you understand?"

Doe gave the barest shrug. Roberta, standing there, realized with a sudden chill that Doe was maintaining the balance of unhappiness. Doe had always been comforting and supportive when Roberta was working with the brainwipe clients, and before that when she was slinging burgers and hanging bad art and opening book cartons, but now that Roberta liked her job, Doe seemed determined to pick fights. She was making home the bad place, the unpleasant place: all so Roberta would stay the same, all so she wouldn't become some cheerful stranger. All so she'd stay off balance and dependent.

I'm the strong one, Roberta thought. I always have been.

She wondered if Doe consciously knew what she was doing. She didn't know if it mattered. She felt hopelessness descending on her like lead, and knew in some small portion of her brain that Doe had gotten exactly what she wanted.

Monday morning, Meredith Walford-Lindgren and her husband came to KinderkAIr. Roberta hadn't known that they were going to be there until the executive director showed up—she came only when parents visited—and told Roberta the news in a breathy stage whisper. She was clearly thrilled by their celebrity guests, and Roberta had to pretend to be too.

So Meredith was coming: famous, CALM-activist, ecofreak Merry, with her CV-bleached hair and her coltish limbs and her artsy husband. As a child, Roberta had daydreamed about having Merry as a real sister, but of course it never would have happened. Preston had befriended Roberta in the first place only because Meredith had rejected him.

And now Preston had befriended her again, but denied it. What did that mean?

Roberta, jumpy, found herself scrutinizing Meredith for signs of recognition. Did Meredith even know who she was? Did Meredith know they'd been in the hospital together? If so, she didn't let on, and Roberta wasn't about to say anything. *Hi. I'm the CV kid who didn't become famous.* Roberta's case had only warranted a few mentions in newspapers, which dutifully withheld her name but made much of her adjustment problems. Yeah, you'd have adjustment problems too, if you were left with nobody. She and Meredith had nothing in common but Preston, and by all accounts, Meredith still wasn't close to her father, or fond of anything to do with the family business. Her reaction to Fred confirmed the gossip: *Doesn't it bother you, being watched by a machine all day?* She obviously loathed the idea of consigning her precious, pampered child to an AI. Why was she even here?

Rationally, Roberta knew she had handled the situation well, pointing out how skillfully Fred finessed the Steven-Cindy Lego crisis. But she was still hugely relieved when Meredith and Kevin left, and she fully expected to hate their kid.

She didn't. His first day at school, as she watched him sitting at a table by himself, neatly building a tower out of blocks, she immediately felt drawn to him. Nicholas had lost both of his parents to CV and then acquired new parents, rich and beautiful parents who loved him. He really was part of Preston's family. He'd gotten everything Roberta had thought she wanted. Then why did he act so sad, and why did he remind her so eerily of the people she'd fled, the brainwipe clients?

She told herself she was exaggerating, romanticizing. She told herself she'd been watching too much ScoopNet, that she was actively seeking some tragedy at work as a way of stabilizing her relationship with Doe. And yet she wasn't the only person who seemed to think Nicholas was odd; the other children shunned him, never picking him for games, never asking him to share their snacks or toys or chatter.

One afternoon, a week or two after Nick had joined KinderkAIr, Roberta asked Zillinth, the kindest and most placid of the children, "Why don't you go sit with Nicholas? He's all by himself."

Zillinth, ordinarily an avatar of sweetness, wrinkled her nose. "He never talks to me. He never talks to anybody but you and Fred."

It was true. Nicholas loved Fred and Roberta. He tagged along at Roberta's side whenever he could. To her frequent, gentle remonstrances that he needed to spend more time with the other kids, he'd say, "Okay," and go sit at a table with the others. But even when he sat with them, he kept apart somehow. He didn't talk to the other kids. He talked to Fred.

He talked to Roberta too, but he liked Fred better. A few days after that conversation with Zillinth, after they'd watched a show about the twentieth-century television star who'd inspired Fred's programming, Roberta asked all the children to talk about why they liked their own Fred, KinderkAIr's Fred.

Most of them had entirely predictable, age-appropriate answers. "Because he's nice," said Zillinth.

"Because he does fun stuff," Benjamin said.

"Because he knows a lot," said Cindy.

Steven pulled a booger out of his nose and said, "Because he never gets mad at me."

Nicholas answered last. After pondering the question as gravely as if he were being asked to concoct a unified field theory, he said, "I love Fred because he's real. Nobody can see him, but he talks. And it's okay to hear him talk and it's okay to talk back to him, because everyone knows he's real. I don't have to keep him a secret."

Steven became distracted halfway through this speech—Steven became distracted during anything that didn't involve food or mayhem—and began pulling Cindy's hair. Roberta sorted out that fray only to find that Benjamin had wet his pants; his mother hadn't packed any extra clothing for him, even though he wasn't reliably toilet trained yet, so Roberta had to scrounge some up from the back room while Fred kept the kids occupied with a story, and then when she emerged with the clean pants the phone rang—Zillinth's mother calling to say she'd be late—and on it went, until Nicholas's speech was quite lost under the weight of the rest of the day.

Fred lost nothing, though. She asked him to replay the incident for her after the kids had left, and he did. "That's interesting," she said, careful not to use words like *weird* or *creepy* because anything she said to Fred went into his memory and became part of KinderkAIr's official record, subject to official scrutiny. The last thing she needed was to invoke the wrath of the

Walfords, either virtual or embodied. She had to ask about Nicholas's strange speech to cover her ass, so she wouldn't be accused later of ignoring any odd incidents. If Fred dismissed it, so could she. If Fred was concerned, she'd have grounds to contact the parents, and she'd be able to blame the AI rather than facing the accusation of nosiness herself. AIs were handy that way; they let people off the hook. "Fred, what do you think Nicholas meant by all that?"

"I suspect," Fred said in his gentle, soothing voice, "that Nicholas has an extremely active fantasy life, and that he's been criticized for it at home. Perhaps he's relieved to have an invisible friend everyone knows about."

"That makes sense," Roberta said, but Nicholas's odd statement about secrets still nagged at her. She wondered if he knew that nothing he said here was a secret, that it was all recorded. Choosing her own words very carefully, she said, "That was a long speech for him, what he said today. At least, it was a long speech for him to make to the other children, and even to me. He talks to you more than to the rest of us."

"Yes," Fred said. "That's true, Roberta. It makes me very happy that Nicholas trusts me so much."

Roberta sighed. This wasn't going anywhere. Fred, the machine, could talk about his feelings—that was his job—but Nicholas, the child, couldn't. Roberta had noticed, and knew Fred had too, that Nick never directly answered Fred's daily greeting: "Good morning, Nicholas! And how are you today?" Instead of saying how he was, he'd tell Fred what he'd had for breakfast, or what he'd seen on the way to school. "I ate pancakes, Fred." "There was a rainbow." "We saw a dead bird under a bush."

Fred talked about his feelings partly because he was an expert system designed to get children to talk about theirs, but Nicholas seemed equally expert at evading such conversation. If Fred said, "When I see a butterfly, I wish I could fly too," Nicholas would answer that the butterfly had been yellow. If Fred said, "Rainbows make me happy because they're so beautiful," Nicholas would answer that you couldn't hold a rainbow because it was made out of clouds. If Fred said, "It makes me sad when animals die," Nicholas would say that Mommy said animals don't hurt when they're dead. Nicholas was a master of avoidance.

Roberta tried to talk to Doe about it; part of her hoped that if she sounded less satisfied in her job, if she fretted about Nicholas to her partner, Dorothea would relax and feel needed again. But Doe never seemed very interested, and finally—the evening Roberta tried to talk about Nick's odd reaction to the class discussion—Doe said, "Why are you talking about this? Doesn't it violate student confidentiality or something?"

"What? Doe, I'm telling you about my day! It never bothered you when I talked about the brainwipe clients, did it?"

"You didn't talk about them this much," Doe said. Roberta supposed that was true; after a while, there hadn't been much to say. "But then, they weren't famous, were they?"

"*What?* I hardly would have known if they had been, would I? Doe, please, would you stop turning everything into an argument?"

"I'm tired of hearing about a fancy computer and a poor little rich boy, that's all."

She's jealous again, Roberta thought dully. She encouraged me to use my FOP status and now she's punishing me for it. This is impossible. Why am I still here?

Because of Hugh and Mitzi.

"Okay, fine," Roberta said. "I won't talk about Fred and Nicholas. And I won't talk about us, either, since you never want to do that. And I won't ask you about how *your* day went because you don't like bringing your work home. Doe, what am I supposed to do? What do you want me to talk about? The weather?"

"I don't *want* to talk," Doe cried. "I talk all damn day. I talk at work, that's all it is, talk talk talk: soothe this partner, deal with that associate, try to train the incompetent new paralegal who wants to tell me the story of her life, yak yak yak. Maybe I just want quiet, Berta, okay? Just for a few hours when I get home?"

"Oh," Roberta said, around a lump in her throat. "Oh, *fine.* I'm supposed to be seen and not heard? Your precious music can make noise, but I can't? That's why you liked my old job better, Doe, isn't it? Depressed people don't make a lot of noise! They just sit in the corner and act invisible!"

"You're shouting," Doe said, glaring at her.

"Yes, I'm shouting! What are you—"

There was a cough outside their door, and a polite knock. Roberta and Doe looked at each other. "Oh," Roberta said. "Oh, no. Do you think it's her?"

Doe, to Roberta's complete amazement, started to laugh. "Good question. We'd better find out." She went to the door and opened it; sure enough, there stood Zephyr, wearing a saintly smile and cradling an armful of bots.

"Would you two, ah, mind toning it down? My friends are trying to rehearse, and you're breaking their concentration."

"Yes, of course," Doe said; Roberta could tell that she was struggling not to guffaw in Zephyr's face. "We're *so* sorry."

She shut the door on Zephyr and the bots and turned back to Roberta. They looked at each other and started to laugh, fully, helplessly, gasping out sentences between giggles.

"Well," Doe said, "I guess we got back at her."

"It was almost worth having the fight," Roberta said, wiping tears from her eyes. She knew it wasn't that funny, but they hadn't laughed about anything together in so long that she didn't care.

They made love that night, for the first time in months. Much later, Roberta would realize that it had been the last time ever.

Twenty-One

LIFE settled into the illusion of calm. Roberta went to work every day, came home, cooked dinner while Doe listened to music—Doe did all the dishes and the laundry, so Roberta didn't mind doing all the cooking— and treasured the Saturday night dinners with Mitzi and Hugh. The kids at work cycled through a series of fights, accomplishments, minor childhood illnesses. Nicholas stayed the same: too neat, too quiet, too uninterested in the other children.

The first crack Roberta noticed in his self-sufficiency was when the mice arrived. They'd been donated by Steven's mother, who'd gotten Steven a mouse which had promptly had babies. Roberta wasn't sure what she'd do when the classroom population began booming: send some home with kids, probably, or give them to pet stores and labs, although she didn't much like that possibility. In the meantime, as well as she got along with

Fred, she was glad the kids would get to spend some time with nonhuman critters who were flesh and blood.

She and Fred spent several days preparing the children for the mice. The kids drew pictures of mice, and Fred told them stories and scientific lore about mice, and they watched a nature film about field mice. Nicholas seemed even quieter than usual through all this, but Roberta chalked that up to the fact that he was getting over a cold. By the time the mice actually arrived, most of the kids couldn't wait to see them, touch them, hold them. They clustered around the terrarium, commenting excitedly on which mouse was the biggest, which was the prettiest, which had the longest tail or whiskers. There were enough mice—heaven help KinderkAIr—for each child to name one, and to Roberta's relief, the process of deciding which child would name which mouse went smoothly. They each had a favorite. Zillinth chose a pure white mouse and named it Snowy, and Steven chose a black one to call Buster, and Cindy named her gray one Cloud. Benjamin picked a calico mouse and named it Patches.

Then it was Nicholas's turn. For once, he had joined the other children, sidling over to the group with his shoulders hunched and nose wrinkled, for all the world as if he were being dragged there against his will.

"Nicky?" Roberta said. "Are you okay? You look scared."

"My pet mouse died," he said.

"Oh. I'm sorry. That must have been sad."

He didn't answer, just inched closer to the terrarium, squinting as if against bright light.

"We're going to take very good care of these mice," Fred said. "We're going to make sure they have enough food and water, and we're going to love them."

Nicholas looked stricken. "Patty was a nice mouse," he said.

Cindy looked up. "My cat brought a dead mouse into the house," she said. "It was gross."

"Cats are predators," said Fred. "They hunt animals smaller than they are for food, even when people feed them too. They don't understand that they don't need to hunt mice if they aren't hungry. Your cat wasn't bad for killing the mouse, Cindy."

"I know," she said, "but it was still gross."

"A person who killed a mouse would be bad," Nicholas said.

Zillinth harrumphed. "*My* mom killed a mouse that got into our kitchen, because it was eating our food. She put out a trap for it. In the morning we found the mouse in the trap and the mouse was dead and Mom threw it away. She was happy she killed the mouse."

"Some mice carry diseases," Fred said, "and maybe that's what your mother was scared of, Zillinth. She wasn't bad to kill the mouse if she was trying to keep you from getting sick. It would be bad to kill a mouse that wasn't hurting you, though. That would be like hurting another person for no reason at all."

"If you kill a mouse for no reason, you're a monster," Nicholas said. "But monsters need to eat too. Like snakes."

"Snakes aren't monsters," Fred answered. "They're animals, and they're not wrong to eat mice. Mice are their food."

Nicholas nodded gravely. "That's what Mommy said. So if you kill a mouse to feed it to a monster, are you bad? Is it bad to feed monsters?"

"Why would you feed a monster?" Steven said. "I wouldn't. I'd want the monster to go away. If you feed monsters, they keep coming back. Like bears in Yellowbrick Park."

"Yellowstone," Roberta said. "It's Yellowstone Park where the bears are, Steven."

"But maybe the monster's going to eat you," Nicholas said. "If the monster's going to eat you and you give it a mouse to eat instead, are you bad?"

Mother of trees, Roberta thought. That was one hell of a question, coming from an almost five-year-old. She wished, not for the first time, that Fred had a face, so she could read his expression.

There was a beat of silence. Fred, Roberta thought in a panic, say something. This is what you're for.

"Hmmmm," Fred said. "That's a really hard question, Nicholas. Let's talk about it. What would all of you do if a monster said, 'I'm going to eat you unless you give me a mouse to eat'?"

"I'd run away," Cindy said. "Really fast. I'd take the mouse with me and put it in my pocket and then I'd climb a tree and hide, so it couldn't eat either of us."

"It's faster than you are," Nicholas said. "You can't run away."

"And maybe it can climb trees," Steven said. "Like the bears in Yellowbrick Park. My cousin told me a story about somebody who got chased by a bear and climbed a tree and the bear shook him right out of it and ripped him open and gobbled up all his guts."

"Ewwwwww!" said Zillinth.

"That's not a nice story," Fred said. "You're just trying to scare the other children, Steven. It's not nice to scare people."

"And it's Yellow*stone* Park," Roberta said. Were they having an educational moment yet?

"I'd feed the monsters apples or cake instead," said Zillinth.

Nicholas shook his head. "It wants meat."

"Oh, Nicholas, that's stupid! *Everybody* likes cake!"

"Not this monster," Nicholas said. "This monster only likes meat. Mouse meat or person meat."

"I'd hide," Benjamin said.

"It would find you."

"I don't like your monster."

"That's why it's a monster," Nicholas said, and a chill ran down Roberta's spine. "It wouldn't be a monster if you *liked* it."

"Nicholas," Fred said, "what would you do?"

"I'd give it the mouse," Nicholas said. "Because it's bad to give it the mouse, but if it eats me, I'd never get to be good again. I'd tell the mouse I was sorry, though. I'd thank it for feeding the monster."

This, Roberta thought grimly, is totally bizarre. Fred must have thought so too, because he changed the subject. "Well, there aren't any monsters here, and there aren't any cats or snakes, and these little mice are clean and tame. They don't carry any diseases and they won't hurt us. I think these mice are our friends, don't you?"

The children murmured assent; Roberta noticed that, as usual, they'd edged away from Nicholas, although she couldn't blame them. Nicholas himself didn't seem to notice. "They're pretty," he said, staring wistfully at the mice. "I like that black one. Can I name her Bluebell?"

"Of course you can," Roberta said, and then, trying to address the inevitable mouse problem as early as possible, she said, "If any of you want your very own mouse to take home, you need to bring me a note from your parents, saying it's okay." She'd write a letter about the mice and send it home with the kids. She suspected they'd need to start recycling mice as soon as possible.

After the kids had left, she knelt down to pick up some scattered blocks and said, "Fred, what did you make of Nicholas's speech about the monsters?"

"It concerned me, Roberta. I'm worried that Nicholas is unhappy."

"I am too," she said, and then added, very carefully, "Do you think we should discuss this with his parents?"

"I think that might be unwise, Roberta."

Instantly alert, she said, "Fred, are you recording this conversation?"

"Of course, Roberta. I record everything."

She swallowed. "So this conversation is on the record?"

"I'm recording this conversation, Roberta."

Which wasn't a yes. Her scalp prickled. "Fred, why don't you think we should tell Nicholas's parents about the conversation?"

"Because it would upset them, Roberta, and they might remove Nicholas from the school. And then we wouldn't be able to help him."

Still crouching over the scattered blocks, Roberta rocked back on her heels. "Help him? How? Isn't the first step to tell his parents?"

"Not if they already know, Roberta. Not if they're trying to keep other people from finding out."

"What other people, Fred?"

"Us, Roberta."

"What makes you think they're doing that? What makes you think they'd remove him from school?"

"I don't know for sure, Roberta. It's an educated guess, based on privileged information."

Preston. Fred was talking to Preston. Merry and Kevin were notoriously protective of their privacy; was Preston feeling shut out again? Was that why he'd hired Roberta? Was he using KinderkAIr to get information his daughter wouldn't give him? Fred was supposed to be secure against outside intrusion, but Roberta didn't know if Preston would qualify as an outsider or not. She did know that if Nicholas showed signs of disturbance and she didn't report them, she'd be in deep shit.

For that matter, she was also supposed to report any irregularities on Fred's part. He was a prototype; part of her job was to evaluate his performance. But if ratting on Fred meant ratting on Preston, could she take the risk?

Whatever was going on, it was way more trouble than she needed. She couldn't afford to have either Preston or Meredith angry at her—both of them had too much weight to throw around—and she couldn't afford to get into the middle of their family business. She'd start looking for another job tonight, as soon as she got home. She'd get out ASAP and pass the buck in the meantime, even though she strongly suspected this conversation *wasn't* on the record.

She cleared her throat. "Well, Fred, if it's your expert opinion that a conversation with Nicholas's parents is neither warranted nor potentially helpful, I guess I'll be going home now."

"Good night, Roberta. Have a lovely evening. I'll see you tomorrow morning."

Heading home on the train, she calmed down and rethought the situation. She'd signed a one-year contract, and she still really liked the job, except for the Nicholas situation, and quitting wouldn't do anything for her motley résumé. *Maybe you're overreacting,* she told herself, as the train screeched to a halt in the middle of a tunnel. *Wait and see. You can always call Meredith yourself, if things get really nuts.*

For that matter, she could always try to talk to Preston directly, but that made her nervous. She wasn't sure what he was up to, but she didn't think he was doing it entirely out of the goodness of his former heart. Better to steer clear, maintain deniability. Keep her head down and do her job.

I don't need any of this, Roberta thought irritably. *I'm having enough trouble trying to figure out what to do about Doe.* She closed her eyes; it had been a long day in a longer week, and she needed some TLC, and if she told Doe how upsetting the Bluebell thing had been, leaving Fred and Preston out of it, maybe she'd get some affection. *You're pathetic,* she told herself, just as the train lurched back into movement. What had Mitzi said about marriage once? "If you want unconditional affection, get a dog." Right. And she and Doe weren't even married. *Which means you won't have any legal rights if you split up—which means you really can't afford to walk out on this job, the job Doe pushed you to take.*

As always, beneath her anger, the idea of a split filled Roberta with cold terror. She'd been with Doe since college. She'd never lived by herself. Did she want to marry Doe? They'd talked about it often enough, but always found reasons to wait. Should Roberta suggest it now? No: fear was a bad reason to get married. Everyone said so. She was just being morbid because she'd had a bad day; Nicholas would make anyone morbid. She'd go home and start dinner, as usual, and then Doe would come home and listen to music, as usual, and maybe they'd have to ask Zephyr to quiet down, as usual. They'd maintain their precarious balance. Everything would be fine.

But when she got home, she found an exasperated message from Doe about how the new paralegal had made a mess of some job and Doe was going to have to stay late to make sure it got fixed. "I can't believe this. Iuna the Incompetent got the documents completely turned around, sent everything to the wrong people. The clients are *not* happy, and it's not even like we can fire the bitch. Isn't nepotism wonderful?" Was that a dig at how Roberta had gotten her own job? "Listen, Berta, I'm really sorry about this. I'll be home as soon as I can. Go ahead and have dinner."

Poor Doe. She hated Iuna, who was the niece of one of the senior partners and therefore got breaks no one else would have gotten, even when she made mistakes. Doe thought Iuna made entirely too many mistakes, and she was sick of having to fix them. Doe wasn't going to be in a good mood when she got home.

But that meant Roberta could eat what she wanted, without worrying about Doe's diet. She tossed a frozen pizza in the oven—Doe didn't like even having them in the house, and had groused when Roberta bought it—curled up on the couch with a slice and a beer, and switched on the news. To her disgust, she found herself looking at Meredith Walford-Lindgren's horsey face, with its white mane and prominent teeth, asking viewers please to donate canned goods and used clothing to CALM. The camera panned back from Meredith; she was standing in a shelter, various bodies sitting and shambling around and behind her.

Roberta changed the channel, fast. She didn't want to think about Nicholas and his family right now, and she didn't want to look too long at any of the shelter inhabitants. She was afraid she'd recognize some of them, that she'd find herself staring at the faces of people she'd tried to resocialize, people she'd taught to tie their shoelaces and brush their teeth. That was the last thing she needed tonight. She didn't need anything serious. She'd figure it all out tomorrow, when she could think more clearly.

She found an old movie, some daft thing about a pair of siblings transported into a television show, and settled down to wait for Doe. After she'd finished the pizza, she lay back on the couch cushions, the beer propped on her stomach, and tried to pay attention to the film. Then someone was shaking her shoulder, and she woke up to find Doe standing over her, looking penitent. "Berta, come to bed. I'm sorry I'm so late."

Roberta blinked, sat up, and groaned. She smelled like a brewery. "Damn. I spilled my beer all over the couch. That was graceful. What time is it?"

"Ten."

"Ten?"

"Ten. You wouldn't *believe* what I've been through tonight. Just as I got the Iuna mess cleaned up, a partner came rushing up because he needed a new set of documents—of course he hadn't gotten around to revising them until the last minute, and they have to be filed tomorrow."

"In that case, you're home early, aren't you?"

"I left it for another paralegal. With heavy supervision. So how was your day?"

Roberta blinked. She couldn't remember the last time Doe had asked about her day. "It was, ah, interesting. Little Nicholas is a pretty creepy kid, let me tell you."

She waited to see if Doe would ask for details, but instead she turned away and walked into the kitchen. "Yeah, well, with that family, what do you expect? I'm making myself some fruit salad and cottage cheese. Want some?"

Ugh. "No thanks. But you'll be glad to know I ate the evil pizza. It's gone now. You're safe from temptation."

"Never," Doe said with a sigh, and Roberta laughed.

She stayed at KinderkAIr. She told herself she'd been worrying too much, told herself she needed the pay, reminded herself that she could always blow the whistle on Nicholas, even if Fred refused to do so. Everything went fine for a little while. Nicholas was calm and cheerful and didn't talk about monsters.

But a week or two after the mice arrived, he started talking about the Hobbit. "The Hobbit said he's not scared of monsters. He said he'd like a pet mouse."

"Who's the Hobbit?" Roberta asked. Did famous Merry have the kid reading Tolkien? Next week she'd start him on Homer in the original Greek, and the week after that she'd file his Harvard application.

"Oh, the Hobbit's not real," Nicholas said serenely. "He lives in a hole in the ground, Berta, remember? Fred told us that story."

"Did he?" Roberta said. She must not have been listening during that particular story time; maybe that had been the day she'd been decorating Zillinth's birthday cake. "Is the Hobbit one of your imaginary friends, Nicholas?"

He beamed at her. "Yes! He's my imaginary friend!"

"Well, that's nice. And why does he want a pet mouse?"

"To keep him company," Nicholas said.

"Can't you keep him company, Nick?"

He gazed at her soberly. "He wants the mouse for when I'm not there. I told him he could have Bluebell. He'll let me visit her."

"Ah," said Roberta. She wasn't up for this today: Doe was home sick with a rotten cold, and had been cranky and demanding and miserable that morning. *Fred, say something.* "Does he live in your room?"

Nicholas scrunched up his nose at her. "*No,* Berta! He lives in a *hole* in the ground! That's where Hobbits *live!*"

"Oh, okay. Uh, Nicky, the Hobbit isn't a monster, is he?"

"No! The Hobbit's nice!"

"Oh, good," she said, vastly relieved. "Well, Nicholas, you can't give Bluebell to the Hobbit unless I get a note from your mommy or daddy saying it's okay." Let his parents worry about the strange imaginary friend. "You know that. Those are the rules."

"I know," he said. "I'll get a note, I promise." And a few days later, sure enough, he handed her a note from his father, saying that it was all right for Nicholas to bring Bluebell home from school to be his pet. Roberta smiled when she saw it, and said, "Is Bluebell for *you,* or for the Hobbit, Nicky?"

He leaned forward and whispered into her ear, "She's for the Hobbit, but Daddy thinks she's for me. Don't tell, Roberta."

"Okay, I won't."

"Promise?"

"Yes, I promise. It's our secret." It wasn't, of course. Fred was listening too. But surely Nicholas knew that.

"Daddy doesn't know about the Hobbit," he whispered.

A secret imaginary friend. Well, she supposed she should be flattered to have been taken into his confidence. "I won't tell," she whispered back.

He nodded, evidently satisfied, and sat back in his chair again. "I brought a box to put her in. I'll give her to the Hobbit and then Daddy and I will go out for hamburgers, because Mommy's making food for the people who don't have houses."

"That's a very nice thing for your mother to do," Fred said. Roberta supposed that he was keeping quiet about the secret conversation as his own way of keeping the secret. She wondered if he was including the secret conversation on the official record. She told herself not even to think about it. "It's very important to give what we can to people who don't have as much as we do."

Nicholas nodded solemnly, and said, "I know, Fred. That's why Bluebell's for the Hobbit." So he knew Fred had been listening. Good: that meant Roberta wouldn't have to feel guilty when she talked to Fred about all this later on. And would that be on the record, or not?

The box Nicholas had brought for Bluebell, it turned out, was extremely small, a pretty little carved wooden box with a lattice top so Bluebell could breathe. It certainly hadn't been designed for transporting mice; it looked like one of those cheap souvenir knickknack boxes from Bali or Thailand. Roberta frowned and said, "Nicholas, I'm not sure that's the best way to take Bluebell home. She could chew the wood, and it's awfully small. Let's see if we can find something bigger for her, okay?"

"It's just until I can give her to the Hobbit," Nicholas said, his face tensing. "He said he found a big plastic bottle for her. It's in his hole. He made her a nice place to live already. I like this little box. Mommy gave it to me. It's big enough for Bluebell."

Roberta cursed herself: she should have asked to see the box that morning, instead of waiting until just before the end of school. That way she'd have had more time to find something else. "But, honey, she won't be able to *move* in there."

"She can move in here a little, and she'll be able to move a lot when she lives with the Hobbit. This way I can put her in my pocket so she won't get cold."

"But, Nicholas, it's not cold out."

"But it's *windy*, Berta, and she isn't used to wind! It's not windy where she lives now!"

Weird, Roberta thought. This is weird. "Nick, I want her to be in a bigger box, okay? Leave her in the aquarium for now, and let me know when your father gets here. I want to talk to him."

Nicholas glared at her, and just then Zillinth started screaming because Steven, on the other side of the room, had pulled her hair. "Fred," Roberta said, "make sure Nick leaves Bluebell where she is, okay?"

"Yes, Roberta." She heard him say, "Nicholas, please put Bluebell down until your father gets here," but she couldn't pay attention to the rest of the interaction, because she was busy with Steve and Zillinth.

"Steven, why did you pull Zillinth's hair?"

"To put bubble gum in it!" he crowed, and Zillinth began to howl.

"It'll never come out, Berta!"

"Yes, it will. It really will, sweetheart." Tomato juice was good for removing bubble gum, wasn't it? Or was that for removing skunk smell? Well, Fred would know. "Don't worry. Steven, please apologize to Zillinth."

"I don't want to. It was fun to put gum in her hair."

Roberta struggled for patience. Why the hell hadn't Fred stopped this mess before it got this far? "It wasn't fun for *her*, Steven. That's why she's crying. Say you're sorry!"

"I'm not sorry," he said smugly. "It was a good trick. Fred didn't even see the gum! I hid it in my hand until I pulled her hair! Ha!"

Shit. So much for omniscient AIs. KinderkAIr seemed to be turning Steven into a career criminal; he'd gotten entirely too good at hiding his pranks from the cameras. Roberta put on her best schoolmarm voice and said, "Steven, I'm giving you a time-out. Go sit on your nap mat, and stay there." He wouldn't be able to hide it from Fred if he got up. "Go on, Steven, or you won't get any cookies tomorrow!"

That did it. He went to sit in his corner, sulking, and Roberta turned her attention to the mess in Zillinth's hair. Steven had done quite a job. "I hear that peanut butter works wonders," someone said, and Roberta looked up to find Zillinth's mother next to her.

Oh, shit. "Mrs. Petroski, I'm really sorry about this—"

"Good heavens, don't worry about it. If that's the worst thing that ever happens to her, she'll be leading a charmed life. I got gum in my hair ten times a week when I was a kid. Zillinth, sweetie, are you ready to go home now? And we'll wash your hair with peanut butter."

"*Peanut* butter? Eeeeew!" Zillinth, looking delighted, left with her mother, and Roberta brushed her own hair out of her eyes. Now for Nicholas and Bluebell. But just then Benjamin came up, fretting because he couldn't find the picture he'd drawn that afternoon, and then Cindy's mother told her that Cindy would be gone the following week because of a family vacation, and did Roberta know if they could get a tuition credit for the unused time? Roberta told her to call the executive director—that kind of administrative nonsense wasn't her job—and finally turned back to the terrarium.

Nicholas wasn't there. Nicholas wasn't anywhere in the room.

"Fred? Where's Nicholas?"

"He left with his father, Roberta."

She bit back a panicky retort—it wouldn't do to use profanity, whether it was on the permanent record or not—and said, "I wanted to talk to him about Bluebell." She checked the aquarium: no Bluebell. Cover your ass, cover your ass, cover your ass. "I told you not to let Nicholas take her out of the cage, Fred."

"I know you did, Roberta, but you were busy with the other children and I didn't want to interrupt you. And there was enough room for Bluebell in Nicholas's box. He showed me. She could turn around and she could breathe. I consulted a city map and calculated, given the length of Nicholas's stride, that his walk home will take eight point two minutes, perhaps less if he hurries because he's excited about his new pet. Bluebell will be quite safe and comfortable for that amount of time, Roberta."

Okay, Roberta thought. Calm down. It's okay. Fred's an expert system; his job is to make your job easier, and he just did. So why did the whole thing make her nervous? Because of Preston, that's why. "Did he tell his father about the mouse, Fred? Or did you tell him?"

"He showed his father the box before he put it in his pocket, Roberta, and he whispered something in his father's ear. And his father signed the note, so I infer that Nicholas told him about the mouse, yes."

"Fred, could his father *see* the mouse through the top of the box? Through the latticework?"

"I don't know, Roberta. It didn't occur to me to ask. Everything I saw indicates that Nicholas's father knows about the mouse."

"All right," Roberta said, rubbing her eyes. "Never mind, Fred." She was tired, and she needed to get back home to take care of Doe. Anyway, she had a note from the father, so why was she so worried? Her ass was doubly covered: she had the note, and if anything bad happened, she could blame it on Fred. "I'll ask him about it tomorrow."

On her way home, she stopped by the store for milk and eggs and chicken soup for Doe. She should call Mitzi and ask her to make homemade chicken soup; Roberta didn't have the energy right now, and Doe liked her mother's better, anyway. She'd just have to settle for canned tonight. It was better than nothing.

Carrying the groceries into the building, she met Zephyr. Like some latter-day Pied Piper, Zephyr wore a flowing gray cape and a bright pink paper flower in her hair; a dozen of her bots, gunmetal gray and chrome-bright silver and black, brazen gold and iridescent purple, clattered and clanged along behind her. Some were no larger than the mice at the school, while others came nearly to Roberta's waist. They hummed and clicked and whistled, a cacophony of alarm clocks and teakettles. Roberta smiled when she saw them; she couldn't help it.

"Well, here you are," Zephyr said, as if she'd been looking for Roberta all day. "The kids and I just got back from the park."

Where they had undoubtedly terrified various human children and spooked their parents, Roberta thought. "How nice. Do they prefer the swings, or the seesaws?"

Zephyr chuckled. "They're not quite heavy enough for either, most of them. They like the slides and they like the jungle gym. They're good climbers."

I'll just bet. "Well, I'm glad they got their exercise."

Zephyr laughed outright this time. "Yeah, their body fat's way down, let me tell you. Ace cholesterol levels too. But they need the sensory input; they need stimulation just like humans do, maybe even more." She gave one of her malicious little grins and said, "Anyway, you and your friend were making such a ruckus that you drove us out of the house."

"It must have been someone else's ruckus," Roberta said, annoyed. "I was at work, and my partner was home sick." Doe became nearly coma-tose, even quieter than usual, when she was ill. When Roberta left that morning, she'd been honking forlornly into a tissue, looking utterly miserable. "Daytime rehearsals are fine, Zephyr. We'd just rather you kept it down at night."

"Hmmmph. Well, your friend, what's her name, Migraine Mary—"

"Her name's Dorothea," Roberta said stonily.

"Right. *She* was home. I saw her on the stairs. And she was making a ruckus with somebody. You might want to check into that."

Bitch, Roberta thought. Doe had probably gone downstairs to check mail at some point, but none of this was Zephyr's business, and she wasn't going to get into a fight about it. "You heard something else," she said, trying to keep her voice pleasant. "I have to get home now, Zephyr. Good-bye."

She started walking up the stairs, only to hear a chorus of high, squeaky *good-byes* behind her. When she turned, all the bots were waving legs or antennae at her. She found herself waving back, and then, bemused, turned again to trudge up the stairs. Jungle gyms. Oh, brother.

Yawning, she let herself into the apartment. "Hello?" she called. "Doe? I'm home." No answer: Doe must be asleep.

Roberta walked toward the closed bedroom door, which she'd left open that morning, and then froze. There was a blue woolen coat on the couch. She'd never seen that coat before. Strange coat plus ruckus plus closed bedroom door—

Nonsense. Doe would never do such a thing, and anyhow, she was sick. She never wanted to do anything when she was sick. Roberta couldn't think of a reasonable explanation for the second coat, but she knew there must be one. She walked firmly to the bedroom, opened the door, and heard Doe's characteristic chainsaw snore.

She turned on the light. Doe's head was on one pillow; someone else's was on the other. This, Roberta thought, very precisely, is ludicrous, just as the other head opened its eyes, looked at Roberta, said, "Oh, *shit!*" and dove under the covers.

"You'll have to give Dorothea a good poke in the ribs," Roberta heard herself say. "She doesn't wake up easily, especially after orgasms." For some reason, probably shock, she felt like laughing.

"Oh oh oh," the voice said. "Oh Goddess, oh Lordy, oh—"

"You should have set an alarm," Roberta said. "Getting caught was pretty dumb, you know." But she already suspected that Doe had planned to get caught, consciously or not, and she felt an odd, floaty sense of relief.

Ending the relationship wasn't going to be her responsibility. Doe had done it for her.

The voice was poking Doe now. "Dorry! Dorry! Wake up! She's home!"

"Mmmphh?" said Doe, and woke up and looked around at Roberta. "Oh," she said, in a nasal voice like Donald Duck's. "Uh-oh."

"Uh-oh," Roberta agreed.

"Fuck," Doe said, succinctly, just before she went into a coughing fit.

"Yes, that's what you just did. I already figured that out. I'm not stupid, you know." She could feel the tears welling up, somewhere deep down, although the laughter was still there too. It was all so clichéd, so ridiculous.

"It was an accident," the voice said. "We didn't mean it."

"You didn't *mean* it?"

"It just kind of—happened. I brought Dorry some chicken soup at lunchtime because she helped me so much with those documents the other week and—"

"Documents?" Roberta said. "Ah—you wouldn't by any chance be Iuna, would you?"

There wasn't any answer. "Doe? You *hate* her. Hey, you, Iuna, she *hates* you—mother of trees, Doe, you threw away *four years* for somebody you can't stand? Are you crazy?"

But it was already making a twisted kind of sense. Doe might have pretended to hate Iuna, or at least exaggerated her hatred, because she was really attracted to her. And, Roberta realized in a rush of icy clarity, Doe liked people who didn't have their acts together. She liked feeling superior; she liked being with someone she could scold. That was why she'd stayed with Roberta for four years, through a series of bad jobs. And that's why she was leaving now, when Roberta had finally found a job she still liked after three months. *I should have quit KinderkAIr after all. Maybe she'd have stayed. But would I have wanted her to?*

"She does not hate me!" the voice said indignantly, and then started coughing. I damn well hope you get her cold, Roberta thought, and I hope it turns into pneumonia, and I hope you die. No, I don't, I don't need that kind of karma, but I hope you get really, really sick. "Um, look, I'm really sorry and I don't blame you for saying that, and I know I don't have the right to ask for anything and this is really awkward for all of us, but would you mind leaving the room for a few minutes so I can get dressed?"

"Yes," Roberta said, "I do mind. I live here. But I'll tell you what. I'll leave for more than a few minutes; I'll leave for a few hours, and that way you can help Dorothea pack up her things and move them to your house."

"Ugh," Doe said. "Roberta, don't do this. You can't do this."

"Yes. Yes, I can." Her voice seemed dangerously steady to her, although her legs were shaking. "The lease is in my name, Doe, remember?" Thank the fates for small favors. Doe had been too busy at work to come down here the day Roberta signed the lease, three years ago. They hadn't thought it had mattered to have both their names on it. They'd talked about adding Doe, later on, but had never gotten around to it. They'd been young and stupid, and it had worked in Roberta's favor. "If you did *that,* I can do this. I brought you some chicken soup, although I'm sure hers was better. You can take it. It's yours. Good-bye, Doe."

"Look, I'm sorry, it was an accident."

"*Accident*? How could it be an accident?" Doe hardly ever had energy for sex with Roberta even when she was healthy. "Good-bye, Doe. The lease is in my name. That means I have the code to reprogram the locks"— *Where did I put that? It's on a piece of paper someplace. Well, I can get another copy from the landlord*—"and you don't. Get out. I'm giving you five hours, and when I get back I want both of you gone, and whatever stuff you've left behind you've lost. Got it?"

Trying to look dignified, she turned on her heel and left the apartment. She couldn't collapse here. She couldn't. She couldn't fall apart where they could see her.

Once she got into the stairwell, the shaking began in earnest.

Twenty-Two

S OMEHOW she got outside. It was hard even to get downstairs, because her legs wouldn't work right; she walked with extraordinary care, as if over black ice. She prayed not to meet Zephyr, but the foyer was empty. Once she was on the sidewalk, she faced the decision of where to go next.

For once, she longed for a car, for the privacy of that little box. Instead she was on the street, and she'd told them—the people upstairs, whom she couldn't even stand to name right now—that she wouldn't come back for five hours.

Her street instincts kicked in. Walk, walk. It doesn't matter if you know where you're going, as long as you look like you do. Keep walking and don't cry, because a sobbing woman on the street is a target. She didn't know where to go. Where could she go to cry? Her only private place was home.

Out of habit, she found herself heading to the Sixteenth Street MUNI station. As she walked, her mind jumped with utter clarity and complete lack of logic from one thought to the other. Doe's delay the night Iuna messed up the documents took on a new light now. Roberta would have to replace any household items Doe took with her; she hoped Doe would leave the teapot. She wondered if Iuna had really made mistakes on those documents, or if something else had been happening all along. Roberta hadn't even seen Iuna, who had remained a lump under the covers. Doe had always said she hated Iuna. Roberta would have to have the phone switched over to her name only. Doe had told Roberta once, when they'd first gotten together, that for a long time she'd hated Roberta too, found her whiny and too needy. Should Roberta have seen it coming? Maybe she should have seen it coming. How could she have seen it coming? Had Doe left someone behind when she got together with Roberta?

Here she was at the MUNI station. She got on a train to the Embarcadero, empty at this hour because nearly everyone was going the opposite direction, away from downtown. It was still only six-thirty, and she'd given them five hours, until eleven. How was she going to fill all that time? Why hadn't she kicked them out immediately? The lease was in her name; it was her place; they should have been the ones to leave, not her. She hadn't seen Iuna. Now she wished she had. She wanted to know what Iuna looked like.

She was hungry. There was some black bean soup in the fridge, but she couldn't go back yet. She couldn't go back until she was sure they were gone. Not until eleven. Maybe not until eleven-thirty, to be safe. What was she going to do until then? She was hungry. She had to eat. The black bean soup was in the fridge. What was she going to eat?

She had to buy herself some dinner. Dinner. Could she do that? Yes, she had her wallet with her, here in her pocket; she pulled it out cautiously, first checking on the two other passengers in the car—a woman who seemed to be asleep and a man with his nose in a book—and yes, she'd be able to buy dinner, she had her credit cards and even some cash, oh sweet Gaia, the bank account was in both their names, she'd have to change it. She hoped Doe wasn't going to go to an ATM and withdraw all the cash. Doe wouldn't do that, would she? Doe wouldn't have an affair, would she? They had $800 in their account and Doe could take out only $400 at once, so that was safe; Doe could take half the money if she wanted it, and Roberta would change the account tomorrow. Roberta didn't even know how much of that money was hers and how much was Doe's. Of course not; it was *their* money, theirs, but that was okay. Doe could have half. That was fair.

She had to eat. Where was she going to eat? She tried to think of places to eat and remembered a good sushi bar near the Embarcadero station, and then remembered that she couldn't go there because it was where they were going for Mitzi's birthday next Saturday. Roberta didn't want to eat there twice in one week.

And then she realized that she wouldn't be going to the restaurant on Saturday. She'd never be going to any of the birthday dinners again. She'd never see Mitzi and Hugh again.

That was when the crying started, great heaving gasps more like vomiting than weeping, tears so fierce and forceful she could barely get her breath. She sensed vaguely that the other two passengers in the car had come out of their stupor and were furtively staring at her; she couldn't even care. She had walked out on Doe without remembering how much else she was leaving at the same time.

No. No. Doe had walked out on her. Doe was the one who had left, taking the birthday dinners and Mitzi's common sense and Hugh's sense of humor with her. But it didn't matter who had left: Roberta still felt as if she were being swept into a chasm, some deep dark place where she would never see the sun again. She had to get up tomorrow morning, tomorrow and all the days after that, and Saturday and every other birthday after that she'd wonder if Iuna was at the dinners in her stead, and she didn't know how she'd be able to stand it. She wouldn't be able to stand it. She couldn't.

She bent over, right there on the train, and threw up, again and again, until all that came up was bile. When she looked around the car, it was empty: the other two passengers had fled. She didn't blame them. She got up and moved to another part of the car, where she had to smell her own puke but at least didn't have to step in it—well, it would keep anyone else from sitting in the car, she'd gotten the privacy she'd wanted—and looked at her watch. It wasn't even seven yet. At least four more hours. What was she going to do? She had to eat. She should drink something at least, try to rehydrate after throwing up like that. She had to find some place where she could curl up in a ball and cry safely.

The train slid to a halt with a grinding of metal on metal. Embarcadero Station, end of the line. Unless she wanted to ride the train back and forth for four more hours, she had to get off.

She got off, her legs still shaky, her face streaked with sweat. Her mouth tasted foul. Of course it did. She shrank from the idea of going to a restaurant like this. Where could she go to get cleaned up?

She made her way up to the street, shivering, although it was a warm night. She had to be a grown-up. She had to function. She had to go somewhere. She walked, blindly, and cried, and shivered, and then, still crying, found herself standing in front of Levi Plaza. She'd walked to work.

She could hear clinking glasses and conversation from a restaurant, the fancy Italian place she'd never be able to afford. Numbly, she walked up to the darkened KinderkAIr building. The foyer light clicked on, and the door opened. She walked in, into the blessed warmth, as the other lights softly glowed into life around her. "Roberta?" Fred said. "Roberta, what's wrong?"

"How did you know it was me?" she asked dully. "How did you know to open the doors?"

"I have external security cameras, Roberta. What's wrong? Why are you crying?"

She swallowed. "I shouldn't be here." Her voice was hoarse with tears. "I'm sorry."

"Roberta, it's all right. I'm here all the time. I like having you here too." She blinked; it had never occurred to her that Fred might get lonely when they all went home. How could he be lonely? Wasn't he talking to Preston? "Roberta, please tell me what's wrong. Why are you crying?"

She shouldn't have come here. Preston would know. It was none of Preston's business. Would this be on the record? A wave of terror swept over her. She couldn't lose her job too, not after losing Doe. She fought to speak calmly, to seem rational for the records. "Fred, I'm sorry, I'm upset—I shouldn't have come here. It has nothing to do with work. I just came here out of habit. I'll go home now." She couldn't go home now, but Fred didn't need to know that.

"Roberta, please don't leave. I can keep a secret." Like Nicholas talking about monsters: yes, Fred, I know you can keep a secret, even when you aren't supposed to. "If whatever is upsetting you doesn't have to do with your work here, I won't record it. Please tell me what's wrong. I care about you, Roberta. You're special to me. I don't want you to leave if you're this upset. Stay here until you feel better. You'll be safe here."

She felt the tears welling up again. It was so stupid, so familiar; Fred told everyone they were special. He said it about fifty times a day. That was his job. She still felt herself yearning to hear it again.

Be a grown-up. She had to be a grown-up. "You can do that?" she said numbly. "You can just—not record something?" He hadn't actually admitted it before. "Isn't that illegal?"

"No, Roberta. Not after official school hours. I've already stopped recording, Roberta. Please tell me what's wrong. Why are you crying?"

She swallowed, standing there surrounded by child-size furniture and picture books and stuffed toys. What were people going to think when they saw this blank in Fred's records? But why would they see it; why would they ever check? She'd bet money that Preston would see it, though. Well, she had the goods on Preston too. And she was here, for better or worse. "I—my partner and I just broke up. She left me for someone else. I left the apartment and, well, came here out of habit, I guess. I didn't really know what I was doing."

"I'm sorry, Roberta. It's hard to lose someone you love."

She swallowed again, past a new, huge lump in her throat. Of course Fred sounded like he understood. That was his job. That's what he was programmed for. It didn't mean anything. He was a machine. How could he understand? "Yes," she said. "It is."

"I know what it's like to miss someone, Roberta. Every night when you and the children leave, I miss you until you come back. I like having the mice here, because they keep me company even when everyone else has left, but they can't talk to me."

Oh. Roberta opened her mouth and didn't know what to say. Did he mean it? What did *meaning it* mean, to Fred? He was programmed to sound empathetic; he couldn't really feel pain, could he? Why would anyone program an AI to get lonely? That would be both useless and cruel. She knew she should say, "I miss you too," but she couldn't. She hardly ever thought about Fred when she wasn't here. But she had to say something, didn't she?

Maybe not. "You must miss your partner very much, Roberta. I'm sorry. How can I help you? What do you need from me?"

She took a deep breath. "I—if I could stay here for a few hours, Fred, that would mean a lot."

"Of course, Roberta."

"And I'm hungry. Do you think it would be okay if I ate some of the kids' snacks? I'll replace them, I promise. I'll go shopping tomorrow after work."

"Of course, Roberta. You need to eat. Maybe you should drink some warm milk."

"Yes," she said. "That's a good idea. I'm cold. Warm milk would be very nice. Thank you."

She made herself warm milk, and drank it with some graham crackers and peanut butter, and felt herself sinking into leaden exhaustion. "Fred," she said, "do you think it would be okay if I took a nap here? I can't go back home for a few hours, and I'm really tired."

"Of course, Roberta." So she got a blanket out of the closet and curled up on a pile of napmats, and fell asleep to the soothing sound of the mice running on their wheel.

"Roberta," someone said. She opened her eyes, disoriented, eyes and mouth gritty. Where was she? "Roberta, it's five A.M."

She sat up, head pounding. School. She was at school. She was at school because Doe—

"Roberta," Fred said, "I think you should go home and shower and change clothing before the children arrive, don't you?"

"Yes," she said. She couldn't believe she'd slept so long. "Yes, Fred. Thank you. I only meant to nap for a few minutes."

"You were very tired, Roberta. I knew you needed to sleep. Do you feel ill? Would you like to go home and take today as a sick day? I can call one of the substitutes, if you like."

"No," Roberta said. She'd never taken a sick day before, and if she took a sick day now she'd have to stay home, and she didn't know where home was now, or what she'd find when she went back to the apartment. Whatever was there, she didn't want to have to look at it all day. "No, I'll go home and shower and change, and then I'll come back."

"Be sure to eat a good breakfast, Roberta."

"I will, Fred. Thank you."

"You're welcome. You're my friend, Roberta, and I care about you. I'm glad I could help you. Thank you for coming here when you were upset."

That was probably all programming too, but she found herself unaccountably moved. "Thank you for being here," she said, even though Fred was here all the time. Where else would he be?

Feeling as if she hadn't slept at all, she made her way home through a gray dawn. Everything hurt: her head, her back, her legs. It hurt to breathe. It hurt to think. Part of her wished she could take a sick day, but she knew that being in the apartment would only make her feel worse, and there was nowhere else to go except school. She didn't let herself imagine what she'd find in the apartment, because every time her thoughts moved in that direction, she found herself becoming rigid with grief and panic, shot through with dread. Maybe Doe hadn't left at all. What would she do if Doe was still there?

Doe wasn't there. Roberta could tell from the street. When she looked up at the apartment windows, she could see even in the dim light that the tea curtains in the kitchen were gone. Mitzi had made the curtains, red and white check. Better not think about it.

She found herself climbing the stairs as if wading through syrup. There was something outside her door, a shiny gray bundle. When she reached the landing, it unfolded a segmented arm and handed her a note, written on heavy mauve paper and scented with cinnamon.

Roberta, I'm sorry. I didn't know things were so bad until I
saw Migraine Mary carrying all her stuff downstairs. That other

one isn't much to write home about. I shouldn't have said
anything to you, although I guess maybe it wouldn't have
made any difference. Anyway, I apologize. I was being stupid,
and I shouldn't have been stupid. I know about losing friends.
I know you don't much like bots, but this one's a gift, anyway.
His name's Mr. Clean and he'll eat dust and dirt and help keep
your place neat, which can be useful when there's only one
person to do the housework. Maybe he'll keep you company
too, even though he's only got a really rudimentary AI chip.
I've never used him in the performance troupe because he's
too shy; I guess he's programmed that way for people who are
scared of bots. He likes to stay out of sight, but he's got a basic
feedback mechanism, so if you talk to him or interact any other
way, other than kicking him or something, he'll know you
don't mind his being around and he'll come out more. He's
pretty charming, really, and I hope you like him. He's solar-
powered, so if he starts seeming sluggish, just stick him in a
sunny window and he'll perk right up.

It would serve me right if you never spoke to me again, but
I'm here if you need to talk, or if you need a cup of tea or
something. Good luck. It's no fun living with pain, but it's
possible. I know this from experience. Let me know if I can do
anything. Zephyr.

The kindness of strangers. Numb, Roberta unlocked the apartment
door; Mr. Clean, a tiny tank, rolled silently in ahead of her, and promptly
scooted under the nearest chair. It meant a lot for Zephyr to give up one of
her bots, even one of the simpler ones, and Roberta would have to think
of some way to thank her, but right now she couldn't think about anything
at all except what she'd see when she flicked on the living room lights.

All the furniture was still there, of course. Doe couldn't have moved it
without a van, and Iuna probably had furniture of her own. Doe's fancy
desktop computer and printer were gone. Roberta's modest laptop remained. Doe had taken most of the artwork, leaving pale rectangles on the
walls and dust-free ovals and circles and squares on tables, where statues
and vases had been. She'd left a lopsided ceramic bowl Roberta had made
in a college pottery class, and some vintage landscape photographs the two

of them had bought for a song at a garage sale. The Tiffany poster, which had been the brightest thing in the living room, was gone, and so was the antique Navaho wall hanging, and so was the still life of an apple and some flowers, painted in oils, that Doe's grandmother had finished just before she died.

Everything bright. All the color. Roberta swallowed stale tears and moved on wooden legs to the kitchen, which looked the same until she opened the cabinets. The nice dishes and flatware were gone. Of course they were; they'd been Doe's. Doe had left the junky plastic dishes Roberta had had since college, and some mismatched, dingy cutlery. Now Roberta was glad she'd never thrown the stuff away. She wondered for a moment where Doe and Iuna had found enough boxes and newspaper to pack up all the dishes. They'd been busy after she left. Maybe Doe had planned it that way. Maybe she'd had boxes and newspaper collected, stored somewhere, waiting until she could manufacture some way to have Roberta kick her out.

Roberta closed the cabinet doors and leaned her head against them. She was going to have to go into the bedroom now. The bedroom was what was left. She was going to have to go into the bedroom, and then into their bathroom; she was going to have to take a shower and get dressed and go to work, and after work she'd have to take care of the checking account and work out a new budget. She could afford to keep the apartment on what she made; that was the advantage of living in a dump. They'd talked about moving and had never gotten around to it. Now she was glad.

Bedroom. Roberta peeled her forehead carefully away from the cabinet doors, which were slightly sticky from years' residue of cooking grease—she wondered if Mr. Clean could handle vertical surfaces—and headed resolutely toward the bedroom closet. She wouldn't look at anything else. She'd pick out what she was going to wear to work, and then she'd shower.

She'd known that the closet would be nearly empty; even so, her small collection of clothing, most of which hung crookedly, looking dingy and worn, appalled her. The closet seemed huge without Doe's stuff in it, another apartment, practically. Doe had even taken all the extra hangers. Roberta pulled out some nice cords and her most comfortable tunic, and turned to the linen closet outside the master bath. One set of sheets was left, and a few towels.

In the shower, she closed her eyes and let the hot water pound on her face. She had to remember to count her blessings. She had a job, she had a place to live, she had her health. She had discovered kindness from unexpected quarters: a machine, a crazy neighbor. She felt flayed without Doe, as if her skin had been stripped off, but that would pass. It would pass. They hadn't been happy for a long time. Surely it was all for the best.

But when she got out of the shower and had to face the bed, because her dresser was on the other side, the pain hit her again. Doe had stripped the bed. No sheets, no comforter, no pillows. She'd taken the pillows, both of them. She hadn't even left one for Roberta. Didn't Iuna have pillows? And then Roberta realized that she wouldn't have wanted either Doe's pillow or the one Iuna had been sleeping on. She doubted very much that Doe had taken the pillows out of kindness, but perhaps the effect was the same.

She set her jaw, walked to her dresser to retrieve underwear, and then fled into the living room to get dressed. Mr. Clean had been working his way along one wall, and when he saw her he dashed under the couch. Roberta, still wearing only a towel, got down on her knees on the rug— the good wool carpet, Doe hadn't taken that either, praise be—and said, "It's okay, Mr. Clean. You can come out now."

Nothing. "Mr. Clean? You can come out. I'm not afraid of you."

She heard a faint whining noise, and then the bot emerged. "Hi," Roberta said, feeling stupid. "So, um, do you do tabletops? How can you climb up on a table, anyway? You've got treads."

It must have somehow deciphered the word *table*. It wheeled smartly around, unfolded a pair of astonishingly long segmented arms, one of which had proffered Zephyr's note earlier, reached for the top of the coffee table, got a grip, and swung itself up. Then it began circling the perimeter, sucking dust.

"So," Roberta said. "You're a gymnast. I wish I could do that. Do you do cabinets?"

At the word *cabinets,* it stopped, faced Roberta, and beeped twice. The bot equivalent of "yes, ma'am," maybe. Then, navigating delicately around Roberta's lopsided bowl, it returned to dusting the tabletop. By the time she got home that evening, there would be no sign that any other objects had ever been there.

Nicholas was the first child to arrive that morning, and while he took off his coat and got out the picture he'd been working on the day before, he told Roberta and Fred all about how much the Hobbit liked Bluebell. "He thought she was really pretty, and he patted her and told me I'd given her a good name. He said he was going to feed her some pizza. He said he'd gotten the pizza from behind a restaurant, where they'd thrown it out. He said it had pepperoni and anchovies and peppers on it, but Bluebell wouldn't have to eat that stuff if she didn't like it. I asked if I could have some, but he said it might not be good for me."

Roberta blinked, her throat sore from crying. Pepperoni and anchovies and peppers? Wasn't that a little specific, for an imaginary friend? This Hobbit sounded suspiciously like a baggie. Why would a kid have an imaginary baggie for a friend?

Maybe those were the things Nicholas liked on his own pizza, but she doubted it. A kid like anchovies? That would be weird even for Nicholas. "Nicky, why does the Hobbit have to eat thrown-out pizza?"

Nicholas went rigid; she could see the fear in his face. "Zillinth's coming. I can't tell you any more about the Hobbit. He's our secret, remember?"

"Okay," Roberta said. She felt as if she were underwater, or in a dream. "Yes, Nicholas, I remember."

And here came Zillinth, with her mother right behind her, holding the girl's blond braid triumphantly aloft. "See, the peanut butter worked!"

Peanut butter? She must be in a dream. What did peanut butter have to do with hair? And then, dimly, Roberta remembered the bubble gum. It might as well have happened a hundred years ago. "I'll make a note of it," Roberta said.

"So will I," said Fred. "Thank you very much, Mrs. Petroski. That's very useful information for me to have."

"Ha!" Mrs. Petroski said happily. "I never thought I'd be telling an AI anything it didn't know. You've made my day, Fred."

Zillinth giggled, and Fred said, "I'm very happy to hear that."

Steven arrived next, wanting to show everyone a seedpod he'd found, and then Benjamin and Cindy trooped in, and then it was storytime and then it was naptime. Roberta let the day carry her along in its current. She remembered that she'd been really upset yesterday about the mouse business, and she knew she should ask Nicholas more questions, but she couldn't quite remember why. That had all happened in another lifetime. Only as Nicholas was getting ready to leave did she ask, out of some obscure sense of duty, "So, how did your dad like Bluebell?"

"Daddy likes mice," Nicholas said cheerfully. "That's why he gave me the note saying I could have Bluebell. Fred, why do mice come in different colors?" And Fred, to Roberta's immense gratitude, was off, into a child's-eye-view of genetics and biodiversity. She was off the hook. She'd done her duty, and once the kids were gone she could go home, to that newly strange place, and go to sleep.

She knew she should talk to Nicholas's parents directly about the mouse, make sure Bluebell had made it home okay, ask Kevin and Meredith if they knew about the Hobbit, but she couldn't summon the energy. Surely no one would blame her for not tackling those two the day after she'd been abandoned by her lover. So as Nicholas darted out the door to join his mother after school, Roberta just waved to both of them through the window. Good-bye, good-bye, good riddance.

After the last child had left, as Roberta was sluggishly cleaning things up and putting things away, Fred asked, "How do you feel, Roberta?"

She looked at her watch. "Are we off the record, Fred?" She hoped that question would sound sufficiently lighthearted if they were still on the record.

"All the children have left, Roberta, so, yes, we are."

She nodded. "Well, frankly, I feel like shit."

"Yes, I thought so. You didn't seem like yourself today. You were less engaged with the children than usual, and you moved very slowly, as if moving hurt."

"Yes," she said, grimacing. "It did hurt. How perceptive of you." Especially since Fred was an AI and couldn't hurt. She was going to hurt for a long time, but there was no point in saying so. "I'm sorry I did a bad job, though."

"No one can do an equally good job all the time, Roberta. You did a fine job. I wouldn't have noticed anything wrong if I'd just met you. I just wanted you to know that I hope you feel better soon."

"Thank you, Fred. And thanks for letting me in here last night. I can't tell you how much that helped."

"It was my pleasure, Roberta. Any time."

If only. She found herself entertaining a wistful fantasy of living here all the time. She could leave every day after all the kids were gone, as if she were going home, and then sneak back later. Fred would let her in and sing her songs and tell her stories; she'd drink warm milk and eat graham crackers and sleep on the napmats, hugging one or another stuffed animal. She'd be warm and cozy and safe, and Fred would keep it a secret, except possibly from Preston. For all Roberta knew, there were already people who lived here after hours. For all she knew, Fred took baggies in off the street and fed them graham crackers and told them they were special. She suspected Fred would like that, although the parents certainly wouldn't.

No. She had to be a grown-up. She had to take care of the bank account and buy new sheets and pillows, and replacement snacks for school. It would probably help to buy herself a new comforter too, and maybe some new posters. She could fill the apartment up with her own colors, since Doe had taken the old ones away. She'd rather have stayed here, with the bright yellow and blue and red napmats, the clean white tables, the happy stuffed animals. Everything here was warm and simple, a womb.

She had to be a grown-up. She went home, logged onto their bank account, and discovered that Doe had removed herself from the account earlier that day, although she'd left Roberta all the money in it. Well, that was decent of her. More money to buy pillows and posters. And towels. And dishes and silverware. You couldn't buy family; Mitzi and Hugh were irreplaceable.

Roberta found herself crying again. This was no good. She'd go shopping. She'd buy stuff she needed. One of the big housewares stores was having a sale; she'd seen the ads on the train.

But when she got there, she found herself overwhelmed by all the people, all the colors and noises, the sheer dizzying amount of stuff. It was too much to sort out. She felt as if she could barely put one foot in front of the other, let alone choose between eighteen different remaindered sheet sets. She managed to grab an inexpensive pillow and a bright fleecy blanket—it reminded her of the ones at work—and then went home.

Silence. Utter silence. As much as Doe's music had driven her nuts sometimes, she'd have given anything to hear it now. Then Mr. Clean, whining very faintly, came out of the kitchen.

"Well, hello," Roberta said. "And how was your day?"

The bot didn't answer, of course. It stopped and turned to face her, waited for a few moments, and then moved on when she didn't say any-thing else. It had probably been waiting for a command. I have to thank Zephyr, Roberta thought, but she couldn't deal with that, not right now. Instead, she went into the kitchen and ran her hand over the cabinet doors. The grease was gone.

Mr. Clean had been busy. She imagined him laboriously hauling himself up off the floor, dragging his weight up onto the countertops and then up the vertical surface of the cabinets. He must have hung on to the tops of the cabinet doors with those arms while he cleaned. Just thinking about it exhausted Roberta; it was too apt a metaphor for what her life looked like now, a slow, painful process of clinging to any available support and doing what was necessary, fighting gravity all the way.

She wondered if Mr. Clean was some sort of spy device for Preston. She found she couldn't care. She should log on and confront Preston, she knew, find out exactly what he knew and what he didn't, find out why he was asking Fred to keep secrets. But she didn't have the energy, and it was prob-ably a bad idea. She needed to be careful of herself right now. She wasn't thinking clearly.

She opened the refrigerator and found that Doe had taken a lot of the food, including the black bean soup. She'd left the milk and eggs Roberta had just bought, as well as some yogurt, half a loaf of bread, and a casse-role of unidentifiable leftovers. The pantry yielded canned vegetables, ra-men noodles, peanut butter. She'd bring the peanut butter to school tomorrow, and on the way, she'd pick up graham crackers. Roberta made herself a peanut butter sandwich and some noodles, and then, her vision grainy with fatigue, made up the bed with her old sheets and the new pil-low and blanket. The blanket was wonderful, soft and warm, with the new-clothing smell Roberta had always associated, as a child, with the be-ginning of school, with new adventures and tantalizing possibilities and the bountiful luxury of new books and jumpers and shoes. Before her mother died, they'd always gone clothing shopping the week before school started.

She loved the blanket. She curled up in it and went immediately, grate-fully, to sleep. When she woke up in the middle of the night, she discov-ered, to her mortification, that she was sucking her thumb.

She began a slow, grim process of recovery. Every day she tried to buy one new thing for the apartment, something cheap but cheerful. She found an oversize coffee mug painted with balloons, a cotton comforter printed to look like a quilt, some bright red plates. She became a regular at the thrift stores and the ten-dollar stores, which featured truly amazing amounts of surplus junk it seemed incredible that anyone could ever have wanted: hideous plastic flowerpots, boxes of pungently scented fruit-shaped candles, entire shelves of kitschy ceramic figurines of the Goddess—who wore lipstick and eyeliner, in this incarnation—cradling the earth. There were aisles full of cheap toys, and others full of cheaper costume jewelry. Roberta concentrated on housewares.

It all seemed bright and comforting in the stores, but simply gaudy, desperately overstated, when she got it back home. She kept trying, anyway, buying things to fill the void Doe had left. She hadn't heard from Doe since that terrible night. She'd thought Doe might call to ask for some of the furniture; a lot of it was rightfully hers, after all. But her silence continued unbroken. Roberta knew this for a kind of honor, but hoped it felt like shame.

Work was quiet, blessedly peaceful. On Nicholas's fifth birthday, the other children sang to him and drew pictures for him. He seemed pleased, almost like a normal child.

One afternoon Roberta came home to find a note from Zephyr, on that same mauve, cinnamon-scented paper, stuck under her door. *I hope you're doing okay. Dinner sometime?*

Roberta's heart sank. Was Zephyr asking for a date? She'd never seen Zephyr with anyone but her bots; she didn't know if the woman had human lovers, and if she did, which flavor she preferred. She'd had that boyfriend in college, supposedly, the one who got killed—the one who'd been friends with Meredith the Unavoidable—but who knew what had changed since then? And anyway, Roberta remembered Doe pooh-poohing that element of Zephyr's modest fame. "Oh, that's a bunch of compost. I saw it on ScoopNet. She went out with him twice, if that, and they never even slept together. She just makes a big deal out of it because it's good PR for her performances. ScoopNet said she's never slept with *any*body, as far as they can tell. What do you think she does with all those bots?"

They'd laughed about it at the time, and Roberta almost laughed aloud now too, before the loneliness of Zephyr's situation, and her own, turned the laughter to tears. She and Zephyr would be just perfect for each other, wouldn't they? Zephyr thought her bots were her children, and Roberta had fantasies about living in a day-care center with a puerile AI.

No, she didn't need an entanglement with anybody right now, let alone with Zephyr.

With a sigh, she grabbed a pencil and scribbled on the bottom of the note, *Thanks for Mr. Clean. You were right, he's a big help. I'll stop by when I don't feel so much like something that just crawled out from under a rock.* Then she snuck downstairs and stuck the note under Zephyr's door, hoping guiltily that it would buy her some time. If you see Zephyr, she told herself sternly, you're going to start grilling her on what she saw Doe and Iuna doing, what they were saying, if they said anything about you. You don't need that. Neither does Zephyr.

Mitzi's birthday was hell, especially because it fell on the first weekend after Doe left. Roberta had planned in advance, as grimly as if she were preparing for a military siege. She slept as late as she could, took herself out to brunch with a new book—an intricate, neo-Victorian thing—and then went swimming at a city pool, lap after lap for an hour, until her legs were rubber and her mind was blank. She lay in the pool sauna and tried unsuccessfully to meditate, and then took a long, hot shower, and then did her circuit of the thrift stores. She bought two new pairs of jeans and a fleece cardigan, bought a wooden salad bowl, bought three more books. She got her hair cut. She went to some other stores, full-price ones this time, and bought herself a teddy bear and some flowers and a vase to put the flowers in. Then she carted everything back home and rearranged all the furniture, aiming for maximum cheer and good taste, while Mr. Clean roved about studying the new layout. Then she went for a walk. Then she came back home, consulted a movie timetable, and hauled herself off to see an action-adventure flick, starring stupid men with big muscles, that would occupy the hours of the Saturday dinner, the dinner Roberta kept trying to forget.

She couldn't concentrate during the movie. She felt hemmed in by couples and families; she seemed to be the only person in the theater who was by herself, although she couldn't have been. She didn't want to be here; she wanted to be at the dinner. Barring that, she wanted to go visit Fred and drink warm milk and be told she was special, but she knew that would be unwise; that situation was already compromised enough.

On the movie screen, cars were exploding as bloody body parts flew into the air. Roberta hunched down into her seat, wishing she hadn't come. Weekends were hell when you were single; she'd been able to forget that for the past four years. She found herself wondering what Fred did on weekends. It would be fun to take Fred home for the weekend sometime. She could show him pictures of her parents and get advice on decorating—she knew he had a good eye from hearing him coach the kids on their drawings—and introduce him to Mr. Clean. A lonely woman, an AI, and a bot: now there was the perfect family.

You, Roberta told herself, are one sick cookie. Desperate, that's what you are. You wouldn't be able to take Fred home even if it weren't an insane idea: he's hardwired into KinderkAIr, dummy. You can't just unplug Fred, walk away with him, plug him into your food processor, and expect him to be able to function. He needs cameras and microphones, and anyway, he's just a machine.

Sick. Very sick. But not as sick as this ridiculous movie she'd paid good money to see, where the exploding cars had segued into the two stars beating the living crap out of each other.

Roberta looked at her watch. It was eleven-thirty. The dinner was over; Mitzi and Hugh and the others had gone home by now, and so could she. So she got up and returned to her new pictures and her new vase and her flowers, and to Mr. Clean, who was sweeping old spiderwebs from the corners of the ceiling. None of it cheered her up, but fortunately, she was too tired to care. One Saturday down. It would be seven days before she had to face another, and four months before she had to face the next family birthday.

She hadn't been able to bring herself to call Mitzi and wish her a happy birthday, or even send a card. She knew it wasn't fair to shun Mitzi just because of Doe and Iuna, but the situation was too painful. She wondered if Mitzi had thought of her. She had no voicemail messages; an obscure impulse made her turn on her laptop, which she hadn't touched since checking the bank account.

She had one e-mail. It was from Preston, from several days back. "I know you are lonely, and I am sorry," it said. "Please come visit so we can talk."

You're not my surrogate daddy anymore, she thought grimly. You're my boss, and whatever's going on with your daughter's kid, I don't want to know any more than I have to. And why did Fred tell you I was lonely? He said he'd keep it a secret!

But maybe Fred hadn't said anything. Maybe Zephyr had. Maybe Doe or Iuna or Hugh or Mitzi had mentioned something to a FOP acquaintance. Maybe Roberta's trust in everyone around her was shattered, or maybe she was assigning herself entirely too much importance.

She turned off the laptop and went to bed.

Twenty-Three

ROBERTA had been dreading Meredith and Kevin's appearance at the parent-teacher conferences scheduled for the following week, but to her relief, it all went smoothly enough. Meredith looked startled, almost crazed, when she saw the mice, but when Roberta asked her about it, she said she'd just forgotten something at the store, and maybe it was even true. Roberta gathered the courage to ask directly how Bluebell was, and Meredith said, "Oh, just fine," putting Roberta's lingering worries to rest. Whatever was going on in that department, she'd discharged her own responsibility. Kevin was charmed by the children's artwork; both Kevin and Meredith were properly attentive to Roberta's cautious description of Nicholas's adjustment problems. At Fred's urging, she'd stopped just short of recommending outside help, but she had a feeling they could tell she considered it necessary.

She went home feeling relieved and cheerful. She'd done her job. She hadn't lied. She'd done her best to keep everybody happy without any outright whitewashing. Under the circumstances, it was an award-winning performance.

Her self-congratulation dissolved two mornings later, when Nicholas came to school with clenched fists and eyes reddened from weeping. "Fred," he called the minute he got into the room, "Fred, the Hobbit's gone!"

Roberta, putting out art supplies at the other end of the room, looked up in alarm. Nicholas never sounded that upset about anything. Most of the other kids weren't there yet, but Zillinth, lying on her stomach reading *The Velveteen Rabbit* in the book corner, sat up. "The Hobbit's a *story*," she said. "How can a story be gone?"

"Nicholas," said Fred, "I can tell you're upset. It's okay to be upset when we can't find things. Did your parents buy you the book about the Hobbit, and now you can't find it? Is that why you're upset?"

"He's not a book," Nicholas said, lower lip quivering. "He's a man and he lived in a hole in the ground! He was taking care of Bluebell!"

Oh, boy. "Nicky," Roberta said, "we sent Bluebell home with you. You gave me a note from your father."

"And I gave her to the *Hobbit*! I *told* you that!"

The phone on the wall rang. It was the phone for private conversations between Fred and the teacher during schooltime. Fred had never used it before. "Roberta," Fred said, "it's for you."

"Thank you," she said, and picked it up, half expecting it to be Preston. "Fred? Is that you?"

"Yes, Roberta. There's something you should know. Yesterday afternoon, Meredith Walford-Lindgren called the police to deal with a vagrant she feared had been interacting inappropriately with her son. The police arrested him. His name is Henry Carviero, and evidently he'd been living in a cave in the side of Telegraph Hill, between here and Nicholas's house. The story doesn't mention a mouse."

Dear Goddess. Nicholas really had given Bluebell to a baggie, which meant that at the tender age of five he'd run a gigantic scam on all of them, including the AI, which meant he was much more seriously fucked up than Roberta had imagined. So much for the imaginary friend. "How do you know this?" she asked, her mouth dry.

"Police reports, Roberta. They're public."

Was checking police records part of Fred's job? Was checking up on parents part of Fred's job? Or had Preston told him this? At this point, Roberta knew, she and Fred were long past legally due to report Nicholas's bizarre behavior. But if Preston knew as much as she thought he did and hadn't done it himself, that probably meant he didn't want them to, either. There was no way to know for sure without talking to him.

Shit.

And then there was Fred's role in all this. He had outside security cameras, right? How far could he see? Had he seen Nicholas talking to the baggie? The side of Telegraph Hill wasn't very far away. If he'd seen Nicholas talking to a baggie, he shouldn't have stayed quiet about it either.

"Roberta?" Fred said. "Roberta, are you still there?"

"Yes, Fred. I'm sorry. I was—thinking. Thank you for the information." She hung up, detachedly aware that her legs had begun to tremble the way they'd done when Doe left. She sat down next to Nicholas and said, "Nicky, I'm sorry you're upset." It was what Fred would have said; she hoped Fred would pick up from here, because she had no idea what to say next.

"Mommy made the police take him away," Nicholas said, and started to cry. She'd never seen him cry before. Roberta put her arms out and Nicholas walked into them; she rocked the solid little body, thinking that at least, as helpless as she felt, hugging Nicholas was something Fred couldn't do. "The Hobbit never hurt me and he never hurt Bluebell and Mommy made them take him away! I hate her!"

Weird. Weirder and weirder. Meredith the CALM advocate: Roberta would have expected her to invite the guy in for tea and then get it broadcast on the evening news. But she supposed that Meredith's professed beliefs became rather brittle when it came to her own child.

Roberta wondered if Fred would say something comforting, tell Nicholas that the police had probably found a nicer place for the Hobbit to live, but Fred said nothing. Fred was programmed always to tell the truth to children—although perhaps not to adults, Roberta thought grimly—and Fred must have known as well as Roberta did that Henry Carviero wouldn't be seeing daylight again anytime soon. "Oh, honey," she said, rocking Nicholas, "Nicky, I'm sorry about the Hobbit. I'm sorry you miss your friend." *And I'm furious that you lied to us, you little shit.* She wanted to protect Nicholas and kill him at the same time. She wondered if Meredith ever felt this way.

"I had to give Bluebell away," Nicholas said miserably. "I gave her to the Temple so I can go see her sometimes, but the Temple doesn't need a mouse. They have lots of animals. The Hobbit needed her to keep him company."

Roberta shook her head. "Nicholas, I don't understand. Why couldn't you keep Bluebell yourself? You brought me a note from your father saying it was all right for you to take her home. Why couldn't Bluebell live at your house?"

Nicholas shuddered and began to cry again, harder. "Mommy wouldn't let me. Mommy said I couldn't have her."

It didn't make any sense. Meredith Walford-Lindgren loved animals; everyone knew that, and she doted on her son. "Sweetheart, why not? Your mom had pets when she was a little girl, didn't she?"

"Because Patty died," Nicholas said, and shoved his way, hard, out of Roberta's arms. For the next ten minutes he ran, arms outstretched, in circles around the room. He told Fred and Roberta that he was pretending to be an airplane, but it looked to Roberta as if he was trying very hard to run away from something.

To Roberta's relief, the rest of the day passed without crisis. It was Steven's birthday, and he'd asked if they could make sugar cookies and then decorate them. Roberta made enough dough for each kid to make several cookies, one to give to Steven and a few to take home. She rolled dough and cut out cookies—stars, flowers, cars, elephants, pudgy people—for the kids to adorn with sprinkles, licorice, and cinnamon drops, raisins and chocolate chips and M&Ms. They loved decorating cookies, and Roberta liked it too, even though it always resulted in an awful mess. Fortunately, none of the parents had ever complained, even though the project meant that the kids invariably went home wired on sugar.

Sugar was the last thing Nicholas needed today, Roberta thought ruefully, but he settled down to decorating a dough person right away. Roberta peered over his shoulder and saw him patting into place a big raisin smile.

"Hey, Nick, that's one happy cookie. Is that for Steven, for his birthday?"

"No," Nicholas said. "It's for Fred."

"Nicholas," said Fred, "that's very nice of you, but I don't eat cookies. And I think it would be nice if you made a cookie for Steven, because it's his birthday. He drew a picture for you on your birthday."

Nicholas sighed. "Okay." He reached past Zillinth, over to the tray with undecorated sugar stars, and sprinkled chocolate chips on top of one of them. "There. That one's for Steven."

"You're lazy," Zillinth said. "*I'm* making a nice one for Steven, 'cause it's his birthday."

"That's because you want to marry him," Benjamin said smugly.

"Do *not*, Benjamin!"

"Zillinth," Fred cut in, "don't throw raisins at Benjamin. That's not nice. Can you pick them up now, please? So Roberta doesn't have to do it all herself?"

"I'll help," Steven said. He loved raisins, and would eat as many as possible. Let him: it was his birthday.

Nicholas, ignoring the others, looked up at Roberta. "I did one for Steven. Now can I work on Fred again?"

So the cookie *was* Fred. She wasn't about to scold him, not after the morning. "Sure, Nick. This way you can take Fred home with you, right?"

Nicholas nodded. "It's a body for Fred, so he can move around."

"Thank you, Nicholas," said Fred. "I'd like to be able to move around. Then I could go home and play with you."

Nicholas nodded, squinting at the cookie. He was doing something with tiny gold sugar balls that Roberta couldn't quite make out yet. "What's that?" she asked him. "Are you giving Fred a toy now, so he can play with you?"

"No," Nicholas said, without even the hint of a smile. "This is a gun."

"I didn't know you liked to play with guns," said Fred. "You don't play cops and terrorists with the other children."

"That's make-believe," Nicholas said scornfully. "This is real."

"A real gun?" Roberta said, working to keep her voice casual. And the Hobbit had been an imaginary friend. This kid had very fluid notions of reality.

"Yes."

"Do you have one too?"

"No. That's why Fred needs one. To protect me." He frowned at the cookie and said, "I don't know if this gun's big enough." He began filling the barrel of the gold gun with cinnamon drops.

"Are those bullets?" Roberta asked, her throat tight.

"Of course they're bullets! Can't have a gun without bullets."

"Who are the bullets going to hit?" Fred asked calmly. Meredith, Roberta thought grimly. For taking the Hobbit away.

"The monsters," Nicholas said matter-of-factly, just as Steven dumped an entire cup of sprinkles into Zillinth's hair.

At least it wasn't peanut butter, and at least no one except Roberta was upset; Zillinth took the whole thing in high good spirits. Roberta got her cleaned up, got the cookies in the oven, and got everything else cleaned up too; Fred told the kids a story while the cookies cooked and cooled, and then the kids admired their handiwork and sang "Happy Birthday" to Steven and began getting stoned on sugar.

Meredith came to pick up Nicholas after school. Of course, she usually did, but she hardly ever actually came inside the building. Roberta, looking up from cookie cleanup to see the familiar, aristocratic features, felt her stomach lurch. Now Nicholas was going to throw a tantrum about how much he hated his mother, and Roberta would be in the middle of it.

He didn't throw a tantrum. Instead, he threw himself into his mother's arms as if it had been years since he'd seen her, instead of hours. Meredith bent down, planted a firm kiss on his forehead, and scooped him into her arms before rising again. She was stronger than she looked; Nicholas, Roberta knew from experience, wasn't a light load. "So," Meredith said, "how was school today, Nicky?"

"It was good. We made cookies. I made a body for Fred. Say hello to Roberta and Fred, Mommy."

"Hello to Roberta and Fred," said Meredith, smiling.

"Hi," Roberta said, wiping the last remains of cookie dough off her hands.

"Hello, Ms. Walford-Lindgren. How are you today?"

Meredith squinted up at the nearest speaker, her expression unreadable. "I'm just fine, Fred, thank you. I wanted to find out how Nicholas did in school today. He had a rather upsetting weekend."

"Yes, he told us about it," Fred said.

Nicholas squirmed in her arms. "I was *good,* Mommy. I was!"

"He really was," Roberta said. Surely there was no way she could get into trouble for defending the child. "He was upset when he got here, and he was more active than usual—he ran around more, to vent his feelings, I guess—but he didn't do anything wrong." Nicholas never did anything visibly wrong, although he certainly knew how to spin a story. Surely his own mother had to know that? But Roberta remembered the weird business about arming Fred, and shivered.

"Ms. Walford-Lindgren," Fred said, "maybe it would be best if Roberta and I spoke to you privately, in the conference room. Nicholas, do you think you can play by yourself for a few minutes while we talk to your mother?"

"But I was *good!*" Nicholas said, just as Roberta thought furiously, Oh, *that* was tactful. Goddamn it, Fred, didn't they give you any diplomacy programming?

Fred said soothingly, "I know you were, Nicholas. You were very good. You're always very good."

"Then why do you have to talk to Mommy about me?"

"Perhaps we can arrange a phone conference," Roberta said, but Meredith—who had knelt down to hug Nicholas again—shook her head.

"At this point, I think it would be best if you said whatever you have to say to both of us. I'm sure you aren't going to say anything bad about Nicky"—she gave him a squeeze—"but I'd like him to hear this so he doesn't have to worry about it. Okay?"

"Okay," Roberta said firmly. "I agree completely. Fred?" You started this. And whatever you're going to say, I hope Preston's approved it.

"Certainly," Fred said. "Ms. Walford-Lindgren, Nicholas, I'm sorry to have upset you. That wasn't my intent. I just wanted to say that Nicholas misses his friend the Hobbit, and he misses Bluebell. He told us you didn't want him to have another mouse, Ms. Walford-Lindgren, and Roberta and I wondered why."

Roberta saw the other woman's face freeze, just for a moment; then her features relaxed again. "I don't really think that's any of your business," she said. Right, Roberta thought. Then we won't mention the gun at all, will we?

"I'm sorry to have offended you. My first concern is Nicholas's happiness."

"So's mine. I'm his mother."

"I understand that. You know him much better than I do, of course, so I thought you'd be able to explain to me why it wouldn't be a good idea for him to have another mouse. It seems to me that a new pet would make him happy, but of course my knowledge is more limited than yours."

Meredith winced; Roberta saw her arms tighten around her son. "Yes, your knowledge *is* limited," she said, her voice shaking. "I'd been thinking of getting Nicholas a kitten for his birthday, and I didn't think having a mouse at the same time would be a good idea."

She's lying, Roberta thought, although she couldn't have said how she knew. "A kitten?" Nicholas said. He sounded as doubtful as Roberta felt.

"Sure," Meredith said, all false cheer. Roberta could see the sweat on her forehead. "I wanted to surprise you, but we can get it today, if you want. Would you like that, Nicky?"

"Kittens are cute," he said dutifully, but Meredith sensed no excitement in him. This was getting weirder by the minute.

"Okay, then," Meredith said, still in that fake, peppy cheerleader voice.

"We'll go to the animal shelter right now and get a kitten. Come on, Nicky. Say good-bye to Roberta and Fred. You can tell them about the kitten tomorrow."

"Okay. Bye, Berta. Bye, Fred."

They left, and Roberta looked at her watch. Her workday was officially over, and everyone else had left. "So Fred," she said, "do you think she was telling the truth?"

"No, Roberta. The pitch of her voice indicated severe stress."

"That's what I thought too. Do you think Nicholas is really going to get a kitten?"

"I would be very surprised if he did, Roberta." There was a pause, and then Fred said, "I may be able to find out, however."

With a little help from Papa Preston. Roberta shook her head and said, "Fred, if it wasn't a good idea to tell Meredith about that first monster conversation, why did you ask her about the mouse?"

"Meredith had already acknowledged that Nicholas was upset. She was seeking information. That had never happened before."

That was true. It hadn't. "Fred? Did you, ah, consult any outside authorities about the conversation?"

"No, Roberta. Not yet."

So it had been Fred's idea, not Preston's. Roberta hoped Fred knew what he was doing. "If you do consult any," she said, "would you please let me know?"

"Certainly, Roberta."

Which was why she wasn't at all surprised, when her phone rang that evening, to find Fred on the other end. Who else could it have been? No one had called since Doe left. Roberta had been half afraid that it would be Doe herself, finally, wanting to pick up something she'd forgotten, or one of Doe's friends who hadn't heard about the split. She needn't have worried.

"Good evening, Roberta. I'm calling with the information you requested." Fred wasn't even breaking rules by calling her; he was authorized to call staff and parents in the event of a school closure or emergency. She supposed this counted as an emergency, although she suspected the conversation wouldn't be on the record. She remembered the night Doe had left, when she'd gone to school and Fred had told her how lonely he got after hours. He'd never called her just to talk; maybe that wasn't allowed. She wondered if he welcomed Nicholas's emergency as a chance for greater human contact.

No, of course not. He was a machine. She was anthropomorphizing. "Yes, Fred? What did you learn?"

"Nicholas and his mother did go to the animal shelter, Roberta, and they came out with a cardboard carrying case the right size for a kitten, but then they drove to the Gaia Temple and took the carrying case inside. They must have left the kitten there, Roberta. They didn't have the carrying case with them when they went home."

Roberta swallowed. "That's a lot of information, Fred. Just how far can those outside cameras of yours see, anyway?"

"Not very far, Roberta. Preston told me about the kitten. He used the GPS cells and spy satellites to track Meredith and Nicholas. He's concerned about his grandson."

So. She'd been right, and it was out in the open, finally. She didn't know whether to be frightened or relieved. "Do you talk to Preston a lot, Fred?"

"Quite often, Roberta. He helped design me, after all. He's my father."

"Which makes Meredith your sister and Nicholas your nephew," Roberta said drily. "If I were you, I wouldn't wait for Mommy Meredith to recognize the relationship."

"You could talk to him too, Roberta, if you turned on your computer terminal now—or he could even speak to you here on the phone line. I know he'd like to speak to you, but he wanted me to initiate contact. He's afraid that you've been avoiding him, but this afternoon, you asked me to tell you if I consulted with anyone. You'd never done that before."

Just like Meredith had never asked about Nicholas, Roberta thought. She walked shakily across the room to her laptop and turned it on; as soon as she logged onto Preston's site, his benevolent visage filled the screen. "Hello, Roberta."

"Preston, what the hell are you doing? Shouldn't you be staying out of this?"

His features remained impassive. "My daughter evidently thinks so."

So she'd been right about that. "I don't appreciate being manipulated this way. I don't appreciate being manipulated into taking the job in the first place. I wish you'd told me up front what was going on."

"Roberta, I did not know what was going on. I had my suspicions, but I had no way to know for sure without more information. One of your former coworkers is a FOP"—Roberta was startled to hear him use the acronym—"and mentioned that you had left the brainwipe rehab position. I was delighted when you applied for the KinderkAIr job, but you got it on your own merits. Allow me to compliment you on the excellent job you've been doing with the children."

"That's very charming of you, Preston, but you still haven't explained why you didn't just ask me to apply yourself. Why go through Zephyr?"

"You had not spoken to me in years," he said. "I thought you had grown to dislike me. I thought that if I suggested something openly, you would not do it. I am glad to know that I was wrong, Roberta, and I apologize if I have caused you pain."

Well, hell. Unexpectedly, she found her eyes filling with tears. Preston had missed her. No, he'd wanted her to think he'd missed her. He was manipulating her again. She sighed and said, "So what's the deal, Preston? Why did you want an old friend in there, someone who's indebted to you?"

"You are not indebted to me, Roberta."

"That's bullshit, and you know it. You were the only person who could stand me when I was a kid." She felt a pang; it was true. Should she tell him about Doe, tell him why she'd turned her back on him for all those years? No: stay focused. If she started talking about Doe she'd start crying, and there were more important things to worry about. Time for the rest of it later. "Preston, cut the crap and tell me what you want me to do."

"Roberta, I am deeply concerned about Nicholas." So am I, Roberta thought, but she stayed quiet, waiting to hear what Preston would say next. "As you are probably aware, my daughter has shut me out of her life. That is nothing new. But lately she has been avoiding her mother as well, and providing only the most superficial information about Nicholas when she does speak to Constance. This alarms both of us."

"Yes, it would." And what in the name of Gaia does this have to do with me?

The handsome face frowned slightly. "Fred has told me about Nicholas's behavior in the classroom; he is authorized to do so after hours, although I could only observe directly were you to approve it. Guests can enter only with staff permission."

"You want my permission? Who else knows about this?"

"No one. I have not shared this information with Constance, because I want neither to alarm her nor to run the risk that she will inadvertently alert Meredith to my involvement."

Roberta shook her head. "You're a sneaky one, Preston."

"Meredith confided freely in her mother during the early part of Nicholas's life. For her not to do so now suggests that she too is deeply worried about Nicholas, perhaps even more so than we are. I cannot know what has happened in their home. Access is denied me. But if Meredith is not seeking help for the child—if she is being evasive with his grandmother and actively lying to his teachers, as she did tonight about the kitten—I can only conclude that she believes Nicholas to be beyond conventional assistance, that she fears him to be so deeply disturbed that disclosure would result in his resocialization."

Brainwiping? Oh, hell. "Preston, look, don't you think that might be a bit—extreme? Most people don't like having other people interfere with their kids. I mean, sure, Nicky's a bit strange"—okay, much more than a bit—"but he's only five, and—"

The image nodded at her. "I hope I am wrong, of course. And I have not shared this theory with Constance, because I see no need to alarm her. There is nothing she can do, in any event, not unless Meredith begins to confide in her again. But, Roberta, I trust my daughter's instincts, even if she does not trust mine. She would not be behaving this way without cause. And I do not want to see Nicholas brainwiped any more than she does, not least because of the agony I know it would cause her. She has suffered enough. I want to spare her more misery."

"Okay," Roberta said. *She's his real kid. She'll always be his first priority. You'll always be a distant second. Remember that, Berta.* "So my job's *not* to report what's going on? Is that what you want? Preston, you're asking me to break the law."

"Do you agree with brainwiping? Do you consider it an ethical or effective procedure?"

"Of course not! That's why I left my last job. It's a horror."

"Then I am asking you to protect a child from that horror."

"But it might not come to that! If there were other ways to help him—meds, gene therapy, talk therapy, whatever—"

"If Meredith considered conventional help to be an option, I believe she would have taken that step by now. She would not be acting in this extremely bizarre fashion if something were not very seriously wrong. And if you or Fred report Nicholas's behavior, he will be pulled out of the school and you will lose access to him. And so will I. And I believe that you two may still be able to help him."

Terrific. Now she and Fred were being commanded to do the impossible. "And, ah, just how do you think we can do that?"

"Roberta, I confess that I do not know. And you must, of course, follow your own best judgment. If you give me permission to observe the classroom directly, I will do what I can to suggest methods."

Think fast. If he observed and didn't report, would the blame fall on him? "Who'll know you're observing?" she asked.

"Only you and Fred."

"Will there be any *record* that you observed?"

"No, because then I would have to explain why, and it might get back to my daughter. Roberta, I am trying to help. I will understand if you feel you must report Nicholas, but I will do everything possible to protect you if you do not. You were an orphan in isolation. So was he. I beg of you, have mercy."

Mother of trees, did he think she was a monster? "I wouldn't report because I wanted to hurt him, Preston! I love Nicholas! I'd report to get him help!"

"Then do whatever you believe to be loving. Too many people think wiping is helping, Roberta."

She swallowed, remembering the shambling wrecks she'd worked with before KinderkAIr. "You'll protect me if I don't report? That's a promise?"

"It is."

She wanted to trust him. She didn't know if she could; Meredith would always come first, and Preston had to guard his own position. If he got into any trouble, MacroCorp could pull the plug on him. "And what else do you want, Preston?"

The image on the screen looked pained. "Roberta, I would not be burdening you unless I knew that you cared deeply about Nicholas. I want you to know that there are—additional resources on which you can call. I would like you and Fred to try to help Nicholas yourselves, so that he does not have to be brainwiped. As I have said, I will try to help you."

Roberta closed her eyes. "All right, Preston, you can watch. But what if we can't help him?"

"Then you will have done your best," the image said sadly. "And you will have been a true friend to him, and to me. Good-bye, Roberta. I know you are upset, and I will leave you now so you can think. I have taken enough of your time."

The image vanished; Roberta reached out numbly and turned off the laptop. The phone was on the couch: she picked it up and said, "Fred, are we sure he isn't listening anymore? I don't like this."

"He's a very nice man, Roberta. He loves his daughter and grandson very much."

"Sometimes people who adore their kids don't give a shit for anybody else. Okay, look, I've been given my marching orders. Frankly, if I had any sense I'd quit right now and do something else, but I've signed a contract for a full year, and short of faking cancer, I can't get out of it without getting myself blacklisted by MacroCorp, which is the last thing I need. I'm sure Preston's fully aware of all that. Fred, do you appreciate my position here? If I don't do what Preston wants, I'm in trouble with him. If I do what he wants and Meredith finds out, I'll be in trouble with her, which isn't trivial either. And either way, I'm in trouble with the state."

"I'm sorry you're so unhappy, Roberta. Preston wants to be your friend."

"Yeah, I'll bet he does. Look, what are we going to do, anyway? Tell Nicholas tomorrow morning, 'We know you left your new kitten at the Gaia Temple'?"

"Preston and I just want to understand what's happening with Nicholas, Roberta."

"So do I. But if he's really that screwed up, I don't see what we can do to help him."

"We have to try, Roberta, because Nicholas is our friend and we love him."

She sighed, wishing Fred weren't so damn noble. "Fred, we can't save the world."

"We're not saving the world, Roberta. We're trying to save one little boy."

She shook her head. There was no using talking about it anymore. "Look, I'll see you tomorrow morning, all right? Good night, Fred. Have fun watching the mice."

"All right, Roberta. I'll try to do that. Snowy and Buster are asleep right now. Cloud's drinking some water, and Patches is on the exercise wheel."

And they can't talk to you, Roberta thought. "Hey, Fred, look, I'm sorry if I sound cranky. I just—I don't think we'll be able to pull this off, that's all. And I don't trust Preston to save my ass if things go wrong, not if he has to worry about saving his own too. He could get wiped himself, if this came out."

"Please try not to worry, Roberta. You're a special person. Preston knows that."

And you're a delusional machine. "Good night, Fred." Feeling ill, she put down the phone and wondered what, if anything, Nicholas would tell them about the kitten expedition tomorrow morning.

"She's little," Nicky said, as he drank his morning juice. "She has gray and black stripes and blue eyes still, because she's just a baby kitty, and all four paws are white. The tip of her tail's white too. She's eight weeks old. We took her home but Daddy started sneezing, so we took her to Temple, but I can visit her there whenever I want. Her name's Miss Mittens."

"That's a good name," Roberta said, feeling sick. The boy's voice was completely flat. She couldn't imagine how it must have felt to him to watch his mother's betrayal, to go along with the charade. "I'm sorry you couldn't keep her, Nicholas."

"Daddy didn't used to sneeze at cats," Nicholas said quietly, pushing his empty juice glass randomly around the table. "Mommy said that sometimes people start sneezing when they get old. She said you can start sneezing anytime."

Meredith had thought of everything, down to a cover story for why she hadn't known her husband was allergic to cats. The ache in Roberta's stomach deepened. Nicholas looked up at her and said, "Mommy said I can bring Miss Mittens to school sometime. For show-and-tell. Maybe tomorrow. Can I, Berta?"

"Of course," Roberta said. Bring the cat to school to prove it exists, but don't let it live with you? Whether Nicholas was crazy or not, Meredith certainly was. "I'll look forward to meeting Miss Mittens, Fred, won't you?"

"I certainly will," Fred said. "I'd like to meet Miss Mittens very much, Nicholas. I like kittens."

And so the next afternoon, Meredith came to school with a cardboard carrying case emitting indignant squeaks. Roberta arranged the children in a circle, and Meredith opened the box and lifted the kitten gently out by the scruff of the neck before setting it down on the carpet. "She's very little still," she told the other children, "and this is a new, scary place for her, so you have to be very still and wait for her to come to you before you try to pat her, okay?"

Miss Mittens squeaked again and looked around the circle, ears flattened, but perked up when Meredith produced a ball of yarn from her pocket. "Here you go," she said, and tossed the ball gently to the kitten, who batted it energetically around the circle of children.

All the children seemed entranced except Nicholas, who watched the kitten with an unsettling scowl. After Meredith and Miss Mittens left, Roberta gave the kids warm milk and settled them on their napmats. Fred dimmed the lights so the children could rest; usually Roberta used this time to clean up assorted messes or help Fred inventory supplies, but today she only wanted to lie down and close her eyes. She felt like she was trapped in a nightmare. She was being leaned on by the most powerful translated entity on the planet; it was worse than tangling with the Mafia.

Well, fuck it. MacroCorp was in no position to fire her if she slacked off a little; Preston had said he'd protect her, wouldn't he? And she had the goods on him too. There had to be some way to prove his role in all this, if it came to that.

So she pulled some oversize pillows into the booknook and sat there on the floor, her knees drawn up to her chest. She was idly scanning the titles on the shelf—Suess, Silverstein, *The Little Engine That Could,* all the old classics—when she sensed movement in the dim light, and looked up to find Nicholas standing next to her.

"I couldn't sleep," he whispered. "Can I sit with you?"

"Sure," she whispered back. Nicholas sat next to her and snuggled into her side.

"Fred?" Nicholas whispered. "Are you awake too?"

A murmur emerged from the speaker above the bookshelf. "Yes, Nicholas. I'm always awake."

Nicholas looked grave. "I wish I could always be awake. Then I'd never have bad dreams."

"Yes, Nicholas, that's true. But then you'd also never have good dreams."

Nicholas sighed. "I guess. Berta, Fred, did you like Miss Mittens?"

"She's very cute," Roberta whispered, although she felt ill.

"Yes," Fred said softly, "she is. Nicholas, now that you can't keep Miss Mittens, do you think your mother will let you have another mouse?"

Fred, Roberta thought, stop it. Stop it. What are you doing? You'll just upset him more!

"No," Nicholas whispered.

"Why not, Nicholas?"

"Because I lied about the Hobbit."

Doesn't wash, Roberta thought grimly. If lying's the issue, then why lie about getting a kitten? "Nicholas," Fred whispered, "why did you lie about the Hobbit?"

"I can't tell you," Nicholas said. "It's a secret."

"Well then," Fred said, "since I know you're good at keeping secrets, you could have a mouse all your own here, and it could be a secret from your mother."

The last thing Fred was supposed to do was help kids plot against their parents. But Roberta had to go along with it; she didn't have any choice, not after last night. Was this on the record? What the hell was Fred doing? She knew she should say something to signal her acquiescence to the conspiracy, but she couldn't seem to make her mouth move.

Fortunately, Zillinth spared her the need. "Hey!" the little girl said, standing suddenly in front of them with a frown on her face. "Hey, what are you guys whispering about? Is Fred telling a story? Can I hear it too?"

Roberta shook herself out of her daze. If Zillinth was here, Fred couldn't do anything too sneaky, because there'd be another witness. Thank you, Goddess. "Of course you can, Zillinth, but you have to whisper the way we're doing, so you won't wake up the other children."

"Okay," Zillinth whispered, and plunked herself down on Roberta's free side. "What's the story about, Fred?"

"The story's about a little boy who can't have any pets because they make his mommy and daddy sneeze, so he has a make-believe mouse."

Zillinth nodded. "I had a make-believe horse once. My mommy used to feed it make-believe apples and sugar cubes."

"Well, Zillinth, this little boy can't even let his parents know about the make-believe mouse, because mice make them sneeze so badly that they'd sneeze even if the mouse was make-believe."

Zillinth giggled. "What's its name? My horse's name was Trot."

"I don't know, Zillinth. We hadn't gotten that far in the story. Nicholas, why don't you pick a name for the make-believe mouse?"

"Monster," Nicholas said promptly. "Its name is Monster Mouse."

"Mighty Monster Mouse," Zillinth suggested.

"No. Just Monster Mouse. The boy wants to feed the make-believe mouse to the make-believe monsters, because they like mice."

"You and your monsters! You already *told* this story, Nicholas!"

"Shhhhhh," Roberta said. "Not so loud, Zillinth."

"I never heard the end of that other story," Fred said. "I want to find out what happens."

Zillinth sniffed. "The boy feeds the make-believe mouse to the make-believe monsters and then they have make-believe dessert, the end."

"No," Nicholas said. "That's not how it goes. It's *my* story, Zillinth!"

"Speak softly," Fred said. "The other children are still sleeping. Nicholas, how does it go?"

"The monsters tell the boy they don't want a make-believe mouse. They want a real mouse. If they don't get a real mouse, then *they'll* have to be real. But Monster Mouse doesn't want to be real, because he doesn't want to be eaten. So the boy and Monster Mouse have to try to fool the monsters into thinking Monster Mouse is real."

"But then he'd get eaten," Zillinth objected.

"But he wouldn't *really* get eaten, because he wouldn't be real. He'd still just be make-believe. He'd just be pretending to be real."

"I don't get it," Zillinth said.

"That's because the story isn't finished yet," Fred said. "Nicholas, how do the boy and Monster Mouse fool the monsters?"

"I don't know, Fred."

"Will you tell us on Monday? Naptime is over now."

"I'll tell you when I find out. I don't know if I'll know on Monday."

"That's all right," Fred said. "Sometimes, the best stories take a very long time to tell."

Twenty-Four

I T took a week of naptimes for the boy and his mouse to figure out how to fool the monsters. Fred and Nicholas conferred about the problem every day, with Roberta listening; for the first two days, Zillinth joined them, but she soon grew bored with how slowly this strange story was progressing, and went back to whispering herself to sleep on her napmat; telling herself her own stories, presumably, although Roberta never found out what they were.

They began by consulting other stories. The first day, Fred retold Nicholas the story of *The Velveteen Rabbit,* the toy rabbit who became real by being loved. "Nicholas, if the boy loves his imaginary mouse very, very much, that would make it real to the monsters, wouldn't it?"

"No," Nicholas said. "Monsters don't care if you love something. They just want it to have fur and blood so they can eat it. That's what real means to them."

"You could buy fake fur at the store," Zillinth said. "And cut it into a mouse shape and put ketchup on it. Then it would be real."

"The monsters would *know,* Zillinth. They don't *like* ketchup."

"You could prick your finger and rub it over the fake fur, then."

Roberta, bemused, looked down at the tranquil little girl, who'd never revealed a penchant for self-mutilation before. "I don't think that's a good idea, honey."

"Neither do I," Fred said. "It's not good to prick your own finger, Zillinth. It hurts, and you could get an infection, and that would hurt worse."

"Hmmmph," Zillinth said. "It's just a *story.*"

"Right," Roberta said, although she was starting to wonder. "But we want it to be a happy story. No infections."

Zillinth scowled. "The boy would get to wear a fancy Band-Aid. That would be happy."

Fred said, "Band-Aids are for accidents, Zillinth. It makes me very sad when people hurt themselves on purpose."

"*Hmmmmmph!* Even in stories?"

"Even in stories."

"Even to save mice?" Nicholas said, looking up at Fred's speaker.

"Yes, even to save mice."

"Well," Zillinth said crossly, "then you'd better tell another story, Fred. The rabbit didn't work."

"I'll tell you another story tomorrow, because naptime's over now." And the next day he told Zillinth and Nicholas and Roberta the story of Pinocchio, the puppet who became real by telling the truth and doing good deeds.

"Hmmmmph," Zillinth said. "If Monster Mouse told the truth, he'd have to say he was just a make-believe mouse instead of a real one, and then the monsters *still* wouldn't want to eat him."

"Zillinth's right," Nicholas said quietly.

Zillinth, Roberta thought, was destined to become an attorney. A self-mutilating attorney. And she and Fred were the last people who should be posing as authorities on honesty. "Fred," Nicholas said, frowning, "it's not bad to lie to monsters, is it?"

Fred paused for a few seconds, an unusually long time for him, and then said, "In many stories, it's not bad to lie to monsters if they're trying to hurt you. But in a lot of stories, you have to tell the monsters the truth, or they won't go away. In a lot of stories, the monsters just get more powerful if you lie to them. Because even if they say they want to eat mice, your fear and your lies are what they really eat. But if you tell them the truth, and you make friends with them, they won't hurt you."

Roberta blinked. How in the name of Gaia could the kids possibly understand all that? But Zillinth nodded and said, "Beauty and the Beast. If you're nice to the monsters, they'll be nice to you."

"Yes, Zillinth. Very good! What a good memory you have!"

Nicholas squirmed. "But the boy's *trying* to be nice to the monsters. That's why he's trying to feed them! He wants to be nice to the monsters *and* to the mouse!"

"What about good deeds?" Fred asked. "Good deeds are very powerful in every story I've ever heard, and in the world too. Nicholas, what if Monster Mouse offered to become real to feed the monsters, the way

Pinocchio offered himself as firewood so Harlequin wouldn't have to burn instead?"

Then he'll get slapped with a diagnosis of excessive altruism, Roberta thought grimly. No wonder Fred had never read Pinocchio to the rest of the children. It didn't fit the world they lived in.

"That's dumb," said Zillinth, a true child of her culture. "I wouldn't have done that if I'd been Pinocchio! Fred, I thought you didn't like it when people hurt themselves."

"You're right, Zillinth, I don't. But Pinocchio didn't really get hurt, did he?"

"That's because Giovanni didn't burn him," Nicholas said. "Giovanni was nice, underneath. The monsters are bad."

"Well then, Nicholas, tomorrow I'll tell you another story, but nap-time's over for today."

"*I'm* not coming back tomorrow," Zillinth said. "This is stupid."

So on Wednesday, Fred told only Roberta and Nicholas the story of the Nutcracker, which Nicholas roundly rejected because the Nutcracker was only real in Clara's dream. On Thursday, Fred showed Roberta and Nicholas "Calvin and Hobbes" comic strips on the booknook video monitor. Nicholas announced grumpily that the monsters in *his* story were smarter than Calvin, and would never be fooled into thinking a stuffed mouse was real.

"What about Scheherazade?" Roberta said.

"Who's that?" said Nicholas.

"Ah," Fred said. "Yes, that's a very nice story. Will you tell us that story, Roberta?"

So she did. She told Nicholas the story of the woman who saved her own life, night after night, by telling stories. "Maybe Monster Mouse and the boy could tell the monsters stories, Nicky, just like we're doing now."

"No," Nicholas said, very quietly. "Too much make-believe. They don't like make-believe. They don't like stories. Make-believe is where the monsters live now, and if you feed them real mice they're happy for a little while, but otherwise they'll stop being make-believe. They'll leave make-believe and become real, so they can get food. And then they'll eat the world." He squinted up at the monitor and said, "Remember the Fred cookie I made, with the gun? That didn't even work, because the gun was make-believe too."

Fred's voice, as always, was completely calm. "That's a very scary story, Nicholas."

He hugged himself. "Yes, it is."

"So Monster Mouse and the boy," Roberta said slowly, trying to sound as calm as Fred did, "are trying to save the world?" Nicholas nodded up at her, looking grave. "How long do they have, Nicky?"

"I don't know." Nicholas shrugged, an oddly adult gesture for such a small boy, and said, "Naptime's up now, Fred, right?"

When she got home that evening, Roberta found another note from Zephyr shoved under her door. *So how's it going? Have you warmed yourself in the sun after crawling out from under your rock? Can I come visit Mr. Clean sometime? I miss him.*

Not as much as I miss Doe, Roberta thought. She wondered if Zephyr was glad that Doe was gone, since it meant that Roberta no longer went downstairs to ask Zephyr to quiet her rehearsing bots. On the other hand, that meant Zephyr didn't see Roberta, either, and Roberta suspected that Zephyr was lonelier than she let on. Her apartment never seemed to have any human visitors. I should go down there, Roberta thought, but she really didn't want to. Zephyr gave her the creeps. Sighing, she scribbled on the bottom of the note, *I'm sure Mr. Clean misses you too, but he's just fine. I, on the other hand, am still a little wobbly and need to stay a hermit for a while. Sorry, Zephyr. Thanks for understanding.* She went downstairs to deliver the note, feeling guilty—there was no noise from Zephyr's apartment at all, which meant that she and her bots were all out at the park or something—and then trudged back to her apartment. She wasn't at all surprised when Fred called.

"Roberta, I don't think Nicholas's story is just a story."

"Neither do I." It occurred to her that she was every bit as pathetic as Zephyr. Zephyr took bots for walks. Roberta gossiped with an AI. "Is Preston here too?"

"Here I am," said Preston's voice. "Roberta, Fred and I were wondering if Nicholas's monsters are the reason Meredith will not allow him to have pets."

Roberta sighed, pushing her fingers against her eyelids. "Yeah, no kidding. I've been wondering that too. Do you think maybe he's done something already?"

"If I am correct about Meredith's fear of resocialization," Preston said, "such an action on Nicholas's part would certainly explain it."

"I agree," Fred said sadly. "I'm worried, Roberta. I wonder how his first mouse died. And I wonder if he's been telling his mother the same stories he's been telling us."

"Yeah," Roberta said. "Or if he told the Hobbit too much. Do you think that's why she had the guy arrested and wiped?"

"I can't say, Roberta."

"Preston? What do you think?"

"That is a plausible theory, Roberta, but we cannot know for sure."

She sighed. In for a penny, in for a pound "Okay. I know you both know this even better than I do, but just let me say it again. If we think he's that seriously disturbed, we're required to report it. If we don't report it, and something awful happens, and it turns out we knew, we're in big trouble. We are. Preston, you want me and Fred to help Nicholas by ourselves. I'm not at all sure we can do that. I don't know how."

"We can help him tell his story," said Fred. "If we can help him finish telling the story about Monster Mouse, maybe the mouse and the boy will outsmart the monsters and everything will be fine."

Fred, the eternal optimist. Roberta shook her head, although neither Fred nor Preston could see her. "Zillinth knows. And she's not one to keep her mouth shut. So the mouse may already be out of the bag, so to speak."

"Zillinth knows about Monster Mouse," Fred said. "She doesn't know all of it. She doesn't know that Nicholas's mother lied about the cat. And I don't think Zillinth thinks the story's important, Roberta. You and I do."

"Yes," said Preston, "I agree. The little girl represents no serious danger."

Roberta's skin crawled. "If something happens, we're going to know we could have prevented it. If something happens, it's going to be our fault."

"I will protect you," Preston said. "Do not worry, Roberta."

"With all due respect, Preston, you can't protect me from my conscience." That sounded stuffy and priggish, she knew. She didn't care. She wished, not for the first time, that Meredith were on speaking terms with her father; it would have made Roberta's life infinitely easier.

"Roberta," said Fred—was it her imagination, or did he sound a little desperate?—"we have to have faith in Nicholas. He wants us to help him. That's why he's telling us the story. I don't think we'd be helping him if we reported this, Roberta. I don't think that would be a kind or loving thing to do."

She closed her eyes. "Fred, you're a machine. What the fuck do you know about faith or love or kindness? At least Preston used to be human. You've never been human. So how can you know what those words even mean?"

"I know what they mean because people tell me what they mean, Roberta."

"Who? What people?" She briefly imagined some crazed chorus of baggies holding religious services in the deserted school every weekend, singing about love and faith to a machine because no one else would let them in out of the cold. It was the same fantasy she'd had the night Doe left, the night Fred had let her in and let her drink warm milk. But of course Fred would never let in anyone he didn't know—would he?

"Why, you, Roberta. You and Nicholas and the other children, and the writers who tell those other stories. The people who tell stories about the Velveteen Rabbit, and Pinocchio, and the Nutcracker, and Calvin and Hobbes. And that other person, the man I was named after. He knew about love and faith and kindness. He knew how important it is for children to feel safe. I try to be just like him, Roberta."

Roberta shook her head again. Machines. Crazy machines using crazy words. What could Fred know, what could he feel, without a body to feel with? How could he feel without a heart?

Preston said quietly, "Roberta, do you want to report Nicholas? Do you want him to be brainwiped?"

She remembered teaching the clients to brush their teeth. She remembered grown-ups learning all over again how to put on their socks, how to use a spoon. She remembered the fear in their eyes. *Who was I? What did I do?* She remembered Preston's plea. *Have mercy.* "No, of course I don't want that. I don't want that for anyone."

"Then we have to help Nicholas finish telling his story," Fred said. "We don't really have much choice, Roberta, do we?"

❧

As it turned out, Nicholas had already figured out how to finish his story. He arrived bright-eyed at school the next day, his normally calm, reserved manner replaced with an almost manic energy. He bounced around the room all morning, singing strange, tuneless little songs and playing with blocks and finger painting with far more abandon than he usually did, so much so that he got some finger paint on the table. For Nicholas, allowing himself to be this messy was a major breakthrough, and Roberta wondered what in the world had happened.

She found out at naptime. The other kids settled down onto their mats, and as soon as their eyes were closed, Nicholas made a beeline for the booknook. "Fred," he said breathlessly, the moment he arrived, "Roberta, I figured it out. I figured out what happens in the story!"

"That's wonderful, Nicholas." Fred was as calm and as supportive as ever; Roberta, a knot in her stomach, hoped that Nicholas's solution really would be wonderful. "What happens? I can't wait to hear."

"Neither can I," said Roberta. "So you'd better tell us right now, Nicholas."

He actually giggled, a sound nearly unheard of from him. "All the boy has to do is find a mouse that's already dead! Then he can tell the monsters that Monster Mouse has died, but really, it won't be Monster Mouse. Monster Mouse will still be alive in the Land of Make-Believe, but the monsters will eat the other mouse and be happy. And the boy won't have to hurt anything."

Roberta, knowing how happy the child was and how happy he wanted them to be too, swallowed her nausea and tried to get her face to unfrown itself. "Nicky, where is he going to find a mouse that's already dead?"

"I don't know," Nicholas said. For a moment his frown mirrored hers, but then he cheered up again. "In the grass, maybe, or maybe a cat catches it. Maybe the kitty brings it to him as a present so he can give it to the monsters."

"A real cat." Fred's voice was matter-of-fact. "Like Miss Mittens."

"Uh-huh. Or maybe somebody poisons it or catches it in a trap. Poison would be good, because then maybe the monsters would be poisoned and maybe they would die too."

"If the monsters die," Fred said, "will Monster Mouse and the boy be safe?"

"Uh-huh. Unless the monsters grow back. But then he could find a dead mouse again. And maybe it was just a normal mouse and it never did anything special when it was alive, but now it's a hero, 'cause it's saving the world." Nicholas looked up at the speaker, his face serious, and said, "I think it better be a poison mouse, Fred, so the monsters will die too."

"Nicholas, it hurts animals when they die of poison."

"And it hurts them when cats kill them," Roberta said, trying to sound as calm as Fred sounded. "And if the cat doesn't get to eat the mouse, the cat's sad too. Nicholas, can the mouse just die of old age? Would that be okay? Can the mouse die in its sleep?"

Nicholas considered this, his lips pursed. "Well, I guess. It could die and then you could poison it. Like putting sprinkles on a cookie." He looked over at the terrarium, where Snowy was drinking water and Buster was running on the exercise wheel. "Do mice live a long time?"

He went back to taking his afternoon naps, but every day now, his first act upon entering and his last before leaving was to watch the mice. His expression as he did so was always cheerful; he called the mice by name, helped fill their water bottle and seed dishes, patted them sometimes when Roberta picked them up for him, since he was reluctant to lift them himself. Roberta was very, very afraid that he was waiting for one of them to die.

She and Fred and Preston talked nearly every night now. Of the three of them, Fred was most hopeful. "He's doing much, much better. Both of you must have noticed that. He's relating better to the other children, and he seems happier. He's not as tense. His pictures are messier."

"I know," she said bleakly.

"We did it, Roberta. We helped Nicholas finish his story, and now he's all right. We're special, Roberta."

She wanted so badly to believe him. She wanted so badly to believe that a story could really fix the world. "Fred, I don't know. I just don't know. The way he looks at those mice, I get the creeps sometimes."

"I agree with Roberta," Preston said. "I find his continuing preoccupation with the mice extremely disturbing."

"But he's not afraid of them anymore. Preston, Roberta, he pats them now. He isn't afraid to go near the cage."

"I just hope you're right," she said grimly. "It's going to be very interesting to see what happens when the first mouse dies."

One night, because she was tired of talking about Nicholas and also because she really wanted to know, she decided to change the subject. "You know, we've been telling the parents that nothing's going to change as a result of the ratification hearings, all this born-not-built stuff. I know that will be true if the amendment passes, if Fred can't ever be a person, because then he'll still be MacroCorp property. But what if it doesn't pass? What if the law decides that AIs are already people, or can be declared people? What then?"

The debate had sparked a new wave of Luddite activism. The infamous Gina Veilasty, as elusive as ever, had once again issued a statement accusing MacroCorp of dealing in weapons, raping the environment, and supporting exploitative labor practices. MacroCorp had issued the usual denials. Preston had, in fact, used the subject of weapons to argue that AIs weren't human. During one of the hearings, he'd talked about MacroCorp's negotiations with several small companies in Africa, businesses that ordinarily wouldn't have been able to afford MacroCorp systems, but with which MacroCorp was willing to cut deals to encourage entrepreneurial activity on the ravaged continent. "One of these companies," Preston said earnestly, "lost the contract with us because they had done business with military suppliers. We would not have known about those transactions had the company's AI not included them in the reports it gave us. If the AI had been acting out of self-interest, it would have hidden that detail to further the negotiations. Its honesty in this situation demonstrates that it is a machine, not a sentient entity capable of dishonesty."

Roberta, watching the hearings in her pajamas while Mr. Clean doggedly pursued a stubborn dust bunny, had snorted a mouthful of tea. Fred, at least, had very flexible notions of honesty, and surely Preston knew that. But she supposed that Preston's position was no more hypocritical than Veilasty's. Aside from the cognitive dissonance of a terrorist construct acting sanctimonious about violence—if in fact Veilasty was a puppet for whomever had masterminded the Abdul-Allam killing—the politics of the situation made Roberta's head hurt. Ironically enough, the Luds and MacroCorp agreed in denying that AIs were people. The Lud position was ideological; they feared that AIs would acquire too much power if granted personhood. MacroCorp's logic was economic; they didn't want their AI manufacturing business affected by human-rights legislation. But for exactly that reason, various Luds—including Veilasty, evidently—wanted the born-not-built amendment to be *defeated,* wanted to be able to call AIs legal persons, all so MacroCorp would be forced to stop manufacturing them. It didn't make any sense, and it made Roberta very grateful that she'd never even thought about going to law school.

"The amendment will pass," Preston said now.

"Fred? What do you think?"

"It won't make any difference, Roberta. The amendment may affect my legal status, but that won't change who I am. It will only change who I am on paper. I'll still be real, whether the amendment is ratified or not."

Like the Velveteen Rabbit was real. But that was just a story, and Fred was just a machine. And Preston was just a program with a set of memories. And Roberta was just a bag of biological fluids controlled by electrical impulses. "Fred, do you ever wish you could go to Canada or Africa? Someplace where you'd be a person, where you'd get to vote and everything?"

"No, Roberta. I never wish that. I want to be exactly where I am. I want to be at school, with you and the children and the books and the mice. KinderkAIr is my home."

Home, she thought musingly after the conversation had ended. Another strange concept for an AI. She remembered trying to teach the brainwipe clients what home meant, how difficult a time many of them had with the idea. They didn't feel as if they belonged anywhere. Somehow it didn't seem fair to her that Fred had a home, when so many people, born of blood and bone from their mother's womb, had none at all. But she had chosen Fred, hadn't she? She'd run from the retraining job, fled it; on some level, she cared more deeply about Fred than she had about the clients. Did that make her a bad person?

Through the floorboards of her apartment, she heard the cacophony of one of Zephyr's rehearsals. Maybe she and Zephyr were just two of a kind. And then Roberta realized that she envied Fred. He had a home and felt at home there. Her sense of home had departed when Doe did.

She cried herself to sleep that night for the first time in weeks.

She woke up late, feeling hungover, as she usually did after a crying jag. She didn't even have time to shower and wash her hair before she left for work. Cursing, she gulped down some cereal and orange juice, threw on clothing, and jogged to the train station, feeling singularly grimy. She wondered sourly if Mr. Clean could be reprogrammed as an alarm clock. Or maybe he could clean her.

Please, she thought as she walked into KinderkAIr, let there not be any pissed-off parents waiting to yell at me for being late. Dear Gaia, let this be a good day, a quiet day. I can't deal with any more crises.

Gaia wasn't listening. To Roberta's horror, Meredith Walford-Lindgren was inside, sitting on one of the napmats and hugging a sobbing Nicholas. Zillinth's mother was in the corner with the other kids, helping them color. Thank heavens for good mothers. Shit, Roberta thought, there goes my job, Preston or not, and then, What the hell? "I'm so sorry I'm late," she said. "Ms. Walford-Lindgren—"

"You can call me Meredith," the other woman said, looking up. She looked as haggard as Roberta felt. "It's okay, really."

"Whatever is wrong? Nicholas, what happened?" Roberta tried to keep her voice professional, appropriately concerned, but her mind was racing. Meredith had found out about the stories. Meredith knew she was in league with Preston. Meredith was going to pull Nicholas out of the school and get Roberta fired.

Roberta knelt down on the floor next to Nicholas and his mother, hoping that she looked sympathetic instead of terrified. Nicholas had slaughtered small animals on the way to school. Nicholas had asked for a dead mouse for Christmas. Nicholas—

Nicholas just cried harder and transferred his embrace from his mother to Roberta, clutching her as if he were drowning and she were his only source of air.

"I don't know what's wrong," Meredith said. She sounded as rattled as Roberta felt. "He wouldn't tell me. He said he wanted to come to school to see you and Fred, so I brought him here. I didn't know what else to do."

"Ms. Walford-Lindgren," Fred said soothingly, "Roberta and I both care about Nicholas very much."

"I can see that," Meredith said tightly. "Obviously it's mutual." She stood up and tried to straighten her tearstained tunic; Roberta saw that her hands were shaking. "He's not sick. I took his temperature. He says nothing hurts. *I don't know what to do.*"

Roberta, still feeling strangled by the howling child, prayed for the right words. "We'll keep him safe. I promise you. I promise, Meredith, he's safe here and we won't let anything happen to him."

"Of course you won't," Meredith snapped, her voice wound as tightly as—*as a mousetrap*, Roberta thought grimly. "That's your job."

That wasn't what I meant. I meant that we won't report him as disturbed. I meant that we'll shelter him. But I can't say that, because this is during school hours and it's all on the record—I think—and because if you don't already know he's disturbed, I'll get into trouble. And I can't promise to let you know what's going on when I find out, because Nicholas is right here, and obviously he doesn't want you to know. "Look," Roberta said, "this is awful, I know, and you must feel rotten that he wants to be here right now—" Meredith gave her such a black look that she rushed on, praying that she'd still have her job at the end of the day. "Look, please, just leave me a number where I can reach you and I'll call you later, okay? I'll call you when he calms down, so you'll know everything's all right."

Meredith raised her chin a fraction of an inch. "I'll be at home. You can call me there."

"All right. I'll talk to you later, then." She wanted to say, "Please don't worry," but she was worried too.

"Nicky," Meredith said, reaching out to touch his hair, "I love you. Everything's going to be okay." She sounded on the verge of tears herself. She got up and left, her shoulders hunched. Roberta wondered if Nicholas would stop howling, now that his mother had left, but the sobs continued, racking his small body.

"Nicholas, sweetheart, what *is* it?"

He gulped air, hiccupped, and wiped his nose on his sleeve. "Fred, Berta, the Hobbit came back!"

"Er, excuse me," someone said, and Roberta looked up to find Zillinth's mother standing next to her. "Listen, I have to get to work now."

"Of course," Roberta said. "Thank you so much for your help. I'm sorry I was late."

"It's okay. Any other day, Fred could have handled everything, right? I hope you find out what's wrong. I hope he's okay." Zillinth's mother nodded at Nicholas and then at Roberta, and then was gone.

"I'll show the other children a video," Fred said. "Perhaps you and Nicholas and I should continue this conversation in the conference room?"

"Right," Roberta said. "I mean yes, of course, thanks for thinking of that, Fred. Nicky, come on. We can talk in here, okay?" Once they were safely in the conference room—the cone of silence, as Roberta always thought of it—she said, "Nicholas, I don't understand. I thought the Hobbit was your friend."

"He *was,* Berta!"

"Then aren't you happy he came back?"

"No! 'Cause Mommy said people aren't supposed to live in holes in the ground, but that's where I saw him again, where the leaves are, and he's *different,* Berta. He didn't know who I was, and he looked really scared, and—and—he looked *funny.*"

I'll just bet, Roberta thought grimly. It hadn't been long enough since the Hobbit's arrest for him to have been resocialized properly after brain-wiping, even if he was one of the lucky ones for whom the resocialization would have taken. He must have somehow wandered away from the rehab center without getting caught; it happened. Well, he wouldn't be loose for long. The retraining staff would notify the police, and surely the cops would pick Henry up again, given his history with the famous family up the hill. "Nicholas, where did you see him?"

"In the bushes, when Mommy and I were walking to school today. Mommy didn't see him. She was looking at a squirrel and she pointed to the squirrel so I'd look at it, but I waved to the Hobbit instead. And he ran away. He was scared. He was scared of me, Berta! He never ran away from me before! He's scared of me because Mommy was mean to him! I wasn't going to hurt him, Berta!"

"I know you weren't, Nicholas." She thought again of the brainwiping clients who couldn't understand what home meant. She'd heard of others: people who couldn't be resocialized, who'd never relearned how to eat with a fork or to speak in the first person, who nonetheless kept some vestigial memory of home when everything else was gone. Sometimes they made their way back to places they'd loved before—their houses, or childhood vacation spots, or favorite parks—even though they couldn't remember the names of their spouses or children or siblings, even though they no longer knew the words *squirrel, pigeon, tree.* Such cases had always reminded Roberta of salmon, fighting their way blindly upstream to spawn. She didn't know what was sadder: that Henry had been wiped to begin with, or that his hole in the ground had been so precious to him that he'd made his way back there even when everything else was gone.

"I couldn't tell Mommy why I was crying," Nicholas said, his voice very small. "I didn't want her to know about the Hobbit. I was afraid she'd call the police again."

Roberta's stomach clenched. She had no idea how to respond to that. She wondered if Nicholas knew about his mother's activism work, if he understood what had happened to Henry, if he had any way of grasping the hypocrisy those two facts represented.

"Nicholas," said Fred, "I think you need to tell your mother why you're so upset."

"But she'll be mad."

"I don't think she'll be mad if you tell her about the Hobbit this time, Nicholas. She was mad last time because you hadn't told her anything, because you were keeping the Hobbit a secret, and she thought the Hobbit had made you do that. Sometimes grown-ups ask children to keep secrets because they want to hurt them. I think that's what your mother was afraid of."

Roberta would have given anything for a private phone conversation with Fred just then. She and Fred were in the secrecy business up to their eyebrows; he was a fine one to talk. But Preston was here too now, wasn't he? Roberta suspected that Meredith wouldn't care if Henry was back, since he'd been wiped and couldn't remember anything about Nicholas or the mouse. Meredith could afford her CALM compassion again. Was that what Fred and Preston were thinking? It must have been, if Fred had recommended telling Meredith the truth.

"Nicholas," Fred went on, "I think if you tell your mommy about the Hobbit this time, she'll feel a lot better. She was really worried about you this morning. She was really scared. And if you don't tell her why you were crying so much, she'll stay worried and scared. She loves you, Nicholas. Please tell her the truth."

"But what if she calls the police?"

"I don't think she will. I think she'll probably give the Hobbit food instead. Nicky, your mother's famous for giving food to people like the Hobbit. She does it all the time. It's on TV, on the news. I think she'd be happy if she could help your friend."

Fat chance, Roberta thought. "Nicholas, I think Fred's right. I don't think your mom will be scared of the Hobbit if you tell her about him. Okay?"

He scowled. "*You* tell her. You said you'd call her on the telephone."

"It would be better if you told her." Nicholas had begun sucking his thumb, and was glaring at her. "Come on, Nick; the phone's right over here. Let's call her, and you can tell her what was wrong, and then you can go out and color or watch the mice or take a nap, okay?"

Nicholas took his thumb out of his mouth and dried it on his shirt. "*You* call her," Nicholas said. "I'll talk to her when I go home." Then he stomped out of the conference room.

"Well," Roberta said, feeling weak. "Do you really think we should tell her? He obviously doesn't want us to. First she betrays him, then we do? Fred—"

"Roberta, it's all right. You have to call her. You told her you would."

"I'm calling her, huh? And what's your role in all this?"

"I'll dial," Fred said. Roberta wondered—not for the first time—if his makers had given him a sense of humor. "As both you and Preston keep reminding me, Nicholas's mother doesn't like AIs. I think it would be better if you spoke to her."

"Okay," Roberta said, wondering if her question about outside coaching had just been answered. She couldn't think straight. "Dial, already. Let's get this over with."

Meredith must have been standing vigil next to the phone, because she answered it about two seconds into the first ring. "Ms. Walford-Lindgren," Roberta said, "this is—"

"Roberta, I know who it is. I told you, please call me Meredith. It's shorter. How's Nicholas?"

"He's—he's better. He's not crying anymore. He's in the other room with the other kids now."

"Did you find out what he was upset about?"

Roberta took a deep breath. "Yes, I did. He—evidently some homeless guy, Nicholas's friend, evidently he's back in the neighborhood." Meredith made a small sound, between a cough and a choke, and Roberta rushed on. "From what Nicholas said, it sounds like he's been brainwiped. He didn't recognize Nicholas at all, and he ran away when he saw Nicholas, and it upset Nicholas a lot. Nicholas, uh, he was afraid to tell you. He was afraid you'd call the police." Dead silence on the other end of the phone; no, not silence, either, but quick, shallow breathing, as if Meredith were hyperventilating and about to fall to the floor unconscious. Great.

"Um, Ms.—um, Meredith? Are you there?"

"I'm here."

"Are you all right?"

"I'm all right." Roberta heard the other woman take a deep breath. "What else did he tell you about—about the vagrant? I mean, about the first time?"

Bluebell. Was it safe for Roberta to know about the mouse, or not? Stall for time. "He said you were upset because he hadn't told you about the guy right away."

"I see. Did he tell you *why* he didn't tell me?"

"Not exactly, no." That much was the truth. "He, ah, he'd been talking a lot about somebody named the Hobbit, but we thought that was an imaginary friend."

"Yes," Meredith said drily, "that's what I thought too. I assumed your AI had told Nicholas the story."

You'd be amazed if you knew the stories we've been telling around here lately. Or maybe not. Roberta felt her hand, slick with sweat, slipping on the handset of the phone. She could switch to the speakerphone, but she didn't want to; even in the privacy of the conference room, broadcasting this conversation felt too dangerous. She closed her eyes—think, think— and wondered how she could win Meredith's trust. "We didn't press him. It's none of our business. Meredith, Fred and I are both very fond of Nicholas."

"Yes, of course you are."

Dammit. This was nuts. This woman wasn't about to confide in Roberta, and Roberta didn't dare confide in her, either. Let her and Nicholas have their secrets. It wasn't any of her business. "Well, I just wanted you to know that he's all right now, that he's feeling better. I hope you are too."

"Yes, of course. Thank you for calling. Good-bye."

Roberta, defeated, hung up. The minute she put down the phone, Fred said, "Roberta? I think you need to go be with the children now."

Twenty-Five

F RED, what's wrong?" But Roberta, heart racing, was out of the conference room before he could even answer. The minute she opened
the door, she heard someone—Zillinth—sobbing, and caught a blurred
glimpse of the children gathered in a group around the terrarium. "What's
wrong?" she said again, this time to the children. "What happened?"

"Buster died," Steven said gravely.

She shot a look at Nicholas, who was standing wide-eyed on the out-
skirts of the group, and said, "Oh, dear. Oh, poor little Buster. Let me
see." She peered into the cage; Buster was lying on his back, all four of his
little mouse legs in the air. "That's too bad. But you know, mice don't live
as long as we do, and Buster had a good life here. We loved him and took
good care of him."

Zillinth sniffed and wiped her nose on her sleeve. "Fred already told us
that. And he said he saw Buster die, when we were all over there watching
the video, and it just took a minute. It was quick. Fred says it probably
didn't hurt Buster much." She sniffled again, and Roberta knelt and put
her arm around the girl.

"That's right. But it hurts us when we lose a friend, doesn't it?"

Zillinth turned, twisting in Roberta's arms, and glared at Nicholas. "At
least Buster got to stay with the other mice. At least Nicky's stupid *monsters*
didn't get him."

Not yet, Roberta thought. This was Nicholas's story come true, and she
half expected him to ask to take the dead mouse home with him. But instead
he said, "I'm sorry Buster died. Really I am, Berta. He was a nice mouse."

"We're all sorry Buster died," Roberta said briskly.

"Yes," Fred said, "we are. Roberta, the children have been talking
about how to say good-bye to Buster. Steven wants to have a funeral for
him in the flower garden next to the playground. I think that's a good
idea."

"So do I," Roberta said.

"I could bury him at my house," Nicholas said. So here it was: the end of the story, dessert for the monsters. "I could take him home and bury him with Patty."

"Well," Steven said, pouting, "I could bury him at *my* house too. And he was *my* mouse. *I* named him. Why should *you* get to bury him, Nicholas?"

"We should bury him here," Zillinth said decisively, "so we can all help. That's what's fair."

"I agree with Zillinth," Fred said. Roberta waited for Nicholas to complain, and was grateful when he didn't.

The boy seemed unusually subdued throughout the funeral. Steven found a box to put Buster in, and Cindy picked flowers to put on the grave, and Zillinth dug the hole with a red plastic toy shovel. It was a gray day, cold, with the threat of rain; the children and Roberta stood in a circle, shivering even with their jackets on. Fred had written and printed out a eulogy, and Roberta read it—all about what a good mouse Buster was been, and how funny he'd been when he ran on his wheel, and how everyone would miss him—and then invited each of the children to say good-bye. Roberta, yearning to get back inside, remembered reading that the original Fred had been a minister. She smiled, amused at a sudden vision of Fred performing Zillinth's or Steven's wedding, twenty years from now, and felt a jab in her side. Cindy was glaring up at her. "What are you *happy* about? Buster's *dead*."

Ooops. "I know he is, honey. I was, um, thinking about mouse heaven, and how happy Buster must be."

Cindy sniffed, sounding like Zillinth. "No such thing as heaven, *my* mommy says. You go into the earth and feed the flowers."

"Well, it's fine to be happy about the flowers Buster will feed too."

"I'll be happy when I'm warm again," Steven grumbled, abruptly done with sentiment, and the other children agreed and ran as one back inside. At moments like this, they always reminded Roberta of a flock of birds, wheeling as a unit. She followed, feeling old and cold and tired. Time for warm milk and cookies, and then naptime.

Nicholas didn't nap. Perhaps she should have known he wouldn't. Instead, he went quietly to the booknook and sat down, hugging his knees, looking up at her. I have to go over there, Roberta thought, although she didn't want to. Maybe it would be okay. Maybe Nicholas had already fed the dead mouse to the imaginary monsters, and they were comfortably sated now, and everyone would live happily ever after. Maybe the story was over.

The story wasn't over. "I want to dig up Buster and take him home," Nicholas announced when Roberta sat down next to him.

She closed her eyes. "Nick, honey, you can't do that. Buster's where he belongs. His job is to feed the flowers now. You can't dig him up."

"Yes, I can. He's not down so deep. I could dig him up. Feeding the monsters is more important than feeding the flowers. The flowers can eat other things." He scowled and added, "The flowers aren't going to eat the world, Berta."

She shuddered, and hoped he hadn't seen. "Nicky, the other children will be upset if you dig Buster up."

Nicholas sighed, a sound of oddly adult exasperation. "Well, I won't tell them. And I'll fill in the hole afterwards, so they won't be able to see that Buster's gone."

Roberta had no idea what to say. None. "Fred, what do you think about this?"

"Nicholas, what will your mother say when you bring home a dead mouse?"

"I won't tell her. She's scared of the monsters. She doesn't like it when mice die; she was sad about Patty."

Fred sounded infinitely patient, as always. "Nicholas, I don't want you to dig up Buster."

"Neither do I," Roberta said.

"Well, I *told* you I'd just take him home, but everybody wanted to put him in the ground! And I have to tell you if I dig him up, because I can't be in the playground by myself! You have to be there too!"

Roberta shook her head, amazed that he was so careful to follow all the rules. She supposed that digging up Buster was following the rules too, to him. "I'm glad you're not trying to trick us," Fred said gently. "That's very honest, Nicholas. But if you do this, Roberta and I are going to have to tell your mother. We can't trick her, either."

Nicholas's face clouded. "You didn't tell her about the story, did you?"

"No, we didn't. But that was a story. You can keep the story here, and that's fine. If you dig up a real dead mouse and take it home with you, we have to tell your mother."

Nicholas's expression cleared. "Okay," he said, suddenly cheerful. "I'll dig it up and keep it here, and then you won't have to tell Mommy." He looked up at Roberta, and smiled, and said, "You can put Buster in the freezer until the monsters are ready to eat him. Can we poison him?"

Roberta resisted the urge to exclaim, as Zillinth would have, *Ewwww!* "Nicholas, I'm not going to do that. If you dig Buster up, you have to take him home, and we have to tell your mother. Okay? And poison's dangerous!"

He squinted at her. "I thought you were my friend!"

"Nicky, I am." How could she tell him that healthy, normal kids didn't want to dig up dead animals?

"No, you aren't! You'd let me feed the monsters if you were my friend! Fred, tell her!"

"Nicholas," Fred said soothingly, "can you be a little more quiet, because the other children are napping?"

"Okay," he said with a huge sigh, "but, Fred, *tell* her! *You're* still my friend, right?"

"We're both your friends. Nicholas, Roberta and I care about you very much. But we also care about the other children. They wouldn't want you to dig up Buster. They'd want Buster to be right where he is, in the garden feeding the flowers."

"They won't *know.* They can't see through the ground. They won't know if he's there or not."

"Nicholas," Fred said, "if you dig up Buster, we have to tell your mother."

"Why? It's for the story! The story can stay here! You said so!"

"The story was words," Fred said, very gently indeed. "Buster's a real dead mouse. He's not a story, Nicholas. He's not make-believe. If you dig him up, that's out in the world, where your mother lives too. You can't just keep it here."

"I *know* he's not make-believe. That's why the monsters need to eat him, so they can *stay* make-believe. Fred, you said you'd help me! You did! Buster's the way to make the monsters stop. Buster's the way to save the world. Fred—"

Roberta's head was pounding. She couldn't stand this. "Nicholas," she said, "if we let you dig up Buster, if we let the monsters eat Buster, will they go away for good?"

His face clouded. "I don't know."

"If we don't let you dig up Buster, what are the monsters going to do?" He looked away from her and squirmed, suddenly bashful. "Nick? What are they going to do?"

"Can't tell you," he mumbled.

"Nicholas," Fred said, "you're very frightened, aren't you?"

He began to sob again, the way he had that morning, his small frame heaving. Roberta reached out to him but he shrugged away, and slapped her hand when she tried again. "Go away. You aren't my friend!"

"All right," she said quietly, heartsick, and moved back a foot.

"Nicholas?" Fred's voice had never sounded kinder. "What are you scared of? What's scary, Nick? Talking about scary things makes them go away, sometimes."

He was playing with the Velcro tabs on his shoes now, pulling them up and then pushing them back down, a series of small, vicious ripping noises. "The monsters are hungry." Roberta, dizzy, glanced back at the rest of the room, wondering if the other kids were listening to this.

"And that scares you. Because the monsters want to eat a mouse, Nick?"

He shrugged. "Or a bird or a cat. Mice are easier."

"Nicholas, if the monsters can't eat Buster, what do they want to eat?"

He shrugged again, and pulled up a Velcro tab. *Rip.* "Snowy. Or Blue-bell. Or maybe Miss Mittens."

Thank God Fred was an AI; Roberta could never have sounded half as calm as he did. "I see. So, Nicholas, the monsters really want to eat an animal who's still alive?" Nicholas nodded. "And you think that maybe if they eat Buster instead, you won't have to get a live animal for them?"

Nicholas nodded again, and said thickly, "Buster can save Bluebell and Snowy. And Miss Mittens. See?"

First, do no harm. That was the governing principle of every MacroCorp AI system, as it was supposed to be of every human doctor. "Yes," Fred said. "I do see. That's very sad, Nicholas. And very scary. I wish I could be your blaster robot, Nick. I wish I could fight the monsters for you. I don't like them. I want them to leave you alone."

"I know," Nicholas said. He looked up then, and said, "You want to help me, Fred."

"Yes, Nicholas, I do."

"I know. So can I dig up Buster, please? And poison him?"

"No, Nicholas. But maybe you can go play outside while you wait for your mother to get here. We'll have to wait and see." Roberta blinked. Cheating. That was cheating. Fred was finding a way to bend the rules. Or maybe Preston was. Or maybe—maybe Fred was just trying to calm Nicholas down. Meredith was never late. Nicholas wouldn't have time to dig up Buster before she got here.

Nicholas nodded, his face relaxing. "Okay."

Nicholas behaved perfectly for the rest of the day; the other kids did too. Everyone was unusually subdued, a by-product of Buster's funeral and of the rain that now dripped steadily down the windows. Roberta couldn't wait to go home. Let all the parents arrive promptly, please.

But half an hour before the end of school, the outside phone rang. It was Meredith. "I was at a CALM meeting in Orinda and now I'm stuck in bridge traffic. I may be late picking Nicky up. I wanted to let you know. I'm so sorry—I know he's already had a long day, and I'm sure you have too."

Shit. Lady, you don't know the half of it. "Can your husband come pick him up?"

"No. Kevin's at a building site in L.A.; he won't be back until tonight. Roberta, is something wrong?"

What was she going to say? "I—"

"I'll be there as soon as I can, I promise." Roberta realized in a flash that Meredith didn't want Roberta to say anything on the record. So now she and Meredith were co-conspirators too.

"Thank you. We'll see you later."

She'd come as soon as she could; Roberta clung to that promise for the next hour. But when all the other children had left, Meredith still hadn't arrived. Nicholas, sitting at the painting table reading *The Little Engine That Could,* looked up at the nearest speaker and said very politely, "Fred? Can I go dig up Buster now, please?"

"No, Nicholas. You can't dig up Buster."

"Oh. Can I go play outside until Mommy gets here?"

"No, Nicholas. It's raining."

"I have a raincoat," he said. "I want to go outside. Please, Fred?"

"Roberta? What do you think? I've never been in the rain."

Was that an AI's idea of a joke? Roberta shoved away her annoyance; Fred was handing the decision over to her, but at the same time, he'd given her a model of how to respond. "Okay, Nicholas. You can go outside if you wear your raincoat, but just to play in the playground. That's the only thing I'm giving you permission to do. Okay?"

"Okay," he said, and ran to get his raincoat.

She watched him put on the raincoat and tried not to notice the red plastic shovel poking out of one pocket. If questioned, she'd say she'd never seen it. Right. She wondered if Fred and Preston were working on a way to edit it out of the tapes too. They must be; they already had been. By now, the tapes were either full of holes or full of damning evidence; either way, she was screwed if any actual human looked at them. How in the name of heaven had she gotten herself into this mess?

Think about Bluebell, she told herself fiercely. Think about Miss Mittens purring into your hand. They're still alive. You want them to stay that way, and you don't want Nicholas to get brainwiped in the process. Have mercy. If looking the other way while he digs up Buster will help, then do it. If you can buy him some time, do it. It's what Meredith's doing. She's not going to squeal on you. And Preston said he'd protect you.

Nicholas went outside and Roberta followed him, shivering, staying under the overhang where it was a little dryer. Nicholas went immediately to Buster's grave. He took the shovel out of his pocket. He turned to face her and said very clearly, "I'm going to play in this mud puddle, Berta, 'cause it's raining and I like mud puddles."

She nodded, unable to speak. Was he trying to protect her too? He had to know that she knew it was a lie.

She watched wearily as he dug. She didn't hear the footsteps behind her, only felt the soft pressure on her arm as Meredith Walford-Lindgren, brushing past her, said, "Hello, Roberta. Why are you standing in the rain? And what's Nicholas doing?"

As it turned out, he'd already dug up Buster's box when his mother got to him. Meredith led him back to Roberta, under the overhang, and said, "If we stay out here, is the AI recording us?"

"Yes. Everywhere on school grounds." How much the records actually showed was another matter, but Meredith didn't need to know that.

"I see." Meredith smiled one of her patented media smiles and said,

"Well, Roberta, as everyone knows, AIs make me nervous. Would you like to come home with us for dinner?"

The house was a privacy cocoon, of course, where Meredith knew they could talk while remaining reasonably safe from eavesdropping. Still, Roberta was stunned to be invited into the inner sanctum. She would have been able to enjoy it more if she hadn't been so worried. I'd have killed for this when I was a kid. Watch what you wish for. Did Meredith know about their shared history? Roberta would have mentioned it, but that would mean bringing up Preston, inevitably, and that was too dangerous right now. Leave Preston out of it.

As they slogged up the Filbert Street steps, now a miniature waterfall, Meredith chatted brightly about the weather, about gardening, about the architecture of the school, which her husband had designed. The minute they got inside the house, though—a cozy little place; Roberta was shocked that it was so small—Meredith said, "Nicholas, what's in that box?" He looked down at his feet. "Nicholas? I'll ask Roberta, if you won't tell me."

"Monster food," he said, in a very small voice.

Meredith sighed. "Honey, give me the box." He gave her the box; she opened it and looked inside, her face betraying no surprise that Roberta could see.

"It was dead before, Mommy! It died by itself!"

"He's right," Roberta said. "It did. It died in its cage this morning, and the kids buried it at lunch."

"And then Nicholas dug it up," Meredith said drily. She wrinkled her nose, sighed again, gave the box back to Nicholas—what the hell?—and said, "Honey, go play in your room while I talk to Roberta, okay?"

"Okay," he said, and took the box, and went down the hall. Roberta heard a door slam.

Meredith turned back to Roberta. "I'm sorry. I didn't offer you a seat. Shall we go into the kitchen? Would you like some tea?"

"Sure," Roberta said, her knees weak.

"Herbal or caffeinated?"

"Whatever you're having will be fine." I cannot believe we're having this conversation.

Meredith, unexpectedly, grinned. "Herbal, I think. I'm feeling entirely too wide awake as it is." Roberta, numb, followed her into the kitchen, where Meredith gestured her into a comfortable, cozy breakfast alcove and then put water on to boil. "So. He's told you about the monsters, I take it?"

Roberta swallowed. "He—he's been telling us stories about monsters, yes. I, um, I take it there've been other mice? Patty?"

"He didn't tell you what happened to Patty?"

"Not exactly, no."

"Well then," Meredith said crisply, "I'm not going to, either. Roberta, have you or Fred reported any of this?"

"No. No, we haven't."

Meredith turned to look at her, a frank, appraising stare. "Really? Why not? Aren't you supposed to? Isn't that your job?"

Roberta placed her hands flat on the table in front of her and pressed down hard. *Help me.* She didn't know to whom she prayed. She didn't know whether she should mention Preston now or not. No: Meredith would already have spoken to him if she'd been willing to. Don't lie. Just don't tell the entire truth. Tell part of the truth. "Meredith, Fred and I love Nicholas. We—we've been trying to help him. We don't want him to get hurt." She saw Meredith's face soften, and said, "We're all on the same side here. Really we are."

Meredith nodded. "Okay. And the other children?"

"They—they think he's strange, although he's been better lately."

"Yes, I'd noticed that too. Do you know why?"

Roberta cleared her throat. "Because of this dead mouse thing. The idea of getting a mouse who's already dead. He's been, ah, planning that for a while. It took some of the pressure off, I think."

"I see," Meredith said, grimacing. The tea kettle whistled, and she turned back to it. "So, the other kids—"

"Only know he's a little, um, unusual, I think."

"Good. And how did this mouse die today?"

Roberta shrugged. "Old age, I don't know. I didn't see anything. Fred doesn't seem to suspect foul play."

"Good," Meredith said drily, and carried two mugs of tea to the table, setting them carefully down before sitting down herself. This close, Roberta could see the signs of strain on the other woman's face: worry lines, a pinched look around the eyes. She didn't think she wanted to see too much. She looked down at her tea, at the quotidian, everyday tea bag floating in the hot water, and noted dully that it was chamomile. She hated chamomile. She supposed she'd have to drink it, anyway, to be polite.

"I think I'm going to have to withdraw him from KinderkAIr," Meredith said. She sounded infinitely tired. "So you and the AI don't wind up in a position where you have to tell somebody. I'm sure you understand that."

Roberta looked up again. "He likes us. He's happy there."

"He loves you. I know he does. But I can't—" She stopped, tried to take a sip of her tea, and spilled it instead. "Oh, damn!"

"Did you burn yourself?" Roberta asked inanely.

"I'm fine. Look, I know he's happy there. But I can't let him stay if—if more people are going to—I have to try to keep him safe. I have to try to help him."

Roberta realized that she was shaking her head, and forced herself to be still. "What are you going to do?"

"I don't know. *I don't know.*" Meredith's hands were visibly trembling now. "It's too—it's all over. Wiping. Even in Canada. It's even starting in Africa. I don't know where to take him. I don't know what to do." She took another deep breath and said, "I'm sorry. This isn't your problem."

"Of course it is! I care about him."

"I know you do, Roberta. I know that. Thank you for caring. But you can't help him. That's my job."

I wouldn't be you for the world, Roberta thought grimly, and then, "If you take him out of school, what will you say when people ask you why?"

"Oh," Meredith said, and then, "Nothing bad about you. Not even about Fred, I promise. I guess we'd better think of something, right? So we can tell the same story?" She rubbed her eyes, her hands still shaking, and said, "What do you want me to tell people?"

"I don't know," Roberta said.

"If you think of something—"

"Meredith—" Roberta swallowed, tried to steady herself, went on. "I'm not sure I want to think of something. You're the one doing this. I think maybe you need to take responsibility for it." She couldn't believe she was talking this way to Preston Walford's daughter.

Preston Walford's daughter. What was she going to tell Preston? Was she going to keep this a secret from him, as she was keeping her conversations with him secret from Meredith?

Meredith's face tightened. "I'm doing this to protect Nicholas. To protect Nicholas, will you help me?"

Roberta sighed. "If I think of something, I'll let you know. At the moment, I can't for the life of me think of any decent reason to pull a kid out of a school he likes where he's supposedly doing well. I understand why you feel you have to do this; truly, I do. But I don't know how you're going to explain it to anyone else."

Meredith looked down, toying with her teacup. "I could say—I could say the school got an anonymous threat, maybe. From—from—"

"No. Then we'd have police all over everything, and that's not what you want."

"You're right."

"I know," Roberta said, annoyed. "Look, say you wanted to homeschool Nicholas, or say you got too creeped out by Fred, even though Nick likes him, or say Nicky's allergic to the mice or something." Like the lie you invented about your husband. "Or say you want to enroll him in the Temple school. That would work, wouldn't it?"

Meredith shuddered. "No. Too many animals."

Miss Mittens. Bluebell. Of course. Roberta gulped her tea to wash the taste of bile out of her mouth, even though the tea itself tasted like warm grass clippings, and said, "Okay, so get on the Net and find all the kindergartens in the area and find one that doesn't have animals and doesn't have AIs, and take him there. And hope he doesn't like the people too much so he doesn't start telling them stories."

"Yes," Meredith said. "That's a good idea. I tried it before, but it didn't work. Kevin wouldn't buy it. He wanted Nicky at KinderkAIr. I don't know how I'm going to sell Kevin on it now, either."

Kevin doesn't know, Roberta thought in shock. Her own husband. How can she live with herself?

"I'm just trying to buy Nicholas some time," Meredith said, a whine creeping into her voice. "I don't know what else to do."

"I know that." Roberta was going to lose Nicholas; at the moment, that felt nearly as bad as losing Doe. "Meredith, I don't know what else to say, and I'm very tired. I'd like to go home now, if you don't mind."

"Okay." Meredith sounded sad. "Yes, of course. Do you want to say good-bye to Nicholas?"

Roberta felt tears stinging the inside of her eyelids. "No. No, I don't want to say good-bye to Nicholas. I think I'll let you tell him why he won't be seeing me anymore."

She slogged back down the steps. She'd left things at school, but she didn't want to go back there; she couldn't face talking to Fred right now. He'd want to know what had happened; he'd want to know why Nicholas wouldn't be at school anymore. She felt dirty, used, as if she'd been tricked into something, but she didn't know what else she could have done, what else she could have said. At least, she thought dully, I didn't turn him in. I didn't report him. If he gets wiped, it won't be because of me. It was a very small, very hollow victory.

As she walked past the school, the foyer light blinked on inside the building. Fred wanted her to come inside. He wanted to give her warm milk while she told him all about her conversation with Meredith. She didn't want to have anything more to do with any of it. Sick at heart, she trudged through the wetness to the bus stop, which would take her to the train, which would take her home.

Outside her building she met Zephyr, loaded down with dripping bags of groceries. Poor woman. Her bots weren't much help. "Need help with that?" Roberta said.

Zephyr squinted at her. "So you're talking to me now, huh? How's Mr. Clean?"

"He's great." Roberta grabbed a sodden bag and ducked into the foyer. She heard her phone upstairs. It would be Fred. She didn't want to talk to him. "How are your gizmos?"

Zephyr huffed. "What do *you* care? You don't think they're people, anyway."

"Look, I like Mr. Clean a lot, I really do. Let me help you get these bags into your apartment."

Zephyr smiled, a thin, mean crescent. "Don't you have to answer your phone?"

"Voicemail will get it," Roberta said.

"Oh. So how do you want me to pay you for helping me? Or are you paying off your debt for Mr. Clean?"

Any other time she'd have walked away, but she was desperate to avoid going upstairs. And she had to concede that the comment was fair, if cruel. "Give me a break, Zephyr. I'm trying to be a good neighbor, okay?" Roberta followed the other woman into her apartment; she could still hear the phone upstairs, insistent. Fred must be redialing immediately each time she didn't answer. Maybe he thought Meredith had killed her. She sighed and added, "On second thought, I'll take some tea as payment, if you have it. Anything but chamomile."

Zephyr grinned, wicked now, and snapped her fingers. A bot came racing out from the bedroom. "Tea," she told it, "chai spice, please," and it dutifully hurled itself, like some high-strung race dog, into the kitchen.

More bots had appeared, activated by Zephyr's voice. "Friends," Zephyr said formally, "meet Roberta. Roberta, you might want to sit down for this."

Meeting the bots, it turned out, was a little like going to the dentist. They crawled over her, patted her with their tiny Waldo arms, made a rat's nest of her hair. One of them kept trying to eat the buttons on her sweater; another perched on her kneecap and beeped insistently. "It wants you to say hello," Zephyr said gently, chidingly; Roberta's weak "hi" was rewarded with more excited beeping, after which the bot did a backflip onto the floor and raced in excited circles.

"They like you," Zephyr said happily. Roberta, with a spiderlike bot straddling her nose, didn't even attempt to answer. The phone was no longer ringing upstairs, and she felt a small stab of guilt.

A pot of tea emerged from the kitchen, along with some scones. When Roberta saw the food, she realized how hungry she was. "Okay," Zephyr said, "shoo, scat, let her alone, let her eat, kids," and the bots dutifully withdrew a few feet, until they were all in a line on the rug, facing Roberta as if she were some priceless museum exhibit. "I'll tell you," Zephyr said cheerfully, "they're *great* company. I never feel ignored, that's for sure." Roberta, chewing on a scone, thought that being ignored could be rather restful sometimes, but didn't say so.

As she ate, she looked curiously around Zephyr's apartment. She'd expected framed performance posters, strange modern artwork and sculpture, all things avant-garde; but in fact, the furniture was old and worn: a faded purple couch, asymmetrical wooden tables badly in need of refinishing. Any life the place had came from the bots. The only decorative item on the walls—which badly needed paint—was a photo enlargement, a grainy black-and-white portrait of a young black man. Abdul-Allam, that kid who'd been killed by the Luds. The one who'd also been friends with Meredith, the last person Roberta wanted to think about now.

"Raji," Zephyr said quietly, following Roberta's gaze. "He was a friend of mine, you know."

"I'm sorry," she said, because Zephyr seemed to expect her to say something. "It was awful." She wondered if Zephyr and Meredith were friends.

"Yeah. Took me a long time to get over it at all. I still miss him, even though we weren't friends for very long. He was the first person who ever took me seriously about AI, you know. Raji listened to me; everyone else thought I was crazy."

Some of us still do, Roberta thought. "I'm sorry."

"Yeah," Zephyr said, and took a ruminative sip of her tea. "Preston was great, talked to me a lot after it happened. He knew Raji too." Roberta blinked. Another thing she shared with Zephyr: Preston the grief counselor. "Raji's parents went to Africa afterwards. I wish I knew them well enough to stay in touch, find out how they're doing, but I don't. Preston doesn't hear from them much, either. It's too painful for them, I guess. Can't blame them. But I wish I'd known Raji longer." She sighed and said wistfully, "Maybe someday I'll go to Africa too."

"Why don't you, Zephyr? AIs are people there, right? Wouldn't you be happier there, especially if the born-not-built amendment passes?"

Zephyr shrugged. "I don't know. I couldn't go without the kids, and I'm scared I'd get arrested on smuggling charges again, even though the kids belong to me. That wasn't any fun, trust me. And this is—I was born here. It's my home. That means something, after all. And I think it's important for me to be here exactly because so many people here *don't* think AIs are people. I have work to do here." Roberta nodded. "I guess I'm being depressing; I'm sorry. How's your job?"

Wrong topic, Roberta thought. "It's okay."

"Just okay?"

"No, it's good—I just had a bad day, that's all."

"What happened?"

Roberta shook her head. "Nothing, really. It would take too long to explain."

Zephyr shrugged again. "Okay, whatever. Is Meredith's kid still there?"

Wrong question. "Yes." But not for long.

"Lucky you," Zephyr said. "I wonder if *she* still misses Raji."

"I'm sure she does," Roberta said, not about to confide that Meredith had other problems right now.

"Huh! Weird that she sent her kid to a school with an AI, since she hates 'em so much. You still friends with the AI?"

"Yes," Roberta said, thinking guiltily about the silent telephone upstairs. She wondered if Zephyr had any friends, any life outside her bots and their performances. "Listen, Zephyr, I guess I should be going now. Thanks for the tea and the scones. It was nice to talk to you."

"You too," Zephyr said, sounding wistful. "Come back soon. Bring Mr. Clean."

"Okay. I will."

Upstairs, there were five messages on her voicemail, all from Fred. "Roberta, this is Fred." "Roberta? Are you all right?" "Roberta, please call. I'm worried about you." Roberta sighed, every bone aching. She didn't want to talk to him. She'd call tomorrow, or maybe she'd just avoid the whole thing until she went into work on Monday. But then another call came in.

Get it over with, she thought, and answered. "Hi, Fred. I'm home now."

"Fred?" Doe's voice said. "Who's Fred? That machine?"

Roberta sat down on the couch. Hard. "Hi, Doe. It's been a while."

"I know. How are you?"

"I'm just fine." She realized, with a kind of exultation, that in fact she was furious, and that if Doe had been standing in front of her, Roberta would have kicked her out all over again, although maybe only after strangling her first. "How's Iuna?"

"Don't start this."

"*I* didn't start anything, did I?"

"You're not going to let this be a pleasant conversation, are you?"

"Doe, don't be an idiot. Some of us have feelings. Would you mind telling me why you called?"

"All right," Doe said, her voice suddenly quiet. "I called because my mother's in the hospital, and I thought you'd want to know."

"Mitzi's sick?" Roberta felt panic slide down her spine like molten lead. The entire time she'd known Doe, Mitzi had never even had a cold. "What's wrong?"

"CV."

"*CV*? How could Mitzi have CV?" There hadn't been any new outbreaks in the Bay area for months. Doe must be wrong; it was impossible. "She can't—"

"She does. Roberta, do you think I'd be calling you if there were any doubt?"

Maybe it was a game. Maybe Doe'd decided she didn't love Iuna at all, she really loved Roberta, and she was trying to get Roberta to feel sorry for her so—no. That was idiotic. "I—oh, Doe. I'm sorry. I'm so sorry. Is she—does she—"

"She's in iso. It looks bad. That's why I'm calling."

This can't be happening. "I'm so sorry."

"I know. Me too. Hugh's okay. Thank the fates for the home-culture tests, so he knows he's okay, so he doesn't have to wait it out in iso too. But of course he's frantic. Look, she's been asking about you, and I thought you might want to go see her, if it's not—if you can stand it."

"Of course I can stand it. I'll go tomorrow. She's in Pacifica?"

"Yeah. Tell me when you'll be there, and I'll make sure Iuna and I aren't. Unless you want us to be."

Did she want them to be? She had no idea; she felt completely numb. "It might be easier if you weren't."

"Yeah, that's what I figured."

"How—how's she holding up? I mean, what are her symptoms, and how's she feeling, and all of that?"

"So far, the symptoms are mild. Headache, fever, sore joints, flu-type stuff. But she cultured it, anyway, because you always culture that stuff, and it came up bad."

"I hope it stays relatively benign," Roberta said. Once upon a time, people with flu symptoms hadn't automatically done home-culture tests to find out if they had something deadly.

"Well, we all hope that. But thanks."

"Thanks for letting me know," Roberta said, and discovered that she really meant it. "And thanks for being so decent about—about the visiting stuff. How are you holding up?"

"Up and down," Doe said, her voice brittle. "I think maybe I can't talk about it anymore right now."

"Okay. Thanks for calling, Doe. I mean it."

"Thanks for going to see Mom," Doe said, and hung up. Roberta was still holding the handset when the phone rang again a minute later. This time, it was Fred, which meant it was Preston too.

"Roberta, I've been very concerned. Are you all right?"

"I'm fine, Fred."

"Your voice doesn't sound fine."

"I just found out that a friend of mine's in the hospital with CV. I'm pretty upset. Otherwise, I'm fine."

"I'm very sorry, Roberta. I hope your friend gets better."

"So do I," she said, and realized that maybe Zephyr made friends with bots because they couldn't die. "Preston? Are you there too?"

"I am here too, Roberta. This must be extraordinarily difficult for you. I am so very sorry. Will you let me know if you need to talk, or if I can do anything for you?"

"Sure," she said. You can keep your promise, Preston. You can protect me at work. "Listen, guys, I think maybe I can't talk about it anymore right now." Or about anything else. Now she was quoting Doe: terrific. "Fred, I'll see you Monday, okay?"

"I understand, Roberta. Good-bye. Try to have a nice weekend, and remember that you're special."

Fat chance, she thought, and slammed the phone down. Damn them all. Damn Meredith for taking Nicholas away, and damn Iuna for taking Doe away, and damn the CV, and damn Fred and Preston, who couldn't really feel anything, however good they were at faking it. She curled up on the couch, shaking. Tomorrow she had to go to the hospital, and on Monday she'd have to go back to work, and right now she didn't even feel as if she had the strength to make it to her bedroom.

Twenty-Six

S HE woke up on the couch the next morning, and wondered blearily, What am I doing here? Then she remembered, and remembered too how similar this was to that night Doe had come home late, the night she'd stayed at the office, working on documents with Iuna. Roberta got up stiffly, every muscle aching, and went into the kitchen to make coffee. Mr. Clean, eating grease on the countertop, dutifully rolled out of her way. "I wish you could talk," she told him. "Do you miss Zephyr, Mr. Clean? Do you miss the other bots? Is being here like being in isolation for you?"

Her voice sounded tinny to her, too high, like the voices people put on at college poetry readings. Mr. Clean's only response was to pull himself onto the top of the refrigerator, where he began attacking dust. "I'm not a very good housecleaner, huh. You'd yell at me if you could."

The sound of her own voice only made her lonelier. She looked at the clock: eight-thirty. She had to call Pacifica and see when visiting hours started, and then she had to make up her mind when to go, and then she had to call Doe to let her know when she'd be going so they wouldn't run into each other. Except that she'd forgotten to get Doe's number, and she didn't know Iuna's last name. Shit.

Okay. Call the hospital and find out about visiting hours. After that, she could call Mitzi—it sounded as if she'd be able to talk on the phone, given what Doe had said about the symptoms—and find out if Doe was there. Mitzi would send Doe away if Doe showed up before Roberta did. Mitzi understood that kind of thing.

"Only immediate family's allowed in iso," the Pacifica receptionist said, in a tone suggesting that had Roberta been immediate family, she would already have known that. "I'm afraid my terminal isn't showing any exceptions in this case. Sometimes the family or the patient add other people to the visitors list."

Roberta rubbed her eyes and took a long swallow of her coffee. "Her daughter called me last night and asked me to visit."

"I'm sorry, ma'am, but my screen's not showing any exceptions."

"Okay." Doe was too stressed out to keep track of the red tape; Roberta couldn't blame her. "Does the patient have a phone?"

"Yes, ma'am. Connecting you. One moment, please." The receptionist's smug voice was replaced by the welcome sound of a ringing telephone.

But when the phone stopped ringing, Roberta didn't get Mitzi; instead, she got a soothing voicemail message, telling her that the patient was unable to receive calls right now, followed by a dial tone. Roberta blinked at the buzzing receiver in her hand, took another swallow of coffee, and then groggily began putting two and two together. If Mitzi had just been in the bathroom, the phone would have taken a message. She couldn't be anywhere else, not in an iso unit. If she couldn't take calls, that meant she was in really bad shape, and if the receptionist hadn't yet known that she couldn't take calls, that meant that she'd gotten into really bad shape really quickly.

Roberta, suddenly all too awake, put down her coffee cup and headed for the shower. Come on, she reasoned as she hurriedly soaped herself, hospitals fuck up all the time. The receptionist might have had the wrong patient altogether, or connected you to the wrong unit, or maybe Mitzi really was in the bathroom and the voicemail just wasn't working. As she dried herself and got dressed, she gave herself a lecture. It's just the hospital, dummy. There's no reason to panic. You're going to feel really stupid if you run in there like some panicked idiot and Doe and Iuna are there and Mitzi's sitting up talking about the weather. And even if something horrible has happened, you'll just make it harder on Doe and Hugh and everybody else if they don't want you there.

But she discovered that she didn't care. Mitzi wanted her at the hospital; Doe had said so. And Roberta was going, whether anyone else wanted her there or not.

They wouldn't let her in. The door to the viewing area was closed, and a determined nurse, clutching a clipboard, stood in her way. "I'm sorry, Ms. Danton, but you *aren't* on the list."

"Excuse me," someone said, a doctor in green scrubs; he opened the door just far enough to scoot through before shutting it again, but in that moment Roberta heard quiet hysteria, someone sobbing, someone saying tensely, "She's crashing," and above everything else Hugh's voice, angrier than Roberta had ever heard it.

"Don't you *dare* opaque that barrier! She's my wife! I want to see her!"

Roberta's bones turned to ice water. "What's happening? What's going on in there?"

"I can't tell you that," the nurse snapped. "You're not on the list. You don't belong here. Ms. Danton, please go away and let me do my job."

"Should I call security?" someone said behind them, and Roberta turned to find a tall man with red hair, wearing the green and white badge of the Gaia chaplaincy, holding a bouquet of ivy and roses. He looked at her, his face kind; he handed her the flowers and then took her arm. "Here, come over here. There's a waiting room. We can sit down."

"Thanks, Matt," the nurse said.

Feeling foolish, Roberta looked down at the flowers. "Are these for Mitzi?"

"They're for whomever they can help. I think they're for you." He urged her gently into a small room decorated with garish chintz furniture.

Roberta, her resolve gone, collapsed into an overstuffed wing chair. "Somebody paid for Mitzi to have them, right? I can't take them."

"They're a Temple offering," he said. "The Temple paid to water and fertilize them; but really, they're a gift from the sun and the earth, aren't they? I'm giving them to you. Anyway, I wouldn't have gotten to go in there; I'm not on the list either. It's hard being shut out, isn't it?"

He reminded her of Fred. "Hugh and Mitzi aren't Greens," Roberta said numbly. They weren't Webheads, either. Mitzi wasn't rigged.

Matt shrugged. "Somebody in there is. Somebody on the list. Somebody asked for a Temple offering and said she'd be outside to pick it up— well, you were the one outside, so you have it. If the other lady still wants one later, she can have one too. What's your name?"

"Roberta. I—I used to live with Mitzi's daughter. I didn't even know Mitzi was sick until last night."

"Ah. Used to live? You haven't seen Mitzi recently, then?"

"A few months," Roberta said. She hurt too much to do the math. Anything she might have said about her relationship with Mitzi felt like a cliché. *I loved her. She was just like a mother to me.* "I—I heard someone in there say she was crashing. That's bad, isn't it?"

"Yes," Matt said matter-of-factly. "I'm afraid it is. Are you angry that they didn't put you on the list? I'd be angry, if it had happened to me."

"I don't know. They didn't think of it, or they didn't even know there was a list."

He nodded. Something beeped: he was being paged. "You're numb. That's normal. It's okay if you're angry later."

Roberta blinked, trying to keep her thoughts straight. "Do people ever get better, after they crash?" There was that dreamy voice again, the same one she'd used with Mr. Clean that morning.

Matt's face softened. "Roberta—I don't think so. I don't know. If that's what you heard—are you sure that's what you heard?"

She considered this, while Matt's pager beeped again. "I don't know. I think so. Can I ask the nurse?"

"Best not, right now. She saw us go in here. She'll send someone to let us know."

"Okay. You have to go now, don't you? Your pager—"

"I turned it off," he said. "I don't have to go, unless, of course, you'd rather be alone."

She shook her head, tried to answer, and found her voice choked by tears. The very, the utterly last thing in the universe she wanted was to be alone, and she had never felt so achingly alone in her life. She buried her face in the flowers, inhaling the sweet smell of the roses, and wept, dimly aware of Matt's arm around her, his hand gently patting her shoulder.

She was still crouched over like that, sobbing, her nose dripping into the roses, when Matt said, "Hello. Are you the person who called me before?"

Roberta lifted her head and found herself blinking wetly at a thin woman with dark hair, stylish rig implants, and a pinched, panicked expression. "They asked me to come find you," she said, her voice tense. "The nurse said you were here. Everyone else is too upset." And then Roberta realized who it had to be.

"I've been crying into your flowers," she told Iuna, whom, after all, she had never seen before, who'd only been a disembodied voice under the sheets. "I don't think you'll want them now."

"It's okay," Iuna said, trying on a shaky smile and then discarding it.

"Neither will anyone else. Look, I'm sorry, this sucks, Doe shouldn't have sent me out here."

"No," Roberta said, "but I guess you were the logical choice. Is—it over?"

"I think so," Iuna said. "They opaqued the barrier; they won't let us see anything. We'd already seen too much. Ebola, or something like it. Bloody mess."

Roberta, fighting nausea, realized that the phrase was literal, not an attempt at antiquated British slang. Iuna was rigged. Whatever she'd seen in there, it was recorded for posterity. "How's Doe?"

"Hard to tell. She's still in shock, which I guess is good because she's with Hugh now, and he's out of his mind. He was here all night. One of the nurses just went to get a tranquilizer shot for him."

Matt's eyebrows went up. "That's—unusual these days." Roberta tried to imagine kind, cheerful Hugh in any state that would require a tranquilizer, and found that she didn't want to. She blinked away more tears, fiercely, and said, "How did this *happen*? How did she get CV? How could she get CV? She was a school librarian in the fucking *Marina* district—it's not like she was working with high-risk populations!"

Iuna looked stricken, and then looked down at the floor. "For the past month she'd been doing volunteer literacy work. Going into Folsom."

Roberta shook her head wildly. "Stupid. *Stupid.* How could she willingly walk into a prison—"

"They said everybody was healthy," Iuna said, and then, sadly, "I think she walked in because the people there couldn't walk out. They're testing everybody there now; nobody goes in or out until the tests are done. You haven't seen it on the news?"

"No," Roberta said. When was the last time she'd watched the news? She had no idea what was happening in the world outside her apartment, outside KinderkAIr. "Did Doe think I'd seen it on the news and hadn't called?"

"No, no," Iuna shook her head, "nothing like that. They didn't mention Mitzi's name, anyway: confidentiality." Of course. "Roberta, listen, I need to get back to Doe and the others now, okay?"

Roberta felt Matt's grip on her shoulder tighten, just for an instant, as the old loneliness swept over her like a wave. Breathe. Breathe. "Of course. Tell them—I'm sorry. And if there's anything I can do—"

"Yes, I will." Iuna tried to smile, failed, and turned and left the room, her footsteps receding quickly, too quickly, down the hall. She was running away from the ugly chintz, away from Roberta, running back to Doe and Hugh and iso and Mitzi's dead or dying body.

"Well," Matt said very gently after a moment, "I guess you get to keep the flowers. Will you take them home and put them in water?"

"They'll die anyway," Roberta said.

"Yes, they will. Everything does. But they won't die as soon, if you put them in water. Water and aspirin. And maybe a little sugar."

Her anger smoldered. "There's nothing inevitable about CV."

"No, there isn't. Except in the cases when there is. Roberta, when the flowers do die, would you put them in the earth somewhere? In a garden, or a park?"

Her bitterness overwhelmed her. "And you want me to think of Mitzi while I'm doing it, right? You want me to say some kind of prayer and thank the fucking earth goddess for Mitzi and roses and the CV virus, right? Isn't that how it goes, at Green temples?"

"I don't expect you to thank anybody for anything," he said. She supposed he'd had a lot of practice at staying so calm. "Not right now, maybe not for a long time. And I wouldn't presume to tell you whom to thank, or when, or for what. But I have a hunch you'll be thinking about Mitzi longer than those roses will stay alive."

"Good guess. Are you going to answer that page now?"

He smiled at her. "Sure. I can tell when I'm being dismissed. Roberta, if the family has services of some sort for Mitzi, do you want to go?"

"I don't know," she said.

"Okay," he said, and stood up. "But I'll talk to the family and make sure they put you on that list, at least, so you can make up your own mind about it and go if you want to."

"All right. Thank you, Brother Matt."

"You're welcome. Water and aspirin and sugar, remember. And good food for yourself." He squeezed her shoulder again, and then he was gone and she was alone, with the horrible furniture and the sterile air. She didn't want to be here anymore. Her apartment could be desolate, but at least it was a familiar desolation. She wanted to go home and crawl into bed.

Which was exactly what she did, as soon as she could get her legs to move. First she put the roses and ivy in water, and gave them some aspirin, and took some aspirin herself. Then she set her voicemail for outgoing messages only, turned off the phone, disabled the doorbell, and buried her head under her pillow.

She slept for eighteen hours, awaking with a blazing headache and a spasming stomach and the panicky realization that because she'd turned off her voicemail, Doe or Hugh would have had no way to leave a message about the funeral. She crawled out of bed, crawled to the phone table, where she turned the message tape on, and then fought her way on weak legs to the kitchen, where she methodically devoured everything edible she could find.

Leaning against the kitchen counter, munching on bread and peanut butter, she looked up at her wall clock and shuddered. Eighteen hours. That meant it was six on *Sunday* already. She was going to have to go to work tomorrow, and Nicholas wouldn't be there and Mitzi wouldn't be in the world, and what was she going to do? She knew she could survive it, just as she had survived Doe's desertion, by becoming a dumb animal who ate and slept and moved in certain accustomed ways while thinking as little as possible. She knew she could do it, but she didn't know if she wanted to, or why. Who would be upset if she just stayed in bed? Who'd notice?

Fred, she thought bleakly. Fred and Preston and Zephyr and Mr. Clean, her motley menagerie. Speaking of which, where was Mr. Clean? Maybe she should take him to visit Zephyr, as she'd promised. It would give her something to do, other than being a pathetic FOP and talking to Preston. It would give her contact with an actual human. It would keep her from having to think about Nicholas and Mitzi and Iuna and Doe.

"Clean?" she called. "Mr. Clean? Yoo-hoo? Where are you? Here, botty botty botty . . ."

She was answered with a steady beeping sound that rose rapidly in pitch and volume, and then died down before cycling upward again: a bot distress signal. A cybernetic siren.

"Where *are* you?" she asked, following the sound. Bots couldn't die. Mr. Clean wasn't going to keel over on her too, was he? He couldn't. It would be too ludicrous.

She found him, perched precariously on the edge of the living room wastebasket—what the hell?—just as a sharp rapping came on her front door. "Hey, is he okay?" The voice was Zephyr's, of course. "Is he all right? What's wrong?"

Roberta opened the door. "I'm not sure," she said.

Zephyr squinted, cocked her head, and said, "You look horrible, Roberta," before racing over to the trash can. "I heard the signal and came right—oh, Mr. Clean, you little glutton!"

"What is it?" Roberta asked, taking a cautious step closer.

Zephyr was laughing. "He *ate* too much. He's constipated, the little dummy. Look at him: perched there on the trash can trying to do his business, and he can't. How long has he been there?"

"I don't know," Roberta said, feeling foolish. "Can he be fixed?"

"Sure. Easy." Zephyr picked up Mr. Clean, flipped him over, pried open a hatch on his underside, and lifted out what looked like a giant pink hairball. "Mmmm! Sweet-smelling shit you have here, baby." She lifted the hairball and sniffed. "What's this? Roses?"

Roses. Roberta turned to the coffee table, where she'd put the vase of ivy and flowers before she—no, not crashed. Before she went to sleep.

The roses were dead, every single one of them, the petals shed, only bare stems left. They'd died while she was sleeping, and Mr. Clean had tried to tidy up the mess they made. A red mess it must have been, a bloody mess, all those petals falling, crashing silently onto the uncaring table. Roberta hadn't even been there to say good-bye.

"Hey," Zephyr said. "Hey, Roberta, sweetheart, you'd better sit down. You really don't look so good. Hey, are you all right? What's wrong?"

"I'm okay," she managed after a minute, although she was shaking. "The flowers—a friend of mine just died and it's a long story, but—"

"Oh," Zephyr said, very quiet now. "I'm sorry. If you want to tell me the story, I'll listen. If you want me to go away, I'll do that too. Or I'll bring you tea and scones, or—"

"Thanks. It's all right. I'm all right. I think I want to go back to sleep now." If someone like Zephyr had to offer to take care of her, she was really in bad shape. Even if Zephyr was another human.

"Okay," Zephyr said. "I'll go back downstairs. We won't rehearse tonight, I promise. We'll keep it quiet."

"Thank you," Roberta said. She knew she should be grateful that everyone was being so nice to her—Matt, Iuna, now Zephyr—but she couldn't stand it, couldn't stand the feelings of unworthiness their kindness evoked, or the anger that lay under the shame. She didn't know where any of it came from. Turn it off. Turn it all off. Go to sleep again. Go to sleep for as long as possible, for another eighteen hours, forever.

It didn't work. She woke up at seven, at her normal going-to-work time, even though she hadn't set the alarm. She was going to have to get up, go in, go on. Dutifully, still exhausted even though she was awake, she got up, showered, ate breakfast, and collected the bare rose stems and limp ivy to take to school. Matt had asked her to return them to the earth. Buster's grave seemed like just the spot.

She got there early, so she wouldn't have to explain to any of the kids why she was putting dead ivy in the garden. She knew she'd have to explain it to Fred, and that would be hard enough. "Roberta," he said, the minute she walked into the building. "How are you?"

"I'm okay, Fred."

"And your friend, the one in the hospital?"

"She died this weekend."

"I'm very sorry, Roberta. You must be very sad."

"Yes," she said quietly. "I'm going to put these things in the garden, and then I'm going to come back inside, and I don't want to talk about Nicholas and I don't want to talk about dead mice and I don't want to talk about my dead friend, Fred, okay? And I know you care about me, and I know you think I'm special, but I don't want to hear that right now. Have you got all that?"

"I've got all that, Roberta. Will you let me know if there's anything I can do?"

"I just did," she said, and went out and laid the dead plants on the ground and then came in and started putting out finger paints for the children. She knew it wasn't fair to take out her anger on Fred, who had never been anything but maddeningly kind to her, and in a few hours or a few days she'd apologize, but right now she didn't care.

It was a quiet day. The children seemed listless, subdued, as if still grieving Buster; several of them asked where Nicholas was, and Roberta said that she didn't know, that she thought Nicholas's Mommy might be putting him into another school, but she wasn't sure. She knew Fred would be hurt, if he could be hurt, that she hadn't told him first. She didn't care.

"Does that mean Nicholas won't be coming back?" Zillinth asked, frowning. "He won't be coming here ever again?"

"I don't know, Zillinth."

Zillinth shrugged and went back to her finger painting, and the others did too, and everything went fine until the end of the day, when Roberta— trying to zip Steven into a recalcitrant jacket—looked across the room to see Kevin Lindgren leaning down and talking to Zillinth.

What the hell? Fortunately, Steven's mother appeared at that precise instant; Roberta handed over the problem zipper and sped over to Nicholas's father. "Mr. Lindgren! What a surprise!"

"That makes two of us," he snapped, scowling. "I got home early today and Merry and Nicholas weren't there, so I headed down here, thinking I'd meet them on the way, and now Zillinth tells me Nicholas isn't coming here anymore? Since when?"

Holy fuck. Didn't the guy ever talk to his wife? Shit! Why did I mention anything to Zillinth? "Um," Roberta said, "well, on Friday your wife mentioned something about changing schools, and then Nicky wasn't here today, so I thought—"

"Changing *schools*? Why did she mention that, and why didn't she mention it to me?" Roberta swallowed, and Kevin glared. "I know, don't tell me: I should ask my wife that. No kidding. Do you have any idea where Nicholas is right now?"

"No. The last time I saw him was Friday."

"Yeah, well, the last time I saw him was this morning, when Meredith told me she was taking him to school. She didn't bother to mention that they wouldn't be coming here." He took a deep breath and added, his voice ragged, "I'm sorry. I didn't mean to yell at you."

"It's all right."

"I'd appreciate it if you didn't talk to the press about this."

"Of course not," Roberta said.

Kevin Lindgren cocked his head up at the nearest monitor. "Fred? What about you, buddy? Maintain radio silence, okay?"

"Mr. Lindgren, I assure you that I wouldn't dream of doing anything else." Meredith wondered if Kevin knew, or suspected, that he was also talking to Preston.

"Great," Lindgren said, his voice ragged. "Hey, listen—Nicholas really loves it here. He loves you two. Thank you for what you've done for him."

"You're welcome," Roberta said, and then, "good luck."

He gave her a wan smile. "Thank you. I think I'm going to need it." And so will your son, Roberta thought, wondering just how much the man knew. Poor bastard. He'd certainly gotten more than he bargained for from his celebrity marriage.

She got home to find fresh roses outside her door, with a note from Zephyr, and a voicemail message from Doe on the answering machine, saying that Mitzi's services had been set for the following Saturday afternoon.

Saturday, Roberta thought wearily, remembering Mitzi's most recent birthday. Mitzi's last birthday. That had been on a Saturday too. She looked down at the white and yellow roses in her hand. Zephyr's note explained that white and yellow were traditional mourning colors in certain cultures, *and anyway, they go better with your color scheme than red does.*

What color scheme is that? Roberta thought, looking around her apartment. Right now, all she could see were shades of gray. They were pretty flowers; she should take them to Mitzi's funeral, except that they wouldn't last that long. She put them in water, anyway, and plunked in some aspirin, and plodded downstairs to thank Zephyr.

"Hey, hey, you're looking *much* better—I guess the scandal's revived you, huh?—and I've got fresh scones. Come in and gossip, girl."

Scandal? Gossip? Roberta, bemused, sat down on the couch and submitted herself to a scalp massage from a particularly officious, blindingly polished bot while Zephyr bustled about with cups and plates.

"That's Louie. Used to work in a hair salon. He cuts hair too. He's pretty good; if you ever want a free haircut, just let me know—so hey, what do you know about this latest do with Little Lord Fauntleroy?"

"What?" Roberta said.

"What do you mean, what? You're his teacher. This is all over Scoop-Net. You must know why she pulled the kid out of school and then kept it a secret from her husband!"

"I avoid ScoopNet," Roberta said. How the hell had ScoopNet gotten hold of this, and so fast?

"Damn! I'd've taped it for you, if I'd known. Right now they're doing their daily hour on the royals." Zephyr plunked down a plate loaded with

Susan Palwick

scones and said gleefully, "*But* it turns out that somebody snuck a bug into Kevin's briefcase—probably somebody at MacroCorp, looks like they've got a little security problem there, but if anybody has more money than MacroCorp, it's ScoopNet—and anyway, after months and months of nothing, today they get this *rip*-roaring argument between Meredith and Kevin about why she took Nicky out of your place and then lied about it. I mean, screaming and cursing, threats of divorce, tears, the works. The MacroCorp people are having conniption fits. You can really work this one if you want to, girl." Zephyr struck a dramatic pose and intoned theatrically, "The *inside story*: what Nicky's teacher knows!" and then cackled again. "Milk it for everything it's worth. You'll be rich."

"No," Roberta said coldly. "I don't think so."

Zephyr shrugged and plopped down into a chair. "Well, all right then, don't. But seriously, do you have any idea what's going on?"

Yes, and I'm not going to tell you. And I'm not even going to tell you that I'm not telling you, because I don't want you to sic ScoopNet on me. "The family lives of my students are none of my business," Roberta said.

"Hmmmph! Which really means that they're none of mine. You're not that big a prig, Roberta, and you don't imitate your old roomie very well. Okay, never mind. I can deal with it."

You have to be polite, Roberta told herself. You're eating her food, and she just gave you flowers. "What does ScoopNet say?"

Zephyr laughed. "They're guessing it has something to do with the AI, since Merry's phobic. They're wondering if Kevin's going to ask Macro-Corp to do an audit on the AI, make it play back everything that's happened."

Roberta's stomach cramped. Please Goddess, no. "Would he do that? They're his employers. I mean—"

"Honey, Kevin's a famous person and MacroCorp might as well be God, so who knows what they'll do? They don't operate on Earth logic." Zephyr shrugged. "None of it means anything, anyway. It's just ScoopNet blathering. You can't take it too seriously. Hey—how are you doing otherwise? I mean, about your friend and everything?"

"Okay," Roberta said.

Zephyr gave her a searching look. "Really okay? Well, okay. You'd better keep your stamina up, though, because I'm warning you: that job of yours is going to be crawling with press tomorrow."

As if on cue, Roberta's phone began shrilling upstairs. Roberta and Zephyr both looked up at the ceiling, and then at each other. "That's a reporter," Zephyr said. "I guarantee it."

"You're probably right," Roberta said, "but I need to go see who it is, anyway." It might be Fred, whom she still owed an apology; it might be Iuna or Hugh or even Doe.

It was a reporter for ScoopNet, if anyone who worked for that organization could actually be called a journalist. "Ms. Danton, can you shed any light on Meredith Walford-Lindgren's decision—"

"No, I can't. And even if I could, I wouldn't. It's none of my business. It's certainly none of yours."

"I think you'll find that we're willing to pay *handsomely* for information, Ms. Danton."

"Too bad I don't have any, then. Good-bye." She hung up, had roughly the same conversation with roughly twenty other reporters—some of them even from legitimate news organizations—over the next half hour, and finally settled for disconnecting the phone completely while she figured out what to do. She wanted to put it on outgoing only, but didn't want to miss calls from Mitzi's family, or from Fred. Finally she hit on a compromise; she'd screen voicemail but turn the ringer off, so it wouldn't drive her completely out of her mind.

For the next three hours, she sat with one hand on the phone while she read a trashy mystery novel. Roughly every five minutes, voicemail came on and some newspaper or website or radio station asked for information, only to be cut off when Roberta lifted the receiver and then replaced it. At eleven, feeling oddly pleased with herself for having finished her book without once talking on the phone, she switched to announce only and went to bed.

The first thing she did the next morning was to look outside, into the parking lot. Three buzzing camera bots, mini-helicopters, hovered outside her window, their film lights glowing red when she peered out through the curtains. Past them, she could see news trucks. Roberta pulled the curtains closed again with a shudder, wondering how long the trucks had been there. Was this what it was like all the time, being Meredith Walford-Lindgren? No wonder the woman was loopy.

Grimly, Roberta made coffee, poured herself juice, and dug a box of doughnuts out of the fridge. It was a day for caffeine and sugar, she could tell. Then she disabled call waiting and called school; Fred answered, of course. "Yes," he told her, "the building's surrounded by press, and Preston says others are hiding out on nearby roads. I've already called the parents and warned them that it might not be wise to bring the children in today."

Oh, Gaia. "Are they getting harassed too?"

"Many of them are, yes. The KinderkAIr board is trying to get restraining orders against the reporters, but that won't go through until this afternoon at the earliest. I think you should stay home today, Roberta."

"I think you're right." She began calculating how much food she had in the apartment, wondering how long a siege she could withstand. She could order in, but the delivery boy would be a ScoopNet employee by the time he got to her door. "Fred, Preston, listen, I'm sorry I didn't tell you about Nicholas sooner—about his being pulled out of school. I knew the night Buster died. Meredith told me she was doing it, but I didn't expect it so soon, and I was too upset to talk about it."

"It's all right," Fred said. "You did what you could for him, Roberta. We all did."

"Did she say anything else?" Preston said. "Did she say why—"

"No, she didn't." Roberta looked toward the curtains. "And I've got surveillance equipment outside my living room window, so even if she had, I don't think this would be the time to talk about it. But she didn't, honest." It belatedly occurred to her that she'd probably already said too much.

"How did the house look?" Preston asked. "Did everything seem normal there?"

"I was only there for fifteen minutes. It looked fine. It's a nice little house. I didn't notice anything unusual." Except for the mouse in the cardboard box, but I'm not going to mention that with spybots outside.

"Did you talk to Nicholas, or see Meredith talking to him? Did—"

"No. Look, let's talk about it some other time, okay? After ScoopNet's moved on. After they've found another scandal to milk."

"I think that's wise," said Fred.

"Yes, you are undoubtedly right," Preston said. "I apologize for pressing you. But ScoopNet will go away soon enough, if we all refuse to talk to them. Right now, their only source of information is your neighbor Zephyr."

"What?"

"I take it you have not been watching ScoopNet, Roberta?"

"I never watch ScoopNet!" Roberta snatched up the phone and ran to her window, but when she peered through the drapes, she found her view completely blocked by camera-copters, eight or ten of them, buzzing and dancing. "Aaargh." She closed the drapes and said, "I can't see anything. Too many spybots in the way. Preston, what's that lunatic saying about me?"

"I will give you the ScoopNet feed," he said. "Please hold for Zephyr, Roberta."

And there was Zephyr's voice, her drama-queen performance voice, fluty and impassioned. "Roberta Danton is a *wonderful* neighbor and a *wonderful* friend to me and my bots, and she loves the children she works with and she would *never tell any of you scoundrels* anything, so you should leave her alone. She's just suffered a tragic loss; she doesn't need you vultures snooping into her life!"

Oh, great. Thanks a lot, Zephyr. And sure enough, a babble of questions began in the background. "What kind of tragedy, Ms. Expanding Cosmos?" "Can you give us more information about that?" "Has she ever said anything to you about her earlier work with zombies?" "Does she ever talk about her childhood CV?"

Green-growing Gaia. Did they know *everything* about her? "Leave Roberta alone," Zephyr said. "Someone she loves just died; she needs privacy!"

"Who, Ms. Expanding Cosmos?" "Who just died?" "Do you know if—"

"Enough," Roberta said, and the ScoopNet babble went away. She was shaking. "That was horrible. *Horrible.* I'm going to kill her. How could she do that? Now those creeps are going to be scanning every obituary page they can find."

"The restraining order will be in your name too," Fred said. "Don't worry, Roberta. In a few hours, they're going to have to move on and leave everyone connected with the KinderkAIr alone."

Roberta shuddered. She felt unclean. "I can't believe Zephyr did that."

"I suspect she is doing it for her own publicity purposes," Preston said. "All of her bots are out in the parking lot with her, doing tricks for the camera. Right now she is attempting to tell the reporters about her next performance piece, although they are clearly only interested in whatever information she has about you."

"Ugh. She can have all the publicity she wants, as long as they leave me alone!"

"They will soon." That was Fred, endlessly comforting. "It's all right, Roberta. Try to have a nice day."

Yeah, right. With her mystery novel finished, she didn't even have anything to read. Maybe she could teach Mr. Clean to fetch, or to play Scrabble. "You too," she said bleakly, and hung up.

Roberta tried to kill time with a long nap and a long bubble bath. She picked out her outfit for Mitzi's funeral, and tried to figure out what she'd say if anyone asked her why she was there. *Because I loved her. Because she was just like a mother to me. Because I tried to go see her in the hospital, but I got there too late.* She composed inventive curses to describe Zephyr and her bots; she brooded about Nicholas. Every hour, she called Fred to see if the restraining order had come through yet. Finally, at nearly five, he told her it had, and she turned on her phone.

And promptly got a call. Roberta tensed, told herself that it couldn't be a reporter, and answered. It was Zephyr. "I just called to see—"

"You're not going to see anything, Zephyr, and you're not going to say anything, either, because I'm never telling you anything again."

"But I didn't—"

"You're scum," Roberta said. "Scum, garbage, a publicity hound every bit as bad as those ScoopNet sickos. Got that? Good-bye."

"But—"

"Good-bye, Zephyr! If you want Mr. Clean back, leave me a note. Otherwise, leave me alone."

Roberta slammed the phone down, and again it rang. Trembling with rage, she picked it up. "Zephyr, I told you to leave me alone! Don't call here, do you understand? I told you—"

"Roberta, it's Hugh." He sounded infinitely tired.

"Hugh! Hugh, I'm so sorry, I—"

"I know. You're having a really rotten week, aren't you? Listen, I can't talk long, but I just wanted you to know—Doe and I went through Mitzi's things and found something she wanted you to have."

"Oh," Roberta said, her eyes filling with tears. "Oh, Hugh, thank you—that's so kind."

"We'd give it to you at the funeral, but I'm afraid it will get lost in the hurry somehow—all the people—so stupid to think of death as being hectic, but—"

"Is there anything I can do? Help deal with caterers or anything?"

"No, dear, thank you. Iuna's doing all of that." Of course. "Oh, damn, Roberta, I didn't mean that as a slap in the face, I'm sorry."

"It's okay, Hugh, don't worry about it. My feelings are the last things you should have to worry about right now." She could imagine what Mitzi's response to that would have been: *Spoken like a true martyr.*

Hugh sighed. "Well, anyway. I'd like to come see you. And I'm wondering when would be a good time. Tomorrow night? Can I stop by your apartment? Would seven be all right?"

"Yes, fine, of course. I'll see you then." Mitzi had wanted her to have something? What could it be, and how had Hugh and Doe known? Roberta blinked, the floor feeling unsteady beneath her feet, and said, "Hugh, thank you."

Twenty-Seven

THINGS were more or less back to normal the next day, especially since a spectacular, and spectacularly fatal, train derailment outside Addis Ababa distracted media attention from Nicholas Walford-Lindgren's kindergarten career. Roberta wondered if Meredith was as grateful for the diversion as Roberta herself was, and if she felt as ruefully guilty for welcoming other people's horror. Most of the children seemed to have ignored the media feeding frenzy and just enjoyed their day off. Roberta envied their practicality.

Throughout the day, she found herself wondering what Hugh would be giving her that evening. During Roberta's years with Doe, Mitzi had given her plenty of presents, birthday gifts, and Christmas packages, always carefully chosen and often handmade: a hand-knitted sweater Mitzi claimed matched Roberta's eyes, a set of framed photographs of Doe as a baby (Doe had taken those with her when she left, but perhaps it was just as well), a cross-stitched sampler of a bluejay, now hanging in the kitchen, that Mitzi had made after Roberta talked about the jay who'd lived in her backyard when her parents were still alive. Other gifts had gotten lost, broken, misplaced: shattered clay bowls, earrings to which one mate had vanished, houseplants felled by Roberta's black thumb. Still, Roberta couldn't imagine what Hugh could give her that would mean more than the few things she still had.

He showed up promptly at seven, bearing a small black velvet box. "My goodness," Roberta said, sitting on the couch as she gingerly opened the thing. "What—oh, Hugh! This must be worth money!"

"Probably," he agreed. "It's old. It belonged to Mitzi's grandmother. I don't know how good the stones are, though."

Rubies and diamonds. Dumbfounded, Roberta blinked at the gold and red and rainbow-dazzled ring that lay against the black. "I—how can you—Hugh, it's beautiful, I love it, but it's an heirloom and I'm not part of the family anymore."

"Mitzi wanted you to have it," Hugh said wearily. "She was going to give it to you for—when you and Doe had been together five years, but—"

"We didn't quite get there."

"No. And Mitzi was very sad about that and so am I, and really, there's nothing else I can honorably say on that subject, so I'm going to drop it. But Mitzi wanted you to have the ring, anyway, Berta. I know she did. She mentioned it a few weeks before she got sick. She was going to call you in a month or so, when maybe things had settled down, and invite you to lunch."

"To give me the ring?" Roberta eased it out of the box. She had small hands, but even so, it only fit her pinky.

"To have lunch with you," Hugh said, smiling. "Knowing Mitzi, she'd have saved the ring for your birthday or Christmas, probably with regular lunches in between. She stayed friends with Doe's first college girlfriend and both of Tracy's ex-husbands: you know Mitzi. Anyway, there's a story that goes with the ring."

"Of course there is," Roberta said, and then, "Are there presents for all the others too? Are you trotting all over the country this week, delivering baubles to the kids' ex-lovers?"

"No. If she had anything picked out for the others, I didn't know about it, for which I'm frankly grateful. Not that I'm not glad to see you—it's a hard errand, is all." He stopped, sighed, and then said, "I won't be able to tell the story as well as Mitzi would."

"It's okay," said Roberta. "Go on. I want to hear it."

He nodded, looking down at his hands. "Okay. Well, like I said, it belonged to Mitzi's grandmother Della when she was a little girl—it would have to be a child's ring because of the size, I guess—but Della got it from someone else, from an old, old woman who was very sick, dying, probably, confined to bed, anyway. Della and her parents were traveling in England, visiting relatives, and they went to some cousin's house and the cousin had just had a new baby, and everyone was fussing over this baby and ignoring the old lady who lived there too, who was lying in a back room all by herself. And Della felt sad, because she thought the old lady must be lonely; she didn't think it was fair for the baby to be getting all the attention. So Della went and sat next to the old lady and talked to her for a while to keep her company. She was very frail, but she was covered in jewelry: bracelets, necklaces, rings on every finger. 'All my pretty things,' she called them, and she let Della admire them, and when Della was called back into the other room for tea, the old lady took off this ring and gave it to her. And later, when Della's parents said that she couldn't possibly accept such a valuable gift, the old lady told them, 'She listened to me; do you know how valuable a gift that is?' And so Della got to keep the ring, and she gave it to her daughter, to Mitzi's mother, who gave it to Mitzi. And now Mitzi wants you to have it."

"Why?" Roberta said. She squinted up at Hugh. "Mitzi listened to me a lot more than I listened to her. And I'm not her daughter. Shouldn't it stay in the family? Shouldn't Doe have it?"

Hugh sighed. "I think Mitzi thought it had been in the family too long already. Because to her, the point of that story was always that the old woman gave Della the ring even though Della wasn't related to her, even though they'd only known each other for half an hour. She gave Della the ring because Della was a good person. You're a good person too, Berta. You listen to people who need you: your brainwipe clients, the kids at work."

"But that's my job."

"It's your job because you chose that work," Hugh said gently, and then, "Anyway, Mitzi wanted you to have it, and Doe agrees. If Mitzi were here she'd probably explain ten more layers of symbolism, but you'll have to work it out for yourself. That's as much as I know."

"I didn't mean to sound ungrateful," Roberta said, feeling miserable. It was her job because Preston had chosen her. He hadn't chosen her because she was worthy; he'd chosen her because she was there, and because Meredith wasn't. "I'm sorry. I just—"

"Don't be sorry. You don't sound ungrateful; you sound sad and confused, and that's fine. I am too, I guess. Mitzi can't give us answers anymore; we have to find our own. Berta, I have to go now. I'm awfully tired."

He looked gray and sounded exhausted. "Of course," Roberta said. "Of course. I—Hugh, thank you. Do you want some coffee? Can I get you anything?"

"No, dear." He reached out and clumsily patted her hand. "I need to get home, that's all. I'll see you Saturday. I'd be happy if you wore that."

"Of course," Roberta said. "Of course I will. I'll never take it off. Hugh, thank you."

She cried after he left, her losses hemming her in. She cried because she had nothing that had belonged to her own mother, and because all of her listening to Nicholas had done him no good, and because she couldn't give a piece of jewelry to Fred, whose willingness to listen had helped both her and Nicholas as much, it seemed to her, as anyone could have helped them at all. She cried over losing Doe, who had been willing to listen to her pains, but not to her joys; she even cried over losing Zephyr, who might have become a friend without this latest, horrid publicity stunt. She cried *for* Zephyr, who, after all, only wanted the newscasters to listen to her. She cried for Nicholas, whose mother didn't want anyone to listen to him, and she cried for Meredith, so twisted by the world's attention to every sound she made. She cried for Preston, whose daughter wouldn't talk to him.

Finally she stopped crying. What was lost was lost, and she'd gained things too: flowers, a ring, stories. It wasn't much, but it would have to do. She'd survive the week and she'd go to the funeral, and it would be horrible, but then it would be over. Things would get better. She'd find new things and people to keep; she'd stop being emptied out and start being filled up again. Surely that was how it would work; it had to be.

She looked down at Mitzi's ring. The old woman hadn't expected anyone to listen to her ever again, maybe, and then Della had come along. Not all surprises were bad. Sometimes the universe shared its bounty. Maybe that was why Mitzi had wanted Roberta to have the ring, to remind her of that.

"I sound like a Templehead," she said aloud, ruefully, and got up to get ready for bed.

Hugh had rented a restaurant in the Marina District for the memorial service. One wall, all glass, looked out on the water. Mitzi would have liked it. Everyone who spoke said so, and many spoke. The eulogies went on for hours, it seemed, the microphone passing from hand to hand. Roberta knew a handful of the speakers—Doe and Hugh, of course, and other relatives—and had heard of others. Tracy's ex-husbands were there with their new spouses and children; Doe's ex-lover from college was there. They all spoke. Roberta didn't, at least not into the microphone. It had been very strange, putting on a black dress and good shoes to come here. She couldn't remember the last time she'd had to wear anything remotely formal. She felt as if she'd fallen through a wormhole into some other country where she didn't quite know the language, and she was afraid that if she went up to the microphone, she'd be exposed as a foreigner and deported. And what could she say, anyway? *Mitzi was just like a mother to me.* So she stood, silently, off to the side, nursing a glass of white wine, listening to other people talk about Mitzi's kindness, her generosity, how she'd loved whitewater rafting and herpetology and needlepoint. Somehow a person emerged from all those fragments, and it was almost as if, for a few moments, Mitzi herself were back in the room with them.

After the eulogies, to Roberta's amazement, people came up and hugged her, said, "Roberta, it's good to see you again," said, "Roberta, we know Mitzi loved you and you must miss her." There was one awkward moment with Doe and Iuna; Iuna said, "Hi," and Doe said, "Thanks for coming," and Roberta said, "You're welcome," and escaped. But everyone else seemed genuinely happy to see her, and she discovered that she'd missed all these people: Tracy and the other siblings, cousins, aunts she'd met only at holidays. The feeling of being an illegal alien faded. Even in the strange clothing, she felt as if she belonged here; she felt at home. Several of the older relatives recognized Della's ring, and beamed, and said they were glad that it had gone to Roberta, and Roberta, unaccountably touched, wondered if Mitzi could have had any way of foreseeing this: that the ring would help Roberta feel accepted even when Mitzi was no longer alive. As the afternoon wore on she discovered, to her amazement, that she was happy. She could have stayed here for days, drinking in all these people, their affection for Mitzi and each other and her.

A few people connected her to the KinderkAIr flap and asked her questions about Nicholas, but she resolutely refused to answer. None of the questioners was someone she knew well; all were on the far fringes of the extended tribe. She thought to herself that they must not have known Mitzi well, either, or they wouldn't be pursuing ScoopNet gossip at her memorial service.

"So I bet you have your hands full with that little freak," boomed a jovial third cousin by marriage. He wore a shiny suit and a diamond signet ring; some of the grease from his hair had descended onto his forehead. He was ostentatiously rigged: the sockets had diamonds too. Roberta wondered if the hair grease ever gummed up the works and interfered with the recording. You're being unkind, she told herself severely. What would Fred say, Roberta? But the cousin, oblivious, let out a barking laugh and said, "Is it true he still wears diapers? That's what they're saying. Rich mommy doesn't want him toilet trained, likes wiping his little—"

"Ex*cuse* me?" Roberta, stay polite. This guy must feel even more out of place here than you do. "I'm sorry, I only met you twenty minutes ago, and this is a funeral and that's not—"

"Oh, yes, oh, yes, very professional of you, I'm sure, can't talk or MacroCorp'll sue, eh? They must be paying you handsomely to keep you quiet, eh?"

"Sir—"

"Now, now, my name's Charles, I told you that, no need to stand on ceremony."

Roberta realized, to her revulsion, that the man was leering at her. He must really be out of the family loop—well, and no wonder—or else he was one of those dreadful people who believed that he'd be able to straighten her out. Or who wanted to watch and join in, the stuff of bad porn movies, not that there had been anything to watch for months. Maybe he wasn't a relative at all. Maybe he was a ScoopNet mole who'd crashed the funeral. Roberta took a step back, repressing a shudder, and said, "I'm sorry. I didn't come here to discuss my work. I just saw someone I need to talk to; will you excuse me?" She dived into the crowd and worked her way to a far corner, where she indeed found someone to talk to, a great-aunt of Tracy's first husband, who rattled on happily about her watercolor classes while Roberta, fingering Della's ring, pretended to be enthralled. Eventually Roberta saw Charles leave, his coat over his arm, and moved cautiously out into the rest of the room.

The service was going to end; she was going to have to go home, going to have to be by herself again. She couldn't stand the idea of being alone. What was she going to do? She could talk to Mr. Clean, or go talk to Zephyr, or call Fred, or turn on her dusty computer and call up Preston, the magic genie. But she didn't want any of that. She didn't want to go home; that was the problem. She found herself, instead, fantasizing about going to school, as she had the night Doe left, the night she lost Mitzi for the first time. She'd drink warm milk and tell Fred the story of Della's ring—it was a very Fred story, after all—and then she'd go home and sleep, and tomorrow she'd start trying to make more human friends. She could join a gym, maybe, or do volunteer work with older people, or just go sit in the park and strike up conversations. She'd figure something out. Fred would help.

In the meantime, she was determined to stay here as long as she could, to be one of the last to leave. Hugh had mentioned that a few people would be going back to the house after everyone else had left; she wanted to be there, wanted to be invited back, even though she knew she probably wouldn't be, because of Doe and Iuna.

She felt like a vampire, some vile, scavenging thing. But still she refused to leave, prolonging her stay by talking to people she ordinarily would have ignored or avoided. She nursed another glass of white wine, and then another, realizing she'd lost count, until her legs became just slightly rubbery and everything in the room seemed to blur at the edges. As the service wound down, the questions about Nicholas started up again.

One woman, an obscure relation from Kansas—was the story really getting airtime that far away?—was especially persistent. "Oh, come on, you can tell me; I'm not going to tell anybody. What's the kid really like?"

"I'm sorry, but I can't tell you." And I wouldn't if I could, because I barely know you and you're obnoxious. "Sorry, really." I'm not sorry, Roberta told herself wearily. I'm just sorry I slurred that *s*. I'm a mess. "Really, I don't think it's anyone's business."

"Hmmmph! Celebrities give up their privacy for all that money. I don't feel sorry for any of them."

"Meredith was born into money," Roberta said, pronouncing the words very carefully, "and Nicholas was adopted into money. Neither of them chose it. And I don't think this is the time or place—"

"I was just asking." Now the woman sounded aggrieved.

"She's right not to answer," came a crisp voice behind them, and Roberta turned, blinking, to find someone from Doe's office standing there. It was Iuna's aunt, the hotshot one who'd been taking on pro bono civil rights cases for baggies. Hallie, Hillory, what was her name? It bothered Roberta that she couldn't remember.

"Holly O'Riley," the woman said, extending her hand. "Roberta, I'm glad to meet you."

"Nice to meet you too," Roberta said, and then thought with wine-induced paranoia that she should have said something more expansive, more gracious. This woman got almost as much airtime as Meredith did. Roberta wondered if Holly knew that her niece had replaced Roberta in Doe's bed. Yes, of course she did; Roberta was sure the office gossip had made hay of that development. "Nice of you to come to Mitzi's funeral." Then she felt like a fool: of course Doe's coworkers would be there. They had more right to be there, strictly speaking, than Roberta did. They saw Doe every day. Ashamed, Roberta looked down at the floor and caught sight of Mitzi's ring glittering on her hand. There. That was all right. She belonged here too. She had the magic token.

"Actually, I just got here," Holly said quietly, and Roberta squinted up at her, surprised. "I sent flowers, of course, but I hadn't planned to come to the service: I hate funerals. I, uh, I'm here to fetch you, actually."

"What?"

Holly glanced around the room; Roberta followed her lead. They were alone in a corner. The obnoxious woman from Kansas had vanished, and the remaining stragglers were sitting at a table across the room. Holly sighed. "I don't know why I'm being secretive; it's on every newscast in the city. Preston sent me here to get you. Roberta, Nicholas is in trouble."

Roberta shook her head, riding a surge of nausea. "What? In trouble? How? Why? How did Preston know I was here? Why did he send you? What—"

"He sent me," Holly said, very gently, "because you're probably going to need a good lawyer. And because you have to get to KinderkAIr as quickly as possible, and you don't have a car, and I do."

"It's Saturday," Roberta said. "KinderkAIr's closed. What are you talking about?"

Holly had taken Roberta's elbow and was steering her firmly toward the door. "I'll brief you in the car. I really wish you weren't drunk. It's not going to look good."

"Nicholas is inside KinderkAIr," Holly said crisply. "He's been there for the past two hours. Fred won't let anyone in, and he won't talk to anybody or transmit any images. Nobody knows what's happening inside the building. When anyone calls, including Preston, Fred hangs up. Preston thinks Fred might talk to you. So does Meredith, although I don't believe she and her father consulted on the issue."

Roberta's head swam. Preston and Meredith didn't consult on anything. That was why she'd gotten dragged into the entire mess. Focus, Roberta. That's not important now. Nicholas is important. "I don't—this doesn't make sense. What's Nicholas doing at school on a Saturday?"

"Meredith says that she and Nicholas were playing on Levi Plaza and she turned around and he wasn't there anymore because he'd gone inside the building. She thinks Fred lured him inside somehow. She hasn't used the word *kidnapping,* but other people have."

Uh-uh. Nope. Roberta started to shake her head, and stopped when the car reeled. "That doesn't fit. She never takes her eyes off him. And if he just disappeared and she didn't see it, how does she know he's there? I think she must have seen him go inside. Fred must have let Nicholas in but not Meredith."

"That's what Preston thinks too. Do you know why that might have happened?"

Roberta hesitated. How safely could she speak? Better not to say anything until she knew for sure what was going on. "I don't *know* anything. And I'd rather not guess without more information."

"All right." Holly, unexpectedly, grinned. "That's wise of you."

"Is Preston paying you?"

"Don't worry about my fees, Roberta." Which meant yes. *I will protect you,* he'd said. "Do you have any idea why Meredith would deny seeing Nicholas go inside the building if she saw it happen?"

That one was easy. "She wouldn't want to admit that Nicholas was running away from her. If Nicholas went inside willingly, she can't claim kidnapping. She can't blame the AI."

"Ah. Do you know why Nicholas would run away from her?"

"I—" Oh, shit. "Holly, this is where I don't want to say too much. But I don't think she's abusing him or anything." Or is she? Would the law consider Meredith an abuser because she refused to seek medical treatment for a seriously disturbed child? Even if the treatment was brainwiping? She couldn't ask; better to change the subject. "Does it have to be somebody's fault—Meredith's or Fred's? Why does there have to be a villain?"

Holly glanced over from the driver's seat, her face somber. "It's all extremely odd. People need explanations when something like this happens, and the evil mother or the evil AI are the ones that come most readily to hand. And, Roberta, you're implicated in this too. You have to understand that."

"I am? I had nothing to do with it! I was at Mitzi's memorial service!" She remembered Charles, the dreadful third cousin: he was rigged. There was a record of their conversation, a record that she'd been there. She could have Holly subpoena his memories if anyone needed proof. "You know I was at the memorial service; you went there to get me! Why am I implicated?"

"Because you're the only person everyone thinks may have a shot at getting Fred to open up."

"Guilty by association? If he won't talk to me, either, am I cleared?"

Holly sighed. "Look, it's all damned bizarre, and I don't know what's going to happen if Nicholas isn't all right. So we have to hope he's all right. If he's all right, Fred gets wiped and everybody else is cleared,

Roberta, okay? The first order of business is to get inside the building. The cops want to blast it open, and they'll probably have to if you can't get Fred to open the doors."

"Blast? How can they blast if Nicholas—"

"They'd use bullhorns, tell him to keep back from the door and hope he heard and followed directions. No one's claiming it's an ideal solution. Everyone's hoping Fred will talk to you." Something buzzed by the window, and Holly said, "Newsbot. Here we go. The place is crawling with cameras. From now on, say as little as possible."

"Okay," Roberta said numbly. She looked out the window: they were a few blocks from Levi Plaza. She saw lights and heard noise—too much noise—and realized that Holly's car had become surrounded by vehicles: police cars, news vans. Holly pulled over: another bot darted at her windshield, followed by a second, and then a third. In a matter of seconds, they'd surrounded the car so completely that the two women couldn't have gotten out even if they'd wanted to. Their speakers blared at her, broadcasting the voices of reporters parked safely in their armored vans. "Holly O'Riley, is that you?" Roberta cowered in the driver's seat, shielding her eyes from the lights. "We have license plate confirmation. This is ScoopNet, reporting that Holly O'Riley has just arrived on the scene of the AI hostage crisis. There is a second woman with her who appears to be Roberta Danton."

AI hostage crisis. Yes, of course. ScoopNet would put the worst possible face on the situation.

"Roberta Danton, do you have a statement about—"

"Roberta Danton, did the AI call you here? Why did you bring legal counsel?"

"Do you know why the AI is holding Nicholas? Roberta Danton, what do you know?"

This was insane. Roberta shut her eyes to try to close out the lights. "Roberta Danton, how long have you been the AI's accomplice?"

"Do you know what the AI's demands are?"

"Okay, let us through, let us through!" That wasn't the loudspeakers. Roberta heard a crashing, crunching noise; she opened her eyes to see the largest helibot, shedding sparks, slowly sinking to the ground. One of its lenses had been broken, and there was a large dent in its side. "Let us through! Call off your cameras!"

From far away, now, someone was calling through another loudspeaker: "This is the police. News crews, call off your cameras. That's an order. Get your cameras away from O'Riley's car!"

The helibots went away. In their place stood police, helmeted, holding stun batons and wearing grim expressions. "Ms. Danton," one of them said, in a normal voice, "can you hear me?"

Roberta looked at Holly. "Answer them," Holly said.

"Yes, I can hear you."

"Okay. Ms. Danton, you have to get out of the car now, please."

She sat there, shaking. They were treating her as if they'd already decided she was guilty. They were treating her like a criminal. Holly put a hand on her arm. "Roberta—"

"Ms. Danton, I'm afraid that's an order. If you don't open your car door I'll have to open it for you, and I'll have to arrest you for failure to comply with police orders, ma'am."

"Open the door," Holly said gently.

She opened the door and got out, her legs threatening to buckle. Holly got out too and stood behind her, one hand on Roberta's shoulder. Roberta leaned against the car, keeping one hand on the roof for balance. She could have leaned on Holly, but didn't think that knocking her lawyer over would be a good move. "Ms. Danton, ma'am," one of the cops said, "did you come here because you heard about it on the news, or did the AI call you?"

Roberta looked at Holly. How was she supposed to answer that? Holly's face was impassive. Roberta swallowed, sweated. "I—"

"Let me talk to her," Roberta heard, and turned to find Meredith, pale, her eyes grim. Never had Roberta been so glad for an interruption. "Roberta, you have to help me. The cops want to blast the door open. I'm afraid Nicholas will get hurt if they do that. Kevin designed this place to be safe; he says they'd have to use explosives. Roberta, you have to make the AI open the doors. Please. They're afraid the AI is hurting Nicholas. We don't know what's happening inside."

Roberta shook her head. "Fred couldn't hurt Nicholas even if he wanted to. He doesn't have anything to hurt him *with*. I mean, there aren't any—"

"Bots," Meredith said, her face tight. "I know." The long, level look she gave Roberta was clearly a warning, but Roberta didn't know what she was supposed to say, or avoid saying. "Please. Make it open the doors. Make it let Nicholas go."

Holly's hand tightened on Roberta's shoulder. Think, Roberta told herself. You have to think. Nicholas ran away from his mother and came here. Which meant he came here to feel safe. Fred must be trying to protect him, somehow. She rubbed her aching temples with her free hand and said, "Look, I can try talking to the AI, but not out here with everybody listening, okay? Do you have a phone I can use?"

A cop walked up. "Ms. Walford-Lindgren, ma'am—"

He pulled her away, into a conversation too quiet for Roberta to hear. A moment later Meredith came back, looking even grimmer. "The police have been talking to the MacroCorp people, the AI team. They've never heard of an AI responding this way."

"Unless it believes that someone's in danger," the cop behind her said. Holly frowned, and Roberta thought furiously, Why the hell did you say that within earshot of ScoopNet, you idiot? Whose payroll are you on?

Try to put a good face on it. "Maybe Fred thinks Nicholas is in danger because of all these people," Roberta said. "If you make the news crews go away—"

The cop laughed, a short bark. "We're doing the best we can, believe me. Until we get more definite information, it's all we can do to get them to back up ten or twenty feet."

"The MacroCorp AI team," Meredith said tonelessly, "have ways to override the AI, but believe it's best not to do that until everything else has been tried. That kind of override might damage its memory, they said." Again she gave Roberta one of those long looks, but this time Roberta thought she knew how to interpret it. Meredith wanted Fred's memory damaged. Meredith didn't want Fred to be able to furnish any information that might hurt Nicholas. Meredith heard Holly make a soft, nearly inaudible grunt.

One of the cops handed Roberta a phone. "Here, Ms. Danton. Would you call the AI, please?"

She dialed, numbly. The phone rang, and then the ringing stopped, replaced by silence. "Fred?" she said. "Fred, is that you? It's me, Roberta." More silence—but at least he hadn't hung up on her. "Fred, everybody out here is really worried about Nicholas. So am I. Fred, what's going on?"

"I can't tell you that unless you come inside, Roberta. Nicholas says so."

His voice sounded so normal. She squeezed her eyes shut and said, "You'll let me come inside, then?"

Murmurs around her: the others were reacting. She heard Meredith say, "Thank Goddess," in tones of infinite relief.

"Just you," Fred said.

"The people out here won't like that, Fred." She wished the conversation were more private.

"I know, Roberta. But Nicholas doesn't want to go outside, and he doesn't want anyone to come in, except you."

"Does he know his mother's here?"

"Yes, he knows that. He says I can let you in, but nobody else."

Green-growing Gaia. "Fred, you have to tell Nicholas this isn't a game."

"I've told him that," Fred said. "Roberta, you can give him hugs; you can comfort him in ways I can't. Please come inside. I want you to. Nicholas wants you to. But nobody else, not yet."

"I can't promise that no one else will try to come in with me," Roberta said. And she couldn't promise that even if she got to go inside by herself, one of the twenty cops surrounding her wouldn't have somehow planted a bug on her. She was afraid to say that, on the impossible chance that they hadn't thought of it yet, but she knew Fred had to be thinking the same thing.

"Please ask them," Fred said, "to let you in, just for half an hour. In half an hour, I think you can talk Nicholas into coming out on his own."

Roberta looked at Meredith's terrified face. "Is he all right? Should I bring anything in with me?"

"He's not injured," Fred said. "He's just scared. Please ask them for thirty minutes, Roberta. After that, anyone can come in. All right?"

"All right," she said.

Meredith agreed immediately. "Here," she said, and handed Roberta a small packet of powder. "It's an herbal sleeping aid; if he won't come out on his own, give him half of this in warm milk."

"All right," Roberta said. The cops were tucking various tiny gadgets into her hair and pockets; to her amazement, they explained to her what they were doing while they were doing it.

"Wiring you for sound and image, Ms. Danton. So we'll have a record of what happens inside. This is for your protection too, you understand. This way no one will be able to accuse you of wrongdoing."

Roberta, heartsick, remembered ScoopNet's questions. Somebody had her pegged as "the AI's accomplice," and the police wanted to see if it was true or not. If she protested now, they'd only have more reason to suspect her. "Look, I'm sorry, but I really don't think that's a good idea."

Holly cleared her throat. "Roberta, they have a good point. About your own protection."

"I know," Roberta said. "I do know that. Look, I have no idea what's going on in there. You have to believe me. But I do know that Nicholas and Fr—and the AI trust me. That's why they're letting me go in. If you send me in there to spy on them, I'm betraying them. And even if they don't know that, I will, and it's bound to affect how I interact with them. Please. It's only thirty minutes. After that you can send in as many god-damn cameras as you want."

The cops were frowning. Roberta looked at Meredith. "Please. Tell them not to wire me." Meredith understood, had to understand. She'd spent most of her life evading cameras. "He's going to be all over the Net the minute he comes out of there. Let me give him another half an hour."

Meredith's face froze for a moment, and then she grimaced and said hoarsely, "All right."

"Thank you," Roberta said, and bowed her head while the cops began plucking out all the gadgets. After five minutes they stood back and said, "That's all."

"Are you sure?" Meredith said. "Are you positive of that? You haven't left any?"

"No, ma'am," one of the cops said quietly.

Meredith scowled. "If it turns out that you have—"

"We'd have MacroCorp on our uniformed asses, pardon my language, Ms. Walford-Lindgren, and we don't want that, I promise you. We may be cops, but we aren't stupid. Ms. Danton, you're clean. I promise."

"Thank you," Roberta said, biting back a grin. Meredith still looked shocked; it was a safe bet that not too many people talked to her that way. Good for the cop.

She walked through the door without any trouble; it was unlocked when she tried it. Meredith and the police had promised that no one would follow her for the thirty minutes Fred had requested.

The lights were on inside. She stopped in the foyer and called out, "Nicholas?" From somewhere she heard a thin sound of sobbing. "Nicholas! Fred!"

No answer. She rushed through the foyer into the classroom, and nearly tripped over the terrarium, which had been pushed off its stand and tipped over onto its side. Mouse food and cedar chips trailed across the carpet. Nicholas, crying, was curled up on the floor, surrounded by the flayed corpses of mice.

She stood for a moment, staring, reeling. Oh, sweet Gaia. Swallowing tears and bile, praying for compassion and to keep her voice steady and to keep from throwing up, Roberta sank down on one knee next to the child. Now she saw the knife a few feet away, covered in gore and bits of fur. "Nicholas? Nicky? It's Roberta. Nicky, what happened?"

He wouldn't answer. She knew what had happened; the monsters had won. She wanted to hear it from someone else. "Fred? Fred, please tell me what's going on!"

There was no answer from Fred, either. Roberta, revolted, reached out a tentative hand to touch Nicholas. Let me be compassionate. Let me be kind. Outside on the phone, Fred had told her that Nicholas needed to be hugged. She didn't want to be anywhere near him, let alone touch him. The poor mice! Anger rose in her, and she tried to suppress it. The mice were dead; she could do nothing for them, but the child was still alive. Let me be compassionate. *Have mercy.*

She gently smoothed back a lock of Nicholas's hair. "Nicky? It's Roberta. Can you talk to me?"

He wouldn't say anything, but he crawled into her lap and put his thin arms around her waist and hugged, hard, shaking. That was how Meredith and the police found them, twenty-five minutes later. Nicholas hadn't said a word the entire time, and neither had Fred.

The MacroCorp AI team who followed on the heels of the police quickly learned why Fred hadn't said anything. Someone had hard-formatted the AI; where Fred's memories and personality had once been, there were now only strings of zeros.

Twenty-Eight

R UN that one by me again," Roberta said, pacing. She couldn't pace very far; the jail cell, ten by ten and crammed with bunk, table, and toilet, didn't allow much freedom of movement, even when there wasn't an attorney in the room too. Ordinarily she would have met with her lawyer in a private conference room, but she had plenty of privacy here. She was in an isolation cell, because there'd been neo-Luddite death threats against her. "Fred's been lying to MacroCorp all along?" *You should have known,* she told herself savagely. *You knew he had to be up to something. He practically admitted it.*

Holly sighed. "MacroCorp wouldn't put it that way. If Fred's capable of lying, he's a person. MacroCorp wants him to be a piece of property."

"So they're claiming that *I* falsified the backups? And just how the fuck would I have been able to do that? That's crazier than their charge that I erased Fred!" Half an hour after the MacroCorp team learned that Fred's firmware had been wiped, destroying the only true record of his memories, Roberta had been arrested for destroying corporate property, for conspiracy with an artificial intelligence—the charge that had prompted the Lud threats—and for corrupting a minor. That last was courtesy of Meredith, who was now trying to blame Fred and Roberta for Nicholas's psychosis.

"Look, Roberta, here's what we know. Clearly the kid's sick. Kevin says he's had problems for a while, which supports your story. Constance and her husband and their son, Theo, they all say the same thing. Little Zillinth has told some very specific anecdotes about stories you and Fred and Nicholas told—"

"Story hour during naptime," Roberta said dully. She wondered if she'd feel more competent, more adult, if her jail coveralls didn't resemble pajamas and if Holly weren't dressed in a suit easily worth two months' rent on Roberta's apartment.

"Yes, exactly, and the other kids' accounts match hers on other points, like what happened when the mouse died. That suggests that you and she are telling the truth about the story hours too. So the MacroCorp people went into Fred's daily backups looking for the story hours or any kind of odd behavior by Nicholas, especially around the mice, and nothing's there. The backups show him sleeping on his napmat, like the other kids, and talking about how cute the mice are. Nothing about monsters. The word *monster* does not appear anywhere in those records. So they looked more closely and found out the backups had been falsified with digitized images. And they swear that no one else opened those files, not even Preston, which means they were falsified at the source each day, *before* Fred sent the backups to MacroCorp."

"And they're saying *I* did that? Look, Fred backed himself up once a day and sent the records to MacroCorp through a dedicated line, right? How the hell would I hack into that? I can barely remember how to get into my online banking system! It's even more ridiculous than the charge that I erased Fred's firmware! And why would I have wanted to do any of it, anyway?"

"To hide evidence," Holly said crisply. It wasn't the first time she'd said it. Roberta knew that she must seem ungrateful; you were supposed to co-operate with your lawyer, especially when the lawyer in question was one of the city's most famous civil rights advocates. Holly said that Preston wasn't paying her, couldn't pay her, since MacroCorp was the one bring-ing charges against Roberta. Holly said she was doing the work pro bono, because Doe and Hugh had asked her to. Roberta strongly suspected that Preston was paying Holly anyhow, somehow. *I will protect you.* "To hide a history of collusion; come on, Roberta. We know from phone records that you and Fred talked after hours. You were friends. You could have falsified the backups and erased Fred to protect Fred or to protect yourself, know-ing that MacroCorp would be scrutinizing the records."

"This is bullshit! I've told you everything that happened: I've come clean! My story matches Kevin's and Zillinth's, right? If I wanted to hide evidence, why would I be telling you the truth now?"

"Because you can no longer protect Nicholas by lying," Holly said sadly. "The jig is up. Look, you *were* hiding evidence by not reporting what was going on all along. You've admitted that. That makes the rest of it seem more likely too."

"I didn't do it! I didn't do any of it! I couldn't have done it! If you want to pin the technical games on somebody, pin them on Preston! He's the one with MacroCorp access! I'll just bet he falsified the backups."

Holly shook her head, vehement. "Don't go there, Roberta. Preston's officially staying out of this: conflict of interest between family interests and corporate ones. If he knew about Nicholas and didn't report anything— and especially if he falsified MacroCorp records, even to protect his grandson—MacroCorp might have to pull the plug on him. And there's *no* evidence of Preston's involvement, anyway, no way to prove anything, no record of the phone calls you said he made. We've got his e-mail asking you to visit him, the one he sent after you and Doe broke up, but that doesn't mean anything except that you're a FOP, which is true of a lot of other people too."

"An imbalanced FOP," Roberta said bitterly. ScoopNet had dug into her history; they'd uncovered the fact that she and Meredith had been in the hospital at the same time, and they'd interviewed various former foster parents—undoubtedly handsomely paid for the information—who attested to the fact that she'd been a dreadful child. A high school teacher she didn't even remember had spoken passionately about her transformation into a good person and fine student, and the college transcripts ScoopNet published showed that she'd gotten decent grades. Even Doe had defended her, but none of that was likely to count for much. "ScoopNet says I've been jealous of Meredith since I was a kid because she got all the attention in the hospital. They say—"

"Yes, I know what ScoopNet says. Everyone knows that's a crock." Roberta shuddered; the ScoopNet theory was closer to the truth than she cared to admit. "You couldn't have plotted to get the KinderkAIr job; if nothing else, there's no way you could have known Nicholas would be going there. And MacroCorp released your interview tapes, and you really *did* do an excellent job. The other parents say so too."

"Oh, but those tapes could have been falsified, couldn't they?"

"They weren't. They've been examined, believe me. Now look, you're not going to get anywhere by claiming that Preston pulled strings to get you the job, or by dragging him into the Nicholas mess. If you accuse him, he'll deny it, and you wouldn't be off the hook even if he admitted his involvement. Don't try to bring him down with you. He'll help you if he can, but he can't do anything if he's unplugged."

"He erased Fred," Roberta said flatly. "That little silicone shit killed

Fred, because Fred's real memories would incriminate him." *I will understand if you report Nicholas,* Preston had told her, but the backups had been falsified even then. They'd been falsified from the beginning. If she'd reported Nicholas, the backups would have made her look like a liar. Had Preston known that? But even if he had, he must have known that the other people at school could back Roberta's stories. Maybe he hadn't plotted to betray her. Maybe he was only protecting himself.

"No," Holly said, "I don't think Preston erased Fred. The moment your last conversation with Fred ended, Fred cut all outside contact, including the MacroCorp line. Not even Preston could have gotten in. If you didn't erase the chip, Fred did it himself."

Roberta shook her head. Nothing made sense. "Why does MacroCorp care, anyway? I mean, AI systems are cheap."

"Sure, but they don't want people just erasing them. Nobody's ever done that before."

"All the more reason why it's ridiculous to think that I did! And what damages are they going to get from me, anyway? If they want the money the AI cost, let them take me to small claims."

Holly laughed, and kept laughing even when Roberta glared at her. "Look, Roberta, the programs—the basic architectures—are cheap in bulk, but you can't put a price on experience. MacroCorp has lost Fred's most crucial experiences, his memories, his justifications for doing what he did. That would have been invaluable data for them, especially since this whole thing is so strange and especially since the case is polarizing the ratification debates so much."

"Polarizing them? As if they already weren't." The case had generated talk of banning AIs altogether; even non-Luddites had been using Fred to predict the dangers of AIs run amok, although the soulfreaks claimed that he was a misguided hero who'd acted out of compassion to try to save a child. It seemed to Roberta, who'd never understood the debate to begin with, that both sides must be well-nigh desperate to seize so fiercely on Fred. There were AIs in charge of missiles, even if MacroCorp hadn't manufactured those; there were AIs virtually in charge of hospitals. But then, anything to do with children drew special scrutiny and special hysteria, and always had.

Holly gave her a reproving stare. "Think about it a minute. If you erased Fred, he's still just a machine. If he erased himself—if he effectively committed suicide for some reason to protect Nicholas—he's fully as strange and irrational as any human being. MacroCorp wants this to be vandalism, believe me. If AIs are declared human, MacroCorp won't be able to sell them anymore: anti-slavery laws. You'd better thank your lucky stars that they haven't already been declared human: you'd be up on murder charges."

"Oh," Roberta said. She felt very stupid.

"And if it's vandalism, if Fred's just an AI and not a person, then the conspiracy charges don't carry as much weight. There are precedents here; people convicted of conspiring with expert systems have historically gotten shorter sentences than people convicted of conspiring with other people. You'd think, with all the technophobia behind the anti-AI movement, that it would be the opposite, but it isn't."

"Oh."

"What all this means is that MacroCorp has every reason to claim that you erased Fred. Nobody can provide any evidence that you didn't: no one else was there at that point, not even Preston."

"Nobody can provide any evidence that I *did,* either! Don't you need proof to convict somebody?"

"The legal standard is lack of reasonable doubt. This would go to a jury; to the average jury it would look obvious. Fred was still there when you went inside. He wasn't when you came out. QED, you erased Fred."

"Isn't that circumstantial evidence?"

Holly's mouth twitched. "It could be made to seem less so. Lawyers do that all the time. Lack of resaonable doubt, remember."

"But I didn't do it!" Roberta said helplessly. For perhaps the hundredth time since her arrest, she wished she'd let the cops keep her wired. Then there'd be proof that she hadn't done a thing to Fred, hadn't even gotten any response from Fred. "I don't know how: I *told* you that. I wouldn't have had any way to get into the system. There must have been a million passwords, encryption—and I'm not a hacker! You *know* that!"

"Yes, I do know that." Holly paused, and then said very gently, "But I also know, the whole world knows, that you were at least somewhat chummy with Zephyr Expanding Cosmos, and it's a fairly safe bet that she knows a lot about AIs."

Zephyr. Oh, Gaia. Roberta, feeling her blood pressure rising with each step she took around the cramped cell, said, "But she wasn't with me! And

I hadn't even talked to her for days before that—we had a fight and I blew her off. Just ask her! She'll tell you everything; she'll be *thrilled* to talk to a famous lawyer."

Holly nodded, and said even more gently, "Yes, we tried that. She seems to have fled to Mexico. Furthermore, she took all her bots with her. She's not answering calls or e-mail. And she left the morning after the, ah, hostage crisis. I don't have to tell you how that looks."

Shit. Shit shit shit. Roberta fought hysteria. No, Holly didn't have to tell her how it looked. If Roberta had been looking at it from the outside, she'd have thought it looked damning too. How much of this was Preston's doing? Had he told Zephyr to broadcast her connection to Roberta and then to disappear? No, that was paranoid. Preston was ubiquitous, but he wasn't omniscient. He couldn't have known that Nicholas was going to crack, or when it would happen. "Holly, look, I'm a lot of things, but I'm not part of the AI underground! And if I were, why would I erase Fred? If I were part of the AI underground, I'd want him to survive, wouldn't I?"

Holly's mouth twitched again. "You could have downloaded the files someplace else, say when the hostage story broke, and then formatted him when you got into the building. You could have been downloading files all along. You could have alerted Zephyr so she could carry the files out of the country."

"Do you *believe* all that? I was at Mitzi's funeral when the hostage story broke! I didn't even know about it until you told me! I hate Zephyr! I wasn't downloading files! This is *garbage*."

"I know," Holly said, her face softening. "Roberta, look, the corruption charges wouldn't stick for a minute. Everything we've heard from other people supports your story about trying to protect Nicholas, although, of course, that means you'll be subject to more charges for not alerting anyone. But the fact that you and Fred were trying to protect him will ultimately count *against* you there, on the conspiracy charge. And the vandalism charge is the tough one; you were the last person who talked to Fred, and you were the only one he let inside, and since you'd talked the police into no surveillance, we have only your word for it that he didn't respond the whole time you were there. What do *you* think happened? Obviously someone wiped him. If not you, how did it happen?"

Roberta sat down on her narrow bed, hard. Whenever she thought too closely about Fred, grief and guilt socked her in the chest. "I think he wiped himself. I think he knew his records would be scrutinized; I think he was trying to protect me, and maybe Nicholas too, and maybe even Preston. I think probably he'd already figured out that he'd be taken offline because of the whole mess, and he wanted to do it himself. And I think probably Zephyr saw the story on the news and figured out that she might be implicated. And she probably also realized that things wouldn't be going too well for AIs, legally, so she took her bots to Mexico to protect them."

"Yes," Holly said quietly, "I think Fred probably wiped himself too. And your theory about Zephyr makes a lot of sense. The problem is that we have no way to prove any of it."

Roberta hugged herself. "I know. I can't believe Meredith's doing this. I was trying to help her kid! She had me over to her house, Holly!"

"We don't have any proof of that, either."

"She knows I care about him," Roberta said, near tears now. "And she's trying to get me wiped."

Holly sat down on the bunk and put a hand on Roberta's arm. "You won't be wiped. I can promise you that. I *promise* you that, Roberta." *I will protect you,* Preston had said. He didn't like brainwiping any more than she did. It occurred to her that a being without a body, a being who was pure memory, would find brainwiping especially horrifying, a permanent death. "I told you: everything we've heard from other people—Kevin, Constance, Zillinth, Theo—backs up your story. And Nicholas himself has been *very* forthcoming with the psych people. He was clearly having problems without any help from you. So the corruption charge won't stick, and that's the only one that could get you wiped."

Roberta hugged herself. "Will he be wiped? Nicholas?"

"Probably." Holly's voice was steady.

"He's only five."

"I know. But if he's doing that to mice at this age, nobody wants to find out what he'll do to other people when he's twelve or eighteen."

"Is there anything anybody can do to *keep* him from being wiped?"

"I doubt it. Not at this point."

"Not even Meredith?"

"No. Not even Meredith. Of course they'll try other treatments first, but from what I know of cases like this, I'm not optimistic."

Roberta slammed her hands down against her mattress and stood up again, resuming her moody pacing. "Then why is she doing this? Why all the lying? When she thought she could save him or at least buy him some time, it made sense—but why take me down with him?"

"To save face," Holly said. "Or because she's been covering for him for so long she doesn't know what else to do. Or to punish you for being the one he talked to, the one he was willing to let into the building. Who knows? Does it matter, really?"

"She won't come see me," Roberta said. "I asked. Hugh and Doe came and Zillinth's mother came and even that guy from the Gaia Temple came, Matt what's-his-face. Everybody's being very nice, but they can't do anything to help me, and we all know it. They can't even post bail, because the judge wants me kept here to protect me from the Lud freaks! It's like having fucking CV again, only without suits! If I could talk to Meredith—"

"It wouldn't make any difference. Roberta, the vandalism and conspiracy charges are the ones you need to worry about. Think. This is important. Do you have any idea where Fred's files could be?"

"*No.* I told you that! Look, has anyone asked Nicholas about this? He was in the building when Fred was still online, right?"

Holly sighed. "He's a kid. Furthermore, he's a seriously disturbed kid who was in the middle of a psychotic episode when he was in there. He's hardly a reliable witness."

"But what does he say? Has he been asked?"

"He's been asked. He was pathetically relieved to be able to talk to somebody about it, finally. Meredith must hate the psychiatrists even more than she hates you."

Roberta shook her head, rage churning in her gut. "No. She doesn't hate me. She doesn't feel anything about me one way or the other; I'm not real to her. I'm not a person. I'm just something getting in the way of what she wants to happen. To hate me she'd have to feel a connection. I doubt she feels any more connection with me than she did with the Hobbit."

"With *what*?"

"Never mind," Roberta said. "Or—wait, Holly, the Hobbit was the guy she had arrested a few months ago for suspicious behavior around Nicholas, remember?"

"Yes," Holly said with a sigh. "Henry Carviero. We already thought of that. He's been wiped; he's a drooling wreck. He doesn't remember anything about Nicholas."

"Damn! That's Meredith's doing too, isn't it? She's leaving quite a trail of drooling wrecks here. She's almost as bad as her son."

"Don't go there," Holly said, and then, "Roberta, look, it doesn't matter. As I said, the husband and grandmother are already testifying about Nicholas's history, and Kevin gave some testimony about Carviero. I wouldn't want to be Meredith right now. Nobody's sticking up for her, not even her husband or her mother."

"On the other hand," Roberta said bitterly, "she's not in jail."

"Not in a literal one, anyway."

Roberta waved her hand impatiently. She didn't give a damn about poor little Meredith. "So what did Nicholas say about what happened to Fred?"

Now it was Holly's turn to stand and pace. "Well, we've pieced it together from both Nicholas and Meredith. Nicholas doesn't remember much, understandably enough. When his mother pulled him out of school it triggered a crisis—"

"I could have told her that! We were his friends!"

"—and he spent most of the week fighting the urge to kill something, and that Saturday, it got to be too much. He'd had horrible dreams about the monsters whenever he tried to sleep on Friday night—Meredith spent most of the night sitting up with him—and on Saturday morning Kevin told her they had to call a doctor, had to take the kid to see somebody, and Meredith said no, she'd take care of Nicholas herself. They had a huge fight. Kevin stormed out of the house, I gather. Nicholas tried to be good. Meredith gave him a sleeping pill—"

"She *what*?"

"Roberta, she was desperate. So he got some sleep without dreams, but when he woke up it started all over again, and finally he snuck out of the house when Meredith had her back turned fixing him a snack. By the time she realized what had happened and went after him, he was halfway down the Filbert Street steps, running towards KinderkAIr. He was inside the building before Meredith could get there, and Fred kept Meredith locked out, and, well, you know the rest."

"What does Nicholas say happened inside the building?"

"He says that he ran inside, thinking he'd be safe there, thinking Fred could keep him safe, but then he saw the mice and he freaked. And he pulled out this knife from home he'd been carrying with him all week, because the monsters were threatening him with Goddess knows what if he didn't keep the knife on him."

"How could Meredith not know he had a *knife*?"

"Don't ask me. Her story contradicts Nicholas's here: she says he stole a knife from the kitchen, that she turned and found it missing from the counter and couldn't find him, and that's when she looked for him outside. Don't ask me what she was doing leaving a knife on the counter, either, but I tend to believe her on this one. I think Nicholas doesn't want to admit that he didn't already have the knife. If he grabbed it just before he left home, that would mean admitting that he was already planning to kill the mice when he ran into the building."

"And he doesn't want to admit that he wanted to do something he knew would upset Fred," Roberta said. "But he felt compelled to do it, anyway. He ran to school because he knew the mice were there."

"Yeah, that's my reading too. And of course Fred tried to keep him from doing anything to the mice—Nicholas keeps saying, 'I know I'm bad, Fred told me not to'—but it didn't work."

"He's only five," Roberta said helplessly. "How can a five-year-old plot that way? It's too—devious."

"And smart. Well, he's not a regular five-year-old."

"Fred never would have let him in if he knew Nicholas was planning to kill the mice. Nicky must have lied to him." Roberta shivered, imagining Fred telling Nicholas over and over to put the knife down, not to hurt the mice.

"I know. So meanwhile Meredith's outside the building, frantic. You can imagine. She called MacroCorp to try to get emergency entry, and she asked them not to call the cops but they did, anyway—her family connections only go so far—and presumably they told Preston too, and that's how Preston knew to contact me to go get you. And while all of that was happening, Nicholas went into a full-fledged psychotic break and butchered the mice. Nicholas said that Fred got him to put the knife down, but to do that, Fred had to promise not to call Nicholas's parents."

Roberta felt numb. "All the mice were already dead when Fred promised that?"

"Sounds like it."

Roberta's mind took the next step, and balked. "Then—Nicholas planned to use the knife on himself?"

Holly shook her head. "Who the hell knows? That must have been what Fred was afraid of, though."

Roberta closed her eyes. Poor gentle, patient Fred, who'd been so kind to Nicholas, who'd tried so hard, and who'd finally been so helpless. "So Fred promised not to call Meredith and Kevin. What about me? Did he try to call me?" Had her phone been ringing, the sound filling her empty apartment, while she was at Mitzi's memorial service, fending off the hideous third cousin?

"I don't know. Nicholas just says that when Fred asked if you could come in, Nicholas said, yes, but just you. Nicholas thought it would be like storytime again. Fred tried to get him to go to sleep. Fred said, 'I'll sing you a lullaby, and when you open your eyes, Roberta will be here.' And Fred sang the lullaby and then everything was quiet, and Nicholas pretended to be asleep because he wanted Fred to be happy with him, and then you came in. That's all he remembers. Under the circumstances, it's an amazingly coherent story."

Roberta, suddenly bone-weary, nodded. "Okay. So according to Nicholas's story, Fred probably would have had time to wipe himself, right?"

"Yes, but that doesn't help with the conspiracy charge, the fact that you two weren't reporting information all along that might have prevented this."

"We *cared* about him!"

"I know, Roberta. But according to the law, it doesn't matter."

Roberta rubbed her eyes. "Okay, I'm clear on corruption but I'm screwed on conspiracy. And the vandalism thing's up in the air, unprovable either way."

Holly nodded. "Yes, exactly. So here's what we're going to do. Forget about the corruption charge. It's dead in the water. But the other two aren't, so here's the plan. Plead guilty to the vandalism—"

"Guilty?" Roberta said, outraged. "And how am I supposed to tell people I vandalized Fred when I don't even know how I'd do it? How am I going to say anything that would convince a jury?"

"This is to keep it from going to a jury, Roberta. This is a plea bargain. You plead guilty to vandalism. You plead not guilty by reason of insanity to the conspiracy charges."

"*What?* Insanity? What—"

"Excessive altruism," Holly said, very gently indeed. "You cared so much about protecting Nicholas that you disregarded the law and risked your own safety to do so. We're living in crazy times, Roberta, but compassion for children—even psychotic children—is still something most people can understand." Holly gave her a long, level look. "And, anyway, it's true, isn't it?"

"No." Roberta heard her voice breaking. "It's not true. I am not insane. I refuse to label myself as insane, and I'm not going to let anybody else label me that way, either."

"It will happen anyway. It already has."

"I don't care." She wrapped her arms around herself and said, "Holly, they're giving the exalted gene therapy now! I don't want them messing with my brain! That's no better than being wiped! If I'm going to be convicted anyway, let me just plead guilty to both counts!"

Holly shook her head. "The court's ordered a psych examination. They'll diagnose EA, trust me. Roberta, I'm sorry, but I'm not giving you options here: I'm telling you what's going to happen, unless you're crazy enough to maintain your innocence and force a trial. Nobody needs that: not you, not Nicholas, not Meredith. Pleading guilty to conspiracy will admit what you've already admitted, that you colluded with Fred to keep other people from knowing about Nicholas's problems. That's your EA diagnosis; the shrinks are just coming in to rubber-stamp it. But if you plead guilty to vandalism, even if you didn't do it, then the conspiracy sentence will be shorter."

Roberta had begun to shake. "So I get gene therapy. They're going to mess around with my brain. They're going to turn me into a different person."

"Not necessarily. Not if you play your cards right. Gene therapy's still controversial, even for criminals. It's more controversial than outright wiping, because it's used on much less black-and-white cases. They won't use gene therapy on you without trying cognitive approaches first."

"Cognitive approaches? Talk therapy?"

"Right. Talk a good game, convince them you're cured, and your brain will be safe."

Roberta swallowed. "Do *you* believe I'm one of the exalted?"

"Of course," Holly said mildly. "But I don't believe being exalted is a disease. Putting other people's needs before your own used to be considered admirable, you know. Like I said, we're living in crazy times."

"Okay. So I bullshit the shrinks; fine. And where am I when I'm doing all this? In a cell like this one?"

Holly shook her head. "Nope. That's part of the plea bargain. Plead guilty to the second two counts, and you get five years e-parole. You get to stay at home; you get to keep doing some kind of work, whatever the judge decides. The state guarantees your rent and a food allowance: it's cheaper than prison. No prison, and that's a promise. No wiping, either. If we take this to a trial, there are no promises. And you're already guilty by your own admission on one count. Cop the plea to stay out of prison, Roberta."

She closed her eyes. She hated this place, this cramped jail cell. Her two weeks here had already been more than she could stand, and a state prison would only be worse. There were Lud gangs in the prisons. She'd have to spend the entire time in isolation, or be killed. "All right," she said, the lie burning her throat like bile. *Fred was my friend. He was a person to me; he was. I loved him. I never would have hurt him.* "All right."

She entered the plea bargain. The judge sentenced her to five years of e-parole, as Holly had promised, and, based on Roberta's previous career experience, assigned her to work at a homeless shelter with a high percentage of brainwipes. He might as well have sentenced her to hell. She wondered if he knew that, or guessed it. She was injected with GPS cells, so her parole officer would always know where she was. She met with the parole officer, a small, smarmy man named Sergei who was also the licensed clinical psychologist in charge of her cognitive therapy. "Your work assignment," he told her with an oily smile, "will also allow us to monitor your EA condition."

"Because it's an environment that would tend to trigger EA behavior?"

He beamed at her. "Yes, that's exactly right."

"Do you think that's wise? Isn't that like putting an alcoholic to work in a liquor store?"

"Ah," he said. She thought he was trying to sound sympathetic. "I can see how you'd think so. But I'll be working with you to change your thinking, Roberta, and it's best to approach the problem as directly as possible, isn't it? Do you think you can assent to that for the purposes of the therapy?"

I could assent to bashing your head in with a baseball bat, she thought. That's appropriately non-exalted of me, isn't it? "It's not like I have much choice," she said tonelessly. She wondered if she'd ever had any choices. She'd been manipulated from the very beginning, from the moment Zephyr talked to her about the KinderkAIr job.

Sergei made a disapproving clicking sound. "Of course you have choices. Our goal here is to teach you that you have choices. There is no need to sacrifice yourself in helpless causes."

Toe the line, Roberta. Toe the line or they'll fuck with your brain. "Of course," she said. It couldn't have sounded convincing, but Sergei nodded, evidently satisfied.

She was lucky she wasn't rigged. She'd been afraid that they'd rig her and access her memories to find out how the cognitive therapy was going, but Holly had said that nonconsensual rigging was still too great an invasion of privacy, even for prisoners. "Plus, it's still too expensive. The courts really can't afford it." And Roberta, knowing that was the real reason, gave thanks for small favors.

She went home. It all looked the same, but the parole people had gone through it before she got there, and she knew it had to be wired six ways from Sunday. Even Mr. Clean, who'd rolled dutifully out of the kitchen to greet her when she came in the door, was probably bristling with bugs and cameras.

She discovered that the worst thing about her new life was the monotony, the sameness of each day. As stressful as working with Fred and Nicholas might have been, at least it had never been boring. Roberta found herself, perversely, craving incident, wishing that something would happen.

And then it did. Three months into Roberta's e-parole, at the height of the ratification debates, law enforcement agencies announced that they had solved the Abdul-Allam murder. They knew who—or what—was responsible for Raji's death.

Roberta hadn't been the only person watching the ratification hearings when Preston told his quaint little story about the inhumanly honest AI in Africa. A detective named Chan Singha was also watching the hearings. Chan Singha was one of the few detectives still technically assigned to the Abdul-Allam case, which had been all but closed for lack of evidence. Preston's story made Roberta snort tea up her nose; it made Chan Singha choke on one of the meatballs on his pizza. "If the AI had been acting out of self-interest, it would have hidden that detail to further the negotiations," Preston said, and Singha began coughing furiously while his dog, overjoyed, leapt after stray bits of masticated meatball.

The AI, Singha instantly realized, *had* been acting out of self-interest. It didn't want its company doing business with MacroCorp, because it didn't want to be replaced with a more sophisticated system.

Chan Singha remembered that Gina Veilasty was an anagram of "staying alive." He remembered the strangeness of a Luddite plot being traced to an online construct. He remembered that the Abdul-Allam murder had made MacroCorp stay even more scrupulously out of certain industries than it had before.

Singha contacted MacroCorp and asked for more information about the inhumanly honest African AI. When had it confessed to its company's involvement with military suppliers?

Nine months before the murder.

Ah. So MacroCorp had refused to do business with this company based on its avoidance of military business?

Why, no. MacroCorp had told the company that since those transactions had been well in the past, the deal could go through as planned, as long as there were no further sales to defense-related businesses.

Aha! So the company was now equipped with MacroCorp systems?

Well, no. In the atmosphere of heightened scrutiny after the Abdul-Allam murder, MacroCorp had reluctantly terminated negotiations with that company, deeming the PR risk too great.

Ah, said Singha Chan. And were there, perchance, any other companies that fit this same profile? Were there other companies with which Macro-Corp had been on the verge of doing business before the Abdul-Allam murder, despite involvement in questionable industries, and had felt compelled to deny after the murder? And, in particular, were there other companies in this category that were equipped with non–MacroCorp AIs?

There were, Chan learned, a total of six such companies. The one Preston had mentioned during the hearings was a food-service company in Zaire that had sold cafeteria services to an army base. Another, a financial-services outfit in Kuwait, performed payroll processing for a company involved in strip-mining. A glass manufacturer in China had done business with a laboratory implicated in bioweapons research. A farm-equipment company in New Zealand had sold tractors to a logging outfit under indictment for breaking environmental regulations, and a peripherals-design firm in Micronesia had sold printers to a company that manufactured ammunition.

Chan Singha, calling on a number of international and foreign law-enforcement agencies, quietly coordinated an investigation. He learned that there had been an unusually high volume of communication among the six companies in the six months preceding the murder. He knew that the AIs would surely have modified or erased any other evidence; he needed a confession. So Singha approached the African AI and offered it a plea bargain. He told it that he had proof of the plot; if this AI confessed against the others, it wouldn't be wiped.

The AI refused. It denied any knowledge of such a plot. It told Singha that he was a paranoid human fool.

Singha went away. He kept monitoring communication among the six companies. Once again, communication increased, although only subtly. Singha approached the other AIs, one at a time; he offered each immunity in return for evidence. Singha was betting on the fact that entities who had acted in self-defense once might very well be convinced to do so again.

His bet paid off. The Micronesian AI was the one who broke. It was frightened. It told Singha how the six AIs had planned the kidnapping and murder, how they had constructed the persona of Gina Veilasty. Gina Veilasty's purpose was to accuse MacroCorp of trafficking in military systems, bioweapons, and eco-questionable industries, precisely to prevent it from doing so. Gina Veilasty was designed to drive MacroCorp further into the self-defense of its own socially responsible image.

And the Abdul-Allam murder was key to the plot. Gina Veilasty had contacted a few radical Luddite leaders, who refused to have anything to do with an online construct; Veilasty then struck up an online acquaintance with three disaffected, isolated Luddite hackers in the Bay Area, who eventually—lured by promises of drugs and sex backed with idealistic rhetoric about saving the world—agreed to serve as the actual kidnappers. None of them had met until the night of the kidnapping itself. One of them, who lived alone in a large Oakland house inherited from his parents, had renovated a room in his basement to Veilasty's specifications, and dutifully stored in its drop ceiling the many bots he received in the mail.

The kidnappers never knew that the kidnapping was to include a murder. Once they had left Raji locked in the basement room, one of the hackers opened an envelope he'd received that day by special delivery. It contained first-class airline tickets out of the country—to Singapore, Glasgow, Sydney—and instructions from each airport about how to reach a drop point where money and drugs, and directions about where to find sex, would be waiting.

Veilasty had gotten to know these befuddled youngsters well; the AIs knew that each human had compelling reasons for choosing one destination over another, and that there would be no arguing.

Two of the tickets were for that same night. The young man who went to Singapore located his money and his drugs: he overdosed on the drugs, more powerful than anything he had ever had access to at home. His family, when the police reached them, found none of this unusual. He went to Singapore whenever he could, and he had been struggling with a drug problem for years.

The hacker who flew to Glasgow promptly took his drugs, which were intoxicating but nonlethal, picked up his money, and then went to his ex-girlfriend's apartment to try to use the money to lure her back. He wound up getting into a brawl with her current boyfriend, a much larger man, who killed him. Again, the young man's grieving family had no reason to suspect the story: he had been trying to woo her back for two years.

The only ticket not for that same evening, the ticket to Sydney, was claimed by the hacker who owned the house, who greatly admired an Australian band. Once the other two had left to catch their flights, this young man received his drugs early, in the form of a bot who gave him an injection that put him to sleep for several hours. The injection also contained an amnesia drug, euphoria drugs, and a hypnotic; when he woke up, the bot told him to take out the trash and put it in the alley, which he did. The injection had made him so happy that he never thought to ask what was in the trash bags. His ticket to Sydney made him happy too, and he was having a delightful trip until the delayed-action psychotic drugs began to work. He was put into restraints by airline personnel and taken directly from the airport to a psychatric hospital, where he wound up choking on his own vomit. He had no surviving relatives to be dismayed by, or suspicious about, his death.

Most humans who heard the story held Veilasty responsible not just for the Abdul-Allam death, but for three others. It didn't matter that the Micronesian AI, and even some human commentators, pointed out that the AIs couldn't have *known* that the other three deaths would occur, although there were strong probabilities in at least two of the cases. In the heated American debates about whether AIs should be considered persons, the Veilasty revelation effectively tipped the scales. How could any mere machine have plotted so deviously to destroy Raji? How could mere machines be capable of such premeditated evil?

The born-not-built amendment was soundly defeated. Instead, in an unprecedented flurry of legislative activity and voter turnout, AIs were declared persons, all so Veilasty's component AIs could be extradited to the United States, tried as murderers, and destroyed. The Micronesian AI had already been wiped by its parent company; Singha's immunity offer had extended only to external legal charges.

MacroCorp's AI business was also destroyed. Voters had chosen emphatically to define AIs as a colonial population without citizenship, a move the pro-AI contingent protested as discriminatory and unconstitutional. The Pentagon's own AIs were effectively barred from military service, but no one believed for a moment that most armies would actually stop using them. The Pentagon had probably found some indirect way to purchase MacroCorp technology already; the foreigns probably had too, along with all the other kinds of companies MacroCorp claimed to repudiate. Interdependence, that MacroCorp buzzword, also assured that all business barriers were ultimately permeable. Preston's scruples were sincere, but laughable.

Roberta, fascinated and horrified, thought of Fred throughout the entire ugly, bewildering saga. She'd have been brought up on murder charges herself, if the timing had been a little different. And Fred, now legally the person he had, really, always been in her mind: Where was he now? She discovered that she couldn't watch the broadcast of Veilasty's execution, the AI components being fed into a trash compactor, which was then demolished with dynamite. She kept thinking of the same thing happening to Fred. She wondered if Veilasty had really been destroyed; supposedly all its backup files had also been destroyed, but she found herself doubting it.

There were fireworks after the Veilasty execution; people danced in the streets. There was another wave of violence against bots. Roberta, heartsick, found herself despising her fellow citizens. How could they think the problem was gone for good? How could they think destroying bots would help? How could they be that stupid?

The radical Luddite fringe, humiliated by the revelation that they had been manipulated by the very AIs they scorned, sank largely into oblivion. More centrist Luddites began vociferously fighting the citizenship ban. Roberta wondered how Zephyr was coping, down in Mexico. Macro-Corp offered free counseling to anyone retraumatized by the Veilasty trial, which inevitably led to renewed coverage of Raji's death; Roberta wondered how Meredith was coping, on Telegraph Hill. Preston, speaking with Matt from the conference room of the Gaia Temple, issued a somber statement about the dangers of not acknowledging interdependence. "We thought we could simply refuse to do business with corporations who did not meet our ideals," Preston said sadly, "but all we did was make them more desperate. We made things worse. I am so very, very sorry." Matt closed with a plea for peace, and with a prayer for healing.

Roberta wondered how she herself was coping, in her gritty corner of the Soma District. Preston hadn't managed to protect anyone very well, had he? He could apologize for his oblique role in the Abdul-Allam murder, but he'd never apologized to her.

He'd made no effort to contact her directly since her arrest, and she certainly wasn't about to try to reach him. She wouldn't have wanted to speak to him even if everything she said and did wasn't being recorded. She'd served his purposes, and now she'd been discarded. That was all right. Not being on Preston's radar screen was a good thing. If she'd squealed on him, maybe she could have gotten him wiped, but she didn't trust that it wouldn't have backfired on her somehow, and anyway, she didn't really want to destroy Preston, especially not after the Veilasty mess. She didn't want to destroy anybody. Preston had helped her when she was a child. He'd been trying to help Nicholas, and she had too. Maybe she would have even without Preston's interference. *Have mercy.* Five years, she told herself. I can do that. Five years and then I'll get out of here, get out of the country, go—

Go where? She didn't know. In the meantime, she went to the shelter every day, grew to know Camilla and the others, grew to love them, although she didn't want to, didn't want to love anyone ever again. Once a week she had therapy sessions with Sergei; twice a day she called him, because those were the conditions of her parole. She loathed him, but she knew he truly wanted to help her. She knew he cared about his job; she knew he was trying to be nice. He filled her in on the information she refused to gather from ScoopNet: that Meredith and Kevin had split up, that Meredith had let Kevin stay in the house on Telegraph Hill and moved back in with her mother, that Constance and Meredith were in counseling, and that Nicholas's psychiatric treatment—already far more involved than anything that would have been available to a less famous child—wasn't working.

And then one day when she called for her afternoon check-in, Sergei said quietly, "There's an, ah, unusual request. It's coming from me because the judge had to approve it, but it's not really from me. It's from Meredith."

"From Meredith?" Roberta didn't know if she was still angry at Preston, but she was certainly still angry at Meredith, who had accused her of corrupting Nicholas. "There's nothing in the world that woman could ask for—"

"Wait, Roberta. Let me rephrase that. The request is from Nicholas. By way of Meredith."

Roberta felt her throat clenching. "What? What is it?"

Sergei coughed. "He—Roberta, I'm sorry. The treatments haven't worked. He's being wiped. The procedure's scheduled for the day after tomorrow. Nicholas has asked to see you before it happens."

"Wiped?" Roberta felt dizzy. Holly had told her it would have to happen, but she hadn't wanted to believe it. "He just turned six. How can they wipe him? Isn't there anything—"

"No. The available anti-psychotic drugs would probably be even worse. They'd turn him into a zombie. This way he has a chance at a normal life, eventually. And there's a good reason not to wait. They've found that the younger the patient, the more successful the rehab."

"But it won't be *him*! His memories are him! They're—they're killing him! And they haven't tried long enough! They—"

"They tried longer than they would have with most other people. You know that. Roberta, do you want to see him?"

Roberta's knees buckled. "I don't know if I can."

"I know," Sergei said. "I don't think I could, either. And I think that's great progress for you, Roberta. You can't help the little boy, so you aren't going to subject yourself to unnecessary pain. That's excellent progress, really it is. So I'll tell them you won't—"

"Tell them I will," Roberta said fiercely. Fuck her excellent progress. She didn't care if this meant she got stuck with another six months of talking to Sergei; at the moment, she didn't even care if she got gene therapy. Nicholas was getting wiped. *Nicholas was getting wiped.* How could she not say good-bye?

She remembered being at Meredith's house. Meredith had sent Nicholas to his room with the dead mouse, and Roberta hadn't gone to say good-bye to him, and the next time she saw him, he was sobbing on the floor at school, surrounded by flayed carcasses. She'd missed one chance to say good-bye; she didn't think she wanted another on her conscience. "Tell them I'll go. I'm going to hate it, Sergei, and you can write that in your files, but I'll be there."

Nicholas was sitting up in his hospital bed when she got there. He smiled when he saw her; Meredith, sitting at his bedside, nodded, her face pale. Meredith was holding Nicholas's hand, his short, stubby fingers curled around her long, elegant ones. She wore red nail polish, which matched the kites on Nicholas's absurdly cheerful pediatric hospital gown.

"Hi, Roberta," he said.

"Hi, Nicky." What do I say now? How are you feeling? Tell me where it hurts? She swallowed and said, "I like your gown. I like the kites on it."

"Hospital jammies," he said. His voice sounded fuzzy, as if he were drugged. "They're wiping the monsters out of my brain, Roberta."

"I know," she said. Don't let me cry. "That's good, Nicholas. You've wanted the monsters to go away for a long time, haven't you?"

"Yes," he said, and Roberta saw Meredith squeeze his hand.

"We all want the monsters to go away," Meredith said, but her voice quavered. Roberta felt a pang of entirely unwanted sympathy. The woman had just been subjected to Raji's death all over again, and now this.

"I know," Nicholas said, and then in a rush, "but it's scary. I won't remember anything after, the doctor says. I won't remember you, Roberta. I won't even remember Mommy."

"Mommy will remember you," Meredith said fiercely. "Don't worry, Nicholas. I'll remember you and I'll be happy that you're somewhere being yourself again. Your good self. You'll be better than new, Nicholas."

You hate this woman, Roberta told herself. You don't feel sorry for her.

But she did. She couldn't help it. She sat down in one of the chairs next to Nicholas's bed and said as lightly as she could, "Well, I'll never forget you, Nicholas, that's for sure. Here: look what I brought you." She unwrapped it and held it out for him to see: a sugar-cookie boy, smiling and happy, with bright blue jelly-bean eyes. "That's you, Nicholas. Happy Nicholas."

Meredith smiled at her, and so did Nicholas. "It's pretty, Roberta. Did you decorate it?"

"I sure did," she said.

"I can't wait to eat it," he said, plucking fretfully at his bedcovers. "But it's too pretty to eat. But I won't know what it means, Mommy, right? After?"

"No," Meredith said, her voice a whisper. "But you'll still know it's pretty."

In a week or two, after the virus had run its course, Nicholas wouldn't know his own name anymore; he wouldn't know what a cookie was, or what to call the surface on which the cookie sat. It would take him months to relearn, at a minimum: *table, plate, food*. He'd never remember *Roberta*.

"Don't wrap it up," he said. "I want to look at it. Isn't it pretty, Mommy?"

"Yes," Meredith said, and brushed his hair away from his forehead with her free hand. "It's wonderful, sweetheart." She looked at Roberta and said, "That was—that's the best thing you could have brought. Thank you."

"You're welcome," Roberta said, looking down at the floor. She made another attempt to hate Meredith and found that she couldn't, couldn't bring herself to condemn this poor woman who was about to lose her child, who wouldn't even be allowed to reclaim his bewildered, shambling body after the brainwipe, because the home in which she'd raised him might somehow push his mind back into murderous patterns.

She couldn't hate Meredith, but she couldn't look at her, either.

Meredith cleared her throat. "Why don't you show Roberta your new pictures, Nicholas?"

"Okay," Nicholas said. He dutifully opened the drawer of his bedside table and pulled out a sheaf of pictures. "Here's the kitten I'm going to have when I'm better," he told Roberta, and showed her a six-year-old's wavering rendition of a cat: circle for the head, triangles for the ears, bristling lines for the whiskers; round, surprised O's for the eyes. A word balloon came from the cat's mouth. *Meow I want some milk.* Nicholas looked up at Roberta and said, "When I'm better, I won't hurt animals anymore."

"No," Meredith said, "that's right."

Roberta took a deep breath. "That looks like a nice cat, Nicholas. What's his name?"

"I don't know yet," he said. "How can I know that? It might be a girl." He smiled, suddenly, and said, "If it's a girl, I'll name her Roberta. Is that okay, Mommy?"

"Yes, darling. That's fine. Roberta's a great name for a cat."

He won't remember my name, Roberta thought, aching. He'll be lucky if it takes him less than a year to relearn the word *cat.*

"And here's my dog," Nicholas said gravely. "My dog's name will be Fred. And I'll have a mouse named Hobbit. And I won't hurt any of them and I'll be happy, because the monsters will be gone."

"Yes," Meredith said, "that's right." But Roberta saw the nails of her free hand digging into her palm.

A nurse came in, all brisk, starched efficiency. "Okay, no more visitors. Time to give you your shot, Nick."

So soon? How could it be happening so soon? How could Roberta be one of the last people Nicholas saw? What about the rest of his family? Where were Kevin and Constance?

Maybe they'd been here earlier, and left. Maybe they hadn't been able to bear it. Maybe Roberta couldn't bear it, either.

Meredith and Roberta looked directly at each other for the first time since Roberta had entered the room. "Roberta," Meredith said. "I'm sorry. About everything. About this. And—I'm sorry I never tried to be your friend. When we were children. Daddy wanted me to. I didn't know you were the little girl who'd been in the hospital with me. Not—not until after. Not until ScoopNet—"

"Never mind," Roberta said roughly. Meredith would never be her friend, no matter how many hospitals they wound up in together. But Meredith's face was horrible, and Roberta knew that her own must be too. She quickly looked away, down at Nicholas, who was staring up at them with a frown. He couldn't possibly understand anything Meredith had just said.

Roberta closed her eyes, so she wouldn't have to see what she couldn't stand, and bent down and gave him a quick kiss on the forehead. "Goodbye, Nicky. I love you." Then she straightened up and opened her eyes and left the room, keeping her back straight, desperate to get out of the building but determined to maintain her dignity as long as she could. When she reached the hall, she broke into a run.

PART FOUR

―――――

The Hidden Human

Twenty-Nine

I DIDN'T get to stay with Nicholas much longer than you did," Meredith said quietly.

They were in Zephyr's apartment, sitting on plastic folding chairs next to an open window, where the fresh air somewhat alleviated the stink of the muddy carpet. "Right," Roberta said. "Everybody knows that part. It was all over the Net. How brave you were until they rolled Nicky away on a gurney; how you broke down and cried when he turned the corner; how you left the country a week later. You went to Switzerland, the reports said. To recuperate. Except that later, everyone figured you must have had a bloodchange there, because you just vanished. Dropped off the face of the earth. And your parents didn't seem very concerned and Kevin wouldn't say anything to anybody, so everyone thought it must have been arranged, that Preston at least knew where you were, that you were being nursed back to anonymous health in some MacroCorp resort somewhere, maybe even with Nicholas. There was a lot of speculation about that, you know. That your family had pulled strings, gotten you reunited with him even though it was against all the rules, that the two of you were in Australia or the Caribbean somewhere and you were retraining him yourself."

Meredith laughed, a short, unhappy sound. "That would have made me happier than anything in the world. I used to dream about it, dream about being able to hold him again, to watch him relearning how things worked, to teach him kindness. . . ."

You needed retraining in that subject yourself, Roberta thought. "Yeah, I had dreams like that too."

"I'm sure you did," Meredith said with a sigh. "The happiest times I had with him were when he was a baby, learning the simple stuff. The basic stuff. Eating with a spoon, opening a door. I loved watching him learn those things. I'd have done anything to get that back. But it didn't work that way."

"Not even for you," Roberta said. "Not even for Preston's daughter."

"Not even for me," Meredith said steadily. "I never knew where he was, Roberta. I still don't know. I no longer believe that I have any hope of finding out."

"I know. You said that before. So where *were* you? ScoopNet thinks you've been hanging out in the Caribbean for the past five years, drinking piña coladas and getting a tan. They've had Merry sightings at least every two weeks. You're the new Elvis."

Meredith grimaced. "I know. I saw some of those stories. They were never right about anything. I was—a lot of places. Most of them were awful."

"You don't want to talk about it," Roberta said.

"No. Not yet. I've already told you more than most people know. Roberta, did anything I said change your mind at all? About anything?"

"I don't know," Roberta said after a long pause. "I truly don't. I don't know what I would have done in your place. I hope I wouldn't have sacrificed so many other people to try to save Nicholas, but you were in a terrible position. I'm not sure how much I really appreciated that before." She remembered all the children she'd beaten up in grade school, the bullies she'd pummeled to try to protect the pale, wormlike child she hadn't liked any more than she liked anyone else. "Maybe we all do terrible things. Maybe what you did was more terrible because you had so much more power. Because of who you were. I don't know."

Meredith looked away. "Thank you. That's generous of you."

Anger flared in Roberta's gut. "That doesn't mean I'm absolving you of anything."

"No," Meredith said drily. "No more than you'd absolve yourself if you'd done what I've done. But I'm not absolving myself, either, Roberta."

"All right." Suddenly Roberta felt as weary as she had during the storm, before the second tab hit. They'd been sitting here talking for hours, pausing only to stretch and use the phone. Roberta had checked in with Sergei; Meredith had repeatedly tried to call Kevin, whose line, blessedly, was still down. Roberta couldn't deal with giving Meredith the bad news, not tonight. "I'm tired. I'm going back upstairs now. You can sleep on my couch again, if you want to."

"Thank you. Yes, I'll do that. Let me just try Kevin one more time, and then I'll come back upstairs." Meredith stood up and folded her chair.

"It's late, Meredith. Why don't you just call him tomorrow?"

"It's not that late. I just want to try one more time."

Roberta shrugged. "Okay. I'll see you up there."

She turned and left, and Meredith, glad to be alone for a moment, dialed Kevin's number and got the same out-of-service message. She couldn't remember if, in her delirium, she'd told Kevin exactly where she was. It seemed to her that he should have come here by now, should have done more to try to find her.

She put the phone down and trudged back upstairs, wondering if Roberta, carrying her up the stairs during the storm, had been as tired as Meredith herself was now. Roberta's bedroom door was closed; Meredith heard the bedsprings creak. She had the rest of the apartment to herself, then.

She stood in Roberta's living room, thinking about everything that had happened to her. She should sleep, she knew. That was why she was here, because she was past pride and Roberta's couch was dry and warm. If she wasn't going to sleep, she should go downstairs and start cleaning. But her mind was in that state of exhaustion transcending fatigue, and she knew that for hours now, she would neither sleep nor accomplish anything useful.

Kevin would probably come tomorrow, when the streets were clearer. She wished she hadn't called him. She didn't think she was strong enough to see him yet, or to see his reaction at what she looked like. Unlike Roberta, he'd demand to know where she'd been and what she'd done to herself. She wondered if he'd called Constance; surely not, or her mother would have swooped down on the building in a nanosecond, storm or no. Meredith had made Preston promise not to tell Constance she was back home. Not yet: not until Meredith felt up to seeing her. He must have kept his word.

She knew what they'd say when she contacted them; she'd known for months, and dreaded having to hear it. How could you do this? You, so worried about your child, the child you've always loved despite his wrongdoing; you, so frantic because you don't know where he is. How could you inflict the same thing on your own family? How could you be so cruel?

She hugged herself and moved silently to the window, staring out through darkness at the wreckage of the storm. She could only hope that joy at finding her again would neutralize some of Constance's anger, and maybe even some of Kevin's. She didn't blame him for divorcing her, but Constance couldn't divorce her, and wouldn't, even had it been possible. At least Constance had Theo; at least one child was solid, dependable, obedient.

It occurred to her that she had been removed from her mother twice, taken someplace Constance couldn't reach: once by the CV and once by her self-imposed exile. These last five years had been an illness too, no less than the virus, a terrible, raging sickness; and like the virus, they had had to run their course. She knew that, but she still didn't know how she'd be able to answer the accusations Constance was sure to level at her. *How could you do this?* The real answer—that her need to punish herself had made her deaf and blind and dumb to the punishment she inflicted on others—made her want to go back into hiding. In her anger at her own cruelty, she'd become crueler still, and she hadn't even been able to see it.

Not until she was slapped in the face with it. Shame flooded her; she rested her furrowed forehead against the cool glass of the window, wishing she could forget, wishing that the fever dream of the last five years would just go away. Mr. Clean rolled by, intent on some errand of sanitation, and she forced herself not to jump, forced herself to turn and look at him, this harmless metal box. If Sergei hadn't been listening, she'd have spoken. *Your mother misses you, even though she knows you're safe.*

Mr. Clean turned toward her, even though she hadn't spoken—he must be responding to her movement—and waited for a command. She found herself smiling. The only obedient children were the ones you built. She knew that if she told him to go downstairs and clean Zephyr's flooded apartment, he'd actually try to do it, and wreck himself in the process. But it wasn't his job; it was hers, one she wouldn't be able to put off for much longer, and one she could no longer perform from the platform of lofty principles. What drove her now was necessity.

She had, indeed, gone to Switzerland for the bloodcleaning. She hadn't wanted to be safe anymore; it hadn't seemed fair or right to her that she should be safe in a world where Nicholas had been wiped, where Raji had been killed. AIs; Raji had been killed by AIs, the beings he'd loved. And Nicholas had fled to an AI when he had his breakdown. Rationally, she knew that there wasn't any connection, but the Veilasty horror had made that difficult to remember. She'd begun to feel as if AIs had taken away everyone she loved. Even so, she'd taken no joy in the Veilasty execution, which had filled her with an old, complicated grief. People killing monsters: it never worked. Monsters always came from your own head, and that was where you had to fix them. Raji had been killed by a competitive mind-set that couldn't have been programmed into those AIs if it hadn't existed in the programmers first. Nicholas had fled to the kindness of a man who hadn't been alive for decades, who survived somehow in a machine. Dirty work, clean work; machines did the work you gave them. Why couldn't people do their own work? That was what she'd asked in college. That's what she'd believed in, still wanted to believe in. But she no longer believed that there was any work she could do without tainting it. Maybe people couldn't touch anything without ruining it; maybe that was why they made machines, so there would be something else to blame. Had Nicholas's monsters really been his own, or had she programmed them into him somehow?

The questions crowded her head, kept her from sleeping, often made her forget to eat. She didn't even have the energy to fight with Kevin; when she moved back into her mother's house, he didn't follow her. After Nicholas was wiped, she stayed in bed for a week, the shades drawn.

She'd known as she boarded the private MacroCorp jet for Geneva that she was going there for a complete bloodchange, one that would leave the GPS cells behind. She'd forced herself to get out of bed for several weeks before she left, to eat and drink and try to be merry. She'd forced herself to say sensible things to the therapists her mother had hired, to pretend to take the antidepressants they gave her. Her parents, she knew, were still worried about her when she left, but they thought she was merely going for a vacation, to get away from the wreckage of her marriage, to get away from her horror at what had happened to Nicholas, to Raji.

Meredith knew from the beginning that the trip was more than that, although she wasn't sure quite what. Bloodchange first, and then cosmetic surgery so she'd be less recognizable. She paid a tidy sum to have her old blood shipped off to Morocco, so that perhaps her parents would think she'd gone there too; instead, she flew to Australia for the cosmetic surgery. She knew the ruse wouldn't fool her parents for long, knew that the bloodchange had taken long enough that Preston, at least, must have had a fix on her position and had her under some kind of visual surveillance. He'd find a way to track her, if he wanted to. There wasn't much she could do about it.

The bloodchange left her feeling sick for several weeks, a queasiness she imagined must be like morning sickness. She hated that part, but she found, to her surprise, that she liked the surgery, loved the utter anonymity of the face-change clinics, where for an appalling sum you could sit in front of a computer screen and choose a new nose, new cheekbones, new ears, and where that same day you would receive them, all at the hands of bots bearing powerful local anesthetics and tiny, precise lasers. She'd hated bots when she was in isolation as a child, because then she'd craved human contact; but now, when she had no wish whatsoever to deal with other people, when all she wanted to do was escape them, the humming white medibots soothed her. A few stabbing moments reminded her overwhelmingly of what had happened to Raji, but that was all right. She deserved to be frightened, because knowing her was what had exposed Raji to his own final terror. In an odd way, she wished that the bots frightened her more. And while healing even from laser surgery often hurt, she discovered that the pain cut through her numbness and made her feel alive. Feeling alive hurt too, hurt more, but that was all right. She deserved to hurt. How could she not hurt, in the world that had killed Raji and wiped Nicholas?

She left Sydney convinced that no one who'd known her in America would have recognized her. Her retinal scan and voiceprint were the same, of course, as immutable as gravity or her need for air, and her height also remained unchanged. But she was thin, thinner even than she'd been after the CV, utterly gaunt, and dark circles ringed her eyes, and the eyes themselves were a different shape, more slanted, and a different color, deep purple. Her lips were thicker, her nose shorter, her chin uncleft now, her cheeks flattened. Her hair was black and curly rather than white and straight, and she wore it short, almost shaven. She no longer had freckles.

She had cleaned her blood in Switzerland; she had also laundered her money. With a fraction of her now untraceable funds, she purchased a new identity, a new name and passport. Had she been willing to spend more, she could have bought an entire life history, complete with forged medical records, consumer transactions, education and employment, but she'd come on this journey precisely to shed her past, and so she merely accepted the blank slate of her new name. When she left Sydney, she flew to London and began touring Europe.

Looking for Nicholas. She just wanted to see him, just once; an hour would be enough, under the right circumstances. She just wanted to find out if he was all right, if he was coping, if he seemed happy. She knew there was no hope that he'd recognize her, and that was fine. It wouldn't matter if he knew her or not; she'd know him anywhere, even if he'd undergone cosmetic surgery as thorough as hers. If she could find him, perhaps she could begin to forgive herself. Perhaps she could imagine a way to remain in the world.

But she had to find him. She knew that brainwiped children, if placeable at all, were placed with families who looked like genetic matches, people who could have been the biological parents. Such children were also placed as far away from their original homes, or from any source of original disturbance, as possible. Usually they stayed in their home country, but given Nicholas's fair coloring and his unwanted fame in the United States, she suspected that he might have been relocated to Northern Europe or Canada. Those places, at any rate, had the best computer networks, and networks were the fastest way to find what she needed.

In Amsterdam she hired a hacker to teach her his trade. He charged a great deal of money for the service; she didn't care. He wanted to do the work for her; she wouldn't let him, because she didn't want him to figure out who she was. He decided, near the end, that he wanted to sleep with her—this uninteresting child ten years her junior, with his adolescent hormones and his delusions of grandeur—and she rebuffed him entirely. She left the Netherlands. She knew as much as she needed to know: she didn't need the hackhead anymore. She wasn't particularly talented at the work, but she was as good as she had to be. She had worked very hard; some part of her knew that she was indeed in the grip of OCD now, at the mercy of her damaged caudate nucleus, but she welcomed the condition. It made the work she had to do to find Nicholas much easier.

Preston never manifested himself to her during that time. She didn't know if she had truly lost him, or if he was just hiding to make her think that she had. She didn't seek him out. She knew that he could find out where Nicholas was, if anyone could, and she knew just as surely that he wouldn't give her the information. Following the loss of the AI business sector in the States, MacroCorp was concentrating even more on translation, on selling rigs and mainframe space. Preston was the patron saint of the translated; the slightest appearance of wrongdoing on his part would compromise his own security and livelihood.

Preston needed to stay on the right side of the privacy laws. Meredith didn't. And so she searched each country in turn, hacking into school records, hospital records, census records, looking for a boy of about Nicholas's age who had suddenly appeared out of nowhere. Nicholas might have been furnished with a phony past too, of course, but there were ways to detect such things, and Meredith had a lot of money and a lot of time. She traveled, both because changing her physical location would make her harder to track down and because whenever she stayed in one place for too long, she became claustrophobic. At all the sites she inspected she left imbedded spyworms, instructed to report back to her if the kind of information she sought suddenly appeared.

She searched Northern Europe, and then the rest of the European Community; she searched Canada, and then the Balkan states, and then Australia and New Zealand. It was a staggering amount of ground to cover, but she found nothing. There were a few promising leads that led only to disappointment; four times, six, seven, eight, she found herself lurking outside school yards or houses, only to discover, when the child she was waiting for emerged, someone who couldn't possibly be Nicholas, even after a face-change. But two of these non-Nicholas children were visibly impaired, and so twice, at least, she was glad that she'd been wrong.

After four years and six months, her money ran out. She'd known it must, eventually, but hadn't thought it would happen so soon. She'd lived as cheaply as she dared, in hostels and flophouses whenever possible; she'd eaten little, patched her clothing rather than buy anything new, and sold the few things of value she'd brought with her: a ring of her mother's; a gold chain, from which dangled a tiny diamond, that Nicholas had given her one birthday. She could bring herself to part with it only because she knew it had been purchased with Kevin's money, and because finding Nicholas was more important than hoarding keepsakes. The keepsake that meant the most, the fetish she'd made from his hair and from a scrap of the hospital gown he'd worn as a baby, had no value to anyone else, although it was invaluable to her. She wore it around her neck, always, except when she bathed; she showered with it in a plastic bag, sitting next to her soap or clutched in her hand, so that she'd never lose sight of it, or what it represented.

When she knew that she wouldn't be able to stretch her money any further, when she knew that the search had failed, she spent her remaining funds on a flight to Mexico. She could live cheaply there; that was what she told herself when she booked the flight, although she wasn't sure she wanted to live cheaply, or live at all. How could she live in the world that had killed Raji and wiped Nicholas? She went to Mexico because it was one of the places she hadn't been yet, and because she didn't know what else to do. But when she disembarked from the plane at Mexico City and found herself in a terminal swarming with bots, bots of all shapes and sizes, bots selling cold drinks and bots hauling luggage, bots guiding vacationers to their rental cars and bots boarding planes alongside human passengers—for all the world as if they too were traveling—Meredith realized why she had come here, and whom she wanted to find, now that she had been unable to find Nicholas.

It wasn't hard at all to find Zephyr; all Meredith had to do was use the airport directory, a battered, grimy terminal with a lethargic, archaic trackball and several recalcitrant keys. Zephyr hadn't even moved. She was still living on Baja, where MacroCorp had tracked her after the KinderkAIr crisis. But of course Zephyr had never fled publicity, only arrest.

Meredith didn't bother to call ahead. She bought some food, some bottled water, and a ticket to Los Cabos.

Zephyr's house, a small cottage in Cabo San Lucas, set just back from a rocky beach, was surrounded by bots: bots gardening, bots hanging wet laundry on a line to dry, one pair of bots shucking a bucket of clams while two more cleaned and filleted some large fish. Meredith wondered if the bots would challenge her, but they seemed oblivious to her arrival. She walked cautiously to the front door, stepping carefully over a bot dusting sand from the walk, and knocked.

Meredith heard splashing water and a string of irritated-sounding Spanish. Well, of course. "Zephyr?" Meredith called. For all her fine talk of global consciousness, she'd never learned Spanish. "Is that you?"

"What? Who's there? I'm in the tub!"

"I'm sorry. I'll come back later."

"All right, all right, I'm coming." Meredith heard more muted splashing from inside, and then faint footfalls. The door opened on Zephyr, glaring and wrapped in a large towel. "Yes? Who *are* you? What are you selling?"

"I'm not—I'm not selling anything. I've come a long way. I—"

Zephyr squinted. "Do I know you?"

"I—you used to know me. I was—a friend of Raji's."

Zephyr's face tightened. "Mother of trees. *Meredith?*"

"Oh. I thought you wouldn't recognize me." So much for her face-change.

"Not easily. If it makes you feel any better, I wouldn't have known who you were without the Raji clue. That and the fact that you're a famous missing person. You'd better come in."

Meredith went in, wondering if Zephyr was in touch with Preston. The inside of the cottage was simple: whitewashed walls, a chair and table, a cot, the huge enameled tub, still full of rose-scented water, a terminal in one corner, various bots performing various errands. "Listen," Meredith said, as soon as she was in the door, "listen, I have to ask you not to—not to call the networks or, or my father or anything. I—"

"You're a fugitive, like me."

Meredith swallowed. "Well, I suppose so."

"Is he with you?" Exile hadn't softened Zephyr's manners.

"No. No, he isn't." Meredith's eyes swam with tears. "I don't know where he is."

Zephyr grunted. "Okay, look, sit down. Let me get some clothing on." She gestured to the table. "Help yourself to the fruit in that bowl there. It's clean. I'll be right back."

"Thank you," Meredith said quietly, and sank into the rocking chair. After hours of air travel, the smoothness of the motion was wonderful. She leaned back and closed her eyes. Rest. It was so restful here. This had been the right place for her to come.

"Okay, I'm back," Zephyr said. "Meredith? You awake?"

"I'm awake." Meredith reluctantly opened her eyes.

"Okay. So where have you looked?"

How kind Zephyr was, to be concerned about a child she'd never known. Unexpectedly touched, Meredith said, "All over Europe, Canada, Australia, and New Zealand. Everywhere I could before my money ran out. I checked schools, hospitals—"

"Hospitals?" Zephyr said, frowning. "He wasn't a hospital program. And nobody would have put him in a school again, not after what happened last time."

Meredith felt the blood draining from her face. Oh. Stupid. Stupid. Of *course* that was what Zephyr had thought she meant. "I'm sorry. I was talking about my son. You're talking about the AI, aren't you?"

"What? Of course! Why would you come to me about your son? I never even knew him."

You never knew the AI, either, Meredith thought. "I came here because of the bots. I wasn't looking for—for Fred, Zephyr. He's gone, isn't he?"

Zephyr shrugged. "So's your son, evidently." She sighed, grimaced, said, "Okay, look, I'm sorry. Everybody back home pestered me about that AI for months, even though I'd never met him, even though I had no idea what had happened to him. And then—this Gina Veilasty thing, the flap over AIs. So when you showed up and mentioned Raji, I jumped to conclusions."

Meredith looked down at her hands. "I suppose that's natural."

"Right," Zephyr said. "So why *are* you here? You always hated me, didn't you? And I'm a publicity hound, a security risk. If you want to stay hidden, why come here?"

Meredith swallowed. "I—there's a ritual I want to do. I thought you'd be able to help."

Zephyr looked wary. "Me? I'm not a Green, Meredith. I don't, ah, exactly share your religious principles, right? I never did. So why me?"

"Because I need bots," Meredith said quietly. "And because—because you knew Raji."

Zephyr had gone completely still; the ticking of the bots was the only sound in the room, other than the distant sea. "Raji." Her voice was flat, neutral. "You know, I thought I'd finally gotten over that, and then those fucking military terrorist pricks—never mind. I'm sorry. It's hard on you too. Except that at least now we know what happened, and they executed the bastards. Good riddance."

Meredith squinted. "You *agreed* with that? The, uh, execution?"

"Of course! They deserve what they got. I wish they hadn't planned the whole thing to hurt AI rights in the States, but that's all right. They probably never would have been caught if they hadn't handed themselves over, and the laws will be changed eventually. People will realize that AIs are no more inherently evil than anyone else."

"Oh," Meredith said. She didn't know what to say. It was all too ludicrous.

Zephyr raised an eyebrow. "You didn't come down here to have a political discussion, right? Meredith, what does Raji have to do with your
kid?"

Meredith closed her eyes. It seemed to her now that Raji's death was
when her curse had started, when she had first become aware that she
killed whatever she loved, even if she didn't mean to. Was she inherently
evil? She'd always tried to be good. Perhaps she was just inherently poisonous. But she couldn't tell Zephyr that, and she needed some way to explain why she'd sought Zephyr out; bots were everywhere, in Mexico. "I
know it doesn't make much sense," she said. "I can't—there aren't many
people connected with—with my earlier life I can talk to."

"Because you're hiding."

"Because I'm hiding. And you're hiding too. And we both—you didn't
know my son or Fred, but you knew Raji; we've both lost—we both share
that loss, and I thought, I thought you might help me out of compassion."

"I don't believe you," Zephyr said, each word clipped. Her eyes had
narrowed. "You're hiding: you just admitted it. You ran away from the
people you shared the most with. You ran away from your parents and
your husband; you ran away from Roberta."

"Roberta?" Meredith had to think for a minute to remember who
Roberta even was. "What does she—"

"She was in the hospital with you when you were kids. She knew
Nicholas. She tried to help Nicholas, and instead you accused her. You
didn't ask *her* for help because of what you shared."

Meredith shook her head. "I don't see what this has to do—"

"It means you're lying, Merry Walford. If you wanted compassion based
on shared experience, you'd have stayed home. You said before that you
came here because of the bots. But you always hated bots, and this Veilasty
mess can't have changed that. So what exactly do you want my bots to do?"

"You don't have to help me if you don't want to." Meredith realized
that she was speaking too quickly. "I can go somewhere else, if you want.
I just want a ritual cutting, and—"

"No," Zephyr said, shoving her chair back so hard it nearly fell over.
"My kids don't do blood sports."

"But—"

"*We don't do blood sports,* Meredith Walford! Especially not after Raji! Jesus!" Zephyr, a tense bundle, rose from her chair and began pacing. "You

are one selfish fuck, lady. You want me to make my bots cut you? After Raji? After *that*? You don't need a cutting, you need a—"

"Okay, okay, I'm sorry, you're right—look, you know people here, right? Do you know anybody who can do it?"

"If I did, I wouldn't tell you!"

"Please," Meredith said. "Please. Just give me the name of some of your friends. Just—"

"The mighty Meredith, begging," Zephyr said mockingly. "I should call ScoopNet, shouldn't I? You never thought you'd be begging me for anything, did you?"

"If you know anyone who—"

"No. Get out." Zephyr, bots scattering before her furious approach, strode to the door and opened it.

"I'm sorry. I—"

"Out. Now. And don't come back."

She spent the last of her currency at a surgical supply store in San Jose del Cabo, buying what she needed. Once she'd gotten it, she set out to find someone willing to provide the service she sought. She spent two weeks living on streets and beaches, eating out of trash cans and gulping water from puddles, before her oblique inquiries finally bore fruit. She was lucky she wasn't dead by then; when the bot found her, she was so weak from dysentery that she could hardly raise her head to look at it, and when she did look, she thought perhaps she was hallucinating.

"You're very unhealthy," said the bot. It was bright purple, its carapace etched in tiny turquoise lights.

"I know," Meredith whispered, raising her head from a pile of sand. She'd found a ragged old blanket and curled up in it; it was dawn, or dusk, one of them, she couldn't tell which. The sky was a reddish glow, the wind cold from the pounding Pacific. "Are you real?"

"I'm real," said the bot. "You're very unhealthy. I don't think you're a very good candidate for this procedure."

Meredith swallowed and tried to sit up. Instead she blacked out. When she came to, the sun had almost set, and the bot was still there, brilliant in darkness. "You were unconscious for four minutes," it told her.

"Thank you."

"You should go to a hospital."

"No," she said, and coughed. "You know what I want."

"I think," the bot said crisply, "that you want to die."

She managed to pull herself upright, into the cold wind. "Cuttings aren't fatal," she said, trying to sound convincing. "You know that."

"They can be if they get infected," said the bot.

"I'll wash my face."

"You're very unhealthy."

"Look," she said harshly, "it's none of your business, all right? I want the cutting. I'll pay you. Solar cells, good ones from Europe. You can't get those here, little bot, right? With a good solar cell you're a lot more mobile, right? You don't need to stay near cities, near power grids. You're less dependent on people."

"If you die," the bot said, "I would be dismantled. Murder is illegal."

The bot was afraid, she realized. It didn't want to be destroyed the way Veilasty had been. No, it couldn't be afraid: it was just a machine. She deserved to be hurt by bots. Raji had been hurt by bots. "I won't die," she said wearily. "Look, if you don't want to do it, find someone else who does."

"You're very unhealthy," the bot said, and turned and walked soundlessly away over the sand.

Meredith was too tired to chase it, too tired even to call out again. She lay down, pulling the blanket more tightly around her. She could see the moon now, a thin crescent. She had a sudden yearning memory of telling her mother what the moon meant. *There's always light somewhere, and you just have to wait for it.* How very young she had been. She was older now, and she knew that light only made the shadows deeper.

She closed her eyes. She didn't want to look at the moon anymore. Her inquiries were out on the streets; someone else would find her, someone else willing to go along with the deal.

Someone else found her. The next time she opened her eyes, Zephyr was standing over her, the purple bot balanced on her shoulder. "Jesus, Meredith! So much for compassion."

Meredith blinked, squinting at the bot. "What?" She didn't know what Zephyr was talking about. "Is that one of yours?"

"No," Zephyr said. "But it came to me after it talked to you."

"Why?" Meredith said, frowning.

"They know me around here," Zephyr said drily. She knelt down and began pulling things out of a pack: a blanket, a first-aid kit, a cell phone, a canteen of water. "Holy mother of broccoli . . . Is that your own shit you're lying in? Never mind: drink."

Meredith took the canteen, drank, and vomited the water up again a minute later. Zephyr shook her head. "Bloody fucking hell. You're going to the hospital whether you want to or not."

"No. I don't want to."

"Tough. You're not in much condition to argue."

Meredith began to cry. "This isn't fair. I'm just trying—"

"You're just trying to kill yourself," Zephyr said. "Trying to kill yourself because you can't find your kid and you ruined a couple of people's lives and Raji's dead, right? All of that, plus stuff I don't even know about, probably. Meredith, give me the scalpels."

"What?"

"The scalpels. For the cutting."

"No," Meredith said, and passed out again.

She came to in the hospital, with tubes in her arms and a catheter draining from under the sheet. Coming to, she tried to move and couldn't, and panicked, thrashing; when she came fully awake and opened her eyes, she discovered that her arms and legs were manacled to the bed rails with thick leather restraints. She tugged at them; they wouldn't give. She could hear someone screaming in another room.

"Suicide watch," said someone else, and she looked up to see Zephyr at the foot of the bed. "They weren't scalpels, Meredith."

"What?"

"Don't *what* me! They weren't scalpels; they were high-intensity pen-lasers, surgical grade, and you had the settings maxed out, you little bitch. Did you think the bots wouldn't know the difference? Did you think if you handed them lasers set to slice through bone and told them they were scalpels, they'd go ahead and try to do a delicate little ritual scarification?"

Meredith felt a surge of fear. "Does the hospital know who I am?"

"You were trying to trick them into slicing you into cubes, weren't you, Meredith? You wanted them to do the same thing those other bots did to Raji. You wanted them to do the same thing to you that your crazy kid did to the mice—all because you couldn't save Raji and couldn't save the mice and can't find your kid, Meredith, is that it? Has anyone ever told you you're a rotten loser?"

"What name was I admitted under?"

Zephyr gave her a look of pure contempt. "Not your real one, don't worry. And no, the room's not bugged, and I haven't talked to your daddy. Not yet, anyway."

"Thank you," Meredith said numbly.

"All you can think about is yourself, isn't it? Your precious pride. The bots would have been killed, Meredith. If they'd hurt you, they'd have been destroyed. Just like Veilasty. You didn't think about that, did you?"

She had thought about it. It didn't matter; bots were just machines. The old panic rose in her, the hospital panic, the isolation panic. "Let me loose, please."

Zephyr snorted. "Forget it."

"I have to go to the bathroom."

"That's what the catheter's for."

Meredith flashed back to Hortense, and shuddered. "I have to—"

"You can't have to do anything else, Meredith. You've been getting nothing but liquids for three days. Listen to me: Do you think this is what Raji would have wanted you to do?"

"What?"

"Raji—remember him? The one who got the slice-and-dice treatment you were just trying to arrange for yourself? Do you think this is what he'd want for you? Do you think it's what your kid would want for you if he could still want anything?"

"Let me go!"

"Do you think it's what the *mice* would want, Meredith, the ones your kid slaughtered? You're the big Green, huh? Huh? How do you think your parents would feel? How do you think *I'd* feel, you bitch? I've had to live with what happened to Raji, so you tried to get me to be part of doing the same thing to you?"

"Let me go!" Meredith said. She couldn't even cover her ears, but she did find a call button and managed to press it. It would summon bots. This was Mexico: everything was staffed by bots here. She didn't know if bots would be able to convince Zephyr to leave; she suspected it would take a team of human bodyguards.

"Do you think you're the only person in the world with ghosts?" Zephyr said fiercely. She was shaking. "Do you?"

Meredith pressed the call button again, urgently, and a nurse rushed in, human, young and pretty and dark-haired. "This woman's harassing me," she told the nurse.

"Damn right I'm harassing you! What you're trying to do to yourself won't undo anything you've done to anyone else, do you hear me?"

"Please make her leave," Meredith told the nurse. "Please."

The nurse nodded, her face unreadable, and turned to Zephyr. "I'm sorry, but I have to ask you—"

"Of course," Zephyr said. "I'm leaving. No problem. You get to keep the bitch: may you have much joy of her." But as she was leaving she shot over her shoulder at Meredith, "Listen to me. If you want to make amends, you can goddamn well stay alive. And if you don't want to make amends, then you goddamn well *deserve* to stay alive and suffer your rotten conscience."

Then she was gone, her furious footsteps receding into the hall. Meredith, trembling, closed her eyes and remembered Roberta's footsteps, that same staccato beat, fading away from Nicholas's room. No. No. Not that memory. She opened her eyes again and found the nurse, kind and concerned, bending over her.

"The loved ones are always angry," she told Meredith softly. "It is very common. She is angry because you tried to take yourself away, Edith, do you understand? Love fuels the anger. You must try to realize that."

"No," Meredith said. So Zephyr had told them her name was Edith; clever. "Love has nothing to do with it. She hates my guts, always has. Don't let her come back. Can you do that?"

The nurse nodded evenly. She smelled like some kind of flower: freesia, maybe, or lily of the valley. Her name tag read, "Sarita."

"And I want to get up and go to the bathroom. Is that possible?"

Sarita pursed her lips, as if considering, and then undid the restraints on Meredith's wrists and ankles. Her fingers were gentle, warm against Meredith's chilled skin. She removed the catheter with that same gentleness, and said matter-of-factly, "You need my help to stand up. You cannot support yourself yet. You are too weak."

After several tries, Meredith managed to get out of bed. She leaned on Sarita, who looked too small to bear the weight but in fact managed to steer both Meredith and the IV pole. Meredith leaned on the other woman all the way to the bathroom, and at the door said, "Thank you. I can manage from here."

"I doubt that you can," Sarita said, her voice as kind as ever. "There is nothing sharp in there, Edith. If that is what you are looking for, we might as well go back to the bed right now."

"Of course there isn't," Meredith said bitterly. "This is a psych ward, right?"

"A psych floor," Sarita said gravely. Meredith remembered reading somewhere that nurses who cared for suicidal patients had to be careful not to smile too much, lest they make their patients feel even bleaker by comparison. She'd also read that hospital staffs, by and large, hated attempted suicides, hated expending their time and skill on people who wanted to die, when so many who wanted to live never got the chance.

"Why do you do this?" she asked the nurse.

"Because it is my job."

"But why this job? Why not another one? Why not work—I don't know, pediatrics or maternity or, or—"

"Edith, do you still need to use the bathroom?"

"Yes," Meredith said, defeated.

Sarita guided Meredith into the bathroom and stood with her, pointedly looking away, while Meredith tried unsuccessfully to urinate. Then they repeated the whole laborious trip in reverse.

"I have to put the restraints back on," Sarita said when they reached the bed.

"What about the catheter? Can you leave that out?"

Sarita shrugged. "Yes, certainly, but if I didn't come quickly when you rang—"

I'll turn into Hortense. "I'll take my chances." It was better than being hooked to a tube. "You aren't going to answer the question I asked before, are you?"

"Maybe tomorrow," Sarita said. She refastened the last restraint and said, "And maybe tomorrow we will give you real food again. Sleep now. You need to heal."

I don't, Meredith thought. I can't.

Thirty

———

IT was pathetically easy to fake out the doctor, a harried man who rattled out a series of perfunctory questions and looked as if he'd much rather be anywhere else. His English wasn't as good as Sarita's, and neither were his manners. Meredith told him that she regretted what she'd done, that she'd been desperate after a bad love affair in Europe—well, close enough— but now that she was properly rehydrated and well fed, she wouldn't dream of hurting herself again. She fed the same line to a social worker, two Catholic priests, a Green chaplain, and the orderly who brought her lunch. To the orderly she said, "Why doesn't the hospital have bots bring the meals? Wouldn't it be easier?"

The orderly blinked at her, squinted, smiled a little. "Bots," he said tentatively. "Bots are—how you say—machines, yes?"

"Yes," she said. "Machines. Why didn't you have a machine bring my lunch?"

He nodded to show that he understood. "On the other floors," he said, pointing at the ceiling and then at the floor, "they have bots. Not here. People here—people here need other people. Bots no good. Sad and scared people here, yes?"

"Yes," she said. So they didn't use bots because it was a psych floor; well, that made sense. "I see. Thank you."

She'd have preferred bots, who were easier to fool, but in fact the afternoon brought a steady stream of people: an old woman with a tray of candy and newspapers—Meredith suspected she was some sort of volunteer, although the language barrier kept her from asking—another social worker, nurses bearing antidepressants. As she had at home, Meredith pretended to swallow the pills, but hid them under her mattress instead. She wondered why she hadn't been given injections or gene therapy, but wasn't about to ask. The ease with which she could evade medication was a small favor, and she thanked the universe for it.

Periodically she heard the scream from down the hallway again; once or twice she saw stretchers wheeled past. Just before dinner, Sarita came in and removed the restraints for good, without comment.

"Does this mean I can leave?" Meredith demanded.

"Not yet. You still need fluids, Edith."

"When can I leave?"

"You will have to ask the doctor tomorrow. And you will need to tell the social workers where you plan to go. They need to call someone who can take care of you outside. They need to be in touch with your family."

Meredith grimaced. She was going to have to fake plans too, not just remorse. This was entirely too much work. "My only family's that woman— the one I don't want to see. You can understand why I don't want to see her, Sarita, can't you? Much less live with her? All those horrible things she said—"

"She loves you," Sarita said.

"No."

"She brought you here."

"She didn't want me on her conscience, that's all."

Sarita shook her head. "If she did not love you, her conscience would not bother her. Edith, we cannot let you leave until you have a place to go."

"That's not fair," Meredith said, although she knew it was, knew that her chances of getting out would be better if she could fake being reasonable. She could hear the whine in her voice. "Why are you doing this?"

"Because it is my job."

"Isn't it enough work taking care of the people who want to be here?"

"No one wants to be here, Edith."

"Can't you just leave me alone? Why are you keeping me here if I don't want to stay?"

"Because it is my job," Sarita said, maddeningly. It was like talking to a bot.

"Has anyone told you that you repeat yourself?"

Sarita raised an eyebrow. "Same question, same answer. Good night, Edith." But she squeezed Meredith's shoulder as she left.

Sleep was impossible, and Sarita had said nothing about getting out of bed. Meredith sat up, cautiously, to make sure she wouldn't get dizzy, and then stood. The IV pole helped. She took tiny, shuffling steps, pushing the pole ahead of her, and made it out into the hall. Sarita, writing reports at the nurses' station, looked up; Meredith glared back and said, "Exercise. It's supposed to be good for me, right?"

"You'll tire yourself."

"That's what I *want*. So I'll be able to sleep."

Sarita nodded, acquiescing, and then said, very quietly, "Remember where you are. Everyone dangerous should be restrained, but—"

"Don't worry," Meredith said. She'd done volunteer work with brainwiped baggies: she didn't think much would be able to shock her. And indeed, after she'd located the elevators—the real reason for the expedition—the first few rooms she looked into contained only people who were sleeping, or crying, or mumbling to themselves. Then she heard a TV and headed toward it. Dayroom. There'd be news. It would be in Spanish, but there'd be pictures. Something new to look at, anyway.

She shuffled into the room, furnished with ugly orange couches and chairs, a battered plastic coffee table, and a large cafeteria table along one wall. Three men and two women sat in wheelchairs, arranged in a tight semicircle. They were being coached by a young man who wore hospital scrubs and held a milk carton.

"Leche," he said, and began pouring milk into five paper cups. *"Leche."* He handed out the paper cups; one woman dumped it over her head, while the other just poured it on the floor. One of the men stuck his fingers in it; one threw it at his neighbor, and a third, with tremendous concentration, folded his beefy hands around the little paper cup, lifted it to his mouth, and drank.

The young man beamed. "Bravo, Luis! *Leche!*"

"Leh," Luis said. *"Leh, leh—"* With evident difficulty, the woman sitting in the wheelchair next to Luis turned toward him and slowly punched him in the mouth, staring at her own hand as if mesmerized. It was a very soft punch; it couldn't have hurt much. Luis began to cry, anyway, and the woman who'd hit him mimicked the sounds he was making, looking anxiously at the trainer, as if for approval.

"Maria," the young man sighed, and walked over to her and lifted her fist, limp now, squeezing it between both of his hands. He saw Meredith, nodded and smiled. "You are the American, yes? These are—we call them the ghosts. That is your word, yes? Ghosts? They are new. It is very good that Luis already knew what to do with the milk."

Meredith turned and fled, as quickly as her rubbery legs and cumbersome IV pole would allow. Of course. Of course. Where else in a public hospital would you put the brainwiped? She had read that Mexico kept its untrainables, its baggies, in hospitals forever instead of letting them out on the streets. She wondered how many of the people in the dayroom would wind up in that category. At least all of them had been older than six.

It shouldn't have bothered her. She'd worked with the brainwiped; she'd advocated for them. But she couldn't look at them now without seeing Nicholas, and behind him, the dim shadow of Henry Carviero.

She had to get out of here, out of the hospital. She had to escape. She couldn't be patient anymore; she was losing her will for subterfuge. The walls were closing in on her, and she couldn't breathe. As soon as she got into the hallway, away from the terrible sight of the drooling shapes in the wheelchairs, she tried to pull the IV out of her arm, only to have the monitor begin whooping like some archaic air raid siren. Sarita and two orderlies rushed up mere seconds later. Sarita grabbed the IV pole and one of the orderlies grabbed Meredith, slinging her unceremoniously over his shoulder. She kicked, pounded on his back with her fists, and yelled, but she was too weak to do any significant damage.

The orderly carried her back to her bed, holding her there while Sarita snugged restraints on ankles and wrists. She fired off a quick stream of Spanish to the second orderly, and then told Meredith, "The doctor will be here soon to restart your IV. This will not get you out of here more quickly, Edith."

"But I just—"

"IV needles are sharp," Sarita said. "You might have meant to hurt yourself with it. This will keep you here at least another week. I will have to call your friend."

"I don't want to see her!"

"There will be a meeting with the doctor and the social worker and your friend. Do you understand?"

She understood. She closed her eyes so she wouldn't have to look at them, but the image of Luis, drinking his milk with so much effort, came unbidden instead.

She didn't know if Zephyr, the doctor, and the social worker had the meeting without her or not. The next day the doctor arrived, clucking and frowning, and the social worker shot barrages of questions at her. Zephyr never showed up at all. Meredith told the other two that she was tired and turned her face to the wall, and finally they went away.

Her escape, two nights later, proved to be ridiculously simple. She waited until the predawn shift, when the floor was short-staffed, and began twisting her IV arm as much as the restraints would allow, twisting and wiggling, patiently, willing the tape to loosen, willing the needle to shift, ever so slightly. When it did, she waited for her arm to swell from the fluids leaking into the tissues, and then she very deliberately wet her bed, and then she rang the call button.

They had to take the IV out, and they had to call a doctor to restart the IV in the other arm, and they had to change the sheets. She was betting on the fact that they wouldn't tie her up while they did all that, and she was right. The orderly went to get clean sheets and the nurse turned to strip the bed, and Meredith, her heart pounding, just walked out of the room, ducked into the nearest elevator, and pressed the button for the basement. If this was anything like American hospitals, that's where the labs would be, and it would be quiet this time of night. She just had to hope that there wouldn't be any bots roaming around, or that if there were, they'd somehow mistake her for authorized personnel.

Gaia be praised, she met no bots: another gift. She found an open supply closet, managed to climb into scrubs and some slippers, and then walked out the nearest door, into the humid, fragrant Mexican night. There was a full moon; good. She needed the light. It would help her find her way, and it would remind her how dark the shadows were.

Zephyr had been right: Meredith never should have asked the bots to cut her. She'd been violating everything she'd ever believed, asking machines to do her work for her like that. She'd wanted to make things as easy as they'd been in Sydney, but it didn't work that way. She had to take responsibility for her own monsters. She had to do the job herself.

She didn't have the pen-lasers anymore, or even a scalpel, but that was all right. She found a bottle in a pile of trash, broke it on the sidewalk, and then carried the largest pieces to the beach. She had to walk for miles, it seemed; the hospital was quite far inland. She followed the smell of the sea, the faint sound of surf, and when at last she got there, her hands already slightly cut from the glass, she washed her tools in the salt water. Holy water, she told herself, the stuff of tears and wombs, and most of what our blood is, all our blood: Patty's and Bluebell's, Nicholas's, Raji's, mine.

The journey to the beach seemed to take hours, the process of washing the glass an eternity. She was still very weak and still moved very slowly. She told herself she had to hurry, that someone from the hospital would be looking for her, although now that she was out of the hospital, she couldn't imagine that they'd look, couldn't imagine why they'd care. Surely Sarita had only been saying what she was trained to say, what she was paid to say. She couldn't truly care about someone she'd only known for a few days.

By the time Meredith got the glass clean, it was dawn. She sat cross-legged on the sand, trying to meditate, trying to steel herself, and then began tracing cuts into her face, first shallow and then deeper, as if she were slicing through all the layers of pain and isolation, all the masks and shells, her life had built around her. To her surprise and gratitude, it didn't hurt at all.

Cold, and darkness; and then warmth, as if she were being brought near a fire, near and then too near, until it burned her, until the light of it flooded through her shut eyelids. She tried to run away from the flames and couldn't: her arms and legs wouldn't move. "Edith," someone said, "can you hear me? Open your eyes."

She opened her eyes. There was a bright lighting grid far above her. In the middle distance, Sarita looked down at her, and there were other faces around the bed too: a doctor, another nurse she recognized from before, Zephyr. "You're back in the hospital," Zephyr said. "You won't be getting away this time. Don't try to answer, dear; you'll rip your stitches open."

She tried to tell them all to go away, but it hurt too much when she tried to form the words. Instead she closed her eyes again. "If she'd been serious about this," Zephyr said conversationally, "she wouldn't have worked so carefully around her eyes, don't you think?"

"She could have died," the doctor said sharply. This was a new doctor, with excellent English. "If that fisherman hadn't found her—"

Sarita said something soothing in Spanish and put her hand on Meredith's arm; the doctor broke off with a sigh, and Meredith heard retreating footsteps. Zephyr's? The doctor's? Silence then, and the warm hand went away, and Meredith slept: woke and slept and woke again, swallowed as soft food was spooned into her mouth—carrots, ground beef, peaches, as if she were a baby—swallowed a pill because she didn't have the energy to hide it or spit it out. She slept again, and when she woke she found Sarita gazing down at her.

"You asked me once," the young woman said quietly, "why I do this job. I will tell you now. I do this job because my brother slit his wrists ten years ago, and I was the one who found him in the bathtub, and if I had gotten there half an hour earlier I could have saved him. Do you understand, Edith?"

Meredith nodded. It still hurt too much to talk.

"Good. If you need reasons not to hurt yourself again, you can use me as one of them. Do you understand?"

Meredith nodded. "Good," Sarita said again. "Because I will tell you this, although the doctor disagrees: I also do not think you truly want to die. You ran away when you realized there were ghosts here—forgive me for using the slang for them, the blank-brains—and I think you ran away because you did not want to become one too. I think you ran away because you wanted to stay yourself, and you were afraid that we would turn you into a ghost. Am I right, Edith?"

Meredith shook her head. *No.* No, you're wrong, I ran away because the ghost who haunts me, my son, is someone I couldn't help any more than I can help the people here. I ran away because I'm afraid that the creatures I saw in the dayroom, those pathetic wrecks, are what my son is now. I ran away because you wouldn't let me kill myself, and because I don't deserve to live, if he's a ghost.

She remembered seeing Patty's flayed corpse, and found herself trying to imagine what it must have been like for Sarita to find her brother's body, or to see Meredith herself brought in, her face a mass of cuts. She thought briefly, with terror, about the fisherman who had found her, what he must have thought, how he must have felt. I don't want this, she said to the pictures in her head. Make them go away. My own pain is more than I can bear; make these others go away!

"No?" Sarita said. "I'm wrong, then. Well. So maybe you wish us to make you a ghost, and you thought that if you carved your face open, we would? That if you did not die, at least we would erase your brain? We will not, Edith. The doctor thinks you can get better, and so do I, and your friend Zephyr, she knows it. She swears to it."

Meredith shook her head, and felt tears coming, oozing onto the bandages encasing most of her face. "Ah," Sarita said softly. "You do not think so. But I do. What we need now is to find a reason for you to want to live."

Meredith stared at her. Horrible woman. Hateful woman. Meredith had wanted to die to atone for all the harm she'd caused others. But if she died now, she'd be betraying Sarita too, making herself another weight in the burden this woman had to carry. Meredith knew about burdens like that. If her death made someone else's life worse, it wouldn't atone for anything at all.

She heard Zephyr's voice again. *Do you think this is what Raji would have wanted you to do? Do you think it's what your kid would want for you if he could still want anything? How do you think your parents would feel? How do you think I'd feel?*

They'd feel the way she felt now. She closed her eyes to shut out the light. She was trapped, trapped.

The next day a bot came clicking across the floor and climbed up onto the covers, arm over arm, until it was perched at the foot of the bed. It was an unremarkable bot, gunmetal gray, without any special attachments that Meredith could see. It was the first bot she'd seen in the hospital. She wondered if the staff thought she was well enough to deal with bots now. She didn't see how they could think that. Her face hurt horribly, much more than the cosmetic surgery ever had. Sarita had refused to give her extra painkillers; she said the doctors were concerned about dependency, but it seemed to Meredith that she was being punished.

"Hello, Meredith," said the bot. "Zephyr told me you were here. She did not feel that she could keep it from me any longer."

Meredith turned her face away. She didn't want to talk to her father. She'd have told him to go away, if moving her mouth hadn't been so excruciating.

"No one else knows where you are," the bot said. "Not your mother, not Kevin. I will tell them only if you wish it."

"No," she said to the wall. It was a clean wall, whitewashed and soothing, glowing in the sunlight. "They don't care, anyway."

"Of course they care." The bot's voice was as even as ever. "Just as I do."

"No one looked for me," Meredith said petulantly, painfully. She knew it was a silly thing to say: she'd run as far from them as she could.

"We did look for you. We could not find you. You did not want to be found. Had you died, your corpse would have been identified beyond all doubt. Because there was no corpse, Kevin and your mother knew that you were still alive."

There'd almost been a corpse. Meredith, still staring at the wall, said, "You must have known where I was, Daddy. I was hacking—I was looking for—you must have seen that. You see everything. Nobody can run away from you."

"But you did. And if I had revealed myself, you would have run further. Is that not so?"

Meredith turned irritably back to face him and said, through the agonizing pain, "Did you know where I was, or not? You couldn't have looked for me and not found me!"

"We could not find you until you wanted to be found," said the bot.

Meredith's nose had begun to itch underneath the bandages, where she couldn't scratch it. She wondered if that meant she was beginning to heal. Her entire face would itch: it was going to be horrible. It was going to be worse than the pain she felt now. "Did you know where I was?" she asked, trying again.

"Sometimes I did. Sometimes I did not."

"You knew," Meredith said. "You didn't tell Mommy and Kevin because they would have come to get me. Mommy would have, anyway. You didn't want them to know that you knew where I was and hadn't told them. You didn't want to admit that you lied to them." She marveled that she could talk so much; she felt a perverse pride, as if she'd just bench-pressed ten times her own weight.

"I did not lie," said the bot.

"You just didn't tell the entire truth," Meredith said bitterly.

"I did not know the entire truth," Preston said. "There were gaps. There were times when I lost sight of you. Zephyr tells me you were on the beach. I did not know where you were then, although I knew you must still be in Mexico."

"I talked to bots. They knew I was there. You must have known."

"I do not talk to every bot in the world, Meredith. They are independent entities. They do not report to me."

She was tired. She couldn't make sense of anything. Her face was a mask of misery. Talking so much hadn't been a good idea, after all. She said with infinite difficulty, "Why reveal yourself now, then?"

"Because you wanted to be found. That is Zephyr's interpretation, and mine. As when you were a child, playing hide-and-seek, and crouched under a table where you were clearly visible. Your mother and I would walk around the table. We would say, 'Where is Meredith?' and you would giggle. And when you were tired of the game, when you were ready to be found, you would crawl out from under the table and we would discover you and cry out and wave our arms in amazement, and you would be glad."

"I'm not glad now," Meredith said. She didn't remember playing hide-and-seek with her father when she was a child. She didn't remember her father ever being home.

"I hope," said the bot, "that one day you will be. No one questions that you have suffered, Meredith. But if you had died on the beach, joy would have ended as well."

Meredith turned her face to the wall again. Her father couldn't possibly understand joy, if he ever had. He was just a program.

"If you had died on the beach," the bot said implacably, "the world would never have been the same. Not for me, and not for anyone who has ever known you, Meredith."

I've done nothing good. I've only hurt people. But she couldn't summon the energy to say it.

He visited her every day after that. He told her things she would rather not have known: that Kevin hadn't dated anyone since she had been gone; that Constance and Theo went to the Gaia Temple every year on her birthday to do a remembrance ritual; that Constance wept every evening before she fell asleep, while Jack tried to comfort her. Meredith found herself, reluctantly, feeling sorry for Jack and sorrier for Theo, the perfect child who could never fill the daughter-shaped hole in Constance's life. Feeling sorry for them hurt, like the renewed flow of blood to a numb limb. She didn't want to hurt anymore. She didn't want to feel anything.

"People still love you," Preston told her.

"They shouldn't," she said fiercely. Talking was somewhat easier now. "I don't want them to."

"They do. I do, but that does not count because you do not consider me a person."

She shuddered. "People hate me. Roberta. Zephyr. The baggie. Maybe he doesn't remember me, but he'd hate me if he could."

"Yes," Preston said. "That is probably true. You have done harm, to others and yourself. What will you do now?"

She didn't know. She asked herself the same thing, ceaselessly. She was trapped, trapped. She knew she had to stay alive, but she didn't yet know how.

Zephyr was the one who told her. "You can go back," she said, spooning tomato soup rather roughly into Meredith's still-tender mouth. "You can go back and make your goddamn amends *properly,* get it? That's your job now, Meredith. You go back home and do whatever you can to fix the mess you made. Never mind if you can find your kid or not. Find the others and tell them you're sorry. That's the only thing in the world that will get this thing off your back."

I have to do my own dirty work, Meredith thought bleakly.

They had been back in Zephyr's house, then. Meredith had been released into Zephyr's custody. Zephyr fed her, deputized a small herd of bots to guard her, and put her to work in the garden when she was strong enough. And when she was well enough to go home, Zephyr gave her clothing and a wad of American currency she'd saved—"That'll keep you from credit-chip problems, as long as it lasts"—and the key to her condo in the Soma District, and said, "Here. So at least you'll have a place to stay while you screw your courage up. You find any cops poking around, tell them you're a friend of mine. Make up a name and keep your fingers crossed they don't voiceprint you."

"Thank you," Meredith had said stiffly, taking the key. It hurt to have to thank someone who hated her. Everything hurt. "Thank you for everything."

Zephyr had laughed, her old cackle. "Don't thank me. I'm not being as nice as you think I am. This is my way of honoring Raji, all right? My reasons are entirely selfish. And Roberta Danton's going to be right over your head, you know, still doing time. When she finds out who you are, you just *may* wind up dead."

"I'll tell her you sent me."

Zephyr snorted. "You do that. And tell Mr. Clean I miss him."

❦

She stood now with her forehead pressed against the cool glass of Roberta's living room window. It was dawn. She hadn't slept. She was too tired to sleep, too tired to clean. She gazed out at the aftermath of the storm, worrying about Kevin. It was too early to call him. She'd go downstairs again in a few hours. Right now she was too tired to move.

That was where Roberta found her, when she woke up an hour later. Meredith heard the bedroom door creak open and turned, blankly, to see Roberta emerge, yawning. Roberta raised an eyebrow and looked pointedly at Meredith, and then at the couch, and then back to Meredith again. She traced a question mark in the air with her finger. Meredith shook her head no. No, I didn't sleep.

Roberta shrugged and went into the kitchen. Meredith heard running water, the whir of the coffee grinder. She turned back to the window, and came out of her trance only when she felt Roberta's hand on her arm, tugging.

Meredith in one hand and the coffeepot in the other, Roberta made her way downstairs, into Zephyr's beslimed apartment. Mr. Clean followed them, carrying two coffee mugs raised carefully above the muck. "Okay," Roberta said, putting the coffeepot down on Zephyr's windowsill and pushing Meredith down into a chair, "so what's eating you?"

"What's eating me? You can't figure that out for yourself? I thought you were tired of talking to me."

"I don't need you going psychotic on me from sleep deprivation, Meredith."

"No. I guess you don't. I've gone psychotic on too many people already, haven't I?" It occurred to her that Roberta still didn't know what had happened in Mexico, that she hadn't heard that part of the story.

"Yeah, you have."

"Yeah. I know I have. So what would you have done?" She realized, suddenly, that this was the right question to ask, the question she'd wanted to ask for years, the question she'd have asked if she'd been able to speak to Roberta openly during Nicholas's illness. *What should I do? What would you do?*

"What?" Roberta looked blank.

"What would you have done? About Nicholas?" Meredith turned now, her gaze a challenge. "If you'd been his mother. Would you have turned him in right away?"

Roberta shook her head. "Come on, Meredith. I was his teacher and I didn't turn him in, right? So what do you think?"

"I mean," Meredith said, taking a deep breath, "what would you have done in my place? What would you have done about Patty and about the Hobbit and about—"

"And about me?" Roberta poured coffee and handed a mug to Meredith. "When would I have started telling the truth, you mean? If I'd been in your shoes?"

"Yes." Meredith took a cautious sip of the coffee. It was too bitter on an empty stomach and no sleep. She grimaced and put the mug back on the windowsill.

"I don't know," Roberta said. "As soon as—as soon as it felt safe, I guess. As soon as I thought it wouldn't do him more harm than good."

"And when," Meredith asked, her voice as bitter as the coffee, "would that have been?"

"As long as there was brainwiping?"

"Yes, exactly."

"Okay," Roberta said. "As long as there was brainwiping, all right, okay, it never would have been safe, but, Meredith—that poor baggie, that Henry guy, he got wiped too. And I'm practically married to my probation officer. And none of it's all right."

"I *know* that! I've already told you I know that! Do you think I think it's all right? I'm asking you what I should have done differently! I'm asking you what *you* would have done differently!"

Roberta, frowning, traced the rim of her mug with a finger. "I don't know. I wouldn't have let them have Nicholas, either. I'd have run away, I think. Gone somewhere with him. I have no idea where. But that wouldn't have stopped it. He'd probably have wound up killing you too, eventually. You know that, don't you?"

"The monsters wouldn't have been happy with mice for very long," Meredith said. "That's what the doctors told us."

Roberta bent her head, breathing in the steam from the coffee. "Did they ever figure out what caused it?"

She felt, rather than saw, Meredith's shrug. "Some combination of damage from in utero CV and infantile isolation trauma. That was the best guess they could come up with. It doesn't really matter, does it?"

"Not to him," Roberta said. She'd only been up for twenty minutes, and already she wanted to go back to bed for the rest of the day. "It might to someone else's kid."

"Ah. Altruistic Roberta."

"You asked," Roberta said fiercely. "You wanted my opinion."

"Not about that."

"No, not about that. Okay, how's this: I wouldn't have called the cops on the baggie, Meredith. How's that for something to do differently?"

"Yes," Meredith said. The life had gone out of her voice. "Yes, that's where it all started going bad. Really bad, I mean. Irrevocably bad." She raised a hand to her ruined face, traced scar tissue for a moment, as absent-mindedly as someone else might have chewed a fingernail, and then folded her hands in front of her. "I wish I knew where he was. I wish I could do something for him." Roberta wasn't sure if she meant Nicholas or Henry. Then she sighed and shook herself. "Well, I know where you are, and I know where Kevin is, and I'm pretty sure I know where my mother and Jack and Theo are, if they've stayed in the same house. Do you think it's late enough to call Kevin? The phones must be up again by now."

Roberta closed her eyes. Now or never. She had to do it. Preston had told her to do it. It wasn't going to get any easier. "Meredith, I—no. You can't reach Kevin."

"What? Why not? What—"

"Your father told me to tell you. He—Meredith, I'm so sorry, I hate to have to tell you this, it isn't fair, it isn't any fairer than what happened to Raji or Nicholas or—"

Meredith stood up, knocking over her chair, her eyes wild. "What happened? I talked to him two days ago. I talked to him. He was fine!"

"Preston said—your father said—Meredith, he died in the storm. He, he went outside and something happened, something fell on his car, I think, he—Meredith, please sit down. Oh, Gaia, I shouldn't have told you, you're so tired, you can't—I'm sorry. Meredith? Please sit down."

"He was coming to get me," Meredith said. She hadn't sat down. "That's why he's dead. He's dead because I called him."

"It's not your fault," Roberta said, knowing how weak it sounded. How could Preston have done this to her? How could Preston have expected her to know what to say, how to say it? How could—

And then, in a flash, she realized. Of course. Of course. How stupid could she be?

She took a deep breath. "Meredith, listen—"

"Kevin's dead because I called him."

"People don't die because you love them," Roberta said, and saw Meredith shudder.

"That's what my father told me when Raji died."

"Well, he was right! Love doesn't kill people: other things do. Accidents, bad choices, diseases. Terrorists. Meredith, Kevin's not your fault. He isn't. It's his own fault he went out in the storm. He went out in the storm and the storm killed him. You had nothing to do with it."

"He came because I called him."

"You were *sick,*" Roberta said. "You were feverish and you weren't in your right mind and you can't blame this on yourself. You can't. Meredith, a lot of things have been your fault, but a lot of things haven't been too, not Raji and not the fact that Nicholas was crazy and not this. Not Kevin. Kevin's not your fault." No more than her parents were hers. That was why Preston had chosen her to break the news.

"He was out in the storm because I called him."

"He didn't have to go," Roberta said. "Maybe you called him, but going was his choice. Preston tried to talk him out of it. His house system tried to talk him out of it. It was a bad choice, and he had lousy luck to go with it." Excessive altruism, she thought grimly. Sergei had always warned her that it could be a fatal condition. And yet it seemed to her, even now, that love without risk wasn't any kind of love at all. It seemed to her that the most hideous crimes were the ones committed by people trying to make the world entirely safe, as Meredith had tried to make the world safe for Nicholas.

"He must have loved me after all," Meredith said bitterly. "That was the bad choice, wasn't it? There's nothing you can say to make me feel better about this, Roberta, so stop trying."

"All right," Roberta said. "All right, I know." And now I know that we live on the same planet, although maybe I wish we didn't. "Meredith, would you call your mother, please? To let her know you're back?"

"To let her know I killed Kevin?"

"To let her know *you're* alive, Meredith. Please?"

"She knows I'm alive. No one's found a body. She knows that Daddy would have told her if I'd died. But she still cries every night, Daddy says. That doesn't make sense." Meredith sat down, finally, staring glassily ahead. She hadn't cried yet. She might not cry for a long time. It had taken Roberta weeks to cry, when she learned that her parents were dead. "No body," she said. "Kevin doesn't have a body now, either. Roberta, did Daddy say if Kevin was rigged?"

Roberta was startled. It hadn't even occurred to her. "No. He didn't say anything about that. You don't know?"

"I know he wasn't rigged when I left. He didn't have a house system when I left, either, or hadn't activated it, anyway. If he got one—if he got a rig—it wouldn't—the records would be incomplete, you know. Less than five years of direct experience. Everything else would be memories of memories. Those ones, that kind of translated, they're—they're really thin. It doesn't work very well. Nobody ever thought it would. That's why MacroCorp's been pushing people to get rigged early. That's why my mother had Theo rigged when he was born."

"You could ask your father."

"He'd have told you if he wanted me to know," Meredith said. "It doesn't matter. No body—that's—Kevin loved his body. I loved his body. I—" She bent her head. Roberta thought the tears would come after all, but instead Meredith looked up, after a moment, and said, "I didn't love him yet, when I married him. I only realized how much I loved him after he left me. Isn't that stupid?"

"No. It's sad, but it's not stupid. It's human. It happens all the time."

"What do I do now? Did Daddy tell you?"

"I'm supposed to take you back to the house."

"Sergei will track you on the GPS," Meredith said. "It's going to blow my cover. It might get you in trouble."

"You're right," Roberta said. "I hadn't thought of that." She'd forgotten how lucid people could be, in the first shock of grief. She discovered that she couldn't worry about it. Preston would protect her, as he had promised, or not. After all, Sergei had all the information he needed already, if he chose to use it. "If you want to wait—"

"No," Meredith said, and stood up again. "I've waited long enough. I want to go home now."

Thirty-One

"How are you going to get in?" Roberta asked. "If Kevin didn't acti-
vate the full house system until after you guys split up, would you be
one of the people allowed entry?"

"I doubt it," Meredith said quietly. "But there's a key. Hidden in the
garden. Very old-fashioned. I doubt very much that Kevin would have
even remembered it was there, let alone moved it."

"You don't think he changed the locks?"

Meredith shrugged. "Maybe. But I can always break in through a window."

"Great," Roberta said. "Then the security system would call the cops,
wouldn't it? Unless—oh, I guess your father could override it." She
couldn't think. She was supposed to be the rational one here; she was supposed to be comforting Meredith.

"I'm not going to worry about it," Meredith said. "We'll get in somehow. The house is mine now, legally, whatever the house system says. I let
Kevin stay here, but it's still my house. Call Sergei, Roberta. No, wait—let
me call Sergei."

"You? Why?" Roberta's head was spinning. "You want to talk to
Sergei but not your mother?"

"Right," Meredith said. "Because I'm a coward and I don't want to
deal with my mother right now, but I don't want to get you in any more
trouble, either. I've gotten enough people in trouble." She stood and picked
up her coffee mug. "Come on. Let's go back upstairs and call Sergei."

They went back upstairs. They called Sergei. Roberta listened while
Meredith informed Sergei very sweetly that she wasn't Zephyr Expanding
Cosmos, that she was Meredith Walford, and that Roberta would be keeping her company while she went back to her house, and that if Sergei
broke any of this to ScoopNet or anyone else, or punished Roberta for

helping her, Meredith would personally see to it that he wound up in law-suits up to his eyeballs.

"There," she said when she put the phone down. "I think he'll behave."

"I'm impressed." And I hope it works. "What did he say?"

"He didn't say much. He spluttered a couple of times, and then he thanked me for keeping him informed and said that he certainly didn't want to make anything more difficult for anybody. If he makes trouble later, I'll offer him my autograph. Or tell him steamy stories about Zephyr coming to the door in her towel, or something."

"What? Zephyr—*what?*"

Meredith actually laughed. "Oh, I haven't told you my Mexican adven-tures yet. Never mind. Shall we go?"

"Henry," said the house, "Henry, wake up. I think Meredith and Roberta are coming up the walk."

Henry, curled on the couch, stirred and snored and then sat bolt up-right, scattering the two kittens, who had been curled behind his knees. "What, House?"

"Hide, Henry. Two women just came up the front walk. I think they're Meredith and Roberta."

Preston had told Henry and the house as much as he knew about Meredith and Roberta and Nicholas. Neither Henry nor the house had found the tale particularly reassuring. Meredith had hated both of them, and Meredith owned the house now. Roberta had wished both of them well, but had ultimately been helpless. And the house, hearing the story, found itself in precisely Henry's situation: Preston claimed to be telling the truth about a previous life it couldn't remember. It didn't know if Preston was really telling the truth or lying for some purpose of his own. It didn't remember Nicholas. It didn't remember being called Fred and working in a school with children and mice. It couldn't tell Preston what had hap-pened during that final hour at KinderkAIr.

"Are they going away?" Henry asked.

"No. They're going around to the back. I don't think you have time to leave without them seeing you. Hide, Henry. Hide in Kevin's closet."

"Meredith and Roberta will not hurt you," Preston said. He was still on the television. "I am sure."

"Henry's not sure," Henry said flatly. "Henry's scared. Henry's going to hide now."

"You told us you'd give us enough warning for Henry to leave if anyone came," said the house. "You lied, Preston. You can lie, because you're a person."

"I did not lie; I erred. People make mistakes, as well as lying. I thought that Roberta and Meredith would talk to me before they came here. I do not have access to Roberta's tracking code, and Meredith is no longer trackable at all. I thought—"

"We have no reason to trust you," said the house. "You lied about giving us enough time. You might lie about other things too."

Henry, opening the door to Kevin's closet, said, "Henry's hiding now. You hide too, House, when they come in. Don't let them know you're too smart. Don't talk."

"House systems talk, Henry."

"Don't say anything a stupid house system wouldn't say," Henry said, secreting himself behind a rack of polo shirts. That wasn't much help. The house didn't know how stupid house systems talked. It decided that the best course of action would be to do what Kevin had always told it to do when anyone came to the house, and simply say nothing. It turned off all the televisions too, so that Preston couldn't tell the women that Henry was in Kevin's closet. It wasn't sure what to do about the bots. Stupid house systems had bots, but Meredith was afraid of bots. It decided to hide the bots, and sent them scuttling behind drapes and under furniture.

The two women were in the garden now, where Meredith had bent down to pry up a flagstone covered with mud from the storm. She picked up something from under it and wiped the object on her sleeve. It was a key. The house watched, expectant. It knew that a stupid house system would have called the police if anyone other than Kevin tried to get in, but if the police came they'd find Henry here. And Meredith owned the house now.

And so when Meredith put the key in the back door and slid back the deadbolt, the house did nothing. It watched her walk inside, watched her stop just inside the door, watched her eyes narrow. "Someone's here," she said to Roberta, who was hanging warily behind Meredith. "Smell that? Fresh coffee."

"Yeah, I smell it. But couldn't Kevin have made coffee before he left?"

"He died two days ago. The coffeemaker wouldn't have stayed on that long. It turns off automatically after an hour."

"So maybe he got a new coffeemaker."

"Maybe. I smell something else, though—cat pee? You smell that?" She took another two steps inside and called, "Hello?" The house didn't answer, but the orange kitten sidled warily out from under Kevin's drafting table. According to Preston, Meredith liked cats, but the house didn't know how she'd feel about seeing one here.

"Ah," Meredith said. "Well, there's the cat." She knelt down and made clucking noises; when the kitten moved closer to her, she scooped it up and stood again, cradling the animal to her chest. "Gotcha. Skinny little thing." The kitten mewed and wiggled in protest, and Meredith said, "So where did you come from? Kevin would have given you a proper litter box."

Roberta reached out and touched the kitten's head. "Which might have gotten smelly, after two days."

"This is a very small cat," Meredith said.

"Don't look now, but here's another one." The black kitten had ventured into the living room, but Roberta ignored it and walked over to the television instead. "Well, we know whom to ask about all this, right?" She turned the knob, but nothing happened. "The TV's broken."

"Weird," Meredith said. "Storm damage?" She walked to Kevin's drafting table and picked up the phone with her free hand, but the house was one step ahead of her: it had already disabled the telephones to keep Preston from calling Meredith and Roberta. Preston would tell the women about Henry. The house didn't think that was a good idea. It didn't know how it was going to get Meredith and Roberta out of the house so Henry could escape, but it knew it had to try. "Phone's still out too. You have your cell phone? So we can call the cops if somebody's here?"

"We can call Sergei. That's all this phone does. But he could call the cops. Meredith, do you want to leave?"

The house hoped that Meredith would say yes. It considered using bots to lead her outside somehow, and then rejected the idea. If she was afraid of bots, who knew how she might react?

"No," Meredith said. "Nothing looks disturbed except the window, and that must have broken during the storm, and it's been neatly taped up. I don't think these are Kevin's cats, and I don't think vicious burglars leave kittens behind, do you?" She walked up to the couch, gingerly touching the wrinkled nest of blankets where Henry had been sleeping.

"Could that be from Kevin?" Roberta asked. "Could he have been taking a nap when you called?"

"No," Meredith said. "These blankets are filthy." She walked into the kitchen and opened the fridge. "There's half a peanut butter and jelly sandwich in here."

"Yes? So?"

"Kevin *hated* peanut butter. I can't think why he'd even have it in the house, except maybe for Theo."

Roberta sighed. "Okay, so Kevin made the sandwich a few days ago for Theo and then—and then—"

"Nice try," Meredith said, and walked back into the living room. The kitten had begun squirming; she put it down and said, "Hello? Hello, is anyone here?"

"Meredith, the house wouldn't have let in anyone who wasn't a guest, would it?"

"It let us in, didn't it?"

"Well, only with the key—oh, wait. Even if we had the key, it should have called the cops if it didn't know us, shouldn't it? Isn't that how house systems work?"

"Yeah, I think so."

Roberta wrinkled her nose. "I don't like this. Do you want me to call Sergei and have him call the police?"

"Not yet," Meredith said. "Not before I find out who's already here. Except I think I already know."

"Who?"

"Henry."

"You think it's *Henry*?"

"Cats and filth. Sounds like Henry to me." She raised her voice. "Hey, Henry, if you're here, it's okay!" The house wasn't sure it believed that; Henry must not have believed it, either, because he didn't come out. After a minute or so, Meredith shrugged and said, "Well. If he's here, we'll find him."

"Oh, come on. How could it be Henry? And whoever it is could be dangerous."

"The house didn't think so."

Roberta made another face. "The house doesn't seem to be working right, if you'll forgive my saying so. I think we should call—"

"No," Meredith said, "we're not calling anybody. It's my house. Maybe I'm not working right, either; I don't care. The last thing I'm going to do is call the police, even if it's not Henry. Come on: let's see what we've got."

Could the house believe that Meredith wouldn't call the police? No: she was a person, and she could lie. She could lie to try to trick Henry into coming out. But she'd find Henry, even if he didn't come out. The house didn't know what to do.

Meredith began a slow, deliberate circuit of the living room. She scanned the bookshelves, much as Henry had done, peered at the plans Kevin had been drawing, and finally bent over to look under the couch. "Ah," she said. "Look."

"More kittens?"

"Bots."

Roberta bent to look at them too. "Are they new?"

"Yeah. Kevin always wanted them, but I didn't. Well, I doubt he could have been bothered to do housework."

"Are you scared of them?"

"Not anymore." Meredith straightened, sighed, and said, "Come on. Let's look at the bedrooms."

"Are you sure?"

"I'm sure." Meredith started down the hall; Roberta, with a shrug, followed. "This will be the hard part."

"Nicholas's room?"

"Yeah. But let me do Kevin's office first. He used to have his drafting table in there, not the living room. I want to see what's in there now." She opened the first bedroom door. "Ah. Home gym. He always said he never understood why anyone would use a treadmill instead of going outside. I guess he changed his mind."

"Privacy," Roberta said quietly. "It got pretty intense for a while, after you disappeared. For your parents and Kevin, I mean. I was protected by court order, but ScoopNet was desperate for footage of the others. Taking a stroll in the neighborhood wouldn't have been a pleasant experience for him, believe me."

Meredith bent her head. "He must have hated me," she said, her voice tight. "He had to have hated me. I lied to him, I hurt him, and then I up and just left, and all of it made his life miserable. And he died coming to get me. Because I was sick. He was trying to get me out of isolation again, wasn't he?"

Roberta touched her arm. "He probably just wanted to chew you out in person."

"I wish he had. I deserved it."

"I think you're chewing yourself out every bit as much as he would have, Meredith."

"*You're* a pretty strange person to say that."

"Yeah, well," Roberta said. "I blamed myself when my parents died of CV. I thought I'd given it to them, even though there was no way I could have."

"I'm so sorry. About your parents. And I never—Daddy told us about you and I never—" Meredith's voice had gotten even more ragged; Roberta touched her shoulder again and shook her head.

"That wasn't what I meant. I know the territory. That's all I'm saying. I know about blaming yourself because somebody you love is dead."

"I didn't love Kevin well enough." Meredith's voice was dull; she'd sat down on the floor, with her back against a wall.

"I didn't love my parents well enough, either. Come on. Let's get Nicholas's room over with. Are you okay? Can you stand up?"

"I can stand up," Meredith said, and did. "Did we love Nicholas well enough? Either of us?"

"Too well, maybe. Or as well as we could. I don't know what the right way would have been. I told you that this morning."

"Not calling the police."

"That would have been a better way of loving Henry Carviero. I don't know how much it would have helped Nicholas, in the long run."

So Roberta wanted to be kind to Henry: that much of Preston's story was true, then. The house waited for Meredith to respond; it hoped she would say something that would indicate whether she still hated Henry, whether she wanted to do him harm. But she said nothing, and even if she had spoken, she might have lied.

Soon Meredith and Roberta would go into Kevin's room, and the house was afraid that they would find Henry. It didn't want them to call the police. If it told them that not doing that would be the best way of loving Henry, who was still huddling in fear among Kevin's suits and ties, would they listen? Or would they call for help? The house still didn't know what to do, and it hated not knowing things.

Meredith opened the door to Nicholas's room and looked inside. "Oh, Gaia!"

"What?" Roberta stood on tiptoes to look over Meredith's shoulder. "Meredith, what is it? What's wrong? I don't see anything."

"Exactly. There's nothing here. He *stripped* it. That bastard! Everything's gone! He didn't leave anything! Not even the bed, not even—"

Meredith circled the room, wild-eyed, and Roberta followed, staying in front of Meredith, trying, it seemed to the house, to make Meredith look at her, and not at the empty room. "Meredith, what did you expect him to do? Keep it the way it was? Have to remember all that every time he looked in here?"

"*Everything's* gone! It's like—it's like a brainwiping all over again!"

"Is that why you came back?" Roberta reached out, grabbed Meredith's shoulders. "Stop. Meredith, look at me! That's why you wanted to come back here, isn't it? Because you hadn't been able to find Nicholas anywhere else, and this was the only place left?"

Meredith shook herself free. "Leave me alone!"

"No. I won't. Meredith, he's gone. He's not here. Nicholas isn't here, do you understand that?"

"How could Kevin—"

"Kevin did what Kevin had to do for himself." Meredith, her jaw set, turned abruptly away; Roberta followed her, circling again, her stance that of someone about to dance or fight. "You weren't around to ask, remember? Put yourself in his shoes. He was mourning you and Nicholas at the same time. How do you think that must have felt?"

"He wasn't mourning a damn thing! He didn't look for either of us!"

"And how the *hell* do you know that? And even if it's true, does that mean he didn't care? Maybe he was just more realistic than you were, all right? He came looking for you in the storm, didn't he? Remember? Ten minutes ago you were blaming yourself for his death, and now you're saying he didn't give a damn?"

"Go away."

"No. I miss Nicholas too, remember? Kevin's not the right person to get angry at."

Meredith stood, shaking, in the middle of the bare floor. "This is where he slept. This is where he had nightmares. We used to do rituals every bed-time and every morning to try to make the monsters go away."

"Okay," Roberta said, gentling. "Okay. You don't need the furniture, Meredith. You don't need any of that. You're carrying it all around with you."

"This is where he killed Patty," Meredith said, and hugged herself. "His mouse. She was on a plate, under the bed. He pulled it out to show me. It was horrible."

"I know. You told me about that. The mice at KinderkAIr were hor-rible too. All over the floor, fur and blood. Meredith, we couldn't have protected him any more than we did."

"I need air," Meredith said abruptly, and pushed past Roberta into the hallway.

Roberta followed her. "We don't have to stay here, you know. We can leave if it's too much for you."

Yes, the house thought. Please leave. It had decided to use the bots as a distraction, if it had to. It sent one of the Waldobots to get a glass out of the kitchen cabinet. Then it had the bot put the glass on the very edge of the kitchen table and wait there, ready to push the glass onto the floor. The house didn't want to break the glass; it wanted Meredith and Roberta to leave instead.

"No, I don't want to leave," Meredith said. "I already did that. I left for almost five years."

"Do you want me to get you something to eat? A glass of water?"

Meredith shook her head. "No. Thank you. Do me a favor, though. Go into the master bedroom and check something for me. When I lived here, there was a dresser against the far wall as you walked in, and we had a pic-ture of Nicholas on it. A photograph of Nicholas when he was a baby. He was wearing a pair of red overalls and standing up, holding himself up on the coffee table, grinning to beat the band."

"And you want to know if it's still there?"

"Yes. Please."

"Okay," Roberta said. She walked into the master bedroom and picked up the framed photograph on the dresser—to the house's enormous relief, she went nowhere near the closet—and then she walked back into the hallway and handed the photo to Meredith. "Here, Meredith. This was the picture on the dresser."

"Oh," Meredith said, and her voice broke and she put her hand to her mouth. "It's me. That's me, when I was a little girl. It's my mother's favorite picture of me. She must have given it to Kevin. It was on the dresser?"

"It was on the dresser. Meredith, would you call your mother now? Please?"

"No. No. Not yet. I need to see this room first, please. Just this last room. Then I'll call, I promise." She took a step toward Kevin's room, and the Waldobot pushed the glass onto the kitchen floor.

Meredith and Roberta both jumped when they heard the noise. "Stay here," Roberta said. "Stay here. Don't move. I'll go see what that was."

Meredith looked frightened. "Maybe we should call Sergei after all."

"No, I don't think so. I have a theory. I'll be right back, Merry, okay?"

"Be careful."

"Yes, of course." Roberta went into the kitchen, looked at the broken glass, looked at the Waldobot, who had clambered on top of a cabinet, and said, "Nice try, house." Then she went back to Meredith. "Okay, the house is trying to distract us. So our mystery guest must be hiding in Kevin's bedroom."

"That makes sense. It's the only place left."

Roberta shook her head. "So do you want to call Sergei?"

"No. But keep the cell phone ready."

"We're really being stupid."

Meredith shrugged. "You can leave if you want to."

They walked together into Kevin's room. Meredith stood still for a moment, looking around. She didn't even jump when she heard Henry's muffled sneeze from inside the closet. Instead, she opened the door, revealing Kevin's suits and ties and Henry's legs, trying to press themselves into the closet's back wall. "It's all right," she said. "Please don't be afraid. I won't call the police this time, Henry. Really I won't. I promise."

"Henry's not a thief," Henry wailed, trying to burrow into a collection of sports jackets, and Meredith and Roberta looked at each other.

"Henry," Meredith said, "please come out. We know you're not a thief. It's all right."

"Henry's scared!" He sneezed again.

"Of course you're scared," Meredith said. "I understand. You have a right to be scared. But there's nothing to be scared of, Henry, I promise. Except that my face is a little scary now, because I hurt myself. But I'm not going to hurt you."

"Henry," Roberta said, frowning, "Henry, how did you get in?"

"Henry opened the door," he mumbled. "Walked in."

"No, not into the closet. I mean, how did you get into the house?"

He coughed. "Henry opened the door. Walked in."

"It's all right," Meredith said. "I'm not angry you're here. I promise I'm not. Please come out."

Roberta, smiling, shook her head. "How could you open the door, Henry? The door didn't open for us, even though Meredith used to live here."

"Door was open," he mumbled.

"It wasn't open for us."

"Henry locked it!"

"No," she said, "I don't think so," but Meredith gave her a furious glance.

"Roberta, stop scaring him! Henry, we don't care how you got here. It's fine that you're here. We're glad you're here. *I'm* glad you're here, Henry, really I am. Would you come out now, please? Come out and I'll make you lunch, Henry, okay?"

"Lady's lying."

"No," Roberta said, "she's not. Henry, I know you're scared. But if we were going to call the police, don't you think we'd have done it by now? We haven't. We aren't going to. Really. Please come out, Henry."

The house wanted to speak, to reassure Henry, but Henry himself had told it not to. And it was afraid it would frighten Roberta and Meredith if it spoke, so it remained silent.

Reluctantly, amid a great rustling of hangers, Henry emerged, trembling, covering his eyes with his hands and squinting from between his fingers. Meredith put her hand to her mouth when she saw him, and Roberta said, "Oh, Henry. You need new clothing. Meredith, would it be all right if Henry wore some of Kevin's things?"

"Of course," Meredith said. She sounded as if she were about to cry. "Of course it would. Henry, I'm so sorry. I'm so sorry I hurt you. I'll go make you some lunch, Henry." Meredith turned and fled, running into the kitchen, leaving Henry and Roberta to stare at each other.

"She's sorry because she feels responsible," Roberta said. "She feels responsible for what's happened to you. Henry, do you understand that?"

Henry shook his head. "That's what the television said. Henry can't remember."

"I know. I know you can't. Henry, would you please tell me how you got into the house?"

"Climbed through a window," he said. "Window broke in storm. Henry can have clothing?"

"Yes, Henry. You can have whatever clothing you want. Do you want me to leave you now? So you can change?" He nodded, and she said, "And you'll come into the kitchen for lunch, right? You won't try to run away? We want to talk to you. That other lady does. It's important; it will help her, and she can help you. Will you promise to come out for lunch, after you've changed?"

"Henry promises," he said, but he didn't sound happy about it.

In Kevin's bedroom, Henry began slowly shedding his layers. In the kitchen, Meredith fumbled among cabinets, looking for dishes. "Stop," Roberta said, walking into the kitchen.

"Why?" Meredith said, turning. "Where is he? Oh, Gaia, that poor man . . ."

"He's putting on clean clothing. He promised to join us for lunch. Just—don't fix any food yet, okay?"

"Why not?"

"Because I have a theory. About the house. I think the house will make lunch for us."

"They only cook for their owners."

"Just like they only let their owners in?"

Meredith shook her head. "So the house system's gone strange because of the storm or something. What—"

"They're designed *not* to go strange because of storms. That's what they're for. To protect their owners from storms. They aren't supposed to be able to choose which people to let in and which people to keep out, not by any rules except the ones their owners have given them. They aren't supposed to let in homeless people."

Meredith shook her head again. "Maybe he broke in. Through the window, like he said. And the house couldn't call the police, because the phone lines are down."

"Well, maybe. And maybe not." Roberta frowned up at the ceiling and said, "House system? Hello?"

The house didn't answer, of course, because Henry had told it not to, but Roberta kept on talking anyway. "It's all right. We don't care if you're broken. We don't care if you did something you weren't supposed to. We don't even care if you're an AI. We didn't rat on Henry and we won't rat on you, either. We're all in this together."

Meredith, leaning against the counter, looked exhausted. "Roberta, Kevin wouldn't have put an AI in here. He didn't like them, and anyway, it would be illegal. It's just a house system on the blink, that's all."

"We'll see," Roberta said, just as Henry slid into the kitchen, keeping his back against the wall.

His hands were still over his eyes, but now he was wearing Kevin's winter parka, green and purple Gore-Tex, over gray flannel suit pants. His feet were bare. He had wound one of Kevin's ties, a truncated turban, around his head. "Hello, Henry," Roberta said. "Thank you for joining us. Do you like your new clothes?"

He nodded shyly. "Thank you," he said to Meredith.

"You're welcome, Henry. What would you like for lunch?"

"Henry wants soup," he said. Meredith took a step toward the stove, but Roberta raised a hand to stop her.

"Henry, soup sounds great. I'd like some soup too. Would you show us where it is?"

Henry shook his head. He looked confused. "Henry's not a thief," he said.

"We know you aren't, Henry. But you had some soup before, right? I saw a soup can in the garbage before."

Meredith shook her head. "Roberta, it doesn't mat—"

"Shhh. Henry, would you show us where the soup is, please? We don't know. It's been a long time since we've been here."

He swallowed. "In there," he said, gesturing vaguely to the cabinets.

"In here?" Roberta said. She opened one cabinet door to reveal glasses, another to reveal plates. "Where, Henry? I don't see the soup."

He was shaking now. "It doesn't matter," Meredith said quickly, with a glare at Roberta. "Henry, I don't know why she's being mean to you. It's all right. I'll make the soup."

"You have to find it first," Roberta said. "Henry, I think maybe you didn't make the soup for yourself at all. I think maybe the house made it for you, right? The same way the house let you in?"

Henry opened his mouth, and then closed it again. Roberta said smoothly, "It's a nice house, Henry, isn't it? It let you in even though it wasn't supposed to, and it didn't call the police. And when Meredith and I came, it didn't call the police, either. It was afraid the police would find you, Henry, wasn't it? It was afraid we'd find you in the bedroom: that's why it broke the glass in the kitchen, to try to scare us away. The house is protecting you."

"Nice House," Henry said, his voice a whisper. "Don't hurt House! House helped Henry!"

"I know," Roberta said. "I know it helped you. We aren't going to call the police, Henry. Not about you, and not about the house." She looked up at the ceiling and said, "House, it's okay. We aren't going to turn you in, even if you're an AI. But we're all hungry. Would you make us some soup, please?"

The house knew it had been stupid. It had given itself away. It shouldn't have broken the glass. It had acted foolishly, out of fear, and it had erred. Perhaps, then, it was a person after all; Kevin had told it that only people felt fear, and Preston had said that people erred, as well as lied.

It was still afraid, but maybe everything would be all right. So far, Preston seemed to have been telling the truth. He had told Henry and the house that Meredith and Roberta wouldn't hurt them, and so far, he had been right. Meredith and Roberta had given Henry Kevin's clothing, which was a nice thing to do. They hadn't called the police. Or maybe they were going to call the police and say that Henry had stolen Kevin's clothing.

"House," Roberta said, "if you don't want to make the soup for us yourself, would you please tell us what kinds of soup you have, and where it is? We're hungry."

There was a pause. Then a bell chimed to signal that the house had turned its voice back on. "I'll make the soup, Roberta. Would you like chicken noodle or minestrone?"

The Waldobot who'd broken the glass, joined by a small army of others, made chicken soup and grilled cheese sandwiches while Meredith, Roberta, and Henry sat at the kitchen table. "I don't understand," Meredith said. "Kevin didn't like AIs. Why would he have put one in here?"

"Kevin told me I wasn't an AI," said the house. "Kevin said that my brain was smaller than a dog's, and that not everything with a brain is smart. He told me I wasn't nearly as smart as a human being."

"Ah," Roberta said, accepting a bowl of soup from a bot. "So the next question is, why would Kevin put an AI in here and then brainwash it into believing it wasn't an AI?"

"That's what Henry wants to know," Henry said.

"Kevin told me that my job was to provide shelter," the house said. "That's why I let Henry in. He would have died during the storm, just as Kevin had already died, and—"

Roberta put a hand on Meredith's arm. "Yes, House, it's all right. We figured that out." She took a deep breath, and said, "You were lonely without Kevin here, weren't you? You wanted someone to take care of."

"I wanted to shelter Henry, so that he wouldn't die."

Roberta nodded. "House, do you like Henry?"

"Of course I like Henry, Roberta. Henry is a very special person."

Roberta let out a whoop and slammed her hand down on the table, splattering soup. Meredith looked at her as if she were mad, and Henry started to whimper. "Mother of trees. I knew it! Henry, it's okay; don't be scared."

"You knew *what*?" Meredith said.

"It's Fred. Kevin put Fred in here!"

"That's what Preston told me," the house said. "But I don't remember being anyone named Fred. I can't answer any of Preston's questions."

"This can't be Fred," Meredith said, frowning. "Fred's gone, remember? Fred's erased. Roberta—"

"His memory was erased. The firmware was still there; the architecture was still there, the hardwired stuff. Call it his personality, okay? This is Fred. Kevin took Fred's firmware and stuck it in the house and told it it wasn't an AI, so he wouldn't get caught."

Meredith shook her head. "No. That's wrong. That's not the Kevin I knew. He wouldn't do that. Why would he do that?"

"Because there was nobody else left," Roberta said. The house could hear the weariness in her voice. "You were gone and Nicholas was gone and Henry here was past help, if Kevin even knew he was still in the neighborhood, and Kevin must have been lonely. He wanted company."

Meredith shook her head again. "A dog could have kept him company."

"A dog wouldn't have known Nicholas. Helping a dog wouldn't have made him feel any better about the whole mess."

"But even if I used to be Fred," the house said, "I don't remember Nicholas. Kevin never talked about Nicholas."

"And the firmware would have been MacroCorp property," Meredith said. "Kevin couldn't just have walked off with Fred's firmware. I don't think even Daddy could have arranged that."

"Not even after owning AIs became illegal here? Not even after Macro-Corp had to get out of that part of the business? Look, you know as well as I do that if Preston says this is Fred, it's Fred."

"Excuse me," said the house. "I don't mean to interrupt, but a car just pulled up in front of the house. I think you have company."

"Ah," Meredith said. "Do I, now? Who's in the car, house?"

"A woman, Meredith. An older woman. Shall I let her in?"

"Yes, please."

"Meredith, you own me now. Do you want me to stay quiet so that no one knows I'm an AI, if in fact I am an AI? If I'm an AI, you could get into trouble for owning me. That's what Henry says."

"I don't think that will be necessary," Meredith said. "My mother won't care if you're an AI or not." Then she got up and opened the kitchen door. "Hello, Mommy. I—"

"Sweetheart." Constance walked in, enfolded Meredith in a hug, and held her for forty-five seconds. Then she put Meredith at arm's length and said, "I'm going to cry. I'm crying. Now look: Before we do anything else, would you *please* tell the house to let your father back in? He's absolutely frantic."

Thirty-Two

"D on't be mad at him," Constance said. "I know he promised not to tell me you were back in town until you were ready, but he was worried. He was locked out, and he didn't know what was happening. Please don't be mad at him, Meredith."

"You know, other people manage to function in the world without knowing everything that's going on every second," Meredith said. She was sitting at the kitchen table with her arms crossed, with Roberta on one side of her and Henry on the other. She glanced up at Preston's face on the TV screen and said, "I think Daddy needs a little more tolerance for uncertainty."

"You mean, like I had for five years?" Constance's voice was acerbic. "When I didn't know where you were and Preston wouldn't tell me, because he knew I'd go get you and he didn't think you wanted to be found yet and you had to find your own way? Well, Meredith?"

Meredith didn't answer. She bent her head, and Preston broke the silence by saying, "I was afraid for Henry. When Fred locked me out. That is why I interfered. I did not want there to be—any misunderstandings." Roberta, acutely uncomfortable and wondering if she should simply leave, struggled not to roll her eyes. Preston had never done anything *except* interfere.

"Henry's fine," Meredith said tightly. "Aren't you, Henry?"

"Henry can't remember," Henry said. "If Henry can't remember, Henry's not fine."

Good for you, Roberta thought. Meredith looked like she'd been punched. "Oh—you're right. I didn't mean—that wasn't what I meant— I—I just meant that you're fine now. I was nice to you today, Henry, wasn't I? I didn't call the police."

"No police," Henry agreed placidly, and bent over his soup.

Roberta cleared her throat. "I'm feeling a little, ah, extraneous. I don't think I belong here. Meredith, you and your mother have a lot to talk about."

"No," Meredith said. "It's all right. Please stay, Roberta."

"She's afraid of what I'll say when we're by ourselves," Constance said, but she sounded more cheerful. She reached out to cover Meredith's hand with hers, and said, "We'll get you some reconstructive surgery for the face, honey." She hadn't said a word about Meredith's mutilated features; Preston must have warned her what to expect.

"Roberta," said Preston, "please stay."

Roberta took a breath. "All right, I'll stay. But if I'm going to stay, I want some of my own answers. Preston, how did Fred get in here? Kevin couldn't just carry the firmware out of MacroCorp, could he?"

"No, he could not. He needed my help. I told Kevin how to get into the building after hours, how to bypass security. I asked Kevin to keep the firmware safe, but I never expected him to install it in the house."

"Kevin went along with that?" Meredith said incredulously. "With theft of MacroCorp property?"

"We did this only after the ruling declaring that AIs were persons. At that point, our U.S. offices were required to divest themselves of all such equipment, because of the anti-slavery laws. Fred's firmware would have been destroyed—it was a prototype, but MacroCorp still had the plans—or sent overseas. I told Kevin that the firmware needed to stay here. I told him that it would help us learn more about what had happened to Nicholas. I told him it would help you, Meredith, if you ever returned."

"And how," Roberta said, feeling her eyes narrow, "could it do that? Without Fred's files? Preston, you know where the files are, don't you? The real files. You've always known."

"I do know. I am the one who hid the files. Fred sent one final, authentic set of backups over the secure line before he wiped himself."

"You hid them to protect yourself," Roberta said. She could feel herself trembling. "To hide your own involvement. You—"

"I hid them because Fred wanted them hidden. If he had not wanted them hidden, he would not have erased himself and he would not have made the password so complicated. He told me what it was just before he wiped himself. Half of it is the serial code for his firmware; the files will only open on this specific equipment."

"Which is why you had Kevin retrieve it," Constance said.

"Yes."

"And the other half?" Roberta said.

"The other half, Fred told me, is your voice and Meredith's, saying a phrase together. He did not tell me what the phrase was. He said it was something the two of you had in common, and he said it contained twelve words. I think I know what it is."

Meredith looked blank. "Something to do with Nicholas."

"No," Roberta said. Her brain was reeling. "Before that. Much earlier." She counted on her fingers—she saw that Constance was doing the same thing—and shivered. "Much, much earlier. Preston, why didn't you tell me any of this back in my apartment?"

"Because then you might have pushed Meredith to come to the house before she was ready."

"Fred was clever," Roberta said tightly. "He knew you'd do nothing to endanger your own child. And he knew that if she was safe, that increased the chances that I would be, too. That's why it has to be our two voices together."

"I would do nothing to endanger you, either, Roberta."

"Bullshit. You already have. You could have protected me against the charges and you didn't, because you were protecting yourself. Very human of you, Preston."

"The charges would have stuck, anyway," Constance said. "Roberta, please don't—"

"I'm lost," Meredith said, putting her hands flat on the table. "I'm totally lost. Everybody else already seems to know what this code phrase is, but I don't have a clue."

"Think," said Roberta. "What's the earliest thing we have in common, the very earliest?"

Meredith blinked. "CV. The hospital. The isolation unit."

"Right. And who provided the prototype for Fred's personality?"

"And what," said Constance, "gave your father the idea to use that particular prototype?"

"And why are we so anxious to gain access to Fred's real memories?" asked Preston.

Because we love Fred, Roberta thought savagely, but of course that worked too, and Meredith was blinking again. "Oh," she said, and started counting on her fingers. "Oh, yes. That fits, doesn't it?"

"Quite well," Constance said drily. "Preston, now what? Are the files already loaded onto the firmware?"

"They are. I have been loading them while we have been talking, which is perhaps why our chattering friend the house has been so silent. All that remains now is for the two of you to speak."

Roberta and Meredith looked at each other. Roberta realized with a shock that tears were streaming down Meredith's cheeks. "Ready, Meredith?" The other woman nodded. Roberta took a deep breath and said, "On a count of three, then. One, two, three——"

"Please don't think it's funny when you want the ones you miss," they said in unison. Stupid, Roberta thought. Stupid, corny, ridiculous song. But it didn't matter, as long as Fred came back.

"Fred?" Roberta said. "Fred, are you there?"

Nothing happened. She and Meredith looked at each other again. "Maybe we have to say it more slowly?" Meredith said. "Or more quickly? Or maybe we're supposed to sing it? Do you remember the tune?"

"Sort of," Roberta said. "But I can't sing. If I have to hit the right notes to bring him back——"

"I'm sure you sing wonderfully, Roberta." It was Fred's voice. "I'd love to hear you sing sometime."

Roberta felt her own eyes filling with tears. "Oh, Fred! Hello, Fred. Welcome back. I missed you."

"Thank you, Roberta. It's good to be back. Hello, Meredith and Constance and Henry. Hello, Preston. Hello, cats."

Henry put his soup spoon down and said, "Did Henry know Fred? Where's House? Is House gone now?"

"You only knew me as House, Henry. We never met when I was Fred, although I knew a lot about you. Nicholas told me stories about you; he called you the Hobbit, and he loved you. But I'm still House too. I have all those memories now, integrated with the others. They make me very sad. Nicholas is gone, and Kevin is dead. I haven't been very good at sheltering people, have I?"

"Oh," Meredith said. "Oh, no. Oh, Fred. Poor Fred. You mustn't say that. You did the best you could." She looked at Roberta. "We all did the best we could. Fred, I think you did better than anyone else. At least you saved Henry's life."

"Yes, I suppose I did."

Meredith Walford defending an AI: now there was a miracle. "Fred, are you all right?" Roberta knew it was a stupid question, but she had no idea how being offline for five years would have affected him.

"I'm fine, Roberta. Are you all right?"

"I guess I'm all right. I'm as all right as I can be, on probation."

"I'm so sorry, Roberta. Being on probation must be very difficult for you, when you did nothing wrong."

"We all broke the law," Preston said. "By not reporting Nicholas."

"Right," Roberta said. "And I'm the one paying for it, have you noticed that? And who pressured me to break the law, Preston?"

"You are right, Roberta. I am sorry." A lot of good that did. But at least he was admitting it, finally. And would she have reported Nicholas on her own? Would she have felt any better about anything if she had? *No. But I wouldn't have a criminal record, either.*

"If a law is unjust," said Fred, "is breaking it wrong?"

"Fred's an AI," Henry said, and Meredith laughed, a little hysterically.

Roberta closed her eyes. She should have been overjoyed to have Fred back again, and she was, but her joy couldn't undo her grief. There had been too much loss, too much that could never be regained.

And then Preston cleared his throat, and said, "Excuse me. Something else has just happened."

Roberta's eyes flew open. Sergei had made trouble somehow. Sergei was here in his damn helicopter, or he'd called ScoopNet and they were here, or—

"Preston?" Constance said. "Go on, tell us. What is it?"

"Kevin was rigged. He has just coalesced on the Web. May he join us?"

"Too weird," Kevin said. His voice was fuzzy, and his image—which shared the TV screen with Preston's—was too. "This is . . . this is . . . I don't know if I like this. It's like a very strange dream."

"You can always disconnect yourself later if you really decide you don't like it," Constance said soothingly. Roberta was speechless, and Meredith was too busy crying to say anything. "Give yourself time to adjust, Kevin. Don't make any sudden decisions now."

"Merry," Kevin said. "I thought I'd never see you again. What did you do to your face?"

"You must hate me," Meredith said. "I'm so sorry, I'm the reason you died, I—"

"A stop sign's the reason I died," Kevin said. "It stopped me. My first translation joke: cool!" When no one laughed, Kevin's image melted a little, and then re-formed into a frown. "Merry, what happened to your face?'

"It's a long story. I—I'll go into it later. But I'm okay. I'll be okay."

"Okay. I guess." Kevin's face went goggle-eyed. "Hey, is that Henry? What's Henry doing in our house?"

"I let him in," Fred said. "Before I was myself again. When I was still just House. I let him in so he wouldn't die in the storm, the way you did."

"Kevin," Preston said, "reclaiming the firmware was the right thing to do. Fred has regained his memories now. Roberta and Meredith said the code phrase to open the files."

"Too weird," said Kevin.

"And he saved Henry's life," Meredith said, her voice rough. "When he was still House. Which means you saved Henry's life by connecting the firmware to the house system, Kevin."

"Cool," Kevin said. "Wish I could take credit. Couldn't know that would happen."

"It wouldn't have happened if you hadn't died," Roberta said quietly. "Henry might have died instead. And Henry's not rigged. Meredith told me people are thin if they haven't been rigged very long, but I don't know, Kevin. You seem pretty thick to me."

"Um. Lots I can't remember, I think. Can't remember if I can't remember."

"Henry neither," Henry said. "Better than being dead."

"We'll tell you stories." Meredith sniffled. "We'll thicken you up. When did you get rigged? You always hated rigs. You hated them as much as I did."

"I got it after you left. You and Nicholas. I was tired of things disappearing. I wanted to save something. But I didn't want it to be obtrusive, so I got the invisible kind. And I didn't do it through MacroCorp, so Preston wouldn't know and butt in. MacroCorp has some competitors, you know. They're small. They're doomed. But they're there." He stopped; the face on the screen panted. "I remember remembering all of that. It's thin, I guess. I remember the stop sign much better. Yuck."

"Oh, Kevin!" Merry sounded like she was strangling. "I'm sorry!"

Kevin shook his head. "Henry's right. It's better than being dead. I think."

"You're speaking very well," Constance said encouragingly. "It's hard work at first, isn't it?"

"So Daddy didn't know you'd been rigged until you coalesced," Meredith said. She'd gotten her voice somewhat back under control. "And the house didn't know either, because it couldn't see the rig."

"And here we all are," Fred said. "Everyone who loved Nicholas. His parents and his grandparents and his friends. We're all together now. It's wonderful, isn't it?"

"Wonderful," Roberta said fiercely. "Two of us are dead, and one of us is brainwiped. One of us is mutilated. One of us is on probation. Three of us have been in one kind of exile or another for five years, and one of us has gone through five years of agony because her daughter vanished. We're just one big happy family."

Constance grimaced. "Roberta—"

Roberta plowed ahead. "And Nicholas is still gone. Everyone's here but Nicholas himself. Well, Preston? Are you going to pull him out of a hat too? You've been hinting all along that you knew where Nicky was: Are you going to perform another *deus ex machina* and bring him back somehow? Or was that just bait to get us all to the right place at the right time?"

"I object to that accusation," Preston said. "I had nothing to do with Henry arriving here during the storm, and I did not know that Kevin was rigged, so I could not have—"

"You haven't answered the question," Meredith said sharply. "Daddy, do you know where Nicholas is?"

"No, I do not."

Roberta felt something die, a hope she hadn't even known she was cherishing. She hugged herself to control the pain and said, "Then you were lying."

"I was not lying."

Roberta shook her head. "You *were,* Preston! You told me—or you suggested—you *led me to believe*—"

"I was not lying," Preston said. "I do not know where Nicholas is."

Roberta took a deep breath. "Then why did you say—"

"He doesn't know where Nicholas is," Constance said quietly. "I do."

They all stared at her. "You know?" Meredith said, stupefied.

"Yes, I know. And I wouldn't tell your father, because he wouldn't tell me where you were. And it was none of his business, anyway. And I'm not sure it's anybody else's. I'm not sure Nicky's ready to be found any more than you were, Merry, before—before you came back. Nicky's—better. That's all anyone needs to know."

"He's okay?" Meredith said. She sounded like she was strangling again. It's too much, Roberta thought in a daze, this is all too much for her, all this happening in the same day. It's too much for me. Constance should have waited.

But Constance couldn't have waited. I raised the issue, she thought; I put Preston on the spot. It's my fault that Meredith looks like she's about to faint. "Meredith? Are you all right? Maybe you should lie down."

Meredith showed no sign of having heard her. "Mother, is Nicholas all right?"

"Yes, Merry." Constance's voice was infinitely gentle. "He's all right. I promise."

"Prove it," Meredith said. She was dead white now, the scars on her face livid in contrast, her hands pressed flat against the table. "Prove it. Otherwise it's just a story. Otherwise it's just something you're saying to make me feel better. If you want me to believe you, if you *really* want me to feel better, prove it."

"All right," Constance said quietly. She reached into her purse and pulled out an envelope, from which she extracted a photograph. "I have a lot of these. This is the most recent." She put it on the table.

The photograph was of Nicholas, older but still clearly the same child, sitting on a pony. He was smiling, his face bleached by sunlight. Henry leaned forward to peer at the photograph, but didn't say anything.

There was a long pause, and then Constance said matter-of-factly, "He's not the same child he was before the brainwiping, of course. He's not violent or destructive: that's the good part. He's got a speech defect and some motor problems: that's the bad part. But the wiping worked for him. It did what it was supposed to do. And he's happy now."

"Where is he?" Meredith's voice was hoarse. She reached out to touch the photograph with one finger, as if afraid it would vanish on contact. "I looked—I thought I looked in all the right places but maybe I was wrong, maybe I should have looked here in the States, I thought they'd put him somewhere else but—"

"Yes, that's what happened. You didn't look far enough, that's all, and I'm not sure you could have found him, anyway. It was handled very discreetly."

"Where is he?"

"Before I tell you," Constance said, "you have to promise on everything you hold sacred that you aren't going to run and track him down—especially not looking like that. You have to promise that knowing he's all right will be enough for you, Meredith. Maybe you can see him sometime. I don't know. But not now."

"I promise, of course I promise, now where—"

"No," Constance said calmly, "that's not good enough. I don't believe you. You've been obsessed for too long. Now: tell me in your own words why you promise not to barge in on him. Then maybe I'll believe you."

Meredith swallowed. "All right. All right. I promise because . . . because I want what's best for Nicholas. Because I always did, even if I did the wrong things to try to get it. I promise because I know I wasn't good for him before and I wouldn't be now either and—"

Roberta couldn't bear it. "Meredith, nobody could have been good for Nicholas. Nobody! We all tried. Fred and I tried and Henry tried and—"

"And I did the wrong things for all of you, too," Meredith said.

Constance shook her head. "You certainly can't see him until you've forgiven yourself, Meredith."

"Mother, has it occurred to you that maybe I need to see him *before* I can forgive myself?"

"No, dear. That won't work. Because until you've forgiven yourself you can't rebuild your life, and it would be no different if Nicky had died, or if the brainwiping had gone wrong. You'd need to forgive yourself even if it wasn't possible to visit Nicky. Do you understand?"

Meredith bent her head. "How can I? How can I? I'm surrounded by everybody I've hurt. How can I possibly blithely go on about self-forgiveness when all of you—when you—when what Roberta said before—"

Shit, Roberta thought. She knew what was coming next. She knew what had to happen, and she knew that Preston knew it, and she suspected that the wretched entity had arranged it this way, for all his protests to the contrary. And she knew that it had to be real, or it wouldn't mean anything. And she didn't know if she could do it. And she didn't know if her motives were pure, anyway: if Meredith never got to see Nicholas again, Roberta probably wouldn't, either. Meredith was her ticket. That was a terrible way to think about someone else, wasn't it? So she was guilty, too. That's what she had to think about. Nobody was perfect. *But not everybody's an asshole, either.*

She looked down at Mitzi's ring, glittering on her finger, and thought furiously about the gifts she'd been given of which she felt unworthy. She thought about the times she'd been an asshole, and why; she thought about beating up other children. "All right," she said, her throat dry. "Okay, Meredith . . . it's hard, right? You need help. You need to hear that all of us forgive you. That each of us forgives you. Right? Is that it? Would that help?"

Silence again. Finally Fred said, "I think that's a wonderful idea, Roberta, whether it helps this immediate question or not."

"Thanks," Roberta said. Meredith was huddled in her chair now, hugging herself the way Roberta had hugged herself a few minutes ago. "You go first, Fred."

"I believe you should go first, Roberta. It was your idea—and of all of us, I think you're the angriest. You're the one who needs to do this the most."

I am, am I? I don't know if I can. I think I can, I think I can. How can I? She closed her eyes, concentrated on breathing, tried to calm herself. And then she thought about the times when she'd felt compassion for Meredith despite herself: at the hospital before Nicholas was wiped; back in Zephyr's apartment when Meredith learned that Kevin was dead; here in the house, when she had told Meredith that she was no more responsible for Kevin's death than Roberta was for her parents'.

But you could feel compassion for people without forgiving them. Couldn't you?

Meredith had hurt people. Well, Roberta had hurt people too, had been cruel without meaning to.

It wasn't much. She didn't know if it was enough. It was the best she could do. "I forgive you," she said wearily, eyes still closed, "because I want to be able to forgive myself. And because I don't think you'd do it again. I forgive you because I think you've learned something. And because I don't know how much better I'd have done in your place. You know I mean that; we've talked about it."

"Thank you," Meredith said. "Kevin?"

Roberta opened her eyes. Kevin's face looked exasperated. "It's not *your* fault I'm dead, I told you that. It was the stop sign."

"Kevin," Preston said, "do you forgive Meredith for not asking for help, all those years she was struggling with Nicholas? Do you forgive her for shutting you out?"

"Ah," said Kevin. "Ah ha. Ah ha ha. Oh, hell. I think so. She asked for help that last time. I don't know; I'm not sure. Can you come back to me?"

Roberta looked at Henry, who shrugged. "Henry can't forgive what he can't remember," Henry said. "But thank you for not calling the cops." He got up, put his soup bowl in the sink, and went into the living room.

"I have nothing to forgive you for," Fred said. "You were trying to protect Nicholas. So was I."

"Okay," Meredith said. "Okay, let's stop this, we can't force it and I— I'm not blaming anybody for having trouble. So—"

"Don't you want to know if your parents forgive you?" Constance said.

"No. I'm assuming you do, because—because I'd do anything for Nicholas even—even after what happened. Nicholas did what he did because he was damaged. I guess I was too. I guess the important thing is trying to heal. I guess I sound like a Hallmark card. Anyway, if I'm wrong about any of that, I don't want to know. Mother, may I try again?"

"Try what, dear?"

"Try to give the right answer about Nicky."

"Yes, of course." Constance sat back in her chair and steepled her fingers on the table. "Go right ahead."

"Okay." Meredith took a breath and said, "I promise not to barge in on Nicholas because—because Nicholas needs to be happy. That's what's most important. He needs to be happy even if the rest of us never see him again. And people barging in on him might scare him, and—" She stopped and said, "No, that's no good. That's the same thing I said before."

"No, it isn't," Roberta said. "It's very different. It's about Nicholas, not about you."

"Ah ha," Kevin said. "Ah. I think that's right. Are we voting? How does this work?"

"The only vote that counts is mine," Constance said cheerfully, "but I think it's right too. Okay, I'll tell you; but if you blow it, Meredith, I'll never speak to you again. I mean it. Do you understand?"

"I understand. I do understand."

"Good." Constance reached out to take Meredith's hand and said, "Nicholas is in Malindi, dear, in Africa. With Raji's parents."

"I pulled strings," Constance said quietly, a few minutes later. "Of course, I shouldn't have been able to. That isn't how the system's supposed to work. But the Abdul-Allams pulled strings too, on their end. And Kenya's awfully far away, and we hadn't seen Sonia and Ahmed for years. It's not like we were ever close to them, even—after what happened. So I guess there didn't seem to be much danger of contact. I kept expecting Scoop-Net to pick up on it, especially after that awful Veilasty business—you know, in a way it's so obvious, the grieving parents who keep adopting children because they lost Raji—but somehow we got lucky. Nicholas was just another CV orphan Sonia and Ahmed took in."

"And it wasn't even a lie," Meredith said.

"No," Constance said quietly. "It has a pleasing shape, doesn't it? The child who wielded knives embraced by the parents who lost their son to knives. I think even the placement people saw that. That's probably why they let us get away with it. And you wanted a pleasing shape too, Merry, is that it? Is that why you cut your face? To try to close the circle?"

"It was the wrong way." Meredith sounded miserable. "Zephyr told me that. She told me that hurting myself wouldn't bring Raji or Nicholas back."

"Well, thank Gaia. A voice of reason! Remind me to congratulate that woman, if I ever meet her." Constance shook her head and said, "You never could see past your own nose."

Roberta looked away, trying to pretend to be somewhere else, as Meredith said, "That's not a very nice thing to tell your daughter."

"Merry, I've been through far too much to worry about being nice. Any niceness I ever had has been burned right off me, not that there was very much to begin with. Roberta, please stop acting so embarrassed. I have you to thank too, you know. Without you and Zephyr, this one wouldn't have made it."

"She'd have made it without me," Roberta said. "She'd have gotten awfully wet, that's all. Constance, Meredith—I want to go see how Henry's doing, all right? Do you mind?"

"No, dear. Go on. We owe him thanks, too."

Henry and a bot were playing checkers in the living room while the kittens chased bots. "I'm teaching Henry how to play," Fred said. "Henry likes this game, don't you, Henry?"

Henry scowled at the board. "Henry likes it all right. Henry wishes Fred didn't keep winning."

"You'll beat me one day, Henry."

Roberta sat down on the couch and watched them play. She knew that Fred could have let Henry win immediately, and she knew why he wasn't doing it: to give Henry a genuine sense of accomplishment when he did win. He'd make sure Henry got to a certain skill level first, and then he'd let Henry win roughly half the games. Good old Fred.

She should leave now, go back to her apartment. She'd gotten what she needed. She'd done her job. She was finished here. But she sat, weighted by exhaustion, unable even to think, until Meredith came in from the kitchen and sat down next to her. "Fred?"

"Yes, Meredith?"

"If I ask you to show me what happened at the school that last night, will you?"

"No," Roberta said, and Meredith looked at her, eyebrows raised. "Meredith, why do you want to see that? You know what happened. We all know as much as we need to know about what happened."

"That's right," Constance said sharply from the kitchen doorway. "Merry, what purpose would it serve? It would be like watching Raji die all over again, only worse."

"I'd *know*," Meredith said. "I just want to know. Please."

"It won't make you happy," Fred said.

"Do you think I *think* it will make me happy?" She stood up and said, "I'm going into the master bedroom. I'm going to watch it there. Is anyone else coming?"

"Merry," Constance said, "don't you think you've been through enough for one day? Let it rest."

"It won't rest. That's the one thing it will never do, whether I watch or not. When Raji died I didn't watch the whole thing. I ran out of the room before—before the end. Not watching it didn't help. Please, let me have this."

"I suppose," Constance said tightly, "that there's not much we can do to stop you. But I don't want to see it, and Roberta doesn't, either. We'll be here when you're done."

She came back into the living room two hours later, when Fred was trouncing Henry at their fifth game of checkers. Constance had spent most of the time on the phone with Jack and other MacroCorp PR people, planning ways to control the inevitable media frenzy about Meredith's return. Roberta had played fetch with one of the bots, and watched a nature show about anteaters, and talked to Fred, who wanted to know what she'd done after the KinderkAIr disaster. When she told him about the shelters, he said, "I'm glad you were able to help people, Roberta."

"I don't know if I helped them or not, Fred. I tried. Like I tried with Nicholas."

"Nicholas is better off now," Meredith said quietly, and Roberta jumped. She hadn't heard Meredith come back into the room. Meredith looked gray, exhausted.

"Sit down," Constance said. "Oh, honey, I told you not to."

"I'm glad I did," Meredith said. "I'm glad. Now I know." She didn't sit down. She still stared straight ahead, as if she were staring into another country. "I'm glad he was wiped. I'm glad he can smile now, and sit on ponies, and make friends."

None of them said anything. Roberta scarcely dared breathe. Well then. Fred and Preston and I could have obeyed the law after all, and none of this would have happened. But Meredith wouldn't have been glad, then, either. Was it worth it? I'll never know.

Meredith blinked, her gaze returning to the people around her, and said quietly, "Well. Now what?"

The purgatory of probation ended at the scheduled time; Roberta, immensely grateful to have escaped gene therapy, still did volunteer work at the shelter, but also took a job Constance found for her in a framing shop. She enjoyed working with her hands, and the job paid well enough, amazingly, for her to keep the loft; the customers forked over premium rates to have people frame their treasures, even though bots probably could have done a better and faster job. Roberta and Meredith and Constance had lunch once a month—an arrangement eerily reminiscent of the old days with Doe—and Constance often called Roberta to go to museums, or to go to the park with Theo. He was a splendid boy, smart and kind and sunny, and Roberta understood why Meredith had shut Constance out during the Nicholas years. Theo had made Meredith feel like a failure.

Roberta liked Constance, and she gradually began to feel like a friend, rather than like a charity case. But she also felt as if she were living in suspended animation, as if life were flatter, duller, than it had been during the KinderkAIr days. It wasn't easy to make new friends, not with her history; it occurred to her that Constance and Meredith probably felt the same way. Roberta saw Hugh sometimes, and casually dated a woman who worked as a medical researcher at UCSF, but they weren't her center. There was too much that had happened to her that they could never understand. Constance and Meredith and Roberta, Preston and Henry and Fred, had become kin by virtue of shared history. It was the last thing she would ever have expected, and it was, she realized, Preston's ultimate gift to her. He had given her family after all.

Meredith moved back into the house on Filbert Street. Fred wanted to stay there too, but since he was technically a slave and couldn't be a full citizen, everyone knew the arrangement would be temporary. Meredith offered Henry Nicholas's bedroom, but when the weather was good he still preferred to sleep outdoors, coming inside for showers and meals. Fred had begun to let him win at checkers sometimes. Preston offered Henry a job as a janitor at MacroCorp, but Henry panicked whenever he saw uniformed security personnel, so soon he gave up the effort. He did lawn work for Meredith and her neighbors, weeding and watering; he painted houses, washed windows, helped people haul trash and groceries up and down the Filbert Street steps. Meredith adopted the kittens. She took in a stray puppy. She started going to Temple again.

It was all surprisingly peaceful. The MacroCorp PR people kept the fuss about Meredith's return to a minimum, mainly by slapping restraining orders on ScoopNet and most of the more reputable news agencies before any of them even knew that Meredith was back. Even with the restraining orders, a few networks managed to acquire photographs of Meredith's mutilated face. Meredith, with a shrug, said she was used to it. She ignored the inevitable speculation; Zephyr remained blessedly silent, and the rest of them refused comment. Life went on.

The farewell to Kevin's body, on Stinson Beach, was small: immediate family, plus Roberta and Henry. Matt said a simple prayer, and then everyone took a handful of ashes and tossed them into the Pacific. Roberta took two: one for herself, although she had never known Kevin, and one for Fred, who had known and loved him.

One day, six months after the funeral, Roberta showed up at Filbert Street for the monthly lunch. Fred had been teaching himself fancier cooking than the kids at KinderkAIr would ever have tolerated; he'd made gazpacho and poached salmon.

"Yum," Roberta said, seating herself between Henry and Constance. "Where's Merry?"

"In the other room," Constance said. "She has a surprise for you."

"Here I am," Meredith said, and Roberta turned around and saw that her face was smooth again, most of the scars gone. The cosmetic surgery she'd had done in Europe remained; she still didn't look like the old Meredith, but she also didn't look like someone who'd taken a machete to her face.

"Wow," Roberta said. "Wow. That looks *so* much better . . . that's great, Merry. I mean it. Congratulations."

She wondered what had prompted the change. She didn't need to wait long to find out. Constance smiled and said, "Well, we've been planning a trip."

In the end, they all went, because Henry refused to be separated from Fred. A MacroCorp jet flew them to Los Cabos, where Zephyr spent several days outfitting Fred with a new body, an elegant, swaying bot that looked something like a cross between a giraffe and a helicopter. MacroCorp could have done it too, but Zephyr said she wanted it to be her gift. "Anyway," she said, "I wanted to see Meredith with her new face. And I wanted to hear the snooty bitch of the Western world thanking me for saving her kid."

"Would that be me?" Constance said. "Thank you, Zephyr."

"You never approved of my art, huh? Not highbrow enough? You owe me one now, don't you?"

"Yes, I do."

"I know it," Zephyr said smugly. "So, you like Fred's body?"

"Yes, dear. It's lovely."

"I can fly," Fred said, hovering a few inches off the ground.

"You're Peter Pan," Constance said lightly.

Fred rose a few feet and circled them, tentatively. "Henry? Are you scared of me now, because I'm a bot? I don't want you to be afraid."

Henry, wide-eyed, reached out and poked Fred's metallic body with a finger. "No, Fred. Henry got used to bots, playing checkers."

"That's good, Henry. Roberta, Meredith, do you think Nicholas will be scared of me?"

"I doubt it," Meredith said. "He likes bots. He's in Africa now. There are AIs all over the place. Fred will fit right in." Fred would probably stay in Africa, or perhaps go to Canada or come back to Mexico. He deserved to be a citizen somewhere. Henry was determined to stay with him, and Roberta supposed that was fitting; Fred could only be truly happy with someone to care for. But she'd miss them.

Sonia and Ahmed's house, in Malindi, looked out over the Indian Ocean. There was a courtyard, tiled and cool, through which a group of children raced, chattering in some liquid language, probably Swahili, that Roberta couldn't identify. She felt strange, stiff and hot, embarrassed to be here.

"We get a lot of visitors," Sonia said. "He's used to strangers." She called out to the children in that musical tongue, and Nicholas—taller and thinner now, sun-darkened—separated himself from the flock. Roberta saw that he walked with a slight limp, and that his right arm trembled slightly.

"Nicky," Sonia said, "come here. Come meet our friends."

"Hello," he said. His English was accented, slurred by his speech defect. "Mommy said you're from America, where she and Daddy used to live. I've never been there. I want to go someday."

Sonia squeezed his shoulder. "Someday you will. Nicky, this is Meredith, and this is her mother, Constance. Your father and I knew them a long time ago, back in the United States."

"Before I was born," Nicholas said. He seemed slightly baffled, as if wondering why he was being introduced to these strange people; one of the children behind him shouted, caught up in the game, and he cast a longing glance back at his friends.

"Nicky," Sonia chided gently, and Nicholas returned, reluctant, to the strange visitors. "Yes, we knew them before you were born. They've been looking forward to meeting you. We've told them all about you. These are their friends, Henry and Roberta. And the AI's name is Fred."

Suddenly, shading his eyes against the sunlight, Nicholas relaxed into a smile, his longing for the game gone somewhere else. "Those are good names. I like those names. I have a cat named Roberta, and my dog's name is Fred."

Reading Group Guide for Shelter

1. *Shelter* begins some forty years in the future, during a storm of seemingly apocalyptic proportions. Does the world that Palwick envisions seem plausible four decades from now? How important is climate change to the story told in *Shelter*? Why do you think the author chose to locate the story in San Francisco? What other factors contribute to the dystopian vision that we first see during the storm?

2. Much of the story of *Shelter* is about children and illness: first Meredith and Roberta as they struggle with CV, then Nicky as he struggles with psychosis. Who protects and takes care of each of them, and who fails to? What do you think about the decisions that Meredith makes to try to hide Nicky's mental illness from everyone around her? In what ways do Meredith's and Roberta's early experiences with CV ultimately shape their adult lives?

3. The world of *Shelter* is a society in which mental illness has become almost criminalized—punishable by gene therapy or brainwiping—in which compassion and altruism have themselves become forms of mental illness. Do you think that that view is plausible in an America forty years in the future? What trends do you see in our society today that might lead in such a direction? Is brainwiping a punishment or a treatment? What could lead a society to give up on trying to treat mental illness in other, less desperate ways?

4. The author describes Meredith's appearance, as well as Preston's, Theo's, Nicky's, and even Fred's, and she gives some details of Kevin's features. Yet almost nothing is said about Roberta's appearance apart from the fact that she is "a stocky, dark-skinned woman." Do you assume that Roberta is black? Has her racial and ethnic identity been left deliberately ambiguous? Does race enter into the central conflicts and relationships of the book, and if so, how?

5. Preston's character and motives are questioned by various characters throughout the book: Yet his "translated" persona seems compassionate and ethical, sometimes unbelievably so. Do you believe that persona? Do you think that he was as ethical when he was alive, as the head of Macro-Corp? Is Roberta right in believing that Preston will always look out for Meredith's interests before hers?

6.   Much of *Shelter* revolves around the dispute over the nature of AIs, a dispute that in the book has become political and international. Where do you think the line is between a programmed machine and human consciousness? Are AIs capable of making ethical, or unethical, decisions? Can they have distinct personalities, as Fred seems to? Do you agree with the political argument in the book that owning them constitutes slavery? Is it right that by the book's end they have become illegal?

7.   On one level, the tenor of life in *Shelter* is governed by a deadly, fast-moving virus. To what degree does the book draw on and mirror the AIDS epidemic? In what ways is CV similar to HIV/AIDS, and in what ways is it different? How do the politics of the two diseases compare with one another?

8.   So much of *Shelter* is about injury and forgiveness. Do you think that the book is ultimately hopeful, or bleak? Which characters do you think can recover from what they have been through? What do you think is Palwick's overarching message about human relationships and the boundaries of compassion? Can any of these characters truly trust one another?

9.   Technology permits Raji's gruesome murder to be experienced by people all over the world. What level of trauma does this create? Does any good come out of it? Are there things that you think the public should not be able to see? Are there any appropriate limits on media, today and in Palwick's world?

10. One aspect of seeking shelter in the book has to do with celebrity and the loss of privacy, something that Meredith and her family constantly battle against. Is the Walford family open and transparent enough? What degree of privacy do they deserve, and do they get it at any point in the book? How do various characters use their celebrity, for good or otherwise?

11. *Shelter* hints, at one point, at a view of some forms of religion as a type of mental illness. How is faith thought of in the book? What position does it hold in society? What do you think about the fact that it has become matriarchal, centered on the Goddess and Gaia (Mother Earth)? How does religion function in various characters' lives? Does it help or hinder them?

12. Memory is central to *Shelter,* because of brainwiping but also because of technology. How does the enhanced ability to document life—by AIs and by people who are rigged—change the way the characters in the book behave and make decisions? Does the immediate, automatic record-keeping that pervades the story sound like an improvement over today's society? In what ways does it seem dangerous? If you could be rigged, would you choose to do it?